PENGUIN BOOKS

LIFE AT THRUSH GREEN

'Miss Read', or in real life Mrs Dora Saint, is a teacher by profession who started writing after the Second World War, beginning with light essays written under her own name mainly for *Punch*. She has written on educational and country matters for various journals, and worked as a script-writer for the B.B.C.

'Miss Read' is married, with one daughter, and lives in a tiny Berkshire hamlet. Her hobbies are theatre-going, listening to music and reading, and she is a local magistrate.

'Miss Read' has published numerous books, including *Village School* (1955), *Village Diary* (1957), *Thrush Green* (1959), *Fresh from the Country* (1960), *Winter in Thrush Green* (1961), *Miss Clare Remembers* (1962), an anthology, *Country Bunch* (1963), *Over the Gate* (1964), *The Market Square* (1966), *Village Christmas* (1966), *The Howards of Caxley* (1967), *The Fairacre Festival* (1968), *News from Thrush Green* (1970), *Tyler's Row* (1972), *The Christmas Mouse* (1973), *Farther Afield* (1974), *Battles at Thrush Green* (1975), *No Holly for Miss Quinn* (1976), *Village Affairs* (1977), *Return to Thrush Green* (1978), *The White Robin* (1979), *Village Centenary* (1980), *Gossip from Thrush Green* (1981), *Affairs at Thrush Green* (1983), *Summer at Fairacre* (1984), *At Home in Thrush Green* and *The School at Thrush Green*. Many of 'Miss Read's' books are published in Penguin, together with three other omnibus editions: *Chronicles of Fairacre*, *More Stories from Thrush Green* and *Further Chronicles of Fairacre*. She has also written two books for children, *Hobby Horse Cottage* and *Hob and the Horse-Bat*, the Red Bus series for the very young, a cookery book, *Miss Read's Country Cooking*, and two volumes of autobiography, *A Fortunate Grandchild* (1985) and *Time Remembered* (1986).

'MISS READ'

Life at Thrush Green

THRUSH GREEN

WINTER IN THRUSH GREEN

NEWS FROM THRUSH GREEN

PENGUIN BOOKS
IN ASSOCIATION WITH MICHAEL JOSEPH

PENGUIN BOOKS

Published by the Penguin Group
27 Wrights Lane, London w8 5tz, England
Viking Penguin Inc., 40 West 23rd Street, New York, New York 10010, USA
Penguin Books Australia Ltd, Ringwood, Victoria, Australia
Penguin Books Canada Ltd, 2801 John Street, Markham, Ontario, Canada l3r 1b4
Penguin Books (NZ) Ltd, 182–190 Wairau Road, Auckland 10, New Zealand

Penguin Books Ltd, Registered Offices: Harmondsworth, Middlesex, England

Thrush Green first published by Michael Joseph 1959
Published in Penguin Books 1962
Copyright © 'Miss Read', 1959

Winter in Thrush Green first published by Michael Joseph 1961
Published in Penguin Books 1975
Copyright © 'Miss Read', 1961

News from Thrush Green first published by Michael Joseph 1970
Published in Penguin Books 1973
Copyright © 'Miss Read', 1970

This collection published as *Life at Thrush Green* 1984
5 7 9 10 8 6 4

Copyright © 'Miss Read', 1984
All rights reserved

Scanned and phototypeset by
Datasolve Information, London
Made and printed in Great Britain by
Richard Clay Ltd, Bungay, Suffolk
Set in Monophoto Bembo

CONTENTS

THRUSH GREEN

To Edie
With Love

Contents

PART ONE

MORNING

---

1. The Day Begins

As soon as he opened his eyes the child remembered, and his heart soared. This was the day he had waited for so long – the day of the fair.

He lay there for a minute, beneath his tumbled bedclothes, savouring the excitement. His mind's eye saw again, with the sharp clarity of a six-year-old, the battered galloping horses with flaring nostrils, the glittering brass posts, twisted like giant barley sugar sticks, the dizzy red and yellow swingboats and the snakes of black flex that coiled across the bruised grass of Thrush Green waiting to ensnare the feet of the bedazzled.

His nose tingled with the remembered scent of the hot oily smell which pulsed from the blaring roundabout and the acrid odour of his own hands, faintly green from clutching the brass post so tightly. In his head rang the music of the fair, the raucous shouting, the screams of silly girls in swingboats, the throbbing of the great engine which supplied the power and, over all, the head-hammering mammoth voice which roared old half-forgotten tunes from among the whirling horses of the roundabout.

At last – at last, Paul told himself, it was the first day of May! And at this point he sat up in bed, said 'White Rabbits!' aloud, to bring luck throughout the coming month, and looked eagerly out of the window into the dewy sunshine which was beginning to shimmer on Thrush Green.

And then, with a horrid shock, the child remembered something else. His heart stopped singing and dropped like a lark to the ground. Would he be able to go? Could he? Would he?

Frantically he clawed at the buttons of his pyjama jacket, tore it open, and surveyed his chest with agonized anxiety.

'The rash has almost gone,' young Doctor Lovell had said to Aunt Ruth the night before. 'If his temperature stays down, I don't see why he shouldn't have an hour at the fair.'

Aunt Ruth had smiled at Paul who had bounced up and down on the mattress with excitement.

'But you've got to take it quietly, young man,' went on Doctor Lovell, 'otherwise, no fair!'

They had left the child in bed and gone downstairs to the cool hall. The front and back doors of the pleasant old house stood hospitably open and the low rays of the setting sun crept in through the back door with the fragrance of the wallflowers which lined the garden path.

'He'll be so pleased if he can go,' said the girl. 'They say that this will be the last time the fair comes here.'

'Oh, you've heard that too?' observed Doctor Lovell. 'Evidently the old lady who runs the thing – Mrs Whatsit –' He snapped his fingers and cocked his long dark head sideways in an effort to remember.

'Mrs Curdle,' prompted Ruth. 'The great Mrs Curdle. Why, I remember her when Joan and I used to come here to stay as children! She always looked about eighty – and as tough as they make them!'

'That's it – Mrs Curdle. They were saying at The Vine last night that she's decided to sell the business.'

'It seems impossible,' said the girl, as they paced slowly down the short flagged path to the gate. 'And what her family will do without her to bully them all I can't think.'

The doctor opened the gate and stood outside. Ruth rested her bare arms on top and they gazed across Thrush Green to the half-dozen or so caravans which clustered at the further corner near the church some hundred yards away. Most of them were gleaming modern beauties, flashing with chromium plating and fresh paint; but two of them were the traditional horse-drawn ones painted gaily with green and red, with yellow wheels and a bucket or two swinging from the axle, and in one of these, Ruth knew, lived the old matriarch who had ruled the fair for so many years.

In the still evening air blue smoke rose from the little tin chimney to the lime trees above. There was a faint whiff of frying onions, and a lurcher dog was sitting close to the caravan, his nose pointed expectantly upward. Nearby two skewbald ponies, tethered to the trees, cropped the new grass.

'Looks the perfect life,' sighed Ruth longingly. 'Just wandering from place to place. Nothing to remind you of things you want to forget –' Her voice trailed away and her companion looked at her quickly. She was uncomfortably pretty, gazing into the distance like that, he thought, and looked much better than she had when he had first met her six weeks before. Then she had been a pathetic little ghost, sitting listlessly in her sister's house, answering politely when addressed, with her heart and mind in some far-distant place.

Damn that fellow! thought young Doctor Lovell savagely, for the hundredth time. And I suppose she'd take him back again if he came crawling, blast his eyes! He fought down his useless anger and spoke equably. The calm evening gave him courage to speak more intimately than he had dared before.

'You will forget,' he assured her seriously. 'Look at the day ahead and never backward. You don't need a caravan for happiness, you know.'

The girl looked at him directly and gave a quick warm smile. The young man laughed with relief and raised a hand in farewell.

'I'll look in tomorrow morning,' he promised, and set off across Thrush Green to his own temporary home.

Thrush Green stood on high ground at the northerly end of Lulling, a small sleepy prosperous town, which had been famous in the days of the wool trade.

The town itself lay some half a mile distant, its gentle grey houses clustered, in a hollow, on each side of the twining silver river, like a flock of drowsy sheep. The streets curved and twisted as pleasantly as the river, but shaded by fine lime trees, now breaking into delicate leaf, instead of by willows, soon to shimmer summer through, above the trout-ringed reaches of the River Pleshy.

The High Street tilted abruptly to rise to Thrush Green. It was a short sharp hill, 'a real head-thumper of a hill' in hot weather, as old Mr Piggott, sexton of St Andrew's, often said. In the grip of winter's ice the same hill was feared by riders, drivers, and those on foot. Years before, a wooden handrail, polished by generations of hands, had lined the high pavement, but the town council had decided that it served no useful purpose and detracted from the charm of the stone-walled cottages perched high on the bank above, and when the handrail had become shaky with age it had been dismantled, much to the annoyance of the Thrush Green residents.

The green itself was triangular, with the church of St Andrew standing at the southerly point. The main road from Lulling to its nearest neighbouring Cotswold town ran along one side of Thrush Green, and a less important lane threading its way to half a dozen or so sleepy little hamlets, skirted the other side. Across the base of the triangle at the northern end ran a fine avenue of horse-chestnut trees, linking the two roads, and behind them, facing towards St Andrew's across the green, stood five sturdy old houses, built of that pleasantly sunny Cotswold stone which reminds one of honeycombs, golden afternoons, and warm and mellow bliss.

It was in the middle house of the five that Ruth Bassett was staying this spring. She had known and loved the house all her life, for it had belonged to her grandparents, and she and her sister Joan had always spent as much time as possible at Thrush Green, escaping from their parents' home at Ealing whenever they could.

It had been wonderful as children to exchange the small garden, the neat tree-lined streets, and the decorous walks in Ealing parks, for the heady freedom of Thrush Green and the big untidy garden that lay behind the old house. Sometimes they travelled with their parents, for their father visited his mother and father as often as his work would allow. But sometimes the two girls travelled alone from Paddington in charge of the guard and it was these journeys that they loved best. Their spirits rose as the train rattled westward, leaving the factories and rows of houses behind. Whatever the season the country enchanted them. They would stand in the corridor of the lurching train, in the springtime, watching the broad fields of buttercups whirling by, glittering like the Field of Cloth of Gold in the May sunshine. In the summer they kept watch for the gay boats on the river, the sunshades, the punt poles flashing with drops in wet hands, and the trailing plumes of weeping willow ruffling the surface. During the autumn the glowing beech woods, gold bronze and red, flared across the hills like a forest fire; and in the Christmas holidays the bare, quiet stillness of the sleeping countryside formed the prelude to the cheerful domestic bustle of Christmas which they knew would welcome them at their grand-parents' home.

Their grandfather had died first. Ruth remembered him pottering about in the garden, a little doll of a man with fluffy white hair and a complexion as softly pink and white as a marshmallow. He had taken a great interest in Lulling's affairs, and the people of Thrush Green were reputed to set their watches and clocks by the old gentleman's punctual appearance at his gate each morning as he set off for his daily walk downhill to the town. He had been a fine cricketer in his day, and during his long retirement he had attended the modest matches at Thrush Green and those more important ones at Lulling's playing field, and those at the neighbouring towns.

One sunny June morning he had returned from his walk a little more breathless than usual after the stiff uphill climb. He had lowered himself into the sagging wicker chair in the shade of the lime tree and had surveyed the fresh beauty of the flaunting oriental poppies and irises which he loved so well. From the house came the welcome smell of lunch being prepared. He had nodded off in the drowsy sunshine, and when they had come to tell him that lunch was ready, he lay there, beneath the lime tree murmurous with bees, in his last sleep.

In the following autumn his widow had died too, and the house had been left to Ruth's father. By this time Joan had become engaged to Edward Young, a Lulling architect in partnership with his father. The two families had been friends for many years and, as a boy, Edward had always been at Thrush Green to welcome the two girls on their visits. He had been a stolid child, even-tempered and quite impervious to the Bassett girls' quips. Ruth had secretly thought him rather dull, but she had had to admit that he had developed into a kindly, reliable man, devoted to Joan and their one little boy Paul, and possessing a remarkably dry sense of humour.

The house on Thrush Green was offered to the young couple by Joan's father, who was compelled to stay in Ealing to be near to his business.

'But the day I retire,' he had threatened his young tenants with a smile, 'you are turned out into the snow on Thrush Green, don't forget! And I move in!'

Meanwhile the house remained much as it was in the grandparents' day. Joan and Edward had changed the dark paint to light and had removed the lace curtains which had shrouded all the front windows in their grandmother's time, but little else had altered, and when Ruth came down to stay, she still felt the same uplift of spirits as she stepped inside the cool hall, and still half-expected to see the pink and white old gentleman and his bustling little wife approach to welcome her.

She always slept in the same bedroom, the one which she had shared as a child with Joan, and the view from its window across Thrush Green never ceased to enchant her. If she looked left she saw the wider road to Lulling, with a few comfortable houses standing well back in leafy gardens. The tallest one belonged to old Doctor Bailey, who had attended to Lulling's ills for almost fifty years, and who had known the Bassett girls since they were babies.

To the right, on the narrow dusty lane, lay the village school behind a row of white palings. A stretch of mown grass lay between the palings and the road and on hot days the children left their stony playground and lay and rolled on the grass just outside. Only if their teacher were with them were they allowed to cross the dusty lane to play on the greater green, for Miss Watson was a timid woman and had no doubt at all that each and every pupil would be run over and either maimed or killed outright if she were not there to keep an eye on their movements.

Beside the school stood the little school house, and beside that a row of small cottages. In the last lived old Mr Piggott, the sexton of St Andrew's. As 'The Two Pheasants' stood next door to his house he was handy not only for his work at the church on the green, but also for his only pleasure. He had been a source of fear to the Bassett girls when they were small. Always grumbling, he had threatened them with all kinds of dreadful punishment if he had caught them walking in St Andrew's churchyard or sheltering in the porch. Now, bent and rheumaticky and crosser than ever, Ruth and Joan found him a figure to be pitied rather than feared, but both agreed that he was an evil-tempered old man and they felt very sorry for his only daughter Molly who kept house for him.

'It's a good thing she's got a job in that pretty little pub in Lulling Woods,' Joan told her sister. 'At least it gets her away from her wretched old father for most of the time. I can't think how she puts up with him. She's so sweet and so terribly pretty – she's bound to get married soon, I suppose.'

And then she had stopped short and had cursed herself fiercely for mentioning marriage to Ruth just then. In the silence which fell upon the room that dusky April evening Joan had cast a swift look at her sister's drawn face and had hastily changed the subject to the plans which she and Edward were making for a few days' holiday. Ruth had offered to mind Paul while they were away, and secretly looked forward to having the peace and comfort of the old house with only the little boy for company. Joan and Edward couldn't have been kinder, she told herself, since the blow had fallen upon her. They had offered hospitality, rest, companionship, and the tranquillity of Thrush Green, all combining to act as balm to a hurt mind and heart, but yet she craved, now that the worst was over, for a little solitude in which to make plans for a timid, sad return to life.

They had driven off on a sparkling April morning and within two days Paul had developed a high temperature and a rash on his chest. Old Doctor Bailey, who just lately had spent most of his time in bed, had sent his young assistant Doctor Lovell across to see the little boy, and Ruth, who had met him soon after her arrival earlier in the spring, had grown to like this quiet young man who had slipped so easily into the ways and the affections of the people of Lulling and Thrush Green. Even Mr Piggott had spoken a grudging word in his favour.

'Pity he don't stop,' he had said to Ruth, nodding across the green at the departing figure. 'The old 'un ain't too good these days. But there – he won't give up till his knifing arm drops off. Still keeps an eye on some of the old patients, ill though he be himself.'

A tapping at the bedroom window above had interrupted this conversation. Paul's woebegone face was pressed to the glass and Ruth had hurried back to the patient.

'All that's troubling him,' old Piggott had called after her, 'is whether he'll be fit to go to the fair!'

When Ruth awoke on the first day of May her first thought, as always, was of that nightmarish scene which had changed her life. The old accustomed horror engulfed her as her mind fought to turn itself away from such bitterness. But, to her surprise, the feeling was not so sharply cruel on this particular day. True, her mind shied from its remembrance like a terrified horse, but it did not plunge and toss, this way and that, in grief-maddened panic, in its efforts to shake off the devil that possessed it. It was as though a veil had been dropped between the dreadful picture and her mind's eye. She could see it all, down to the smallest detail, but the picture was dimmed, the impact was gentler, and her own feeling less agonized.

Could it really be true that time healed everything, Ruth

wondered? For six weeks now she had woken daily to a sickening sense of loss and humiliation, and this was the first time that she had felt any lessening in the misery that engulfed her.

The clock of St Andrew's struck seven and she could hear movements from Paul's room across the landing. The first of May! The day of Thrush Green fair. No wonder that he was awake early. If the rash had gone and his temperature remained normal she felt sure that he would be allowed to go to the fair. Doctor Lovell would be along as soon as possible, she knew, to put the little boy out of his suspense.

She sat up and reached for her slippers. The sun was already striking rainbows from the dewy grass and gilding the roofs of the caravans on Thrush Green. As Ruth thrust her feet into her slippers she was struck once again by a second marvel. The thought of seeing young Doctor Lovell again had sent the faintest flicker of warmth into her sad heart. She sat on the side of the bed and considered this phenomenon dispassionately. To have the searing pain lessened at all was remarkable enough for one morning, but to find a little warmth among the dead ashes of her day-to-day existence was even more extraordinary.

Wondering and bemused, shaken with a vague sense of gratitude for mercies received, she went to the bedroom door. And clutching this crumb of comfort to her she made her way across the sunlit landing to see Paul.

2. The Great Mrs Curdle

Mrs Curdle heard St Andrew's clock strike seven as she lifted the boiling kettle from her diminutive stove. She had been up and about for over an hour, moving slowly about her caravan, straightening the covers on the bunk, shaking the rag rug, and even giving the brass on her beloved stove an early rub with metal polish.

The stove was the delight of her heart and had been built especially by a friend of her late husband's to fit neatly into the end of her tiny home. The top was of gleaming steel which Mrs Curdle rubbed up daily with emery paper, hissing gently to herself like a groom to a horse, as her busy hand slid back and forth, back and forth across the satin of the surface.

A circular lid could be lifted off and the fire then sent up its released heat to Mrs Curdle's kettle, stew-pot, or frying-pan. When the food was cooked, or the teapot filled, it could be kept hot by standing it farther along the hob, and frequently the top of the little stove was filled with a variety of utensils each giving off a rich aroma, for Mrs Curdle was a great cook.

The front of the stove was black but decorated with a great deal of brass. The knobs and hinges of the tiny oven door gleamed like gold against the jetty blacklead. Another door, covering the bars of the fire, could be let down and formed a useful ledge. It was here that Mrs Curdle heated her great flat-iron, propping it up on its back with the ironing surface pressed to the glowing red bars.

But this morning the stove, despite its comforting warmth and beauty, failed to cheer Mrs Curdle's troubled heart. She had known, as soon as she had woken, that this was going to be one of her bad days, for the burning pain in her back and stomach had already begun to torment her.

'Dear, oh, dear!' had muttered poor Mrs Curdle, heaving her back painfully from the narrow bunk. She had sat there breathing heavily, for a full ten minutes, rubbing her enormous stomach as rhythmically as she did the gleaming stove top, and talking aloud to herself as was her custom.

'And only a morsel of fried liver and onions for me supper! Never touched the cheese and never wetted me lips with nothin' stronger than tea all yesterday. An' there's no doubt about it – I'll have to turn it all in – turn it all in!'

She had gone slowly about her toilet, wiping her strong brown face with a damp cloth and giving her neck and magnificent bosom a perfunctory wipe afterwards. She dressed herself in her black stuff dress, put on a dazzling flowered overall, and pulled on a red and grubby cardigan. Her hair she combed through carefully with soapy water and braided it into shiny sticky bands, with two loops hanging at each side of her head, each encircling an ear. Gold drop ear-rings, the wedding gift of her husband, had glittered against Mrs Curdle's weather-beaten cheeks for over fifty years and these, with the exception of a gold brooch with the word MIZPAH embossed upon it, were the only ornaments that the old lady wore.

She had been a handsome girl, tall and beautifully proportioned, with plentiful black hair and lustrous dark eyes. And now despite her seventy-odd years and her great girth she was still a fine-looking woman, with her jutting haughty nose and compelling gaze beneath the thick arched brows. She had treated her husband as an equal, in business affairs, in their domestic life, and as the father of their eight children. She had been as strong physically as he, for he was a slight man and they had shared the heavy manual work needed in setting up and taking down the equipment of their business. When he had died, as the result of a fall from the framework of his own swing-boats, at the age of fifty, Mrs Curdle had mourned him deeply. She had lost not only a husband, but her dearest companion and co-partner in a flourishing concern.

But Mrs Curdle had not mourned for long. The three oldest children were of an age to help in the fair, but there were five smaller ones, the youngest hardly able to walk and still needing the board across the doorway of the caravan to protect her from falling head-long down the three wooden steps that led precipitously to the great world beyond her tiny home.

She was determined that nothing should part her from the fair which she and her husband had built up over the years, with back-breaking effort. Two men, both distant relations of her husband's, remained to help her, and these two she ruled as strictly as she did her own struggling brood. Instant obedience was expected, and on the rare occasions when it was not forthcoming Mrs Curdle's mighty arm would swing, or her cruel tongue would lash, and child or fair-hand would meekly acknowledge his master.

Those who knew her but slightly marvelled that the children, as they grew old enough to earn their own livelihood, elected to stay with one so ruthlessly overbearing. But despite her matriarchal severity Mrs Curdle was scrupulously just and uncommonly warm-hearted, and her family adored, as well as feared her. She had no room in her life for loafers, grumblers, or petty thieves; but an honest man or woman who had fallen on evil times or needed advice in trouble found in this indomitable old lady kindness, sympathy, and the wisdom born of experience.

Mrs Curdle had many friends and very few enemies in the half a dozen or so counties which her caravan traversed in the southern part of England. She was known to three generations in villages and towns, and when the rumour had gone round that the great Mrs Curdle was thinking of selling her business and that the fair would be no more it came as a sad shock. Grandparents in the water-meadows of Wiltshire, fathers and mothers in the grey Cotswold villages, and little children playing among the wooded upper reaches of the Thames Valley all felt the same pang of regret at the possibility of this annual joy passing from them for ever.

'It doesn't seem possible,' old Doctor Bailey had said to his wife, the week before Mrs Curdle's visit was due. 'May the first, without Mrs Curdle on Thrush Green – why, the whole idea's absurd! It just *isn't* May the first without Mrs Curdle!'

'We shall miss the flowers,' said his wife. She was sitting in an armchair in the window of the patient's bedroom which looked across Thrush Green to the village school. The doctor was comfortably propped up against his pillows in the evening sunshine. He had spent the warm afternoon pottering about in his garden, smelling the lilac, admiring his tulips, and watching a blackbird flutter back and forth, her beak full of wriggling insects for her nestlings nearby.

But now he was tired and quite content, as the April day cooled, to be helped back into his comfortable bed and to read or gossip lazily with his wife.

'Those flowers!' said the old man, shaking his head. 'A bigger and brighter bunch each year it seems.'

Mrs Curdle's annual bunch of flowers constituted something of a problem in the doctor's house, for they were artificial and lasted for ever. They were indeed works of art, great mop-headed beauties made from finely cut woodshavings which curled into unbelievable shapes. Mrs Curdle had learnt this handicraft as a young girl and was an expert. When the flowers had been made she dyed them yellow, pink, orange, and scarlet and mounted them among evergreen twigs of laurel. They made a dazzling bouquet, not without charm, but the bunch which was presented each May Day by Mrs Curdle in person to the doctor was of such gargantuan proportions that Mrs Bailey was hard put to it to find a suitable place for it.

Each year Mrs Curdle asked to see how the previous year's bouquet had worn, so that the doctor and his wife were in honour bound not to destroy these offerings.

'Do you realize, my dear,' said the doctor, 'that we've had a bunch of Curdle blooms ever since 1915?'

'Forty-odd years with the top shelf of the pantry occupied,' commented Mrs Bailey. 'And then having to remember to unearth them before the day! Really, I shan't know myself.'

'I don't like the idea,' responded the doctor with vigour. 'To think of that caravan drawn up in some buttercup field under the lee of the same hawthorn hedge for ever, with grass seeding over the wheel-tops, and the shafts down, rotting – no, I tell you! It's against nature. Mrs Curdle's too game to let that happen. Surely, she'd never let it happen!'

But there was a query in the old man's tone and silence fell upon the room. Outside, the blackbirds scolded and the sound of children playing on the green, glorying in the first few outdoor games of spring, could be faintly heard. Mrs Bailey stole a glance at her husband. His blue eyes were gazing far away and his wife knew that he was thinking of that distant evening when he and Mrs Curdle had first met, on just such an April evening, many years ago.

Doctor Bailey was then a young man in his twenties, newly qualified and recently married and settled in this his first practice. The tall house on Thrush Green had been but sparsely furnished for the young couple had great aspirations but little money, and most of the furniture was solid Victorian stuff given by their parents. The large room to the left of the graceful hooded front door was young Doctor Bailey's surgery. Later, as his family came into the world, it was to be the dining-room and a new surgery was built at the side of the house, but when Mrs Curdle first knew him the doctor and his wife dined in a sunny little room at the back of the house, conveniently near to the kitchen.

They had been at supper on that far distant evening when Mr Curdle, white with panic, had drummed madly on the glass of the hall door. The little maid-of-all-work had been disdainful, telling the wild-eyed rough-looking man that Doctor Bailey had finished his evening surgery and was not at home.

At this the sorely-tried husband had broken into such cries of frustration and wrath that the good doctor had thrust aside his plate and gone out into the hall to discover what all the hullabaloo was about.

'It's me missus, sir,' had said Mr Curdle, clutching the doctor's arm. 'It's on the way – afore time. Ain't never seen her this way afore!'

'I'll come,' had answered the doctor, picking up his bag from the hall table. The maid had retired, tossing her head at the thought of such low people as them gyppos having the sauce to interrupt the master at his supper.

The two men had crossed the green to the small caravan. The husband was voluble with anxiety.

'This makes the fourth,' he had told the doctor, 'and never a minute's worry with any on 'em! Be as strong as a 'orse, me old gal; but never see her this way!'

The doctor had entered the tiny caravan which was stuffy and evil-smelling after the fragrance of the April evening outside. It seemed packed with humanity, for as well as the patient, writhing and moaning in the narrow bunk, there were two women, administering advice and pungent potions, as well as three small children.

'Get them all outside,' the doctor had said curtly, and the crowd had melted away leaving him with his patient and her husband hovering anxiously at the door. After a brief examination he had scribbled a note and handed it to the husband.

'Run across to my house with that and tell my wife to lose no time,' he said.

'What's it for?' stammered the man.

'For the ambulance. We must get her into the county hospital straight away.'

The man had vanished at once, but the patient had burst into hysterical screaming at the word 'hospital'.

'Ah, don't 'ee send me there, doctor dear! Please don't send me to that place, doctor. I'll die – that I will! I'll die!'

'You'll die if you don't go, young woman,' the doctor had said honestly. The straight words had shocked her into silence and she lay quietly until the ambulance had arrived. It was a high, dignified vehicle, the pride of Lulling Cottage Hospital, and the outcome of many fêtes and jumble sales in the neighbourhood.

Doctor Bailey never forgot that ten-mile journey to the county town. He had sat inside watching his patient, directing the husband who was now in tears, to sit in front with the driver. It was one of those typical April evenings, showery and sunny in turn. The sky was a purplish-grey with heavy storm clouds and against this background the young green of the new leaves gleamed goldenly. As the ambulance lurched along through the scented odd-coloured evening the doctor was struck, for the first time, by the memory of Millais' Picture of 'The Blind Girl'. The artist had caught the same bizarre colouring exactly, and enhanced it by the addition of that unforgettable, glowing, auburn hair.

Young Mrs Curdle had clung pathetically to the doctor's hand throughout the journey. He had promised her that all would be well, that the hospital staff wanted to help and not to frighten her, and that if she did all that she were told the baby had every chance of being born alive and of flourishing. She had listened silently, tears rolling helplessly from her dark lovely eyes, but she knew, before the agonizing journey was over, that here was a true friend and counsellor.

The child had been born the next day after a gruelling period of pain. It was a delicate boy and the mother was ill for over a month after the birth. She was moved to Lulling Cottage Hospital where Doctor Bailey saw her each day and grew to like this gallant young woman whose spirits returned slowly with her strength.

No one could guess how much hospital life oppressed the girl. She lay in her bed on the veranda and gazed listlessly at the neat rose-beds, each trim bush bearing a tidy label with its name, and she craved for the sight of a spray of pale wild roses tossing in the fresh breeze on the open downs, for the splash of rain on her face, and the whistling of the wind through her hair.

She ate the grey tepid food on the clean white plates obediently, and yearned for the mingled smell of woodsmoke and hare broth and the clatter of her own metal spoon and platter. The one bright spot of her arid day was the visit of young Doctor Bailey. To her he was god-like. Without him she would have died, and her son with her.

Every Sunday her husband came from whichever of the nearby towns the little fair was working. He came dressed in his best black and sat, monosyllabic and ill at ease, among the white counterpanes, the flowers, and the rustling nurses.

Mrs Curdle questioned him sharply about the business and the children, but that done conversation languished, and each was secretly relieved when the visiting time was up and he made his sheepish farewells, too shy to kiss her before strangers and too loving to go without pain.

Early in the July of 1914 Mrs Curdle and the baby had joined the fair again in a windswept Berkshire village, but not before Mrs Curdle had given her thanks to the young doctor and promised to show him the baby on her next visit to Thrush Green at the beginning of the following May.

'And take care of him,' the doctor had said. 'He's a fine boy and I shall look forward to seeing you both next May.'

But it was not to be, for within a month war had broken out in Europe and the doctor was fighting in France when Mrs Curdle had called with her baby and the first of many bunches of lovingly-made flowers. It was Mrs Bailey, herself by now the mother of a young son, who admired the child and accepted the bouquet; and it was not until George Curdle (named after the King) was a sturdy child of five that he first saw the doctor who had helped to bring him into the world.

And now, on this May morning more than forty years from those far-off days, Mrs Curdle thought again of Doctor Bailey. She would go to him for medical advice, for the second time in her life. She had come to this decision slowly and painfully, and only at the promptings of prolonged and terrifying suffering.

For months now the pain in her stomach had made her even more dictatorial than usual. Many a sharp word to her large family had called forth muttered blasphemies from growing grandchildren less willing to show the meek respect which their parents had done to the head of the tribe.

Old Mrs Curdle was too proud to consult her daughters, or even women friends of her own age, about her ailments. She suffered the burning pain, the nausea, and the headaches without complaint, and only her growing impatience and tired eyes gave a hint that she was not a healthy woman.

Secretly she had made up her mind that she was the victim of cancer. She had heard enough of this enemy to fear it, and she visualized this creeping evil groping about the tender members of her body with deadly tentacles. On one thing she was determined. If Doctor Bailey discovered a growth within her, then within her it would remain. Nothing, she swore, would be as terrifying to her as hospital and the surgeon's knife. She would carry her pain back to the caravan, and bear it as best she could, as she had done for so many months, until the good God released her from its clutches. She was used to it now and could settle down with it philosophically, like a mother with a bad-tempered child.

She took her cup of black tea to the doorway and settled down on the steps of the caravan. The air blew deliciously cool upon her face and the warm tea soothed her pain. The camp was astir. Water was being emptied on to the grass, young mothers pegged baby clothes on improvised lines, and over by the village school Mrs Curdle could see her favourite grandson Ben, George's only child, a boy of twenty, buying milk from the van which delivered daily on Thrush Green.

Her old heart warmed towards him. He was just like his father, just as tall, just as dark, just as quick and handsome. The old pang gripped her as she thought of George, as she always did when she came to Thrush Green, virtually his birth-place. His photograph, in uniform, stood in the very centre of the tiny mantelshelf. He smiled at her from it as he had smiled so often, and would never smile again. For George, her dearest, had been killed in France three weeks before the Second World War ended, and his timid little wife and young Ben had been left in Mrs Curdle's care.

She had turned all her fierce maternal love upon this child who returned her affection, and when his mother had been offered a second marriage by a grocer in one of the small towns which the fair had visited, old Mrs Curdle had insisted that Ben remain with her. This suited both the grocer and the colourless little woman who had once made George so happy, and thus it was that Ben was brought up by his grandmother.

She looked at him now as he brought back two bottles of milk across the dewy grass, and the pleasure which the sight of him gave her turned suddenly to unhappiness as a spasm of pain and sad remembrance gripped her.

Ben might look like George, but he'd never be the man his father was if he carried on as he had done during the last few months! Mooning about, sulking, answering back! Mrs Curdle didn't know what had come over him lately. Where was the fun they used to have together? Never heard him sing these days or crack a joke or laugh hearty.

Mrs Curdle sighed and watched him pass beyond one of the caravans. She struggled to her feet and swayed against the door as the pain stabbed her.

Ah, well! Another day to get through. Another day nearer the end of the poor old fair, she told herself, looking at the bustle around her. A pity for it to go. If young Ben were more like his dear father and had the life and go he used to have, why, she'd be glad to hand the reins over to him – but there, it was no good thinking of that these days.

She looked at the table in the dusky corner of the caravan. There lay the largest bouquet of wood-shaving flowers she had ever made. It might well be the last, she knew.

Tonight, after surgery hours, she would call, an annual pilgrim, on old Doctor Bailey and tell him all her troubles. And from that kind old friend she would, at last, learn her fate.

3. Ben Curdle Meets His Fate

Ben Curdle walked back from the milk van, across the wet grass, a bottle dangling from each hand. He was conscious of his grandmother's morose eye upon him, and averted his own gaze. His dark young face looked surly, but his heart was bounding joyfully about in his breast like a clockwork toy.

He knew where she was! He knew where she was, he sang to himself! For two pins he would have turned cartwheels down the length of Thrush Green and back. This was the finest day in his life, the finest day the world had ever known. He had found his girl.

He had met her exactly a year ago, when the fair had visited Thrush Green. It had been a cold, blustery day, but lit with such warm radiance for young Ben Curdle that he would never forget it. He had seen Molly Piggott, first, very early in the morning. She had emerged from the cottage next to 'The Two Pheasants' armed with a bucket and scrubbing brush, and had plumped herself down to scrub the red-brick doorstep. She wore a frock with blue flowers on it, Ben remembered, and a red woollen jacket. Her pretty legs were bare and she wore white sandals. She had a mop of curly hair as dark as his own, and when he had called 'Good morning' to her from the doorway of his caravan she had flashed such a smile at him that his heart turned over. The sleeves of the red jacket were thrust up above her elbows and the water from the scrubbing brush ran down her milky arm and trickled to the ground.

For a year now Ben had remembered her like that at will. They had spent three or four hours of that enchanted day in each other's company, and though Ben remembered it all and hugged the memories to him desperately, it was that first glimpse of her that stayed most clearly in his mind and had given him mingled comfort and torment for so many barren months.

At that time, and ever since she had left school three years before, Molly Piggott had been living at home, looking after her father, that crotchety widower, cooking his midday meal, her own life largely governed by his sexton's duties. In the afternoons, after washing-up at the shallow slate sink in the tiny scullery, she walked across Thrush Green to the Bassetts' house.

Here she ironed or mended linen, mostly for young Paul, who adored her, until quarter to three, when Paul's after-dinner rest ended. It was then her duty and pleasure to get him up and take him out for an hour or so, returning to nursery tea, followed by a game, bath-time, and bed. Between six and seven she returned to her own cottage and spent most of the evening alone whilst her father drank gloomily in the pub next door.

Molly had been quite content with this placid life, despite the constant grumblings of the old man. Luckily, he was out of the house for a large part of the day, pottering about the church and churchyard, occasionally digging a grave and tidying it after the sad ceremony or ringing a wedding peal and sweeping up the confetti and gay little silver horseshoes afterwards. His demeanour remained exactly the same whatever the function. He hauled on his striped furry sally as each young couple emerged, starry-eyed, into the dazzling sunshine of Thrush Green, with the same gloomy expression of a disgruntled tortoise, with which he wielded his mattock to lift the first sod for some boyhood friend's grave. Life was sour for old Mr Piggott, and he made sure that everybody knew it.

The afternoon was the happiest part of Molly's day. She did her ironing or mending in the quiet stone-flagged kitchen whose windows looked out upon the garden in which old Mr Bassett had pottered and finally died. She loved this tranquil hour in the hushed early afternoon. Thrush Green was somnolent in its after-dinner nap, and the old house dozed around her. Paul was in his bed upstairs playing, looking at his books, or sometimes merely lying there in that blissful state between sleeping and waking, where dreams and reality merge imperceptibly and the cry of the cuckoo from the lime tree might well be the chime of the clock on the wall of the dream-room into which one has just floated.

Molly's kitchen was fragrant with the smell of freshly ironed linen and she felt her satisfaction mounting with the pile. Paul's small shirts and vests, his minute trousers and his handkerchiefs, bright with nursery rhymes, all received especial care. And later, as she sat in the low wooden armchair, with the needle flashing in and out of the clean clothes, she would plan the walk that she would take him when the time came to lift young Paul, warm and heavy, smelling faintly of Vinolia soap, from his rest.

In the winter they kept to the roads, or, if the earth were hard with frost they might play on Thrush Green with a bat and ball in view of Paul's home. Occasionally they walked down the steep hill to Lulling to shop for something which Joan had forgotten. But more often they took the little leafy lane which led from Thrush Green to Upper Pleshy, Nod, and Nidden, the lane that threaded half a dozen or more sleepy thatched villages, like hoary old beads upon its winding string, before it emerged upon the broad highway which led to Stratford-upon-Avon.

Sometimes their expeditions were more adventurous. Molly and Paul knew all the true joys that were within an hour's walking time of Thrush Green. There was the pond that lay, dark and mysterious, along the lower road to Lulling Woods, mirroring the trees that stood around it. Sometimes in the summer Paul had taken a bright wooden boat on a string and floated it there, beating at the water's edge with a fan of leaves to make waves. In the spring vast masses of frogs' spawn floated just beneath the surface, like submerged chain-mail cast there by some passing knight. And on one day of hard frost Paul and Molly had slid back and forth across the shining ice, screaming with delight, watched by a bold robin who sat fearlessly nearby on a low bare branch preening the pale grey feathers that edged the bronze of his breast.

There were other places that they loved which were accessible only in the summer. There was the steep path through Lulling Woods, cool as a cathedral, even on the sultriest day. There was the field path to Nod, where the grass brushed Paul's shoulder in high summer and he looked at marguerites and red sorrel at eye-level. A bower of brier roses guarded the final stile that led into Nod and, in later life, Paul never smelt that sharp breath-taking sweetness of the wild rose without remembering the languor and warm happiness of those golden afternoons with Molly Piggott.

She was the perfect companion for a little boy, placid, good-tempered, and ready to answer endless questions.

'Why can't I fly, Molly?'

'Would you be terribly, terribly sad if I died, Molly?'

'Why don't all animals have horns?'

These were a few of the simpler questions that Molly faced daily. When Paul started to attend Sunday school at St Andrew's and, later still, listened to Miss Watson's Scripture lessons at the village school, the queries grew more difficult.

'Did John the Baptist always have a headache?' he asked at tea-time one day.

'Never knew he had one,' said Molly equably, spreading jam for him.

'Well, he said he wasn't fit to stoop down and tie up shoe laces,' pointed out Paul reasonably, cutting the bread and butter energetically. And later on, as Molly tucked him into bed he had asked:

'Who is the Holy Ghost, Molly?'

Molly pushed her hair back from her forehead, screwing up her eyes in an effort to solve this teaser.

'I don't rightly know, Paul,' she answered slowly, 'but he was a friend of Jesus's.'

'What I thought,' answered the child, butting his head into the pillow, and, satisfied, was asleep in two minutes.

When Paul was five and had started school Molly feared that her services might not be needed at the house on Thrush Green, but Joan Bassett had reassured her. The two had been together in the big kitchen, one December afternoon, Molly with her mending and Joan icing the Christmas cake, while Paul rested upstairs.

'You know that Paul starts school in the New Year,' Joan had said, intent on her sugar rosettes, 'but we all hope you will stay with us for as long as you want to.'

Molly had kept her head bent above her sewing but her heart leapt at the news.

'He ends school at half past three each day, so that you can have tea with us as you've always done and help with the linen and run a few errands—'

Joan paused as she negotiated a tricky edge with her icing tool. Molly said nothing, speechless with relief. Joan wondered if the girl might have other plans and began again with some diffidence.

'Of course, I know you'll want something with more scope now that you're getting older, and we'd never stand in your way, Molly. You must feel quite free to go to any other post if you are offered one.'

'Oh, no!' Molly exclaimed from a full heart, 'I don't *ever* want to leave here!'

And, at that moment, she really meant it.

And so the winter months had slipped by, with Paul bursting from school at half past three and running home across the green bearing a paper mat woven erratically from bright strips, or a wallpaper bookmark still damp from the paste brush, as a souvenir of his day's labours.

He was ecstatically happy at the little school. Both teachers he had known from babyhood. Miss Watson he saw but little, for she took the older children, and after morning prayers and a Scripture story she retired to her own classroom and was seen no more by Paul. But Miss Fogerty, the infants' teacher, he adored, and she began to share Molly's place in his heart. She had been teaching at Thrush Green school as long as the Bassett girls could remember and had not changed a scrap in all the years. Small and mousy, with very bright eyes behind gold-rimmed spectacles, she darted about the classroom and playground still wearing the silver pencil on a long chain about her neck that Joan remembered from her own childhood glimpses of Miss Fogerty.

Molly missed the companionship of the child on the afternoon walks. She often ran an errand nowadays for Joan at the time when she had formerly taken out Paul. She was a reliable shopper and Joan found that she could give her increasing responsibility in choosing food and drapery from the shops in Lulling. By Easter-time Molly was doing a large part of the catering for the household at Thrush Green, keeping an eye on the larder and making intelligent suggestions to Joan for the evening meal when Edward would be home.

Joan began to hope that Molly would indeed stay for ever, as she had so ardently promised. But on the day of Thrush Green Fair

young Ben Curdle had walked into Molly Piggott's life, and by the
time the harvest was being gathered, things had changed at the house
on Thrush Green.

It had been a cold, wretched day that year for the first of May.
The gusts of wind shivered the young lime leaves about the caravans
and the sky was as grey as the canvas tent which housed the 'Marine
Wonder' hard by.

Molly had spoken a few words, during the morning, to the dark
young man who was busy erecting the scaffolding for the coconut
shies opposite her cottage. She had liked him from the first moment
that she had seen him when she was scrubbing the doorstep. She
liked his soft voice and his crinkly, wiry hair and the odd shape of his
dark eyes. If she had been drawing his face, she thought to herself,
she would have put triangles for his eyes. Molly liked drawing and
Miss Watson had often pinned her sketches on the school-room wall
for her fellow-pupils to admire.

He had called to her when she emerged to go shopping for old Mr
Piggott's dinner with her basket on her arm. He was squatting down
in the wet grass, his hair upswept in the wind, looking intently at
something on the ground.

'Come and see,' he invited, giving her a crooked smile, his head
on one side. Molly had crossed the road and gone to look. A young
frog, speckled and yellow, crouched between Ben's shoes, its throat
pulsing, its starfish front feet turned in. For a dreadful moment
Molly feared that he might kill it, as she had seen other stupid
country boys do when they were displaying their manly bravado
before the girls, but with relief and pleasure she watched him gather
it in his grimy hands. He rose in one graceful movement and crossed
to the railings of the churchyard where the grass grew tallest. He
deposited the creature there and returned to Molly wiping his hands
down his black corduroy trousers.

'Coming to the fair?' he asked.

Molly nodded, her face alight with mischief.

'And bringing a boy,' she quipped. Ben's face clouded and Molly
was unaccountably stirred.

'Only a little one,' she said, laughing. 'Lives over there.' She
nodded across to the Bassetts' house, hitched her basket further up
her arm, and set off for the butcher's shop.

'See you later then,' Ben called after her; and Molly had trotted away, conscious of his eyes upon her back.

That afternoon Joan had asked her to collect some eggs from Dotty Harmer's and Molly had joyfully accepted the basket and the money, for the way lay close to the coconut shies.

Dotty Harmer was an eccentric old maid who lived alone in a ramshackle cottage in one of the meadows which bordered the path to Lulling Woods. Her father had been a history master at the local grammar school and Dotty had kept house for the old man until his death, when she sold their home, bringing some of the furniture, all the books, four cats, two dogs, and a collection of medicinal herbs to her new abode. The herbs flourished in her tiny garden, with roses, peonies, lilies, and carnations which were the envy of all the gardeners in Lulling. Dotty concocted alarming potions from the herbs and these she pressed upon her unwilling neighbours and friends if they were unwary enough to admit to any slight ailment in her presence. So far, she had killed no one, but the vicar of St Andrew's had once had to call in Doctor Bailey as he was in agony with severe stomach pains, and had had to admit that he had taken tea and sandwiches with a peculiar and pungent filling, at Dotty Harmer's a few hours before. The Doctor had dismissed his troubles airily, diagnosing, 'Dotty's Collywobbles', a fairly common Lulling complaint, and had warned him about accepting further hospitality at that lady's hands.

As well as herbs and flowers Dotty reared some fine chickens and sold eggs to a few favoured friends. Molly often called there and enjoyed the old lady's garrulity.

That afternoon, as she had hoped, the dark young man was loitering by the coconut shies, as she approached.

'You busy?' he asked.

'Only going to get some eggs. It's not far,' she replied. There was a pause. Molly did not like to stop for she felt that she might be seen from the windows of the Bassetts' house. Her father, too, might catch sight of her. He was in the churchyard, clipping the edges of the grass paths, but she was afraid that he might rise from the sack on which he knelt and shout at her if he caught her talking to this stranger.

'Can I come?' said Ben suddenly.

'Can't stop you, can I?' said Molly, swinging her basket and smiling at him. 'Come on then. We go this way.'

Between 'The Two Pheasants' and the Piggotts' house was a narrow path which led gently downhill to the meadow where Dotty Harmer lived. Ahead, to the right, could be seen the massive leafy slopes of Lulling Woods, and the rushing of the wind in the turbulent branches could be clearly heard.

As they emerged from the passage-way between the buildings and dropped down the sandy path through the field they were suddenly sheltered from the tormenting wind.

'Peaceful, ain't it?' said young Ben, stopping still and looking at the view spread before him. 'Let's sit down.'

They sat on the cropped grass at the side of the path and talked slowly and shyly. Molly told him of her job at the Bassetts', about Paul, about her father, and about her daily round. He listened attentively, chewing a piece of grass, and nodding occasionally.

'But what do *you* do?' asked Molly. 'My word, you've got some luck, going about, seeing all these different places!'

'I like it right enough,' agreed the young man, 'but it wouldn't suit everybody.'

'It'd suit me,' said Molly forthrightly, then blushed as she thought of the construction Ben might put upon these bold words. She need not have worried. Ben answered her gravely.

'It's a rough life,' he said candidly, and he went on to tell her of the hardships and the discomforts and, finally, of old Mrs Curdle who ruled them all so firmly.

'But she's a grand ol' gal,' he asserted. 'She says sometimes she'll take me in as a partner. Ah, I'd like that – but there, you mustn't count your chickens.'

Molly rose and took up her basket.

'Chickens reminds me,' she said, and together they wandered across the meadow to the distant cottage, oblivious of the cold wind that whipped their hair and very contented in each other's company.

The children were streaming out of school when they returned to Thrush Green, and Paul flew across to her.

'That your young man?' asked Ben, looking at Molly with that engaging crooked smile.

Molly nodded.

'Reckon I shan't be jealous of 'ee!' said Ben. A harsh voice
came floating upon the wind from a nearby caravan. It was Mrs
Curdle's. She loomed, large and impressive, in the doorway of her
home.

'See you tonight,' promised young Ben and hurried back to his
duties.

Joan and Molly had taken the excited Paul to the fair as soon as it
opened after tea. His bedtime was postponed time and time again at
his own urgent pleading, but at last St Andrew's clock struck seven.
Paul was led home, protesting still, by his mother, and Molly walked
to the cottage which was her home.

She had spoken again to Ben, but only briefly, and he had whispered to her urgently:

'You coming back? On your own?'

'When I've give my dad his supper,' she promised him swiftly.
'He goes off to pub soon as he's had it and I'll slip over again.'

She had been as good as her word and by half past eight she was
back, her curly hair brushed into a dark cloud and her eyes shining.
The blue and white frock which she had worn at their first meeting
had been changed during the day for a yellow one, spotted with
white, and she looked even more gipsy-like.

Ben put a young cousin in charge of the coconut shies and took
Molly round all the side-shows of the fair. Molly had never had an
evening like this before. They had turns on the swing-boats, roundabouts, switchbacks, dodgem cars, and helter-skelters, without pause,
and Molly was dizzy not only with exhilarating motion but with the
exciting companionship of this amazing young man.

At ten-thirty the fair began to die down, much to the relief of
those residents on Thrush Green who were hoping for an early
night. As the stalls began to pack up and the crowds started to thin
out, Ben took Molly to a little jewellery stall close by the roundabout.
A few people were having a last long ride and the raucous music
blared out a sentimental ballad.

'Choose what you like,' said Ben to Molly, nodding at the dazzle
displayed on the stall. There were necklaces, bracelets, ear-rings, and
cuff-links, all cheap and tawdry in the cold light of day, but under
the electric light and the flashing of the revolving mirrors of the

roundabout nearby everything seemed exquisite to young Molly, dazed and bedazzled by a hundred sensations.

She chose a modest brooch in the form of a cornflower and Ben pinned it solemnly at the neck of the yellow spotted frock. The noise of the roundabout was deafening, but Molly saw Ben's lips move and thought she heard him say, 'Can you be true?' and she had nodded and smiled.

In the months that followed she often wondered about that half-heard question. Had he really said that? And, if so, had he meant to ask for her loyalty to him, or was he merely asking the silly sort of question that needed no answer, and which the voice from the roundabout was shouting too? Or had he said: 'Can *it* be true?' or had she misheard him altogether? Those four words were to puzzle and torment poor Molly for a whole year.

'I must get back to my dad. He'll be kicking up a fuss!' said Molly breathlessly. Ben had ambled at her side, past the stalls which were now packing up, to the cottage on the green.

They stood on the red-brick doorstep which the girl had scrubbed that morning.

'We're off first thing, so I'll say good-bye now,' said Ben. 'Had a good time?'

'Lovely,' breathed Molly. There was so much to say and somehow no words to say it. They stood in embarrassed silence for two long minutes, while the lights of the fair dimmed.

'Might get over if I can,' said Ben at last. 'Depends, though.'

'There's always the post,' suggested Molly.

Ben kicked moodily at the bricks.

'Bain't much of a fist at letter-writing,' he muttered.

From inside the cottage they could hear the scrape of chair legs on a stone floor.

'My dad!' whispered Molly in alarm. 'Good-bye, Ben. It's all been lovely.'

She reached up and gave his cheek a hasty peck. Then she turned the door handle and slipped inside the cottage before he could answer.

Bemused, young Ben wandered back to his caravan beneath the rustling lime tree; while, upstairs in the cottage, Molly, in her petti-coat, put away the cornflower brooch in a shell-encrusted box and prepared for bed with a singing heart.

But circumstances had combined against poor Ben. An alteration in the fair's accustomed route and his grandmother's ill-health had prevented him from getting within visiting distance of Thrush Green. To his deep shame he could not write, for he had had very little schooling, and apart from signing his name he could do little. He had mastered the technique of reading, and, though he was slow, he enjoyed browsing through the newspaper and an occasional paper-backed thriller.

His pride forbade his asking a friend to write to Molly for him, and in any case he could not have put into words the deep feelings which rent him, and to ask for help in expressing such emotions was unthinkable.

And so Ben suffered throughout the months that followed. Would he see her next May? Would she still be at Thrush Green? She might have got another job and gone away. Supposing another man had found her? This thought was so appalling that Ben's mind shied away from it only to be confronted by a worse horror.

Suppose she was dead? Killed, say, on the roads? Hundreds of people were each week. Or crippled? Or beaten by her horrible old Dad? Thus Ben tortured himself and roamed, restless and distraught, about his duties until it was no wonder that old Mrs Curdle, herself a prey to morbid fears, lost patience with her mooning grandson and compared him, more and more unfavourably, with that adored son buried in France. Ah, if only he had been alive, she told herself, throughout that worrying year, she would never have to think of giving up the fair, for there would have been a man – a real man – to carry on for her.

And now, a year later, Ben stood on Thrush Green once more. He had learnt that Molly still lived at the cottage, but not for all the week. Part of the time she was to be found at 'The Drovers' Arms' on the heights of Lulling Woods where she was now employed for four days a week.

Ben had made his inquiries cautiously of the milkman. He had called at the cottage the night before but no one was there. He had asked a postman, going home from late duty, if he knew where she was, and he had not known. After that Ben had not dared to ask anyone too closely connected with Thrush Green for he feared that old Mr Piggott might hear of his inquiries and vent his annoyance on

Molly. He had gone to bed much troubled, but was determined to track her down as early as possible next day.

The milkman had been most forthcoming.

'Ah! Up Lulling Woods, me boy. Helps in the house and then the bar Tuesdays to Fridays. Some chap takes over week-ends and Molly gets back then. Yes, still does a bit at Bassetts' now and again.'

He started up his ancient van with a roar, and shouted above the racket.

'You'll find her, me boy! Up Lulling Woods! She'll be in the bar till two, but free till six, I knows that 'cos I sometimes gives her a lift into the town from there. You'll find her all right!'

He rattled off, the milk bottles clashing and clattering in the metal crates, as the van shuddered its way down the hill to the town.

And thus it was that at half past seven one May Day young Ben Curdle found the moon and stars joining the morning sun in a crazy heart-bursting dance over an enchanted Thrush Green.

4. Thrush Green Astir

By nine o'clock the sun was shining strongly from a cloudless sky. The light mists that had spread a gauze over the water meadows of the River Pleshy had now dispersed. As the dew dried in the gardens of Lulling the scent of narcissi and hyacinths began to perfume the warm air.

The birds were clamorous. Blackbirds alternately fluted and scolded as they bustled about in search of food for their nestlings. Thrushes ran to and fro upon the tender grass which bent beneath their fragile claws, stopping abruptly every now and again, to peer intently with a topaz eye at the ground before them. From gardens, woods, and parkland a dozen cuckoos called to one another with thrilling liquid notes.

The buds of the trees had cracked imperceptibly during the last week or so. Already the sycamores had frothed into yellow leaf and the elms, until recently covered with a rosy haze of tight buds, now showed a curdy mass of pale breaking leaves. Only the beeches it seemed were loth to emerge from their winter sleep, for still the long slender buds remained furled, upthrust and glinting in the sunshine like the bronze tips of spears.

On Thrush Green life was now well astir. Little Paul, still in his bedroom, and pyjama-clad, had finished his breakfast of boiled egg and bread and butter, and had watched his school-fellows running to school. Some had waved and called to him, and he had shouted back that his spots were gone but the doctor was coming, so he wouldn't be at school today.

Bobby Anderson, a lumpish child with a perpetually damp nose, pointed to the end of the green where the fairground men were erecting scaffolding.

'Comin' tonight?' he bawled up at the window.

Paul nodded.

'Who said? Doctor?'

Paul nodded again.

'You better then?'

Paul nodded a third time.

'Oughter be over school then,' said his fellow-pupil severely, and terminated this one-sided conversation by leaping upon a friend of his, knocking him to the ground, and pummelling him in an affectionate manner. The school bell rang out, the boys got up, dusted themselves down in a perfunctory way and ambled across to the playground with their arms across each other's shoulders, with never a backward glance at the little figure watching from the bedroom window.

Doctor Bailey too was still pyjama-clad and had just finished his breakfast in bed. The remains of toast and marmalade lay on the tray on the side-table.

The sound of the school bell floated across Thrush Green and Doctor Bailey put aside *The Times*, pushed his reading glasses up on to his forehead, and gazed through the window at the blue and white morning.

He could see a spiral of smoke from the chimney of Mrs Curdle's caravan and a few gaunt spars as the men began to erect the framework for the swing-boats. He could hear their cheerful voices and the creak of timbers being hauled and strained. There were heavy thuds as mallets rammed supports into place, and the occasional

high-pitched squeal of a fairground child. Doctor Bailey sighed and
drew up his thin legs between the sheets.

If the rumours were true then this would be the last time that he
would hear the sounds of the fair. It seemed unthinkable that the first
day of May should find Thrush Green as empty and quiet as on the
other mornings of the year. What must the old lady be feeling, he
wondered, as he watched her smoke curling delicately against the
background of the fresh lime leaves. Where would she be next May?
And where, for that matter, thought the doctor, would he be?

He faced this nagging problem afresh. For months now he had
lived with it and he knew that he must find a solution, and the
sooner the better. He knew, only too well, that he would never
recover the strength and health which he had rejoiced in for seventy
years. Well, he told himself, he had had a good innings and he
supposed he should give up the practice and go and live in some
confounded cottage where the roof was too low, and play bridge
with other old dodderers every Wednesday afternoon, and do a bit
of fishing when the weather allowed, remembering to wear a panama
hat in case of sunstroke!

Pah! The doctor tossed his legs rebelliously and *The Times* slid to
the floor. He'd be damned if he gave up! Give him another fortnight
and he'd be back taking his surgeries and paying a few visits. There
was still plenty he could do – it was just that he tired easily. No
doubt about it, if he intended to continue in practice he must take a
partner.

He heard the bang of the surgery door. It always caught the wind
if there was a sou'-wester. He wondered how many patients young
Lovell would have calling today. Doctor Bailey looked approvingly
at the small silver clock on the mantelpiece. Only five past nine and
that young man was well down to it! Yes, if a partner was needed
then he would be quite content to have young Lovell in harness with
him. He had watched him closely for six weeks, and he had listened
to the gossip about his work. He was liked, not only for his youth,
but for his quiet and sympathetic manner. The older patients were
delighted to find a new audience for their complaints, describing
their symptoms with a wealth of nauseating detail which old Doctor
Bailey would have cut short ruthlessly, as well they knew.

'Proper nice chap, that new assistant,' they said to each other.

'Hope he stops. Listened to me 'eart and that 'orrible rumbling in me stomach, as nice as pie, and what's more, give me a good bottle of medicine. Ah! A proper nice chap!'

A twittering, and a flash of black and white across the bedroom window, roused the doctor from his ruminations. The house-martins were up and doing, and so must he be, he told himself. It was going to be a perfect day. He would potter about in the garden and get some sunshine. Nothing like fresh air and exercise for giving you strength! He had told enough people that in his time, and he knew that it was true. He would follow his own advice and he would try and come to some decision about this proposal to young Lovell. He believed he would jump at the chance and somehow he felt that Thrush Green would suit him.

He thrust his long thin legs out of bed and stood up. Now he could see the bustle of fairground preparations and the sight warmed him.

The first of May again! There was always excitement in the air on Thrush Green then – and a bunch of flowers to come, he thought wryly, looking with affection at Mrs Curdle's caravan. As good a day as any to make a decision. Who knows, he might even ask that young fellow today.

With a light heart Doctor Bailey donned his dressing-gown and went, whistling, to the bathroom.

Mrs Bailey, sitting downstairs in the sunny little back room which had once been their dining-room, heard her husband whistling, and smiled. It was good to hear him so cheerful. He was getting stronger daily.

The whistling changed to singing and Mrs Bailey listened attentively.

> 'I think that we shall have
> A very, very lovely day:
> Very, very warm for May.
> Eighty in the shade, they say
> Tra la la –'

With an uprush of spirits Mrs Bailey remembered that night, over forty years before, when she and her husband had gone up to London to see *The Arcadians*. A visit to town was a rare treat in those days and they had enjoyed every minute. She had worn a lilac chiffon frock, she remembered, bought specially for the occasion, and shoes to match with diamanté buckles. What a shining, glorious time of life that had been, when everyone had seemed as young and as happy and hopeful as themselves!

Mrs Bailey set down the shopping list she was engaged upon and looked out into the sunny garden. An early butterfly was abroad, hovering among the velvet wallflowers. They were so very lucky, Mrs Bailey told herself for the thousandth time, to have had their lot cast in such a pleasant place. Just suppose that the doctor's practice had been in one of the great industrial cities! She would have been looking upon a small soot-blackened garden, or – dreadful thought – upon no garden at all, and instead of Lulling's sleepy tranquillity they would have had to face the clamour and killing pace of life in a large town.

She had loved Thrush Green from the first moment that she saw it, and had grown fonder of it as the years passed; but she wished at times that it were easier to get to London, for she missed the theatre and the gay restaurants sorely. Had London really been as wonderful as she remembered it just before the First World War, or was it the natural nostalgia, born of passing years, which made it appear so enchanting in retrospect? People nowadays seemed too busy for gaiety, and, what was worse, appeared to frown upon innocent enjoyment. Life was too dreadfully real and earnest these days, thought Mrs Bailey, and all the young people were middle-aged at twenty. And look at the dreary and revolting books and plays they wrote, about the most brutal and depraved creatures who didn't know their own minds, even when they had them!

The strains of *The Arcadians* floated from the bathroom strongly. Ah, there was fun for you, thought Mrs Bailey! If only people would realize that light-hearted and gay things were not any *less* significant than the violent and brutish, what a step forward it would be. Because a song, a book, a play, a picture, or anything created was gay, it did not necessarily follow that it was trivial. It might well be, mused Mrs Bailey gazing into the moving sunshine with unseeing eyes, a finer thing because it had been fashioned with greater care and artifice; emotion remembered and translated to give pleasure, rather than emotion remembered and evincing only an involuntary and quite hideous howl.

The gurgle of water from the bathroom pipes brought Mrs Bailey back to her duties. She looked again at her shopping list. Should she add liver, and make a casserole of liver and tomatoes for the doctor's lunch? It would be particularly nourishing, and she could bake potatoes in the oven, which he loved. And while the oven was on she might as well make an egg custard, and perhaps she would put in a plum crumble-top to go with it. In which case, Mrs Bailey told herself, it would be sensible to make a really large amount of shortbread mixture so that she could make two tins ready for tea-time.

At this point in her housewifely manoeuvres Mrs Bailey caught sight of a wood pigeon on the lawn, its opal feathers glinting in the sunshine and its coral feet wet with the dew. All Mrs Bailey's good intentions dropped from her.

She would go out into this glorious morning. To salve her conscience she would walk down to Lulling and take her frock to the cleaners, and she would buy some ham and tongue and salad for lunch. It was far too wonderful a morning to spend in a hot kitchen, and against all natural laws on the first of May.

Despite her sixty-odd years, she ran upstairs with the agility of a girl, singing as she went:

> 'Very, very warm for May,
> Eighty in the shade, they say,
> Tra la la –'

And to the doctor, drying himself in the bathroom, she sounded as youthful and happy as when they had first heard that light-hearted ditty so long ago.

Across the green, in the infants' room, Miss Fogerty was trying to teach the words of 'There is a Green Hill Far Away' to an inattentive class.

'But *why* hadn't it got a sitting wall?' persisted Bobby Anderson, his youthful brow criss-crossed with perplexity.

Above the noise of scuffling feet and the scraping of diminutive wooden armchairs Miss Fogerty attempted to explain that 'without' here meant 'outside', but before she could make herself heard, another child tugged at her arm and whispered urgently in her ear.

'But had all the other green hills *got* sitting walls? And why had all the other green hills got sitting walls?' clamoured Bobby Anderson vociferously.

Miss Fogerty clapped her hands for silence, the urgent child was dispatched hurriedly across the playground, the clock on the wall said nine-thirty and Miss Fogerty took her noisy rabble to the door in readiness for a physical training session.

And thus it was that Bobby Anderson was doomed to go through life with the hazy impression that the green hills of the Holy Land have, in the main, walls built round them – walls, moreover, not of the usual standing variety, but of a mysterious type called 'sitting'.

Old Mr Piggott leant over the iron railings of St Andrew's and surveyed the activity of the fair with a morose countenance.

'Goin' to keep fine?' inquired a brawny man, wielding an oil rag over the traction engine. He jerked a massive black thumb at the shimmering view behind him.

Mr Piggott was not to be wooed by honeyed words. He didn't hold with the fair and he didn't care who knew it.

'Can pour down for all I cares,' grunted old Piggott sourly. 'Might drown some o' your durned racket later on!'

''Ere, 'ere! 'Oo's 'urtin' you!' began the oily man truculently. He doubled his great fists, stepped down from the wheel of the engine, and advanced threateningly towards Piggott.

Mr Piggott stepped farther back from the railings, out of arm's reach, but he did it in a carefully casual manner to show that he was not intimidated. From a safe distance he replied.

'Two churchings at six-thirty,' he grumbled, 'and all that blaring racket goin' on outside. 'Tisn't reverent, I tell 'ee!'

And spitting forcefully into the laurel bushes, making a swift, flashing arc over the remains of one Ann Talbot, Virtuous Wife, Devoted Mother, and Esteemed Friend, he retired towards the protection of the church while the going was good.

5. Doctor Lovell's Patients

Young Doctor Lovell was interviewing his last patient in the surgery, and finding it heavy going.

Ella Bembridge was a formidably hearty spinster of fifty-five who had lived, with a wilting friend of much the same age, in a small cottage on the Lulling corner of Thrush Green for the past ten years. It was generally agreed that Ella ruled the roost and that 'poor Miss Dean' had a pretty thin time of it.

Deborah Dean had been nicknamed Dimity, so long ago that the reason for the diminutive had been lost in the mists of time. Now, at the age of fifty-odd, the name was pathetically incongruous, calling up as it did someone fresh, compact, and sparkling, with an air of crisp, but old-world domesticity. Dimity nowadays resembled a washed-out length of grey chiffon, for she was a drooping, attenuated figure with lank, mouse-grey locks and a habit of dressing in shapeless frocks, incorporating unpressed pleats and draped bodices, in depressingly drab shades. Doctor Lovell, who knew both women slightly, suspected that she was brow-beaten by the dominating Ella now before him, and would have liked to try the effects of an iron tonic on Dimity's languid pallor.

He was beginning to wonder just how quickly he could bring Miss Bembridge's monologue to a close. She had come to consult him about a skin complaint affecting her hands and arms.

'I said to Dimity, "Looks like shingles to me. Better go and see the medico, I suppose, for all the good that'll do!"' Here Miss Bembridge laughed roguishly and Doctor Lovell felt positive that she would have dug him painfully in the ribs had not the large desk providentially stood between them. He gave a faint smile in acknowledgement of this witticism, and glanced across the shimmering summer glory of Thrush Green to the Bassetts' house.

Miss Bembridge followed his gaze.

'I thought I might have picked up something from young Paul. Dim and I were there to tea a day or two ago and then the little horror came out in some repulsive rash or other. Not that I'm saying a word against Ruth! Heaven knows she's had enough to put up with, and naturally her mind is full of things other than a child's rash, but I do think it was just the *teeniest* bit careless to invite us there when the child was infectious.'

Doctor Lovell rose impatiently. His lean young face still wore a polite professional smile, but it was a little strained.

'Paul's rash,' he said steadily, 'did not appear until after your tea party. I was called in as soon as it was found.' He felt his dislike of this tough ungainly woman growing minute by minute. She had sat there for almost a quarter of an hour, her massive legs planted squarely apart to display the sturdiest pair of knickers it had ever been Doctor Lovell's misfortune to observe. In shape and durability they had reminded the young man of his father's Norfolk breeches used in the early days of cycling, and the silk shirt and Liberty tie added to the masculine impression.

It was an odd thing, mused Doctor Lovell, that it was Ella who was the artistic one of the pair. Dimity ran the house, it appeared, and it was her slender arms that bore in the coal scuttles, the heavy shopping baskets, and the laden trays, while Ella's powerful hands designed wood-blocks, mixed paint, and stamped the lengths of materials which draped their little cottage.

Occasionally Ella took the train to town with a portfolio of hand-blocked patterns, and usually she returned, blown but jubilant, with a few orders from firms who appreciated her strong shades of olive green, dull beetroot, and dirty yellow madly ensnared in black mesh. It was the paint, Doctor Lovell had surmised, which was causing the present rash on his patient's hands, and he had given her a prescription for a curative lotion and recommended the use of rubber gloves for a few days whilst handling her artistic materials. She had clutched the prescription in a pink spotty hand and had continued to sit stolidly in the chair. Poor Doctor Lovell, who was not yet completely versed in getting rid of lingering patients, resigned himself to another few minutes of Miss Bembridge's comments, delivered in a booming voice that would have been an asset in a shipwreck. He had heard all about Miss Dean's fancied ailments after he had listened to the more pressing ones of Miss Bembridge, and he felt more and more like the unfortunate Wedding Guest who encountered the Ancient Mariner.

From outside came the sweet scent of the old-fashioned pheasant's-eye narcissi which Mrs Bailey massed against the wall beneath the surgery window, and the thump of Ben Curdle's mallet as he rammed home stake after stake. Doctor Lovell longed to be out in the freshness

of Thrush Green's morning, but Miss Bembridge continued re-
morselessly.

'I tell her a good blow is what she needs. Get rid of the cobwebs.
But no, every afternoon she says she must have a rest on her bed!
Unhealthy, I tell her. But then, dear old Dimity always was a one for
imagining she'd every ill under the sun. This back-ache now, she
complains of —'

Doctor Lovell cut her short.

'Too much lifting, I expect. You'll have to see she gets help with
the heavy work. And tell her to call one morning. I'll have a look at
her.'

Miss Bembridge looked startled.

'Oh, there's nothing really wrong! That's what I'm trying to tell
you. Sheer imagination! Now, my hands are quite a different kettle
of fish —'

He had let her run on for one more minute exactly, his eye on the
round silver clock which had been Mrs Bailey's mother's. It was then
that Ella Bembridge had begun the sly comments about Ruth
Bassett's shortcomings as an aunt which had made Doctor Lovell
realize, with sudden passion, that he could not bear to remain in this
wretched woman's presence for one split second more.

The cries of the junior class as they emerged into the stony playground, there to bound breathlessly about as galloping horses,
reminded the doctor that it must now be Miss Watson's physical
training session and therefore almost ten-thirty. He strode resolutely
to the surgery door and held it open.

'I mustn't keep you,' he said firmly, and watched Miss Bembridge
heave her bulk from the armchair, cross the threshold, and depart,
still booming and not a whit perturbed, down the flagged path.

Doctor Lovell returned to the surgery to tidy his papers, shut
drawers and files, and collect his bag.

He closed the surgery door behind him and stood for one minute
savouring the fragrance of the May morning. The air was cool and
sweet. A spiral of blue smoke curled from Mrs Curdle's gaily painted
caravan, the children laughed and called from the school yard, and
on the highest point of Doctor Bailey's roof a fat thrush poured out a
stream of shrill-sweet trills, his speckled breast throbbing with the
ardour of spring.

No less enchanted, young Doctor Lovell went through the gate, his eyes upon the house where Ruth and Paul were to be found, and, crossing the shining grass of Thrush Green, prepared to make the first visit of the day.

Paul was standing on his head on the pillow of his bed. His pyjama-clad legs rested comfortably against the wall, and, apart from a slight discomfort of the neck, Paul was feeling very pleased with himself.

He had remained poised in this upside-down position for a full minute and this was easily the longest time he had managed so far. The room, he observed, really looked much more attractive this way, and the colours were definitely brighter. This fact so interested him that he lowered his legs with a satisfying bounce and looked again at his surroundings the right way up. They certainly looked duller. He adopted his former topsy-turvy position and gazed with fresh rapture at his transfigured world.

An early fly hovered around the central light and Paul wondered how it must feel, swooping aimlessly here and there. Surely the ceiling would seem like the floor to the fly, and he would think it the most ordinary thing in the world to have chairs and dressing-tables and tallboys hanging from the ceiling. Paul pondered about this until the crick in his neck caused him to drop his legs, climb off the bed, and wander to the window.

The school playground was empty and he wondered what his friends were doing under the red-tiled roof of the village school. A pigeon rattled out from the chestnut tree nearby and flew across to the school, its coral claws gripping the ridge of tiles as it landed. Paul caught his breath with envy. To be able to fly – just like that! Could anything be more wonderful than flying from roof to roof, from wood to wood, over fields and rivers, looking down upon Thrush Green and the whole of Lulling's chimney-pots? Why, if that pigeon peeped through a crack by his curling claws he might see all the children at their lessons!

It was a pleasant thought, and Paul turned it about in his mind as busily as his fingers were now twisting and untwisting the bone acorn which hung at the end of the window-blind's cord.

He would like to be a giant bird, decided Paul, as he watched the pigeon. He would be so strong that he could lift the roofs right off all the houses in Lulling and then fly over the town and see everything that was happening inside. Aunt Ruth had read him the story of *The Princess and the Swineherd* and he remembered the magic saucepan which allowed the princess to know just what was cooking in every house in the kingdom. Paul thought his idea was a better one. Much better to see than to smell, decided Paul, twirling the blind cord. He would lift the school roof first.

Down below him he would see the round heads of his friends, black and brown and yellow, with here and there a bright hair ribbon. He would see the long wooden desk-lids and the plaited wicker circle which was the top of the waste-paper basket, and Miss Watson, curiously foreshortened, standing by the blackboard. It must be past ten o'clock Paul reckoned, so that she would be taking a geography lesson on this particular morning. The map would be hanging over the easel, giving out that faint oily smell which always emanated from it as soon as it rolled, released, from its bright pink tapes. From his lofty vantage point he would listen to the far class-room sounds – the scuffling of fidgeting feet, an occasional cough, the lilt of Miss Watson's voice, and the tap-tap of her pointer against the map. He would replace the roof, silently, magically, as easily as slipping the lid back on to a box, and fly over to St Andrew's Church.

What would he find there, Paul wondered, gazing through the bedroom window to the building which loomed large behind the clustering caravans, against the dazzle of the morning sky. Probably only Mr Piggott would be in the church at this time. How small he would look from such a high roof! Paul could see him, in his mind's eye, shuffling slowly up and down the long nave with the pews stretching in neat lines on each side, like rulings on the two pages of an exercise book, one each side of the central fold, with hassocks like little blobs of red ink here and there. He would be no bigger than a black beetle, and so far away that his grumblings and snufflings would be lost in mid-air long before they reached the vasty heights where the lone Paul-bird hovered unseen.

He would swoop next, down and down, to lift Mrs Curdle's painted roof. Paul thrilled at the thought of it. He would touch it very gently, he told himself, for it was as old as it was beautiful, and as awe-inspiring as it was gay. Molly had told him all about Mrs Curdle and gipsies' ways. She would be standing by her glittering stove, cooking hedgehogs, Paul had no doubt. He had once, fearfully, climbed the three steps to Mrs Curdle's caravan and had gazed, fascinated, at the glory within, the half-door had been shut, but by standing on tip-toe he had seen the shelves, the tiny drawers, the cupboards, the gleaming brass and copper, and the rows of vivid painted plates as breathtakingly lovely to the child as the bright birds which he had seen the week before at the Zoo, sitting motionless upon their perches, in a splendour of tropical plumage.

· No one had been in the caravan. Only a clock ticked and a saucepan sizzled, now and then, upon the diminutive stove. Molly had stood beside him and had pointed out one particularly small drawer close by the door. It had a curious brass handle, embossed with leaves and fruit.

'She puts the money in there,' had whispered Molly, in the child's ear.

'What money?' Paul had asked.

'The fortune-telling money. See, she leans over this door and reads your palm and you pays her a bit of silver, sixpence say, or a shilling, and she pops it in this little drawer just beside her. Real handy, isn't it, Paul?'

He had nodded, open-mouthed, and would have liked to have stayed longer, just gazing at the beauties, but Molly had hurried him away.

'And would we have seen a sixpence or a shilling if we'd opened that little drawer?' he had asked her later, as she bathed him.

Molly's eyes had grown as round as an owl's.

'It would have been *stuffed tight* with silver. And gold sovereigns too, most like. And too heavy to move, ten to one.'

Paul had been most impressed, so that now, on his astral travels he looked at the interior of Mrs Curdle's caravan with the eye of reverence. There would be so many things to see that it would be hard to distinguish separate objects. It would be like looking into his own toy kaleidoscope, a glory of shifting colour, winking lights, shimmering reflections, and endless enchanting patterns.

Would Mrs Curdle be there at nearly ten-thirty in the morning? Paul shivered at the thought of seeing her, even if he himself could remain invisible, for Molly had told him that gipsies could cast spells, just as witches did.

She might, thought Paul, pleasurably apprehensive, be making a

little clay doll to stick with pins, so that the real person it was meant
to be would suffer pains. Supposing she *knew* he was watching without having to look up? Supposing the doll was meant to be Paul
Young?

The crick in his neck came back unaccountably and Paul threw
away his idea of being a giant bird. It wasn't as good as he'd first
thought.

He ran to the door and opened it, suddenly in need of company.

The smell of coffee brewing floated from downstairs and the
sound of Aunt Ruth singing happily to herself as she clack-clacked
across the stone-flagged kitchen in her high-heeled sandals.

'Aunt Ruth, Aunt Ruth!' he called urgently. 'Come and watch
me stand on my head!'

The sense of mercies received, to which Ruth had woken that
morning, remained with her as she worked about the house. She was
astonished at this new inner peace, bewildered but grateful for the
strength which had ebbed back to her. It was as though some throbbing wound had miraculously healed overnight and the scab which
had formed over it could be touched without dread. For the first
time Ruth found that she could recall the whole tragic affair dispassionately.

She had become engaged to Stephen Gardiner just over a year ago
amidst general approval. Only her father had looked coolly at the
young man and had remained unaffected by the fair good looks and
charming boyish manner which won Stephen so many friends. He
was employed in a firm of tea and coffee importers and went daily
by Tube train to the City. His income was comfortable enough to
support a young wife, his health was excellent, his family background
very similar to that of the Bassetts, and he was head over heels in love
with his pretty Ruth and there was no reason for her father to refuse
his consent. Nor did he. But he could not whole-heartedly like this
young man. For some reason Stephen's straight blue gaze, his
deferential manner, and his ease with the ladies of the Bassett household aroused a small, nagging distrust in Mr Bassett's heart, and
Ruth was aware of it. She had taxed him once when they were alone
together.

'What is it that you dislike in Stephen?' Her father had answered
her honestly.

'I don't know, my dear, I just don't know. If he's your choice, I'm content to abide by it. But one thing I would like to ask you.'

'And what's that?' she had answered.

'Don't marry too soon. Stephen tells me you'd like to marry this summer. Well, don't, my dear. Leave it until next spring, and I shall feel a lot happier.'

She had smiled and told him that she would talk to Stephen about it.

'We don't want to see you go, you know,' her father had said, smiling back at her.

And so the wedding had been fixed for the first week in March, and the young couple had planned to go away for their honeymoon in Italy just before Easter.

Early in the year they had found a flat in Kensington. It was the top floor of a Victorian house, in a quiet leafy road, shabby, but comfortable, with big rooms and broad windows. It would be convenient for Stephen's journey to the City and for Ruth's office job in Ealing which she proposed to continue after marriage. They spent their evenings painting walls, choosing curtains, planning their furnishings, and dreaming of the future. Ruth never for one moment had any doubts about their happiness together. She moved towards her wedding day with serenity, unmoved by the bustle of activity accompanying her. Her mother's complicated plans for the wedding breakfast, the invitations, the presents, the cake, the organist, the bell-ringers, the bridesmaids, the trousseau, and all the other paraphernalia of a suitable wedding left her unperturbed. All would be well, she knew. Nothing could alter the unshakeable fact that she and Stephen would be married and living together in the adorable flat before the end of March.

Looking back on that halcyon period, after the blow, Ruth became aware of numberless small things which should have warned her of Stephen's waning affections. He was a man who was accustomed to success in every undertaking. He approached his goals directly and with ease, and the long engagement was particularly frustrating to one of his impatient and ambitious calibre. Would all have been well, Ruth sometimes wondered, if they had married earlier, or, as her father had suspected, would Stephen's deflection have occurred in any case, and then had more serious consequences? It was one of those unanswerable problems which were to torture poor Ruth for many sad weeks.

But at the time only one small incident had ruffled her calm. Stephen had been offered a position in the firm which made it necessary to take charge of their office in Brazil for two or perhaps three years. He had told her this news one rainy spring evening as they sat on the floor of the empty dining-room at the flat, painting the skirting board. Ruth had not even bothered to look up from her work.

'It's out of the question, of course,' she had said, drawing her brush carefully along the wood.

'It's promotion, and we could do with it,' Stephen had answered, so shortly, that she had put down her brush and gazed at him. His cheek twitched with a tense muscle and she realized, with a sharp stabbing pain, that he had looked strained and tired for some time. She spoke gently.

'If you honestly think we should –' she had begun.

'What's there to stay for?' he had answered.

'Why, this!' she had responded, waving her hand at the new paint around them.

'Four frowsty rooms in a scruffy little backwater,' he had scoffed. ' "Caged in Kensington." What a title for a domestic tragedy!'

Perplexed and hurt, Ruth had tried to answer him. She had told him that if he felt like that then they would certainly go to Brazil together. She made him promise to see his doctor about the headaches that had been plaguing him. She was positive that he needed glasses. That direct, intense gaze, which fluttered so many hearts, might well be due to short sight and nothing more glamorous, but he had a great aversion to wearing spectacles and brushed away her suggestions of a visit to the oculist.

Later, he had comforted her, called himself a brute, a selfish pig, promised her that all would be well when they were married, and had begged her to forget all about Brazil. They would be far better off as they were for the first year or two of their married life, and other opportunities would crop up he knew.

But Ruth was not entirely comforted, and although she seemed as tranquil as before, she watched Stephen secretly, conscious that he was working long hours under strain. But it was a transitory malaise, she felt certain, which would pass away as soon as they were married.

One morning, four days before the wedding, Ruth's dress arrived, a misty white armful of chiffon and lace, which emerged from a cocoon of rustling tissue paper. The post had arrived at the same time and her father sat at the breakfast table, gazing fixedly at a short note written in Stephen Gardiner's hand. He rose from the table and looked across at his daughter and his wife.

Ruth was pirouetting about the room, the fragile frock swirling as she held it against her. Mrs Bassett's face was alight with wonderment.

'My dear,' said Mr Bassett, in a husky voice, 'leave that child to her own devices for a minute and come and help me on with my coat.'

The two went into the hall and Mr Bassett closed the door. Then he handed the note to his wife. Her face crumpled as she read, but she made no sound. The letter bore the address of a Swiss hotel and began without preamble.

> I've made a hopeless mess of everything. Tell Ruth it's no use going on with the wedding and better to part now. She'll get a letter by the next post, but tell her not to think too badly of me. She's always been too good for me in any case. Forgive me if you can.
>
> Stephen

'He's ill. He's not himself,' whispered Mrs Bassett at last, raising tear-filled eyes. Her husband looked grim.

'I'll try and book an air passage today,' said Mr Bassett, 'to see the fellow.'

'And Ruth?' faltered his wife.

'Break it to her before the afternoon post arrives,' answered Mr Bassett, transferring the burden with customary male ability. 'You'll do it better than I can. I'll see her when I get back.'

He kissed his wife swiftly, crammed the letter in his pocket, and escaped through the front door.

Ruth had received the news later that morning with amazing tranquillity. Her reaction had been the same as her mother's. Stephen was not himself. This sudden flight, the agitated note, the panic before the ceremony, were all symptoms of intolerable strain. The appalling thought that Stephen might really leave her and that the wedding might never take place hardly entered her head. The plans were made, the guests invited, the beds in the house were already made up awaiting elderly aunts from Cheltenham, a Scottish cousin, and a school friend from Holland. The wedding was as inevitable to Ruth as the approach of dawn, and though her heart was wrung with pity for Stephen, she felt none for herself. There was no need.

It was she who calmed her mother that day. She read her letter from Stephen, which arrived that afternoon, in her bedroom, with the white wedding dress at her side. It added little more to the one her father had received, except that the post in Brazil was mentioned. He urged her to forget him, to forgive him, to waste no time in regrets. Better by far to part now, was the gist of the distracted communication, than to find out their mistake too late.

Ruth felt that she should go at once to Switzerland to see Stephen, but her mother insisted that she should await her father's return the next day. Both women slept little that night. Mrs Bassett knew instinctively that Stephen would never be persuaded to return. Besides her grief on Ruth's account her racked mind agitated itself with plans for the cancellation of the ceremony. At three o'clock she rose and paced distractedly about the quiet house, and Ruth joined her, equally distraught, but not for herself. She grieved for her unhappy lover, her agitated mother, and her father's journeyings. She longed for his return which she was positive would bring good news, and possibly Stephen himself.

And so the blow for Ruth was all the more annihilating. When her father returned, grey-faced and weary, to tell her that there was no hope at all of a reconciliation, that Stephen had already accepted the post in Brazil and was to fly out on the day that was to have been his wedding day, and that he never wished to see Ruth again, the girl collapsed. Even then the tears refused to come. She lay in bed, white and small, dark eyes roving restlessly about her room, unable to eat or speak, while the dreadful news was dispatched to the invited guests, friends, neighbours, caterers, and all.

When she was fit to travel her father had driven her down to stay with her sister Joan, still numb with shock, a woebegone little ghost.

And there, throughout the slowly unfolding spring, amid the kindly scents and sounds of Thrush Green, her frozen heart thawed again.

The sound of her nephew calling from upstairs roused Ruth from her musings. She left the coffee brewing and ran upstairs to see the little boy, pausing at the landing window to look at the golden glory outside.

The horse chestnut trees were beginning to break, their palmate leaves looking like tiny green hands bursting from sticky brown gloves. She could see the children running about in the playground, their hair flying in the wind, their arms and legs gleaming like satin in the morning sunshine.

Miss Bembridge was coming from Doctor Bailey's house and Ruth watched her sturdy figure stump along the road to the cottage on the corner. The surgery door opened again and young Doctor Lovell stood for a moment upon the threshold, before setting off across Thrush Green. Ruth watched his advancing figure with growing comfort.

'Paul!' she called, hurrying across to the bedroom. 'Doctor's coming!'

Paul was scrambling into his tousled bed as she opened his door. He looked up at her, open-mouthed.

'Aunt Ruth,' he said in astonishment, 'your eyes are shining.'

6. Coffee at 'The Fuchsia Bush'

Mrs Bailey was enjoying a cup of coffee in 'The Fuchsia Bush', Lulling's rendezvous for the ladies of that small town. She had left the doctor in the garden, happily slicing the edges of the flower beds with a formidably sharp new edgecutter, and more full of zest than she had seen him for many weeks.

She had tripped lightfoot down from Thrush Green, rejoicing in the sparkling morning and the exhilarating sounds of the fair's preparations. But now, with the shopping safely in her basket, she was quite pleased to sit alone, watching the inhabitants of Lulling pass by on their lawful occasions, before facing the long uphill pull to her house.

'The Fuchsia Bush' prided itself on its appearance. Its architect had done his best to make a building which would harmonize with the surrounding Cotswold stone and yet suggest the 'cosy-chintzes-within' atmosphere which his clients had insisted upon. An enormous bow window with several of its panes devoted to a bottle-glass effect, kept his clients happy, and later their customers, for it was generally accepted in Lulling that the appearance of one's friends gazing through the bottle-glass panes was a never-to-be-forgotten experience. Like gigantic carp they goggled and gulped and when embellished with hats, or, better still, spectacles, even the handsomest of Lulling's inhabitants could strike fear and awe into the beholder's marrow.

Mrs Bailey stirred her coffee slowly and read the new placard outside the chapel opposite. It said:

THE WAGES OF SIN IS DEATH

which Mrs Bailey found more grammatically irritating than thought-provoking. She suddenly remembered that, years ago, she had heard of a firm that had written across its delivery van:

MAYS WAYS PAYS ALWAYS

'And at least', thought Mrs Bailey, snatching comfort where she could, 'I was never forced to see that!' She turned her attention to the interior of 'The Fuchsia Bush'.

Apart from two elderly men in mufflers, who sipped their coffee noisily and discussed chess, Mrs Bailey was the only customer. Two girls, in mauve overalls with cherry-coloured cuffs and collars, did their best to emulate fuchsia flowers, and certainly drooped silently against the grey walls quite successfully. A stack of mauve- and cherry-striped boxes stood on the glass counter in readiness to hold the excellent home-made cakes which were already cooling in the window, adding their fragrance to that of the coffee. A beam of sunlight fell suddenly upon Mrs Bailey's hand, the first real warmth for months, she thought delightedly, and her spirits rose at this token of the summer to come.

What fun Lulling was, she told herself for the thousandth time! She looked affectionately at the old men, the lackadaisical waitresses, the chapel notice, the leisurely moving few people walking outside on the wide pavement beneath the whispering lime trees. I suppose

I'm so fond of it because I'm really part of it, she mused to herself. 'Attached to it,' she added, echoing Eeyore as he mourned his lost tail; for Mrs Bailey's mind was a rag-bag of snippets, some of which she drew out for herself to admire and delight in, and some of which fell out of their own accord, gay unconsidered trifles which she had long forgotten, as in the present case, but which afforded her infinite joy when they reappeared.

The door swung open and interrupted Mrs Bailey's ponderings. Ella Bembridge blew in, her felt hat jammed low over her brow, followed by Dimity Dean bearing a laden basket. The room, which had seemed so large and peaceful, suddenly shrank to half its size and became a battleground of conflicting noises as Ella Bembridge thrust her way between wheel-backed chairs, booming cheerful greetings. It was at times like this that Mrs Bailey had the feeling that she had at last grasped Einstein's theory of relativity, but it was always a fleeting glimpse of Olympian clarity, and almost at once the clouds would close over that bright vision and Mrs Bailey would realize that she was still in her usual woolly-minded world of three dimensions.

'Anyone with you? Coming, I mean?' shouted Ella.

'No. No one,' responded Mrs Bailey, lifting her basket from a chair and smiling at Dimity who collapsed upon it gratefully.

'Just been to get –' began Dimity in an exhausted whisper.

'My prescription made up,' roared Ella.

'The fish,' added Dimity.

'For my rash,' boomed Ella.

'For lunch,' finished Dimity.

Mrs Bailey was quite used to this dual form of conversation and nodded politely.

'Think that young Lovell knows what he's up to?' asked Ella, planting her sturdy brogues well apart and affording the assembled company an unlovely view of the formidable underclothes which had offended Doctor Lovell earlier that morning.

'I'm sure he does,' answered Mrs Bailey equably. She wondered how many more questions Ella would ask.

'How's your husband? Taking a partner yet?' went on Miss Bembridge, feeling in her jacket pocket.

'Much better,' said Mrs Bailey, answering the first, and ignoring the second question. Ella produced a worn tobacco tin, undid it, took out a cigarette paper from a small folder, pinched up a vicious-looking dollop of black tobacco from the depths of the tin, and began to roll a very untidy cigarette.

'Oh, do let me do it for you, darling,' said Miss Dean, leaning forward eagerly.

'Don't fuss so, Dim,' said her friend brusquely, raising the limp tube to her mouth and licking the edge of the paper with a thick wet tongue. She lit the straggling tobacco which cascaded from one end, inhaled strongly, and blew two terrifying blasts down her nostrils. Mrs Bailey was reminded of the rocking-horse which had lived in her nursery sixty years earlier, and would have liked the leisure to recall its half-forgotten beauties, the dappled flanks, the scarlet harness bright with gilded studs, and its worn hospitable saddle. But no one mused in Ella's company.

'Hell of a time that girl takes getting the coffee,' said she, in far too carrying a voice for Mrs Bailey's peace of mind. One of the drooping fuchsias detached herself from the wall and drifted towards the kitchen.

'We oughtn't to be too long –' began Dimity timidly, hauling up a watch on a long silver chain from the recesses of her bodice.

'Doesn't matter if we fry it!' responded her friend. Dimity looked tearful.

'But you know it doesn't –'

'Agree with me?' boomed Miss Bembridge menacingly. 'Of course it does! Fried fish is the only way to eat the stuff.'

'But the doctor said only this morning that you shouldn't touch fried food, darling, with that rash. It's for your own –'

Ella broke in mercilessly, tapping her cigarette ash forcefully into Mrs Bailey's saucer.

'My own good! I know, I know! Well, I've said we'll have it in parsley sauce, much as I detest it, so let's forget it.'

Dimity turned apologetically to Mrs Bailey.

'I do feel fish is so much more wholesome in a mild white sauce. So pure and nourishing, and so light too. But it takes longer to cook of course. I said to Ella this morning, "A little light fish, or perhaps a boiled egg, while you've got that rash, will be the most *wholesome* thing you can have."'

Mrs Bailey smiled and nodded and thought of Mr Woodhouse, her favourite Emma's father, who also recommended boiled eggs. 'An egg boiled very soft is not unwholesome. Mrs Bates, let me propose your venturing on one of these eggs.' And she wondered, looking at Dimity's pathetic anxiety, if she might be driven by it to go even further and suggest 'a small basin of thin gruel', which was all that Mr Woodhouse could honestly recommend, if Miss Bembridge's rash persisted. For the sake of the friends' domestic harmony Mrs Bailey prayed that Doctor Lovell's prescription would be speedily successful.

It was at this moment that Dotty Harmer fumbled her way into 'The Fuchsia Bush'. Her steel spectacles were awry, her woollen stockings lay, as always, in wrinkles round her chicken-thin legs, and her hair sprouted at all angles beneath a speckled grey chip-straw hat.

The less languid of the attendants went forward to greet her.

'Just one of your small stone-milled loaves, please,' murmured Dotty, peering into the glass cabinet that held the loaves.

The girl replied with considerable satisfaction, that all the small ones had been sold, but there was most providentially, just one large one left. This threw Dotty into the greatest agitation. She dumped her string bag on the floor, thrust her hat farther back upon her head, and began to pour out her troubles.

'But I can't possibly use a large loaf! Living alone as I do a small one lasts me three days at least, and even if I make rusks of the last bit for the animals it is really more than I can manage. And in any case, now that the weather has turned warm I shan't need to light the stove and so there will be no means of making the rusks!'

The girl suggested a small white loaf. Dotty's agitation was now tinged with horror.

'A *white* loaf?' squeaked Dotty, with such repugnance, that one might reasonably have supposed that she had been offered bread made from fine-ground human bones. 'You should know by now my feelings about *white* bread. It never, never appears in my house!'

'Dotty!' bawled Miss Bembridge, at this point, in a voice that set the crockery rattling. 'Get them to cut it in half!'

The girl cast Ella a look so deadly that it was a wonder that Miss Bembridge's ample form was not shrivelled to a small dead leaf. Dotty's face, however, was alight with relief.

'Dear Ella! How sensible! Yes, of course,' she said, turning to the assistant, 'just cut the large wholemeal one in half.'

The girl flounced off to the kitchen, lips compressed, and returned

with a bread board and knife. She cut the loaf in two and held the
board out for Dotty's inspection.

'Oh, dear,' said Dotty, her face clouding again, 'I wonder if I
really need half. It's quite a large amount, isn't it? I mean, for one
person?' She peered anxiously at the girl's face for some help, but
received none.

After some tut-tutting she lifted first one piece of bread to the
light, and then the other. She then sniffed at each, tasted a crumb or
two which had fallen on to the board, and began to shake her head
doubtfully.

Mrs Bailey became conscious that the bread knife still remained
within the grip of the silent waitress, and felt that the time had come
to intervene.

'There are always the birds, Dotty dear,' she pointed out. 'Take
the crustier half and come and have coffee.'

Dotty nodded and smiled. The girl flung one half into a paper bag
and handed the bread board to her colleague with a long-suffering
look. The knife, Mrs Bailey was relieved to see, she set aside on a
shelf, while she stood watching Dotty fumble among a dozen com-
partments of a large black purse for the money. Dotty's fingers,
stained with many a herb, scrabbled first here, then there, and the
girl's foot began to tap ominously on the shining linoleum.

At last Dotty raised a damp worried gaze from her labours and said:
'I appear to have only a coat button, my door key, and an Irish
sixpence. Unless,' she added, drawing forth a very crumpled piece of
paper, 'you can change a five-pound note!'

Ben Curdle, stripped to the waist in the morning sunshine, sat
on the grass with his back propped against one wheel of his caravan
and a bottle of beer from 'The Two Pheasants' propped between
his knees.

He had been hard at work now for over four hours. The main
stands were all erected and Ben had just finished helping his cousin,
Sam, to hitch the swing-boats into place. It was heavy work, for the
boats were old and cumbersome though they looked gay enough, he
admitted, with the fresh paint they had put on during the winter. If
he had his way, thought Ben, he'd scrap them and get some of those
new light ones. Just as safe and not so back-breaking to heave about.
But with Gran as she was, what was the good of suggesting it?

He watched his cousin Sam who was sitting on the steps of his caravan with his flashy young wife. Ben had never liked either of them. He'd never trusted Sam since he had found him boasting one day of some shirts which he had stolen from a line in some cottage garden. It was not the sort of thing the Curdles did. If his old Gran had ever heard about it Sam would have been given his marching orders, Ben knew. The incident had occurred many years before and Ben had made it pretty plain just what he thought of such goings-on, putting up with the tauntings of the older man in dour silence.

A few months later Sam had married. Mrs Curdle did not approve of the match. The girl, she told Sam bluntly, 'had been anyone's' in the small Thames-side town from which he had brought her, but providing she buckled-to and worked her way with the fair old Mrs Curdle was agreeable to her joining them. The girl, Bella, had had the sense to keep out of the old lady's way as far as was possible, but she deeply resented the matriarch's caustic remarks about her thatch of hair, as yellow and brittle as straw from frequent dousings with peroxide, and the comments on her wardrobe to which she gave considerable thought and expenditure. Sam bore the brunt of his wife's resentment in the privacy of their small caravan, and he often thought sadly to himself that although she was a real smart bit her tongue could fair flay a man. Three children had been born to them, whining and wet-nosed, but all three dressed extravagantly in the bright and shiny satins to which their mother was addicted.

Ben watched the family now, and wondered, not for the first time, just how Sam managed to dress all that lot. There was fat old Bella in that red frock – a new one bought in the last town, he knew. And she had flaunted a watch under his nose last week that she'd told him Sam had bought for her. She'd said he'd been lucky with the horses, but you didn't have to be a wizard to know that horses let you down more often than they came home, mused young Ben.

He drained his bottle, wiped his mouth on the back of his hand, and leant forward upon the warm comfort of his knees under their black corduroy covering. He felt pretty sure that Sam was getting money dishonestly, and he could guess where. He knew, as did all the great Curdle family, exactly how much each of them received each week, for on Friday night the ritual of paying out took place.

The heads of each family and the single members, such as Ben, who were still under age and under Mrs Curdle's direct protection, assembled in the old lady's caravan as soon as the lights of the fair had gone out. All the money from that night's stand was put into a great brass bowl ready to be transferred to a battered attaché case which was kept at the foot of Mrs Curdle's mattress and was the Curdle Bank. Meanwhile the old lady had counted the week's takings already in the case and had allotted them with scrupulous justice to all concerned. Those with children had more, naturally, than those without. Mrs Curdle would tell the company how much had been earned and would then call out each name in turn. The piles of money stood stacked before her on a small card-table, which she had used to support her crystal in earlier days. The wages varied, of course, from week to week, according to the size of the town which the fair was visiting, the weather, rival attractions, accidents to gear, and so on. But each man knew that the fierce old lady whose hawk-gaze terrified him was absolutely, ferociously, searingly honest, and if the handful of coins was pitifully small, as sometimes it was, without any doubt he had his right and proper share. There had been one or two members of the family who had demurred at this despotism in their time. They had been given their choice – to go or to stay willingly. Two had gone, and no one had ever heard of their fortunes, nor had Mrs Curdle made any inquiries about them. They had left the Curdle family, therefore Mrs Curdle had no further interest in them. The others elected to stay, and they spoke no more heresy.

There were two ways, Ben knew, in which Sam could help himself to money. In the first place he could secrete some from his own takings and pay in the rest after each day's work. This was not as easy as it seemed, for many eyes were about, the helpers on his stand would soon become suspicious, and, in any case, the old lady, after years of experience, had a fairly shrewd idea of the amount to be expected. There was a second way. Mrs Curdle had become increasingly careless of late in the disposal of the money. She was ill, she was old, she was habitually tired, and to heave up the mattress to put away odd sums of money in the case was becoming a burden. Quite often, Ben knew, she thrust it into the little drawer by the side of the half-door, or into a pewter tea-pot which stood on the mantelpiece beside the photograph of his dead father. Usually she roused herself to transfer it to the case, but Ben had seen, only the week before, notes and silver stuffed into the narrow dresser drawer, which hitherto had only held a shilling or two for a passing beggar or for the purchase of a loaf or a bottle of milk from some travelling tradesman that the caravans might meet in the lanes.

The family came and went to its head's caravan a dozen times a day, and it would be the easiest thing in the world to abstract money from the drawer in Mrs Curdle's absence. Sam made bets almost daily, and lately they had been heavier, Ben knew.

St Andrew's Church chimed the half-hour and Ben stirred himself. Half past eleven already! He leapt to his feet, stretching his arms luxuriously above his head. His corduroy trousers slipped, cool and comfortable, round his bare waist and the light breeze played across his naked shoulders refreshingly.

He thought, with sudden joy, of his Molly. By half past one he hoped to see her again. As soon as he had had his dinner with Gran, he would set off alone, through Lulling Woods to 'The Drovers' Arms'. She would be in the bar then, and with any luck would be free from two o'clock. He could hardly believe his good fortune in finding her again.

He became conscious that Sam was calling to him to give a hand with the bell-tent which housed the small menagerie. Another hour's hard work would see the fair ready and waiting for the evening's fun. And then, Ben told himself, he had two more jobs ahead. To find Molly – that was the first and all-important one; and to keep a sharp eye on the movements of his cousin Sam to confirm his suspicions.

'Coming, Sam!' he called, and went methodically about the first of the tasks ahead.

After coffee the four ladies had returned together up the hill from Lulling. It was soon after twelve as they stood making their farewells on the corner of Thrush Green near the church. The sun was now overhead in a cloudless sky of powdery blue. The rooks were wheeling above the clump of elm trees by the path which led to Dotty Harmer's cottage, the dew had vanished from the grass, and the shadows of the trees in the horse-chestnut avenue lay foreshortened, like dark pools, at the foot of the trunks. Later they would creep, longer and longer, across the grass until they almost reached the edge of the green opposite Doctor Bailey's house, and then, Mrs Bailey knew from many years' experience, that meant that it was almost time for the music of the fair to begin.

The heat shimmered above the caravans and along the white road to Nod and Nidden. The school-children were skipping and darting home to their dinners.

Dotty Harmer, her half-loaf clutched against her chest and the bulging string bag dangling at her side, was the first to leave the group and vanish down the narrow passage between the Piggotts' cottage and 'The Two Pheasants'.

'And I wonder what *her* lunch is!' said Miss Bembridge. 'Fried frogs with dandelion sauce, I expect. Poor old Dotty!'

The mention of lunch threw Dimity Dean into extreme agitation.

'We simply *must* fly,' she said to Mrs Bailey. Her watery eyes, screwed up against the sunshine, turned to St Andrew's clock, which gave her small comfort.

'Darling,' she squeaked, in horror. 'Look, ten past twelve and the fish still to be done!' She tugged ineffectually at Ella Bembridge's bolster-like arm. So might a fluttering fledgling have attempted to pull off a branch.

Miss Bembridge gave a sigh that rustled the tissue paper over the lettuce in Mrs Bailey's basket.

'Needs must, I suppose, when the devil drives!' she boomed, and the two friends set off to their cottage leaving Mrs Bailey to cross the grass to her own home.

A piquant smell of fried pork chops and onions wafted from Mrs Curdle's caravan as the doctor's wife passed nearby. The old lady was preparing lunch for herself and for Ben. Mrs Bailey thought wryly of the bouquet which no doubt already lay in the matriarch's home, awaiting its bestowal, and she remembered, with a pang, that this might well be the last time that she would smell Mrs Curdle's midday meal and receive a bunch of flowers, garish and gaudy but made with love and in a spirit of steadfast gratitude, from those gnarled dusky hands.

Mrs Bailey paused with her hand on her gate and looked back at the morning glory of Thrush Green. Would it ever look like this again on the first day of May, so blue, so golden, so breathtakingly innocent?

She looked with affection at the cheerful bustle of the little fair-ground, the tents, the flapping canvas, the blue smoke spiralling from a camp fire, and the brightly clad fair folk moving among it all. They were as gay as butterflies, thought Mrs Bailey, and as ephemeral. By tomorrow the fair would be over, and only a ring of cold ashes and the ruts made by wooden wheels would remind them of their visitors. The mellow enduring houses, which sat like sunning cats, four-square and tranquil, around the wide expanse of Thrush Green would have it to themselves again after tonight's brief bonfire-blaze of glory.

'A pity!' said Mrs Bailey, with a sigh, looking across at Mrs Curdle's caravan, blooming like some gay transient flower against the grey background of St Andrew's. 'We've weathered a lot together.'

PART TWO

AFTERNOON

———

7. Noonday Heat

Thrush Green drowsed under the growing heat of the midday sun. It was that somnolent time, soon after one o'clock, when everything lay hushed. In cottage kitchens, where the midday dinner had been served an hour before, the plates had been washed and returned to their shelves, the tables had been scrubbed, the checked cloths spread upon them, and the potted plants placed to the best advantage. After the hubbub of the morning the kitchens showed their peaceful afternoon faces, while their owners dozed in the armchairs by the hob or settled down to enjoy a quiet cup of tea.

The steady ticking of a clock, the sizzle of a kettle, or the rustle of a slowly read newspaper were the only sounds to be heard in that tranquil haven of time between the two tides of morning and afternoon.

But in the big sunny kitchen at the Bassetts' Ruth and Paul had only just finished their meal. Much to Paul's joy Doctor Lovell had said that he could get up, and providing that he had an hour's rest later in the day he could go to the fair for a short while.

'And you'll be fit for school on Monday,' he had pronounced. Paul, young enough still to dote on this institution, was energetic in his thanks.

He had eaten well, demolishing a plate of cherries, bottled earlier by his mother, and now rattled on gaily as he counted his stones.

Ruth sat beside him still in a state of bemusement at the inner peace which now engulfed her. Her gaze was fixed upon the sunlit garden, and she hardly heard the little boy.

'Mummy says girls count their stones to see who they'll marry, and boys count to see what they'll be,' chattered Paul busily. 'So I'll tell you what I'm going to be.'

He counted slowly, nodding his way through the rhyme:

> Tinker, tailor, soldier, sailor,
> Rich man, poor man, beggar man, thief,
> Tinker, tailor—'

He paused and sighed heavily.

'A tailor, Aunt Ruth! Hear that? A tailor! I wouldn't want to be a tailor, would you?'

Ruth roused herself.

'I'll tell you another rhyme,' she said, taking the spoon from her nephew. She leant over the plate and recited slowly:

> 'Soldier bold, sailor true,
> Skilled physician, Cambridge blue,
> Titled noble, squire hale,
> Portly rector, curate pale.
> Soldier bold, sailor true—'

'How's that?' she inquired, looking at him.

'Sailor true,' Paul nodded with immense satisfaction. 'Much better. I'd like that!'

Ruth put down the spoon and was about to collect the plates but Paul stopped her.

'Your turn, Aunt Ruth. I'll see who you're going to marry. Say it with me.'

Together they chanted slowly, pushing the wine-coloured stones along the rim of the blue and white plates.

> 'Soldier bold, sailor true,
> Skilled physician, Cambridge blue,
> Titled noble, squire hale,
> Portly rector, curate pale,
> Soldier bold, sailor true,
> Skilled physician—'

Ruth put down the spoon hastily as she came to the last of the stones.

'What's that?' inquired Paul.

'A doctor,' said Ruth, brushing the stones into one plate.

'Like Doctor Lovell?' asked the child.

'Or Doctor Bailey,' said Ruth evenly. She rose and took the plates to the sink.

'He's too old,' objected Paul, 'and Mrs Bailey might not want you. But Doctor Lovell would do.'

'If I'd had one less cherry, Paul, I might have married you,' said Ruth, smiling at him. But the child was not to be put off his train of thought so easily, Ruth noticed wryly.

'Doctor Lovell's very nice,' persisted the child. 'Would you marry him?'

'Of course not!'

'Why not?'

'For one thing he hasn't asked me,' Ruth said lightly. 'Now, would you like to play in the garden while I wash up?'

The child ignored this suggestion and fixed his remorseless blue gaze upon his aunt. Ruth could not help feeling like a mother bird who has trailed a wing before some particularly dogged hunter only to find her wiles are of no avail.

'But if he did!' insisted Paul, clinging to the side of the sink, and staring unblinkingly at his victim. 'The stones *said* a skilled fizzun and that probably means Doctor Lovell. And he is a real *nice* man. You *ought* to marry him if the stones say you ought. It's what —'

Ruth cut him short impatiently.

'Oh, don't fuss so, Paul! It's only a rhyme and doesn't mean a thing. Out you go now, while I wash up.'

The boy disengaged himself slowly. It was obvious that his thoughts were wholly of the signs and portents of the cherry stones, but, child-like, he turned the situation to his own advantage.

'Can I go and see Bobby Anderson, before he goes into school?'

Ruth hesitated. She did not like the child to roam Thrush Green unaccompanied, but he could not come to much harm if he were within sight of the house, and she felt the need of a few minutes' solitude to collect her wits. The child, watching her, guessed her thoughts, but felt that all would fall out as he wished.

'Just for a little while then. But come back when the school bell goes at a quarter to two.'

'Can I show him the postcard Mummy sent?' This was a fascinating picture of a cat with large glass eyes which rolled about in the most enchanting manner, and had given the bed-bound Paul immense joy.

'Of course you can,' said his aunt. 'But put on your linen hat, and don't forget to keep in sight of the house. I may want you before a quarter to two.'

The child rushed from the kitchen and Ruth heard him bounding up the stairs in search of his postcard.

'And let's hope it puts other ideas out of his head,' muttered his aunt aloud. But, as she disposed of the cherry stones which had caused so much discussion, she could not help but notice that the 'other ideas' continued to flicker and dance in her own mind like the warm sunbeams that sparkled and twinkled about her as she splashed water into the bowl.

Paul, clutching his postcard and crowned, obediently, with his linen hat, ran down the path to the green outside.

The hush which enveloped Thrush Green threw its spell over the excited little boy and his pace slowed as soon as he emerged from his own garden. There was no breeze now. The bright caravans, the trees, the daisy-spangled grass of Thrush Green lay, like a painted back-cloth, motionless and unreal. It was an enchanted world, doubly arresting to the child who had been housebound for several days.

He looked, with new wonder, at the blossoming cherry tree, which overhung the low stone wall of the next-door garden. For the first time he noticed, with a thrill of joy, the delicate white flowers suspended by thread-like stalks to the black tracery of the boughs. Those threads, he realized suddenly, would dangle cherries later where the flowers now danced, and he would be able to hang them over his ears and waggle his head gently from side to side for the pleasure of feeling the firm glossy berries nudging his cheek. It was a moment of poignant discovery for young Paul, and he felt a thrill of pride as he realized that he knew now exactly how the cherries came to be. In future they would be doubly beautiful, for he would remember the glory of that pendant snow even as he sensuously enjoyed the feel of the fruit against his face and the cool freshness in his mouth as he bit it.

He found Bobby Anderson lying on his stomach, a daisy stalk between his lips and legs waving idly, for even this vociferous youngster had succumbed to the spell of midday sloth.

'Smashing!' was his verdict on the treasured postcard.

Paul glowed in the sunshine of his hero's approbation.

'You comin' in then?' asked Bobby, nodding towards the school.

'Monday, not now,' answered Paul casually. It was wonderful to be able to dismiss school so airily.

'Bet you've been sucking up to ol' Doctor Whatsit,' grumbled Bobby enviously. Paul was stung.

'No, I didn't then,' he protested indignantly, 'but I've got to have a rest this afternoon.'

Bobby Anderson contorted his features into a hideous travesty of a crying baby.

' "Got to have a rest," ' he mimicked, in a maddening, mewing squeak. 'You and your rest!' he continued, in normal tones of extreme scorn. 'In your soppy ol' hat!' he added, tipping it off with an adroit blow.

Paul was about to join battle inflamed by this last insult, but Miss Watson appeared in the school doorway, and instantly Bobby fled to her across the playground, crying urgently as he went:

'Can I ring the bell, miss? Miss, miss, please let me!'

Paul watched his friend and tormentor vanish into the porch. Two seconds later the bell above the steep-pitched roof gave out its cracked message, and Paul knew that Bobby's sturdy frame was swinging lustily on the end of the bell-rope hidden within.

Nearly a quarter to two already, and he hadn't done half the things he had intended, thought Paul mournfully. He turned his back upon the school and looked, with some awe, upon Mrs Curdle's distant caravan. As he watched, he saw the old lady emerge, carrying a bucket. There was an arc of flashing water as she tossed its contents into the sunshine, and then she stood motionless, a massive, majestic figure against the dazzling sky.

Paul saw that she was watching somebody who was crossing the grass towards him. As the figure approached him Paul recognized it joyfully. It was Ben – his Molly's Ben – and he was waving to him!

'How do, Paul?' asked the young man, smiling down at the little boy.

'Very well, thank you,' responded Paul, flushing at this unexpected honour.

'Bet you don't remember me,' said Ben. His voice held a slight query and he seemed unaccountably anxious. Paul hastily reassured him.

' 'Course I do. You're Ben Curdle and you took my Molly to the fair last time.'

Ben laughed, and Paul noticed again how crinkly his eyes were. No wonder Molly had missed him. She had said only a little to Paul, about the young man, as they took their excursions, but it had been enough for the child to realize that she had taken an uncommon liking to this fleeting visitor.

'Are you going to see Molly?' inquired Paul. Ben bent down to pick a stalk of grass and his face was red when he straightened up.

'Ah, maybe!' he answered, with carefully assumed indifference. Such cavalier behaviour annoyed young Paul.

'Well, you *did ought*!' he maintained stoutly. 'You never wrote, and you never wrote, and Molly looked out for a letter for *weeks and weeks*. She thought you were real mean, not writing.'

Ben's eyes widened at this vehement attack, but he answered equably enough.

'I'll look her up, Paul. Don't you fret.' He dusted down his black corduroys, and gave a sudden swift grin at the boy.

'Comin' to the fair tonight?' he asked.

'Yes, rather!' said the boy warmly.

'See you then,' nodded Ben. He sketched a salute and set off, with long rapid strides towards the lane which led to Lulling Woods, leaving Paul standing gazing after him.

The child watched until the energetic black legs, the dazzling white shirt, and the bright neckerchief vanished between 'The Two Pheasants' and the Piggotts' cottage.

He's got his best clothes on, thought young Paul sagaciously. And he's going the right way!

And, savouring these very satisfactory portents, he returned slowly to his gate.

Ben's heart was light as he swung along through the meadows that lay before the heights of Lulling Woods. In the sunshine the buttercups were opening fast, interlacing their gold with the earlier silver of the daisies. For the sheer joy of it young Ben left the white path and trod a parallel one through the gilded grass, watching his black shoes turn yellow with the fallen pollen.

The field fell gently downhill to his left, tipping its little, secret, underground streams towards the River Pleshy, a mile distant. Dotty Harmer's cottage was the only house to be seen here, basking among the buttercups like a warmly golden cat.

Dotty herself was in the garden, a straw hat of gigantic proportions crowning her untidy thatch of hair. She waved to the young man and called out something which he could not catch.

He waved back civilly.

'Nice day, ma'am,' he shouted, for good measure.

'Rum ol' trout,' he added to himself, noting her eccentric appearance. 'Not quite the ticket I should think. Or else gentry.'

He forgot her as soon as the cottage was behind him. A bend in the path brought him to a stile at the entrance to Lulling Woods. It was nearly a mile of steep climbing, he knew, before he would emerge on to the open heathland where 'The Drovers' Arms' stood.

His spirits were buoyant. So she'd missed him! She hadn't forgotten him! Everything pointed to happiness. He forged up the narrow path, slippery with a myriad pine needles, as though his feet were winged.

It was very cool and quiet in the woods after the bland sunshine of the meadows. Above him the topmost twigs of the trees whispered interminably. An occasional shaft of sunlight penetrated the foliage and lit up the bronze trunks of the pines, touching them with fire. A grey squirrel, spry after its winter sleep, startled Ben by scampering across his path. It darted up a tree with breathtaking ease, and the young man watched it leaping from bough to bough, as light and airy as a puff of grey smoke.

The primroses were out, starring the carpet of tawny dead leaves, and the bluebells, soon to spread their misty veil, now crouched in bud among their glossy leaves in tight pale knots. The faint, but heady, perfume of a spring woodland was to stay with Ben for the rest of his life, and was connected, for ever, with a lover's happiness.

At last, exhausted by his own fervent speed, Ben was obliged to rest, and it was then that his feverishly high spirits suffered their first check. What had that boy said? Molly thought him 'real mean' not to write? His heart sank like a plummet, and he kicked moodily at the log upon which he had sunk.

Suppose she was fed up with him? Suppose she refused to see him because he hadn't bothered to get in touch with her? She was a real pretty girl, and in a pub she'd have plenty of followers. Back flocked his familiar fears to torment him with renewed savagery.

And if she did speak to him again, what of it? What could he offer her? It was a poor sort of life he led in the caravan. A decent girl, used to service in a great house like the Bassetts', and living in a snug little cottage on Thrush Green, wouldn't be likely to take up with a travelling-fair man. Might just as well mate up with some good-for-nothing tinker or scissor-grinder, thought Ben gloomily, now as dejected as he was formerly elated.

Be different, he told himself, rubbing salt into his wounds, if there was any chance of Gran taking him into partnership, as she had once suggested. But what hope of that now? Hardly spoke to a chap, he thought morosely, remembering their almost silent dinner together an hour or two before.

Suddenly overcome with despair he let his unhappy head fall into his hands. His fingers knotted and writhed in and out of his wiry black hair and he groaned aloud. An inquisitive robin settled on a twig nearby and surveyed his agony with an unfeeling bright eye.

What should he do? What should he do? he begged himself as he rocked his hot head this way and that. Go on and be humiliated, or turn tail and slink back to Thrush Green like the coward he was? He looked up and caught sight of his companion whose beady eye was still cocked upon this strange creature's sufferings.

It was at this moment that two thoughts combined to make poor Ben's way clear.

'She missed you!' came one comforting whisper. And hard upon its heels came a great cry from Ben himself, as he jumped to his feet.

'I've got to see her! Just to see her! Whatever comes of it, I'll see her first!'

He took to the uphill path again, but now his feet were leaden. Only his fierce single-minded passion to see the girl once more helped him to ignore the swarm of doubts which stung and plagued his progress.

He drew towards the edge of Lulling Woods and emerged from their dusk into the clear sunshine of the open heath. Bees hummed among the gorse flowers and two larks vied with each other as they sang a duet high in the blue air.

Not fifty yards away, where four modest tracks met, 'The Drovers' Arms' stood waiting for him behind its neat strip of mown grass. The door was shut, no smoke rose from the chimneys, and not a soul was in sight. Only two grey and white geese rose menacingly from the shade of a low hedge, and advanced, with necks stretched out ominously, towards the unhappy young man.

But the windows were open, he noticed, and, very faintly, he could hear the sound of dishes being clattered in the kitchen at the rear of the house. A young clear voice began to sing, and Ben's heart turned over.

He took a great shuddering breath, raised his head, and set off to meet his fate.

8. A Chapter of Accidents

'Not bad! Not bad at all,' pronounced Ella Bembridge, dabbing parsley sauce from her chin with a hand-woven napkin.

Pink with praise, Dimity Dean carried the empty dish into the kitchen, returning with bananas in custard. The two friends hitched their wheel-back chairs to the table again and continued their meal and their gossiping.

'I must say,' said Ella, between succulent mouthfuls, 'that Winnie Bailey wears well. What must she be? Nearly seventy?' There was a slightly grudging note in her voice which did not escape her sensitive friend's notice.

'Oh, hardly that, dear,' she answered, in mollifying tones. 'And of course she's had a very *sheltered* life, being married, you know.'

Ella nodded, somewhat comforted.

'Time he gave up, if you ask me. That young fellow could do worse than settle here, and he seemed fairly competent, I thought. Inclined to take himself a bit seriously,' added Ella, remembering her hasty dismissal from the morning surgery. 'Likes to think he's the only one with any work to do – but there you are! That's the way with everyone today.'

'It might be rather dull for a young man at Thrush Green –' began Dimity, but was cut short.

'*Dull?*' boomed her friend. 'What's *dull* about Thrush Green? And anyway, if I'm not a Dutchman, he'll be marrying before long. He's been making sheep's eyes at Ruth Bassett ever since the cocktail party Joan and Edward gave this spring.'

'Now, Ella darling,' protested Dimity, with ineffectual severity, 'that's really too naughty of you! I'm sure you're imagining things. Ruth has been much too upset to look at anyone else.'

'Doesn't stop him looking at her, does it?' persisted Ella stoutly. She pushed aside her plate, took out the battered tobacco tin, and rolled one of her monstrous cigarettes. Dimity considered this possible romance as her friend blew smoke upon the remains of the food. It might well be true. Darling Ella was wonderfully astute in matters like this. It would be the best possible thing for poor little Ruth, thought Dimity, her eyes filling as her sympathetic heart was pleasurably wrung. For once Ella noticed her friend's over-bright eyes, and remembering Doctor Lovell's remark about heavy lifting, she spoke with bluff kindness.

'Here, young Dim, you get along to bed and have your rest. I'll wash up today. You look a bit done-up.'

Such unaccustomed consideration caused the tears to hover perilously at the brink of Dimity's blue eyes.

'Are you sure, darling? You're so good to me.'

'Rubbish!' roared Ella cheerfully, crashing plates together like tinkling cymbals. The custard spoon fell with a glutinous thwack upon the rush mat at their feet and the water jug slopped generously upon the polished table, as Ella bent her back, grunting heavily, to retrieve the spoon.

'Soon have everything ship-shape and Bristol fashion,' she said heartily, emerging red-faced from her exertions. 'Up you go for an hour.'

'But what about that stuff you wanted to dye? Can you manage it alone?' quavered Dimity, hovering about the table.

'Easily!' replied Ella, screwing the linen table mats into tight balls before thrusting them into the table drawer. Dimity averted her gaze. Dear Ella, so good-hearted, but so clumsy! Depend upon it there would be as much work to do clearing up after Ella's ministrations as if she had done the job herself, thought Dimity. But she mustn't be disloyal, she told herself, and really it was uncommonly thoughtful of Ella to offer to do these chores she so hated.

'Very well, dear,' she said gratefully. 'I'll go up, if you insist! But do put on your rubber gloves!'

She mounted the creaking stairs to the little bedroom above and turned a stoical ear to a dreadful crash, followed by a muttered imprecation, which shook the cottage.

'As long as it isn't mother's fruit bowl,' thought Dimity anxiously, and climbed resignedly under the eiderdown.

Having washed up the glass, silver, and china, and carefully stacked the sticky casserole, caked with parsley sauce, a saucepan equally encrusted with mashed potato, a parsley cutter, a stained board on which the herb had been cut, and various other utensils used in the preparation of the meal, all upon the draining-board to await Dimity's ministrations later, Ella felt aglow with righteousness.

It was really rather pleasant to have the kitchen to herself, she decided. She filled an enormous two-handled saucepan with water and set it on the gas-stove ready for the dyeing. The rubber gloves annoyed her. They were slippery, and her hands felt clumsy in them, but she realized that she had better obey Doctor Lovell's injunctions if she were going to handle her painting materials.

She set about mixing the dye in an old enamel bowl. It was a beautiful deep red, and by the time it had been added to the hot water, it looked as luscious as wine.

Ella tested a scrap of the natural-coloured linen she proposed to steep in it. It came out a satisfyingly rich shade and Ella sighed with pleasure. Little by little she let the length of stuff slide into the bubbling brew until it was all submerged.

As she stood by it in the quiet kitchen waiting for the allotted time to pass she became conscious of the sounds of the fair. She could hear the occasional shout of one man to another as they rigged up the booths or steadied machinery. There was a steady chugging noise which she guessed was the engine which provided the power for the roundabout and switchback. Everything was tested carefully before the evening, and Ella could well imagine Mrs Curdle making her rounds, ebony stick in hand, as she had done for so many May-days before the fair opened to the customers on Thrush Green. It would be a pity if the rumour proved true, thought Ella, stirring her cauldron like some stout, preoccupied witch.

Time was up. Ella turned the gas off, cursing the rubber gloves which added to her habitual clumsiness. She surveyed the great pot with a doubtful eye. It was very heavy, she knew from long experience, and usually Dimity helped her lift it into the sink.

It was on the tip of her tongue to hail her unsuspecting friend above her with her usual hearty exuberance. Dimity, she knew, would come readily tripping down the stairs, only too anxious to be of use. But today, with the milk of human kindness still pulsing its somewhat bewildered way through her veins, Ella decided, generously, to manage on her own. Giving a tug to her maddening rubber gloves Ella approached the stove. She gripped the two handles and gave a mighty heave. It certainly was heavy and she wondered, for a split second, if she should replace it.

But pride overcame caution. She gave a determined stagger towards the sink before disaster overtook her. Whether, as she afterwards maintained, the confounded rubber gloves slipped along the handles and shot the contents downward, or whether she caught her foot in the coconut matting, or whether, in fact, both calamities occured, she was never quite clear. But, in one agonizing moment, the pot overturned, and fell upside-down to the floor, cascading boiling dye down poor Ella's legs and draping her ankles and feet in searingly hot wet linen, which acted like some ghastly cleaving blood-red poultice.

Her screams brought Dimity pell-mell downstairs to stand aghast at the scene. Ella was disengaging herself from her fiendish encumbrances, her face contorted with pain.

'Oh, Ella, Ella!' was all poor Dimity could say, putting her thin arms around her suffering friend's shoulders. It was Ella herself who directed operations.

'Give me a hand getting my skirt and stockings off,' she ordered, gasping painfully. She stumbled to the kitchen chair, once white but now mottled with claret-coloured splashes, and began to fumble at her shoes. They were filled with the hot liquid and the metal eyelet holes were searing her flesh. Dimity collected her wits and helped her to strip off her garments, but as soon as she saw the scalded flesh, already beginning to blister, her face crumpled.

'Oh, poor Ella, poor darling Ella! I'll run and get Doctor Lovell. You simply must have a doctor!'

'He's out,' panted Ella, still struggling with a mammoth suspender, 'and anyway, we're going to wash this dye off before anyone starts messing about with my legs. Get some stuff out of the medicine chest, for pity's sake!'

Dimity fled to the bathroom and returned with the tiny first-aid box.

'There's this lotion that Dotty Harmer made up for your hands. D'you think that would help?' she asked, holding up an evil-looking green liquid in a shaking hand.

'Talk sense!' snapped Ella, with pardonable irritation. 'D'you want gangrene to set in?'

Dimity rummaged frantically again, tears falling from her eyes.

'Which it may well do, anyway,' went on Ella morosely, surveying a crimson ankle. 'And I'll be stumping about Thrush Green on my knees for the rest of my life,' she continued, warming up to her theme, and becoming garrulous, now that the first shock was over and she had a sympathetic audience.

Dimity could bear no more.

'I'm going now,' she exclaimed. 'You can't possibly see to that alone. I'll help you to the bathroom and you can swab it with cotton wool if you like, but you must have proper medical attention. Shall I ring the hospital for an ambulance?'

'Good God, Dim!' shouted Ella, shocked at this ruthless suggestion. 'Do you want to kill me?'

For Ella's conception of hospitals was two-fold. In the first place, she looked upon them as large, disinfectant-reeking establishments, provided by society, for the hygienic segregation of those about to quit this world; and secondly, as convenient and practical schools for medical men who literally had their raw material at their finger-ends. The thought of entering one alarmed her far more than the actual accident.

Together the two women struggled to the bathroom, which was situated, luckily, on the ground floor. Dimity fetched Ella's dressing-gown, established her on a stool by the bath, and left her friend to bathe her legs and feet in tepid water. She was not at all happy about this, but Ella, now secretly near to tears with pain, shock, and the truly awful suggestion of hospital treatment, was becoming voluble and obstreperous.

'I'm sure we should be putting oil, or a paste of bicarbonate of soda, or something like that on it,' protested poor Dimity, one distracted hand ruffling her hair. 'If only I could remember what I learnt during the war! I used to know it all so well – and now I can only remember how to deal with incendiary bombs! Poor Ella!'

'If you're going for the doctor, then go!' burst out her much-tried companion. And, without another word, Dimity fled for help.

Doctor Bailey was dozing in the sunny garden when Dimity pealed agitatedly at the bell.

Dimly, through the comfortable wrappings of slumber which surrounded him, the doctor became conscious of women's voices in the hall. Someone was pouring forth a torrent of words while his wife was doing her best to soothe the visitor. Rousing himself from his chair Doctor Bailey went in from the sunshine to investigate the commotion.

'It's Ella!' burst forth Dimity, as soon as he came in view.

'She has had an accident,' put in his wife swiftly. 'I'm going along to see if I can help. There's no need for you to be disturbed.'

'She's most dreadfully scalded –' began Dimity, in a tearful gabble.

'Scalded, eh?' interjected the doctor. 'I'll come along.' He reached for the black bag which always stood in readiness on the hall table. His wife made another attempt to return him to his disturbed rest.

'Let me go first, and if we need you I promise I'll come back,' she said, laying a hand on her husband's arm. He disengaged it gently.

'It's no distance, my dear, and we mustn't neglect an old friend like Ella when she's in trouble.' He lifted the bag and made for the front door, followed by Dimity twittering her thanks and fears. Mrs Bailey, knowing when she was beaten, wisely said no more, but watched them make their way to the gate through the warm flower-scented garden.

Ella was still sitting in the bathroom when the doctor arrived. He took one look at his patient whose teeth were now chattering with cold and shock, and said firmly:

'Bed for you, my dear. Come along.'

'What, on a lovely afternoon like this?' protested Ella.

'Yes, indeed. Dimity, put the kettle on and make a cup of tea for both of you.' He turned to Ella. 'I'll help you upstairs and Dimity can give you a hand later on. Those legs want dressing straight away.'

Slowly they mounted the stairs. Ella's massive arm was thrown round the doctor's shoulders and it was as much as he could do to support her weight up the crooked staircase, across the landing, and into her bedroom.

Dimity, having put the kettle on, returned to help her friend undress and put on her nightgown while the doctor unpacked his bag.

'And she'll want that dressing-gown too,' ordered the doctor. 'Keep her warm, my dear.'

An ear-splitting whistle from below warned the company that the kettle was boiling and Dimity moved away leaving Ella to the ministrations of their old friend.

The kitchen was in an unbelievable condition of chaos, as poor Dimity saw as she set out teacups upon a tray. She lifted the soaking linen into the sink and put the great saucepan outside the back door. The mat was ruined and the walls, chairs, and scrubbed table-top spattered with crimson dye. There was an hour's hard work waiting for her here, decided Dimity sadly.

As she lifted the tray her eye fell upon the mound of revoltingly sticky utensils which Ella had left at lunchtime. She sighed bravely and made her way to the door. It was perhaps a good thing that domestic martyrdom was a commonplace in Dimity Dean's life.

'She'll do,' said Doctor Bailey ten minutes later. 'Not as bad as I first thought – but you're to stay there until Lovell's had a look at you. A shock like that takes more out of you than you realize.'

He turned a shrewd and kindly eye upon Dimity.

'And you'd better have an early night too,' he said. 'Get as much sleep as you can. Both of you.'

'On May the first?' cried Dimity. 'You know the fair keeps us all awake for hours! Really, I do think it's too bad to allow that dreadful noise to go on as it does!'

'Only once a year, Dim,' pointed out Ella from the bed. 'And probably the last time anyway.'

'I hope not,' said Doctor Bailey, gathering his things together. 'Stuff your ears with cotton wool, if you must! But don't forget – early bed!'

He parted from Dimity at the front door.

'There's nothing to worry about,' he assured her, noticing her anxious face. 'Ella's got the constitution of a horse.'

He waved farewell, and, somewhat comforted, Dimity Dean returned to the upheaval in the kitchen.

The dazzle of Thrush Green after the shade of Ella's bedroom was almost too much for the doctor. His head bumped strangely and the trees and caravans and busy fair-folk blurred together in a giddy whirling motion.

He stopped by a fence and steadied himself against it. His bag seemed uncommonly heavy and he set it down carefully, closing his eyes in case vertigo overcame him.

'Damn, damn, damn!' swore the doctor furiously to himself. 'Twenty yards' walk, one simple case, and I'm useless!'

He leant dizzily against the fence, praying that his wife should not happen to look out from their gate and see his helplessness. Another minute and he would be perfectly all right, he told himself.

A voice spoke, so close to him that he was startled.

'You all right, doctor?' It was Mr Piggott, lately come from 'The Two Pheasants' which had shut its doors some half-hour or so before. A smell of beer and plug tobacco emanated from him, so strongly that the doctor was partially revived by it.

'Yes, yes. I'm all right, many thanks, Piggott. Found the sunshine a bit dazzling, that's all.'

He was surprised, and touched too, to see the expression of concern on the old rapscallion's normally surly countenance, and even more surprised when he lifted up his black bag for him and accompanied him to his gate.

'Well, that's very kind of you, to be sure,' he said, when they arrived. For want of anything better to say he waved towards the fair.

'Are you going tonight?'

'Me? Not likely,' growled Piggott, with his usual venom. 'I'll be glad to see the back o' this lot, I can tell 'ee. Nothing but a set of rogues and thieves. Be a good riddance when they clears out tomorrow.' He hitched his trousers up viciously and ambled away through the offending collection of caravans to his work, leaving the doctor pondering on this exhibition of both sides of his neighbour's nature.

'How was she?' first asked his wife. And then, in the same breath: 'You shouldn't have gone. You're over-tired.'

The doctor roused himself to speak calmly.

'Ella's not too bad. I've left her in bed and the burns will keep till Lovell can see her in the morning.'

He had put down the black bag, as he had done so many times, upon the hall table; but this time his hand remained resting upon it as he faced his wife.

'Come and sit down,' urged Mrs Bailey. 'You really shouldn't have gone.'

'I'm glad I went,' replied the doctor steadily, patting the bag as one might a much-loved dog. 'It's helped me to come to a decision.'

'About Doctor Lovell?'

'About Doctor Lovell,' agreed the doctor. 'I shall offer him a partnership tonight.'

9. At 'The Drovers' Arms'

Molly Piggott sang as she washed up the glasses in the back kitchen of 'The Drovers' Arms'.

She was alone in the house, for as soon as the bar had shut at two o'clock, Ted Allen, the landlord, and his wife Bessie, had driven off to Lulling, in their twenty-year-old Baby Austin, to do the week-end shopping.

'We'll be back in an hour or so, love,' fat, rosy Bessie had called from the car, 'in time to let you get away real early, as it's fair day. Keep your eyes open for the laundry van. He's supposed to be calling about three – but you know what he is!'

They had rattled off leaving Molly to enjoy the peaceful kitchen on her own. She was glad of her own company for she was in a state of great excitement.

Molly had been born at the little cottage on Thrush Green and, for her, May the first had always been the highlight of the year. The travelling fair had become associated for Molly with the most be-witching time of the country year, when hope, warmth, and colour flooded fields and gardens, and the hearts of men could not fail to be quickened by the glory around them. And this year the fair-day held a particular significance for Molly Piggott.

The memory of that lovely evening with Ben had warmed Molly throughout the year. She had been more attracted by the young man than she had realized, and she was astonished at her own disappoint-ment when she had failed to hear from him.

She had continued to go about her daily affairs looking as cheerful and as bustling as ever, but at heart she was sadly perplexed. She cooked and cleaned, washed and mended, weeded the garden and fed the hens, enduring the surly company of her father with less equa-nimity than usual, and escaping as often as she could to the haven of the Bassetts' house across the green. Paul was an enormous comfort to her, and although she was careful not to let too much slip out about the dark young man who had taken her to the fair, Paul's pertinent questions and shrewd guesswork soon uncovered her secret.

He was genuinely sympathetic to poor Molly and hated to know that she was in any way upset. Touched to the heart by his warm-hearted solicitude Molly still tried to treat the whole affair light-heartedly, but Paul was not to be so easily put off.

'You should write to him,' said Paul decidedly, as they walked together one afternoon to Dotty Harmer's to get the eggs. The rain was slanting across the field, shrouding Lulling Woods in a grey veil. Paul strode through the puddles in his gumboots. His sou'wester dripped upon his shiny oilskins in little rivulets. One hand was thrust in his pocket and the other comforted Molly's with a warm wet grasp.

'He may be a real nice man,' he continued judicially, ignoring the torrents about him, 'but he can't know you're worrying about him, or he'd come and see you.'

'I'm not worrying,' Molly had said, with a very good imitation of a light laugh. 'And I can't write to him if I don't know where the fair is, can I? Even if I wanted to – which I don't!' she had added hastily.

'He should come,' maintained Paul stoutly. 'He must be a friend because he gave you that brooch and he took you to the fair. He should come and see you. Or he should send you a picture postcard of wherever the fair is.'

'Perhaps he's ill,' suggested Molly, making excuses for Ben against her will. 'Or maybe old Mrs Curdle don't like him wasting his time writing to girls. She's a proper ol' pip, they say, at keeping 'em all working.'

Paul, with a child's black and white conception of right and wrong, and having no interest in or recognition of those forgiving shades of grey with which adults confuse the issue, would have no excuses made for poor absent Ben.

He asked Molly whenever they met if she had heard from Ben, so that Molly grew more and more alarmed at the interest taken in her affairs, and dreaded lest the child should let fall some chance remark at home or anywhere else on Thrush Green. She knew, only too well, how quickly rumours spread in a small community and was horrified to think how a spark, so innocently dropped by sympathetic young Paul, would blaze a trail from Thrush Green to Lulling, to Nod and Nidden and all the little hamlets that clustered near the River Pleshy. As for her father, if he should come to hear of the evening out, let alone anything further, he was quite capable of making her life a misery with braggart threats and mean-spirited mockings.

'Don't you say a word now,' she had said severely to Paul one day when he had questioned her once more about the errant Ben. 'It's a secret, see? I wish I'd never said a word about him to you. I don't care all that about him anyway,' protested poor Molly, tossing her head.

'Then why do you wear that cornflower brooch every day?' Paul had answered mildly. For two pins Molly could have slapped the child, torn as she was between exasperation and affection. She did her best to speak calmly.

'Well, he was kind to me, Paul, and I likes to wear it to remind me of a lovely time. But there's no call for you to think I'm fretting, you know. And don't forget – what I've told you is a secret. Promise?'

'Promise,' echoed Paul solemnly, and he had kept his word.

But Molly had grown increasingly perturbed as the year slid from summer into winter. Her father's boorishness, his bouts of morose drinking, and her own disappointment over Ben's silence combined to make her life depressing. She almost dreaded going to the Bassetts' house in the winter months for then she and Paul were together indoors, often in the company of Joan and Edward, and Molly trembled lest Paul should forget his promise and reveal her feelings unintentionally. It was during the autumn that she heard about the post at 'The Drovers' Arms'.

'They wants a girl as'll help in the bar and give them a hand in the house,' the milkman had told her one day. He was a cheerful fellow who always stopped for a word, and was fond of any lively buxom girl like Molly. He was a great favourite with most of the ladies on Thrush Green, though Dimity Dean had found him 'detestably familiar' once when she had been obliged to answer the door in her dressing-gown.

'Why tell me?' Molly had asked, with genuine interest.

'You're too good to waste away under this roof,' the man had said shrewdly. 'You'd see a bit of life up there. The Allens is real nice and homely. Food's good, pay's good, and home here for the week-end if you still wants to see old Happy Face!' He had jerked a thumb in the direction of Mr Piggott who was stirring up a bonfire in the churchyard.

'They won't want me,' said Molly. 'I've never done bar work.'

'You go and see 'em,' urged the milkman, patting her arm. 'I told 'em you'd be just the right sort of gal if they could persuade you. You think it over. Tell 'em I sent you up.'

She had turned this amazing offer over in her mind as she had gone about her duties that day, and had almost decided not to go. But that evening her father had been unbearable. He had pushed the piece of steak that the girl had cooked for him this way and that across his plate, prodding it with a fork and grumbling about its toughness, its meagre dimensions, and his daughter's poor cooking. That decided the matter for Molly. She had stood enough.

She said nothing at the time, but the next day she walked through the autumn woods to 'The Drovers' Arms' and faltered out her willingness to take the post.

Ted and Bessie Allen were a boisterous, kindly pair, who took at once to the pretty girl whose character had been given them by the milkman. It was all quickly arranged. Molly was to live there from Monday night until Friday afternoon each week, and the week-ends were her own as Mrs Allen's brother came down from town each week-end and liked to help in the bar to earn his keep.

Mr Piggott was too flabbergasted at this *fait accompli* to make much comment. Joan Bassett was glad for the girl's sake for she knew that her home conditions were wretched, but glad too to know that Molly would come to help her at week-ends if ever she were needed.

And so the winter and spring had slipped by and Molly's spirits had risen as the good company and good living at the little pub had had their effect. She was willing, lively, and glowed with good health and fun, and became a great favourite with the customers.

No one would have thought that Molly Piggott had a care in the world. Her eyes sparkled, her curly hair sprang crisply above her clear white brow, and she tripped lightly about her business.

But the cornflower brooch was always pinned on her dress, and at night when she put it carefully away in the shell-encrusted box which had accompanied her to 'The Drovers' Arms' her eyes would cloud as she remembered the young man who had asked her to be true but, alas, had forgotten to be true himself.

As May had approached she had become more and more excited. At least she would see him again. Not that she was going to run after him, she told herself! If he liked to come and find her – well, that was different.

And if he didn't come? Then she had her plans ready. There were several young men who called at the pub who had already suggested that she might honour them with her company at Thrush Green fair. To all she had given an evasive answer, praying secretly that Ben would have called for her long before the fair opened. But if he didn't come – and at this dreadful thought her spirits fell like a plummet – then she would go with the first young man who asked her, and she would see Ben again, and speak to him too. And woe betide that dark young breaker-of-hearts if he failed to clear up the mystery of a silence which had lasted a year!

All through the sparkling morning Molly had hoped and wondered, plotted and surmised. Ben would not be able to see her much before tea-time, she reckoned, for she knew that it took most of the day to prepare the fair and Mrs Curdle would see that there were no defaulters.

She had looked out the yellow spotted frock which she had worn the year before, and had polished her new black shoes with the high heels. She had tried a yellow ribbon across her dark hair and had approved of her reflection in the dim mirror in the little attic bedroom under the thatch. The ribbon lay now, beside the spotted frock, across the white counterpane.

Molly sang at the thought of the pretty things awaiting her upstairs. She would wash up, and then she would take up a jug of warm rainwater to her bedroom and wash herself in the blue-and-white bowl on the corner washstand. She would brush her hair till it frothed round her head and then tie the yellow ribbon smoothly across. And then, she told herself with a beating heart, dressed and freshly clean, she would sit in the sunshine and wait.

She glanced through the window at the trim garden. Heat waves shimmered across the pink-and-white apple blossom, and a few fragile petals fluttered down, in the heat, upon the forget-me-nots that clustered below. It was all so beautiful that Molly's song ceased abruptly as she stared.

She rested her plump arms along the edge of the sink. Soap-suds popped softly on the creamy skin. Her red frock, so soon to be changed for the immaculate yellow one above, was wet with her energetic splashings, and her curls clung damply against her brow.

'He'd have to come, a day like this,' whispered Molly to herself, gazing bemused at the view before her.

And, at that moment, Ben knocked upon the back door.

*

Outside, in the scorching sunshine, Ben waited anxiously. The heat beat back from the worn paint of the door. A blister or two had risen here and there, and in the vivid light Ben noticed minute iridescent specks freckling the paintwork, reminding him of the sheen on a pheasant's throat.

He was never to forget that endless moment of waiting, in the full murmurous beauty of May Day, the acrid smell of the hot paint-work mingling with the fragrance of the spring garden.

He heard the singing stop. There was a sudden silence, and then the sound of footsteps on the stone-flagged floor. The door opened, and Ben's heart turned over.

There she stood, prettier than ever, her eyes sparkling with such radiance that Ben knew instantly that he need never have doubted his welcome.

'Ben!' breathed Molly rapturously, all preconceived ideas of a frigid approach to the errant young man melting at once as their eyes met.

Ben was unable to speak, but stood gazing at the cornflower brooch at her neck.

'Ben!' repeated Molly, holding out two soapy hands and a striped tea towel. 'Come in out of the heat!'

Obediently, Ben stepped over the threshold into the cool shade of the kitchen. He was still speechless with joy and wild relief. But if his tongue was useless his arms were not. And throwing them round the tea towel, the wet frock, and his plump, lovely Molly, he hugged her until she gasped for breath.

After the first joy of meeting, Ben took another tea towel and helped the girl to wipe the glasses.

'And then we're going out,' he said firmly.

'But I can't, Ben, honest, I can't!' pleaded Molly. 'There's no one here to see the laundry man and there's the chicken-food to cook up, and the –'

Ben cut her short.

'Stick a note on the door for the laundry, and put the chickens' grub over the side of the hob. That won't hurt. We'll go up the common for a bit.'

'I've got to be here about five, though, just to see the others in. Then I'm free.'

'You must come and see my old Gran before the fair starts,' persisted Ben. 'I wants her to see you. You'll like her all right.' He gazed admiringly at Molly, whose brow was furrowed with trying to work out an afternoon's programme which gave her as much time as possible with Ben and yet saw her duties done.

'And what's more,' went on Ben, 'she'll like you!'

It all sounded alarmingly fast for Molly trying to keep her head amidst this sudden whirl of events.

'I'll go and change my frock first,' she said, hoping to escape to the peace of her bedroom for a few minutes in order to collect her scattered wits. But Ben would have none of it. They'd been apart for a year and now he had found her again he had no intention of letting her out of his sight.

'Come out now,' he urged. 'You look fine in that red frock.'

'But it's all wet –' faltered Molly, displaying the splashes.

'Sun'll dry it,' said Ben firmly, spreading the tea towel over a chair back. He turned, and, arms akimbo, surveyed the girl as she stood thoughtfully by the sink, looking down at her damp dress.

'Change your frock when you come back to the fair with me,' suggested Ben. Molly looked up, and catching sight of his crinkly dark eyes smiling at her, regained her usual sparkle.

'I didn't say I was coming to the fair, did I?' said Molly, turning wide eyes upon him. 'Not with you anyways. There's plenty of other young men have asked me lately, and I haven't said "Yes" or "No" to any of 'em.'

Ben was not to be foiled by these womanly wiles. After the months of doubting fears, culminating in the anguish of mind as he had walked through Lulling Woods in the heat of the day, it was as though he were now inoculated against all further torments. He knew, with a deep sense of wonder and inner comfort that was to remain with him all his life, that the girl before him was his for ever, to be as essential to him, and as much part of him, as his hand or eye.

It was this knowledge that gave him a new-found strength and gentleness. Nothing now could go wrong, he told himself, anywhere – ever – in the whole world!

He took the girl's hand and led her, laughing, to the door.

'Other men!' he scoffed exultantly. 'To hell with them! You're coming with me!'

And together they made their way out into the sunshine.

The common, which surrounded 'The Drovers' Arms', rose at one point to a cluster of beech trees which served as a landmark for miles around.

It was towards the trees that the two climbed through the dry fine grass, and when they reached the first welcome shade thrown by the outspread branches they sat down to talk.

From the little hill they had a clear view of the four roads that met at 'The Drovers' Arms', for Molly, despite her excitement, was still conscious of her mistress's injunction about the laundry and about 'keeping an eye' on the place. By settling here she salved her conscience enough to be able to give young Ben the major part of her attention.

The heat waves quivered across the view spread before them. A myriad winged insects hummed in the warm air, and far away, so high above that it was lost in blue air, a distant aeroplane droned drowsily.

Ben rested his arms on his knees, a grass between his teeth, and observed the mighty hulk of a steam-roller, drawn up in a clearing at the side of the road directly below them. A froth of Queen Anne's lace had grown up round the rusty wheels, and the sun glinted on the brass horse which ornamented the front. Soon its winter rest would come to an end, for with the May sunshine would come the time for tarring, and the sleeping monster would be tugged from the clinging greenery which softened its primitive and grotesque lines and be roused into life by fire kindled in its belly. With the rumbling of the giant about the quaking lanes the people of Lulling would know that high summer had really come.

Tired with their climb, and with all that had happened to them, Ben and Molly spoke little at first, content to be in each other's company and enjoy the quiet loveliness that echoed their own bliss. But gradually their tongues loosened and they began to exchange news of the long year behind them.

Ben listened with pity and anger to Molly's account of life at the cottage on Thrush Green, and admired secretly the sturdy common sense with which she had faced her difficulties, devoid of any self-pity for her conditions. But his heart smote him even more poignantly when she put a hand upon his sunburnt arms and said:

'And then you never came! And, worse still, you never wrote! I did think you'd send a letter, p'raps.'

Ben took a deep breath. The shameful secret would have to be told, and better now than later on.

'I can't write, Moll, and that's the truth,' he said looking away from her. A yard away the blue broken shell of a bird's egg had become speared upon a tall grass, and swayed gently, like some exotic harebell.

'Can't write?' echoed Molly in amazement. He turned to her swiftly, and Molly's heart was shaken at the pain in his face.

'Well, I never had much schooling. Being with the fair, see. We was always on the move. I can read a bit, but all the schools I went to seemed to do different writing and somehow I never sort of mastered it.' His fingers plucked nervously at the grass and Molly covered them with her own.

'You don't want to worry about a little thing like that,' she said stoutly. 'I knows dozens as can't write. And anyway I can easy teach you. 'Twouldn't take you more than a week or two to get the hang of it.'

'I'd like that,' nodded young Ben earnestly. 'And Gran'd be pleased.'

He went on to tell her about the old lady and the hopes he had of being taken into partnership. He told her about the work of the fair, the earnings he had, and the improvements he would make if he had any say in the future running of the business.

Molly listened intently. The life of the fair had always attracted her, and the account of the hard work which lay behind the glitter held no fears for her. If that were to be her life, she would relish it. She was used to tough conditions, she welcomed change and move-ment with the natural excitement of youth, and she knew too that wherever the young man before her chose to go she would want to go too. But she was, nevertheless, a little taken aback to hear him describe the alterations he would make to his caravan for their future comfort.

'But, Ben,' she protested, 'you're taking a lot for granted.'

He looked at her bewildered face and, for a moment, all his old doubts assailed him again.

'Maybe I'm asking too much,' he said soberly. 'Girls like you, with a steady job and a home and that, would find our everlasting traipsin' the roads a come-down. 'Tisn't fair perhaps to ask you to take on a rough chap from a fair, and never have no comfort.'

He was lying full length upon the grass, his chin propped on his fists, and now he looked up with such utter misery at Molly that she caught her breath.

'But, Moll,' he pleaded, 'what'll I do if you won't come?'

There was a little silence, stirred only by the summer murmuring about them, while poor Ben waited for his answer.

'I'll come,' promised Molly, at last.

10. Sam Curdle is Tempted

While Ben Curdle lay, lapped in bliss, upon the grassy heath above Lulling Woods, his cousin Sam was facing a domestic squall at Thrush Green.

His wife Bella was in a fine fury. She confronted him now, her eyes flashing. Her massive bosom heaved under the tight red dress as she railed. As usual it was money that she demanded.

'I tell you, Bella,' protested Sam, 'I'm broke. I give you your whack last week. What you done with that lot?' His face was as red as his wife's.

'You had plenty yesterday morning,' screamed Bella. 'You hand some over. It's for your kids' clothes – that's all I'm asking for! D'you want to see 'em barefoot?'

Sam swore softly under his breath, but put a grimy hand in his pocket.

'That's the lot!' he growled, flinging two filthy pound notes on to the table. Bella swooped upon them and rammed them into her shiny black handbag.

'About time,' was her comment. 'We gets paid tonight anyway – no need for you to be mean all of a sudden.'

She put her head out of the doorway and yelled to her three children who were playing with a skewbald pony in the shade of the lime trees.

'Give over! We're going down Lulling. Come and get your faces wiped!'

She turned to have a parting shot at her husband. He was kicking moodily at the table leg and his face was black as thunder.

'If you're short of money, why don't you ask the old girl for more? You earns it, don't you? You're all the same, you Curdles! Afraid to say a word for yourselves against her. Under her thumb, the lot of you, under her thumb!'

And, still heaving with indignation, Bella descended the steps of the caravan to find her brood.

Sam lay back upon the garish cretonne cushions which Bella had made for the long wall-seat of the caravan, and cursed his luck. He cursed Bella and her tongue, the children and their everlasting wants, and his own feebleness in parting with the two pound notes.

These had been earmarked for the afternoon's betting, and now the outlook seemed hopeless. Sam gazed blackly at the ceiling above him where two flies waltzed erratically around Bella's pink-fringed lamp-shade. Give her her due, Sam admitted, as his temper cooled and the peace of the afternoon crept upon him, she kept the place nice, nag though she did.

His eyes wandered to the flowery curtains that matched the cushions below his head, to the pink rug that she had made, and the new plastic tablecloth with its scarlet-and-black design. When you thought that it had once been an old bus, Sam mused, it hadn't turned out a bad little home. Bit cramped, of course, now, with the three kids, but if the horses did their stuff maybe they'd be able to get a bigger caravan to live in – a real flash job, with plenty of chrome and a bay window with latticed panes.

The thought of the horses reminded Sam painfully of his predicament. He sat up and pulled the newspaper towards him morosely. Running a black-edged finger-nail down the racing column his gloom returned.

Yes, there they were, all right! Both the beauties that young chap had tipped him, Rougemont and Don John. One in the three-thirty and the other in the four-thirty, and here he was with ninepence halfpenny in his pocket! Sam swore anew.

The fair had stopped for two days, earlier in the week, at South Fenny, a village in Oxfordshire famous for its racing stables. In the pub Sam had been in conversation with one of the stable lads, an Irishman whose eloquence had impressed Sam deeply.

'Can't go wrong, my boy,' he had said earnestly to the traveller. 'They've both been readied for the Newbury meeting, and I know for a fact the stables are backing 'em. Remember the names now. Rougemont and Don John!'

'Don John!' Sam had said derisively, anxious to appear as knowledgeable as his adviser. 'Why, he ran like a cow at Lingfield!'

The Irishman brushed this aside with a testy wave of his hand.

'But I'm telling you, they were saving him for Newbury, getting him down in the handicap. Put all you can find on 'em, and you'll never regret it. Don't forget now – Rougemont and Don John. They're worth a fortune to you!'

Sam had bought him a drink for luck and had written the two names down on the edge of a newspaper. And now, here they were, both of them, running on the same afternoon and he had nothing to put on them.

He rose to his feet and went outside into the quivering sunshine. Across Thrush Green he could see the small stone house where Ernie Bender lived and worked, and where he laid bets for the lucky ones who had the money to take to him.

Ernie Bender's house stood next door to that belonging to Ella Bembridge and Dimity Dean. It stood well back in a garden shady with plum and apple trees, and in the front window a notice said:

E. BENDER
BOOT AND SHOE REPAIRS

The inhabitants of Thrush Green were glad of Ernie Bender. He ministered to heels and soles, footballs, harness, handbags, and suitcases. In fact, as he was quick to tell his customers, he would 'have a go at anything made of leather – but it must be leather, mind! I won't waste my time on your plastic stuff!' Over the years he had stitched Doctor Bailey's black bag, Paul's pram hood, the netballs at the village school, saddles and bridles for Joan and Ruth when they were small, and kept in trim the footwear that passed and repassed his window as the various owners went about their business on Thrush Green.

He was a tiny gnome-like man who wore half-spectacles made of steel and peered over them at the view through his window as he sat on a high stool at his bench. Not much escaped those long-sighted eyes and he had been known to summon a running child to tell him that his sole was worn through and that his mother had better let him see to it right away.

His passion was horse-racing and he had an account with a bookmaker in Lulling. Many of his customers took their bets to Ernie Bender along with their boots, and found he was always ready to talk about racing memories or prospects for a coming race day, his eyes gleaming as brightly as the steel spectacles which rested on his diminutive nose.

Sam knew him well. It was there that Sam had proposed to go, sauntering casually behind the screen of caravans and booths to dodge Bella's and the old lady's eye, to put ten shillings each way on both Rougemont and Don John.

The bright sun mocked his despair and the peaceful scene before him only infuriated Sam still further. He cast round in his mind for any hope of a loan from one or other of the Curdle tribe, but it was hopeless, he knew.

In the first place this was Friday afternoon when purses and pockets were almost empty at Curdle's fairground. Tonight was pay-night, the brightest spot in the week. If only Rougemont and Don John had been entered on tomorrow's card, thought Sam!

As if to emphasize the callousness of time, St Andrew's clock let fall three silvery notes. Sam's fury flared anew. Another half-hour and Rougemont would be off!

'And he'll go like an arrow, my boy,' the Irishman had sworn solemnly. 'Nothing can stop him. He can't fail!'

The words echoed in Sam's ears infuriatingly. And he'd probably start at odds of eight to one, too, Sam told himself. And where was his money? Snug in Bella's bag. It was enough to make you take to wife-beating, that it was!

He looked up at the implacable face of St Andrew's clock and made a decision. He'd done it before and no one was any the wiser. He'd do it again. What if it did seem like stealing? If old Gran was too mean to pay him right, then she deserved to have a bit pinched now and again.

No, not pinched, he told himself hastily, as a vision of the tribe-leader's awe-inspiring face floated before him. Borrowing, let's say – just a little advance on what would be given him by right tonight. He could slip it back in the drawer sometime, just as easy as he could slip it out.

His stomach was queasy at the thought of his mission, for Sam was the most chicken-hearted of the Curdles. Only his passion for betting could render him brave enough to undertake the deed.

Old Ma, he knew, would be inspecting the fair, to see that all was in order before the evening opening. She did the routine job thoroughly, tugging at guy ropes, surveying the prizes, straightening notices, and going the rounds of each booth and stall minutely. The little menagerie was inspected with particular rigour, for Mrs Curdle was fond, as well as proud, of the pets exhibited and their food and comfort dare not be neglected.

Sam made his way as casually as he could across the grass. He did not walk directly towards Mrs Curdle's caravan, but wove his way, with seeming indifference, between the caravans clustered near the church.

Sitting on the steps of one of them he discovered Rosie, his young cousin. She was feeding her baby, patting its back gently and humming to herself as she rocked to and fro. She might have been the incarnation of spring itself, with her fair hair and pink-and-white skin, but Sam had no time to waste on aesthetic matters.

'Seen Ma?' he asked urgently.

The girl looked up at him dreamily.

'Saw her going in the animals,' she answered vaguely. 'Couldn't say when though. I been busy.'

She returned her gaze to the infant's face, smiling at it so blissfully that Sam knew he was forgotten at once.

The clock said ten past three. Sam slipped like a shadow among the booths, taking care to avoid his fellows, and came warily towards his goal.

Mrs Curdle had indeed started on her round of inspection that afternoon, but she had not completed it.

The burning pain, which now seemed to be her constant companion, had attacked her with spiteful severity soon after the silent meal with Ben.

After he had gone she had rested a little, and then had roused herself to wash up. She had been too engrossed with her own sufferings to give much heed to Ben, but as she flung the washing-up water into the sunlight she had caught sight of his slim figure striding across the shining grass, and all her old love for him had suddenly welled up.

He was George all over again, as straight, as handsome – the apple of her eye! Her pain forgotten, she watched him as he spoke to a little boy.

'Time he had one of his own!' she thought to herself and mused on the idea of her young George being a grandfather. She watched him turn towards the sun and set off purposefully towards the lane that led to Lulling Woods.

She could see now that he was dressed in his best, and she could see too, now that the sun shone full upon his face, that it was alight with excitement. Instantly, she knew the answer to those long silences and dark moods which had estranged them for the past months and marvelled that she had not guessed before.

'So it's a girl,' nodded old Mrs Curdle to herself, returning to the caravan. 'Just as simple as that – a girl!'

She had pondered upon this, sitting heavily on the side of her bed and watching a finger of sunlight pick its way over the gleaming plates on the dresser.

She felt both sadness and delight at this revelation – sadness because she knew that Ben could never be hers again, as he had been for almost the whole of his twenty years, and delight because it meant happiness for the boy.

Despite his youth she knew he would want to marry almost at once, as his father had done. She only prayed that he had chosen more wisely. If he had – if she were a girl with courage and gaiety, it would be the making of Ben.

'This'll change his ways,' the old lady told herself. 'Nothing like love for brightening up a young man. He'll work twice as hard with a wife to keep.'

She saw, shrewdly enough, that Ben's well-being would react on the fortunes of the fair and her heart was comforted by the thought that the business which she loved so well might yet flourish.

She heaved herself upright, took her ebony stick in hand, and set out upon her rounds.

Inside the menagerie tent Mrs Curdle found only one person attending to the animals' needs. Rachel was twelve years old, sister to Rosie, the young mother who nursed her baby in the sunshine near at hand.

Their father was Mrs Curdle's nephew, a blond giant of a man, for whom she had little respect. It was he who should have been at hand, for he was in charge of the menagerie; but, more often than not these days, Rachel was left to attend to things.

She was a willing child and Mrs Curdle was fond of her. She spoke affectionately to her now, peering through the murk after the vivid light outside.

'And how's my Rachel?'

'Fine, Gran,' answered the child. She held up a jug and Mrs Curdle nodded approval. The girl was going methodically from cage to cage filling the water bowls. The faintly acrid smell of animals hung in the air.

'Where's your dad?' asked Mrs Curdle.

'Don't know.'

'He been in yet?'

'No. Over "The Two Pheasants", I think.'

Mrs Curdle snorted and bent to inspect the toy house in which a frenzy of white mice lived and loved.

'Not enough sawdust,' was her comment.

'I can't find none, Gran,' confessed the child earnestly. 'I been looking all over. Dad said he'd get some this morning–'

'Your dad wants sorting out,' broke in the old lady. 'Leaving you to do his job!'

Her voice had a steely ring and the child trembled.

Mrs Curdle took a deep breath as though to continue her tirade, when suddenly she crumpled and fell forward. The ebony stick dropped from her hand, and, to the child's horror, the old lady slumped into a massive heap on the trampled grass.

The child fell on her knees beside her.

'Gran, Gran!' she whispered in terror, staring at the closed eyes.

Mrs Curdle's lips moved. From very far away, it seemed to the girl, her voice could be heard.

'I'm all right, my dear. Don't 'ee be frightened. I'll be better in a minute. Here, hold my hand.'

She gripped the child's hand in a grasp so fierce that the girl almost cried out.

'I'll get Dad! I'll get Rose! Gran, let me go, and I'll get someone!'

'You'll stop here,' said the small voice, but there was an implacable note in it that told the girl that she must stay.

A dreadful silence pervaded the stuffy tent. Only the small squeaks and twitters from the animals and the heavy laboured breathing of the prostrate woman could be heard. Gradually strength returned to Mrs Curdle. She opened her eyes and sat up, though her head dropped in an alarming manner.

'Get us up, girl,' whispered the old lady, releasing her at last.

The child put her frail arms round the massive shoulders and gave an ineffectual heave.

'Give me my stick,' ordered Mrs Curdle, 'and both your hands!'

With much grunting and moaning she at last struggled to her feet, and stood, swaying slightly, in the gloom.

'Not a word about this to anyone, mind!' said Mrs Curdle, shaking the stick at Rachel.

'All right, Gran,' she whispered.

'Help me back home. Round behind the tents, my dear. Don't want no fuss. It's nothing serious.'

The two made their way into the sunshine. Mrs Curdle leant heavily upon her stick with one hand and rested the other upon Rachel's bony shoulder.

When they reached the caravan Mrs Curdle patted the child's cheek kindly.

'You're a good girl,' she told her. 'Better than your dad, by far. And don't forget – not a word about this. 'Tis only wind round the heart – nothing to worry anyone about.'

She dismissed Rachel with a wave of the stick, hobbled ponderously up the three steps, and sank gratefully upon the bed.

Mrs Curdle lay there very quietly. The sudden nausea which had overcome her had passed away and she was content to let thoughts of Ben, and the future of the fair, flutter through her quiescent mind.

Three o'clock chimed distantly and the sun shone through the caravan door, slanting across the dresser and the money drawer, and throwing Mrs Curdle's bed into deep shade.

She became conscious of furtive footsteps approaching and a shadow fell athwart the money drawer. Mrs Curdle lay very still. There was something menacing, something intensely suspicious, about that motionless shadow. It remained there for a full minute and Mrs Curdle knew that someone waited there, alert and listening, for her movements.

At last she could bear it no longer. Rolling from the bed, she advanced to the door, calling as she went:

'Who's there? What d'you want?'

Outside stood her nephew Sam. His air was unconcerned, but it did not deceive Mrs Curdle. He collected his wits and tried to speak casually.

'Bella says you got such a thing as a inch-tape?' he asked glibly. 'She's making somethin' for the kids.' Mrs Curdle looked steadily at him, and beneath that hawk-like gaze Sam felt his legs turn to water.

'Tell Bella,' said Mrs Curdle with terrible emphasis, '*when she comes back*, she's already borrowed my inch-tape.'

'Must've forgot,' muttered Sam, backing hastily. 'Thanks, Ma,' he added, and took to his heels.

Mrs Curdle watched him vanish behind the switchback and then turned to the drawer.

'So that's where it's been going,' muttered the old lady to herself grimly. 'And serve me right for leaving it there.'

She opened the drawer, scooped out a note or two and a handful of silver, and stood with it in her hand, gazing at the end of the bed where the Curdle Bank caused a substantial hump at the end of the mattress.

'Can't lift that now,' she told herself, shaking her head ruefully.

She crossed to the mantelpiece, lifted down the pewter teapot, and stuffed the money in with that already stored there. Then very carefully she replaced the teapot and took down the photograph of her smiling son which stood beside it.

'I could do with you now, George, my boy,' she said soberly.

11. Mrs Bailey Visits Neighbours

Ruth Bassett lay in a deck-chair in the shade of the lime tree which her grandfather had loved.

The afternoon post had brought a letter which lay opened upon her lap. Paul had scooped it joyously from the mat, on his way up to his enforced rest. Ruth had tucked him in and carried the letter to the peaceful garden knowing she would not be interrupted.

But the letter had contained disturbing news. It was from the head of the firm where Ruth worked, and it said:

Dear Miss Bassett,

It seems a long time since you were with us, and I can assure you that we all miss you at the office. There has to be a certain amount of reorganization in the next few months, and I am writing to know whether we may look forward to your return soon. I need hardly add that we should welcome it, but if you have other plans, I should be glad if you would let me know your decision.

We don't want to hurry you in any way, but naturally we should have to advertise for your successor in the unhappy event of your non-return here, and this should be done within the next fortnight if we are to get things settled before June 1st.

We all send our best wishes and hope to see you back among us very soon.

Well, there it was, thought Ruth, a fair offer that could not have come at a better time. Now she must make a decision, and her new-found strength would help her.

She stretched her arms above her head and looked up into the young leaves above her. Somewhere, high aloft, two sparrows skirmished among the branches and Ruth wondered if they too had problems to face. Did the siting of a nest, the choice of building materials, grass, moss, twig, and feather, perplex those grain-small brains as hers was now perplexed?

Of one thing she was certain. She could not, under any circumstances, go back to the office. There would be many plans to make and they must be made carefully and soon, but the first step was quite clear. She could not go back.

At this moment, Ruth heard the click of the garden gate at the side of the house and saw Mrs Bailey approaching.

She crossed the grass, letter in hand, to meet her.

'You couldn't have come at a better moment,' she cried. 'Come and give me some advice.'

Mrs Bailey looked at Ruth over the top of her reading glasses. The letter lay upon her lap. She had read it through twice, with no comment, and now fixed the girl with a speculative eye.

'And are you going back?' she asked, after a pause.

Ruth wriggled unhappily, making the deck-chair creak with her movements. A ladybird crawled busily along her bare arm and she bent her worried gaze upon the scarlet speck.

'I hardly know how to tell you,' she said. 'It seems cowardly, I suppose, but – well, somehow I can't.'

Mrs Bailey nodded sympathetically.

'Poor darling,' she said gently. 'Of course, I understand.'

'Oh, don't pity me, for heaven's sake!' burst out Ruth, flinging the ladybird violently from her. 'Or you'll make me cry – and I haven't cried once today! It's really rather a record,' she added, with a crooked smile.

'I wasn't pitying you,' responded Mrs Bailey, with professional briskness. She had had a lifetime's experience with agitated patients and Ruth's tremors did not perturb her unduly. 'At least, not in the way you think. I was just feeling rather sorry that you had such a decision to make so quickly.'

Ruth made no answer for a little while, but picked a grass at her feet and nibbled idly at it. A cuckoo called in the distance, and somewhere, far away, some lambs bleated in the fields beside the Upper Pleshy road.

Their trembling young voices brought back with sharp clarity a picture of that lane which was a favourite walk of Ruth's. Only a few days before she and Paul had wandered between its quickening hedges and trodden the springy grass of the roadside verges, so soon to be miller-white with a froth of cows' parsley and the powdering from a myriad overhanging hawthorn flowers.

It was the thought of the beauty yet to come, the beauty that would flood the countryside in her absence, that tore Ruth's heart. She tried to explain it, in a small apologetic voice, to the doctor's wife.

Mrs Bailey, with her eyes closed against the sunshine, nodded sympathetically.

'You see,' finished Ruth, 'it's not so much that I dislike going back to town as finding that I simply cannot bear to leave the country. Joan and I always loved it – but, somehow, since Stephen left me, it has meant much more. More than a lovely place, more than a way of living, and something more than just a comfort. All I know is – I can't do without it now.'

Mrs Bailey did not reply for a minute. She was thinking that, at last, she had heard the girl speak of Stephen. It was the first time that she had said his name, and to hear her talk, calmly and dispassionately, of the absent lover, gave the older woman much satisfaction. There was now no doubt about it. Ruth Bassett's wound had healed.

'Is there any need for you to do without it?' asked Mrs Bailey. 'There must be work in Lulling that you could do. And I know Joan and Edward hope that you will stay here. They have told us so many a time.'

'They've been wonderful,' replied Ruth warmly, 'but I don't feel that I should stay here, in this house, any longer. But if I could get a tiny flat, or a cottage, somewhere nearby, I believe it would be the answer.'

'I'll keep my eyes and ears open,' promised the doctor's wife. 'Both for posts and somewhere to live.'

She leant forward and placed a hand on the girl's knee.

'You are quite right, and so wise, to see that the country is the only home for you. Some people might think that you are trying to flee from society, that you can't face the fun and fury and stimulus of a crowded life. But I know you better than that.

'Follow your instincts. You've found refreshment here and you'll continue to, I know, for I have too.'

She paused, thinking of that morning's delight in her May garden and her delicious walk down the hill to Lulling while the dew still glittered on Thrush Green. It had taken almost all her life to realize, consciously, how much the country sights and scents around her had contributed to her inner happiness and had provided zest and comfort in turn.

'As one gets older,' she continued slowly, 'so many things get in the way of one's instincts. There's duty to one's children, the necessity to consider a husband's needs and feelings, the knowledge too that one's strength may not be great enough to do what one would like. All sorts of stupid little things too – like wondering what the children would think, or whether a doctor's wife should really do this or that – all these things one considers in relation to a fine, rapturous in-stinctive desire, and, so often, that fine, rapturous, instinctive desire is gently smothered and its little fire dies under a wet blanket.'

She smiled across at the girl.

'Young people, like you, are much freer. When they see what they want, they cut through difficulties and take it. Just stick by your decision. Make a new life here, and you know that we shall all help you.'

'I'll do that,' promised Ruth gravely. 'When Edward and Joan come back next week we'll talk things over. He offered me a secretarial post in his own firm – and I might begin with that, I think.'

Mrs Bailey smote her substantial thigh a resounding whack.

'Good girl! But do you know what I really came for? To borrow some magazines for poor Ella, and I'd almost forgotten.'

She related the details of Ella's accident, and added that her husband seemed to have realized at last that he must have more help.

'He's resting now,' she said, 'and making very light of his weakness; but he was quite done up when he got back from Dimity's. I thought I'd take Ella something to read. She may turn a page or two and give poor Dimity time to clear up the mess.'

'I'll go and fetch some,' said Ruth, jumping up.

'Not the ordinary women's magazines,' implored Mrs Bailey. 'It's not a bit of good giving love stories to Ella, as you know; but anything with designs and furnishings she'll look at, and even if they only make her blow her top off, it'll keep her attention from her scalds.'

Ruth vanished into the house leaving Mrs Bailey to wander in the warm sunshine of the garden, and to ponder on the girl's vital change.

Now she looked forward, her back turned for ever upon the dark miseries which had held her prisoner for so long.

Mrs Bailey's next visit was to Ella's, and as she crossed Thrush Green, bearing Ruth's carefully-vetted magazines and a bunch of mixed daffodils from the Bassetts' garden, she came face to face with Mrs Curdle.

The old lady was standing by her bright caravan and Mrs Bailey was shocked at the change in her appearance. Still massive, and still commanding, there was now something pathetic about her. There was a droop about the shoulders and a dullness in those dark eyes which the doctor's wife had not seen before.

The women greeted each other cordially.

'And how are you, Mrs Curdle?'

'Very middlin', ma'am,' answered the old lady. 'Very middlin' indeed. And gets next to no help from my family these days.' She shot a venomous glance in the direction of Sam's caravan.

'But how's your good man?' she continued. 'I hear tell he's been took to his bed for some time past.'

'He's been very poorly, I'm sorry to say,' said Mrs Bailey. 'But improving daily.'

'The years is too much for us,' said Mrs Curdle, with heavy solemnity. She looked across to the doctor's house with a grave face.

'I be coming to see him, after his surgery time, I expect,' went on Mrs Curdle.

'We'll be very pleased to see you,' answered the doctor's wife warmly. 'But he isn't taking surgery at the moment, so just come whenever you can fit it in most conveniently.'

'I'll see the show started, and then be over,' promised Mrs Curdle.

'I hear,' began Mrs Bailey, rather diffidently, 'that you are thinking of retiring. Is it true? We all hope not, you know.'

Mrs Curdle turned a sombre glance upon her.

' 'Tis true I be thinking of it. There's times I feel I can't go on for pain and trouble. But between ourselves, ma'am, I reckons 'twould break my heart to give up.'

She put a dusky hand against the gay paintwork of her caravan, tracing a yellow cut-out leaf, warm in the sunshine.

'Maybe your good man can help me,' went on Mrs Curdle. 'He's been a real friend to me. And you too, ma'am, and that's true.'

'You come and have a word with him,' said Mrs Bailey. 'It'll do him good to see you, I know.'

She made her farewells swiftly, for she did not want to leave her husband alone too long, and Ella had yet to be visited.

But when she had rung Ella's bell and was waiting on the doorstep of the corner cottage, she looked back at the dark figure standing motionless by the gaudy caravan, and felt that she had never seen such loneliness before.

Dimity answered the bell, her hands incarnadined.

'She'll be so pleased to see you,' she twittered, leading the way up the stairs. Mrs Bailey followed her red-speckled legs and scarlet-soled slippers aloft.

Ella Bembridge was an awe-inspiring sight in bed. Her short grey hair stood in a fine shock as she had run her fingers through it in her agitation. A bright red dressing-gown, no less vivid than the dye which bespattered her friend, was pinned at her neck with a gruesome grey monkey's paw, and contrasted strongly with the white bandage which enveloped one scalded hand.

Dimity had erected a tunnel, made with considerable ingenuity, from a bow-fronted fireguard, in order to keep the bedclothes from pressing too heavily upon poor Ella's painful legs, and this great mound, covered with a patchwork quilt of Ella's own making, added to the bizarre effect.

'Nurse is bringing a proper leg-cage later,' said Dimity, gazing with pride at her own handiwork, 'but she's at a baby case at the moment.'

Mrs Bailey admired the present appliance and inquired about the patient's sufferings.

'Simple ruddy torture!' responded Ella with energy. 'If it hadn't been for your husband I'd have taken a meat-axe to my lower limbs. Couldn't have hurt much more than they do now,' she added, with gloomy relish.

Dimity uttered a horrified squeak.

'Now, darling, don't be so naughty. It'll only make your rash worse.'

'And if you toss about,' warned Mrs Bailey, 'you'll capsize the tunnel.'

'Might just as well give up and die, I suppose,' boomed the patient, with a heartiness that belied her words. 'What about some tea, Dim?'

'Not for me,' said Mrs Bailey hastily, 'I must be getting back. I just wanted to see you and to leave these things.' She put the magazines carefully at Ella's side, well away from the sufferer's hurts, but even so the patient winced away and let out a bellow that set the washstand ringing.

Mrs Bailey tried to look contrite, and Dimity rushed to the bedside.

'Keep back! Keep back!' shouted Ella energetically, like a policeman with an exuberant crowd to control. The two women stood respectfully away from the bed and surveyed the vociferous patient.

'Don't worry,' said Mrs Bailey. 'We'll keep right over here away from your legs. Perhaps I can put these flowers in water for you?'

Dimity hurried away and returned with a large glass jug.

'I can't reach anything else in the kitchen,' she confessed, 'but they should look lovely in that. I must go down again. There's someone at the door.'

She fluttered off again and quietness fell upon the room. Mrs Bailey took the jug and flowers to the washstand, and began to arrange the white and gold daffodils carefully.

Their fragrance crept about the room, adding their breath of spring to the scents and sounds that came through the open window. The rooks wheeled and called above the elms nearby, and from Ella's flower-beds could be heard the chattering and scolding of half a dozen starlings who were busily demolishing her velvety polyanthus flowers. An early bee droned against the pane, his scaly brown legs tap-tapping against the glass like the frail twigs of the jasmine nearby.

Ella watched, in one of her rare silences, as Mrs Bailey moved the blossoms, standing back every now and again to survey her handiwork. The glass jug had been a happy choice, for the soft green beauty of the stalks and leaves could be seen. A myriad tiny air bubbles studded their length, like crystal beads, and Ella, whose gruff exterior hid a discerning sensitivity to loveliness, was moved to speak.

'They're perfect, Winnie. Don't muck 'em about any more. They're just absolutely right in that jug.'

'Clever of Dimity to get it,' murmured Mrs Bailey, still engrossed.

'I must say,' went on Ella, now emerged from her brief spell of quietness, 'it's a real pleasure to see flowers allowed to arrange themselves comfortably against the side of a vase, instead of being threaded through an entanglement of squashed-up chicken wire, or that wadding stuff the Lulling Floral Club will foist on its members.'

'Oh, come,' protested Mrs Bailey, advancing upon Ella with a pheasant-eye narcissus flower which had broken off. 'I think you must have some help sometimes for flowers. Think of nasturtiums or cowslips!'

She held out the flower to Ella to smell, but she made such violent gestures of dismissal, rocking the fireguard perilously, that Mrs Bailey tossed her the flower and returned to the washstand. Ella raised the blossom to her heated face and continued her harangue between violent sniffs at its snowy petals.

'Well, I've got no time for the Floral Club, as I've told you all before. It doesn't matter which house you go into within a radius of six miles, you can always tell if the mistress goes to the Lulling meetings.' She flung a bolster-like arm in the direction of Mrs Bailey and pointed an accusing finger at her.

'You know what I mean. You do it yourself. *April!* Everybody's got some prissy little workbox fished out from the attic and stuffed up with primroses and moss. *May!* Dam' great boughs of cherry blossom, impaled on wire, and perched up above eye-level somewhere where they're bound to get blown down. *June!* One iris, Japanese fashion, in a "cool-grey" or "celadon-green" vase!'

Mrs Bailey, shaking with laughter at her friend's vehemence, tried to protest, but was brushed aside.

'*July!*' continued Ella, warming to her theme. 'Three gladioli in a horrible flat white object, and arranged like a one-masted barque, with one up in the middle, and the other two horizontally fore and aft! And as for Christmas—'

Ella took a large breath, and turned a reddening, ferocious face upon her convulsed friend.

'I tell you plainly – now, in ample time. If you're thinking of concocting some horrible great table decoration out of plastic fern, dried grass, two dusty old sprigs of left-over Cape gooseberries, some ghastly artificial flowers from the haberdasher's, topped up with the bunch of violets you've worn to Lulling funerals for the past ten years, plus three poor little Roman hyacinths – like waifs among the corpses – then you can think again! I can face up to silver-painted holly, if that's what you people have in mind, with the rest of you – but I'm damned if I'll thank anybody, even you, Winnie dear, for a monstrosity like that. Or for an armful of frosted beetroot leaves!'

'Darling,' said Mrs Bailey, wiping her eyes, 'I promise you that I'll give you nothing floral at all when Christmas comes.'

She bent towards her old friend and gently kissed her good-bye.

Ella, her spirits as much restored by her own loquacity as by the flowers and the company, beamed her farewells. She had stuck the narcissus behind one ear, like a Pacific Island maiden. Its fragility contrasted strongly with the weather-beaten cheek against which it fell, and gave an added rakishness to her raffish appearance.

A large tabby cat, which was the adored pet of the house, crept in as Mrs Bailey opened the bedroom door. It glided to the bedside, gathered itself together, and leapt heavily upon its mistress's lap. Mrs Bailey, who had been powerless to forestall it, waited for screams and imprecations to rend the air. None came.

'Dear old puss,' cooed Ella lovingly, enveloping the creature in an embrace of red dressing-gown. 'Come to see your poor old mum, have you?'

Mrs Bailey closed the door quietly upon their reunion, and crept downstairs. At least, she told herself with amusement, she could let her husband know that one patient was well on the way to recovery.

12. A Family Fight

Curdle's Fair was now in readiness for its grand opening, soon after six, in about two hours' time.

It was not a large fair, it is true, but to its owner and its admirers in Thrush Green and dozens of other villages scattered across half a dozen counties, it had everything that was essential for an evening of delicious noise and heady vertigo.

The roundabout was the centre-piece. Its brass winked in the sunshine, and the dappled horses, legs stretched and nostrils aflare, galloped in eternal fury. A switchback, a trifle shabby about its red plush seats, but capable of dizzy speed, stood nearby; while eight swing-boats, painted red and blue, provided more sensation, and hung now, idly swaying beneath the striped furry sallies of their ropes. Later, as darkness fell, the youths of Lulling would tug with sweating palms at those hairy grips, vying with each other for speed and height and causing their terrified passengers to scream with mingled fear and ecstasy. What could be more exhilarating than the music of those faint screams, tribute to one's manly strength, added to the wild rush of night air as the boat swept up and back in a breathtaking arc, with the glare of the fair's lights swirling below and the pale stars glimmering above? The swing-boats were rarely idle once the fair began, but now, in the heat of the afternoon, they seemed to drowse, like boats at anchor in some serene harbour, swaying gently, in that lovelier element than water, above the rippling green grass.

The marquee that housed the menagerie was now in readiness. Rachel, shaken but obediently silent, had finished her ministrations there and now sat plaiting her hair on the steps of her home.

The coconuts stood poised upon the red-and-white striped posts that Ben had rammed home that morning. Five or six stalls – rolling pennies into a square, toy ducks to be caught with a magnet, the wheel of fortune, and the like – awaited their customers. Above each stall, festooned against a glitter of mirrors, hung teddy bears, dolls, teapots, cushions, kettles, crockery, watches, knives, and a host of prizes to dazzle covetous eyes.

A shooting range, with playing cards pricked with a thousand pin-marks, displayed similar prizes and some of a humbler type, pottery figures of dogs, gnomes, and unsteady baskets, doomed to break, chip, and peel in less than no time and to find a merciful end in a cottage dustbin.

A few small booths completed the fair. Some old sweets, great humbugs as big as a child's fist, vast flat tins of treacle toffee that cracked beneath the stallholder's metal hammer like brown enchanted glass, and billowing clouds of pink-and-white candy floss. Hanging at the side of one stall from a great hook, was a wonderful silky skein of sweet sugar floss which was pulled and twisted, looped and tossed, by dusky hands which were a seven-day wonder to the open-mouthed children and a shocking affront to their elders.

Two of the smaller booths flashed like Aladdin's cave with a galaxy of cheap jewellery. It was from one of these that Molly's much-loved cornflower brooch had come. Bracelets, necklaces, ear-rings, powder cases, and jewelled pins for scarf and hair sparkled with rubies, sapphires, diamonds, emeralds, pearls, and topazes, no less dazzling because they were of glass. They twinkled in the brilliant sunshine, reflecting its light from a thousand facets. Later they would flash even more brightly beneath the harsh lights set against the mirrored roof above them.

They expressed the very essence of the fair, garish but gay, seduc-tive but innocent, phoney but fascinating.

And in many a cottage home next day, one of those sparkling trinkets would be treasured as the souvenir of an enchanted evening, when hearts were as young and light as the newly broken leaves that whispered on Thrush Green's trees.

The infants had already straggled out of school. They had sung their grace, led by Miss Fogerty's quavering soprano:

> 'Thank you for the world so sweet.
> Thank you for the food we eat.
> Thank you for the birds that sing,
> Thank you, God, for everything.'

Some were sharp, some flat, some growled tunelessly, but all took it along at a spanking pace, determined to get out into the exciting canvas world of the fair, which had sprung up so miraculously since morning.

Shouting, running, trailing coats too hot to wear on this golden afternoon, they had vanished from Miss Fogerty's sight.

Sighing with exhaustion the teacher bent down and loosened her shoelaces. There was nothing more tiring to the feet than a sudden burst of warm weather, she told herself. Tomorrow, if it lasted, she decided, as she locked her desk and swept the snippets of coloured paper which littered it into the waste-paper basket, she really must look out her Clarks' sandals and be comfortable.

At the same time Molly and Ben were descending the steep path through Lulling Woods on their way to Thrush Green.

The laundry van had called early, and Ben had persuaded Molly that the main reason for lingering at 'The Drovers' Arms' had now vanished.

'Give us the chicken food,' he had directed, 'and I'll chuck it over while you tidies up.'

'But what about my missus?' Molly had said, pretending to be anxious.

'Leave her a note. You can write, can't you?' he said, with a wry smile. Molly gave him a sudden hug, delighted that he could now joke about something that had worried him so recently. The hug was returned warmly, and would have been prolonged indefinitely had not Molly broken away, thrust the chicken's bucket into her lover's hand, and run upstairs to put on the yellow spotted frock and hair ribbon.

Within half an hour they had emerged from the cool greenery of the woods into the golden meadows below. They walked slowly, arms round each other's waist, stopping every few paces to kiss or gaze with wonder at each other. After a year of doubt, loneliness, and despair the sudden revelation of their true feelings overwhelmed them. They were in the grip of the age-old spell of first love, and moved like beings entranced.

Ben had never felt so buoyant, so confident, and so invulnerable before. All the world was his, and there was nothing that he could not attempt now that he knew Molly was his.

But Molly, despite her happiness, felt apprehensive about the meeting with old Mrs Curdle. She had been a figure of awe-inspiring majesty to the girl all her life, and the thought of those black eyes scrutinizing and criticizing her was indeed a fearsome one.

'I could give you a cup of tea at our house,' she said shyly. 'The key's under the mat, and you'll have to meet my dad some time.'

'I daresay,' answered Ben, stopping again and holding his girl at arms' length. He knew all that was passing in her mind and laughed aloud to think that she should fear to meet old Gran.

'But I'm taking you straight to Gran's, and she'll give you more than a cup of tea. She'll give you the biggest welcome you've ever had. You'll see, she'll be that pleased!' promised young Ben earnestly, and Molly took what comfort she could from his assurances.

It was at this moment that they became conscious of a distant voice calling to them. Dotty Harmer, at the end of her garden, one hand clamping the enormous sun hat to her head and the other holding up a basket, was trying to attract their attention. They left the dusty path and waded through the sea of buttercups to her hedge, Molly hastily detaching herself from her companion's grasp.

'You wait here,' she urged. 'I won't be a minute.'

She approached the low hedge.

'Good afternoon, Miss Harmer,' she said demurely.

'Molly, be a good girl and take these few things in to Miss Bembridge. Have you heard about her accident?'

'No, indeed!' exclaimed Molly, and listened to the tale. She took the basket and lifted it over the hedge. Inside were various bottles and jars huddled under a dishevelled bunch of wilting primroses.

'I can't get up to Thrush Green myself,' went on Dotty, speaking of the place as though it were in another hemisphere, 'as the cat's kittening and she does like a little support at these times.'

She cast an inquisitive glance at the distant Ben.

'And who is the young man?' she inquired.

Curious old cat, thought Molly rebelliously, why should I tell her? But Miss Harmer, despite her scarecrow appearance, still occasioned a vestige of respect and a certain amount of pity too, so that the girl answered civilly.

'He's Ben Curdle, from the fair.'

The sound of anguished mewing floated from the shed nearby and Dotty turned away hastily.

'Many thanks,' she called as she went. 'Just drop it in, Molly.'

She vanished from sight and Molly rejoined Ben.

'She potty?' inquired the young man, nodding towards the cottage.

'Not really,' replied Molly tolerantly. 'Just had too much book learning.'

Together they resumed their interrupted progress to Thrush Green.

Meanwhile, Sam bit his nails and sat, glowering, on the steps of his caravan. The heat of the day and his own black temper caused him to sweat profusely. He untied his gaudy neckerchief and threw it behind him on to the floor of the caravan.

Well, that put paid to the horses for the afternoon, he told himself morosely. The old girl was back in the caravan and not likely to budge again. He remembered the cold, glittering look which she had cast him and Sam's craven soul shuddered at the remembrance.

The church clock chimed the first quarter, the silvery sound floating down through the sunny air as lightly as the summer insects that made the air murmurous about him. In fifteen minutes, thought Sam savagely, Rougemont would be setting off to win – and not a penny would he have on him.

He leapt to his feet, unable to sit still any longer under such provocation, and prowled behind the canvas enclosure of Ben's coconut shies. It was very quiet.

Not a soul was in sight, although he could hear the voices of women in a neighbouring caravan and the cries of the school children making their way home across Thrush Green.

At that moment he saw Mrs Curdle. She descended the steps of her caravan and made her way steadily in the direction of the menagerie tent. The old lady was about to continue her disturbed inspection. Sam noticed how heavily she leant upon her ebony stick, but it was not pity which moved his heart. A searing flash of hope caused it to throb. Talk of luck, he told himself! There still might be a chance!

His fears forgotten in the excitement of a flutter and a race against time, Sam moved swiftly towards the caravan. Its doorway faced away from the centre of the fair and he entered unobserved.

He wasted no time in investigating the drawer or the teapot, but crept to the end of Mrs Curdle's bed and heaved frantically at the mattress which enveloped the Curdle Bank.

Ben and Molly approached Mrs Curdle's caravan from the rear.

Molly had delivered Dotty's basket into Dimity's hands, had received her profuse thanks, and had inquired with real sympathy after poor Miss Bembridge. Molly had received many kindnesses from both ladies and felt for them affection mingled with some pity for their maiden state.

Her errand done, she returned to Ben with a fluttering heart, for now the time had come to face his formidable grandparent.

'Oh, Ben,' she said, suddenly faltering on the verge of Thrush Green, and turning beseeching eyes upon him.

Ben gave her that crinkly smile that turned her heart over, squeezed her hand, and said nothing. Together they threaded their way behind the booths and stalls, occasionally passing one of the Curdle tribe who glanced interestedly at Ben's companion but said nothing. Only a fair-girl, feeding her baby, and humming blissfully to herself in the drowsy sunshine, nodded to Molly and smiled at Ben. He paused for a moment to chirrup to the child and to flick his cousin's light hair, but they did not speak.

As they neared the caravan they could hear the sound of movement inside. Ben stopped, arrested by a sudden thought.

'I best make sure Gran's all right,' he said to Molly. 'She has a laydown sometimes of an afternoon. Wait half a minute for me.'

Molly nodded so eagerly and thankfully at this brief reprieve that Ben, now that no eyes were upon them, gave her a swift fierce hug and kiss that left her breathless.

Still laughing, he left her standing in the sunshine and ran lightly round the caravan and up the steps.

The scene that met Ben's astonished gaze needed no explanation. After the dazzle outside, the interior of Mrs Curdle's caravan was murky, but Ben saw enough to justify his swift action.

The bunk bed lay tumbled, and upon the crumpled quilt was the

Curdle Bank. The lid of the battered case was open, displaying a muddle of banknotes and silver and copper coins.

Sam, on being disturbed, had cowered as far as he could into a corner by the glittering stove. One hand he held up as if to ward off a blow, and the other was hidden behind his back.

His eyes were terrified as he gazed at the intruder who barred his only way of escape. His mouth dropped open, and a few incoherent bubbling sounds were the nearest that he could get to speech. Not that he was given time to account for himself, for Ben was upon him in a split second, gripping his arms painfully.

Sam twisted and heaved this way and that, trying to hide the notes in his hand, but Ben jerked his arm viciously behind him, and turned him inexorably towards the light. The notes fluttered to the floor.

Ben gave a low animal growl of fury and Sam a shrill scream of sudden pain. He lunged sharply with his knee. The two men parted for a moment, then turned face to face, and locked in a terrible panting embrace began to wrestle, one desperate with fear and the other afire with fury.

They lurched and thudded this way and that within the narrow confines of Mrs Curdle's home. Ben's shoulder brought down half a dozen plates from the diminutive dresser. Sam's foot jerked a saucepan from the hob, and the hissing water added its sound to the clamour which grew as the fight grew more vicious.

Molly, aghast at the noise, ran to see what was happening and, appalled at the sight, fled to get help. The flaxen-haired girl, still holding the baby to her breast, was wandering towards her.

'It's a fight!' gasped Molly. The girl looked mildly surprised, but uttered no word, merely continuing in an unhurried manner, to approach the source of the uproar.

Molly ran round a stall and was amazed to see a number of the Curdles converging rapidly upon her. There were about a dozen altogether, including several young children, whose eyes were alight with pleasurable anticipation at the thought of witnessing a fight.

The bush telegraph of the fairground was in action. These first spectators hurried past Molly, and, in the distance, she could see others, jumping down the steps of their caravans, calling joyously to each other of this unlooked-for excitement and scurrying to swell the crowd which was fast collecting round Mrs Curdle's caravan.

Emerging from one of the tents Molly saw the great lady herself.

A small fair-haired girl tugged agitatedly at her hand, urging her to hurry. The old lady's face was grim. She bore down upon the shrinking Molly like some majestic ship, and passed her without even noticing the trembling girl.

Emboldened by the example of this dominating head of the tribe, Molly braced herself, and like a small dinghy following in the wake of a liner she crept after Ben's grandmother and back to the scene of battle.

The spectators who had been vociferous, quietened as their leader stalked into their midst.

It was a tense moment. Ben had forced Sam to the doorway and they grappled and swayed dangerously at the head of the steps. They made a wild and terrifying sight, bloodied and dishevelled.

There was a sudden convulsive movement, a sickening crack as Sam's jaw and Ben's bony fist met, and Sam fell bodily backwards to the grass. He rolled over, scattering some of the crowd, groaned, twitched, and lay still.

A great sigh rippled round the onlookers, like the sound of wind through corn, and Mrs Curdle strode to the foot of the steps. She spared no glance for the prostrate man at her feet, but looked un-blinkingly at Ben, who swayed, bruised, and dizzy, against the door frame. A trickle of blood ran across his swelling cheek, and blood dripped from his broken knuckles upon the dusty black corduroy trousers.

Nobody watching the old lady could guess her feelings. Her dusky face was inscrutable, her mouth pressed into a hard thin line. Ben looked down upon her forlornly and broke the heavy silence.

'He asked for it, Gran,' he said apologetically.

Mrs Curdle made no sign, but her heart melted at the words. Just so, she remembered, had George looked, so many, many years ago, when she had caught him fighting another six-year-old. He too had swayed on his feet, and had looked outwardly contrite, whilst all the time, as she very well knew, he had secretly gloried in his victory. The sudden memory stabbed her so sharply, and filled her with such mingled sorrow and pride, that she continued to gaze at George's son (who might be George himself, so dearly did she love him) in utter silence.

Ben's eyes met his grandmother's and in that long shared look he knew what lay in her heart. He had proved himself; and to that love which she had always borne him another quality had been added. It was reliance upon him, and Ben rejoiced that it was so.

'Gran!' he cried, descending the steps with his arms out-stretched. But the old lady shook her head and turned to face the crowd. And Ben, content with his new knowledge, waited patiently behind her.

It was at this moment that Bella and her three children came upon the scene. She had been told the news as she struggled up the hill from Lulling, and now arrived, screaming, breathless, and blaspheming, her yellow hair streaming in the breeze, like some vengeful harpy. At the sound of her voice, Sam groaned, and struggled into a sitting posture, his aching head supported by his battered fists.

Mrs Curdle raised her ebony stick and Bella's torrent of abuse slowed down. Beneath the old lady's black implacable silence she gradually faltered to a stop, and began to weep instead, the three children adding their wails to their mother's.

At last the old lady spoke, and those who heard her never forgot those doom-laden words. Thunder should have rolled and lightning flashed as Mrs Curdle drew herself up to her great height, and, pointing the ebony stick at Sam, spoke his sentence.

'You and yours,' she said slowly, each word dropping like a cold stone, 'go from here tomorrow. And never, never come back!'

She turned her solemn gaze upon the gaping crowd, and, with a flick of the ebony stick, dismissed them. Two men assisted Sam to his feet and amidst lamentations from his family he hobbled to his caravan.

Mrs Curdle watched the rest of the tribe melt away and turned to question Ben at the foot of the steps.

But Ben was not there. She looked sharply about trying to catch sight of him among the departing spectators and suddenly saw him. He was some distance off, talking earnestly to a pretty young girl, beneath a tree.

As Mrs Curdle watched, she saw him take the girl's hand. They advanced towards her, the girl looking shy and hanging back. But there was nothing shy about Ben, thought Mrs Curdle, shaken with secret laughter and loving pride.

For, bruised and bloody, torn and dusty as he was, Ben radiated supreme happiness as he limped towards her across Thrush Green; and Mrs Curdle rejoiced with him.

PART THREE

NIGHT

---

13. Music on Thrush Green

The sun was beginning to dip its slow way downhill to hide, at last, behind the dark mass of Lulling Woods.

The streets of Lulling still kept their warmth, and the mellow Cotswold stone of the houses glowed like amber as the rays of the sun deepened from gold to copper.

On Thrush Green the chestnut trees sloped their shadows towards Doctor Bailey's house. The great bulk of the church was now in the shade, crouching low against the earth like a massive mother hen. But the weathercock on St Andrew's lofty steeple still gleamed against the clear sky, and from his perch could see the River Pleshy far below, winding its somnolent way between the water meadows and reflecting the willows and the drinking cattle which decorated its banks.

Although twilight had not yet come the lights of the fair were switched on at a quarter past six, and the first strains of music from the roundabout spread the news that Mrs Curdle's annual fair was now open.

The news was received, by those who heard it on Thrush Green, in a variety of ways. Sour old Mr Piggott, who had looked in at St Andrew's to make sure that all was in readiness for the two churchings at six-thirty, let fall an ejaculation, quite unsuitable to its surroundings, and, emerging from the vestry door, crunched purposefully and maliciously upon a piece of coke to relieve his feelings.

Ella Bembridge, who had eaten a surprisingly substantial tea for one suffering from burns, shock, and a rash, groaned aloud and begged Dimity to close the window against 'that benighted hulla-baloo'. Dimity had done so and had removed the patient's empty tray, noting with satisfaction that she had finished the small pot of quince jelly sent by Dotty Harmer that afternoon. In the press of events, she had omitted to tell Ella of Dotty's kindness, and now, seeing the inroads that her friend had made into Dotty's handiwork, she decided not to mention it. Ella could be so very scathing about

Dotty's cooking, thought Dimity, descending the crooked stairs, but obviously the quince jelly had been appreciated.

Paul, beside himself with excitement, was leaping up and down the hall, singing at the top of his voice. Occasionally he broke off to bound up to Ruth's bedroom where she was getting ready. The appalling slowness with which she arranged her hair and powdered her face, drove her small nephew almost frantic. This was the moment he had been waiting for all day – for weeks – for a whole year! Would she *never* be ready?

To young Doctor Lovell, returning from a visit to Upper Pleshy in his shabby two-seater, the colour and glitter of the fair offered a spectacle of charming innocence. Here was yet another aspect of Thrush Green to increase his growing affection for the place. Throughout the day he had found himself thinking of his happiness in this satisfying practice. He could settle here so easily, he told himself, slipping into place among the friendly people of Lulling, enjoying their company and sharing their enchanting countryside.

He drew up outside Doctor Bailey's house, and, resting his arms across the steering wheel, watched the bright scene with deep pleasure. This was the first time he had seen Mrs Curdle's fair. It would probably be the only time, he told himself grimly, for Mrs Curdle might not return next year, and if she did, who was to know where he would be?

The thought was so painful that Doctor Lovell jerked his long legs out of the car, slammed the door, and moved swiftly towards the surgery to find solace in his work.

Mrs Bailey heard the familiar noise of the surgery door, and looked over the top of her spectacles, just in time to see young Doctor Lovell vanish inside.

She was sitting in the window seat, sewing, and enjoying the last rays of the sunshine which had transfigured the whole day.

Doctor Bailey lay comfortably on the couch attempting to solve *The Times* crossword which lay upon his bony knees. He had recovered from his afternoon's bout of weakness and, to his wife's discerning eye, he appeared more serene and confident than he had for many weeks – as indeed he was. For having resolved to offer young Lovell a partnership in the practice his mind was at rest. That agonizing spasm in the brilliant sunshine of Thrush Green had taught him a sharp lesson and he was a wise enough man to heed it.

His decision made, at terms with himself and the world, the old doctor was content to let his body and mind relax, awaiting the end of surgery hours when he could put his proposal to his new young helper. That he would accept it, Doctor Bailey had no doubt at all.

The room had been quiet, with that companionable silence born of mutual ease. When the music of the fair blared out it made no difference to the peace of the two listeners. It was the first of May on Thrush Green, and music was its right and fitting accompaniment.

It was also the overture to Mrs Curdle's annual visit, remembered Mrs Bailey. She let her needlework drop into her lap and looked at last year's bunch of wood-shaving flowers which she had conscientiously put into a tall vase ready for Mrs Curdle's polite inspection later.

Her mind flew back to her first view of young Mrs Curdle, with baby George securely fastened to her hip by an enveloping bright shawl, holding the first of many mammoth bouquets. Poor George, thought Mrs Bailey, so loved, so dear, so soon to leave his adoring mother to be killed in battle. What a tragic loss, not only for inconsolable Mrs Curdle, but for their fair and, for that matter, the country as a whole.

Mrs Bailey's thoughts slipped back, as they so often did, to those lost young friends of both wars, and she wondered, yet again, if the world would have been different had they lived. It would have been enriched, of that she had no doubt, for all those lives had something of value – some facet of truth and beauty – to offer, that would have illumined other men's lives as well as their own. The world we must accept as it is, she recognized that fact philosophically, but it did not stop one from pondering on its limitless possibilities if those others, untimely dead, had had their way with it.

Her husband's voice recalled Mrs Bailey from 'old unhappy, far-off things, and battles long ago' to the present.

'Dairycats,' he was saying speculatively. 'An anagram. Any idea?'

'Caryatids,' responded Mrs Bailey, without hesitation. Beaming, the doctor filled in the clue in his neat precise hand. Now that the spell of silence was broken Mrs Bailey told her husband about her meeting before tea with old Mrs Curdle.

'And she looks quite desperately ill,' she said. 'And as far as I could gather, she wants to consult you. I did hint gently that Doctor Lovell would be taking the surgery tonight—'

'She won't take that hint!' pronounced Doctor Bailey emphatically. 'In any case, I should like to see her myself, and I don't think she would allow anyone else to examine her.'

'Well, I certainly hope you'll find her fit to carry on,' said Mrs Bailey. 'I can't imagine May the first without that background!'

She nodded her head in time with the raucous and distorted rendering of 'Happy Days are Here Again' which floated through the open window.

'She'll keep going if there's half a chance,' prophesied the doctor. 'She's a grand old girl. She won't want to give up any more than I do.'

He wriggled himself into a more comfortable position, then wagged a solemn finger at his wife.

'You know what? Mrs Curdle and I are in the same boat. We're old and we don't like it. I think we shall both feel better when we've faced that uncomfortable fact. Now, my dear, give me your advice. Should you say that "Knickerbocker Glory" was an anagram?'

Across the road, on Thrush Green itself, the head of the fair moved methodically from one stall to the next. Mrs Curdle's dark eyes missed nothing, and as the members of her tribe saw her approach they straightened up the prizes, flicked the dust from mirrors and brass, and renewed their shouts of encouragement to the few customers already exploring the attractions.

Tonight, particularly, after the scene of Sam's shame, her family were on the qui vive. Ma, on the war path, was a figure they had cause to fear, and this was pay day too. Curdle's Fair was at its most efficient.

Sam was at his post, by the switchback, despite a bruised face, a swollen jaw containing two loose teeth, and a headache which normally would have kept him in his bunk bed.

He knew well enough that he would have more to suffer if Mrs Curdle found him malingering on his last day in her employ.

Bella, to his amazement, had said little, too confounded by the shock of dismissal and Sam's disgrace to remonstrate further. She had, often enough, he remembered bitterly, nagged him to leave the fair. Well, now he had no option but to go. He leant his aching back against the painted support of the switchback, his dizzy head whirling as madly and as noisily as the machinery behind him. It said much for Mrs Curdle's discipline that Sam never for one moment considered approaching her for forgiveness or change of heart. From that implacable matriarch nothing, he knew, would be gained. Go he must, and in the early light of dawn, when Mrs Curdle's retinue took the high road towards the north, on its way to join a large fair at an ancient market town near Oxford, Sam's family would be missing from the procession. He knew, from experience of other family outcasts from the Curdle tribe, that he would never be spoken of again.

He straightened up as he saw the old lady bearing down upon him. She looked better than she had done all day. She carried the ebony stick, but leant upon it less obviously, and her flashing eyes above the jutting haughty nose had a fire in them which had been missing for many a long day. It was as if the fight had given her new strength. Many a woman, the victim of robbery and treachery in her own family, would have been shaken with shock, but Mrs Curdle was made of lusty stuff and had thrived all her life on just such battles. Firmly she approached the switchback and the trembling, unhappy Sam.

She gave a grim searching glance at the circling contraption, her hawk gaze passing over her nephew without a flicker. He might have been one of the gnats that hovered in her path, so little notice did she take of him. Neither by word nor gesture did she acknowledge his presence. He was no longer part of Mrs Curdle's world.

She passed on, leaving Sam even more wretched than before. The thought of a drink at 'The Two Pheasants' floated ravishingly into Sam's dizzy head, and was instantly rejected. Sam knew when he was beaten, and watched this tyrant continue her regal progress towards the coconut shies, where Ben, with Molly beside him, exhorted the customers to greater efforts.

And, to his chagrin, Sam saw the old lady's grim mouth soften into a warm smile as she approached the pair.

It had been an extraordinary tea party in Mrs Curdle's caravan that afternoon, and Molly was never to forget it.

When Sam had departed, and the crowd had vanished as quickly as it had formed, Ben had found her half-way home. Already under considerable strain from the emotion of the day, and strung up at the thought of meeting Ben's formidable grandmother, poor Molly had found this sudden, fierce, silent fight absolutely unbearable. She had determined to slip back to the cottage and to venture forth later when the rumpus had died down.

Ben, bleeding and dishevelled, was a fearsome figure when he caught up with her, but his dark eyes shone and his voice was gentle as he pleaded with her to return with him. She could not refuse him and he had led her back to that awe-inspiring figure at the foot of the caravan steps. Mrs Curdle had watched in silence as they approached and it was Ben who spoke first.

'Gran, this is Molly. She lives over the green. I've brought her to tea.' He wiped a hand across his cheek, and looked with some surprise at the blood on his fingers.

Mrs Curdle turned a smile upon the girl, so quick, so warm, and so like Ben's that Molly's fears fell from her.

'You be very welcome,' said the old lady, graciously, inclining her head with a royal gesture. She turned to Ben, who stood beaming upon them both.

'And if you be coming to tea too you'd best wash that muck off yourself,' she ordered. Ben pulled himself together and began to brush the dust from his corduroy trousers.

'I'll get cleaned up, Gran,' he promised and set off towards his caravan. Mrs Curdle watched him go with a smile.

'He's a good boy,' she murmured, as if to herself. 'A real good boy. His dad all over again.'

For a moment she seemed to have forgotten Molly and to have slipped away to some time or place of which the girl knew nothing. But, after a long minute, she sighed and turned politely to her guest.

'Come you in, my dear. And if we're going to get a cup of tea – well, maybe you'll give me a hand tidying up the mess them young fellows have made.'

The two women had mounted the steps and faced the turmoil. Molly was used to creating order from chaos and wasted no time on useless bewailing. Old Mrs Curdle sat on the edge of her tumbled bed and began returning the scattered money to the attaché case, whilst the girl swept up broken china, replaced the pots and pans that littered the floor, and mopped up the water that had been spilt round

Mrs Curdle's shining stove. The old lady watched her deft movements with approval.

'You known my Ben long?' she inquired shrewdly.

'Since last year,' said Molly, looking up from her mopping. She
wrung out a dripping cloth into an enamel bowl and set to again. It
was easier to talk with her hands occupied in such familiar tasks and
her qualms were leaving her under the kindly scrutiny of the old
lady on the bed.

'He's a boy you can trust,' Mrs Curdle said soberly. 'No fly-
by-night, young Ben. But he wouldn't stand for any flirting,
mind!'

Molly flushed.

'There's no need for him to,' she retorted. 'I ain't the flirting kind.'
The thought of her year's unhappy vigil pricked her into speech
again, for the old lady's words rankled.

'I been waiting to hear from him for a twelve-month, and refused
a-plenty, and that's flat!'

She rubbed energetically at a tarnished streak on the side of the
stove. Her mouth was rebellious and Mrs Curdle stretched down a
dusky hand to the curly head that bobbed so near her knee.

'You don't need to take on, my dear,' said Mrs Curdle very
gently. 'Ben won't look at no one else. And I hope yes, I do hope –
as you'll see fit to stick to our Ben. You're the one for him.'

The girl sat back on her heels, still clutching the wet cloth, and the
two women exchanged a look of complete understanding. Mutual
affection, respect, and the love which they both bore Ben united
them in that instant. The bond was never to be broken.

'How old be you?' asked Mrs Curdle, resuming her tidying.

'Near enough eighteen,' answered Molly, rising to her feet. She
rested the enamel bowl easily against her hip and old Mrs Curdle
looked her up and down approvingly.

'I had my first at eighteen,' said she, nodding sagely. ''Tis a good
thing to start a family young in our line of business. They helps as
you gets older and the big 'uns brings on the little 'uns.'

Molly was momentarily disconcerted at this calm acceptance of
the position.

'My dad don't know nothing about Ben. I keeps house for him
really. He'll have something to say if I tell him.'

'Ben'll call on your dad tonight,' pronounced Mrs Curdle finally.

'There's no call to be flustered. I don't doubt Ben'd rush you off to church tomorrow if he had his way. Ben's always hasty, and his dad was the same. But, at eighteen, going steady's no crime for a bonny girl like you, and your dad can like it or lump it.'

'He won't like it, that I do know,' said Molly emphatically. 'He don't like travelling people. He'll say I'm –' She hesitated, anxious not to hurt the old lady's feelings by putting the ordinary settled man's suspicions of the nomad into words.

Mrs Curdle gazed at her shrewdly.

'He'll say you're throwing yourself away on a gipsy, who ain't got two ha'pennies to rub together. Is that it?'

The girl nodded unhappily. There was a silence in the little caravan, broken only by the fluttering of an early butterfly against the sunny caravan window.

'Do you think you are?' asked the old lady at length. The girl's face lit up.

'Never!' she said softly. Mrs Curdle sighed happily.

'There's time for your dad to get used to the idea of your marrying a gipsy boy. Won't hurt you two to wait a few months and start your married life when we're resting for the winter. And besides –'

She paused as though wondering if she should add what was in her mind. The girl waited, with her head on one side, looking down at that dark thoughtful face.

'And besides,' continued Mrs Curdle, 'what your dad don't know is that Ben's no pauper, but a chap with a grand business behind him. He needn't fear his daughter'll starve while Curdle's Fair is going strong.'

At that moment, Ben had appeared in the doorway, washed and clad in clean clothing.

'Ain't you two women had time to put the kettle on with all that talking?' he inquired. And grabbing the empty vessel from the side of the hob he went, whistling, to remedy their omission.

And now, as the sunset did its best to rival the gaudy splendour of the fair, Mrs Curdle finished the tour of her little world with her spirits restored. Every booth and side-show and every piece of machinery was in order and buckling to its daily business. The clamour, the shouting, the throbbing of motors, and the oily smell that emanated from them and was as incense in the nostrils of the old lady who owned them, filled the warm evening air.

Up the steep hill from Lulling in the south, across the western golden meadows below Lulling Woods and down from the north-lying hamlets of Upper Pleshy, Nod, and Nidden, came the country folk to enjoy the brief pleasures of the glittering fair.

For tonight Thrush Green throbbed and beat like a great heart, pulsing out its message to the countryside around, and there were many who answered the call, remembering, with a pang, that it might be the last time that they would hear it.

With a heart as bright and indomitable as the fair itself Mrs Curdle stood at the doorway of her home and surveyed the bustle. It had been a good day, she told herself, trash thrown out and a bit of real gold found, she fancied, thinking of Ben's fine girl. Well, there it was, her fair, her whole world, spinning away as usual, and quite capable of looking after itself for an hour or two while she took time off to face the last job of this long, bright day!

She turned her back upon it resolutely and began to prepare herself for her visit to Doctor Bailey.

14. All the Fun of the Fair

Paul's happiness was complete. At last he was in the midst of that glorious world which he had seen being created, that morning, from his bedroom window. It was even more intoxicating than he had remembered it. Were there ever such lights, such music, and such a galaxy of pleasures?

He gripped his aunt's hand, but was unconscious of her presence. His eyes and mouth formed three great O's, and he was oblivious of everything but the splendour which surrounded him. His school-fellows hailed him, grown-up friends spoke to him, but he was too entranced to notice them. This was a magic world and he was in its spell.

Ruth led him towards the roundabout, for she knew that this was his favourite attraction of the fair. He clambered up the steep wooden step and edged purposefully towards an ostrich, a creature resplendent in pink and green plumage, that lived in remarkable amity with the galloping horses beside it. It was this beast which he had ridden last year, and his affection for it had remained constant.

Ruth hoisted him aloft and mounted the horse beside him. From her perch she looked down at the faces of those watching below, many of them known to her since childhood. The feel of the smooth wood between her knees, and the curly cold brass pillar between her hands, gave Ruth the same thrill that she remembered feeling years ago. Tonight, with her decision to stay at Thrush Green still fresh in her mind, the fact of being here on the day of the fair possessed an added poignancy.

For better or for worse, she was part and parcel of this small world, and content to be so. Her spirits rose as the roundabout began to turn, and the music blared deafeningly from its centre. An archaic contraption, of organ-like appearance, emitted the noise, and Ruth watched Paul's admiring gaze fixed on the mirrors and jiggling marionettes which embellished the machine. She had wondered if violent motion would upset the child, but there was no sign of anything but holy ecstasy on her nephew's countenance.

The roundabout whirled faster and faster, and now the outside world was just a coloured blur, and Ruth and Paul had all they could do to stay on their flying mounts. As Paul soared up on his glorious ostrich, Ruth sank low upon her horse, and as the positions reversed Ruth caught glimpses of oily, creaking machinery, jerking and jumping, in the semi-darkness below the glittering organ. It looked remarkably rickety, and she turned her eyes hastily away.

One of the Curdles approached her, swaying easily among the heaving horses, and held out a black hand for the money. He shouted some pleasantry at Paul, but the noise was so deafening that the words were lost in the tumult. He flashed a smile at Ruth, dazzlingly white amidst the murk of his countenance, and continued his rolling progress.

At last the roundabout slowed down. The coloured blur, which had surrounded them, became individual figures; the houses, the church, the chestnut avenue, and the white palings of the village school ceased chasing each other and settled again into their appointed places, and Ruth and Paul descended, a trifle wobbly at the knees, but greatly exhilarated.

The ride had woken Paul from his earlier trance and now he dragged Ruth from one attraction to the next, chattering excitedly.

'Let's go on the switchback,' he cried. But Ruth felt that one dizzy ride was enough for a little while, and also, looking at the morose and battered Sam Curdle who was in charge, felt some repugnance.

'Look! Coconut shies!' carolled her nephew, tugging energetically at her arm. They hastened in the direction of the crowd which had collected there. Several youths, their shirt sleeves rolled up, hurled the small wooden balls savagely towards their target. The crack of wood against the wooden stands of securely placed coconuts alternated with the thwack of the balls against the taut canvas background. Very few coconuts fell off, despite the onslaught, but there were plenty of customers encouraged by Ben's lusty approval and Molly's pretty face.

'There's Molly!' shrieked Paul with joy, and, breaking from Ruth's grasp, fled across the battlefield in the thick of flying balls to join his friend.

'Oy!' shouted Ben, laughing. 'You'll get your 'ead knocked off for a coconut!' – which sally Paul thought the very essence of humour. He recognized Ben, despite a swelling cheek and some discoloration of the eye, as Molly's particular friend, and looked suddenly up at her with a questioning glance.

'He said he was coming to see you?'

'He did,' said Molly, nodding reassuringly at the little boy. He had known her feelings from the first and she did not intend to try and keep secrets from him now.

'Then it's all right?'

'It's all right,' repeated Molly, with such a delicious smile that Paul hugged her round the waist, in a sudden embrace that showed his joy, relief, and congratulations in one swift movement.

'Going to try your luck?' asked Ben, approaching.

'Please,' said Paul, and Ruth handed over sixpence. Ben gave Paul three balls and took him to the half-way line. While he took his stance solemnly and eyed the tempting coconuts, Molly inquired about the little boy's parents.

Ruth gave her news of their return in two days' time, and they exchanged gossip about their families. All the time, Ruth noticed, Molly's eyes followed the figure of the young man.

At last, as though wishing to share her pent-up happiness, Molly spoke rapidly to Ruth.

'I been to tea with Mrs Curdle today. That's her grandson, over there – Ben, his name. Paul knows about him, and p'raps you do too.'

'I don't, you know,' said Ruth, 'but he looks very handsome.'

Molly flushed with pride.

'He's a lot handsomer than that really, but he had a bit of a fight before tea.' Molly made it sound as though physical conflict before a meal was the most natural thing in the world, but she rattled on before Ruth could go further into this interesting disclosure.

'We've got to see my dad later, and I must say I don't relish it, but Ben don't show a bit of fear.'

'Does this mean you're thinking of leaving us?' asked Ruth tentatively.

'Not yet,' answered the girl, 'but I reckon I'll be gone before the winter.'

'Oh, Molly, we shall miss you!' said Ruth, putting out a hand with genuine concern. Molly smiled gaily at her.

'I'll be back next May the first,' she promised, 'with Curdle's Fair. Shall I look out for you, or will you be gone by then?'

Ruth shook her head slowly and returned Molly's smile.

'I'll be here,' she said.

At that moment Paul ran up, appealing for another sixpence.

'I hit one but it didn't fall off. Did you see? I hit one. Were you looking? I *actually* hit one! This time I'll knock it right off!'

'That's right,' said Ben. 'He'll get one this time, you see.'

Ruth handed over another sixpence and the two departed to try again. This time Paul's shots went wider than ever, but Ben spoke to Molly before returning to his customers and she vanished into a corner, returning with a coconut which she presented to the astounded Paul.

'But I didn't hit it!' he protested.

'Sh!' said Molly, one eye on the customers. 'It's what's called a consolation prize. You tried hard so Ben's give you this. Save a bit for me!' She gave the child a swift pat on the cheek, waved farewell, and returned to Ben's side.

Bearing the hairy trophy like some sacred relic, Paul, enraptured, led the way towards the swing-boats.

One of Mrs Curdle's daughters, as massive and dark, but not a quarter as majestic as her mother, greeted them boisterously.

'Come along, my ducks. 'Op in now and give yerself a treat!' She

lifted a long plank that was attached to the gear and applied it as a
brake to the bottom of a scarlet boat. It slowed down abruptly, much
to the vociferous annoyance of two young ladies who Ruth recognized as two of the genteel assistants at 'The Fuchsia Bush'. Their
refined accents had vanished under stress of circumstance and been
replaced by a more plebeian, and far less painful, mode of speech.

They clambered out, displaying a prodigious amount of leg, and
Paul began to climb the wobbly step-ladder that stood beside the
swaying boat.

Ruth suddenly felt that she could not bear the motion of the
swing so soon after the roundabout and the general noise which
surrounded her.

'Can you work it alone? I'll wait here,' promised Ruth. Paul
nodded his agreement, settled himself importantly on one red cushion, gripped the furry sally, still warm from the clutches of one of
the young ladies, and began to haul himself into glorious motion.

'The young gentleman'll be all right, mum,' said Mrs Curdle's
daughter heartily. 'If you gets nervous lift this 'ere stick, or 'oller for
me. I'll be 'andy!' She bustled off to another client, leaving Ruth
very content to stand alone enjoying the rush of air as Paul's boat
beat its rhythmic way back and forth above her.

For Paul, had she known it, this solitary splendour was the highlight of his day. Always, for months and years now, he had longed to
ride alone in a swing-boat, to be master of this flying craft, with no
one to fuss about him or to slow his progress.

This, he told himself, as he soared blissfully above the trees on
Thrush Green, this really was flying! He remembered his imaginary
flight of the morning when he had peered inside the school, the
church, and all the pleasant corners of Lulling. How much more
satisfying was this heady swooping! He hauled vigorously, thrilled
with his own prowess, and as the boat curved skywards he could see
the pale lane that led to Nod and Nidden, and the buttercup fields
that lay behind the little yard of the village school.

He must be nearly as high as the weathercock on the steeple, he
told himself ecstatically. The light was beginning to thicken now, so
that the sleepy grey town below the hill was indistinct, but in bright
sunshine he was sure he could have seen every roof-top and chimney,
and perhaps, still farther afield, the sea and glimpses of those foreign
lands he so wanted to visit when he was a grown man.

He paused in his pulling for a moment, for his young arms were aching, and was content to swoop tranquilly back and forth while he mused upon those distant places that were beginning to welcome the sun which had now slipped away from Thrush Green. At this very minute, thought young Paul, there were people there laughing and playing – swinging perhaps, as he was, but on bright tropical trees that grew by seas as blue as the swing-boat that lay idle beside his own.

It was a game that he often played when he was alone, letting his mind dwell on things that were happening all over the world at the same moment, and today the motion of the swing-boat and the unaccustomed height added to the range of his fancies. A gleam of distant water caught his eye, and he knew that it was the River Pleshy where he picnicked and paddled on summer days. And now, as he swung on Thrush Green and over the sea those brown gay people played under their flowered trees, among the watery weeds of his much-loved river the minnows would be wavering in shoals, all headed up-stream, their eyes gleaming like jewels. And far away, in waters much more cold and turbulent, the great sharks would be splashing and diving. And farther still, sharks and a myriad other fishes, cruel or benign, slid mysteriously among the forests and caverns of the sea which helped to make this colourful round ball of a world the wonder that it was.

This power of transporting himself elsewhere was never to leave Paul. It came from a sympathy and kinship with all forms of life, and from an awareness of the smallness of the world around him. At the moment Thrush Green was his real world. He saw that the people there knew and relied on each other. It was a closely knit community of individuals, each sensitive to the other and related by ties of kinship, affection, dislike, or work. With the eyes of a six-year-old, Paul looked down upon the small familiar green face of his little world. In later years, after much travelling, he was to find the greater one about it very much the same.

Doctor Lovell had very few patients at his evening surgery, which did not surprise him. There is a therapeutic quality about a one-day fair that works more healing than a visit to the doctor.

Tomorrow, as he well knew, the sad familiar faces would line the walls of the waiting-room, but meanwhile, those that could forget their aches and pains had taken themselves and their children to enjoy the fun.

A message about Ella Bembridge's accident had been left on his desk and, now that the last patient had gone, he decided to walk along to the corner cottage.

The sky was a glory of colour, pink, gold, and mauve, with here and there a tinge of apple-green that told of the clear skies which had smiled all day upon the first of May.

Doctor Lovell stood by the gate enjoying the air and the lively scene. At his side stood a young lilac tree, its buds now so tightly furled that they looked like bunches of red currants in the rosy light. Soon it would be adding its heady fragrance to the wallflowers and narcissi at his feet.

A man passed by with a bundle of stout bean poles balanced across his shoulder, and Doctor Lovell felt a pang of envy as he saw him, so confident that he would be here in Thrush Green to enjoy his beans in July and August, so secure in his plans and his provision for the future.

It was going to be hard to leave Thrush Green, if that were to be his fate. His eyes strayed to the Bassetts' house and his thoughts turned again to Ruth, as he had found them doing so often lately.

He opened the gate and turned left to pay his visit to Ella. The clamour of the fair blew like a blast from the green across the road, but above its noise a shrill voice could be heard.

'Look at me, doctor! Look at me!'

His first patient of the day attracted his attention. He waved cheerfully to the small flying figure, and would have passed on, but at the same instant he saw Ruth waiting patiently below.

With a heart behaving in a most unorthodox way for the property of a medical man, Doctor Lovell left the path of duty and joined the girl.

15. Mr Piggott Gives His Consent

Dimity Dean, a little weary in body, sat in the creaking wicker armchair in the corner of her patient's bedroom.

To the observer it would have appeared a serene domestic scene.

Dimity was engaged in knitting a grey jumper, to enhance her mouse-like appearance the following winter, while Ella, propped against her pillows, perused the magazines which Mrs Bailey had left.

The reading-lamp beside the bed shed its light upon the fading narcissus flower still perched over one ear. The large cat had settled itself comfortably upon the bed, and soon the curtains would be drawn against the night which was beginning to envelop Thrush Green.

The noise of the fair was muted by the closed window, but the bright lights of the revolving roundabout and switchback passed and repassed across the low ceiling of the little room.

The scene may have looked peaceful but Ella's stringent comments on her reading matter contrasted strongly with her tranquil surroundings.

'Now, here's a damfool idea!' protested Ella energetically, folding back the thick magazine with a loud cracking noise. 'Sticking something you've broken together again, painting the cracks with scarlet lacquer, and giving it away to a friend! Wouldn't be a friend for long, I'd say! Can you beat it?'

She glowered upon the picture with some relish, before turning over.

'And this is even worse! Listen to this, Dim. "How to make a set of dainty table mats." And how I do hate "dainty"!' gibbered Ella, in a frenzied aside.

'How do you?' asked Dim equably, genuinely interested.

'I'll tell you,' said Ella, with fiendish satisfaction in her tone. 'You cut up pieces of lino that you have no further use for –'

'Like that bit in the shed,' exclaimed Dimity, eyes brightening.

'Like that bit in the shed,' conceded Ella grimly. 'That is if you *really want* dinner mats made of lino covered with mildew like prussian-blue fur, or even just made of lino *without* the prussian-blue fur –'

'Well, go on,' said Dimity.

'I *am* going on,' shouted Ella rudely, 'but you keep interrupting.'

'You'll upset the fireguard,' warned Dimity.

'Do you, or do you not, want to hear about these infernal mats?' inquired Ella furiously.

'Why, yes,' cried Dimity. Ella turned back to the magazine and continued truculently.

'Then you cut out sprays of flowers from plastic material. And then you stick these horrible sprays on to the lino mats, varnish the lot and there you are. As evil a set of vicious-looking table mats as ever saw the dim religious light of any church bazaar!'

She leant back upon her pillows contemplating these innocent suggestions as if they had been some dreadful rites connected with Black Magic. Dimity hastened to change the subject.

'I think it's time you had a dose of medicine for your rash.'

Ella continued to watch the lights revolving dizzily across the ceiling for a minute. When she spoke it was in a changed tone.

'D'you know, Dim, I feel quite extraordinary. Whether it's those dam' lights, or something I've eaten, I don't know, but I feel jolly queasy.'

Dimity, with a guilty start, recalled Dotty Harmer's quince jelly.

'Could be that ghastly fish in parsley sauce,' continued Ella speculatively. 'Never could stomach the stuff. Might as well eat whitewash or that muck they make you swallow before X-rays.'

She turned a searching glance upon the wilting Dimity.

'You feel all right? You ate it.'

'Well, yes,' faltered poor Dimity. 'I feel quite fit, but—' She hesitated, wringing sad limp hands still rosy from the dye.

'But what?' asked Ella. Her face was contorted with a sudden spasm of pain and she put a hand upon her capacious stomach.

Dimity took a brave deep breath and made her confession.

'I forgot to tell you — that quince jelly, dear. It was made by Dotty. She sent it up this afternoon.'

Groaning, Ella sank back upon the pillows.

'You're a fine friend!' she said roundly, but her gruff tone held a hint of kindliness. 'You know Dotty. She probably put a cupful of hemlock in to give it a bit of a kick!'

'Oh, Ella darling!' moaned poor Dimity, 'I wouldn't have had it happen for worlds. What shall we do?'

'Don't suppose it'll be fatal,' answered Ella morosely. 'Though with all I've got at the moment death would be a mercy, and that's flat! I'll get young Lovell to give me some jollop when he comes.'

She looked at her friend and gave her a sudden warm smile.

'Cheer up, Dim, it might be worse! Pull the curtains and shut out those vile lights. That'll help.'

Dimity crossed to the window and looked out upon the bustle and glitter of Mrs Curdle's fair across the road.

'Why,' she exclaimed, 'there is Doctor Lovell! And it looks like Ruth he's talking to! Yes, it is. I can see Paul running up to them.'

'Time that child was in bed,' snorted Ella. 'Ruth should know better, keeping him up while she philanders with her young man.'

'Oh, Ella, really!' protested Dimity.

'It's been sticking out a mile for weeks,' said Ella firmly, her pains momentarily forgotten. 'If they don't make a match of it before the year's out, I'll eat my hat. But not tonight,' she added hastily, as Dotty's jelly made itself felt.

'He's coming this way,' said the watcher at the window suddenly. 'He must be calling here.'

'Then for pity's sake get him up here quickly,' urged her friend. 'He'll find plenty to do.'

Sure enough, within two minutes the knocker was being attacked and soon young Doctor Lovell confronted his patient. Although he could not take to this brusque ungainly woman, yet so warm and radiant is the power of love that the doctor found himself feeling a new sympathy. The unaccustomed sparkle in his dark eye and his gentle manner only confirmed the suspicions of his tough spinster patient. Here indeed was a man in love.

He examined the scalds and the rash and listened sympathetically to Dimity's incoherent confession. This was not his first encounter with Dotty's handiwork. He smiled benignly as he scribbled down a prescription on his little pad, and took out two white pills from his case.

'These will help at the moment,' he promised Ella. 'Nurse is coming with the cage for your legs and I really think you'll feel much better tomorrow.'

'I should hope so,' responded the patient feelingly. 'What a day! I never thought so much could happen to me in one day.'

'Nor me,' agreed the young man warmly, but his tone held a wonder lacking in his patient's. He stood for a moment as though his thoughts were engaged elsewhere on Thrush Green. The sardonic gaze from the bed brought him to his senses.

'I'll see you in the morning,' he said hastily, collecting his belongings. 'You're a pretty straightforward case, you know. Burns, shock, dermatitis, and now this last disease.'

'D'you know what it is?' asked Ella.

'Unique to the district, ma'am, so I understand,' said young Doctor Lovell, smiling from the doorway. 'Dotty's Collywobbles!'

From among the noisy activity of the coconut shies Molly Piggott watched young Doctor Lovell emerge from Miss Bembridge's house and make his way briskly back to Doctor Bailey's.

'Wonder how he found the poor old dear?' thought Molly to herself, descending from the rapturous heights which she had inhabited for the last few hours for a brief visit to the everyday world of Thrush Green. But on such an evening the affairs of anyone as mundane as Ella Bembridge could hold Molly's attention but momentarily, for here, beside dear Ben, accepted by his grandmother, and with the future glittering as brightly as the fair itself, enchantment lay.

But despite her joy, one shadow remained. Her father had yet to be informed of her plans and Molly dreaded the encounter for Ben's sake. She had cast anxious eyes towards the cottage for the past two hours, but the windows had remained dark. The master of the house was still enjoying his leisure under the hospitable roof of 'The Two Pheasants' next door.

At last Molly saw a light in the window and her heart sank. Now she was for it, she told herself. Best cut across home, fry the old boy's supper and rasher and egg, and break the news as best she could. She turned to Ben and put a hand upon his arm. The noise was deafening about them, and although the girl put her mouth within an inch of Ben's bruised ear, she could not make herself heard. Only by nodding in the direction of the cottage did she make her meaning clear.

Ben took her arm, calling as he did so to Rachel's father who was leaning dreamily against a booth negligently picking his teeth with the end of a feather.

'Take over, Bob, will you, for a bit?' shouted Ben. 'Be back in half an hour.'

Bob nodded casually, and strolled towards the coconut shies.

'Won't make a fortune there for the next half-hour, I'll lay,' said Ben grimly. 'But never mind, my gal, let's get over and see your dad.'

Molly stood still and looked at Ben with eyes dark with worry.

'Hadn't I best go back alone? I always gets his supper, see, my nights off, and I could easy tell him a bit about us, without your botherin'. He can be a bit nasty – short-like, you know, if he's surprised or anything. I don't want no unpleasantness, not on a lovely day like this has been.'

'This is my business, Moll, as well as yours and his. If there's any unpleasantness I'm the one to stop it. You needn't fear I won't behave civil in your father's house. My Gran's learnt me proper manners, you know, but this 'ere's a man's job. You cook his supper and I'll break the news while you breaks the eggs. How's that?'

He put his head on one side and gave her his crooked smile. Molly nodded silently, too moved with relief and love for speech.

Together they crossed the soft spring grass towards the cottage. The blare of the fair faded behind them and the rustle of the trees in the warm night air could be heard again.

'This is Ben, Dad. Ben Curdle – from the fair,' said Molly. She was smiling bravely, but her heart fluttered in a cowardly way.

'Oh, it is, is it?' grunted her father. He had been rooting in the table drawer when they had entered and now faced them with a pointed knife in his hand and an expression of extreme disgust upon his sour old face.

' 'Evening, sir,' said Ben pleasantly. Mr Piggott turned his back and continued to rummage in the drawer.

'I'm trying to rustle up a bit of grub for meself,' grumbled the old man. 'Most nights I has to fend for meself, but Fridays I reckons to find a bit ready for me after a hard day's work.'

'I'll get you something,' broke in Molly swiftly. 'Bacon and egg I was going to do. You sit down and talk to Ben.'

'What for?' asked Mr Piggott looking at the young man with loathing. 'I never had no truck with gyppos all me life and I don't intend to start now. What you bring him in the house for, I'd like to know?'

Molly's blue eyes began to blaze.

'Ben here's a friend. And we don't want no talk about gyppos neither. Ben and me –'

'It's all right, Moll,' said Ben, with disarming gentleness. 'You go and see about the supper.'

'And who might you think you are?' shouted Mr Piggott with a belligerence born of six pints of beer on an empty stomach. 'Whose house is this? Yours or mine? You clear off over the green, where you come from. Sticking your nose into decent folks' houses and laying down the law –' He raised his right elbow threateningly, the dinner knife wavering dangerously near Ben's throat.

Ben grabbed the older man's wrist and lowered him forcibly into the wooden armchair that stood by the table. Mr Piggott sat down with a jerk and Ben quietly removed the knife from his grasp.

'God help us!' exploded Mr Piggott, attempting to bounce to his feet again. Ben's hand on his shoulder thwarted his efforts, and something about the glint in the young man's eye, despite his steady smile, seemed to flash a warning to Mr Piggott's beer-fuddled sense. He took refuge in pathetic bellowings to Molly in the kitchen.

'Here, Moll, what's all this about? Your poor old dad beaten up by this young gyppo – ted then, if you don't like gyppo,' he added hastily, as the grip on his shoulder tightened. 'Molly, who is this chap? You come on in here and see what he's a-doing!'

Molly put a mischievous face round the door and she and Ben exchanged a swift smile.

'I told you, Dad, it's Ben Curdle. You and him's going to have a little talk while I cooks your supper. Two rashers, Ben?' she asked.

'He's not having no rashers,' stormed her father. 'Not a morsel or bite of my hard-earned bread passes 'is lips –'

'Now, Dad,' remonstrated Molly, advancing further into the room. 'Ben's as hungry as you are. You'll talk better together over a meal.'

'If you take it easy, sir,' put in young Ben, 'maybe a drop of something from next door might help the meal along.'

Mr Piggott's black visage was softened into the near-semblance of a smile.

'Now that's talking sense, boy. Double X for me, unless you fancies something stronger yourself. Get the boy a jug, Moll, and get a move on, will you?'

He settled back in his chair and watched Ben vanish round the door. From the kitchen came the fragrance and sizzling of frying rashers and the sound of a daughter hard at woman's work.

Mr Piggott licked his wet lips and sat back well content.

By the time Ben returned Molly had set the cloth and was bearing in three plates. Mr Piggott had bestirred himself to the extent of lifting down from the dresser two thick glass mugs, souvenirs of the

Coronation of Her Majesty Queen Elizabeth II, and placing them expectantly upon the table.

His eyes brightened as Ben deposited a foaming jug of draught beer by the cruet and he became even more jubilant when Ben pulled a half-bottle of whisky from his pocket and put it deferentially before him.

'Now that's very handsome of you, me boy,' said Mr Piggott, his voice husky with emotion. 'Very handsome indeed. Maybe you ain't so black-hearted as you looks.'

This, Molly knew, was as honeyed a speech as would ever fall from her parent's lips, and the only hint of apology that Ben could expect. They broached the meal with relish. Molly was surprised to find how hungry she was, and her father's unlovely open-mouthed mode of mastication for once failed to nauseate her.

Ben prudently waited until the plates were empty and his host's first mugful had been drained before approaching the business in hand. Then, characteristically, he came directly to the point.

'Molly and me's hoping to get wed some day, Mr Piggott.'

'Oh, ah!' said Mr Piggott carelessly, refilling his glass. He appeared oblivious of the importance of this remark, but fixed all his attention on the billowing head of froth that wavered at the brink of the mug.

Ben spoke a little louder.

'We've been friends like for a year now.' He looked across at Molly with a quick smile, and she nodded, smiling, in reply.

'That's right, Dad,' she said earnestly. A look of annoyance crossed her pretty face as she saw the complete absorption of her father in his brimming mug. Her voice became tart.

'You listening? Ben's trying to tell you something important. I shan't be here to cook your suppers much longer.'

This practical attack on his creature comforts had the desired effect. Mr Piggott raised his rheumy eyes and his habitual expression of truculence reappeared.

'What say? Not be here? What's all this?'

'I been saying,' Ben said patiently, 'as Molly and I wants to get married—'

'Too late!' asserted Mr Piggott, in his sexton's voice of authority. 'Dark now. Can't get married this time o' night. Besides I've swep' up the church.'

'We wasn't thinking of tonight, sir,' said Ben, trying to control the laughter in his voice. 'This summer, say – later on, before we lays up the fair for the winter.'

Mr Piggott, slightly glazed, looked a little more mollified.

'Can't stop you, I suppose. People gets married day in and day out – no reason why you and Molly shouldn't.'

His gaze wandered to the whisky bottle and his eyes widened pleasurably.

'What say we puts a dash o' this in along o' the beer?' he suggested enthusiastically to Ben. Molly shook her head violently at the young man.

'Oh, I wouldn't broach it now,' said Ben with studied carelessness. 'It's a little present for yourself. You open it sometime when I'm not here.'

Mr Piggott considered this suggestion earnestly, the mug at his lips and his eyes still caressing the whisky bottle.

'Ah, you got something there, boy,' he said at last, with the hint of a hiccup. 'I'll have more on me own. Have the lot, eh? Do me good, won't it?'

'Hope so,' said Ben briefly.

'Dad,' said Molly, leaning across the table and putting one hand upon her father's. 'D'you know what we've said? We wants to get married and I hopes you'll say you're pleased.'

'Oh, I'm pleased all right – I'm pleased!' gabbled Mr Piggott in a perfunctory manner. 'You get married any time you like – summer or something you said, didn't you? Suits me. I'll get the church spruced up. Don't make no odds to me. All part of the day's work getting the place ready for weddings. Funerals too, come to think of it.' He turned a speculative eye upon the young pair.

'Wedding'd be more in your line, I reckons,' he conceded. 'If I was you I'd wait a bit for the funeral.'

With a sudden sigh he put his arms round his mug and the beloved whisky bottle, and, pillowing his head upon the empty greasy plate, fell instantly asleep.

Ten minutes later Molly and Ben, with the washing-up done and stacked away, stood at the open door.

Ben looked back at the snoring figure at the table.

'I suppose you might say we've got your father's consent,' he said to Molly.

And putting his arm round her waist he jumped her lightly from her doorstep and led her back to the joyful brightness of the fair.

16. Doctor Bailey Asks for Help

Doctor Lovell returned from Ella's to Doctor Bailey's house.

His eyes wandered over the crowd that now thronged Curdle's fair, but Ruth and Paul were hidden somewhere among the mass.

It was a perfect evening, he told himself, and it had been a perfect day. The air was still warm, and scented with a myriad blossoms of spring; and in the bright light shed by the strong electric bulbs of the fairground the small young leaves fluttered like yellow mimosa against the dark-blue sky.

It was heady sort of weather, young Doctor Lovell thought. Heady enough to make anyone think of love. Half-defiant, half-amused, and wholly happy he surveyed his present plight and found it good.

He was hurrying back to see Doctor Bailey in response to a note left on the surgery desk. It had said:

Spare me a few minutes during the evening, will you? Any time after surgery to suit you.

D.B.

It was probably about a new case, thought the young doctor, or a message from the hospital delivered in his absence. He enjoyed these little encounters with the older man and never tired of hearing his salty and wise comments on the Lulling characters he was beginning to know almost as well as Doctor Bailey himself.

He walked into the hall, and tapped lightly on the sitting-room door.

He found Doctor Bailey sitting on the sofa, his thin legs covered with a dashing tartan rug and *The Times* crossword, almost completed, on his lap.

Mrs Bailey put aside her needlework and rose to greet him.

'Come and keep Donald company,' she said, indicating her chair.

'No, no,' protested the young man, 'I'll sit over here.'

'I'm just going to do some telephoning and sort out magazines for the hospital,' said Mrs Bailey. 'You couldn't have come at a better moment.'

She smiled conspiratorially at young Doctor Lovell as he held the door for her and went about her affairs.

'Come and get us both a drink,' said Doctor Bailey, removing his spectacles and flinging *The Times* to the floor.

The young man poured two glasses of sherry carefully at the tray standing ready on the side-table and brought them to the sofa.

'To Mrs Curdle and her fair!' said Doctor Bailey, nodding his head towards the window before sipping his wine.

'Mrs Curdle!' echoed young Doctor Lovell solemnly, sipping too. He put his glass carefully on the hearth and looked expectantly at the old man.

'How are you enjoying it all here?' asked Dr Bailey.

'Love it,' answered Doctor Lovell emphatically.

'That makes it easier for me then. I've at last made up my mind. It's taken me weeks of shilly-shallying, but now it's done I feel a good deal happier.'

He looked shrewdly across his glass to the young man.

'You know what I'm talking about?'

'I think so,' said Doctor Lovell soberly. His thin dark face was grave, for his heart was filled with pity and admiration for the older man. One day, he thought, I shall be facing this.

Doctor Bailey watched the young man closely and liked what he saw. There was no thought of self in that serious face, but an appreciation of a job to be bravely done. He spoke more freely.

'It's like this. I realize I shall never be able to do much again. If I can take four or five surgeries a week and attend a few of the real old folk who prefer to have me – well, that's about all I can hope to do. The point is – would you be willing to come in with me and bear the larger part of the practice on your shoulders?'

'There's nothing I'd like more, sir,' answered the young man earnestly. Doctor Bailey gave a gusty sigh of relief.

'Thank God for that! I'll tell you frankly, there's no one I'd like better to have with me and no one hereabouts better liked by the people. You'll fit in ideally.'

A thought seemed to strike him and he leant forward, peering intently at his companion.

'But look here, boy, I don't want you to make your mind up too hurriedly. Think it over. It's a big step to take, you know. Winnie always says: "Sleep on it," and she's usually right. Let me know in the morning.'

Doctor Lovell smiled for the first time in the interview. It was a slow warm smile that illuminated his long dark face and made it suddenly youthful.

'It's the finest offer I've ever had in my life. I was beginning to wonder if I could ever bear to leave Lulling – and now, this! It's perfect.'

Doctor Bailey raised his glass.

'To our practice, then.' They drank together, and Doctor Bailey replaced his glass with fresh energy.

'Now, the position is this. This particular practice is really just about big enough for a man and half. That's fine at the moment. You have to be the man, and probably a bit more, and I'm your half a man.' He smiled wryly, but cheerfully.

'As you know, the other four chaps in partnership in the town cover most of the southern area, but although our district is sparsely populated I believe you'll find that you'll have enough for two men here in time. There's a new estate going up at Nidden and a batch of council houses along the main road to the north. So that if you decide to settle here you should find a growing practice and could take a partner in with you.'

'That's a long way ahead, I hope,' said young Doctor Lovell.

'I shan't last for ever,' said old Doctor Bailey, 'but I know this. I'll last a dam' sight longer with you to carry most of the load for me.'

'Then we're both satisfied,' said the young man. And sitting back he basked in the glow born of his good wine and his good fortune.

Twenty minutes later, having bidden the older man good night, young Doctor Lovell sat alone in the surgery. He had called in to collect some papers, but enjoyed the opportunity of complete privacy to savour to the full the wonderful news which he had just received.

Earlier in the day he had realized how much Thrush Green and his work there had really meant to him. Now, in a few minutes, he had been offered his life's happiness – work which he knew he could do well, in a place and among people dear to him.

Outside the fair throbbed and spun merrily, and its cheerful raucous music found an echo in the singing in his own heart. May the first – a day of enchantment. He would never forget it, he told himself! He remembered the doctor's first toast to Mrs Curdle and her fair. Long may she reign, thought happy young Doctor Lovell, and bring as much joy each first of May as she had done today!

He took a cigarette from his case and was surprised to see that his fingers shook. He crossed to the window and looked out upon the gay scene spread beneath the dark curve of the night sky.

Over in the Bassetts' house an upstairs light was burning. It was the landing light, young Doctor Lovell observed, which meant that his first patient of the day was now safely in bed after all his excitements, and his aunt would be free downstairs.

Suddenly young Doctor Lovell felt that he must tell someone of the good news which fermented and bubbled within him. He had meant to follow Mrs Bailey's habitual advice and 'sleep on' his secret before he made it known, but now, young, lonely, and bursting with excitement, he knew that he must go to Ruth and let her share his happiness.

Who knows, thought the young man as he crossed the grass with the clamour of the fair ringing in his ears, this very day may prove to be the start of a new life for us both at Thrush Green?

The gate clanged noisily behind him, and for a moment he leant with his back against it, watching the lighted hall through the glass door, suddenly half-fearful of approaching the girl.

As he stood there, his heart throbbing as madly as the fair behind him, Ruth opened the door with a wide welcoming gesture.

'How lovely to see you,' she cried. 'Come in, come in!'

And Doctor Lovell knew that his happiness was complete.

Upstairs Paul had been in bed for an hour, but found it impossible to sleep. So much had happened in the day. He had been pronounced cured of his illness, which meant that he could go back to school on Monday, and would be free to play all day tomorrow, which was Saturday, and to watch the departure of Mrs Curdle's fair if he were awake in time.

He had seen Molly united with her Ben and knew that her worries were ended. But, best of all, his sleepy memories were those of the glittering, noisy, spinning fairground, home of that near-deity Mrs Curdle, and Ben, who now shone as a hero in Paul's eyes, for he had overheard two gossipers discussing the fight and had noticed the scars borne by both men.

Tomorrow, or Sunday, he knew that his father and mother would be home again and his heart leapt at the thought. He turned over and felt the cool pillow against his flushed cheek. Across the mirror on his wardrobe the lights of the fair twinkled, signalling across the darkness their message of gaiety and shared excitement, both tonight and in the future.

From the landing came an equally comforting light through the half-open door. If the flickering lights in the mirror spoke of dizzy excitement the one from the landing spoke of loving care and security. Between the two Paul felt himself swinging gently towards sleep, the lilt of the music from the fair in his ears and the motion of the swing-boat, rocking beneath the stars, still stirring in his veins.

The clanging of the gate caught him back to consciousness again, and he heard Aunt Ruth open the front door.

'Come in, come in!' he heard her cry, so happily, so warmly, that he knew his young aunt's troubles had vanished as swiftly and suddenly as Molly's had done.

Everything would be right now, Paul thought dreamily, eyelids drooping again, and his last clear thought was – what more would you expect of May the first? Everything was bound to turn out right on such a magical day.

Within two minutes he was asleep, and for him the splendid day was ended.

17. Doctor Bailey Gives Help

Through the little window of her caravan Mrs Curdle saw the light in the surgery suddenly vanish, and, a minute later, she observed Doctor Lovell's tall figure crossing the grass towards the Bassetts' house. She took a deep breath, and tried to calm the fluttering of her heart. She must muster all the courage she could and make the dreaded visit, which the young doctor's comings and goings during the past hour or so had delayed for her.

Not that Mrs Curdle had been idle while she had waited with one eye cocked on the tall grey house of her old friends. When she had returned from her routine inspection of the fair she had settled herself on the red plush stool which stood by the stove and had set about her usual Friday-evening business of putting out the wages for her workers. This she would do, she told herself, before making herself clean and tidy for her annual visit to the doctor. Who knows what shape she might be in on her return? What news of fearful illness she might bear back with her? More frightening still, supposing that the doctor took her straight to that dreaded hospital of terrible memories?

Mrs Curdle, old and in pain, felt her fears thronging round her like a flock of dark evil bats, mis-shapen, mocking – the arbiters of doom. But, old and frail as she was, her grim courage remained, a tiny impregnable fortress standing sturdily against the onslaughts of a myriad doubts and fears. She thrust them resolutely away from her, and fetching the old card table which had once held her crystal, she set it up as she had done every Friday night for over thirty years.

She pulled out the battered case, which had caused so much trouble that afternoon, and began to count out notes, silver, and coppers, licking a dusky thumb every now and again, and saying the amounts to herself aloud.

Mrs Curdle needed no list to help her in her task. She had no account book, no notes, no jottings, to confuse or help her calcula-tions. Beneath the coils of black hair Mrs Curdle's shrewd mind knew to a penny just what was due to each man, woman, and child under her management. The piles were stacked methodically in lines on the table, little heaps weighted with neatly piled silver and copper, with Sam Curdle's final earnings in their accustomed place in the row.

Mrs Curdle put the malefactor's dues ready with neither resent-ment nor pleasure. All her life she had, of necessity, been decisive and forward-looking. There had never been time in her busy life, nor had she ever had the inclination, to look back unnecessarily. What was done, was done; and remorse and regrets had never played much part in the old lady's life. Sam had failed her. He must go. It was as simple as that.

From time to time she looked across at Doctor Bailey's house. She had seen his young helper go in and later had caught a glimpse of him through the surgery window. With half her mind she welcomed his presence there for it postponed her own going.

She put out the large brass bowl on the minute dresser. It stood, twinkling and flashing, as it caught the light from the hanging oil-lamp above the table, awaiting the rustle and clatter of that evening's takings when the Curdles arrived later to tip in their contributions and collect their wages. Then she covered the laden table with a multi-coloured shawl of vivid brightness to keep the money safe from prying eyes and any draughts which might remove a stray note. Mrs Curdle's business arrangements were completed once again and she turned to her personal preparations.

The surgery light still shone as Mrs Curdle washed her massive arms and shoulders at the diminutive basin near the stove. She washed her face and neck and gazed at her reflection sadly as she dabbed herself dry with a small striped towel.

The little mirror, at which her husband had shaved so many years before, gave Mrs Curdle a dim and distorted copy of her features, but she was comforted to see that she had some colour in her cheeks, and that though black shadows lay like sooty smudges beneath her eyes, the eyes themselves were as bright as ever.

Her gold ear-rings looked as fine as the day on which her bride-groom had given them to her, and after combing and replaiting her hair, Mrs Curdle donned her best black satin frock, a new black cardigan, and her largest checked shawl, and looked again from her window.

The light vanished and Mrs Curdle's throat constricted with sudden fear. Almost at once she saw young Doctor Lovell hasten down the path and emerge upon Thrush Green.

Mrs Curdle took a last look at her caravan. All lay in readiness for her return, all was in order. The diminutive stove seemed to wink encouragement, the lamp swung as though nodding a kindly fare-well, and all the small dear objects which had shared her tiny home and her long life seemed to return to their troubled mistress some of that love which she had given them.

With the bunch of flowers – the largest and most beautiful she had ever made – in one hand, and the ebony stick in the other, Mrs Curdle descended the steps of her home, and with slow dignity approached the house of Doctor Bailey.

★

Mrs Bailey came from the little back room, where she had been packing up the magazines, to answer the door. Mrs Curdle, tall and imposing in her best black, stood on the doorstep with the bright lights of her fair behind her and the great bouquet before her.

'With my compliments, ma'am, as always,' she said, graciously inclining her head, and handing in the dazzling blooms.

'They are more magnificent every year,' said Mrs Bailey truthfully, ushering in her guest. She looked with genuine admiration at the great mop-heads fashioned with such skill and patience. Scarlet, orange, pink, and mauve, they flaunted their gaudy beauty like some tropical exotic blooms compared with the modest narcissi that sent their gentle perfume from the hall table.

'Come and see how well last year's bunch has worn,' said Mrs Bailey. 'The doctor's looking forward to seeing you.'

She led the way into the sitting-room and Mrs Curdle followed, her dark eyes glancing round the hall as she went. Houses made Mrs Curdle ill at ease. There was so much space, so many bare places on the walls, so far to walk. It seemed to the old lady that there was nothing home-like about such a place. Her own caravan, with everything within arm's reach, fitted her as snugly as a snail's shell. The sight of so much floor to sweep and walls to clean appalled her, and the lofty ceilings made her feel lost and unsafe.

'Might as well live in a church,' thought Mrs Curdle to herself, as she picked her way gingerly over the unaccustomed carpet. ''Twould never do for me.'

The doctor came forward to greet her, both hands outstretched and a welcoming smile on his lined old face.

'Come and sit down, Mrs Curdle. We've been looking forward to seeing you all day. It wouldn't be May the first, you know, without a visit from you.'

He drew forward a straight-backed armchair, and Mrs Curdle seated herself regally. Mrs Bailey brought forward last year's bouquet for the old lady's inspection.

'It do seem to have kep' very nice,' agreed Mrs Curdle, with satisfaction. 'It pays to use a good dye, I always say. And you takes good care of them, I can see that,' she added politely.

They talked of many things, the fortunes of the fair, the news of

Lulling and Thrush Green friends, the death of one of the nurses who had attended her so long ago at Lulling Hospital, the floods which the overflowing River Pleshy had caused earlier in the year, and other general matters.

'I hope that you are not thinking of giving up,' said the doctor. 'We've heard all sorts of rumours, you know.'

Mrs Curdle's face grew grave.

'There's times I think I must,' she said slowly. 'I been none too good lately. I was going to have a word with you about it all.'

Mrs Bailey rose quietly.

'I'll leave you to talk, and I'll go and cut some sandwiches.'

Mrs Curdle looked alarmed.

'None for me, ma'am, thanking you kindly. My stomach's been that queasy, I can't tell you, and I'll have a sup of something later on before I gets to bed.'

'That doesn't sound too good,' said Doctor Bailey, as his wife retreated to her magazine-packing, closing the door firmly upon the tête-à-tête which she knew to be so important.

He hitched his chair nearer to Mrs Curdle's and looked closely at her.

'Let's see your tongue,' he said suddenly. Mrs Curdle put it out obediently.

'Horrible!' said the doctor with professional relish. 'Tell me all about this trouble and then I'll have a real look at you.'

Mrs Curdle gave a sigh, half of bewilderment and half of relief. Now that she was actually under the doctor's roof, with his reassuring presence so close at hand, her fears seemed suddenly less potent. She began to talk falteringly.

'It's been comin' on a long time now – best part of five years, I'd say. Catches me, sir, back and front.' She gripped the small of her back bending forward and fixing anguished dark eyes upon the doctor. He nodded sympathetically.

'Makes me dizzy,' went on Mrs Curdle, warming to her theme. The relief of pouring out her long-pent-up troubles gave her an unaccustomed eloquence.

'I has to sit down, my head gets that giddy. And today I had it that bad I fell right over – fainting, you might say. It's the pain, Doctor, a burning kind of pain, that flares up in me middle.'

She knotted a gnarled fist and pressed it fiercely against the jet buttons of her cardigan.

'And can you eat?' asked Doctor Bailey, remembering her prodigious appetite in earlier times.

'Scarce a morsel,' asserted Mrs Curdle, with mournful pride. 'I takes no breakfast these days, though I cooks for young Ben regular. Just a drop of tea, and maybe a bit of bread if the pain ain't too nigglin'.'

'What time did you faint today?' inquired the doctor. Mrs Curdle wrinkled her brow with concentration.

''Twould have been after dinner some time. I was taking a look round the show, I knows that.'

'Ah!' said Doctor Bailey. 'After your dinner, eh? And what did you have?'

'Pork chop and fried onions,' said the old lady. 'With a bit of good strong cheese to follow. Nothing rich or heavy like.'

The doctor looked with an experienced eye at his patient's drawn face and the hint of yellow about the eyes that told of biliousness. He could guess the sort of diet that Mrs Curdle's ancient stomach was called upon to digest day after day. The old lady had always been a great frying-pan cook, as of necessity were most of the tribe, and her tea, as the doctor remembered with an inward shudder, was of a strong Indian variety which was reckoned to be at its best after half an hour's stewing on the little hob. It was small wonder that her overtaxed digestive system had begun to rebel after more than seventy years of such treatment.

But there might be more to it than faulty diet, thought the old doctor, gazing speculatively at the earnest face before him. Mrs Curdle had lost her sparkle. There were mental as well as physical troubles to be blamed for that pinched unhappy look about her mouth and eyes. The doctor determined to know all, and set about it with his customary guile and kindly delicacy.

'I think we'll have to give you a little help over your diet, my dear. I'm positive that that's all that's wrong and you've nothing to worry about at all. Less fat, very little tea — and that weak — less bread and fried foods, and you'll be fighting fit in no time.'

Mrs Curdle bridled slightly.

'I eats next to nothing—' she began, in a hurt tone.

Doctor Bailey leant forward and patted her knee.

'I know you do, I know you do. But it's probably the wrong sort of food for you now. I'll write it down for you and you need not worry any more about it.'

Mrs Curdle looked mollified, and the doctor continued gently.

'You see, we're both getting older, Mrs Curdle, and our poor old bodies can't cope with the food – nor life itself quite as bravely as they did when we first met. Why, for the last few weeks I've practically lived on milk.'

'You looks peaky,' agreed Mrs Curdle sagely. 'Maybe it's good food you needs.'

The doctor began to feel that he was making little headway, but he brushed aside her comment, and approached nearer to his objective.

'And because our bodies are old and tired, we begin to worry about them and that makes them worse. So it goes on. And when any little troubles arise – money matters, say, or quarrels in the family – they all seem so much worse than they really are.'

He noticed that a gleam had kindled in Mrs Curdle's eye, and she nodded her dark head in agreement.

'That's very true, sir. I've been that way myself this year with our Ben – dear George's boy, you remember?' The doctor nodded, fearful of speaking and breaking the flow of words which would help his old friend far more than any of his bottled medicine could.

'He's fair broke my heart, these last few months,' confessed the old lady. She settled her great bulk more comfortably against the back of the chair and told her sympathetic friend of all that she had endured. She told of Ben's moodiness, his sullen silences, his inexplicable neglect of the job which he had always taken such delight in, and the barrier which had grown up between them.

Out it all poured, the doctor listening intently to this simple but poignant tale. She told of her increasing depression, the more frequent attacks of pain, the silence which she kept, imposed upon her by her innate pride of spirit, which only aggravated the misery of both body and mind. She told of all her hopes of making young Ben a partner in the business which was the very essence of her being, and how those hopes had dwindled as the sad frustrating weeks had gone by.

Through it all, the doctor noticed, ran the strong double thread of her great love for Ben and the fair. They were both of her creating.

They were as much part of her as the dusky right hand which smoothed the black satin to and fro, to and fro, over her massive knee as she spoke. If she lost either her life would be lopped of its vital force and purpose, and she would surely dwindle and die.

For want of breath Mrs Curdle paused, and the doctor gave what advice he could.

'I'm afraid it's all part of getting old, Mrs Curdle, this anxiety about keeping our affairs going well and wondering if the young ones will ever keep the boat afloat as well as we did. It's a right feeling, I suppose, but it does mean that we have to decide what is the right thing to do and the right time to do it. I've been having the same thing to face here.'

'You have?' said Mrs Curdle in surprise, projected momentarily from her inward-looking at her own troubles to those of her fellow, which was precisely what the wise doctor had wanted.

'You see,' said Doctor Bailey, smiling, 'I'm old too – older than you are, my dear – and very much more tattered and torn I'm afraid. I've been clinging to the hope that this illness would pass and that I would be quite able to continue as I always have done with my doctoring, but nature has said "No". It's been saying "No" for a long time,' admitted the doctor ruefully, 'but I've been too pig-headed to listen. But today I did listen, and I've made my decision.'

'And what's it to be?' asked Mrs Curdle.

'It's to be sensible. To face the fact that I'm growing old, that I must have help if I'm to be of any use to my patients. And another thing I've found out today. I am not indispensable. My young partner can do the job as well, and perhaps better, than I ever could do it.'

There was a sadness in her old friend's face that moved Mrs Curdle strangely although she had not fully understood all that the doctor had told her.

'You been the best doctor in the world,' she said stoutly. 'I never knew a better doctor – never!'

Doctor Bailey, knowing that he was the only one that had ever attended her, could not help being secretly amused, as well as touched, by her faith in him.

'Don't think I'm unhappy about it,' said the doctor truthfully. 'I'm glad. The work goes on, that's the comfort. I only wish I'd realized that years ago and saved myself a mint of heart-searching.'

He turned to the old lady.

'And that's what I want you to face, as I did. You must have help. Let someone share the load and you'll be of some use. Be too proud to ask for it and you'll go down under it. We're both in the same boat, my old friend.'

Mrs Curdle nodded thoughtfully. The doctor, seeing her engrossed in thought, imagined that she was trying to choose, from among her tribe, one best suited to her purpose.

'If Ben doesn't seem the man for it –' he began. But the old lady cut him short.

Eyes flashing, and back as straight as a ram-rod, Mrs Curdle answered indignantly:

'Who said Ben wasn't the man for it? There's nothing wrong with my Ben now. You never let me finish the tale!'

Humbly and hastily Doctor Bailey begged Mrs Curdle's pardon, secretly delighted at this flash of her old spirit.

And within five minutes he had heard of Ben's transfiguration, of his proposed marriage with young Molly Piggott, and, best of all, of Mrs Curdle's decision to take him into partnership that very day on her return to the caravan.

'We shan't forget this May the first, either of us, Mrs Curdle,' said the doctor, when he had heard her out. 'You'll see. My practice will go on, and your fair will go on.'

'They'll both go on!' agreed Mrs Curdle, with great satisfaction.

The two old friends looked at each other and smiled their congratulations.

'And now,' said Doctor Bailey briskly, 'I'm going to have a look at you.'

Later, Mrs Curdle, with a light heart, crossed the road again. She had made her parting from the Baileys in the hall, but now with her feet on the grass of Thrush Green she turned to look once more at the house where she had received such comfort of body and mind.

Silhouetted against the light of the open doorway stood the doctor and his wife, their hands still upraised in farewell. Mrs Curdle waved in return and turned towards her home.

In her cardigan pocket lay some pills and a simple diet sheet, but it was not of these that Mrs Curdle thought. She was thinking of Doctor Bailey whose good advice had never failed her throughout her long life. Her way now was clear.

With a tread as light as a young girl's, Mrs Curdle, her fears behind her, hurried to find Ben.

He should hear, without any more waste of time, of his good fortune and the future of the fair.

Meanwhile, the doctor and his wife had returned to the sitting-room. Mrs Bailey had carried in a tray with soup, fruit, and a milky drink, for, with their visitors, supper had been delayed and the hands of the silver clock on the mantelpiece stood at a quarter to ten.

They supped in silence for a while. Then Mrs Bailey, putting her bowl down, said:

'And does the fair go on?'

'Yes,' said the doctor. 'I'm thankful to say it does.'

The music surged suddenly against the window with renewed vigour, and they smiled at each other.

As Mrs Bailey stacked the tray she noticed that the doctor's eyes strayed many times to the gaudy bouquet which flamed and flared like some gay bonfire.

'I'll take those flowers to the larder shelf,' said Mrs Bailey, advancing upon them.

'No,' said her husband, and something in his voice made her turn and look at him. He sat very still and his face was grave. 'I'd like them left out.'

Mrs Bailey could say nothing.

'We shan't see the old lady again,' said Doctor Bailey. 'I doubt if she has three months to live.'

18. The Day Ends

At half past ten the lights of Mrs Curdle's fair went out and the music died away. The last few customers straggled homewards, tired and content with their excitement, and by the time St Andrew's clock struck eleven Thrush Green had resumed its usual quietness.

A few lights, mainly upstairs ones, still shone from some of the houses around the green, but most of the inhabitants had already retired, and dark windows and empty milk bottles standing on the doorsteps showed that their owners were unconscious of the happenings around them.

The church, 'The Two Pheasants', and the village school were three dark masses, but a small light twinkled between the two latter. It shone from Molly Piggott's bedroom where the girl was undressing.

The blue cornflower brooch lay on the mantelshelf and beside it a small ring.

'You shall have a proper one, some day,' Ben had promised, 'not just a cheap ol' bit of trash from the fair.' But to Molly it was already precious – a souvenir of the most wonderful day in her life.

She had parted from Ben only a few minutes before, when he had told her of his new status in the business, and she had promised to be up early in the morning to see him again before the caravans set off on their journey northwards.

She clambered into the little bed, which lay under the steep angle of the sloping roof, keeping her head low for fear of knocking it on the beam above.

Carefully she set her battered alarm clock to five o'clock, wound it up, and put it on the chair close beside her. Then, punching a hollow in her pillow, she thrust her dizzy dark head into it and was asleep in two minutes.

In the next bedroom Mr Piggott, asleep in his unlovely underclothes as was his custom, stirred at the thumpings made by his daughter's bed and became muzzily aware of her presence in the house.

Vague memories of a young man, a bottle of whisky, and Molly's future swam through his mind. No one to cook for him, eh? No one to clean up the house?

'Daughters!' thought Mr Piggott in disgust. 'Great gallivanting lumps, with no idea of doing their duty by their poor old parents!'

He relapsed into befuddled slumber.

Ruth Bassett's light still shone above the bed. She sat propped against the pillows, a book before her, but her attention was elsewhere.

Doctor Lovell had left an hour or so before and the memory of their pleasant time together warmed her unaccountably. She had scrambled eggs in the kitchen while he had supervised the toast, and together they had sat at the kitchen table enjoying the result, brewing coffee, and talking incessantly.

She had never felt so at ease in anyone's company and the thought that he had sought her out to tell her his wonderful news touched her deeply. Plainly, he was as devoted to Thrush Green as she was. And who can blame him? thought Ruth, as a distant cry from one of the Curdle tribe reached her ears.

It had cured her of her misery and given her new hope. It had, as it had always done, provided her with comfort and contentment. Her decision to make her home there filled her with exhilaration. To-morrow, when Joan and her husband returned, they would make rosy plans.

For a moment her mind flitted back to the cause of this decision. The figure of Stephen, tall and fair-haired, flickered in her mind's eye, but, try as she would, she could not recall his face. It seemed a shocking thing that one who had meant so much could so swiftly become insubstantial. The ghost of Stephen had vanished as com-pletely as the man himself and, Ruth observed with wonder, her only feeling was of relief.

She put her book to one side, switched off the light and settled to sleep, secure in the knowledge that the dawn would bring no tortur-ing memories, but only the wholesome shining face of Thrush Green with all it had to offer.

Young Doctor Lovell was writing a letter to his father, telling him of Doctor Bailey's offer, asking his advice about the financial side, and explaining the future possibilities of the practice.

He wrote swiftly in his neat precise handwriting and covered two pages before he paused. Then he lit a cigarette and stared thoughtfully at his landlady's formidable ornaments on the mantelpiece.

It is not in the nature of young men to open their hearts to their fathers and to tell them of their private hopes and feelings, particularly when a young woman is involved, and Doctor Lovell was no excep-tion. But he was fond of his father – his mother had been dead for ten years – and he wanted him to know that this offer meant more to him than just a livelihood.

His thoughts turned again to Ruth. He knew now, without any doubt, that she would always be the dearest person in the world to him. As soon as she had recovered sufficiently from her tragedy to face decisions again he would ask her to marry him.

Life at Thrush Green with Ruth! thought young Doctor Lovell, his spirits surging. What could anyone want better than that?

Smiling, he picked up his pen and added the last line to his letter:

I know I shall always be very happy here.

He sealed it, propped it on the mantelpiece against a china boot, and went whistling to bed.

In her cottage nearby lay Miss Fogerty from the village school. She was fast asleep. Her small pink mouth was slightly ajar, and her pointed nose twitched gently over the edge of the counterpane, for all the world like some small exhausted mouse.

It had been a tiring day. The children were always so excited on fair day, and Friday afternoon meant that she had to battle with her register amidst the confusion of twenty or so young children playing noisily with toys brought from home – a special Friday-afternoon treat.

Her last thought had been a happy one. Tomorrow it was Saturday. If it were as lovely and sunny as today had been her weekly wash-day would be most successful, she told herself.

Her Clarks' sandals were prudently put out underneath the chair which supported her neat pile of small-clothes. Miss Fogerty was a methodical woman.

'No need to set the alarm,' she had said happily to herself as she folded back the eiderdown. 'Saturday tomorrow!'

And with that joyous thought she had fallen instantly asleep.

Ella Bembridge and Dimity Dean had taken the advice of Doctor Bailey and settled to sleep early.

Dimity had fallen into a restless slumber disturbed by confused dreams. She seemed to be standing knee-deep in a warm crimson pond, stirring an enormous saucepan full of parsley sauce, while Mrs Curdle and Ella stood by her, wagging admonitory fingers, and saying, in a horrible sing-song chant: 'Never touch the stuff – it's poison! Never touch the stuff – it's poison!'

Ella found sleeping impossible. Her legs hurt, her rash itched, and the shooting pains in her stomach, though somewhat eased by Doctor Lovell's white pills, still caused her discomfort.

Morosely, she catalogued the day's tribulations, as others, less gloomily disposed, might count their blessings.

'Visit to the doctor – a fine start to a day. Blasted parsley sauce. Rubber gloves. That boiling dam' dye. Dotty's collywobbles. Two more visits from doctors, to top the lot – and Mrs Curdle's hurdy-gurdy for background music! What a day!'

She glowered malevolently at Mrs Bailey's daffodils, a pale luminous patch in the darkness. One ray of hope lit her gloom.

'At least May the second shouldn't be quite as bad as May the first has been!'

Somewhat comforted, Ella moved her bulk gingerly in the bed, for fear of capsizing the leg guard, and waited grimly for what the morrow might bring forth.

Away in the fields below Lulling Woods the creator of poor Ella's latest malady lay in her bed.

Dotty Harmer's room was in darkness, lit only by the faint light of the starlit May sky beyond the grubby latticed panes.

Dimly discernible by Dotty's bed was a basket containing the mother cat and one black kitten. Much travail during the golden afternoon had only brought forth one pathetic little still-born tabby, sadly mis-shapen, and ten minutes later this fine large sister kitten. Dotty had buried the poor dead morsel in the warm earth, shaking her grizzled head and letting a tear or two roll unashamedly down her weatherbeaten cheeks.

The survivor was going to be a rare beauty. Dotty could hear the comfortable sound of a rasping tongue caressing the baby between maternal purrs, and cudgelled her brains for a suitable name.

'Nigger, Blackie, Jet, Night, Sooty – too ordinary!' decided Dotty, tossing in her bed.

She thought of the glorious day that had just passed and remembered the spring scents of her garden as she had awaited the birth.

'Should be something to do with May,' pondered Dotty. '"May" itself would have done if it had been a pale kitten, but somehow – a dark little thing like that –' She resumed her meditations and the memory of Molly and her dark young man came floating back to her.

'Gipsy!' thought Dotty, groping towards the perfect name. She felt herself getting nearer. Something that was dark, magnificent, and connected with May the first, she told herself. It came in a flash of inspiration.

'Mrs Curdle!' cried Dotty in triumph.

And with the rare sigh of a satisfied artist, she fell asleep.

Gradually the lights dimmed in the old stone houses round Thrush Green, but still one shone in Doctor Bailey's house.

The good doctor himself was asleep. He had had the busiest day of his convalescence and had retired more exhausted than he would admit to his wife.

The last sad interview with Mrs Curdle had been a great strain – greater because his grief had to be kept hidden behind his kindly professional mask in front of the old lady. Her case, he knew, was hopeless, and when her fair came to rest for the winter that year he had no doubt that she who had ruled its kingdom for so many years would be at rest too.

It gave the old doctor some consolation to know that he had helped her to assure the future of her little world, and that when next May Day came the full-blooded music of Mrs Curdle's fair would still shake the young leaves on Thrush Green and all its innocent pleasures would be there again in the capable young hands of Ben Curdle.

The thought that his own affairs too were as squarely arranged as Mrs Curdle's own gave him a deep inner peace. He had woken that morning with a battle to fight, and now that battle was over. Whether he had won or lost, the doctor was not sure, but now that the heat of it was over he could retire from the field with his duty well done.

The good old man slept easily.

But his wife could not sleep.

Her mind turned over the happenings of that sunlit day and refused to rest. She remembered the glory of her dewy garden, the coffee party with those dear odd creatures, the wonderful change in poor little Ruth, Ella's mishap, which had been a real blessing for it had forced her husband to make his decision, and – last of all, to her the most poignant happening of that long crowded day – her husband's disclosure of Mrs Curdle's doom.

She heard St Andrew's clock chime the quarter after eleven o'clock. Would she never sleep? Carefully, she crept from the great double bed and made her way to the kitchen to warm herself some milk. Sometimes this calmed her active mind and she hoped that the old-fashioned remedy would work now.

She carried her steaming mug to the sitting-room, switched on the small reading-lamp and sipped slowly.

The three or four street lamps round Thrush Green had gone out at eleven o'clock, for country dwellers are early abed. Through the window she could see the dark shapes of the caravans against the starlit sky. One or two still showed lights, for the Curdles had been busy since closing time collecting their weekly wages and putting their personal belongings together ready for an early start on the morrow.

Mrs Bailey looked with affection, and with infinite sorrow, at the ancient caravan which housed her good friend. Its old beautiful lines showed plainly against the clear night sky and its small window glowed from the lamp within. The light quivered and blurred before Mrs Bailey's tear-filled eyes, and she turned hastily away.

There was nothing to weep about, she told herself with as much firmness as she could muster. Mrs Curdle's long life neared its end, but her work would thrive and her family too. She would never be forgotten while they endured.

The peace of the sitting-room and the comforting warmth of the milk began to soothe Mrs Bailey. She looked at the loved things around her and suddenly realized what riches were gathered there together in one lovely drop of time.

There on the side-table stood the blue-and-white bowl, a wedding present from a long-dead friend, filled with narcissi which had forced their fragile beauty from the dark prison-house of earth so recently to delight her. An orange, which had travelled the far seas, touched its reflection in the black polished beauty of the Chinese chest on which it stood. The chest had been brought back in a tea-clipper by a sailor great-uncle of Mrs Bailey's, and its perfection had always stirred her. The mug from which she sipped had been a christening present to her son. That son, she remembered, who was much the same age as Mrs Curdle's dear George would have been.

She took a deep breath and looked with new eyes at her familiar treasures. All these lovely things had come from all over the face of the earth to offer her their particular solace. Some had intrinsic beauty of their own. Some had the beauty of association and long use, but all offered comfort to her troubled heart.

Mrs Curdle would pass, as she and her dear husband must pass before long; but the world would go on, as bright and enchanting, and as full of quiet beauty for those that used their eyes to see it, as it had always been.

Mrs Bailey turned off the light, went quietly back to bed and composed herself to sleep.

The houses round Thrush Green now lay in darkness, crouched comfortably against the Cotswold clay like great sleeping cats, their chimneys like pricked ears. Only from two or three of the caravans that huddled together in the centre of the green shone a few small lights from some humble oil lamp or candle flickering there.

Sam and Bella Curdle were thinking of their future. At one end of the caravan lay their three children in heavy slumber, and their parents spoke in low tones.

Sam's last earnings at Curdle's fair stood in a pile on the chair beside their bunk bed. Bella, already in bed, dressed in a shiny pink nightgown of gargantuan proportions, surveyed the money grimly. She had been doing her best to prise from her morose husband his plans for their future livelihood, but without success.

She watched him now, tugging his shirt moodily over his head. His face emerged, battered from the afternoon's fight which had caused his downfall, and sullen with his wife's questionings. She attacked the goaded man again in a shrill whisper.

'Well, tell us, then. What are you going to do when that little lot's gone? See us all starve?'

Sam finished undressing before he spoke. Then he answered her slowly.

'There's a farmer-chap up the Nidden road wants his sugar beet hoeing. I done it afore. We could take the caravan that way and settle there for a bit.'

'How long will that take?' asked Bella stiffly. Her pride quivered at the thought of her husband undertaking such low work. Worse was to follow.

'Three or four weeks. And you could do some too!'

Bella gasped at the shock.

'And what about the kids?' she protested.

'Won't hurt them either,' said her brute of a husband. He turned out the oil lamp and clambered into bed beside her.

'And you'd get some of your fat off,' said Sam savagely, hauling at the bedclothes, and adding insult to injury.

Much affronted, his wife turned her face to the wall. The fumes from the oil lamp crept uncomfortably about the darkness and Bella's misery grew. Two tears of self-pity rolled down to the pillow.

Bella had never liked work.

Ben Curdle heard St Andrew's chimes ring out the half-hour as he was propping a snapshot of Molly above his bed.

He ought to be asleep, he told himself. There was plenty to do in the morning, clearing up the show and setting off on the road again, besides seeing his girl.

So much had happened that he was too excited to think of sleep.

He had accomplished the two tasks he had set himself that morning as he had rested on Thrush Green's dewy grass. He had found Molly and he had confounded his cousin Sam, the thought of whose mean treachery still made Ben's hot head throb with fury.

But more than that had happened to Ben, the full significance of which he barely realized yet. He looked back to that solemn meeting with his grandmother earlier that evening and marvelled again.

She had returned from her visit to Doctor Bailey with renewed vigour. Ben had not seen her eyes so bright or her bearing so resolute for many a long month. She had closed the door of the caravan, had motioned him to sit, and had taken her own majestic stance upon the red plush stool by the fire. Then she had begun to talk to him as she had never done before.

Out it had all poured. She spoke of his dear father, in words that moved him unaccountably; she spoke of her love for Ben himself, which had touched him so much that he had forgotten all embarrassment, and then she spoke of her own health and disabilities and her need for his help.

She did what Ben had never thought possible. She put into words all that that telling glance had said when they had confronted each other immediately after the fight. She spoke to him, not as one in authority, but as a partner who asked for help and knew that it could be given. Ben was accepted as joint master of the Curdle business and he vowed that he would see it thrive.

The old lady had turned to practical matters. She had shown him her rough and ready ways of calculating expenses, and had given her reasons for following certain routes year after year. She had warned him against certain districts, against unwelcoming councils, and against doubtful members of the Curdle tribe itself.

Ben had listened fascinated. Much he already knew, but much he learnt that night. His happiest moment had been when the old lady praised his Molly and told him that she would welcome her to the family.

But his most triumphant moment had come later, when Mrs Curdle had put a chair beside her own at the card table, and they had sat side by side with the weekly wages arranged before them. The Curdle tribe, awaiting their rewards, had goggled at the sight.

Mrs Curdle had presented Ben to them with much the same air as the monarch presents his prince to the people of Wales.

'Ben,' she said proudly, her hawk gaze raking the assembled company, 'is my partner now. Any orders he gives are to be obeyed, as mine are.'

There was a murmur of assent, for this had been long expected, and young Ben was popular.

'Won't be long,' continued Mrs Curdle, 'before I'm dead and gone. Ben'll carry on for me.'

Ben had gazed modestly at the green baize of the table while his grandmother spoke and had waited for her next remark.

It had come with her habitual tartness.

'Stop gawking and pay out!' she had snapped, nudging him sharply. And Ben, partner and heir, had meekly obeyed.

Now, in the stillness of his own caravan, he tried to realize his overwhelming good fortune, but it was too great to understand.

Dizzy with happiness, he flung his clothes into a corner, took a last look at Molly's photograph, turned out the light, and fell almost immediately into deep sleep.

Only one light glimmered now upon Thrush Green.

Old Mrs Curdle had set her candle on the chair by the bed and its small flame flickered in the draught from the half-door.

The old lady leant upon the sturdy lower half and gazed meditatively at the sleeping world about her.

The skewbald ponies were tethered nearby and she could hear them cropping steadily at the grass. Far away an owl hooted from Lulling Woods and, nearer in a garden, a love-sick cat began its banshee wailing.

The air was still and deliciously warm. Summer had begun with that sunny May day and Mrs Curdle thought of those happy busy months which lay ahead.

Within a few hours her little home would be rumbling along the lanes again between the flowery verges and the quickening hedges.

Her mind roamed ahead visualizing the villages she knew so well, rosy-red brick ones, some with whitewashed walls and grey or golden thatch, and some, like dear Thrush Green, built of enduring Cotswold stone.

Ah, a travelling life was the best one, thought old Mrs Curdle happily. With Ben beside her, and her fears put to rest by her old friend Doctor Bailey, she felt she could face the leisurely jolting miles of summer journeyings. All would be well.

She took a last long look at Thrush Green. The old familiar houses slept peacefully awaiting the dawn. The last light, in the doctor's sitting-room, had gone out and she alone was still awake.

High above her St Andrew's clock chimed midnight, and then the slow notes telling the passing of another day floated upon the night air.

'Twelve,' counted Mrs Curdle, straightening up. 'Time I was abed.'

She closed the top of the door slowly.

'I've never been to Thrush Green yet without feelin' the better for it.'

She climbed heavily into bed, sighing happily.

'Ah, well! I've had a good day,' said Mrs Curdle, and blew out the light.

WINTER IN THRUSH GREEN

To Peg and Clare
With Love

Contents

PART ONE

THE COMING OF WINTER

---

1. The Newcomer

Autumn had come early to Thrush Green. The avenue of horse-chestnuts, which ran across its northerly end, blazed like a bonfire. Every afternoon, as soon as the children at the village school had finished their lessons, they streamed across the wet grass and began to bombard the trees with upthrown sticks as their fathers had done before them. The conkers, glossy as satin, bounced splendidly from their green and white cases and were pounced upon greedily by their young predators.

In the porch of 'The Two Pheasants', next door to the village school, swung a hanging basket filled with dead geraniums and trails of withered lobelia. All summer through they had enlivened the entrance, but now their bright day was over, and the basket was due to be taken down and stored in the shed at the back of the little inn until summer came again to the Cotswolds.

Chrysanthemums of red and gold glowed on the graves in St Andrew's churchyard, while Mr Piggott the gloomy sexton swept the bright pennies of dead leaves from the paths and cursed fruitlessly as the wind bowled them back again into his newly-swept territory.

The creeper, which climbed over the walls at Doctor Bailey's house and the cottage occupied by two old friends, Ella Bembridge and Dimity Dean, had never flamed so brilliantly as it did this October. The sparkling autumn air, the unusually early frosts and the heavy crop of berries of all sorts made the weather-wise on Thrush Green wag their heads sagely.

'We'll be getting a hard winter this time,' they said in tones of mingled gravity and satisfaction. 'Best get plenty of firing in. Mark my words, it'll be a real winter this one!'

Mr Piggott straightened his aching back, clasped his hands on top of the broom, and surveyed Thrush Green morosely. Behind him lay the bulk of the church, its spire's shadow throwing a neat triangle across the grass. To his right ran the main road from the Cotswold

Hills down into the sleepy little market town of Lulling, which Thrush Green adjoined. To his left ran a modest lane which meandered northward to several small villages.

Within fifty yards of him, set along this lane, stood his cottage, next door to 'The Two Pheasants'. The village school, now quiet behind its white palings in the morning sunshine, was next in the row, and beside it was a well-built house of Cotswold stone which stood back from the green. Its front windows stared along the chestnut avenue which joined the two roads. The door was shut, and no smoke plumed skywards from its grey chimneys.

The garden was overgrown and deserted. Dead black roses drooped from the unkempt bushes growing over the face of the house, and the broad flagged path was almost hidden by unswept leaves.

Mr Piggott could see the vegetable garden from his vantage point in the churchyard. A row of bean poles had collapsed, sagging under the weight of the frost-blackened crop. Below the triumphant spires of dock which covered the beds, submerged cabbages, as large as footballs, could be discerned. Onions, left to go to seed, displayed magnificent fluffy heads, and a host of chirruping birds fluttered excitedly about the varied riches of the wilderness.

Mr Piggott clicked his false teeth in disapproval at such wicked waste, and shook his head at the FOR SALE board which had been erected at the gate the week before.

'Time someone took that over,' he said aloud. 'What's the good weeding this 'ere if all that lot's coming over all the time?' He cast a sour look at the leaves which still danced joyously in his path. Everlasting work! he thought gloomily.

The clock began to whirr above him before striking ten. Mr Piggott's face brightened. Someone came out of 'The Two Pheasants' and latched the door back to the wall hospitably. The faint clinking of glasses could be heard and a snatch of music from the bar's radio set.

Mr Piggott propped his broom against the church railings and set off, with unaccustomed jauntiness, to his haven.

Across the green Ella Bembridge was also looking at the empty house. She had just made her bed, and was busy hanging up her capacious tweed suit in the cupboard, when the sight of a small van drawing up by the FOR SALE board, caught her eye. She folded her sturdy arms upon the window-sill and gazed with interest.

Two men emerged and Ella recognized them. They worked at the local estate agents and lived, she knew, at the village of Nidden a mile or two from Thrush Green. She watched them go inside the gate and start to wrench at the post supporting the board.

'Dim!' called Ella, in a hearty boom, to her companion downstairs. A faint twittering sound came from below.

'Dim!' continued Ella fortissimo, 'they're taking down the board from the corner house! Must be sold!'

Dimity Dean entered the bedroom and joined her friend at the window. A slight, bedraggled figure, clad in an assortment of grey and fawn garments, she was as frail as Ella was robust. She peered short-sightedly at the activity in the distance.

'Isn't that young Edwards? The boy who used to help in the garden?'

'Yes, that's Edwards,' agreed Ella watching the figure heaving at the post.

'Then he's no business to be doing such heavy work!' exclaimed Dimity, much distressed. 'That poor back of his! You know I always wheeled the barrow for him after he slipped that disc.'

'More fool you!' said Ella shortly. 'Bit of exercise will do him good, lazy lout.'

Dimity shook her head mournfully, her eyes filling with sympathetic tears. Of course dear Ella was probably quite right, but Edwards had been such a sweet boy, with an ethereal pale face which quite made one think of Byron. She was relieved to see the board suddenly lurch sideways and the two men carry it out to the van.

'Well,' breathed Dimity, 'I suppose we can look forward to new neighbours now. I do hope they'll fit in at Thrush Green. Quiet people, you know – like us.'

'People who like whooping it up aren't likely to come to Thrush Green,' pointed out Ella, turning her back upon the sunshine. 'Tell you what, we'll see if Winnie Bailey's heard anything when she comes in this morning.'

Dimity clapped a skinny hand to her mouth to stifle a scream.

'Oh, Ella, what a blessing you mentioned her! I'd quite forgotten. I must rush down and get the coffee ready!'

She scuttled down the stairs like a startled hen leaving Ella to speculate upon the future owners of the empty house.

Winnie Bailey was the wife of Doctor Bailey who had been in practice in Lulling and Thrush Green for almost half a century. He still visited a few old patients and occasionally took surgery duty, but since he had retired through ill-health, his young partner Doctor Lovell did more than three-quarters of the work and throve on it.

Life was good to Winnie Bailey. Now that her husband was less busy she found more time for informal visiting, for reading and for the quiet cross-country walks which did so much to refresh her happy spirits.

Thrush Green had changed little since she came first to it as a young wife. True, there were new houses along the lane to Nidden and a large housing estate further west, and in Lulling itself there were twice as many inhabitants. But the triangular green, surrounded by the comfortable Cotswold stone buildings, had altered very little. Winnie Bailey had known those who lived in them, had watched them come and go, grow from children to men and women, and followed their fortunes with an interest which was both shrewd and warm-hearted.

As the wife of a professional man she knew the wisdom of being discreet. Many came to Winnie Bailey for advice and comfort. They went away knowing full well that their confidences would go no further. In a small community discretion is greatly prized.

She too that morning noticed that the board had gone from the corner house and speculated upon its new owner, as she selected some apples to take to Ella and Dimity who owned no apple trees. She hoped it might be a chess player. Donald, her husband, had so few people to play with these days, and she was no match for him. She picked up a Cox's Orange Pippin and smelt it luxuriously. What a perfect thing it was! She admired its tawny streaks, ranging from palest yellow to glowing amber, which radiated from the satisfying dimple whence its stalk sprang.

She rubbed it lovingly with the white linen cloth, now so old and soft that it crumpled in her hand like tissue paper, and put it carefully in the shallow rush basket among its fellows. Ella would appreciate the picture she was creating, she knew, for beneath Ella's crusty and well-upholstered exterior was a fastidious appreciation of loveliness, which expressed itself in the bold, and sometimes beautiful, designs which she printed for curtains and covers. It was strange, thought Winnie Bailey, that those thick knobbly hands could execute such fine workmanship, while Dimity's frail fingers coped so much more successfully with lighting fires, baking cakes and cleaning the cottage.

The doctor's wife delighted in this incongruous pair. She had known them now for over twenty-five years, and despite their oddities and Ella's brusqueness, was grateful for their unfailing friendship.

She looked at the kitchen clock, which said a quarter to eleven. Donald Bailey was still in bed resting after an unusually busy day. His wife ran up to see him before she set forth with her basket, reflecting as she mounted the stairs on the uncommon devotion of Ella and Dimity.

'I really don't think anything could ever part them,' commented the doctor's wife, addressing the tabby cat who minced past her, *en route* to the kitchen from the doctor's bed.

But, for once, Winnie Bailey was wrong, as the oncoming winter would show.

'Well, tell us all the news,' said Ella, half an hour later. She leant back in the sagging wicker armchair, which creaked under her weight, raised her coffee cup and prepared to enjoy her old friend's company. 'First of all, how's your husband?'

'Very well really. Rather tired from yesterday. Old Mrs Hoggins wanted him to see a grandchild who is staying with her, and he insisted on going as she's such an old friend, but it rather knocked him up.'

Dimity fluttered between them, proffering first the sugar, then biscuits. From Winnie Bailey she received smiles and thanks; from Ella a fine disregard.

'And what have you heard about the corner house?' queried Dimity, settling at last in her chair, after her moth-like restlessness. 'Who's taken it? Have you heard?'

'Only in a roundabout way from Dotty Harmer,' said Winnie. She stirred her coffee serenely, as though the matter were closed.

Ella snorted, drew out a battered tobacco tin from her pocket and began to roll a very untidy cigarette. The tobacco was villainously black and Mrs Bailey knew from experience that the smoke would be uncommonly pungent. She noticed, with relief, that the window behind her was open.

Ella lit up, drew one or two enormous breaths and expelled the smoke strongly through her nostrils.

'Well, come on,' pressed Ella impatiently. 'What did Dotty say?'

'Nothing actually,' said Winnie, enjoying the situation.

'Then who did?' boomed Ella, jerking her shoulders with exasperation. The coffee cup tilted abruptly and spilled the rest of its contents into Ella's lap.

'Darling,' squeaked Dimity, rising to her feet. 'How dreadful! Let me get a cloth.'

'Don't fuss so, Dim,' snapped her friend, taking out a grubby handkerchief, and wiping the liquid from her lap to the rug with perfunctory sweeps. 'It's your fault, Winnie, for being so perfectly maddening. Do you or do you not know who is coming to the corner house?' She pointed a tobacco-stained forefinger at her guest.

'No,' said Winnie.

Ella threw her handkerchief on the floor with a gesture of despair and frustration. Dimity, anxious to placate her, hastened in where angels would have feared to tread.

'Winnie dear,' she began patiently, 'do you mean "No, you *don't* know" or "No, you *do* know who is coming"?'

'For pity's sake,' roared Ella, 'don't you start, Dim! If Winnie sees fit to drive us insane with her mysteries, well and good. One's enough, in all conscience. For my part, I don't wish to hear who is coming, or not coming, or what Dotty said or did not say, or anything more about the corner house *at all*.'

Exhausted with her tirade she leant back again.

'Any more coffee left?' she asked in a plaintive tone. Dimity hastened forward.

As she filled the cup, Winnie Bailey relented.

'Then I'll just tell Dimity what I've heard, dear, and you need not listen,' she said gently. Ella growled dangerously.

'Betty Bell, who helps Dotty, as you know, has been keeping the corner house aired since the Farmers left, and she has seen most of the people who have looked over it. Three men with families have been, someone from the B.B.C. —'

'Television or sound?' asked Ella eagerly. 'Our television's appalling lately. Everything in a snowstorm or looping the loop. I must say it would be jolly useful to have someone handy to see to it.'

'Oh, not that sort of *useful* person,' exclaimed Winnie, 'just a producer of programmes or an actor, I think.'

'Pity!' said Ella, losing interest.

'Well, who else called?' asked Dimity.

'Several middle-aged women who all found it too large and inconvenient –'

'Which it is,' interrupted Ella. 'D'you remember that ugly great wash-house place at the back? And the corridor and stairs from the kitchen to the dining-room? The soup was always stone cold at Mrs Farmer's parties.'

'And two middle-aged young men, as far as I can gather, who had something to do with ballet,' continued Mrs Bailey, closing her eyes the better to concentrate, 'and then this last man.'

'And what did he do?' pressed Dimity.

'Nothing. I mean he had retired,' said Winnie hastily, as Ella drew a deep breath ready for a second explosion.

'From what?' asked Ella, ominously. 'The army, the navy, the church or the stage?'

'None of them, so Mrs Bell says. I think he's been abroad. Hong Kong or Singapore or Ghana. Maybe it was Borneo or Nigeria, I can't quite recall, but *hot* evidently. He was worried about getting his laundry done daily.'

'Done daily?' boomed Ella.

'Done daily?' quavered Dimity.

'The man must be mental,' said Ella forthrightly, 'if he thinks he's going to get his washing done *daily*. In Thrush Green too. What's wrong with once a week like any other Christian?'

'I don't suppose he really expects to have it done daily *now,*' explained Winnie carefully. 'I imagine that he may have mentioned this matter – the habits of years die hard, you know – and it just stuck in Betty Bell's memory because it seemed so outlandish to her.'

'Seems outlandish to me too,' said Ella. 'When's he coming?'

Mrs Bailey raised limpid eyes to her friend's gaze. She looked mildly surprised.

'I don't know that he is. Betty Bell only told Dotty about the different people who had looked at the house. He was the last, but

there may have been more since then. I haven't seen Dotty since last
Thursday when I called for my eggs.'

Ella uncrossed her substantial legs, set her brogues firmly on the
stained rug and fixed her friend with a fierce glance.

'Winnie Bailey,' she said sternly, 'do you mean to say that you
have been going through all this rigmarole – this balderdash – this
jiggery-pokery – this leading-up-the-garden – simply to tell us *in the
end* that you don't know who is coming to the corner house?'

In the brief silence that followed, the distant cries of children,
released from school, floated through the open window. It was
twelve o'clock. Winnie Bailey, not a whit abashed, rose to her feet
and smiled disarmingly upon her questioner.

'That's right, Ella dear. As I told you at the start, I simply do not
know who has taken the corner house. You'll probably know before
I do, and I shall expect you to let me hear immediately. There's
nothing more maddening,' continued Winnie Bailey serenely, collecting her rush basket from the window-sill, 'than to be kept in
suspense.'

'You'd have been burnt for a witch years ago, you hussy,'
commented Ella, accompanying her to the door. 'And deserved
it!'

2. Wild Surmise

Ella and Dimity were not the only ones interested in the fate of
'Quetta', the official name of the empty corner house. Built at the
turn of the century for a retired colonel from the Indian army, the
house had its name printed on a neat little board which was planted
in one of the small lawns which flanked the gates. Apart from young
children, who delighted in jumping over it, the name was ignored,
and the residence had been known generally for sixty-odd years as
'the corner house'.

The Farmers had lived there for over twenty years and moved
only when age and illness overtook them and they were persuaded
by a daughter in Somerset to take a small house near her own. Their
neighbours on the green missed them, but perhaps the person who
mourned their disappearance most wholeheartedly was Paul Young,

the eight-year-old son of a local architect who lived in a fine old house which stood beside the chestnut avenue within a stone's throw of the Farmers'.

Ever since he could walk Paul had been free to call at the corner house and, better still, free to roam in the large garden. Old Mr Farmer was a keen naturalist, and finding that the young child was particularly interested in birds and butterflies he encouraged him to watch their activities in his garden and the small copse which adjoined it. Beyond the copse the fields dropped away to a gentle fold of the hills where Dotty Harmer, an eccentric maiden lady much esteemed in Thrush Green and Lulling, had her solitary cottage and flourishing herb garden.

In the distance lay Lulling Woods from whose massed trees many a flight of starlings whirred, or jays called harshly. Paul loved to stand in the little spinney gazing at the fields below or the wooded slope beyond them. His own garden was large, a flat sunny place with trim lawns and bright flower-beds, with here and there a fine old tree which his grandfather had enjoyed. But there was no mystery there. It was all as familiar and everyday as his own pink hands, and although he loved it because it was his home, his growing imagination and delight in secret things made his neighbour's domain far more attractive.

He had said good-bye to the Farmers with much sadness, waving until their car had sunk below sight down the steep hill to Lulling. The sight of Betty Bell closing the gates and returning to the empty house gave him a sense of desolation which he could scarcely endure. He went home dejectedly.

'It's no good fretting, Paul,' his mother said gently, observing his pale face. 'We must hope that the next people will be as nice as the Farmers.'

'It isn't just that,' answered Paul. 'It's the garden, and the birds. There were eleven nests in their copse last spring, and there's red admirals galore on their buddleia. We never get red admirals in our garden.' He kicked morosely at the leg of the kitchen table.

His mother, who was peeling carrots, put one silently before him and watched her sorrowing son find some comfort in its bright crispness. She spoke briskly.

'Well, you know, Paul, you mustn't go into the Farmers' garden now. It's bad luck, but there it is. Perhaps the new owner will let you watch the nests next year, if he sees you don't do any harm. But you mustn't trespass while the house is empty, you understand?'

Paul nodded unhappily. He told himself afterwards that he had not given his word to his mother. He hadn't opened his mouth, he protested to his guilty conscience. Nodding didn't really count, he was to tell himself fiercely many times in the next few weeks.

But Paul was not at ease. For despite his mother's embargo, Paul intended to visit the garden as often as he could. There was more to the Farmers' garden than the red admirals and the birds. There was Chris Mullins.

Christopher Mullins had first burst into Paul's small world in the early summer. At Easter, Paul had left his adored Miss Fogerty who taught him at the village school, and in May began to attend a reliable preparatory school in Lulling.

The new school was much the same size as his earlier one, but to wear a uniform, to carry a satchel, to be taught by masters, and to know that the headmaster was a very great man indeed, impressed Paul considerably.

He knew many of his fellow pupils, for Lulling was a friendly little town and his mother's family and his father's had lived there for many years. In consequence he was not unduly awed, and addressed the bigger boys with less ceremony than some of the newcomers did. When one has shared garden swings, Christmas parties and chicken pox, in a small community, the ice is for ever broken.

But with Christopher Mullins it was different. He had only just arrived from Germany when term began and the attraction of foreign things hung about him. He was bigger, better-looking, older and altogether more interesting than the other boys in Paul's form, and he made it understood that he was only with them because he needed to accustom himself to English methods of education before rising rapidly to the form above – or even the form above that – where he would find his rightful sphere.

Most of the boys treated his superior airs with complete indifference or mild ribaldry, but Paul found them enchanting. He admired Chris's sleek dark hair, his unusually tidy clothes and his superb wrist-watch which had a large red second hand which swept impressively round its shining face. Paul was dazzled by this sophisticated stranger, and the older boy, lacking friendship, was secretly grateful for such homage. When, one day, Paul offered him half his ginger biscuits at morning break, the friendship was sealed and Paul's happiness soared.

Christopher's father was in the army and the family lived in part of an old house on the main road from Lulling to the west. Their garden ran down to the fields near Dotty Harmer's cottage, and it was easy for Christopher to approach Thrush Green from this direction. A path ran through the meadows from Lulling Woods which emerged on to Thrush Green by the side of Mr Piggott's cottage near 'The Two Pheasants'. Sometimes the boy came this way, but more often than not he climbed the grassy hill to the Farmers' copse and there met his jubilant friend.

They had kept their meetings secret, partly because Chris was trespassing, but largely because it made the whole affair deliciously exciting. Between the spinney and the herbaceous border was a thick growth of ox-eyed daisies which formed a background for the lower-growing plants. Here, in this hidden greenness, the two boys had made their headquarters. There was nothing to show that it was a place of any importance, only two small chalked letters on a tree trunk – a C and a P side by side – which would escape the Farmers' old eyes or the occasional glance of Mr Piggott when he 'obliged' two or three times a year.

Their activities were innocent enough. They exchanged news of nests, animals, friends or relatives, in that order of importance. Sometimes they sat amicably in the damp green hide-out and ate liquorice boot-laces or a fearsomely sticky hardbake which was sold in one of the back streets of Lulling and was much prized for its staying qualities. Once they smoked a cigarette which Paul had brought from home, but they did not repeat that experiment.

They met in all that summer about six times, and the place had grown very dear to young Paul. At school, before the other boys, they said nothing about their secret meetings. It was this delicious intimacy which Paul mourned on the departure of the Farmers.

With the coming of autumn the meetings had become less frequent. Not only was it too cold to sit crouched in the green gloom behind the daisies, but the frosts had thinned them sadly, so that small boys might be observed far too easily. They decided that in future they must shift their headquarters to the spinney itself where there was more cover.

And Paul, rebelliously crunching his carrot, was determined to keep his trysts with Chris Mullins despite his mother's words and the uncomfortable stirrings of his own conscience.

After the removal of the signboard early in October, the inhabitants of Thrush Green renewed their energies and attacked the autumn jobs that pressed upon them. The air was exhilarating, the sun shone with that peculiar brilliance which is only seen in a clear October sky, and the autumn leaves added to the bright glory.

Apples were being picked, potatoes dug, and herbaceous borders tidied, and Sam Curdle's ancient lorry creaked and shuddered under the loads of wood which it bore down the lane from Nidden to prudent householders who were filling up their store sheds against the winter's cold.

Sam Curdle lived in a caravan a mile or two from Thrush Green and eked out a living from various types of piece-work for local farmers, by selling logs or acting as carrier in the district. For over two years now he had supported himself and his wife Bella and their three children in this way, and he was now part of Thrush Green's life; but the good people of that place remembered his dismissal from the great Mrs Curdle's Fair, on the last May Day that that amazing old lady had seen, and were careful not to trust Sam with anything of particular value. Mrs Curdle had found that he was a thief. Thrush Green, who had known Mrs Curdle for over fifty years, knew that she was usually right, and did not forget.

It was noticed, too, that Mrs Curdle's grave which lay in St Andrew's churchyard, at her own request, was never visited by Sam or his family, and though this was understandable when one remembered the nature of their parting, yet it was not easily forgiven. As the landlord of 'The Two Pheasants' was heard to say:

''Tain't right that the only relative living near should neglect the old lady like that – never mind what passed between them! If young Ben weren't away with the Fair he'd keep it fit for a queen, that I don't doubt. A proper mean-spirited fellow that Sam. I don't trust him no further than I can see him!' And that expressed, pretty correctly, the feelings of the rest of Thrush Green.

Nevertheless, he had to be lived with and he seemed willing to make a useful contribution to village life, so that people spoke civilly to Sam, gave him their custom and odd jobs to do, and kept their misgivings to themselves.

One bright October afternoon Winnie Bailey had engaged Sam to sweep up dead leaves and make a bonfire, which he did with much energy. The blue smoke spiralled skywards filling the air with that sad scent which is the essence of autumn.

Winnie Bailey hoed vigorously round the rose bushes in the front garden which looked upon Thrush Green. From Joan Young's garden she could hear the sound of a lawn mower doing its final work before the grass grew too long and wet. In the playground of the village school Miss Fogerty was taking games with the youngest children, and their thin voices could be heard piping like winter robins' as they played the ancient singing games.

The doctor was having an afternoon nap and Mrs Bailey was intent on finishing the rose-beds before tea-time. Her hair had escaped from its pins, her face glowed with fresh air and exercise, and she was just congratulating herself upon her progress, when Ella's hearty voice boomed from the gate.

'Can you do with some sweet williams?'

Winnie Bailey propped the hoe against the wall and went to greet her.

'Come in, Ella.'

'Can't stop, my dear. I'm off to get Sam Curdle to leave us some wood.'

'He's here, this minute, in the garden,' said Winnie. 'So you'd better come in and save yourself a trip.'

Ella thrust an untidy bundle of plants wrapped in newspaper into Winnie Bailey's arms, and opened the gate.

'They're wonderful,' said Mrs Bailey with genuine enthusiasm. 'I'll put them in as soon as I've finished hoeing. Sam's at the back, if you'd like a word with him.'

Ella stumped resolutely out of sight. Voices could be heard above the scratching of Winnie's renewed hoeing, but within five minutes Ella returned.

'That's done. Good thing I looked in. Ever had any wood from Sam? Does he give you a square deal? Always was such a blighted twister, it makes you wonder.'

Winnie Bailey thought, not for the first time, that it was amazing how well Ella's voice carried, and wished that if she could not moderate her tones she would at least refrain from putting her opinions into such forceful language. She had no doubt that Sam had heard every syllable.

'As a matter of fact I had a load of logs from him last year, and they were very good indeed,' answered Mrs Bailey in a low voice, hoping in vain that Ella would take the hint. 'I didn't mention it to Donald, for he abominates the fellow, as you know, after the way he treated old Mrs Curdle, so say nothing if it ever crops up.'

'Trust me!' shouted Ella cheerfully.

She made her way to the gate, paused with one massive hand on the post, and nodded across to the corner house.

'Any more news?'

'None, as far as I know,' confessed Mrs Bailey.

'I did my best at Johnsons' cocktail party last week,' said Ella. 'Got young Pennefather in a corner and asked him outright, but you know what these estate agents are. Came over all pursed-lips and prissy about professional duties to his client!'

'Well –' began Winnie diffidently.

'Lot of tomfoolery!' said Ella belligerently, sweeping aside the interruption. 'Anyone'd think he'd had to take the hypocrite's oath or whatever that mumbo-jumbo is that doctors have to swear. I told him flat – "Look here, my boy, don't you come the dedicated professional over me. I remember you kicking in your pram, and you don't impress me any more now than you did then!" Stuffy young ass!'

Ella snorted with indignation, and Winnie Bailey was hard put to it to hide her laughter.

'Relax, Ella. We're bound to know before long, and I should hate to have to wake poor Donald up to attend to an apoplectic fit in the front garden.'

Ella's glare subsided somewhat and was replaced by a smile as she wrenched open the gate.

'Don't think it will come to that yet,' said she, and set off with martial strides to her own house.

Half an hour later Mrs Bailey made her way across the green to St Andrew's church with the last of the roses in her basket. It was her turn to arrange the flowers on the altar and she wanted to get them done before the daylight faded.

Mr Piggott was trimming the edges of the grass paths with a pair of shears. He knelt on a folded sack which he shifted along, bit by bit, as the slow work progressed.

Mrs Bailey went over to speak to him, and the sexton rose painfully to his feet, sighing heavily.

'Anything you want?' he asked with a martyred air.

'Nothing at all, Mr Piggott,' said Winnie cheerfully, 'except to ask how you are.'

'Too busy,' grunted the sexton. 'Too busy by half! All these 'ere edges to clip and more graves to keep tidy than I ought to be asked to do. Look at old lady Curdle's there! What's to stop Sam keeping the grass trimmed? My girl's husband Ben won't half be wild if he finds his old gran's grave neglected, but there's too much here for one pair of hands.'

Winnie Bailey stepped across to the turfed mound against the churchyard wall. A neat stone at its head said simply:

ANNIE CURDLE
1878–1959

The little stone flower vase at its foot was empty except for a little rainwater which had collected there. Mrs Bailey selected half a dozen roses from her basket and put them in one by one, thinking as she did so of the dozens of bunches of flowers she had received from the old lady during her lifetime.

Mr Piggott watched in morose silence, scraping the mud from his boots on a convenient tussock of coarse grass. He steadied himself by resting his weight on a mossy old tombstone. The inscription was almost obliterated by the passage of years and the grey lichen which was creeping inexorably across the face.

'Ah, we've got all sorts here,' commented Mr Piggott with lugubrious levity. 'They say this chap was shipped back from Africa in a barrel of rum.' He patted the tombstone kindly, and his face brightened at the thought.

'I can't believe that,' expostulated Mrs Bailey, coming round the stone to peer at the inscription. 'Oh no, Piggott! This is Nathaniel Patten's grave. I'm sure he'd never have anything to do with rum. He was a strict teetotaller and a wonderful missionary, I believe.'

'Maybe he was,' said old Piggott stoutly, 'but in them days bodies was brought home from foreign parts in spirits. That I do know. I'll lay a wager old Nathaniel here ended up in rum, even if he didn't hold with it during his lifetime.'

'I must ask the doctor about it, if I can remember,' replied Mrs Bailey, picking up her basket and making her way towards the church. 'And I really must find out more about Nathaniel Patten one day.'

As she entered the quiet church intent upon her duties, she little thought that Nathaniel Patten, born so long ago in Thrush Green and now lying so still beneath his grassy coverlet, would be the cause of so much consternation to his birthplace.

3. Miss Fogerty Rises to the Occasion

One Monday morning in October Miss Fogerty arrived at the village school on Thrush Green at her usual time of twenty to nine.

Her headmistress, Miss Watson, took prayers with the forty-odd pupils at nine o'clock sharp, and Miss Fogerty, who took the infants' class and was the only other teacher at the establishment, liked to have a few minutes to put out her register and inkstand, unlock the cupboards and her desk drawer, check that the caretaker had filled the coal scuttle and left a clean duster, and to be ready for any early arrivals with bunches of flowers which might need vases of water for their refreshment.

She had enjoyed her ten-minute walk from lodgings on the main road. The air was crisp, the sun coming up strongly behind the trees on Thrush Green. Zealous housewives, who had prudently put their washing to soak on Sunday night, were already busy pegging it out and congratulating themselves upon the fine weather. Miss Fogerty, whose circumstances obliged her to do her own washing on Saturday morning each week, was glad to see their industry rewarded. Unless one was prepared to get one's washing out *really early* in October, she told herself, as she trotted along briskly, then one might as well dry it by the fire, for the days were so short that it virtually didn't dry at all after three or four in the afternoon. Unless, of course, a gale blew up, and that did more harm than good to clothes, winding them round the line and wrenching the material. Why, only on Saturday, her best pair of plated lisle stockings had been sorely twisted round the washing line and she greatly feared the fibres had been damaged.

With such matters had earnest little Miss Fogerty busied herself as she hurried along. There were very few children about, and when she reached the school only half a dozen or so were at large in the playground. Punctuality was not a strong point at Thrush Green, and Miss Watson's insistence on prayers at nine sharp was one of her methods of correction. Latecomers were not allowed in, and were obliged to wait in the draughty lobby. While their more time-conscious brethren received spiritual refreshment for the day, Miss Watson hoped that they would meditate upon their own shortcomings. In fact, the malefactors usually ate sweets, redistributed the hats and coats of the pious, for their future annoyance, among the coat-pegs, and played marbles. They were wise enough to choose a large rubber mat by the door for this purpose, for experience had shown them that the uneven brick floor made a noisy, as well as unpredictable, playing ground, and Miss Fogerty had been known to slip out during the reading of the Bible passage to see what all the rumbling was about. Hardened latecomers were prudent enough to play marbles only while the piano tinkled out the morning hymn, for then Miss Fogerty, they knew, would be at the keyboard and Miss Watson leading the children's singing. After that it was as well to compose their faces into expressions of humility and regret, and to hope secretly that they would be let off with a caution, as the congregation returned to its studies.

The school was empty when Miss Fogerty clattered her way over the door-scraper to her room. That did not surprise her, for Miss Watson lived at the school-house next door, and might be busy with her last-minute chores. She usually arrived about a quarter to nine, greeted her colleague, read her correspondence and was then prepared to face the assembled school.

Miss Fogerty hung up her tweed coat and her brown felt hat behind the classroom door, and set about unlocking the cupboards. There were little tatters of paper at the bottom of the one by the fireplace, where the raffia and other handwork materials were kept and Miss Fogerty looked at them with alarm and suspicion. She had thought for some time that a mouse lived there. She must remember to tell Mrs Cooke to set a trap. Mice were one of the few things that Miss Fogerty could not endure. It would be dreadful if one ran out while the children were present and she made an exhibition of herself by screaming! After surveying the jungle of cane, raffia and cardboard which rioted gloriously together, and which could well offer a dozen comfortable homes to abundant mice families, Miss Fogerty firmly shut the door and relocked it. The children should have crayons and drawing paper this afternoon from the cupboard on the far side of the room, she decided. Mrs Cooke must deal with this crisis before she approached the handwork cupboard again.

The clock stood at five to nine, and now the cries and shouts of two or three dozen children could be heard. Miss Fogerty made her way to the only other classroom, and stopped short on the threshold with surprise. It was empty.

Miss Fogerty noted the clean duster folded neatly in the very centre of Miss Watson's desk, the tidy rows of tables and chairs awaiting their occupants, and the large reproduction of Holman Hunt's 'The Light of the World' in whose dusky glass Miss Fogerty could see her own figure reflected.

What should she do? Could Miss Watson have overslept? Could she be ill? Either possibility seemed difficult to believe. In the twelve years since Miss Watson's coming she had neither overslept nor had a day's indisposition. It would be very awkward if she called at the house and Miss Watson were just about to come over. It would look officious, poor Miss Fogerty told herself, and that could not be borne. Miss Fogerty was a little afraid of Miss Watson, for though she herself had spent thirty years at Thrush Green School, she was only the assistant teacher and she had been taught to respect her betters. And Miss Watson, of course, really was her better, for she had been a headmistress before this, and had taught in town schools, so large and magnificent, that naturally she was much wiser and more experienced. She was consistently kind to faded little Miss Fogerty and very willing to show her new methods of threading beads and making plasticine crumpets, explaining patiently, as she did so, the psychological implications behind these activities in words of three or, more often, four syllables. Miss Fogerty was humbly grateful for her goodwill, but would never have dreamt of imposing upon it. Miss Fogerty knew her place.

While she hovered on the threshold, patting her wispy hair into place with an agitated hand and looking distractedly at her reflection in 'The Light of the World', a breathless child hurried into the lobby, calling her name.

'Miss Fogerty! Miss Fogerty!'

He rushed towards her so violently that Miss Fogerty put out her hands to grasp his shoulders before he should butt her to the ground.

The child looked up at her, wide-eyed. He looked awestricken.

'Miss Watson called me up to her window, miss, and says you're to go over there.'

'Very well,' said Miss Fogerty, calmly. 'There's no need to get so excited. Take off your coat and hang it up. You can go to your room now.'

The child continued to gaze at her.

'But, miss,' he blurted out, 'Miss Watson – she – she's still in her nightdress and the clock's struck nine.'

Miss Watson's appearance when she opened the side door alarmed Miss Fogerty quite as much as it had the small boy.

Her nightdress was decently covered by a red dressing-gown, but her face was drawn with pain and she swayed dizzily against the door jamb.

'What has happened?' exclaimed Miss Fogerty, entering the house.

Miss Watson closed the door and leant heavily against it.

'I've been attacked – hit on the head,' said Miss Watson. She sounded dazed and vaguely surprised. A hand went fumbling among her untidy grey locks and Miss Fogerty, much shocked, put her hand under her headmistress's elbow to steady her.

'Come and sit down. I'll ring Doctor Lovell. He'll be at home now. Tell me what happened.'

'I can't walk,' answered Miss Watson, leaning on Miss Fogerty's frail shoulder. 'I seem to have sprained my ankle as I fell. It is most painful.'

She held out a bare leg, and certainly the ankle was mis-shapen and much swollen. Purplish patches were already forming and Miss Fogerty knew from her first-aid classes that she should really be applying hot and cold water in turn to the damaged joint. But could poor Miss Watson, in her present state of shock, stand such treatment? She helped the younger woman to the kitchen, put her on a chair and looked round for the kettle.

'There's nothing like a cup of tea, dear,' she said comfortingly, as she filled it. 'With plenty of sugar.'

Miss Watson shuddered but made no reply. Her assistant switched on the kettle and surveyed her headmistress anxiously. Her usual feeling of respect, mingled with a little fear, had been replaced by the warmest concern. For the first time in their acquaintanceship Miss Fogerty was in charge.

'The door-bell rang about half-past five, I suppose,' began Miss Watson hesitantly. 'It was still dark. I leant out of the bedroom window and there was a man waiting there who said there had been a car crash and could he telephone.'

'What did he look like?' asked Miss Fogerty.

'I couldn't see. I said I'd come down. I put on my dressing-gown and slippers and opened the front door –' She broke off suddenly, and took a deep breath. Miss Fogerty was smitten by the look of horror on her headmistress's face.

'Don't tell me, my dear, if it upsets you. There's really no need.' She patted the red dressing-gown soothingly, but Miss Watson pulled herself together and continued.

'He'd tied a black scarf, or a stocking, or something over his face, and I could only see his eyes between that and his hat brim. He had a thick stick of some kind – quite short – in his hand, and he said something about this being a hold-up, or a stick-up or some term I really didn't understand. I bent forward to see if I could recognize him – there was something vaguely familiar about him, the voice perhaps – and then he hit me on the side of my head –' Poor Miss Watson faltered and her eyes filled with tears at the memory of that vicious blow.

The kettle's lid began rattling merrily and Miss Fogerty, clucking sympathetically, began to make the tea.

'I seem to remember him pushing past me. I'd crumpled on to the door mat and I remember a fearful pain, but whether it was my head or my ankle, I don't really know. When I came round again the door was shut and he'd vanished. It was beginning to get light then.'

'Why didn't you get help before?' asked Miss Fogerty. 'It must have been about seven o'clock then. He will have got clear by now.'

'I was so terribly sick,' confessed Miss Watson. 'I managed to crawl to the outside lavatory and I've been there most of the time.'

'You poor, poor dear,' cried Miss Fogerty. 'And you must be so cold, too!'

'I couldn't manage the stairs, otherwise I should have got dressed. But I thought I would wait until I heard you arrive, and then I knew I should be all right.'

Miss Fogerty glowed with pleasure. It was not often, in her timid life, that she had been wanted. To know that she was needed by someone gave her a heady sense of power. She poured out the tea with care and put the cup carefully before her patient.

'Shall I lift it for you?' she asked solicitously, but Miss Watson shook her head, raising the steaming cup herself and sipped gratefully.

'The children –' she said suddenly, as their exuberant voices penetrated the quietness of the kitchen.

'Don't worry,' said Miss Fogerty with newly-found authority. 'I'll just speak to the bigger ones, then I'll be back to ring the doctor.'

'Don't tell them anything about this,' begged Miss Watson with sudden agitation. 'You know what Thrush Green is. It will be all round the place in no time.'

Miss Fogerty assured her that nothing would be disclosed and slipped out of the side door.

The children were shouting and playing, revelling in this unexpected addition to their pre-school games time.

Miss Fogerty leant over the low dry-stone wall which separated the playground from the school-house garden. She beckoned to two of the bigger girls.

'Keep an eye on the young ones, my dears. I'll be with you in a minute, then we'll all go in.'

'Is Miss Watson ill?' asked one, her eyes alight with pleasurable anticipation.

Miss Fogerty was torn between telling the truth and the remembrance of her promise to her headmistress. She temporized wisely.

'Not really dear, but she won't be over for a little while. There's nothing for you to worry about.'

She hastened back to her duties.

Her patient had finished her tea and now leant back with her eyes closed and the swollen ankle propped up on another chair. She opened her eyes as Miss Fogerty approached, and smiled faintly.

'Tell me,' said Miss Fogerty, who had just remembered something. 'Did the man take anything?'

'He took the purse from my bag. There wasn't much in it, and my wallet, with about six pounds, I believe.'

Miss Fogerty was profoundly shocked. Six pounds was a lot of money for a schoolteacher to lose even if she were a headmistress.

'And I think he may have found my jewel box upstairs, but of course I haven't been up there to see. It hadn't much of value in it, except to me, I mean. There was a string of seed pearls my father gave me, and two rings of my mother's and a brooch or two – but nothing worth a lot of money.'

'We must ring the police as well as Doctor Lovell,' exclaimed Miss Fogerty.

'Must we?' cried Miss Watson, her face puckering. 'Oh dear, I do hate all this fuss – but I suppose it is our duty.'

Miss Fogerty's heart smote her at the sight of her patient's distress. It reminded her too that she should really get her into bed so that she could recover a little from the shocks she had received. She sprang to her feet, with new-found strength, and went to help her head-mistress.

'Back to bed for you,' she said firmly, 'and then I'm going to the telephone. Up you come!'

Five minutes later, with her patient safely tucked up, Miss Fogerty spoke to Doctor Lovell and then to Lulling Police Station. That done, she went over to the school playground to face the forty or more children for whom she alone would be responsible that day.

Normally the thought would have made timid little Miss Fogerty quail. But today, fortified by her experiences, feeling six feet high and a tower of strength, Miss Fogerty led the entire school into morning assembly and faced a host of questioning eyes with un-accustomed composure and authority.

For the first time in her life Miss Fogerty was in command, and found she liked it.

As Miss Watson had feared, the word had flown round Thrush Green with exceptional rapidity. It was too much to hope that the visit of Doctor Lovell, and later, the sight of a policeman walking up the path to the school-house, should pass unnoticed, on a fine Monday morning, in Thrush Green. Neighbours shaking mats, pegging out the week's washing or simply gossiping over the hedges, saw the signs and spread the tales.

'Probably got a touch of this 'ere flu that's going round,' said one, as Doctor Lovell strode briskly towards the school-house door. 'It's gastrical this year,' she added, airing her medical knowledge.

'Hasn't looked well for weeks,' said another. 'Very tiring life, that teaching. Everlasting bawling at the kids – must knock you up in the end.'

'Poor Miss Watson, wonder what ails her? At a funny age, of course, for a spinster,' commented a third matron, taking a swipe at her screaming ninth and youngest, and feeling unaccountably superior at the same time.

Within ten minutes of Doctor Lovell's appearance Thrush Green had burdened Miss Watson with every ill from ear-ache to epilepsy, and felt for her an all-embracing sympathy.

Within half an hour the policeman arrived. He was hot and breathless, having pushed his bicycle up the steep hill from Lulling. He vanished inside the house and the temperature rose again on Thrush Green.

'If it weren't that Doctor Lovell's so very particular I'd say she'd been assaulted,' said one neighbour earnestly to another, damning in one breath the morals of the rest of the medical profession and Miss Watson's modest charms.

'Could be attempted suicide,' said another, her eye brightening. 'Teaching's enough to turn your head at times. You can't wonder with children round you all day.'

'That's true,' agreed her crony, nodding her head sagely. 'Poor Miss Watson's probably come over violent and Doctor's sent for the police. Unless, of course, she's done something real bad and just confessed it to the doctor –'

The tongues wagged gaily. By the time the children came out to play at ten-thirty Thrush Green had Miss Watson convicted of every crime from forgetting to renew her television licence – this was the most charitable suggestion – to slitting young Doctor Lovell's throat with the bread-knife whilst in the grip of a violent brainstorm brought on by twelve years' non-stop teaching. This was the opinion of those who allowed their thoughts to be coloured by the recent reading of their Sunday newspapers. There was certainly enough to keep Thrush Green pleasurably amused for many happy days, and by the time Doctor Lovell had departed, and the policeman had stowed away his pocket-book with poor Miss Watson's statement in it and a detailed description of the missing purse, wallet – and, alas – the jewel case and a small gilt alarm clock, there were enough rumours flying round the green to last a year.

As Ella Bembridge said afterwards: 'It never rains but it pours,' for before the children returned to school at ten forty-five prompt, another momentous happening shook Thrush Green.

A large Daimler car glided to the gate of the corner house. Out stepped a tall military figure who stood looking about him, just long enough for the watchful eyes of his future neighbours to notice his sunburnt face and white moustache, before taking out a door-key, hurrying up the path and letting himself into his new home.

For a brief moment Miss Watson's blaze of glory was extinguished in the dazzling light of this new event.

At last, the corner house was occupied.

4. Plans for a Party

Some days after this excitement, Ella and Dimity sat at the dining-room table writing invitations. It would be more truthful to say that Dimity was doing the writing, while Ella conned a list and occasionally thumped a stamp on the addressed envelopes.

'About time we did this,' commented Ella, watching Dimity's careful pen inscribing SHERRY in the left-hand corner. 'How long since we gave a blow-out, Dim?'

'Quite two years,' said Dimity, selecting an envelope. 'I know it was in the summer, soon after Mrs Curdle's fair came. The last time we saw her,' added Dimity, her eyes beginning to look misty.

Ella stirred herself to be bracing. Much too sympathetic, poor old Dim! Ought to have had a husband and six children to lavish all that affection on, thought Ella, not for the first time.

'Grand old girl,' agreed Ella heartily. 'Well, she had a good run for her money, you know, and the fair's still going strong under young Ben. I hear he's coming to Thrush Green for Christmas with Molly, to see old Piggott.'

As she had intended, this diverted Dimity's attention.

'That will be nice. I'd like to see Molly Piggott again – Curdle, I mean.' Dimity smiled at the thought and attacked the stack of cards again.

'Who have we done now?' she asked Ella, who was ticking the list.

'The Baileys, the Youngs, the rector, the Lovells, Dotty, and the three Lovelock sisters. Only four more to do. I can't see where we're going to put them anyway in this cottage.'

'People shrink at cocktail parties,' Dimity assured her. 'It's because they stand up and are packed together neatly. At tea parties their legs are spread all over the floor.'

'Awful lot of women,' mourned Ella surveying the list.

'I wouldn't say they're awful,' said Dimity, sounding shocked.

'No, no,' replied Ella testily. 'They're *not* awful. There's just too many of them.' Her face brightened.

'Dim, we've forgotten to put down the new man. Write one quickly.'

'But we don't know him,' objected Dimity. 'We haven't called yet.'

'I have,' said Ella briefly. Dimity looked at her with her mouth open.

'You didn't tell me.'

'I forgot. I took the parish magazine in and he was in the front garden. Seems a nice man.'

Dimity looked a little affronted, but obediently inscribed a card and put it in an envelope. She looked up, pen hovering.

'What is he called?'

'Harold Shoosmith,' said Ella promptly. 'With an "o" instead of "e" in "Shoo". And an "o" for Harold, I'm glad to say, not "a". If there's one thing I can't abide it's a Harald with an "a". Like "Hark the Harald Angels Sing",' added Ella facetiously.

Dimity's pen remained poised in mid-air. She ignored Ella's weak joke with unaccustomed severity.

'Is he retired army or navy?' she asked.

'Search me,' said Ella. 'Winnie Bailey says he's a Lieutenant-Commander, Joan Young says he's a Major, and Ruth Lovell heard he was a Squadron-Leader. As far as Thrush Green's concerned after a week's acquaintanceship I should say "Esq." would fit the case perfectly.

She watched Dimity write the address and sighed happily as it was pushed over to her to stamp.

'I must say it's a real pleasure to have an unattached man at one of our parties. Can't remember the last time we had one under our roof, can you, Dim?'

'The rector comes often enough,' pointed out Dimity, a little tartly.

'Well, you can't count the rector,' said Ella reasonably, 'poppet though he is. Besides, he's a widower.'

'So may Harold Shoosmith be,' said Dimity, writing rather fast. Her mouth was pursed, and Ella could see that she had not been completely forgiven for having met the newcomer before her friend. She watched the hurrying pen with mingled guilt and amusement.

Dimity completed the card and looked across at Ella meaningly.

'Or even married!' she said with emphasis.

And she might just as well have added 'So there!' thought Ella, stamping the envelope in silence, from the hint of triumph in her voice.

Ella's lively interest in Harold Shoosmith was shared by the rest of Thrush Green. It was said that he was retired from the army, the navy, the air force, the civil service and the B.B.C. He had been a tea-planter in Ceylon, a cocoa-adviser in Ghana, and a coffee-blender in Brazil. It also appeared that he had owned a sugar plantation in Jamaica, a rubber plantation in Malaya and a diamond mine – quite a small one, actually, but with exceptionally fine diamonds – in South Africa.

Thrush Green was sorry to hear that he had never been married, had been married unhappily and was now separated from his wife, had been happily married and lost his wife in childbirth and (disastrously), still married, with a wife who would be coming to live with him at the corner house within a few days.

The inhabitants of Thrush Green were able to gaze their fill at the stranger on the first Sunday after his arrival, as he attended morning service in a dove-grey suit which was far better cut, everyone agreed, than those of the other males in the congregation. The rector and one or two other neighbours had called upon him already and pronounced him 'a very nice man' or 'a decent sort of fellow' according to sex.

To the rector's unfeigned delight the newcomer was among the very few communicants at the altar rail at the eight o'clock service on the following Sunday. About half a dozen faithful female Christians kept the rector company at early service usually, and these included Dimity Dean – but not Ella who went to church less frequently – and Dotty Harmer. It did the rector's heart good to see a man among his small flock, and he hoped that others might follow his example.

Betty Bell was the chief informant about Harold Shoosmith for she had been engaged for three mornings and three evenings a week. The morning engagements Thrush Green could readily understand, for a man living alone could not be expected to polish and clean, to cook and scrub, and to wash and iron for himself; though, as Ella pointed out, plenty of women lived alone and did all that with one hand tied behind them, and often went out to work as well into the bargain, and no one considered it remarkable.

The evening engagements were readily explained by Betty Bell herself. She went for an hour and a half to give him a hot cooked dinner, which she had prepared in the morning, and to wash up afterwards.

'He's a very clever kind of man,' said Betty to her other employer, Dotty Harmer, one morning. 'He wants to learn to cook for himself. Being out in those hot countries, you know, he's never had a chance to learn. The kitchen's full of black people falling over themselves to do the work, and he's never been allowed to see his own dinner cooking, so I hear.'

'I should have thought he could have managed a fried egg,' said Dotty cutting up quinces at the table. 'Ah, Betty,' she sighed sadly, peering up at the girl through her thick glasses, 'this means the real end of summer, you know. When I make quince jam I know it's the last of the season. It'll soon be November, Betty, and winter will be here.'

'That's what I told Mr Shoosmith,' agreed Betty, returning to her present consuming interest. ' "You want to know how to cook a meal for yourself, in case I can't get here one winter's day," I said to him. So I've shown him how to fry bacon and egg and sausage, and how to make a stew. He's real quick at picking things up, I must say.'

'Poor man,' said Dotty, 'he'll miss the sun, I dare say. Would you like to take him a pot of my jam when it's done?' Her face brightened at the thought. She had introduced herself to the newcomer after early morning service and had been glad to welcome such an attractive addition to the Thrush Green circle.

Betty accepted the offer guardedly and made a mental note to warn the unsuspecting recipient against eating it. Dotty, as a keen herbalist and dietician, could never refrain from adding a few sprigs of this, and a drop or two of that, to her dishes in order to give them added vitamin content, and the number of people who had been attacked with 'Dotty's Collywobbles', as a result of her cooking, was prodigious.

At that moment the postman appeared at the kitchen window and handed in an untidy parcel and one letter.

'This must be my dried coltsfoot and the other things for my winter ointments and cough cures,' said Dotty excitedly, dropping the quinces and tearing at the parcel with sticky fingers. Some strongly-smelling dead foliage fell upon the kitchen table and the black cat who was sunning herself upon it near the jam-making operations. Outraged, she leapt down and stalked towards the stove, tail quivering erect with indignation.

'There now,' said Betty, 'you've been and upset Mrs Curdle; and her expecting too.'

Dotty was now reading the card which she had extracted from the envelope. The scattered herbs lay unheeded where they had fallen.

'Oh, how lovely!' exclaimed Dotty, her wrinkled face alight with pleasure. 'Miss Bembridge and Miss Dean are giving a sherry party on October 31st. Now, isn't that nice?'

'All Hallows E'en,' commented Betty, bending to stroke Mrs Curdle's ruffled dignity. She had been named after the famous old lady because she had been born on the day that Curdle's Fair visited Thrush Green over two years before. The cat shared with her famous namesake some of her dark magnificence and queenly dominance. She now allowed Betty to smooth her fur, but turned her back upon her thoughtless mistress.

'So it is,' cried Dotty. 'A party on All Hallows E'en! Well, well, I must certainly go to that!'

She picked up some of the quinces, together with a few stray herbs from the parcel, and dropped them into a saucepan.

As she stirred she peered closely into the bubbling brew, and Mrs Curdle, suspecting that food might be forthcoming, deigned to return to her mistress's side.

'Proper witches' party it will be, and no mistake,' thought Betty Bell to herself, surveying the scene. 'And I'll take care not a morsel of that quince jam ever passes the innocent lips of poor dear Mr Shoosmith! My, that man just doesn't know what he's letting himself in for – coming to live at Thrush Green!'

Meanwhile, Miss Watson's assailant remained undetected. The police had very little to go on. Miss Watson could tell them no more than she had at first, and there were no helpful footprints or finger-prints to help in the search. The weather had been brilliant and dry for over a month, and even if footprints had been left, the arrival of several dozen children at the school an hour or so later meant that a large number of them would be effaced. There seemed to be no doubt that the man had worn gloves, and indeed Miss Watson thought that she recalled that the cosh was gripped in an iron-grey woollen glove bound with leather.

She racked her aching brain for several days trying to pin down the faint sense of recognizing those gloves and the man himself, but all was in vain. In the end she had given up worrying about it, and was content to take Miss Fogerty's good advice and 'let the matter rest'.

Miss Watson confessed that she could not have managed without Miss Fogerty's boundless help. Every morning the good little woman had arrived at eight o'clock to give her her breakfast in bed, until at the end of the week Miss Watson had insisted on returning to school again. There she had found everything in apple-pie order. The ac-counts had been kept, correspondence had been answered, fresh flowers decked the two classrooms and even the calendar had been torn off daily.

Miss Watson was much troubled by her assistant's kindness and ability. Lying in bed for two or three days had given her, at last, time to dwell on the sterling qualities hidden beneath Miss Fogerty's mouse-like exterior. For twelve years she had taken the older woman for granted, and on many occasions had felt impatient with her timidity and out-of-date methods. At the end of each day she had bade farewell to Miss Fogerty with something akin to relief. Now it could never be quite the same again. Miss Fogerty had proved herself a friend.

As the headmistress limped about her school in the next few weeks she became increasingly aware of Miss Fogerty's newly found confidence which had flowered during her own absence. The nervous acquiescence which had so often irritated Miss Watson had now vanished, and they discussed school problems on equal terms.

Misfortune had united and strengthened them both, and the school at Thrush Green was all the better for it.

The burglary had created some unease in the neighbourhood. People who had never locked a door in their lives now looked out forgotten keys and turned them in the locks before departing to Lulling for a morning's shopping. Those who had been in the habit of hiding their keys under upturned flower-pots or their door-scrapers now decided that it would be prudent to change these well-known hiding-places for new ones.

'I'm leaving my key under the mat in the back porch,' Mrs Bailey told her closest friends. 'Everyone knows about the ledge over the door.'

'We're putting ours behind the paraffin can in the shed now,' said Dimity.

Mr Piggott, who had a door key of ecclesiastical design weighing a good three-quarters of a pound, fixed it to a stout belt round his waist, and put up with the inconvenience of its sundry blows as he bent about his business in the churchyard. The burglary had impressed him considerably, and he made no bones about expressing his disgust with the police.

'What we pays them for I don't know,' he grumbled over his glass at 'The Two Pheasants'. 'Folks on Thrush Green going in fear of their lives – and what's done about it, eh? I'll lay I could find the chap that done it, if I was given half a chance!'

'That's right,' said the landlord, winking secretly at his other customers. 'You turn Sherlock Holmes, see – and show the police where they get off.'

As the last days of October slipped by, the press of autumn life caused the robbery to slip into the background. There were borders to be dug, wallflower plants to be put in, and all the outside preparations for winter which the kindly weather encouraged. Before long, Thrush Green would be enveloped in the cold rains and fogs of a Cotswold winter. If the weather prophets proved correct there would be snow too. Wise householders made the most of this respite, and the excitement of the newcomer to their midst and the attack on Miss Watson soon shook down into place with other matters.

But for old Mr Piggott the robbery was of major importance. He had lived alone ever since the departure of his daughter Molly with young Ben Curdle, and he had plenty of time to let his beer-befuddled imagination dwell on the mystery. As he pottered about his damp little cottage, or performed perfunctorily his simple duties as sexton of St Andrew's hard by, he dreamt wonderful day-dreams, envisaging himself as the sleuth of Thrush Green, the man who showed the police how to do their job, and the hero of his admiring and grateful neighbours.

'I'll show them,' muttered old Piggott, slashing viciously at a bed of nettles which threatened to engulf the headstone of Nathaniel Patten. 'I'll show them all – that I will!'

5. Nelly Tilling

The day of the party dawned cold and blustery. Ella and Dimity sat at their breakfast table watching the bright leaves whirling to the grass. A spatter of rain rattled on the windowpane and Dimity shivered.

'Do you think we ought to light the paraffin stove in the sitting-room as well as the fire, dear?'

'Wouldn't be a bad idea to have it alight this morning, but we're not keeping that thing going all day. It'll smell the place out. Nothing like a strong reek for killing the party spirit.'

'But it doesn't smell!' protested Dimity.

'No woman thinks her own paraffin stove smells,' said Ella emphatically, dousing the stub of her cigarette in the dregs of her tea-cup. This detestable habit would have caused a less devoted companion to have left Ella long before, but Dimity daily shuddered and forbore to speak of her pain. 'It's a natural phenomenon,' continued Ella, blandly unaware of her friend's revulsion, 'like being unable to hear your own voice.'

Ella settled back comfortably, crossing one massive leg over the other, and seemed prepared to expand this interesting theory. But Dimity, conscious of the work to be done in preparation for the party, rose hastily and began to pack up the breakfast dishes.

'I think I'll get out Mother's little silver bon-bon dishes and polish them. They'll do beautifully for the salted nuts,' she began busily.

'They'll get tarnished,' objected Ella. 'What's wrong with saucers.'

'Saucers?' cried Dimity in horror. 'At a party?'

'I meant the *best* ones,' said Ella, trying vainly to bring down Dimity's heightened temperature.

'Quite out of the question!' replied Dimity, with unusual severity. 'We must use the silver dishes, and I am quite prepared to polish them after the party.'

She might have added that no one in the household besides herself ever did do any polishing, but Dimity was used to holding her tongue and did not give way to temptation on this occasion.

Ella lumbered to her feet, sighing.

'Just as you say, Dim. You know best. Let's go and have a look at the decorations by daylight, and we'll see if we need the stove lighted.'

The two friends crossed the small hall to their sitting-room which they had embellished the previous evening. The fact that they had arranged the party for All Hallows E'en dawned on the two ladies soon after they had posted the invitations and Ella had put her ingenuity and skilled hands to work on the decorations.

A flight of witches, cut from stout black paper and dangling from threads, flew diagonally across the room, twisting and turning in the draughts in the most spirited manner. Their hair streamed behind them from their pointed hats, and Ella had stuck on green sequins for the eyes of her creations, which glittered balefully as they caught the light.

Two great copper jars filled with autumn leaves and Cape gooseberries glowed from the corners of the room, and on the mantelpiece stood a golden pumpkin. This had been presented by Dotty Harmer and Ella had hollowed it out, cut out two round eyes, a triangle for a nose and a crescent for a mouth, and put a night-light inside it. This, when lit, caused the hollow globe to glow and the whole effect was deliciously sinister.

Dimity looked at her friend's handiwork with genuine admiration.

'It's simply wonderful, Ella darling. I wonder if it would be a good idea to play a few Hallow E'en games – bobbing for apples, you know, and that kind of thing!' Dimity's faded eyes shone at the very thought, but her friend damped her ardour abruptly.

'Be your age, Dim! People are coming for a civilized glass of sherry and to meet their friends. They won't thank you for cold water down their bodices, ducking for green apples – and double pneumonia by the end of the week, ten chances to one.'

Her tone changed as she noted her friend's crestfallen face.

'We're all getting too long in the tooth for those capers,' she said more kindly. She patted Dimity's arm with a massive hand. 'Let's get the stove going for an hour or so, and check up on the drinks. Got any lemons, by the way?'

'Three,' said Dimity. 'Sevenpence each.' Her voice was still subdued and Ella wished she had been less brutal about poor old Dim's suggestion for games.

'It should be quite a cheerful crowd,' said Ella, trying to make amends. 'I'm glad the new man's coming.'

She led the way back to the dining-room with Dimity fluttering behind, and still looking like a kitten that has been kicked.

'Don't forget to look in the mirror when you brush your hair tonight, Dim,' continued Ella, with heavy jocularity. 'They say you see your husband on All Hallows E'en!'

The unconscious association of ideas in Ella's remarks might have struck an astute observer, but both Ella herself and Dimity were unaware of anything remarkable. To the two friends only one thing was apparent – the olive branch was being offered by one and gratefully accepted by the other.

With their arms affectionately entwined they approached the drinks cupboard.

The rain and wind increased as the morning wore on. The honey-coloured houses that clustered round Thrush Green grew a deeper gold as the rain lashed their glistening walls. Thousands of drops ran from one Cotswold stone tile to the next, down the steep roofs to the waiting gutters which gurgled and spluttered with their un-accustomed load. Rainwater butts, which had stood almost empty for the past few weeks, rumbled and bubbled in their stout wooden bellies; and the thirsty gardens drank up the bounty and gave forth a blessed fragrance by way of grace.

Umbrellas bobbed down the hill to Lulling, and cars sent up flashing fountains from the long puddles by the side of the green. The horse-chestnut trees flailed their branches, sending down the last few leaves to join their fellows in the mud below.

The wind howled among the chimneys of Thrush Green, and the sign-board of 'The Two Pheasants' leant away to the south at a steep angle. Two tea towels in the little yard had twisted round and round the line until they looked like two bright giant caterpillars clinging there.

Above St Andrew's steeple a flock of rooks swayed and dipped in the airy tides. They looked like fragments of burnt paper eddying in the current from a bonfire, and now and again, above the roaring of the wind about them, a faint harsh cry could be heard.

Far below them, beneath the windy steeple, beneath the humming belfry with its singing louvres, and beneath the draughty chancel, Mr Piggott, like some earthy mole, laboured in the stoke-hole.

Here was no sound of wind and storm, no icy splash of rain. The great boiler gave forth a pungent heat and whispered quietly as it digested its coke.

Nearby stood its guardian. Mr Piggott had two clothes pegs in his mouth and his spare shirt in his hands. A row of garments sagged from a small line and steamed gently in the heat.

Mr Piggott's wash-day took no account of the weather. The heat which he engendered to warm the worshippers might just as well dry his clothes, argued the sexton to himself, as he pegged the shirt on the line.

Standing back, he surveyed his clothes with pride. They might not be as white as those of his neighbours which he saw billowing on their lines, but here, among the coke, they looked all right to Mr Piggott.

He took out a large watch and squinted at it short-sightedly. Surely they must be open by now! He saw, with pleasure, that the hands stood at ten-thirty.

With remarkable agility Mr Piggott mounted the steep stone stairs from the stoke-hole, and prepared to face the weather.

The noise above ground surprised him. There was a menacing hum high in the lofty dimness above him, and a general confused roaring from the trees outside the church. Mr Piggott made his way up the long aisle, bending here and there to pick up a stray dead leaf or morsel of confetti which the wind had flung in from outside. While he was thus engaged he became conscious of other noises nearer at hand. He heard the metallic click of the porch door, the clanking which betokened heavy feet on the wire foot-scraper and the gasping of a breathless wayfarer.

'Treading in the dirt all over my flagstones,' muttered Mr Piggott, inhospitably, opening the heavy church door with a venomous tug. There was a squeal of surprise as the newcomer turned to face him, her hand on her capacious bosom.

'Lor, Albert, you give me a fright!' puffed the lady. 'Never 'ad no idea of you being in there. Came in out of the wet for half a minute. All right, is it?'

She darted a quick look at the sexton from small dark eyes well embedded in rosy flesh. Beneath her sodden head-scarf a few dark curls protruded, sparkling with rain-drops. She seated herself on the stone bench and began to peel off her wet gloves.

Mr Piggott watched sourly. He had known Nelly Tilling most of his life, and they had shared the same desk at the village school for a term or two. Kept her looks, she had, observed Mr Piggott privately, if you like them plump. Why, she must weigh nigh on twelve or thirteen stone, he ruminated, casting an eye experienced in assessing the weight of a pig, over his old school-fellow's bulk.

'Don't want to sit on that stone,' advised Mr Piggott, dourly. 'Strikes up.'

'Well, it does a bit,' confessed the lady, heaving herself to her feet. 'But I'm real whacked, walking against this wind.'

'Best come inside, I suppose,' said Mr Piggott, grudgingly, but he made no move to open the door. He found his visitor a nuisance. Should he invite her down to the stoke-hole to dry out, he wondered? Thoughts of his dangling underclothes dismayed him. He had no desire to be the butt of Nelly Tilling's derision. His own cottage was cold and he did not want his neighbours to see him taking the buxom widow into it, for Nelly Tilling was reputed to be looking for a second husband after burying her first the year before, and Mr Piggott disliked appearing ridiculous. If he invited her to 'The Two Pheasants' he would have to pay for her, and that, of course, was unthinkable.

On the other hand, Mr Piggott was surprised to feel a tiny glow

within him as he watched Mrs Tilling shaking her gloves and brushing the drops from her enormous coat. After all, they had been to
school together, it was a beast of a day, and the poor toad was likely
to catch her death if she sat about in those clammy things without a
sup in her. And, say what you liked, she was a fine-looking woman
and Mr Piggott realized, with a shock, that he had felt lonely for a
long time. Somewhat to his horror, he heard himself saying :

'Come and join me in a drink. I was on my way to "The Two
Pheasants".'

The lady's reaction to this innocent suggestion was alarming. Her
rosy face became redder than ever, her dark eyes flashed fire, and
indignation swelled her heaving breast to such an extent that her coat
buttons strained from the cloth. She reminded Mr Piggott of a
bridling turkey-cock.

'I joined the Band of Hope the same day as you did, if you can cast
your mind back that far, Albert Piggott! And what's more, I ain't
never broke the pledge yet – which is more than you can say from
what I hear!'

She advanced upon the shrinking sexton to wag a massive finger
in his face. Mr Piggott backed away nervously until his greasy cap
knocked against a bland cherub who stared sightlessly from the porch
wall. Nelly Tilling, in anger, was an awe-inspiring sight. She seemed
akin to the natural elements which raged so furiously around her,
and though taken aback at her onslaught, Mr Piggott found himself
admiring her spirit.

'No need to act so spiteful then,' returned the sexton, with unusual
mildness. He rubbed his knocked head while he reviewed the situation.

Nelly Tilling calmed down a little after her outburst and withdrew
to study the weather from the doorway. Behind her sturdy shoulders
Mr Piggott caught a glimpse of the inn's signboard as it groaned and
creaked in the gale. His thirst returned.

'Well, gal, if you don't want a drop, I do,' he said ungallantly.
'Make yourself at home here, while I slip over. Stoking's thirsty
work, and I ain't never made no boast about taking the pledge!'

He made to edge past her, but the lady turned to face him, barring
his way. Her red mouth was curved in a delicious smile. Albert
Piggott found it both alarming and bewitching.

''Ere, let me –' he began weakly.

'Albert, I wouldn't say no to a nice cup of tea, if I was to be asked over to your house. How about it?'

Mr Piggott's fear of his neighbours' interest must have made itself apparent in his apprehensive face.

' 'Twould only be civil, a day like this,' pressed Nelly Tilling. 'I wouldn't stop more than a minute or two – just while the rain's so heavy.'

Mr Piggott's expression lightened a trifle, but his mouth still turned down at the corners.

'I can't stop long in any case,' pursued Nelly, winningly. 'I've left a sheep's head boiling on the stove.'

Mr Piggott allowed a half-smile to soften his severity.

'Sheep's head!' he whispered huskily. 'Why, I haven't had a bite of sheep's head since my Molly got wed!' His rheumy old eyes gazed unseeingly into the windy distance behind Nelly's head.

Mrs Tilling gave a violent shiver and a very creditable imitation of a sneeze.

'I'm in for a cold if I don't get a hot drink soon,' said she, pathetically. Her dark eyes gazed at her old school-fellow with all the wistful appeal of a beaten spaniel's.

Mr Piggott succumbed.

'Come on over then,' he said bravely, opening the porch door. A vicious burst of wind almost buffeted the breath from them and the rain danced like spinning silver coins on the old flagged path.

'Put your head down, Nell, and we'll run for it,' shouted the sexton.

Wind-blown and panting, Mrs Tilling thankfully accepted the armchair which Mr Piggott indicated.

'I'll just tidy these up,' said her host, stuffing a dozen or so unwashed socks behind the grubby cushion. Mrs Tilling viewed the proceedings with some misgivings, but sat herself down gingerly on the edge of the seat.

'Make yerself at 'ome,' said Mr Piggott, passing her an out-of-date copy of the parish magazine. 'I'll put on the kettle.'

He moved into the little kitchen which led from the sitting-room and soon Nelly could hear the tap running. Her eyes wandered round the unsavoury room. If ever a house cried out for a woman's hand, thought the lady dramatically, this was it!

She noted the greasy chenille tablecloth which was threadbare where the table edge cut into it – a sure sign, Nelly knew, that the cloth had been undisturbed for many months. Her eyes travelled to the dead fern in its arid pot, the ashes in the rusty grate, the festoons of cobwebs which hung from filthy pelmets to picture rails and the appalling thickness of the dust which covered the drab objects on the dresser.

The only cheerful spot of colour in the room was afforded by St Andrew's church almanack which Mr Piggott had fixed on the wall above the rickety card table which supported an ancient wireless set.

Mrs Tilling, who began to find the room oppressive and smelly, left her sock-laden armchair (from whence, she suspected, most of the aroma emanated), and decided to investigate the kitchen.

Mr Piggott was standing morosely by the kettle waiting for it to boil. It was typical of a man, thought his guest with some impatience, that he had not utilized his time by putting out the cups and saucers, milk, sugar and so on, which would be needed. Just like poor old George, thought Nelly with a pang, remembering her late husband. 'One thing at a time,' he used to say pompously, as though there were some virtue in it. As his wife had pointed out tartly, on many occasions, she herself would never get through a quarter of her quota of work if she indulged herself in such idleness. While a kettle boiled she could set a table, light a fire, and watch over a cooking breakfast. Ah, men were poor tools, thought Mrs Tilling!

The kitchen was even dirtier than its neighbour. A sour fustiness pervaded the dingy room. In a corner on the floor stood a saucer of milk which had long since turned to an unsavoury junket embellished with blue mould. Beside it lay two very dead herrings' heads. A mound of dirty crockery hid the draining-board, and the sight of Mr Piggott's frying pan hanging on the wall was enough to turn over Mrs Tilling's stout stomach. The residue of dozens of past meals could here be seen embedded in grey fat. Slivers of black burnt onion, petrified bacon rinds, lacy brown scraps of fried eggs and scores of other morsels from tomatoes, sausages, steaks, chops, liver, potatoes, bread and beans here lay cheek by jowl and would have afforded a rich reward to anyone interested in Mr Piggott's diet over the past year.

'Where d'you keep the cups?' asked Nelly Tilling, when she had regained her breath. Her gaze turned apprehensively towards the pile on the draining-board. Mr Piggott seemed to sense her misgivings.

'Got some in the other room, in the dresser cupboard,' he said. 'My old woman's best,' he explained. 'Molly used 'em sometimes.'

'You get them while I make the tea,' said Mrs Tilling briskly. 'This the pot?' She peered into the murky depths of a battered tin object on the stove.

'Ah! Tea's in,' said Mr Piggott, making his way to the dresser.

The kettle boiled. With a brave shudder Nelly poured the water on the tea leaves, comforting herself with the thought that boiling water killed germs of all sorts.

Five minutes later she put down her empty cup and smiled at her companion.

'Lovely cup of tea,' she said truthfully. 'I feel all the better for that. Now I must go over to Doctor Lovell's for my pills.'

'It's still pouring,' said Mr Piggott. 'Have another cup.'

'I'll pour,' said Nelly. 'Pass your own.'

'It's nice to have someone to pour out,' confessed Mr Piggott. He was beginning to feel unaccountably cheerful despite the disappointment of missing his customary pint of beer. 'This place needs a woman.'

'I'll say it does!' agreed Nelly, warmly. 'It needs a few gallons of hot soapy water too! When did your Molly see this last?'

'About a year ago, I suppose. She's coming again Christmas-time – she and Ben and the baby. Maybe she'll give it a bit of a clean-up then.'

'It wouldn't hurt you to do a bit,' said Nelly roundly. 'Chuck out that milk and fish, for one thing.'

'The cat ain't had nothing to eat for days,' objected her host, stung by her criticism.

'That don't surprise me,' retorted Nelly. 'No cat would stay in this hole.'

'I got me church to see to,' began Mr Piggott, truculently. 'I ain't got time to –'

'If Molly comes home to this mess at Christmas then I'm sorry for her,' asserted Mrs Tilling. 'And the baby too. Like as not it'll catch something and die on your very hearth-stone!'

She paused to let the words sink in. Mr Piggott mumbled gloomily to himself. The gist of his mutterings was the unpleasantness of women, their officiousness, their fussiness and their inability to let well alone, but he took care to keep his remarks inaudible.

'Tell you what,' said Mrs Tilling in a warmer tone. 'I'll come up here and give you a hand turning out before Christmas. What about it?'

Mr Piggott's forebodings returned. What would the neighbours say? What was Nelly Tilling up to? What would happen to his own peaceful, slummocky bachelor existence if he allowed this woman to have her way?

Nelly watched the thoughts chasing each other across his dour countenance. After a few minutes she noticed a certain cunning softness replacing the apprehension of his expression, and her heart began to beat a little faster.

'No harm, I suppose,' said the old curmudgeon, grudgingly. 'Make things a bit more welcoming for Molly, wouldn't it?'

'That's right,' agreed Mrs Tilling, rising from her chair and brushing a fine collection of sticky crumbs from her coat. 'One good turn deserves another, you know, and we've been friends long enough to act neighbourly, haven't we, Albert?'

Mr Piggott found himself quite dazzled by the warmth of her smile as she made for the door, and was unable to speak.

The wind roared in as she opened the front door, lifting the filthy curtains and blowing the parish magazine into a corner. Might freshen the place up a bit, thought Nelly, stepping out into the storm.

'Thanks for the tea, Albert. I'll drop in again when I'm passing,' shouted the lady, as she retreated into the uproar.

Mr Piggott nodded dumbly, shut the door with a crash, and breathed deeply. Mingled pleasure and fury shook his aged frame, but overriding all these agitations was the urgent need for a drink.

'Women!' spat out Mr Piggott, resuming his damp raincoat. 'Never let a chap alone!'

His mind turned the phrase over. There was something about it that made Mr Piggott feel younger – a beau, a masher, a man who was still pursued.

'Never let a chap alone!' repeated Mr Piggott aloud. He pulled on his wet cap, adjusting it at an unusually rakish and dashing angle, and made his way, swaggering very slightly, to his comforts next door.

*

'Do you know,' said Dimity Dean, looking up from polishing the silver baskets ready for the evening's festivities, 'do you know that Nelly Tilling has just come out of Piggott's house?'

'Nelly Tilling?' repeated Ella, looking up from rolling an untidy cigarette. 'Which is she?'

'You know,' said Dimity, with some impatience. 'The fat woman who's supposed to be looking for a second husband!'

'Hm!' grunted Ella shortly. 'She's welcome to old Piggott!'

6. All Hallows E'en

At six-thirty Ella and Dimity awaited their guests. Both ladies were dressed in the frocks which had been recognized by Thrush Green and Lulling as their cocktail clothes for the last decade, and both exuded the aroma of their recent baths, lavender in Dimity's case and Wright's Coal Tar soap in Ella's.

Dimity's grey crêpe had a cowl neck-line which had been rather fashionable just after the war and a full skirt which a more sophisticated woman would have supported with a stiffened petticoat. Over Dimity's modest Vedonis straight petticoat, however, the fullness draped itself limply, ending in a hem so uneven that it was obviously the work of the cleaners rather than the couturiers. A rose of squashed fawn silk at the waistline strove unavailingly to add dash to this ensemble.

Ella, in a plain black woollen frock decorated only with cigarette ash on the bodice, looked surprisingly elegant. Released for once from their brogues her feet were remarkably neat in a pair of black suède shoes, low-heeled but well-cut, which drew attention to the fact that despite Ella's bulk she still showed an attractive pair of ankles.

The fire crackled and blazed hospitably giving forth a sweet smell of burning apple wood. The golden pumpkin glowed on the mantelpiece, its grotesque face beaming a welcome. Ella counted the bottles briskly and busied herself with bottle opener, lemons and glasses, while Dimity fluttered hither and thither putting little dishes of salted nuts and other savoury things first here, then there, surveying the effect with much anguish.

'All I want,' said Ella, squinting at her companion over the cigarette smoke which curled into her eye, 'is a private dish of olives behind the azalea. I've seen that young Lovell at parties before, wolfing 'em down. By the time I've got the drinks circulating he'll have had the lot,' said his hostess forthrightly.

'Oh, Ella dear,' protested Dimity, 'I'm quite sure he doesn't behave like that! He's a very well-brought-up young man.' But she obediently put one dish of olives behind the azalea plant near Ella, nevertheless. Ella took three, clapped them into her mouth, like a man taking pills, and crunched with relish.

'I'll bet you sixpence in the Cats' Protection box that Dotty arrives first,' said Ella rather indistinctly.

'Of course she'll be first,' said Dimity. 'It's not worth betting on. Besides,' she added, looking thoughtful, 'I don't know that we ought to bet like that. The rector was saying, only the other day, that betting is on the increase.'

'Bless his innocent old heart,' cried Ella, wiping her olive-wet palm smartly down the side of her skirt, 'what on earth is he doing then when he holds a raffle for the organ fund?'

'It's not quite the same –' began Dimity primly, when the bell rang and both ladies hurried to meet their first guest. It was, as they had surmised, their old friend Dotty Harmer, clad in her familiar seal-skin jacket. This archaic garment had been her mother's, and had an old-world charm with its nipped-in waist and a hint of leg-of-mutton about the upper part of the sleeves.

'Come in, come in,' shouted Ella hospitably, throwing open the door with such violence that the house shook.

'I'll just take off my boots on the step,' said Dotty, bending over. 'It's absolutely filthy along my field path after all the rain. What a day – what a day!'

'You come in,' said Ella, in a slightly hectoring manner. 'It's perishing in this wind, stripped out as we are. Besides, we'll have the fire smoking.'

Thus adjured, Dotty pressed into the little hall and the front door was shut against the roaring night.

'They're my *new* boots,' explained Dotty proudly. 'I put them on *over* my shoes, you see, and then I can just step out easily and I don't dirty people's carpets.' Her wrinkled old face was flushed with excitement. She might have been six years old in her unaffected delight.

'How awfully sensible,' said Dimity kindly, watching her friend tugging ineffectually at one boot while she balanced precariously on the other. 'Can I help?'

'I'll just sit on the stairs,' said Dotty. 'They're a bit stiff.'

'Come inside,' implored Ella, rubbing her hands for warmth. It was apparent to her that Dotty would be stuck on the stairs in everybody's way, puffing and blowing over her infernal boots, for some time to come. 'Or upstairs to the bedroom.'

'But that *entirely* defeats the purpose of my boots,' protested Dotty. 'I shan't be a moment.'

She bent down again, her face becoming purple with her efforts.

'Let me –' began Dimity, but Dotty waved her aside.

'No, no, no! It's just their being new,' puffed Dotty, resting one thin leg across the other knee and displaying an alarming amount of undergarments to the glass front door. Really, thought Ella irritably, she carries eccentricity too far. In two shakes we shall have the others arriving – the new man among them – and it's enough to frighten a stranger out of his wits to see old Dotty mopping and mowing in her seal-skin coat with one boot in her ear. Her irritation, coupled with the draughts in the tiny hall, gave Ella inspiration.

'Take the whole thing off, Dotty, shoe and all. Then you can pull your shoe out afterwards.'

The other two ladies gazed at her with respect. Dotty obeyed, the shoes were retrieved, her jacket taken from her, and Dotty stood revealed in the brick-coloured dress and coral necklace whose fine divergence of shade had delighted the neighbourhood for so long.

'Oh, my jacket!' wailed Dotty, as she was being ushered into the sitting-room. 'I've brought you some of my quince jam, dears. It's in the pocket.'

'How kind,' said Dimity. 'I'll put it in the kitchen at once.' She fluttered off on her errand, leaving Dotty to exclaim over the metamorphosis of her pumpkin.

Guests now began to arrive thick and fast and the little sitting-room was soon filled with chatter and laughter. All those present had known each other for years and more than half of them had met before during the day as they went about their daily rounds. Harold Shoosmith had not yet arrived and Ella wondered if he could have forgotten, as she bore her tray of drinks round the room.

The small clock on the mantelpiece was striking seven when the door-bell shrilled and Ella and Dimity hurried to answer it.

Harold Shoosmith entered in a gust of wind and a shower of apologies. The telephone had rung as he was about to leave – a long-distance call – an old friend in trouble – on her way north and had shattered her windscreen – might call at his house later. The words gushed out as Ella took his coat and scarf so that it was some minutes before she could introduce him to Dimity who stood looking pink and expectant at the sight of such a handsome – and unattached – man actually under her own roof.

Harold Shoosmith gave Dimity a smile that turned her heart over, murmured some polite words and followed his hostesses into the sitting-room, smoothing his white hair, which the wind had ruffled, as he went. His dark suit was impeccably cut, his linen snowy, his tie discreetly striped, and denoted, both ladies felt sure, a school, college or regiment of the finest quality. They felt very proud of their distinguished guest as they led him to their friends and Dimity felt, for the first time, that it was a pity that Thrush Green men did not take the same pains with their dressing. Why, young Doctor Lovell, she noticed now, was actually wearing a dog-tooth checked jacket with leather patches on the sleeves! But, of course, she chided herself hastily, he may have come straight from a patient's sick bed. One must be charitable.

The newcomer was soon happily settled with a gin and tonic and Doctor Bailey and the rector to talk to. Very soon Doctor Lovell and his brother-in-law Edward Young, who was a local architect, drifted towards the group and Ella saw, with some resignation, that the sexes had divided into two camps as usual.

She made her way to the ladies' end to replenish Violet Lovelock's glass. The three Miss Lovelocks had seated themselves on the window-seat, their silvery heads nodding and trembling, and their glasses, as Ella expected, quite empty.

These three ladies, now in their seventies, lived in a Georgian doll's house in Lulling's High Street. There they had been born, their wicker bassinette had been bumped down the shallow flight of steps to the pavement by their trim nursemaid, young men had called, but not one of the three tall sisters had emerged from the house as a bride. They lived together peaceably enough, busying themselves with good works and their neighbours' affairs, and collecting *objets d'art* for their overcrowded gem of a house with a ruthless zeal which was a byword for miles around.

Many a hostess had found herself bereft of a lustre jug or a particularly charming paper-weight when the Misses Lovelock rose to leave, for they had brought the art of persuasive begging to perfection. Continuously crying poverty, they lived nevertheless very comfortably, and the inhabitants of Lulling and Thrush Green were wary of these genteel old harpies. Tales were exchanged of the Lovelocks' exploits.

One told of their kind offer to look after her garden while she was away and how she came back to find it stripped of all the ripe fruit and the choicest vegetables. 'Such a pity, dear, to see it going to waste. We knew you would like us to help ourselves, and it does keep the crop growing, of course. We must let you have a bottle of the raspberries – so delicious.'

Neighbours who were unwary enough to let the Misses Lovelock look after the chickens in their absence rarely found any eggs awaiting them on their return, and in some cases a plump chicken had died. 'Terribly upsetting, my dear! It was just lying on its poor back with its legs stuck up and a dreadfully resigned look on its dear face! We buried it in our garden as we didn't want to upset you.'

The ladies now smiled gently upon Ella as she retrieved their glasses. All three were drinking whisky, barely moistened with soda water, with a rapidity that had ceased to startle their friends. Ella noticed, with some alarm, that their eyes were fixed upon the silver basket which Dimity was proffering.

'Do you like salted nuts, Bertha?' asked Dimity anxiously of the youngest Miss Lovelock. Bertha, Ada and Violet took two or three daintily in their claw-like hands. Their eyes remained appraisingly upon the gleaming little dish.

'What a charming little basket!' murmured Violet.

'We have its brother at home,' said Ada, very sweetly. 'I believe this should be one of a pair.'

'I can see we shall have to ask Dimity to take pity on our poor lonely little dish at home!' tinkled Bertha, laughing gently.

Ella broke in with bluff good humour.

'Better bring your lonely one up here! We've got a couple to keep it company, haven't we, Dim?'

The three sisters tittered politely and took refreshing gulps of whisky, while Dimity cast a grateful look at her protector and made her escape to young Mrs Lovell, clutching her mother's silver basket to the fawn silk rose.

Ruth Lovell was a great favourite of hers. Dimity had known her since she was a little girl and had shared Thrush Green's delight at her marriage with Doctor Lovell a year ago.

Ruth looked young and glowing with health. Dimity remembered her wan sad demeanour some years before when the poor girl had been cruelly jilted and she had come to recuperate with her sister Joan Young, and, soon after, had found consolation with Doctor Bailey's new junior partner.

'What a long time since we've met, Ruth,' said Dimity, sitting down beside the girl. 'And how pretty you look in that pink blouse! I like the way you young things wear your blouses loose over your skirts or trousers. It's really most becoming. And I really believe you are putting on a little weight, my dear, which suits you so well.' She patted Ruth's knee encouragingly.

'It's only to be expected, Dimity,' replied Ruth, smiling. 'You know we're looking forward to a baby at Christmas-time. That's why I'm in this enormous smock. Nothing else fits!'

Dimity's eyes grew round and she grew pink with pleasure and embarrassment.

'How perfectly lovely, my dear! Do you know, I hadn't heard a word of it. Now isn't that extraordinary? But I do so hope the men didn't hear me making such thoughtless remarks to you.' She looked anxiously towards the other end of the room where the men stood in a cloud of blue tobacco smoke making an immense amount of noise.

'Don't worry,' said Ruth. 'They're far too engrossed. Now, you must promise to be one of the very first to see the baby. I shall look forward to seeing you particularly.'

Dimity nodded delightedly and, looking conspiratorial, went to see how the men were faring.

'It was one of the reasons why I chose Thrush Green to live in,' Harold Shoosmith was saying. 'I've the greatest admiration for Nathaniel Patten, and to find a house for sale in his birth-place seemed too good a chance to miss.'

'A wonderful person,' agreed the rector. The round blue eyes in his chubby face gazed up at his new parishioner's great height. The rector of Thrush Green bore a striking resemblance to the cherubs which decorated his church and his disposition was as child-like and innocent as theirs. He was a man blessed with true humility and warm with charity. From the top of his shining bald head to the tips of his small black shoes he radiated a happiness that disarmed all comers. Thrush Green was rightly proud of the Reverend Charles Henstock, and watched his tubby little figure traversing his parish, with much affection.

'You know, of course,' said Harold Shoosmith, to the group at large, 'that it's the hundredth anniversary of Nathaniel's birth next March.'

'I didn't know,' said Edward Young honestly.

'Nor me,' said Doctor Lovell. 'Tell me, who was the old boy?'

'Now that's quite shocking,' chided old Doctor Bailey laughingly. 'Nathaniel Patten is a public figure. He was a most zealous missionary. Am I right?' he appealed to Harold Shoosmith.

'Indeed you are,' said he. 'He founded a wonderful mission station in the town where I worked overseas. They were making great plans for all kinds of festivities in March. They hope to add a wing to their hospital on the occasion.'

'We really should do something ourselves,' said the rector, wrinkling his brow. 'I must confess I hadn't given it the thought I should, though I certainly intended to put a brief note in the parish magazine for that month.'

'He was an amazingly fine person,' said Harold Shoosmith. 'It seems a pity if his anniversary goes by unnoticed in his birth-place. It won't elsewhere, I can assure you.'

'We might consider putting up a small plaque,' suggested Edward Young. 'In the church perhaps, or on his house.' He looked suddenly thoughtful. 'If anyone knows which house he was born in,' he added doubtfully.

'I think you'll find it is one of the cottages by "The Two Pheasants",' said Harold Shoosmith. 'Doesn't the sexton live in one there somewhere?'

'Indeed he does,' agreed the rector. 'I must find out more about Nathaniel Patten. It is shameful to know so little about Thrush Green's most distinguished son.'

'I've collected a few notes about him,' said the newcomer. 'Call in any time and I'll let you have them. I do feel that it would be an excellent thing to remind Thrush Green of Nathaniel's place in the world. I should be very glad to do anything to help in the way of celebrating his anniversary.'

The rector thanked him and promised to call. Edward Young wondered if Piggott's cottage would stand up to a ladder against it, if a plaque were to be affixed on its ancient face. Doctor Lovell made a mental note to ask his wife if she had ever heard of this old missionary fellow who had made so deep an impression on Harold Shoosmith. Doctor Bailey turned his mind back to his early days at Thrush Green, and tried to remember, unavailingly, if Nathaniel Patten's daughter had once been among his patients, and if so, what her married name was. He must ask Winnie, he told himself, when they were home again.

Meanwhile, Dimity, who had hovered on the edge of the group listening to the conversation, now found a chance to collect the men's glasses.

'This is a delightful room,' said Harold Shoosmith, as he took the tray from her grasp and carried it towards Ella. 'And this is the happiest evening I've had since coming to Thrush Green.'

Suddenly, for Dimity, the fire crackled more gaily, the pumpkin beamed more brightly, and the glasses tinkled and sparkled with twice as much gaiety. It was a perfect party, she told herself, with an upsurging of spirits. Let the wind scream outside, let the rain lash the window panes! Here within, was warmth and colour, the comfort of old friends, and the excitement of new ones.

7. The Newcomer Settles In

Harold Shoosmith soon found, as all newcomers to a village find, that there was plenty to do. During his busy working days abroad, he had occasionally dwelt upon the peaceful bliss of his retirement in England. He imagined himself pottering about an English garden, discussing with an enthusiastic hard-working gardener the planting of new rose beds or an embryo orchard, or the best way to train an espalier pear on the south wall. He dallied with the idea of collecting china – possibly the attractive little houses used for burning pastilles, for which he had always felt a great affection – and had seen himself, in fancy, picking his entranced way among the well-dusted shelves in the drawing-room which housed his purchases.

He looked forward to entertaining in a modest way, a simple supper for his friends, or perhaps a tea-party for those with children. He realized that domestic help might be difficult to find, but in all these rosy dreams there lurked somewhere in the background a competent but self-effacing servant.

His decision to settle in Thrush Green was prompted, as he told the vicar, by his admiration for Nathaniel Patten and the fortuitous advertisement about the corner house which was published at a time when he was beginning to feel anxious about finding a suitable resting place. The matter was arranged quickly, and his dreams seemed to be very near at last.

Reality came as a shock. The garden, which was in an appalling state of neglect by the time he arrived, looked like staying that way for all the help Harold Shoosmith was likely to find. He was not averse to digging, weeding, hoeing and pruning, but he knew that the job was much too large for him to tackle alone, and also he needed the advice of some local person about soil, drainage, and reliable sources of plants, shrubs and garden needs such as manure, leaf-mould and so on. An advertisement in the local paper brought two replies. One was from a middle-aged lady in riding breeches, with metallic yellow hair sporting a wide dark parting, whose appearance so startled Mr Shoosmith that he felt quite unequal to considering her application. He told her suavely, and untruthfully, that the place was already taken, and had many uncomfortable meetings with her later at various cocktail parties. The second applicant was so old, so shaky, and had so rheumy and red an eye that he had difficulty in supporting himself in Mr Shoosmith's presence, let alone a gardening tool, even of the lightest construction.

Diligent enquiries among his neighbours at Thrush Green and Lulling brought forth nothing, and in the end Harold Shoosmith realized that he must consider himself lucky if that old rogue Piggott deigned to call in for an hour or two to make a little extra beer money.

As for help in the house, that too, he found, was practically nonexistent. The deft and devoted cook and housemaid whom he had been prepared to engage – provided that their references were first-class, of course – were replaced by Betty Bell, and he knew that he was fortunate to have her somewhat slap-dash ministrations. He was a sensible man, who soon realized that he had been living in a fool's paradise, and he accepted his present mode of living very cheerfully, becoming very fond of chatty Betty Bell and quite resigned to the fact that any collection he might make would be comfortably covered with dust unless he set to and dusted it himself.

Picking up pastille houses on his travels for a shilling or two, was yet another dream that was abruptly shattered. The price of any worthwhile small piece was beyond Harold Shoosmith's straitened means, he discovered. As for entertaining, his plans for simple supper parties of two or three well-cooked courses soon evaporated, and he was content to offer a drink and a cigarette to his neighbours, in the usual Thrush Green manner.

His time was much taken up with small domestic chores for which he found he had some natural aptitude. He chopped firewood, carried coal, swept the paths, painted the gates and fences, and found himself extremely busy. By the time evening came he was often quite tired and prepared to go up to bed by ten o'clock. If life in England did not have the leisurely nineteenth-century flavour which he had so fondly imagined might still exist in its rural backwaters, yet it was very pleasant, nevertheless, and Harold Shoosmith faced his years of retirement contentedly enough.

The number of local activities brought to Harold Shoosmith's notice, in the first few weeks of his residence at the corner house, as in need of his support, staggered him. In Thrush Green and Lulling were to be found Guides, Scouts, Brownies, Cubs, a Church Guild, a Chapel Youth Centre, a Mothers' Union, a Women's Institute, and no end of functions instigated by various sporting clubs.

He found himself giving clothing to three minute Brownies with a hand-cart for their jumble sale, lending his ladder to the Scouts for the repair of their Den roof and giving half-crowns to various worthy people who called with a collecting tin. On one occasion he even agreed, under pressure, to parting with a newly-baked chocolate sponge which Betty Bell informed him he had promised as his con-tribution to the Sunday School party.

This was not all. He was urged by the rector, Doctor Lovell, and many other residents to join the committees of at least a dozen local bodies. Their pleas were so ardent that Harold Shoosmith wondered how on earth they had managed to get along at all without his help for so many years. The most pressing need, it seemed, was that of Thrush Green's Entertainments Committee which, the rector said solemnly, 'was in need of new blood'.

He had called upon Mr Shoosmith one wet November evening, splashing through the puddles of the newly-gravelled drive in the early darkness.

The bright blaze of October had changed to a succession of dreary days in November, each bringing hours of heavy rain which soon turned the green into a quagmire and sent rivers gurgling continuously along the gutters. Wellingtons and mackintoshes were the daily wear, the men working in the fields were soaked daily, and at the village school a row of wet gloves steamed on the fireguard every morning. Gardeners stood at their windows fuming at their neglected gardens. The heavy clay soil of the Cotswolds became impossible to turn in its glutinous condition. The last of the flowers lay battered on the sodden ground and the cows in the fields stood patiently, backs to the wind and rain, with water trickling steadily from their glistening coats. The water ran so continuously from the thatched roofs of one or two of Thrush Green's cottages that the stones beneath were scoured as clean as if they were in the bed of a trout stream. Tempers grew frayed as wet day followed wet day and washing had to be dried by the fire. The women were at their wits' end to keep up with the demand for dry clothing, and the windows were opaque with steam both by day and night.

'Appalling weather,' said Harold Shoosmith, settling his friend by the fire. His eye was caught by the rector's sodden shoes which squelched as he moved. The soles, he observed, were in sore need of mending. The fellow wants looking after, thought Harold Shoosmith.

'Would you like to borrow some slippers? We could dry your shoes while you're here.'

The rector's cherubic face became pinker and he looked concerned.

'I do so hope I haven't made a mess on your carpets. I quite forgot how dirty it was outside.'

His companion reassured him on this point but was unable to persuade him to part with his disgraceful foot-gear which steamed gently in the glow from the fire. The rector settled back in his leather armchair and looked with pleasure about the room.

'You've made it all uncommonly cosy,' he remarked. Betty Bell's ministrations were apparent in the gleaming copper kettle on the hearth and the array of silver cups which reflected the firelight on the sideboard opposite the hearth. Harold Shoosmith had been something of an athlete in his younger days, and this was another bond that the two men had, for Mr Henstock had once coxed his college eight in the years when he had weighed seven and a half stone.

He found Harold Shoosmith's comfortable house and his friendly welcome particularly cheering. The Reverend Charles Henstock, although he did not realize it, was much lonelier than he imagined. The death of his wife, some years before, had been borne with great courage. His religion was of the greatest comfort to him, for he was sustained by the knowledge that he would meet his wife again as soon as he left this world for the next. The affection and kindness of his parishioners never ceased to amaze him. The thought that his own shining honesty, modesty and goodwill might be the cause of his neighbours' esteem never entered his head. He was welcomed in all the houses in his parish, but felt some hesitation in staying too long. Fathers were coming home from work, children from school, wives from shopping. He, who had no wife and no child in his home, found the company of the newcomer to Thrush Green much to his liking. They were roughly the same age, enjoyed the same pleasures and had plenty of time on their own. It was natural that the rector began to call more and more frequently at the corner house. For his part, Harold Shoosmith liked his pastor more each time they met.

'I've been thinking about the memorial to Nathaniel Patten,' said the rector, warming his hands at the fire. 'The subject came up at the last meeting of the Entertainments Committee.'

'How did that come about?' asked Harold, much amused.

'We were discussing the arrangements for the Fur and Feather—' began the rector earnestly.

'The Fur and Feather?' ejaculated his friend, looking up from poking the fire. 'What on earth's that? A pub?'

'No, no! "The Fur and Feather *Whist Drive*," I should have said,' the rector explained. 'We have one every Christmas in the village school.'

'But why "Fur and Feather"?' persisted the wanderer in other lands. 'What's the significance of calling it that?'

The rector began to explain patiently that the prizes for this particular type of whist drive were of poultry or game. His friend's brow cleared.

'I see. Thank you. But how does this tie up with Nathaniel?'

'Well, you know what village meetings are – everything is discussed except the points on the agenda. I find it very helpful in my parish work. I always get to hear who is ill or in trouble of any sort. It's most necessary for a parish priest to be on committees. I really don't know how I'd manage without them.'

'Is the idea acceptable, then?'

'Indeed it is. General feeling seems to be in favour of a really worthwhile memorial. I suggested a seat on the green, but most people seem to think that a statue is the thing.'

'Pretty expensive, I imagine. And it might turn out to be hideous.'

'We might get someone in the neighbourhood to do it,' said the rector vaguely. 'Miss Bembridge is very artistic.'

'Good God!' said Harold, startled into strong language. 'D'you mean she'd do it?'

'She hasn't been approached, of course,' replied Mr Henstock. 'But I believe it has been suggested.'

A heavy silence fell upon the room. The rector was trying to remember just what it was that he meant to ask his new friend to do for him. Harold Shoosmith, glumly surveying the crack which he had just widened so successfully in a large lump of coal, was blind to the delights of the hissing gaseous flames which fluttered like yellow crocuses in the crevices. A memorial to his beloved Nathaniel Patten was one thing – a ghastly monstrosity created by the intimidating Ella was another. He shuddered to think where his first innocent suggestions might lead.

A particularly vicious spattering of rain against the windowpane roused the rector from his chair.

'I must be getting back,' he said, sighing. 'There was just one thing that I wanted to ask you – but I seem to have forgotten it.' He looked about the snug room, so different from his own bleak drawing-room which no amount of firing seemed to make habitable.

'Anything to do with committee work?' asked Harold Shoosmith resignedly. He was already a member of the Cricket Club, Football Club, British Legion, Parochial Church Council and the local branch of the R.S.P.C.A., after a residence of less than two months.

The rector's wrinkled brow became smooth again.

'How clever of you!' he cried. 'Yet, it was. The Thrush Green Entertainments Committee asked me to invite you to join them. We make most of the arrangements for our local activities. This business of the memorial will probably be dealt with by the T.G.E.C.'

Harold Shoosmith thought quickly. He felt as though the shade of Nathaniel Patten hovered anxiously at his elbow, pleading for justice and for mercy. If he accepted the committee's invitation, at least he would hold a watching brief for his long-dead friend and could do his best to see that his memorial would be a worthy one.

'I'd be very glad to join the committee,' said Harold honestly, as he opened the front door, and let out the rector into the inhospitable night.

'Very good of you indeed,' said the rector warmly. 'You will be more than welcome. The Entertainments Committee needs new blood. It does indeed!'

Beaming his farewells, the rector splashed bravely, in his wet shoes, towards the gate.

8. Sam Curdle is Observed

Rain continued to sweep the Cotswolds throughout November and the wooded hills were shrouded in undulating grey veils. The fields of stubble, which had lain, bleached and glinting, under the kind October sun, were being slowly and patiently ploughed by panting tractors which traversed their length and turned over rib after rib of earth glistening like wet chocolate.

Young Doctor Lovell found his hands full. Coughs, colds, wheezy chests, ear-ache, rheumatic pains, stomachic chills and general depression kept his car splashing along the flooded lanes of Thrush Green and Lulling. In this, his first practice, he was a happy man. Thrush Green had brought him not only work, but also a wife, to love. The thought of their child, so soon to be born, gave him deep satisfaction. It was no wonder that Doctor Lovell whistled as blithely as a winter robin as he went about among his ailing patients. Some viewed his cheerfulness sourly.

'Proper heartless young fellow,' they grumbled, revelling in their own miseries.

But most of them were glad to greet a little brightness among the November gloom.

His senior partner in the practice, Doctor Bailey, did very little these days and found the weather particularly trying. Like most of Thrush Green's inhabitants he kept the fire company while the rain poured down.

Winnie, his wife, viewed his condition with secret alarm. He seemed to have difficulty with his breathing, and she did her best to persuade him to take a holiday abroad where they would find some sunshine.

'Can't be done, my dear,' wheezed the aged doctor. 'Costs too much, for one thing, and young Lovell's got too much to do anyway. At least I can take surgery for him now and again. He'll need to feel free to go and see Ruth when the baby comes.'

He caught sight of the anxiety in his wife's face, and spoke cheerfully.

'Don't worry so. I've been fitter this year than I have for ages. It's just this dampness. It'll pass, I promise you.'

'You must take care, Donald. Keep in the warm and read – or better still, shall I see if Harold Shoosmith is free for a game of bridge this afternoon?'

The doctor's eye brightened. The newcomer to Thrush Green had many attributes which his neighbours approved. That of a fair-to-average bridge player made him particularly welcome in the Baileys' household.

'Good idea,' agreed Doctor Bailey, sounding more robust at once. 'And maybe Dimity and Ella will come as well.'

He watched his wife bustle from the room to the telephone and lay back, contentedly enough, in the deep armchair. He was more tired than he would admit to her. The thought of sunshine filled him with longings, but the effort of getting to it he knew was beyond his strength. Better to lie quietly at Thrush Green, letting the rainy days slip by, until the spring brought the benison of English sunlight and daffodils again.

The room was very quiet. The old man closed his eyes and listened to the small domestic noises around him. The fire whispered in the hearth, a log hissed softly as its moss-covered bark dried in the flames, and the doctor's ancient cat purred rustily in its throat. Somewhere outside, there was the distant sound of metal on stone as a workman repaired a gatepost. A child called, its voice high and tremulous like the bleating of a lamb, and a man answered it. Doctor Bailey felt a great peace enfolding him, and remembered a snatch of poetry from 'The Task', which he had learnt as a small boy almost seventy years ago.

> Stillness, accompanied with sounds so soft
> Charms more than silence.

He was blessed, he told himself, in having a retentive memory which tossed him such pleasures as this to enhance his daily round. He was blessed, too, with a wonderful wife and a host of good friends. Half-dozing now, he saw their faces float before him, friends of his boyhood, friends of his student days, friends among his patients. Most clearly of all he saw the face of the great Mrs Curdle whose burial he had attended at St Andrew's two years before. The flashing dark eyes, the imperiously jutting nose and the black plaited hair delighted his mind's eye as keenly as ever. He fancied himself again inside her caravan home, sipping the bitter brew of strong tea with which she always welcomed him. He saw again the dazzling stove which was her great pride, the swinging oil lamp, and the photograph of George, her much-loved son, whose birth might well have caused the death of his mother had young Doctor Bailey not acted promptly so many years ago. Bouquets of gaudy artificial flowers floated before the old man's closed eyes – each a tribute to his skill, a debt paid yearly by the magnificent gipsy woman he was proud to call his friend. Dear Mrs Curdle, whose annual fair had welcomed in each May at Thrush Green – there would never be another like her!

The door opened and his wife stood before him.

'They'll all come,' she said, smiling.

'Thank God for good friends,' said the doctor simply, turning from those in the shades to the living again.

If Harold Shoosmith was welcomed as a bridge player at the

Baileys' he was just as warmly welcomed as a next-door neighbour by Miss Watson and Miss Fogerty at the village school.

It is essential for anyone in charge of children to have tolerant neighbours. The number of balls that fly over fences and have to be retrieved is prodigious. There are those who answer the timid knocking, rather low down, at the front door with an exasperated mien which strikes terror into the heart of the importuners. The newcomer was not one of these. Nor did he toss the balls back into the playground so that they rolled hither and thither to be picked up by any joyous passing hound.

If the children were at play he would hand their property to them with a smile. He went further. If he came across the bright balls in the grass or among his plants when school was over, he took the trouble to go round to Miss Watson's house and present them to her with the small old-fashioned bow and charming smile which caused so many female hearts to flutter at Thrush Green.

Miss Fogerty spent many evenings in Miss Watson's company these days, and it was natural that the two ladies should discuss the good fortune of having such a pleasant neighbour.

Miss Watson's sprained ankle still gave her pain although the stick had been discarded. On the few November evenings when the rain stopped, Miss Fogerty helped her friend to dig the flower border which ran along the communicating stone wall between the school garden and Harold Shoosmith's. After their labours they would retire into the school-house living-room and have a light meal of sandwiches and fruit.

Miss Fogerty relished these companionable hours. She had lived for years in her prim and somewhat dismal lodgings, with very few friends of her own. Miss Watson's invitations gave her great happiness, and the thought that her headmistress too might have felt the pangs of loneliness did not enter the modest little woman's head. She was glad to have been of use in a crisis and rejoiced now in the pleasure of Miss Watson's friendship.

Over the cheese sandwiches one evening Miss Watson spoke of yet another of their neighbour's kindnesses. It was a year when the apple crop had been a bumper one, and Harold Shoosmith, appalled at the thought of eating apples in some guise or the other for the rest of the year, had presented the schoolchildren with a sackful which stood at Miss Watson's back door.

'We are lucky to have him next door,' agreed Miss Fogerty.

'He must be missed by his firm,' continued Miss Watson, pouring coffee.

'With a firm?' echoed Miss Fogerty. 'I heard he had been in the Army.'

'And the Navy and Air Force,' said Miss Watson, a little tartly. 'People spread these rumours about in the most terrible way!' From her manner one might have thought that there was something shameful about all the Services.

'He very kindly gave me a lift up from Lulling the other day and talked about his work in Africa quite openly. I've no idea why people think he makes a mystery of his past, I'm sure.'

'He may have felt that he could confide in you,' suggested Miss Fogerty, her moist devoted eyes fixed upon her new friend. Miss Watson looked gratified.

'Well, I don't know about that—' she began in the sort of deprecating tone people use when they secretly agree with a statement made. 'But he certainly told me quite a bit about himself. He was with Sleepwell's for over thirty years, evidently. He was manager for all Africa — a most responsible position, I should think.'

'Sleepwell?' echoed Miss Fogerty in bewilderment. 'You mean the stuff you mix with hot milk?'

'Of course,' said Miss Watson. 'People need to sleep in Africa, I imagine, as well as in England.'

'But hot milk,' protested her friend. 'In Africa! It seems so wrong. Surely they would prefer fruit squash or something cooling.'

'I believe the nights are quite chilly,' said Miss Watson, with as much conviction as she could muster. She was a little shaky about the climatic conditions in the darkest continent and felt it would be as well to steer the conversation to surer ground.

'Anyway, Sleepwell seems to be a very popular drink there,' she continued, 'otherwise Mr Shoosmith wouldn't have stayed there for all that time.'

'Whereabouts in Africa was his business?' enquired Miss Fogerty. 'My cousin's family came from Nairobi. He may have met them.' She spoke as though Africa and Thrush Green were of approximately the same size.

'Somewhere on the west coast, I gather.' Miss Watson furrowed her brow. 'At a place with a name like Winnie Khaki. It's where

Nathaniel Patten started his settlement, you know. He began with a little mission school for the native children, and now, Mr Shoosmith says, there's a village with a church, and school and a magnificent hospital.'

'It's strange to think,' said Miss Fogerty musingly, 'that Thrush Green sent Nathaniel Patten to Africa, and Nathaniel Patten has indirectly sent Mr Shoosmith back to Thrush Green.'

'And a very good thing for us that he did,' said her friend briskly, collecting the débris of their simple meal. 'He's a great asset to the place.'

Together they repaired to the kitchen sink to wash up before Miss Fogerty made her way home to her lodgings.

To little Paul Young and his crony Christopher Mullins, Harold Shoosmith appeared in a different light. He was a man to be avoided, outwitted and feared. Needless to say, he had no idea of this.

The two boys had shifted their headquarters from the thinning greenery of the ox-eyed daisies to a tree on the side of Harold Shoosmith's spinney furthest from his house. This decrepit elm had been cut off some twelve feet above the ground in the early days of the Farmers' residence at the corner house. Half-hearted attempts had been made to remove the hollow stump, but it had defied its molesters and still stood firmly, overlooking the small grassy valley where Dotty Harmer lived.

Bushy young growth sprouted from its battered crown and concealed the boys from sight. They had cut rough footholds in the mouldering interior of the split trunk and could climb up easily enough to this exciting new hide-out. It was unlikely that the new tenant would discover them, and unlikely that he would seriously object even if he did so, but the two boys found it more thrilling to pretend that poor Harold Shoosmith was a monster, and persuaded themselves easily enough that he would shout, brandish a stick, report them to their parents, the police and their headmaster, with dire consequences, should he ever stumble upon their whereabouts on his premises. This, naturally, gave their meetings a delicious fillip.

One misty Saturday afternoon in November the two friends sat aloft in their eyrie, unknown, of course, to their parents.

'Chris Mullins has asked me to play,' Paul had said to his mother, and she, in her innocence, had imagined that he would be playing in the Mullins' garden.

'Paul Young's asked me to play with him,' Christopher had said to his mother, who had fondly thought that her son would be safely on the Youngs' premises.

By such simple strategy have boys, throughout the centuries, accomplished their nefarious ends.

Paul had arrived first and watched his friend emerge from the green garden door in the wall across the valley. He watched him run up the grassy hill and warbled an owl's cry as he approached. This was their secret sign, and the fact that an owl warbling in daylight might arouse suspicions, had not occurred to the boys.

Chris arrived quite breathless at the tree and Paul tugged him up the rough stairway joyously.

'I've brought a Mars bar and some transfers,' he announced proudly when his friend had found a precarious seat.

'I've only got two apples,' confessed Chris. 'It's all we seem to have in our house,' he continued bitterly. 'Apples, apples, apples!'

Paul sympathized. There is a limit to the number of apples even a small boy can eat. This year's crop was proving an embarrassment.

'My mum,' went on Christopher, 'says that they clean your teeth, and chocolate ruins them. Been reading something in the papers, I expect.' He spoke with disgust. Paul found such contempt of parents wholly wonderful, and broke the Mars bar carefully in half. A few delicious damp crumbs fell upon the leg of his corduroy trousers and he licked them up thoughtfully, running his finger-nail down the grooves afterwards to collect any stray morsels which might have become embedded there. They munched in amicable silence. From their perch they commanded an extensive view. Far to the west Paul could see a white ground mist veiling the lower part of a distant hollow. Only the tips of the bushy scrub protruded from the drowned field – like rabbits' ears, thought Paul idly – and he watched a distant hedge becoming more and more ghostly as the mist wreathed and swirled through it. As yet their own little valley had but a slight mistiness, but it was obvious that fog would engulf all by nightfall.

'Let's see your transfers,' said Christopher, wiping his sticky hands down his trousers perfunctorily. Paul fished in his pocket and handed over a crumpled booklet. He watched his friend anxiously. Would he think they were babyish? Some of the transfers were of toys – a ball, a kite and a doll. He could not bear to be ridiculed by his idol.

To his relief Chris seemed pleased with what he saw. He tore out a Union Jack, placed it carefully face downward on the back of his hand and licked it heavily with a tongue still dusky with chocolate. Paul chose a picture of a football boot – it seemed a manly choice – and licked as heartily.

'Seen old Shoelace?' asked Chris as they waited for the transfers to work. This nickname was considered by both boys to be the height of humour.

'Not a sign,' said Paul. 'Must be out, I think.' Even as he spoke there was a cracking of twigs on the other side of the spinney.

'Get down!' whispered Chris urgently. The two boys cowered low among the scanty brushwood. Paul could hear his heart beating under the green jersey Aunt Ruth had knitted him. His nose was so close to the transfer on his hand that he could smell the oily pungency from it. The silence became unendurable. Suddenly a blackbird chattered loudly and flew from the little wood. Silence fell again, and after a few more breathless minutes the boys straightened up.

'Gosh!' breathed Chris, 'I thought we'd been found that time.' They sat listening intently for a few more minutes, and then Paul sighed with relief.

'No one there, Chris. Let's peel off our transfers. You first.'

'No, you first,' said Christopher, punching his friend affectionately on the arm. 'Mine'll take longer to do with all the lines on the flag.'

'What about all the twiddly bits on my boot?' objected Paul. 'All right, all right,' he added hastily, as his friend's fist was raised again. 'I'll do mine first.'

Carefully he raised the corner of his damp transfer. His tongue protruded with the effort as he began to peel it gently away from his pink hand. Half-way across the picture began to disintegrate.

'Press it back again quick,' urged Christopher. 'And huff on the back. You ought always to huff on transfers. The wet in your breath keeps it the right temperature.' He watched anxiously as Paul obeyed.

They rested their hands on their knees and breathed energetically upon the back of the transfers. Paul tried again, gingerly peeling the damp paper away. He was rewarded by an almost perfect picture of the football boot.

'Only one of the laces a bit wonky,' he said proudly. 'Not bad, is it?' He held up his hand for Chris to admire, but his friend was much too busy revealing his own masterpiece. The result was disappointing. Only half the Union Jack adhered to Christopher's hand.

Paul tried not to look too smug. Christopher he knew, liked to excel at everything, and could be violent when things went wrong.

'D'you know why mine didn't take?' demanded Chris belligerently. 'I'll tell you,' he continued, without giving his apprehensive friend time to answer. 'It's because I'm so much *stronger* than you are! That's why!' He thrust an aggressive face towards Paul's.

'Stronger?' faltered the smaller boy.

'Yes,' said Christopher. 'See the back of my hand? Smothered in hairs, isn't it?' He held up his grubby paw, and against the light, one or two faint hairs were discernible. 'That shows I'm strong. Like Samson, remember? Well, transfers won't take on a hairy hand, naturally. You have to have sissy smooth hands like yours for transfers to work. It's a kid's game, anyway.' He tossed the book back to Paul who put it silently back in his pocket. The afternoon was not going as it should, and Paul began to wonder how he could put matters right.

It was at this uncomfortable moment that they saw the man.

He came into their line of vision as he swung down the hill towards Dotty Harmer's garden. He had evidently come from the lane that led to Nod and Nidden from Thrush Green, and he was about two hundred yards from the tree where the boys watched him.

He reached the low gate in Dotty's hedge, leant upon it and looked around him. Apart from Dotty's cottage no other house looked out upon this little valley. Harold Shoosmith's view was obscured by the projecting curve of the spinney, and, as far as the man could see, he was unobserved. He opened the gate, walked to the hen-house and disappeared inside.

There was no movement from the house as the cackling of hens made itself heard. In fact, Dotty was busy shopping in Lulling at that moment, and the house was deserted except for Mrs Curdle, Dotty's black cat.

Within a few minutes the man emerged carrying a brown-paper carrier bag. He latched the hen-house door, and departed up the hill again with swift easy strides. The boys could see his face quite clearly as he vanished over the brow of the hill towards the lane.

'That was Sam Curdle,' said Paul. 'Do you reckon he was taking things? Eggs, say, or even a chicken?' He looked rather shocked and alarmed. Christopher, who did not know the history of the Curdle family as well as his friend did, was less impressed.

'He didn't look as though he was doing anything wrong. P'raps someone asked him to feed the chickens for them.'

'Might have,' admitted Paul doubtfully. 'But he's an awful thief, Chris. Everybody says so. D'you reckon we ought to tell somebody?'

'If we do,' pointed out Chris, 'they'll ask us what we were doing here, and that's the end of the camp for us.'

'I hadn't thought of that,' confessed Paul unhappily. They sat in silence for some time turning the problem over in their minds. Paul felt sure that Sam had been up to no good; but Chris was right in saying that they could not afford to disclose what they had seen. Of course, Paul told himself, Dotty might have asked Sam to look at her chickens, as Chris had said. It might all have been above-board. He hoped it was – more for the sake of keeping their hiding place secret than from anxiety on Dotty's behalf.

But he was far from happy about the matter. He watched the white mist thickening in the distant hollow and saw that it was beginning to seep along towards their own valley. Suddenly the afternoon seemed chilly and wretched. Everything had been horrid. The transfers had failed, Chris had hit him far harder than was necessary for real friendship, he felt slightly sick with too much chocolate, and sicker still at the thought of keeping all he had seen a guilty secret from his mother.

All at once he wanted to be at home with her – to be warm and dry, to see the fire dancing and to hear his parents talking. A great distaste for the camp, for old Shoelace, and for the wet mustiness of the decaying tree suddenly suffused the boy.

'I'm going home,' he said abruptly, and slithered rapidly to the ground.

Chris, astonished and silent, followed him.

'See you Monday,' said Paul shortly, setting off for home on the west side of the copse. Without answering, Christopher plunged down hill in the opposite direction through the thickening mist. As he ran he became conscious of a stickiness on the back of his hand. Exasperatedly he clawed the remains of the unsuccessful transfer from it with his finger-nail.

Altogether, he thought bitterly, it had been a beast of an afternoon.

As the melancholy month of November wore on Dimity and Ella found themselves getting to know the newcomer quite well. As well as meeting him at the occasional bridge party, and coming across him on their walks abroad, the rector, who had always been a frequent visitor to their cottage, now often came accompanied by his new friend.

Both ladies were delighted. As Ella said, there were far too few unattached men about Thrush Green and their company was quite refreshing after all their single women friends.

Harold Shoosmith went at first with some reluctance to the cottage, but had been pressed to do so when returning with the rector from a country walk on one or two occasions. He was welcomed so warmly that his shyness deserted him. He found too that the two women held an attraction for him. He was sorry for Dimity, considering her outrageously treated by her domineering friend. It needed the rector's wise words to point out that Dimity's life of service was also her crown of glory, and that she was completely happy.

Harold Shoosmith's feelings towards Ella were mixed. Her outspokenness half-shocked and half-amused him. Her physical clumsiness revolted him. Her generosity and warm-heartedness compelled his admiration. But overriding all these feelings was one of fascinated horror at her artistic creations. He was a man who liked recognizable patterns. His shirts were striped or checked. His ties were plain, striped or of a traditional paisley design. His curtains carried fleurs-de-lis and his chair-covers matched them.

Ella's strong blobs of colour, irregularly placed on a background of nobbly black broken checks, appalled his sense of order. The very idea of letting her loose on the memorial to Nathaniel made him quake.

It was the preoccupation with this possibility that led Harold Shoosmith to visit the cottage so often. So far he had heard no more about Ella's part in the project. A meeting had been held in the school to see what Thrush Green felt about the plan. Wholeheartedly the inhabitants had agreed to mark the occasion of Nathaniel's centenary with a suitable memorial. They had, furthermore, voted that

the proceeds of that year's Fur and Feather Whist Drive be devoted
to the fund. The rector had then exhorted them to go home to put
their minds to work on the best type of memorial to their greatest
son, and to put their suggestions in the box provided in the church
porch. Another meeting to vote on the results was to be held early in
December.

Harold Shoosmith found the suspense almost unbearable. The two
ladies never spoke about it, and he found that he could not bring
himself to broach so painful a subject. He comforted himself with the
thought that Ella must surely have mentioned the matter if she had
been approached. It was too much to expect that such a forthright
person would be so delicately reticent.

Meanwhile he made a point of being particularly kind to timid
little Dimity. His attentions were much appreciated by that modest
lady and did not go unnoticed by Ella Bembridge – nor, for that
matter, by the good rector.

Even sour old Mr Piggott felt a certain warmth towards Thrush
Green's latest resident, for he was the means by which the sexton
resumed his role of detective.

On the last day of the month he went to the corner house to cut
back the laurel hedge that grew just inside the communicating wall
between the school-house garden and Harold Shoosmith's.

He slashed lustily with a small bill-hook, for the laurels were
grossly overgrown. The glossy green leaves fluttered to the ground
around him. After one particularly vicious onslaught a small object,
which had lodged in a crook of a bough, fell at his feet. Bending
painfully, old Piggott retrieved it and held it up in the waning light.

Joy coursed its unaccustomed way through his hardening veins. It
was a wallet – and without a doubt it was the one which Miss
Watson had lost on the night of the burglary. It was empty, but that
was only to be expected.

'The first clue!' chortled old Piggott, pocketing it carefully. 'I'll
get 'im yet!'

And, much encouraged, he bent to his task again.

PART TWO

CHRISTMAS AT THRUSH GREEN

9. The Memorial

The meeting to decide upon Nathaniel Patten's memorial was well attended. The infants' room at the village school was almost uncomfortably full. Small thin people squeezed into the desks at one side of the room, and the more portly sat sedately on the desks themselves or on the few low tables upon which the babies usually pursued their activities. A pile of minute bentwood armchairs remained stacked in the corner, for not even Dimity could have folded her small stature into such a confined space.

The rector sat at Miss Fogerty's desk as he was chairman. Harold Shoosmith found himself sharing a desk top with Ella and wondered, somewhat unchivalrously if it would bear their combined weight.

As the latecomers drifted in, to prop themselves against the partition or the ancient piano, Harold gazed idly at the notices pinned to the wall. They were written in large black letters and were obviously the work of Miss Fogerty. 'MY BIRTHDAY,' said one, 'IS TODAY.' Below this dramatic announcement two names, Anne and John, had been inserted into a slot provided for the purpose.

'MONITORS THIS WEEK,' said another, 'John, Elizabeth, Anne.'

'WE FORGOT OUR HANDKERCHIEFS,' the third confessed frankly. Only John appeared to be culpable.

'That chap John seems to lead an active life,' observed Harold to Ella. 'And Anne for that matter,' he added.

'They're all called Anne or John,' explained Ella kindly. 'Unless they're Amanda or Roxana or Jacqueline or Marilyn or Somesuch.'

'I see,' said Harold, light dawning. 'Seems a pity the old names aren't used,' he mused. 'My sisters had friends with good old names like Bertha and Gertrude.' He paused, and appeared to rack his brain for more, but failed to add to the list. 'What's wrong with Bertha and Gertrude?' he added rhetorically of his neighbour.

'Plenty,' said Ella simply.

At this point the rector banged the desk with Miss Fogerty's safety inkwell and the meeting began.

'I must thank you for the excellent suggestions which have been put into the box,' began the rector. 'We have had five put forward – well, four, really, I suppose. I'll just read them out and if there are any more ideas we can then add them to the list.'

He adjusted a pair of half-glasses upon his snub nose and peered at the back of *The Quarterly Letter to Incumbents* upon which he had written his notes. The glasses gave his chubby face an oddly Pickwickian look. His hearers watched him with affection.

'What about putting up the suggestions on the blackboard?' suggested a bright youth perched on the nature table beside the winter berries.

'An excellent notion,' agreed the rector. Miss Fogerty hurried forward from the side of the piano.

'Oh, do let me put it up for you,' she fluttered, beginning to tug the easel from its nightly resting place against a map of the Holy Land.

Harold Shoosmith and the bright youth politely disengaged Miss Fogerty from the unequal struggle and she returned, pink with pleasure, to her place by the piano to watch the men's efforts with the board pegs.

'If I might suggest –' she began timidly, as the youth exerted all his pressure upon a peg too large for the hole, 'the one *above* is easier.'

The board leant at a drunken angle as the boy adjusted the awkward peg. He and Harold hoisted it one jump higher and stood back to admire their handiwork. Miss Fogerty's neat printing told a simple but poignant tale upon the blackboard's face.

> NED IS IN BED
> HIS LEG IS BAD
> NED'S PET TED BIT NED'S LEG.
> BAD TED TO BITE NED'S LEG!

All eyes were riveted upon the board with an attention which must have warmed Miss Fogerty's heart had she been less flustered. One or two enchanted members of her elderly class read the words aloud with slow absorption.

The rector, seeing his parishioners' attention deflected so wholeheartedly, sighed resignedly and took off his spectacles, preparing to wait.

'There's a case in point,' observed Harold to Ella. 'Ned! You simply never hear of a Ned these days.' He scrutinized the blackboard carefully.

'Or Ted, even. Used to be dozens of Teds when I was a boy. Proper names, I mean, not hooligans.'

Ella did not reply as she was trying to attract Dimity's attention. Dimity had found a resting place on a low table beneath the window and was idly unscrewing the bone acorn attached to the window blind.

The rector coughed apologetically and called his wayward flock to the business in hand.

'May we rub out your lesson, Miss Fogerty?' he enquired kindly.

'Oh, yes, indeed. Please do,' quavered the lady. The bright youth eagerly accepted the proffered blackboard cleaner and dashed away at the writing amidst clouds of chalk and general regret.

'The first suggestion,' said the rector resuming his glasses, 'is a sundial.'

'Shall I put it up?' asked the boy, fingering a lovely long stick of chalk handed to him from Miss Fogerty's store.

'If you please,' said the rector.

Rather crookedly the word was written in a passable copperplate. As an afterthought, the boy added the figure 1 in front of it.

'Secondly,' said the rector, 'a fountain. I suppose that means a drinking fountain,' he added doubtfully.

'Not at all,' said the oldest Miss Lovelock. 'I envisaged plumes of water flashing in the sunlight. Like Versailles, you know.'

'I see,' said the rector gravely.

'Be the devil of a job laying the water across the green,' observed someone in the front row.

'Remember them a-laying of them electric light wires?' reminisced his neighbour. 'Cor! That were a proper Fred Karno affair, that were! Best part of the summer –'

'*Please*!' said the rector beseechingly. 'We must get on. Discussion later, please.'

There were apologetic growlings and the vicar consulted his list again.

'A Celtic cross comes next.'

'Celtic!' burst out Ella, in a booming voice that set a wire humming inside the decrepit piano. 'Why Celtic? What's wrong with a decent plain *English* cross for Thrush Green? Too much altogether of this twilight-of-the-gods and Deirdre-of-the-sorrows nonsense!'

The rector turned a look more anguished than angered upon her, and Ella subsided with a gruff 'Sorry!'

'How do you spell "Celtic"?' asked the boy at the blackboard, waggling the chalk in hesitant fingers.

Several people told him several versions. More by luck than judgement an accepted spelling was finally inscribed, with a neat 3 in front.

'There were a number of slips of paper,' continued the rector, 'bearing the suggestion that a statue of Nathaniel Patten should be erected.'

A warm buzz went round the room. It was obvious that this idea was most welcome.

'Statue,' said the youth, pressing unduly upon the chalk and snapping it in two. His finger-nails scratched the board and there was a hissing as several people drew in their breath sharply.

'Puts your teeth on edge, don't it?' said old Mr Piggott glumly.

'Not so bad as a slate pencil,' said his elderly neighbour.

'Ah! It's walking on a stone floor in me socks that touches me up,' said someone else conversationally. 'Specially if your feet's a bit damp-like. Fair turns your teeth to chalk that does.'

'Sorry all,' said the boy cheerfully, diving to retrieve one of the pieces from under the pedal of the piano. The rector, seeing his meeting stray once again, rapped smartly with the inkwell once more.

'There are several modifications of this last suggestion,' he said in a firm voice, looking severely over his half-glasses at old Piggott who was embarking upon a long rigmarole about the reaction of false as against natural teeth when they were being set on edge. Reluctantly Piggott rumbled to a halt.

'Some have put "life-size", some have said the kind of material they prefer, such as "bronze" or "stone", and one rather charming suggestion wonders if Nathaniel might be surrounded by a group of African children for whom he did so much.' The rector's kindly gaze seemed to stray towards Dimity who twisted the acorn with such agitation that it fell off and rolled under a radiator.

'Let me,' said Harold Shoosmith, kneeling down with an alacrity and suppleness which the rector envied. Not even a knee-crack, noted the rector wistfully, remembering the reports, which habitually punctuated the services, from his own stiffening joints.

The acorn had rolled as far as it could into the murk under the radiator. Harold lay down at full-length and pulled out a toffee paper, part of a jig-saw puzzle, a rusty drawing-pin, two beads and a handful of grey fluff.

'Really!' said Miss Watson, turning pink. 'I must speak to the cleaner.' She looked most annoyed. She had not been too pleased to see Miss Fogerty's archaic reading lesson made so public. There were plenty of bright modern readers in the cupboards, specially recommended by the new infants' school adviser for the area. It gave such a wrong impression to see all that stuff about Ned's bad leg on the board. Fond as she was of dear Agnes there was no doubt about it she was just a shade behind the times. And now all this rubbish being brought to light! Really teachers had enough, one way or another, to drive them quite mad, thought poor mortified Miss Watson, tugging at her cardigan.

Harold retrieved the acorn and scrambled nimbly to his feet, smiling at Dimity. The rector, collecting his wits, returned to the fray.

'Are there any more suggestions?' he asked. The heavy silence which met this remark was only to be expected. People lowered their eyes to inspect the desk lids or their own shoes. Somebody blew his nose like a trumpet, and the boy by the blackboard, who had been studying his broken finger-nail with close interest, now bit it off briskly with a decisive snap.

'Well, shall we take the suggestions in turn?' asked the rector. 'How do we feel about the sundial?'

'Not bad,' said Edward Young cautiously. 'It would look rather well on the green, I think.'

Eyes were turned respectfully on the young architect. After all, he should know something about these things with all those years of training behind him.

Doctor Bailey rose to his feet from a desk at the back.

'It was my suggestion. I felt it wouldn't be too expensive, nor too big – I can't help feeling that a statue might dominate our small green rather too much – and might be useful too.'

'Thank you,' said the rector. 'Any comments?'

'Well, we've got a clock on the church already,' pointed out old Piggott sourly. 'And that tells the time fair enough, rain or shine, which is more'n you can say for a sundial.'

'True,' agreed the doctor equably. There was a long pause broken at last by the rector.

'Shall we go on to the next item? The fountain?'

'Wouldn't never work,' said someone dourly.

'Get frozen up come winter,' said another heavily.

'All the kids would come home sopping wet,' came a woman's voice from the back. 'Might even get drowned. You know what kids are!'

Murmurs of gloomy assent greeted this cheerful remark. The rector looked apologetically at the oldest Miss Lovelock, who continued to smile and nod her trembling head with unconcern.

No further comments being made the rector consulted his list again.

'Now we come to the Celtic cross,' said he.

'Well, you know my feelings on *that*,' boomed Ella heartily. She hoisted her bulk round to face the assembly. 'Whose idea was it anyway?' she asked forthrightly.

There was no reply to her belligerent question. Harold Shoosmith, half appalled and half amused, could not help feeling that it would be a brave man indeed who admitted to such folly before that stalwart Amazon. As a matter of fact, it had been Ruth Lovell's innocent suggestion, but although Edward Young, her brother-in-law, knew this, he kept silence. Ruth, at home on the sofa, at that moment enduring the belabourings of her unborn babe, would have been amused at the scene.

'Then I take it there are no further points?' queried the rector, hurrying to safer ground. 'And that brings us to the statue.'

Released from the tension of Ella's making, tongues now began to wag more readily.

'That's the best idea of the lot,' said one.

'The *only* thing,' said another downrightly.

'A real good big 'un,' suggested another. 'Don't want nothin' mean-lookin'!'

There was quite a hubbub in the little room and the rector was forced to thump again with the red inkwell.

'I really think the time has come to take a vote on these suggestions,' he said. 'Shall we raise hands? Those in favour of the statue?'

Almost all the hands in the room seemed to be aloft. The rector stood up, the better to do his counting, then turned to Harold.

'Shoosmith, my dear fellow, would you check for me?'

The two men stood at the front of the classroom on tiptoe, their mouths slightly open, their foreheads slightly wrinkled in concentration. On the wall the great clock ticked in the sudden quietness, and outside in the wet December night a distant car splashed along the muddy lane to Nod and Nidden.

'Thirty-seven,' said Harold Shoosmith.

'Thirty-seven,' agreed the rector. 'I think there's no doubt that the statue will be our choice, but it would be wise to vote upon the others in turn. Now, first of all, the sundial!'

A few hands went up, including Edward Young's.

'Seven,' said Harold.

'Eight,' said the rector.

'Sorry,' said the bright youth who had perched himself again on the nature table. 'I was scratching under my arm.'

'Seven it is then,' said the rector. 'Now the fountain!'

Only three hands were raised in support of Miss Lovelock's suggestion. The delights of the flashing plumes in summer sunlight were obviously overborne by the thought of the trench-digging and freezing possibilities put forward by the killjoys earlier.

The Celtic cross fared even worse, whether by reason of Ella's contumely, natural patriotic pride, or plain apathy, no one could tell, but only two hands were raised aloft, one of them belonging to the nail-biting boy.

'Well,' said the rector. 'That seems to be that.'

An excited buzz ran round the room. There seemed to be general pleasure at the verdict. Above the hum the sound of St Andrew's church clock could be heard, striking eight.

The rector rapped again, after looking at Harold Shoosmith and Edward Young.

'Perhaps while we are all here together we might go a little further into this question of the statue.'

'Time's getting on,' said the woman at the back. 'My husband wants to get down to "The Two Pheasants", but he's minding the baby.'

'Do him good,' said Ella robustly. 'Don't you hurry back.'

There was general laughter.

'Ah maybe!' replied the woman grudgingly. ''Tis all right for you single 'uns to talk, but us poor married toads has to keep the boat up straight!'

'It does seem,' said the rector, ignoring the interruption and secretly fearful of being drawn into this incipient argument, 'that there are a number of points to bear in mind. First of all, I think Mr Young will tell us, a life-size statue of Nathaniel Patten will be an expensive affair. Not only are there the materials to pay for, but the sculptor too.'

'I don't see why Miss Bembridge can't be given a chance,' said someone at the back. 'We'd all be proud to see her work on our green.'

'Good Lord!' exclaimed Ella. 'I've never done anything like that!' Her eye began to gleam with a dangerously creative light. 'But I wouldn't mind having a bash,' she added, with growing enthusiasm.

Harold Shoosmith trembled. He had settled himself beside Dimity, after screwing back the acorn, and she looked at him with sudden anxiety as their shared table-top shook.

The rector, with an aplomb born of many similar village crises, spoke smoothly.

'I'm sure we can come to some arrangement later about the person we ask to undertake the work, but first of all I think we should decide what medium we want. Bronze has been suggested or stone of some sort.'

'A nice bit of pink granite,' suggested old Piggott, 'well shone up.' Edward Young shuddered.

'I like copper myself,' said his neighbour. 'Goes that nice green shade in time.'

'We'd get it pinched,' commented the bright boy. 'Copper fetches ten bob a lump these days. A *small* lump. Come to that, any sort of metal statue's going to cost a packet. Specially life-sized.'

This sound piece of sense brought forth a few grunts of agreement, and a small speech from Dimity.

'In this connection, perhaps I could withdraw my first suggestion about a group of figures,' she began breathlessly, her earnest gaze fixed upon the rector's encouraging face. 'It did seem to me that *children* should be part of the memorial, but why not have *Nathaniel* as a child? After all, he played on the green as a little boy, and the statue would be much smaller and less expensive.'

'It's a very sensible and charming idea,' agreed the rector gently. Taking heart from his support, Dimity continued rather breathlessly.

'And it could be *most attractive*. I mean, look at Peter Pan! What could be sweeter? Perhaps the same person would do it?'

Edward Young opened his mouth as though to speak, thought better of it, and subsided.

'We will certainly bear that in mind, Miss Dean,' nodded the rector, watching Dimity resume her place beside Harold.

'Then we must choose our sculptor,' went on Mr Henstock, 'one who can work in the medium of our choice, and give us a memorial which suits its surroundings and which we all are proud of.'

His plump face began to pucker with worry.

'It occurs to me that we must, of course, get planning permission from several authorities if we want to put up the statue. Really, there is a great deal to consider.'

Edward Young then spoke up.

'Perhaps you would allow me to make enquiries about prices and possible sculptors on behalf of us all here? I should be delighted to be of some service, and I think I could advise you too about the best way of approaching the necessary authorities.'

A hum of agreement ran round the room. The rector looked mightily relieved.

'It is most kind of you. Would someone propose that Mr Young should undertake this particular set of enquiries?'

'I will,' said Miss Watson briskly.

'And I'll second it,' added Doctor Bailey.

'That really is a great comfort,' said Mr Henstock gratefully. 'I am sure we are all much indebted to you for offering your professional help so freely.'

He turned over *The Quarterly Letter to Incumbents* and scrutinized it closely.

'Just one more thing,' he continued, looking at the assembled company over his glasses. 'A good friend of Thrush Green, who wishes to remain anonymous, has said that he would like to defray half the expense of this project. I think you might like to register your approval of this most generous offer.'

Loud clapping and a few foot-drummings demonstrated the fervour with which this announcement was met. As it died down, Edward Young spoke again.

'That is wonderful news, sir. I just wondered if it might not be a good idea to form a very small committee, representing all assembled here tonight, to go further into this statue business. For one thing, we shall want it unveiled presumably on Nathaniel's birthday, some time in March, I believe.'

'That's right,' said Harold. 'The fifteenth!'

'Then in that case, we must work quickly,' went on Edward. 'It might be rather nice if one of Nathaniel's descendants could unveil his memorial.'

'His daughter's dead,' said a very old man, who was leaning against Miss Fogerty's weather chart and smearing the black umbrellas and yellow suns most carelessly. 'Died soon after she were married. I knows that 'cos my sister and she used to send each other Christmas cards for years. There were a boy though, I do recollect.'

'That's most interesting,' said Mr Henstock. 'We'll follow that up. Now, what about Mr Young's very sound suggestion? Shall we appoint someone – or two perhaps – to help him?'

'Yourself, sir,' suggested the bright boy.

There was a murmur of agreement.

'I shall be most happy,' said the rector. 'Doctor Bailey, do you feel that you could join Mr Young and me?'

Doctor Bailey shook his silvery head.

'I'd rather someone else took it on, if you don't mind. I'm not as reliable these days as I'd like to be. What about Mr Shoosmith?'

The name brought forth such a burst of warm assent that the normally self-possessed newcomer looked almost shy.

'I should be very glad to be of any use,' said Harold politely.

And so it was left. The three men would look further into the matter and let Thrush Green know more about their findings later.

It was almost nine o'clock when the company dispersed into the wet darkness.

'Keeps mild, don't it,' said the old man, who remembered Nathaniel's daughter, to Mr Piggott as they made their way to the brightly-lit pub.

'Ah!' responded old Piggott morosely. 'You know what they say about a green Christmas? Makes a full churchyard. And that makes more work for me, I may say.'

'I don't know as I believes that,' replied the old man with a flash of spirit, 'but that's as may be. What I do know is these meetings give a chap a rare thirst. You come on in and have a pint with me, my boy.'

At this generous invitation old Piggott's face softened a little, and, united in a common bond, the two crossed the welcoming threshold of 'The Two Pheasants' and left the dark behind them.

10. Albert Piggott is Wooed

Nelly Tilling kept her word. She paid three visits to Mr Piggott's cottage, carrying with her each time a stout rush basket bearing a scrubbing brush, house flannel, and a large packet of detergent whose magic properties had been dinned into her by television advertisements. Nelly was a firm believer in the educational value of television, and took everything she saw as gospel truth.

Her set was an old one, given her by the landlord of 'The Drovers' Arms', not far from her own cottage, where she worked two mornings a week scrubbing out the bar. Kindly Ted and Bessie Allen, for whom young Molly Piggott had once worked, felt very sorry for Nelly Tilling when her husband died and had decided that their old television set would be just the thing to cheer her lonely evenings.

They were quite right. Nelly was an avid watcher and took great delight in telling her employers all about the programmes – which they had seen for themselves the night before – in meticulous detail.

One morning, soon after the meeting about the memorial, Nelly made her way round to Mr Piggott's back door, her basket on her arm and her spirits raised at the thought of the work before her. Nelly was a fighter. She chased dirt as she chased and routed any weakness for strong drink or dubious entertainment. Brought up by militant evangelistic parents Nelly continued, in ripe middle age, to practise those precepts learnt in her youth. She knew where to draw the line, and even switched off the television set if any of the dancers appeared too lightly clad for her sense of propriety.

She intended this morning to attack Albert Piggott's kitchen. This task would have daunted many a woman, but Nelly, armed with the magic detergent and the stout scrubbing brush, really looked forward to the job.

She found Albert Piggott gazing intently into a small triangle of looking-glass propped on the window-sill. He greeted her glumly.

'Got summat in me eye,' he said.

'Here, let's see,' said the fat widow, putting her heavy basket on the floor and advancing upon him. Albert turned a watery pale blue eye in her direction.

'That reminds me,' said the lady, pulling her handkerchief from her coat pocket and screwing the corner into a workmanlike radish, 'I've brought a cod's head for your cat.'

Mr Piggott grunted, by way of thanking her, and looked with alarm at the handkerchief.

'It'll come out on its own, I don't doubt –' he began. But his protests were of no avail. He found the back of his head held firmly in Nelly Tilling's left hand while she swiped shrewdly at his eye with the formidable weapon in her right one.

Nelly Tilling had plenty of experience in dealing with refractory children. She had brought up three of her own, all scrubbed and polished like bright apples, and had the knack of grabbing a reluctant child behind the neck and whisking a soapy flannel round its face and ears before it had time to protest. Although all her children were now grown up, Nelly's hand had not lost its cunning. Within two seconds Albert was released, and the eye was freed of its foreign body.

'Well!' gasped Albert, flabbergasted but impressed. 'That was a smart piece of work, I will say!'

''Twas nothing,' said the widow, looking gratified nevertheless. 'While you're over the church, Albert, I thought I'd set this room to rights today, and maybe we could share a bacon pie, like I promised. I've got it in my basket here. I'll just hot it up for midday.'

Albert's eye brightened. For all her running him round, which he was inclined to resent, a bacon pie was a bacon pie, particularly when such a delicacy was virtually unobtainable to a man living alone.

'I'll pick a bit of winter green,' said Albert, with unaccustomed vigour, 'it's doing well this year. Give us the enamel bowl, my girl, and I'll go down the garden.'

He departed, whistling through his broken teeth, and Nelly set about heating some water for her campaign, well pleased with the way things were going.

Two hours later Nelly sat, blown but triumphant, on the kitchen chair and surveyed her handiwork.

She had cause for pride. A bright fire glowed behind gleaming bars, and the bacon pie was already in the oven beside it and beginning to smell most savoury. The thin little cat, her repast spread on a newspaper in the corner, dug her sharp white teeth into the cod's head, closing her eyes in bliss the while.

The floor, the walls and the wooden table had all been lustily scrubbed. Albert's dingy sink had been scoured to its original yellow colour, and the window above it gleamed and winked with unaccustomed cleanliness.

Taking a steady look at it, thought Nelly to herself, easing off her shoes for greater comfort, it wasn't such a bad little house, and certainly very much more conveniently placed for shopping than her own cottage at Lulling Woods.

Two rooms up and two rooms down would be just a nice size for Albert and herself, and her own furniture would look very handsome in these surroundings. The few poor sticks that Albert had collected over the years were fit for nothing but firewood.

She allowed her mind to dwell for a minute on her old schoolfellow in the role of husband. True, he was no oil painting, but she had long passed the age of needing good looks about her, and anyway, she admitted to herself with disarming frankness, her own beauty had long since gone.

And, of course, he was a miserable worm. But, Nelly pointed out to herself, he had some justification for it. The drink had something to do with it, no doubt, but lack of a decent woman in his house was the real cause of the trouble. She cast an appraising eye over the clean kitchen and listened to the music of the sizzling pie. With a cheerful place like this to come home to, thought Nelly, 'The Two Pheasants' would lose its appeal. And if by any chance it didn't, then Nelly Tilling would put her foot down – for hadn't she seen, with her own eyes, young Albert Piggott in a Norfolk jacket much too small for him, signing the pledge all those years ago?

The advantages of the marriage were solid ones. Albert earned a steady wage, was a good gardener and could afford to keep a wife in reasonable comfort. There would be no need for her to go out to work. 'The Drovers' Arms' was a pleasant enough place to scrub out, but Nelly disliked seeing people drinking. She would not be sorry to give up the job there, despite Bessie and Ted's goodwill towards her.

At Thrush Green she would be able to pick and choose her employers. Miss Ruth or Miss Joan, as she still thought of Mrs Lovell and Mrs Young, could probably do with a hand. She remembered the great flagged kitchen floor at the Bassetts' house and her heart warmed.

Or better still, there was the village school practically next door! The thought of those yards of bare floorboards, pounded day in and day out by scores of muddy boots, fairly crying out for a bucket of hot suds and a good brush, filled Nelly's heart with joy. There was a cloakroom too, if she remembered rightly, with a nice rosy brick floor that really paid for doing. And there was something about a large tortoise stove, freshly done with first-class blacklead and plenty of elbow-grease, that gladdened your eyes. She had heard that Miss Watson wasn't best pleased with the present cleaner. A word dropped in the right ear, Nelly told herself, might bring her the job if she decided to earn an honest penny at Thrush Green.

She heard the sound of Albert's footsteps approaching, heaved her bulk from the chair, and opened the oven door. A glorious fragrance filled the room. On top of the hob the winter greens bubbled deliciously. The mingled scents greeted Albert as he opened the back door.

'Cor!' breathed Mr Piggott with awe, 'that smells wholly good, Nell.'

His face bore an expression of holiness and rapture which his habitual place of worship never saw. Albert was touched to his very marrow.

Nelly was not slow to follow up this advantage.

'Sit you down, Albert,' she said warmly, 'in a real clean kitchen at last, with a real hot meal to eat.'

She withdrew the fragrant dish from the oven, and put it, still sizzling, before the bedazzled sexton.

'There!' breathed the widow proudly, setting about her wooing with a bacon pie.

Albert Piggott's cottage was not the only house in Thrush Green where thoughts of matrimony disturbed the air.

On the same day, across the green, Ella Bembridge mused upon the married state. She was alone in the house, her work materials spread out upon the kitchen table. She was busy hand-printing a length of material for Dotty Harmer's new summer skirt, and for once the dishes of paint, the jar of brushes and the chunky wood block failed to please her.

Dimity was out with Harold Shoosmith in the large Daimler. She would be more than adequately chaperoned, for about six cars were with them. The Lulling Field Club was off to see a Saxon church, much prized by antiquarians, resembling a stone bees' skep, and smelling strongly of damp. Ella had decided to forgo this pleasure and to get on with one or two orders while the kitchen was unoccupied.

But her heart was not in the work. The possibility of either of them marrying had been thought of when the two friends had joined forces many years before. As they grew older there was, naturally, less likelihood of marriage, and their lives had been filled with many interests and a cheerful affection for each other which most successfully kept the bogey of loneliness away.

All these thoughts buzzed about Ella's head as she thumped her wood block steadily down the length of cloth before her. The kitchen seemed stuffy, the pattern second-rate and the printing patchy. At last, unable to bear it any longer, Ella downed tools, grabbed her coat from the back of the kitchen door, and marched out for air.

It was one of those still, quiet days of winter, when everything seems to be waiting. No breeze disturbed the plumes of smoke from Thrush Green's chimneys. The trees stood bare and motionless. On the hedges small drops of moisture hung; no breath of wind disturbed them, no beam of sunlight lit them to life. The sky was low and of uniform greyness.

'Might as well be in a canvas tent,' thought Ella gloomily, turning her steps towards the lane to Nod and Nidden.

About half a mile along the quiet road she came to a low wall of Cotswold stone, built by a craftsman years before, stone upon stone, so skilfully, that although no mortar had touched it the dry stones had weathered many a gale and blizzard and remained untouched.

Ella leant upon its comforting roughness, took out the battered tobacco tin which accompanied her everywhere, and began to roll herself one of the shaggy vile-smelling cigarettes for which she was noted. Lighting one untidy end she drew in a refreshing breath of strong smoke. Before her, in December haze, stretched mile upon mile of Cotswold country, ploughed fields, grazing pastures, distant smoky woodland, valleys and hills. Here, in this quiet lovely place, Ella knew that she must put her thoughts in order.

Better to face it, she told herself, there was nothing on earth to keep Dimity from marrying if she were asked. What sort of a life did Dim have, when you looked at it squarely? She was bullied and shouted at, did most of the work and got no thanks for it.

'It's a wonder she's stuck it as long as she has,' said Ella aloud to a fat blackbird who had come to see what was going on. With a squawk, her companion fled, and Ella, in her present state of self-chastisement, did not blame him.

And there was no doubt about it that Harold Shoosmith seemed fond of her. He had taken to calling in several times a week and Dimity was unashamedly delighted to see him. He would probably make a very good husband, thought Ella magnanimously. Poor state though matrimony was, it obviously appealed to quite a number of people.

She supposed that they would live at the corner house. Suddenly, Ella found the whole idea peculiarly painful, and tossed her cigarette irritably into a tuft of wet grass. Could it be jealousy, she asked herself? Any man would say so, many women would not. Ella tried to look at the matter soberly again.

Quite honestly, Ella decided, it was not jealousy that made her feelings so acute. She had no desire for marriage herself, though she knew that Dimity's more gentle nature would flower in the married state. Her own mental life was vigorous and creative and afforded her greater satisfaction with every year that passed. Marriage for Ella would be a distraction. She was too selfish not to resent any interruption in her own way of life. For Dimity's happiness she rejoiced. It was just, thought Ella with a wince of pain, that she would miss Dim so much – the shared jokes, the companionship in the little cottage, the modest expeditions and the fun of discussing things with her.

Life was going to be very different with Dim across the green. Could the cottage be endured without her company, Ella wondered? Or would it be best to uproot herself and go elsewhere? It might be fairest to both of them, she decided. Whatever the future held she must let Dimity have her way. She must not be selfish and tyrannical – for too long Dimity had suffered her own over-bearing ways. If this should prove to be Dim's chance of happiness, then, Ella decided, she should take it and she herself would do all in her power to promote it.

Ella took a deep breath of damp Cotswold air, and having cleared her mind, felt a great deal better.

She gave the stone wall a friendly clout with her massive hand, and turned her face towards Thrush Green again.

But still her heart was heavy.

11. Christmas Preparations

The little town of Lulling was beginning to deck itself in its Christmas finery. In the market square a tall Christmas tree towered, its dark branches threaded with electric lights. At night it twinkled with red, blue, yellow and orange pinpoints of colour and gladdened the hearts of all the children.

The shop windows sported snow scenes, Christmas bells, paper chains and reindeer. The window of the local electricity showroom had a life-size tableau of a family at Christmas dinner, which was much admired. Wax figures, with somewhat yellow and jaundiced complexions, sat smiling glassily at a varnished papier mâché turkey, their forks upraised in happy anticipation. Upon their straw-like hair were perched paper hats of puce and lime green, and paper napkins, ablaze with holly sprigs, were tucked into their collars. The fact that they were flanked closely by a washing machine, a spin dryer and a refrigerator did not appear to disturb them, nor did the clutter of hair dryers, torches, heaters, bed-

warmers and toasters, beneath the dining-room table, labelled
ACCEPTABLE XMAS GIFTS.

The rival firms of Beecher and Thatcher which faced each other
across Lulling's High Street had used countless yards of cotton
wool for their snowy scenes. Some held that Beecher's 'Palace of
the Ice Queen' outdid Thatcher's tableau from Dickens's *Christmas
Carol*, but the more critical and carping among Lulling's inhabitants deemed the Ice Queen's diaphanous garments indecent and
'anyway not Christmassy'. Both firms had elected to have Father
Christmas installed complete with a gigantic pile of parcels
wrapped in pink or blue tissue paper for their young customers. A
great deal of explanation went on about this strange dual per-
sonality of Father Christmas, and exasperated mothers told each
other privately just what they thought of Beecher and Thatcher
for being so pig-headed. The psychological impact upon their
young did not appear to have dire consequences. Country children
are fairly equable and the pleasure of having two presents far out-
weighed the shock of meeting Father Christmas twice on the same
day – once in the newly-garnished broom cupboard under Thatcher's main staircase, and next in the upstairs corset-fitting room,
suitably draped with red curtaining material, at Beecher's establishment.

With only a fortnight to go before Christmas Day Lulling people
were beginning to bestir themselves about their shopping. London
might start preparing for the festival at the end of October; Lulling
refused to be hustled. October and November had jobs of their own
in plenty. December, and the latter part at that, was the proper time
to think of Christmas, and the idea of buying cards and presents
before then was just plain silly.

'Who wants to think of Christmas when there's the autumn digging to do?' said one practically.

'Takes all the gilt off the gingerbread to have Christmas thrown
down your throat before December,' agreed another.

But now all the good folk were ready for it, and the shops did a
brisk trade. Baskets bulged, and harassed matrons struggled along
the crowded main street bearing awkward objects like tricycles and
pairs of stilts, flimsily wrapped in flapping paper. Children kept
up a shrill piping for the tawdry knick-knacks which caught their
eye, and fathers gazed speculatively at train sets and wondered if

their two-year-old sons and daughters would be a good excuse to buy one.

At the corner of the market square stood Puddocks', the stationers, and here, one windy afternoon, Ella Bembridge was engaged in choosing Christmas cards.

Normally, Ella designed her own Christmas card. It was usually a wood cut or a lino cut, executed with her habitual vigour and very much appreciated by her friends. But somehow, this year, Ella had not done one. So many things had pressed upon her time. There were far more visits these days, both from the rector and from his friend Harold Shoosmith, and the vague unhappiness which hung over her at the thought of change had affected Ella more than she realized. Today, in Puddocks', reduced to turning over their mounds of insipid cards, Ella felt even more depressed.

But, depressed as she was, she set about her appointed task with energy. She made directly towards the section marked 'Cards 6d., 9d., and 1s.' and began a swift process of elimination. Ballet dancers, ponies, dogs, anyone in a crinoline or a beaver hat, were out. So were contrived scenes of an open Bible before a stained-glass window flanked with a Christmas rose or a candle. It was amazing how little was left after this ruthless pruning. Ella, coming up for air, looked at the throng around her to see how others were faring.

She envied the stout woman at her elbow who picked up all the cards embellished with sparkling stuff and read the verses intently. She had plenty of choice. She admired the way in which a tall thin man selected black and white line drawings of Ely Cathedral, Tower Bridge and Bath Abbey with extreme rapidity. She watched, with bitter respect, a large female who forced her way to the desk and demanded the ten dozen printed Christmas cards ordered on August 22nd, and promised faithfully for early December. Here was efficiency, thought Ella, returning to her rummaging.

At last, she collected a few less obnoxious specimens, paid for them and thrust her way through the mob to the comparative spaciousness of the pavement outside. The clock on the Town Hall pointed to ten past five and Ella decided to try her luck at 'The Fuchsia Bush', Lulling's most genteel tea-shop.

'The Fuchsia Bush's' contribution to Christmas consisted of a charming scene arranged on the sideboard just inside the door. Whitewashed branches, from which white and silver bells were suspended, spread above a bevy of white-clad angels. Unfortunately, the whole had been lavishly sprinkled with imitation frost which blew about the shop in clouds every time the door opened. Discriminating customers chose cakes which could easily be shaken free of the glitter and eschewed the iced sticky buns which were normally a fast-selling favourite at The Fuchsia Bush.

At a table near by Ella was delighted to see her old friend Dotty Harmer, her grey hair lightly spangled with blown frost. A cup of tea steamed before her and on a plate lay three digestive biscuits.

'Well, Dotty, expecting anyone?' boomed Ella, dragging back the only unoccupied chair in the tea-shop.

'No, no,' replied Dotty, removing a string bag, a cauliflower and a large paper bag labelled 'LAYMORE' from the seat. 'Bertha Lovelock was here until a minute ago. Do sit down. I'm just going through my list once more. I think I've got everything except whiting for Mrs Curdle. It's usually rock salmon, you know, but I think she's expecting again and whiting must lie less heavily on the stomach, I feel sure.'

'Tea, please,' said Ella to the languid waitress who appeared at her side.

'Set-tea-toasted-teacake-jam-or-honey-choice-of-cake-to-follow-two-and-nine,' gabbled the girl, admiring her engagement ring the while.

'No thanks,' said Ella. 'Just tea.'

'Indian or China?'

'Indian,' said Ella. 'And strong.'

The girl departed and Ella unwound the long woollen scarf from her thick neck, undid her coat and sighed with relief.

'Wonder why it's "Indian or China"?' she remarked idly to Dotty. 'Why not "Indian or Chinese"? Or "India or China"? Illogical, isn't it?'

'Indeed yes,' agreed Dotty, breaking a digestive biscuit carefully in half. 'But then people *are* illogical. Look at Father's man trap.'

Ella looked startled. Sometimes Dotty's conversation was more eccentric than usual. This seemed to be one of her bad days.

'What's your father's man trap got to do with it?' demanded Ella.

'I just want it back,' said Dotty simply. She popped a fragment of biscuit into her mouth and crunched it primly with her front teeth. The back ones had been removed. She had the air of a polite bespectacled rabbit at her repast.

'Oh, come off it!' begged Ella roughly. 'Talk sense!' Dotty looked vaguely upset.

'You know Father gave his valuable man trap to the museum. It was quite a fine working model used in the eighteenth century by Sir Henry – a great-great-grandfather of the present Sir Henry. Father used to demonstrate it to the boys at the grammar school when he was teaching history there.' She paused to sip her tea, and Ella, fuming at the delay, began to wonder if that were all Dotty would say.

Dotty replaced her cup carefully, patted her mouth with a small folded handkerchief, and continued.

'Well,' she said, 'now I could do with it.'

Ella made a violent gesture of annoyance, nearly capsizing the tea tray which the languid girl had now brought.

'What on earth do you want a man trap for?' expostulated Ella. Dotty looked at her in surprise.

'Why, to catch a man!' explained Dotty. Ella made a sound remarkably like 'Tchah!' and began to pour milk violently into her cup.

'I suspect,' continued Dotty, unaware of Ella's heightened blood pressure, 'that someone is stealing my eggs. I could set the man trap at dusk and let the police interview him in the morning.'

'Now, look here, Dotty,' said Ella, in a hectoring tone, 'don't you realize you'd probably break the chap's leg in one of those ghastly contraptions – ?'

'Naturally,' replied her friend coolly, 'a man trap works on that principle, and ours was in excellent condition. Father saw to that. He would be quite safe in it till morning. I get up fairly early, as you know, so he wouldn't be in it more than a few hours.' She spoke as though she would be acting with the most humane consideration, and even Ella was nonplussed.

'But man traps are illegal,' she pointed out.

'Fiddlesticks!' said Dotty firmly. 'So are heaps of other traps, but they're used, more's the pity, on poor animals that are doing no wrong. This wretched man knows quite well he is doing wrong in taking my eggs. He deserves the consequences, and I shall point them out to him – from a safe distance, of course – as soon as I've trapped him.'

There was a slight pause.

'You know what?' said Ella interestedly. 'You're absolutely off your rocker, Dot.'

Dotty flushed with annoyance.

'I'm a lot saner than you are, Ella Bembridge,' she said snappily. 'And a lot saner than those chits of girls at the museum who won't let me have Father's property back. I very much doubt if they are legally in the right about refusing my request. After all, Father left all his property to me, and as I say, that man trap is exactly what I need at the moment.'

'You forget it,' advised Ella, rolling a ragged cigarette. 'Pop up to the police station instead and get Sergeant Stansted to keep his eyes skinned. And, what's more,' she added, for she was fond of her crazy friend, 'don't tell him you want the man trap back, or you're the one he'll be keeping his eye on.'

She drew a deep and refreshing inhalation of strong cigarette smoke. This was an occasion, she thought to herself, when a woman could do with a little comfort.

Meanwhile, at Thrush Green, Dimity and Winnie Bailey were busy in the cold and draughty church of St Andrew's.

They were getting the crib ready and had decided that the open-fronted stable, containing the cradle and the figures, really needed re-thatching. They were hard at it, ankle-deep in straw, by the font, as the clock above them chimed half-past three.

Already the church was getting murky. Above their bent heads the tattered remains of regimental flags moved gently in the draughts, and round their cold feet the straw whispered along the tiled floor. The chancel, distant from them, looked ghostly and incredibly old, a place of shadows and mystery.

'I never knew it would be so difficult,' confessed Winnie Bailey, trying to fold refractory straw into a neat bundle. 'We ought to have asked a proper thatcher to do it for us.'

'Never mind,' said Dimity, standing back to survey their handi-work, 'it looks very spruce from a distance. Only this corner to do and then we've finished.'

She gazed ruefully at her small hands.

'I'm full of splinters,' she said. 'When we've finished the roof, let's clear up and have some tea. It's getting too dark to see properly anyway.'

'Lovely!' agreed Winnie with enthusiasm. 'And we'll wash the figures at home.'

In five minutes all was done and the two weary friends were collecting stray wisps of straw when the door opened and the rector came in.

'How goes the work?' he asked. Dimity and Winnie indicated the golden roof with modest pride.

'Experts both,' exclaimed the rector admiringly.

'And very tired ones,' said Winnie. 'We're just going to have tea.'

'Come too,' insisted Dimity, making her way to the windy porch; and the three set off through the winter dusk to Ella and Dimity's home.

After the bleak loftiness of the church the low-ceilinged sitting-room appeared very snug.

The fire glowed with a steady red warmth and the table lamps cast comfortable pools of light on the polished surface of the bookshelves which flanked the hearth. The room was filled with the scent of early Roman hyacinths. A magnificent pale pink azalea caught the rector's eye, and he admired it.

'Isn't it lovely?' agreed Dimity, rolling her gloves together neatly. 'Harold Shoosmith brought it over for us. The fire's just right for toasting and there are some crumpets. Sit down while I fetch the tray.'

The rector seated himself obediently, while the two women departed to the kitchen, and held out his cold hands to the fire. He seldom saw an open fire these days, he realized with a slight shock. His housekeeper preferred him to use the electric fire as it saved her work, and the good rector was only too willing to fall in with her plans. But, until this moment, he had not realized how much he missed the companionship of a real fire. Here was a living thing that talked with crackling tongues of flame and responded to tending. He really must persuade Mrs Butler to light his fire again. Even if he cleared it up himself in the morning, the rector decided, it would be well worth it.

He leant back into a soft armchair that enfolded him comfortably and looked with pleasure about the little room. How pretty it was, how warm, how welcoming! This was Dimity's work he knew, and how well she did it – timidly, unobtrusively, but with love. His eye lit upon the pink azalea and a small pang shot through the rector's enveloping sense of well-being. Harold Shoosmith, now he came to think of it, also had the knack of making a place comfortable. It wasn't money alone that did it, the rector mused rather sadly, although Shoosmith was a wealthy man compared with himself. It was an ability to choose and place the most suitable objects together, to plan lighting, to attend to small details. The rector thought of his great barn of a rectory, the cold corridors, the lofty Gothic windows and the everlasting cross-draughts from them, and he sighed.

At this moment, Dimity and Winnie returned bearing the tea-things, and the rector seeing a pile of crumpets, took the proffered toasting fork, set about his primitive cooking and felt much more cheerful.

'What news of the statue?' asked Winnie, during the meal.

'Edward's doing very well,' answered the rector. 'He has asked several people to submit designs and we should be able to commission one of them very soon. We've also tried to find Nathaniel's grandson, but we're having some difficulty.'

'What about the daughter?' asked Dimity, pouring tea.

'Nathaniel's daughter? Dead, I fear. She married rather a ne'er-do-well and lived in great poverty somewhere in the West Country. But we hope to trace the son. He should be a man in his thirties now. We all feel that he should be consulted in this business of a memorial to his grandfather. And, as Edward suggested, it would be extremely pleasant if he could unveil it in March.'

'Do you think it will be ready?' asked Winnie doubtfully. Thrush Green was not noted for its punctuality.

'I'm sure of it,' said the rector sturdily. He withdrew a black and smoking crumpet hastily from the fire, blew out the flames and looked at it dubiously. 'Perhaps I'd better keep this one,' he suggested. The ladies agreed with somewhat unnecessary fervour, the rector impaled another crumpet, and tried again.

'I can't think why Ella is so late,' exclaimed Dimity. 'She must have stopped for tea somewhere. I hope she comes back before you go.'

But Ella did not. By the time she had finished her tea at 'The Fuchsia Bush', said farewell to Dotty, whose mind still ran dangerously upon the man trap, and stumped up the steep hill to Thrush Green, Winnie Bailey and the rector had departed.

In the hollow the lights of the little town twinkled in the clear night air, and the rector, walking across to his house looked down upon them with affection. He was much attached to Lulling, and even more to Thrush Green, finding delight in their many aspects. Tonight, snug in its valley, with the dark hills girding it around, the small town appeared particularly endearing.

He gave it a last look before opening his heavy front door and stepping inside.

The house was silent and struck him as cold and damp as he closed the door behind him. He went into his study, switched on the light and looked about him.

The electric fire stood cold and gleaming. Above his desk upon the wall hung a crucifix. The paint was a pale green which gave the room a sub-aqueous look and did nothing to add warmth to the rector's surroundings. The roof was uncomfortably high, and the thin curtains moved restlessly in a continuous draught from the lofty narrow windows.

The rector, remembering the cosiness he had just left, sighed at so much bleakness and switched on the electric fire. It had all been so different when his dear wife had been alive. Life sometimes seemed as forlorn as this study, he reflected.

Then he caught sight of the cross upon the wall, chided himself, and sat down at his desk to work.

12. The Fur and Feather Whist Drive

Miss Fogerty, looking at her restless class of infants, thanked her stars that it was the last afternoon of term. The last day of any term was exhausting, but the one which ended the autumn term, less than a week before Christmas, was enough to try the patience of a saint, particularly if one had the misfortune to be looking after the infants.

Beside themselves with excitement they had fidgeted and squealed, giggled and wept until Miss Fogerty had clapped her hands and said sternly:

'Heads down!'

And when the last head had subsided on to fat young arms folded across the little desks, she had added, for good measure:

'No story until you have been absolutely quiet for five minutes!'

Only then had comparative peace descended upon the classroom, and Miss Fogerty had felt her sanity return.

She walked to the window and looked out at the darkening sky. It was nearly half-past three on the shortest day of the year. Beyond the little playground the fields dropped away to the gentle valley where the path ran to Lulling Woods and where Dotty Harmer's solitary cottage lay. Sheep were grazing on the slope and one sat, chewing the cud, so near the hedge that Miss Fogerty could see it plainly, looking like Wordsworth, with its long nose and benign expression. Blandly surveying the landscape, rotating its jaws in placid motion, it gave Miss Fogerty a blessed feeling of calm.

She turned back to look at the class, much refreshed in spirit. The children lay in varied positions of torpor. Above them hung paper chains in rainbow hues, and here and there a Chinese lantern dangled, swaying gently in the breeze from the windows. Around the room went a procession of scarlet-coated Father Christmases, with white beards made of cotton wool and shiny black paper boots. Normally, all these garnishings would have been taken down before the end of term, but the Thrush Green Entertainments Committee had asked for the decorations to be left up as the school would be in use for the Fur and Feather Whist Drive in the evening.

'We will take down everything,' Mr Henstock had assured the two teachers, and the ladies had been truly thankful.

The great wall-clock ticked on past the half-hour and Miss Fogerty returned to the high teacher's chair ready to read the promised story. She looked down upon the bowed heads, ranging in colour from gipsy-black to flaxen, of the class before her. On each desk lay the fruits of the term's industry waiting to be taken home. Spinning tops made of cardboard, calendars, shopping pads, paper mats and Christmas cards jostled together. Soon they would be carried to cottage homes as treasured presents for the families there.

'You may sit up now,' said Miss Fogerty graciously, from her perch.

Thirty-odd flushed faces turned eagerly upward. Three heavy heads remained in sleep upon the wooden desks and Miss Fogerty wisely let them remain there. She opened her little book and raised her voice:

'Once upon a time there was an old pig called Aunt Pettitoes. She had eight of a family; four little girl pigs –'

The children wriggled ecstatically and settled down to hear yet again the tale of the Christmas Pig – Pigling Bland.

Later, that evening, the paper chains swung above the parents and other inhabitants of Thrush Green and Lulling.

The Fur and Feather Whist Drive, whose posters had fluttered bravely from gatepost and tree trunk during the past few weeks, was in progress. The glass partition between Miss Fogerty's and Miss Watson's classrooms had been pushed back with ear-splitting protests from its steel runners. The desks and tables were stacked at one end and upon them lay the prizes. Pride of place went to a large turkey, its snow-white head and scarlet wattles adding a festive touch. Ranged neatly on each side were chickens, pheasants and hares, and everyone agreed that it was a fine show.

The rickety card tables were packed closely together, the tortoise stove was red-hot, and there was a pervading odour of warm bodies and drying country clothes. Faces glistened with the heat, the unaccustomed concentration and the excitement of the chase after the dead game.

At half-time a halt was called for refreshments and the assembly drank coffee or tea from the thick white cups owned and loaned by Thrush Green Sunday School. Conversation was brisk as the brawn sandwiches and sausage rolls were munched, and Nelly Tilling, who dearly loved a whist drive, let her dark eye rove round the company.

Albert Piggott, she decided, was softening up nicely. He had protested against accompanying her to the whist drive, but she had persuaded him 'to look in' towards the end.

'Making me look a fool!' he had muttered audibly. 'What'll people say, seein' you hangin' round me day in and day out?'

'No more'n they're saying now,' retorted Mrs Tilling, with spirit. 'Let their tongues wag. What cause have you to bother?'

He had said no more. He was fast discovering that Nelly Tilling pursued her course very steadily, and it would need a cleverer man than he was to deflect her from it.

She was enjoying her evening. The cards had been in her favour, and already her score was high. With any luck she should carry home one of the plump birds before her. She appraised them with an experienced eye. The magnificent turkey apart, she decided that she would choose the brace of pheasants to the right of it if she were lucky enough to have the choice.

Meanwhile, with an eye to the future, she heaved her formidable bulk from the chair and made her way to Miss Watson's side.

The headmistress knew Mrs Tilling only slightly, but as she had been sitting alone she imagined that the plump widow had taken pity on her plight, and so was unusually welcoming.

'Terrible hot in here,' began Nelly, throwing off a small fur tippet but lately released from its moth-balls. 'I'd say that stove of yours draws too strong.'

'Indeed, not always,' responded Miss Watson. 'The wind has a lot to do with it. It must have gone round to the north, I think, to pull the stove up like that. Unless the caretaker has put too much on, of course.'

Mrs Tilling permitted herself a perturbed clucking noise.

'Need a lot of knowing, those stoves,' she replied. 'Want several trips a day really to see they're all right!' This was a master stroke as Nelly knew quite well that the present caretaker lived at Nidden and could only attend to the stove once a day. She was delighted to see a pang of anxiety cross Miss Watson's face.

'Can be real dangerous, you know,' she continued smugly, following up her attack. 'I knew a man once as was blown to smithereens by one of them things exploding. He was never the same again.'

'I can imagine it,' said the headmistress.

'And, of course, with children,' Nelly went on forcefully, 'you simply can't be too careful. Especially,' she added, as a happy touch, 'when they're not your own.' She spoke as though the sudden disintegration of one's own offspring could be borne comparatively lightly.

'Oh, I really don't think that would ever happen—' began Miss Watson, a shade doubtfully.

'How often does the caretaker get in?' asked Nelly, with assumed concern. 'I can see by the floors and the paint and that it can't be very often.'

Miss Watson bridled slightly, and Nelly wondered if she had gone too far. Best tackle it slowly, she told herself, if she wanted this job in a month or two.

'Mrs Cooke comes in for an hour or so every evening,' said Miss Watson with a touch of *hauteur*, 'and works very well.'

'Mrs Cooke?' queried Nelly, with wonder. 'Would that be Ada Cooke I was at school with? She used to be in service at Lady Field's place. Always worked well, I heard. Leastways she did before she had that row of children. Must tie her – can't do what you used to with a gaggle of kids under your feet, of course.'

Privately, Miss Watson wholeheartedly agreed with Mrs Tilling about Ada Cooke's decline in reliability, but wild horses would not have dragged agreement from her. She looked about her, hoping to catch sight of someone to whom she could retreat.

Nelly Tilling's dark eyes saw all and she shot her last arrow before her quarry escaped.

'It's a lovely job for her here, I must say. I fairly envy her and that's flat. Plenty of scrubbing and polishing is just what I can tackle to, as anyone'll tell you. I'd be proud to help you out, Miss Watson, should Ada ever be took bad.'

Miss Watson smiled graciously, murmured her thanks and fled to the other side of the room. Nelly, watching her agitation, was well content.

'Will you return to your tables, please?' shouted the rector, who was acting as Master of Ceremonies, above the clatter of cups.

The second half was about to begin.

The trouble started an hour later when the whist drive was over. The snow-white turkey had gone to a stranger who lived quite four miles away, Nelly Tilling, rejoicing, had collected the coveted pheasants and the rest of the prizes had been distributed, when the rector gave his customary little speech of thanks to all who had helped.

'You will all want to know how much this evening has brought in,' he added. 'I'm delighted to say that five pounds ten shillings and ninepence will be added to the Nathaniel Patten Memorial Fund.'

There were polite exclamations and a little clapping, but above this pleasant noise rose a belligerent voice. It belonged to Robert Potter, a pork butcher in Lulling, renowned not only for the excellence of his chipolata sausages but also for his fiery temper.

He was a formidable sight as he shoved back his chair with one huge red hand and faced the rector, his red face flaming above the bull neck.

'I'd like to know why the money's going to this Nathaniel Patten fund and not to the Children's Home as it always has done. Us folks in Lulling had no say in the matter.'

He thrust his face forward and shouted even more loudly.

'And what's more, I speak for plenty of others who don't hold with their money being grabbed by a lot of Thrush Green layabouts to spend. Nathaniel Patten's as much Lulling's property as Thrush Green's. We'd a right to be consulted at our end of the town.'

The rector surveyed his critic soberly. Inwardly he was shaken by this attack. Outwardly, he appeared unruffled. Not even the few cries of agreement which arose, somewhat sheepishly, from various quarters of the packed room, seemed to perturb him. When he spoke it was with quiet authority.

'I'm sorry to hear that there is this feeling about. The posters stated quite plainly that the proceeds would be devoted to the Memorial Fund. I can't help feeling that it would have been better to have spoken earlier about this disagreement.'

The rector's reasonable tone went a little way to calming Robert Potter's choler, but he still spoke truculently, and obviously relished the support of those who had voiced their resentment.

'Well, there it is! I don't hold with the money going to the Fund. Nathaniel Patten may have been a good man – I'm not saying he wasn't – but as a strong chapel-man I don't like to see a statue raised to a churchgoer when it's my money involved. Straight speaking never done no harm, they say, and that's what I'm doing now.'

There were cries of 'Hear, hear' and 'Good old Robert!' from a few men desirous of showing off before the women.

The rector suddenly found himself wishing that Harold Shoosmith were there. In the midst of his mental turmoil he was surprised to find how much he was coming to rely on the good sense of this new friend. But he was used to facing trouble alone and braced himself in the thick of parochial battle.

'I will report your objection to our committee, Mr Potter,' he answered courteously. 'Meanwhile, I suggest that we say our fare-wells in the spirit of goodwill which should be present at this time.'

He smiled cheerfully at his flock as they collected coats and hats, scarves and gloves and made for the door. There they were, the good meek sheep, the silly ones, and the one or two black ones. His eye caught sight of Robert Potter's thick red neck and he wished that he had a shepherd's crook in his hand to catch away that infectious member of his flock from the rest.

'I will have a word with you after the next committee meeting,' said the rector politely.

'Hmph!' grunted Robert Potter, and departed stiffly.

The next morning Mr Henstock looked in at the school again. A band of helpers was busy taking down the paper chains and the Chinese lanterns, and the village school was beginning to look more like itself again. In a day or two's time Mrs Cooke from Nidden would set about her scrubbing, her younger children left in charge of those of riper years.

The rector helped for a short while and then wandered into the playground. The blue smoke from a winter bonfire blew across from Harold Shoosmith's garden next door, and there, in the distance, he could see his friend vigorously forking garden rubbish on to the blaze.

Without more ado the rector made his way there and told Thrush Green's latest resident what had occurred the night before. Despite his light tone Harold Shoosmith noticed that the rector seemed worried. His response was heartening.

'Forget it until after Christmas. Ten to one it will all blow over. We can mention it at the next meeting in the New Year, but if my guess is correct there will be no more heard of Mr Potter's objec-tion.'

He bent down to collect a wet armful of dead leaves and branches, tossed them upon the bonfire, and sniffed happily.

'Smells wonderful, doesn't it?' he said to the rector. 'I've been looking forward to a great smoky winter bonfire for thirty years.'

'And I've been looking forward to a winter holiday somewhere abroad for about the same length of time,' confessed the rector. 'I suppose the truth of the matter is that we're none of us ever com-pletely satisfied.'

A woman's voice, calling shrilly from the house, caused them to turn their heads.

'That means coffee,' said Harold Shoosmith, giving a last loving poke to the fire with his fork. 'Betty will have one ready for you too, I'm sure.'

'It will be very welcome,' said the rector politely, following his host to the back door.

13. Christmas Eve

Dusk fell at tea-time on Christmas Eve at Thrush Green. There was an air of expectancy everywhere. The windows of St Andrew's church glowed with muted reds and blues against the black bulk of the ancient stones, for inside devoted ladies were putting last minute touches to the altar flowers and the holly wreath around the font.

Paul Young and his friend Christopher lay on their stomachs before the crackling log fire in the Youngs' drawing-room. They were engaged in fitting together a jigsaw puzzle, a task which Paul's mother had vainly hoped might prove a sedative in the midst of mounting excitement. They were alone in the room and their conversation ran along the boastful lines usual to little boys of their age.

'I never did believe in Father Christmas,' asserted Christopher, grabbing a fistful of jigsaw pieces which Paul had zealously collected.

'Here!' protested Paul, outraged. 'They're all my straight-edged bits!'

'Who's doing this?' demanded Christopher belligerently. 'I'm a visitor, aren't I? You should give me first pick.'

There was a slight tussle. Christopher twisted Paul's arm in a business-like way until he broke free. Panting, Paul returned to the subject of Father Christmas.

'I bet you did believe in him! I just bet you did! I bet you *went on* believing in Father Christmas until I told you. So there! Why, I knew when I was four!'

'So what? I bet you still hang up your stocking!' bellowed Christopher triumphantly. Paul's crimson face told him that he had scored a hit.

'So do you,' retorted the younger boy, not attempting to deny the charge. They fell again into a delicious bear-hug, rolling and scuffling upon the hearthrug, and finally wrecking the beginnings of the jigsaw puzzle which had been so painstakingly fitted together.

The sound of carol singing made them both sit up. Dishevelled, breathless, tingling with exercise and the anticipation of Christmas joys, they rushed into the hall.

The carol singers were a respectable crowd of adult inhabitants of Thrush Green, all known to the boys. So far this year the only carol singers had been one or two small children, piping like winter robins at the doors of the larger houses on Thrush Green for a few brief minutes, and then dissolving into giggles while the boldest of them hammered on the knocker.

The boys watched entranced as the carol singers formed a tidy crescent round the doorstep. Some held torches, and the tall boy who had written on the blackboard at the meeting to decide about the memorial, supported a hurricane lamp at the end of a stout hazel pole. It swung gently as he moved and was far more decorative in the winter darkness, as it glowed with a soft amber light, than the more efficient torches of his neighbours.

Joan Young opened the front door hospitably, the better to hear the singing, and the choir master tapped his tuning fork against the edge of the door, hummed the note resonantly to his attentive choir, and off they went robustly into the first bars of 'It came upon the midnight clear'.

Their breath rolled from their tuneful mouths in great silver clouds, wreathing about their heads and the sheets of music clenched in their gloved hands. In the distance the bells of Lulling Church could be faintly heard, as the singers paused for breath.

The smell of damp earth floated into the hall, and a dead leaf scurried about the doorstep adding its whispers to the joyful full-throated chorus above it. The bare winter trees in the garden lifted their arms to the stars above, straining, it seemed to young Paul, to reach as high as St Andrew's steeple.

The boys gazed enraptured, differences forgotten, strangely moved by this manifestation of praise. It seemed to be shared by everything that had life.

★

A mile away, Doctor Lovell's wife Ruth roamed their small sitting-room restlessly. Her husband was tinkering with the car in the nearby garage, and she wondered whether she should call him or not.

She felt extraordinarily shaky and rather light-headed. The baby was not due for another week, but babies do not wait upon their coming, as Ruth as a doctor's wife well knew. She leant upon the mantelshelf and ran her mind over the preparations she had made.

Everything awaited the baby upstairs. One of the Lulling doctors, an old friend called Tony Harding, was to attend her, and her daily help had promised to live in for a fortnight when the birth took place. Her sister Joan would be with her much of the time and keep an eye on the house-keeping.

Luckily, she remembered, she had stuffed the turkey and had prepared a delectable trifle. The cupboard was crammed with food, the beds had been changed, the laundry awaited collection, the flowers were fresh and the house had been garnished especially well for the Christmas festival.

Ruth heaved a sigh of relief. She could afford to forget her household cares and think of this momentous happening after so many weeks of weary waiting.

A particularly vicious spasm gripped her, and when it passed the girl made her way to the window and opened it. The cool night air lifted the fair hair from her hot forehead. The faint sound of Christmas bells floated from afar on the refreshing breeze.

'John!' called Ruth, 'I think you'd better fetch Tony Harding.'

A small black car, rather shabby and sagging a little at the springs, was drawn up outside Albert Piggott's cottage. It had travelled a long way throughout the short winter day.

Inside the house, Ben Curdle and his wife Molly, sat at table with Mr Piggott eating fried bacon and eggs cooked by Molly. Upstairs, in the room which had been her bedroom, her small son slept in a drawer pulled out from the chest, and stowed neatly on the floor at the foot of his parents' bed.

Molly's eyes took in the shining stove, the clean walls, the scrubbed brick floor and the scoured sink. It was quite apparent to her that a woman had been at work, and one who knew her job well. Her father had been grudgingly welcoming an hour ago, but had made no mention of anyone helping him in the house. She looked across the tablecloth at him, munching as morosely as ever.

'Place looks nice, dad,' she said.

'Ah! I does what I can,' said Albert, never raising his eyes from his plate.

'What about your cooking?' enquired his daughter.

'I gets by,' said Albert flatly. Molly caught her husband's twinkling eye upon her, and winked mischievously.

'I've brought a chicken ready for the oven,' said Molly, 'so you'll have a good meal tomorrow. How's the stove drawing these days? D'you ever sweep the flues?'

'Now and again,' answered Albert, polishing his plate slowly with a piece of bread guided by a grubby forefinger. 'I got me own work, you know. That church don't get no smaller.'

Ben shifted his long legs and spoke.

'I went over to have a look at Gran's grave when we arrived. Looks a bit neglected. Don't no one ever see to it?'

Albert Piggott grunted.

'Can't get it all done by myself,' he muttered.

'I'll tidy it up tomorrow,' said Ben steadily. 'That's not right to see the old lady under half a peck of hay. Not seemly, to my way of thinking. Who's responsible for the graves then?'

'Those as want regular clipping, and the plants on 'em tended proper, pays me a bit extra,' said Albert. He put the piece of bread in his mouth and chewed it noisily. Ben watched him levelly.

'I'll see you're paid,' he said quietly.

Molly seemed about to speak, but a rapping on the door checked her. As they looked up, startled by the noise, the door opened and Nelly Tilling's face, rosy and arch, peered round it.

'Oh my law! You 'ere again?' said Albert Piggott, with a groan.

Construing this ejaculation as a welcome, the stout widow came into the room, closed the door behind her, and dumped a laden basket on the table.

'There!' she panted breathlessly. 'Your Christmas dinner, Albert dear!'

Molly drew in a sharp breath. So this was the answer to her secret questioning! This was the mysterious scourer and scrubber, the cook and companion! And just how far had this gone? Molly asked herself with unreasoning fury. Before she could speak, Ben put a large brown hand over hers and pressed it warningly. Molly held her tongue, and waited, as quietly as Ben, to see how her father would respond.

A dusky flush had crept over his unlovely features and his jaw dropped. To say that Nelly Tilling had taken the wind out of his sails was to put it lightly. He was staggered at her effrontery. He had made quite sure that she knew she would not be wanted while his daughter stayed in the house, and this was open defiance. But what could a chap do, he asked himself, when a woman set her cap at him so boldly and brought a square meal with her into the bargain? He took refuge in truculence.

'We ain't that short of food, Mrs Tilling,' he answered gruffly. 'Don't know what brought you on this errand, I'm sure.'

Nelly Tilling's dark eyes flashed dangerously.

'Ho ho!' she said, bridling. 'Very hoity-toity, some of us, aren't we? And since when 'ave I been Mrs Tilling to you, Albert Piggott? It's been Nelly all right these last few weeks while I've been cleaning up this pigsty for you.'

She hoisted the basket to her arm again belligerently.

'Seeing as I've had this flung back in my face I may as well leave you for good,' she continued. 'Leave you to your swilling and swearing and the filthy ways you was used to before I put you straight!' She paused to get her breath, her ample bosom rising and falling violently beneath her tightly-buttoned coat.

Suddenly Molly felt sorry for her. It must have taken her hours to prepare all the good things that she could glimpse under the snowy cloth which covered the basket. And she had trudged all the way from Lulling Woods carrying that weight, thought Molly, for what thanks! She found that all her old disgust at her father's mean ways was returning fast. First his behaviour in the matter of old Mrs Curdle's grave, and now this betrayal of Nelly Tilling's kindness, inflamed Molly's sense of fitness. She rose from the table and took the infuriated widow's arm.

'You come and sit down, Mrs Tilling,' she said gently. 'I think it was real nice of you to think of Dad at Christmas-time. We're just making a pot of tea, so have some with us.'

Somewhat mollified, Nelly sat down on a chair by the door, her basket by her feet. Albert, dumbfounded by this unexpected alliance against himself, decided to retreat.

'Want somethin' a bit stronger, lad?' he asked Ben, hoping in this way to assert his independence before Nelly and Molly, before taking flight.

'If you like,' said Ben politely.

'Come on next door then,' said Albert, rising hastily from the table.

He was past Nelly and through the door in half a minute. Nelly looked grimly down her nose, her massive arms folded upon her chest.

Ben paused by her chair and touched a large shoulder gently. He smiled at her, his eyes crinkling in the way which had so charmed his wife. Nelly looked less grim.

'I'll look after him for you,' said Ben gently, and was rewarded with Nelly's grateful smile.

There was silence for a short time in the little room, broken only by the singing of the kettle on the shining hob. Then Molly said shyly:

'Thank you for looking after my dad. He's not much of a hand at housework and all that.'

Nelly permitted herself a gusty sigh.

'That he ain't,' she said honestly. 'Don't go thinking too much of this, Molly. I've only been acting neighbourly, and it fair cut me to the quick to see him so short with me just now. More than 'uman flesh and blood can stand, it was.'

'He's a bit awkward,' confessed Molly, in sublime understatement. 'The place looks beautiful. I could see someone who knew what she was doing had been at it.'

Nelly gave a gratified smirk and accepted her tea graciously. She loosened her coat and prepared to enjoy this tête-à-tête. After ten minutes' polite conversation she rose to go, and Molly decided that now was the time to show Nelly that she was her friend.

'Would you like to see my baby?' she asked.

'I'd love to,' said the widow, following Molly up the narrow stairs so recently brushed down by her own sturdy hand.

The baby lay deep in slumber, his eyes screwed tightly shut and his small mottled fists clenched each side of his mop of black hair. Nelly clucked maternally.

'Eh, what a little love!' she wheezed rapturously, after the steep ascent. 'Don't he favour his dad? You're a lucky girl, I must say.'

She rummaged in her handbag, drew out half a crown and slipped it gently beneath the sleeping child's small fingers.

'Oh no!' protested Molly.

'Ah yes,' said Nelly firmly. 'It'll bring me good luck to cross your baby's hand with silver. And, believe me, I can do with it!'

She made her way on tiptoe to the door and descended the narrow stairs, followed by Molly.

'I'll leave the basket,' she said, as she stood in the doorway outlined against the darkness of Thrush Green. 'Use what you want, and I hope you'll all have a very happy Christmas.'

'But won't you come and join us for dinner?' asked Molly, now genuinely fond of Nelly after her appreciation of the baby.

'No, dear,' said Nellie firmly. 'It's real nice of you, but Christmas is a family time.'

She turned and made her way into the darkness.

'I'll be seeing Albert afterwards,' she said, and in her tone was something which brooked no good for that backslider.

It seemed to Molly, as she closed the door, that her father had met his match in more ways than one.

Ella and Dimity were spending the evening by the fire. Both women were tired with the bustle of the day. Dimity had made one trip to Lulling in the morning, only to find, on her return, that she had forgotten several urgent articles needed during the Christmas holiday, which meant another journey down the steep hill and up again, during the afternoon.

She was touched by Ella's offer to make the second trip, but had refused, for dear Ella had been very busy delivering Christmas presents of her own making to nearby friends.

Now they sat comfortably enjoying the peace after the storm. Ella smoked one of her rank shaggy cigarettes, her sturdy brogues propped up on a string stool, while Dimity knitted placidly a matinée coat for Ruth Lovell's coming baby. Upstairs, carefully packed in one of Thatcher's dress boxes was a thick ribbed cardigan for Ella's Christmas present, only finished just in time, for Dimity had been obliged to work at it only in Ella's absence from the room, as she intended it to be a surprise.

Ella, too, had packed a garment in one of Thatcher's boxes for Dimity's Christmas present, but it was not of her own making. She had bought a soft fluffy blue dressing-gown for her friend on one of her trips to London. Too long, she decided, had Dimity wrapped her thin form in a shabby grey flannel garment which she admitted to buying long before the war. Since Ella's heart-searching, by the Cotswold stone wall on her lonely walk, she had done her best to be less selfish, and it had not gone unnoticed.

'I thought we'd have eggs for supper,' said Dimity, letting the knitting fall into her lap. 'Boiled or scrambled, Ella dear?'

'Boiled,' replied Ella. 'Less bother. No filthy saucepan to clean up either.'

Dimity began to wind the wool round the needles, but Ella got up before her.

'You stay here, Dim. You look a bit done up. I can do boiled eggs easily enough.'

'Oh, Ella, you're much too kind! You're tired yourself!'

'But I'm not going to early service tomorrow, don't forget.'

'I feel I must,' said Dimity, clasping her thin hands earnestly. 'The rector does so like to have a full church at early service. Harold's going I know.'

Ella stubbed out her cigarette violently. She seemed embarrassed at the mention of their new friend's name, thought Dimity, somewhat bewildered.

'He's a good chap,' said Ella gruffly, and stumped towards the kitchen.

Left alone, listening to the crashing of saucepans from the kitchen, Dimity pondered on Ella's generous heart. She had been even more thoughtful lately, she told herself – more gentle, more sympathetic. She remembered Ella's unusual embarrassment when she had spoken of Harold Shoosmith. They said that love often had a mellowing influence, and certainly Ella had always thought highly of the newcomer. Could Ella's recent gentleness have anything to do with affection for their handsome friend? asked Dimity in wonderment.

Darkness thickened over Lulling and Thrush Green. The Christmas tree twinkled and blazed in the market square dwarfing the stars above to insignificance.

Excited children for once went willingly to bed, stockings clutched in their rapacious hands and heads whirling with delirious thoughts of joys to come. Exhausted shop assistants sat at home soaking their aching feet in warm water. The patients in Lulling Cottage Hospital thought of the long gruelling day ahead, complete with boisterous surgeons carving turkeys, paper hats, hearty nurses singing carols and all the other overwhelming paraphernalia of Christmas in the wards, and they shuddered or smiled according to temperament. House-wives, flopping wearily in armchairs, congratulated themselves upon remembering the decorations for the trifle, the cherry sticks for the drinks and other last minute details until they were brought up short by the horrid thought that in the pressure of so much unaccustomed shopping they had completely forgotten salt and tea, and now it was too late anyway.

But away from the lights and worries of the town the quiet hills lay beneath a velvety sky. No wind rustled the trees and no bird disturbed the night's tranquillity. Sheep still roamed the slopes as they had that memorable night so long ago in Palestine, and low on the horizon a great star, bright as a jewel, still held out an eternal promise to mankind.

14. Christmas Day

'It might almost be September instead of Christmas Day,' exclaimed Dimity, as they walked down their garden path on the way to the Baileys' house. 'Look, Ella, there are still some marigolds out!'

It was certainly mild, and the midday sun had a slight warmth. Ella snuffed up the fresh air like an old war-horse and nodded her shaggy locks with approval.

'Something to be thankful for, anyway,' she responded. 'I can't say I relish these Dickensian Christmases with snow up to your knees and a lot of wild skating parties. Far more likely to make a full churchyard, they are, than a nice seasonable green Christmas – whatever old Piggott may say!'

Winnie Bailey was at her door to meet them.

'Happy Christmas,' she said. 'You're the first to arrive. It's just an *elderly* party. And a very small one.'

It was a punctual one too, for Ella and Dimity had only just greeted the doctor when Dotty Harmer, the rector and Harold

Shoosmith arrived together. The doctor dispensed drinks and the chatter began.

'Doctor Lovell rang up a few minutes ago,' confided Winnie to Ella quietly. 'The baby is due to arrive today.'

'Bad luck,' said Ella. Winnie Bailey's eyebrows rose.

'Only because it will have its birthday on Christmas Day,' explained Ella hastily. 'Always tough on children, I think. Who's with her?'

'Joan, and the daily, and young Lovell's mopping and mowing about, I gather. Mrs Burridge, the aunt who stayed here during the war, was going to come, but decided she couldn't. Do you remember her?'

'Do I not!' said Ella explosively. 'I'm not a womanly woman, as well you know, but the way that cat used to leap to her feet when Dim and I came into the room, and then guide us solicitously to the nearest chair as though we were senile, used to make my blood boil. She must have been a good ten years older than we were anyway!' Ella's normally rosy face had turned quite purple with wrath at the memory.

'Even Donald admitted that she was the embodiment of malice,' agreed Winnie calmly. She became conscious of the rector's mild eye turning upon her, as he overheard this remark, and went over to speak to him. Dimity and Harold were at the window watching the world of Thrush Green taking the air in readiness for Christmas dinner. They appeared happily engrossed and Ella, turning from the sight abruptly, found Dotty Harmer at her elbow. She seemed agitated.

'I don't want to be too long,' she whispered to Ella. 'I've left a pumpkin pie in the oven. It's an American dish – I had an American cookery book given to me some time ago and I thought I'd like to try something rather different for Christmas Day.'

'If it's anything like marrow,' said Ella firmly, 'you're welcome.'

'It's a great delicacy,' insisted Dotty. 'The Americans have it on Thanksgiving Day, I gather. Though why they should want to give thanks for losing touch with their mother country, I never could imagine,' added Dotty, with a touch of *hauteur*. 'My father always referred to what the Americans call "The War of Independence" as "The American Rebellion". The new headmaster was quite unpleasant about it, and he and Father had words, I remember.'

'Ah well,' replied Ella, in a conciliatory tone, 'it all happened a long time ago, and the Americans seem to be struggling along quite nicely without us. Can't expect your children to cluster round your knee for ever, you know.'

Dotty did not appear completely persuaded by this philosophy, but allowed Doctor Bailey to take her glass to be refilled, and then fluttered after him to change her mind. Ella remained alone on the sofa and all her old unhappiness suddenly flooded over her.

To all appearances this annual sherry party was like all the others. There was the blue and white bowl filled with Roman hyacinths and sprigs of red-berried holly. There was Winnie, as pink and white and gay as ever, wearing the deep blue suit that she had worn last year. And, she supposed, she herself presented the same tough leathery aspect that she always did.

But what a change had occurred in the last year! What a cataclysm had gone on in her heart! Nothing was the same, nothing was stable. Life had been turned topsy-turvy, and turmoil and conjecture tossed her to and fro. She looked again at the serene room, her old friends, and the placid indifferent countenance of Thrush Green through the window, and Ella could have howled like a dog with abject misery at the hopelessness of ever trying to explain how different all her loved and little world was to her this Christmas Day.

At half-past one, in Albert Piggott's cottage, Molly was washing up the débris of the Christmas feast. Her father and Ben were accustomed to taking their main meal of the day at twelve o'clock for they were early risers, and Molly too had risen soon after six after feeding her baby.

Ben wiped up vigorously, and his father-in-law leant in the doorway considerably impeding the progress. Occasionally Ben thrust a piece of crockery into his unwilling hands for him to put away in the cupboard. Conversation was carried on above the clatter at the sink and the cries of young George above who was impatiently awaiting his two o'clock feed. The child had been named after Ben's father, the favourite child of old Mrs Curdle, who had lost his life in the war. Doctor Bailey, to whom Molly had proudly shown her son that morning, maintained that he was the image of that baby he had delivered almost fifty years before.

'We'll leave you in peace this afternoon,' said Molly. 'Ted and Bessie Allen want to see the baby and we'll be there till they open the pub at six.'

'No need to hurry back on my account,' answered Albert sourly, squinting at a glass mug, in an unlovely way, to see if Ben had polished it sufficiently.

'Must be back by then,' said Molly firmly, 'to put George to bed. But if you want to go out – to see Nelly Tilling, say – don't wait about for us.'

It was pure mischief that had prompted Molly to speak of the widow, and Albert rose swiftly to the bait.

'Don't go getting ideas in your head about Nelly Tilling,' he growled. 'She be a rare one for chasing the men, as I've no doubt you knows well enough. She ain't 'ad no encouragement from me, that I can say.'

'More fool you,' said Ben cheerfully. 'You'd be lucky to get her. Look after you well, she would.'

'Too dam' well,' grunted Albert. 'Never let a chap forget 'e signed the pledge before his mother's milk 'ad dried on 'is lips.' He sniffed noisily. 'I 'opes I've got more sense than to put me 'ead in that noose!'

'Well, it seems to be expected,' said Molly lightly. 'Miss Watson asked me about her when I took the baby past her house this morning.'

'Miss Watson? That old faggot?' shouted Albert, shaken to his marrow. 'What call 'as she got to go linking Nelly Tilling and me?' He breathed heavily for a minute.

'She ain't never been right since she got hit on the head a month or two back,' he continued. 'Must've left her a bit dotty.'

'First I've heard of it,' said Ben. 'What happened?'

Albert gave a garbled account of the robbery at the school-house in the autumn.

'And the police,' he said, banging his hand on the dresser for emphasis, 'is fair scuppered. As a matter o' fact, I'm on the look-out for the chap meself.'

'Well, I hope you find him,' said Molly, undoing her apron. 'Poor old soul! Fancy hurting an old lady like Miss Watson! Why, she must be over fifty!'

Albert looked at himself in the kitchen mirror, and smirked.

'That ain't so old,' he said, with unusual jauntiness, brushing his damp mouth with the back of his hand. He caught the eye of his son-in-law and gave a watery wink.

Miss Watson, happily ignorant of the furore she had caused, was sitting snugly in the schoolhouse parlour, spending her Christmas afternoon in writing letters of thanks.

She was engaged in giving a long account of the morning's service at St Andrew's to Miss Fogerty whose Christmas holiday was being spent with an octogenarian aunt at Tunbridge Wells.

'The church,' wrote Miss Watson in her precise copperplate, 'looked lovely, decorated with holly, red and white carnations and Christmas roses on the altar. You would have enjoyed the singing, and the rector's sermon was very fine, on the theme of generosity. Very much to the point, I thought, in a community like Thrush Green, where back-biting does occur, as we know only too well. It made me feel that I really must try and *forgive*, even if I cannot *forget*, that wretched man who attacked me.'

Miss Watson put down her pen for a moment and gazed thoughtfully out upon Thrush Green. The room was tranquil, and she was enjoying her holiday solitude. Now that she had time to collect her thoughts Miss Watson had gone carefully over and over the incidents of that terrifying night, but further clues escaped her. From the first she had felt that her attacker was someone that she knew. In the weeks that followed she scrutinized the men of Lulling and Thrush Green to no avail. But she had not, and would not, give up hope. One day, she felt certain, she would recognize the brute and he would be brought to justice.

The winter sun was beginning to turn to a red ball, low on the horizon. Above it, long grey clouds, like feathered arrows, strained across the clear ice-blue sky. Somewhere a blackbird sang, as though it were a spring day, and Miss Watson, suddenly finding the room stuffy, opened her window the better to hear it.

A family passed near by, crossing the green, no doubt bent upon taking tea with relatives. That indefinable Christmas afternoon atmosphere, compounded of cigar smoke, best clothes and new possessions crept upon Miss Watson's senses, as she watched the father bending down to guide the erratic course of his young son's new red tricycle. Screaming with annoyance, the child beat backwards at his father's restraining hand. The mother's protests, shrill and tired, floated across the grass to the open window.

'There are times,' said Miss Watson smugly to the cat, 'when an old maid has the best of it.' And she turned, with a happy sigh, to her interrupted letter-writing.

While Miss Watson finished her letter and her neighbours slept or walked off the effects of their Christmas feasting, Ruth Lovell looked, for the first time, upon her daughter.

She weighed seven pounds and two ounces, had a tiny bright pink face mottled like brawn, and from each tightly-shut eye there protruded four short light eyelashes. But to Ruth, to whom good looks meant a great deal, the most alarming thing was the shape of her daughter's head, which rose to a completely bald pointed dome.

'Will she always look like this?' asked Ruth weakly of Tony Harding, who was busy packing his bag neatly. She did not like to seem ungrateful for his ministrations, but she was beginning to wonder, in the daze that surrounded her, whether he had not helped her give birth to a monster.

'Heavens, no!' was the brisk reply. 'That head will have gone down in a day or two. Believe me, you're going to have a very pretty little girl.'

Ruth smiled with relief and settled the baby more comfortably in her arms.

'It was too bad of me to bring you out on Christmas Day,' she said apologetically. 'I'm terribly sorry.'

'Think nothing of it,' replied the doctor, straightening up. 'All in the day's work.'

He made for the door.

'There's a very good precedent, you know,' he said cheerfully, and vanished.

The red sun had dropped behind the folds of the Cotswolds, and the short winter day was done by the time Albert Piggott shuffled across to St Andrew's to ring the bell for evensong.

Two or three bicycles were already propped against the railings, and a figure moved hastily away from them as Albert approached.

'Who's that?' asked Albert, switching on a failing torch. By its pallid light he recognized Sam Curdle.

'Bike fell over. Just proppin' it up,' volunteered Sam, a shade too glibly. Albert looked at him with dislike and suspicion. He wouldn't mind betting Sam had been looking in the baskets and the saddlebags for any pickings, but as far as he could see the fellow held nothing in his hands. Albert grunted disbelievingly.

'Got yer cousin staying at my place,' he said at last. Sam did not appear delighted.

'Don't mean nothing to me,' he said spitefully. 'Ben and me never had no time for each other. He can go to the devil for all I care.'

'Well, that's your business,' said Albert, shuffling on again. 'I'll say good night to you.'

'Good night,' replied Sam shortly, and set off in the direction of Nidden. Albert, pausing on the church path, looked after his disappearing figure. A growing conviction shook his bent frame with excitement.

'If that fellow didn't do poor old Miss Watson,' thought Albert to himself, 'I'll eat my hat!'

And taking that greasy object from his bald head, he entered the church and made his way towards the belfry and his duty, highly elated.

PART THREE

THE NEW YEAR

---

15. A Bitter Journey

On New Year's Day the rector and Harold Shoosmith set out on a long journey.

Four letters and a telegram, with a prepaid answer, had all failed to elicit any reply from Nathaniel Patten's grandson. His address had been found with the help of many people, and it appeared that William Mulloy lived in a remote hamlet in Pembrokeshire.

'The only thing to do,' Harold said, 'is to call on the fellow and try to get some answer from him. We'll stay the night somewhere. It's a longish drive and we may as well do it comfortably.'

After a few demurrings on the part of the conscientious rector, who had various meetings to rearrange in order to leave his parish for two days, the two men had decided that the first day of the New Year, which fell on a Friday, would suit them both admirably.

It had turned much colder. An easterly wind whipped the last few leaves from the hedges, and dried the puddles which had lain so long about Thrush Green. People went about their outdoor affairs with their coat collars turned up and their heads muffled in warm scarves. Gardeners found that digging in the cruel wind touched up forgotten rheumatism, and children began to complain of ear-ache. In Lulling the chemist displayed a choice selection of cough mixtures and throat lozenges. Winter, it seemed, was beginning in earnest.

The two men breakfasted very early, Harold Shoosmith in his warm kitchen on eggs and bacon, and the rector walking about his bleak house with a piece of bread and marmalade in his hand, as he did his simple packing. It had seemed selfish to expect his housekeeper to rise so early, and she had not suggested it. She wished him a pleasant journey before retiring for the night and said she would take the opportunity of washing the chair covers in his absence. With this small crumb of comfort the rector had to be content.

He felt rising excitement as he crossed Thrush Green from his gaunt vicarage to the corner house. The Reverend Charles Henstock had few pleasures, and an outing to Wales, albeit in January and in the teeth of a fierce easterly wind, was something to relish. It was still fairly dark, only a slight lightening of the sky in the east giving a hint of the coming dawn. One or two of the houses around the green showed a lighted window as early risers stumbled sleepily about their establishments.

The dignified old Daimler waited in the road outside Harold's gate. Its owner was busy wrapping chains in a piece of dingy blanket, and stowing them in the boot.

'Just in case we meet icy roads,' said Harold, in answer to the rector's query, and Charles Henstock marvelled at such wise foresight.

The car was warm and comfortable. After talking for the first few miles the two settled down into companionable silence, and the rector found himself nodding into a doze. He was happy and relaxed, pleased to be with such a good friend, and relieved to leave Thrush Green and its cares behind him for two days. He slumbered peacefully as the car rolled steadily westward.

Harold Shoosmith was glad to see him at rest. Nothing had come of the protest at the Fur and Feather Whist Drive, and it had been generally decided to press on with the arrangements for the memorial. But the rector had worried about it considerably, Harold Shoosmith knew. To his mind, the rector had a pretty thin time of it, and if he himself had ever been saddled with the sort of housekeeper Charles endured he would have sent her packing in double-quick time, he told himself. There were some men who were born to be married, and who were but half-men without the comfort of married estate. The good rector, he realized, was one of them, and he fell to speculating about a possible match for his unconscious friend. It would seem, as he reviewed the charms of the unattached ladies of distant Thrush Green, that the rector's chances were slight, thought Harold unchivalrously.

He braked suddenly to avoid a swerving cyclist and his companion woke with a start.

'Good heavens! I must have dropped off,' exclaimed the rector, passing a hand over his chubby face as if to brush away the veils of illicit sleep. 'Where are we?'

'Just running into Evesham,' replied Harold. 'You finish your kip.'

'No, no indeed,' protested the rector, yawning widely. 'I'm not in the least tired.'

He straightened himself and watched the neat bare orchards roll by. The sky above was an ominous dark grey and a wicked wind caught the side of the car now and again, making it shudder off its course. By the time they reached Hereford heavy rain, pitilessly cold, swept the streets, and here they stopped for lunch.

'A real beast of a day,' commented Harold, as they waited for their mutton chops. Through the window of the hotel they watched the rain spinning like silver coins on the black shiny road. 'But as long as it rains it won't snow,' he continued. 'I've a feeling we'll see plenty of that later on this winter.'

'I'm no weather prophet,' confessed Charles Henstock, 'but Piggott says we're in for several weeks of it. I hope he's wrong.'

'Piggott's a gloomy ass,' said Harold. 'Never so happy as when he's miserable, as they say. I shouldn't take his prognostications too seriously.'

'He's often right about the weather though,' said the rector, rubbing his cold hands. He held them to the meagre warmth of the one-bar electric fire with which the hotel hospitably welcomed its visitors to a lofty dark dining-room of tomb-like chill. Three paper roses in a tall glass vase, one pink, one red and one yellow, decorated each table, standing squarely in the middle of the frosty white tablecloth.

'Make the most of the place, don't they?' commented Harold ironically, surveying the scene.

'It looks very clean,' ventured the rector charitably, and indeed, used as he was to bleak surroundings, his present circumstances seemed comparatively cosy.

Luckily, the soup was hot and the mutton chops succulent, and the two friends continued on their journey much refreshed. Soon they were among the dark Welsh mountains, whose majesty was veiled in curtains of rain.

'We shouldn't have much trouble in finding a room tonight,' said Harold, driving through a water splash that covered the windscreen momentarily. 'There won't be many people out in this lot.'

'I hope Piggott will keep the stoves well stoked,' said the rector, his thoughts turning again to Thrush Green. 'It's choir practice to-night, and there are so many colds about.'

'What's a cold here and there?' asked Harold robustly, stopping at a level crossing.

'I always think my poor wife died of a neglected cold,' mused the rector, as though to himself.

'I'm sorry,' said Harold, chiding himself. There was silence in the car. In the distance a faint whistle told of the approach of the train. 'You must miss her very much,' went on Harold, trying to make amends.

The rattling of the train across their path prevented any response. The great gates were swung back by a fat little Welshman with a wet coat draped over his head and shoulders and the car moved over the rails to continue its journey.

'I miss her more than I can say,' said the rector at last. He looked sadly at the road before him, but his friend had the impression that he was glad to talk of this matter which he had kept to himself for so long. He made a sympathetic noise, but no verbal comment.

'It's a strange thing,' continued the rector, 'that one doesn't remember how the dead looked during the last months of their life. When I think of Helen it is always as a young woman.'

His voice grew more animated.

'She was so gay. She sang, you know, about the house. And she made it so cheerful with flowers and fires. We had a little cat too, but Mrs Butler doesn't like animals, and when it died I thought it best not to get a kitten.' His voice died away, and they drove for almost a mile before he spoke again.

'Somehow the house too seems dead now,' he added, almost apologetically.

'If you don't mind my saying so,' said Harold, 'you'd be better off without that housekeeper of yours.'

'Mrs Butler?' asked the rector, astonished. 'I really think she does her best for me. Why, she's even taking the opportunity of washing the chair covers in my absence.'

'That's as may be,' said Harold stubbornly. 'She does a bit, I dare say, but she could do a lot more. You never have a decent fire, for one thing, and it's my belief she skimps on the cooking.'

Such plain speaking rendered the rector temporarily dumb. But on turning over the words in his mind, he admitted to himself that there was a great deal of truth in them.

'But what can I do?' asked the rector pathetically. 'If I complain, she'll go, and it really is an appalling job to get anyone else suitable. I shudder when I think of some of the applicants I interviewed. There was the young woman with pink hair –' He stopped, arrested by the memory.

'Don't I know,' sympathized Harold. 'I've had it too, don't forget. Enough to make me think of marrying, it was at times,' he said lightly. 'And I'm not a marrying man, I fear.'

The words were said so cheerfully and in such a matter-of-fact tone that their full impact did not dawn on the rector for some minutes. But later he was surprised at the warm glow of delight that suffused him. Could it be possible that his friend had no matrimonial designs upon any one of the ladies of Thrush Green whose hearts he had so pleasurably fluttered since his advent?

'Some are the marrying sort, and some not,' continued Harold, looking at three small children fighting in a village street. 'Frankly, I would say that you are.'

'I think you may be right,' agreed the rector, in a small voice. 'But I've very little to offer a woman.'

'Don't come that modest-martyr stuff over me,' implored Harold. 'You think about it. That's my advice. And think about sacking Mrs Butler too, or at least tell her to pull her socks up.'

'I really don't think I'm equal to it,' confessed the rector. But whether he was referring to his hopes of matrimony, or the dismissal of his housekeeper, no one could say.

They stayed the night in a small Pembrokeshire town within a few miles of their quarry.

'How did you sleep?' asked the rector, at breakfast the next morning.

'Apart from some Welsh-speaking plumbing that was woven around the room, I heard nothing at all,' said Harold. 'I feel ready for the hunt. One thing, the rain's stopped.'

It was true, but the sky still had a steely greyness about it, which boded no good, and the wind still blew evilly from the east. The dining-room, however, was a little more comfortable than the one in which they had lunched, and two electric bars warmed a smaller room, there was a modest carpet and a real fern on an intricately carved stand in the window. Two moth-eaten heads of deer graced the wall above the marble mantelpiece, and the rector, who abhorred blood sports, averted his gaze from the glassy eyes above him.

By ten o'clock they were approaching the little hamlet where they hoped to find William Mulloy. The rector looked forward to the meeting with interest, but Harold Shoosmith felt considerable excitement at the thought of coming face to face with the grandson of the man he had esteemed for so long. Would there be any facial resemblance, he wondered, as the Daimler threaded its way in a gingerly manner down a narrow rough lane? He had been looking out ancient photographs and the copy of a portrait of Nathaniel for the proposed sculptor's benefit, and he had become very fond of the plump Pickwickian countenance of the good old missionary.

'We should be there,' observed the rector, looking about him. 'We've taken the left-hand fork and gone about a quarter of a mile. Now, where is the pair of cottages?'

They stopped the car, studying the rough sketch map that the waiter at the hotel had given them. The bare fields stretched away on each side, and from the tussocky bank near by a thrush whistled, surveying them with a bright inquisitive eye.

A small girl with a very dirty face appeared suddenly in the lane. She was carrying an empty milk bottle.

'Could you tell us where Mr William Mulloy lives?' asked Harold politely.

'Behind the trees,' answered the child, in a sweet sing-song, nodding to a clump near by. Now that their attention was directed there, the two men saw a wisp of smoke rising from a hidden chimney.

'Thank you very much,' said Harold, preparing to get out of the car. The child smiled and continued her journey towards the larger road, still clutching the milk bottle.

'I suppose the milkman leaves milk at the top of the lane,' said the rector, genuinely interested in these domestic arrangements. 'This lane must peter out eventually. What a deserted sort of place.'

They collected the few papers about the proposed memorial from the back of the car and made their way on foot to the cottage. It was one of a pair, both ramshackle in appearance, with every window tightly closed. Harold knocked at the front door with some difficulty, for the knocker was rusty and was stiffly encrusted with ancient paint.

There was a sound of footsteps, then a bolt was drawn back, and a struggle began within to tug the door from its fast-clinging frame. At last a breathless voice called to them:

'Step round to the back, will you? The door's stuck.'

Obediently the two men traversed a narrow concrete path which skirted the house so closely that Harold had difficulty in remaining upon it.

At the back door waited a small pale woman with hollow cheeks. She wore an overall and a pair of fawn carpet slippers.

'Are you from the insurance?' she asked. She spoke with a strong Welsh accent and looked alarmed.

'Indeed, no,' said Harold reassuringly.

'We're looking for Mr Mulloy,' said the rector gently. 'Are you, by any chance, Mrs Mulloy?'

'Well yes,' said the woman doubtfully. 'In a manner of speaking, I am.'

'That's splendid,' said Harold heartily. 'We wondered if your husband could spare us a few minutes.'

'He's not here,' said the woman, and for a moment it looked as though she were about to shut the door.

'Now please –' began Harold in an authoritative voice, but the rector motioned him to keep silence, and spoke instead. His experienced eye had noticed the sudden pain which had caused the woman to draw in her breath sharply.

'We won't bother you for more than a moment,' he assured her gently, putting a plump hand on her thin arm. She looked at him and gave a small smile. The rector noticed that she had very few teeth, which accounted for the hollow pinched look of her sad face.

'We wrote to your husband several times,' he continued, 'but I fear the letters must have gone astray.'

'No, they're all here,' said the woman unexpectedly. 'You'd better come in out of the wind.'

As they followed her through a small kitchen to the living-room at the front of the house, the rector became conscious of someone following him. The small girl, now holding a full milk bottle, was entering too.

'My little girl,' said the woman. 'Put the milk in the cupboard, Dulcie.'

'Dulcie!' exclaimed Harold. 'Named after her grandmother perhaps? That was Nathaniel's daughter's name.'

'That's right,' said the woman, without much enthusiasm. She closed the door between the kitchen and living-room and motioned the men to sit.

'We'd better explain,' began the rector, and gave a brief account of Thrush Green's plans.

'So you see,' broke in Harold, 'we would like to see how your husband feels about it. Does he work on a Saturday morning? We had hoped to find him at home.'

The woman answered dully.

'He don't call this home any more. The truth is, he's left me.'

'Left you?' echoed the rector, with compassion in his voice.

'Left you?' echoed Harold, with dismay in his. What if the wretched fellow had left the country altogether? A fine wasted journey they would have had, thought Harold Shoosmith with disgust.

Mrs Mulloy took four letters and an unopened telegram from the mantelpiece and handed them to Charles Henstock.

'I kept them thinking he might be back. The first came the day after he went. But he's never come.'

'I'm so very sorry,' said the rector. 'We had no idea of this, naturally.'

'Do you know his address?' asked Harold practically. Mrs Mulloy's face took on a mutinous look, and the rector spoke hastily.

'You see, we've come such a very long way, and I have to be back tonight ready for my Sunday services tomorrow. It would be so kind of you if you would tell us where he is. We might be able to see him if he is not too far away.'

The woman's face softened as she looked at the rector's cherubic countenance. The man need have no fear, thought Harold watching her, of not having any charm over women. It's partly that child-like look and partly his genuinely kind heart, he decided, content to leave the negotiations in his friend's competent hands.

'He's left me for a low common woman I wouldn't demean myself to speak to,' burst out Mrs Mulloy. 'He's at her house now, no doubt. Two miles up the valley, and the name is Taylor. It's a farmhouse. Anyone will tell you.'

She stopped suddenly, and the rector saw that her eyes were wet.

'Does he provide for you?' he asked.

'Not a penny,' she said bitterly. She was talking to the rector as though no one else were present, and Harold sat very quietly. 'I'm to go to court next week.'

'How do you manage?' said the rector.

'I've got a job at the big house. Dulcie comes there after school for her tea, then we come home. I don't go Saturdays, unless I'm wanted specially.'

'I see,' said the rector. He put the letters in his pocket, and held out his hand. 'We won't worry you any further, Mrs Mulloy,' he said. 'But I think we will try to see your husband, while we're here. I will write to you, if I may, when I return, and perhaps I can be of some help. I hope so.'

The woman held his hand trustingly and gave him a watery smile. Harold rose to make his farewells and they made their way through the kitchen to the bleak garden. Dulcie was cutting up cabbage in a business-like way with an enormous fierce-looking knife. The scene quite terrified the rector.

'Here,' said Harold firmly, at the door, 'buy something for the little girl from me.'

'Thank you, sir,' said the woman, almost sketching a bob, as she took the note. 'And I hope you both have a good journey back.'

'How brave of you to give her money outright like that,' said the rector, when they were back in the car. 'I just couldn't do it!'

'You did the real dirty work,' answered his friend. 'She'd have told me nothing. Now let's go and find the malefactor.'

The farmhouse, by Cotswold standards, was a humble affair. It consisted of a two-storey box, which had once been white-washed, with a grey slated roof. A jumble of outhouses, made of corrugated iron and rough timber, clustered at its side, and the sound of animals could be heard coming from them. They drove the car up a steep track, axle-deep in mud, as near to the house as was possible, before picking their way on foot to the front door. A black and white sheepdog, tied to a post with a stout rope, barked hysterically at them, standing on its back legs and pawing the air in its frenzy.

Before they had time to knock, the door was opened by a young woman with a cigarette in her mouth.

'Yes?' she asked shortly, squinting at them through the smoke that curled into her eye. 'You from the insurance?'

Harold Shoosmith began to wonder if all strangers in Pembrokeshire were welcomed in this way. What was it, he wondered, about their appearance which suggested that they were con-

nected with an insurance company? Or why, for that matter, were
the householders of Pembrokeshire so anxiously awaiting the arrival
of insurance men? It seemed a pity that he would never know the
answer.

'We've called to see Mr Mulloy,' began the rector diffidently.

'He's here. Come in,' said the woman without preamble, and
they followed her into a small smoky room almost filled with a
gigantic three-piece suite upholstered in shabby black leather. It
reminded Harold Shoosmith of the railway station waiting-rooms
of his boyhood as he looked at the buttons dimpling the back of
the couch.

From the depths of one of the chairs a massive man arose. His shirt
collar was open and he wore no tie. His creased grey flannel trousers
were tied round his vast stomach with a dressing-gown cord. His
hair was long, his eyes bleary, his teeth were stained brown with
tobacco smoke and Harold Shoosmith judged that his last shave took
place three, or possibly four, days before. If this were Nathaniel's
grandson then he was glad that the spruce old man could not see his
descendant.

'Mr Mulloy?' he asked abruptly, disappointment sharpening his
tone.

'That's right,' said the man. 'My wife send you?'

'She told us the way,' replied Harold. 'But we came to see you,
not your wife.'

'Take a seat,' said the woman, removing a pile of newspapers from
one end of the couch and tossing them pell-mell into the corner of
the room. A startled mew gave evidence of a cat's presence in the
murky corner, but it remained in hiding. 'I'll clear out if you're
going to talk business.'

'Really, there's no need,' protested the rector. 'It's just a little
matter of a memorial.'

'Who to? The wife?' asked the man, guffawing loudly. 'I'd give
you a bit towards that, wouldn't I, Ethel?'

The woman smiled grimly, but made no comment. The rector
looked disconcerted, and not a little shocked.

It was Harold who took command at this interview, and in a few
curt phrases outlined the purpose of their errand. William Mulloy
slouched forward as he listened, his stomach heavily pendulous inside
his grubby shirt, sucking his revolting teeth and swallowing noisily.

The gentle rector, almost overcome by the rank smells of the stuffy room, prayed that their visit would be brief.

'What d'you want me to do about it?' asked William Mulloy, when Harold finished. 'Want money, do you, to put up this 'ere statue? You'll get not a farthing from me, I can tell you. I heard enough about that old bundle of misery from my mother – she was just such another Holy Joe – and I want nothing to do with it.'

Harold Shoosmith's face so openly expressed the disgust he felt that the rector decided that he had better intervene.

'We had no intention of asking you to contribute towards your grandfather's memorial. We simply wished to find out if you were interested. We felt that it was common courtesy to get your opinion on our venture.'

'Well, my opinion, gents,' said William Mulloy, with a shrug of his massive shoulders, 'is that the lot of you are plain barmy. But if you like to throw good money away by sticking up some tin-pot effigy to that dismal old sky-pilot, why, you're welcome. But don't expect me to take any interest in it. My life was made a misery with his ideas. If it hadn't been for my dad giving me a good time now and again I reckon I'd have gone loopy the way my mother kept talk, talk, talk about what grandad would have said.'

'He was a very fine man,' said Harold, with controlled passion. 'A man who did so much good in his life that he is remembered with affection and respect all over the world.'

'Aw! Stow it,' yawned William Mulloy. 'You and my ma would have made a good pair.' He heaved his great bulk from the chair and held out a sticky fat hand.

'I'll say good-bye. Sorry you've had a long journey for nothing. But you've got my blessing for this crack-brained scheme, if that's what you came for. If there's any money over, you might think of the old chap's descendants, you know.'

Harold Shoosmith could not bring himself to take the extended hand, and contented himself with nodding and hastening to the door; but the rector shook it politely and murmured his farewells to them both.

The sheepdog kept up its insane barking as they backed away from the house and regained the lane. Harold seemed speechless with fury and disappointment, and the rector spoke with some diffidence.

'He obviously takes after the ne'er-do-weel father,' he commented. 'Not a very attractive person, I thought.'

'What I thought,' remarked Harold grimly, 'is unprintable.' He pulled the wheel round savagely and set off on the long journey home.

They stopped only once, and that was at Ross, for a late lunch. By that time their disappointment and shock had somewhat evaporated. The rain had ceased and the wind had dropped, so that they were able to enjoy the winter beauty of the wooded countryside.

The air was iron-cold and hurt the lungs. The sky's menacing greyness was tinged with the slight coppery colour which precedes a snowstorm, and the two men were glad to regain the warmth of the car after the walk from the hotel.

Darkness fell earlier than usual and they drove for several hours through the ominously still blackness. As they climbed the last steep hill to the haven of Thrush Green the first few snowflakes began to waver across the windscreen.

'Hello,' said Harold, 'here it comes at last.'

They got out of the car stiffly and stretched themselves luxuriously. Around them the snow whispered its way to the ground, although as yet, it failed to cover it.

'It's been a wonderful break,' said the rector, by way of thanks. 'Though disappointing perhaps.'

'At least we know where we are,' replied Harold. 'We certainly don't need Mr Mulloy's help in the unveiling ceremony. Come inside and get warm.'

The rector held his face up to the whirling snowflakes as Harold fumbled for the key. It was good to be back again at Thrush Green. He remembered, with sudden pleasure, the conversation on the way down and realized, with deep happiness, that more had been resolved, for him, than simply the unveiling of Nathaniel Patten's memorial.

16. Snow at Thrush Green

The inhabitants of Thrush Green woke on Sunday morning to find an eerie lightness reflected from their ceilings and a hushed white world outside their windows.

Snow was still falling, steadily and gently, and had settled by breakfast-time to a depth of two or three inches. The steep Cotswold roofs, white beneath their canopies, showed sharp and angular against the leaden sky which promised more snow. A light powdering had settled along the branches of the chestnut trees, and round the many bird-tables of Thrush Green the footsteps of dozens of small birds made hieroglyphics as they came seeking charity.

The reactions of the Thrush Green folk to their changed world varied considerably. Paul Young, waking to see the whiteness on his ceiling, leapt from his bed with wild delight and rushed to the window. Heaving it up, he scraped the new snow from the sill and crammed it rapturously into his mouth. The crunch with which it clove deliciously to the roof of his mouth, before melting into icy nothingness, entranced him. In the distance he could see the milkman, trudging to each house from his van and leaving a neat row of footprints to each door. The sight of Thrush Green stretching smooth and virginal, in all its wide spaciousness, offered a challenge to run and jump, to roll and frolic, and to make that vast anonymity his own, signed with his own ecstatic markings. Shaking with excitement, he thrust himself into his clothes.

Albert Piggott's response was typical as he gazed morosely from his bedroom window.

'Would 'appen on a Sunday. All that muck trod into the coconut matting in the aisle when the folks come to morning service! This'll take some clearing up!'

Gloomily, he stumped down the narrow stairs to prepare his breakfast.

Nelly Tilling, in her distant cottage near Lulling Woods, took one look at the snow, another at the threatening sky, and went barefoot and in her vast nightgown to check her provisions. There was flour in plenty in the enamel bin. Sugar, butter, tea and rice gave her silent comfort from one shelf, and bottled fruit and jam of her own preparing from another. Onions dangled from the beam above her head, jostled by a bunch of dried herbs. A shoulder of mutton waited to be cooked and there were eggs and cheese in plenty. She could live comfortably for a week at least, she decided.

But firing was a different matter. There was some coal, but that was lodged in a small shed at the end of the garden, together with logs which needed splitting for kindling wood. Nelly, suddenly conscious of the chilly floors, returned to the bedroom to dress. She must collect as much fuel as she could manage to store indoors before the snow engulfed the little shed.

Dotty Harmer, in her solitary cottage in the hollow behind Thrush Green, was also up betimes. Her spirits had soared as she surveyed the dazzling purity of the fields which surrounded her. Snow had always delighted her. She remembered the tobogganing parties which she and her small friends had enjoyed on the sledge made for her one Christmas by her school-master father. How well he had fashioned it and of what stout stuff was proved by the fact that it still hung in Dotty's lean-to at the side of her house. Two or three winters before she had dragged home her shopping on it from Lulling in just such weather, she recalled, and had later lent it to her neighbour to draw fodder to some cattle at the end of the small valley.

Unlike Nelly Tilling she did not think of her own provisions, but her first anxiety was for her chickens at the end of the garden, and for Mrs Curdle and the new kittens. She put on a man's overcoat and a pair of wellington boots and made her way through the scrunching snow, with a double measure of corn in the zinc dipper.

The chickens were delighted at this largesse and pecked at the yellow grains which studded the unaccustomed whiteness of the run. Dotty threw a large groundsheet over the wire roof, so that the snow should not get too thick. She thrust a bundle of straw into the hen house for extra warmth, and cut three large winter cabbages from the patch. These she shook free of snow and dropped into the run. She could do no more, she decided, filling the water bowl. They were well provided for.

As she bent to her tasks, she was conscious of an ache across her chest as she breathed. For the past week she had been troubled by a cold and a cough which kept her awake at night.

'It's this cold air,' said Dotty to the hens, who were almost delirious with joy at so much food at one time. 'I'd better take some of my coltsfoot and raspberry cordial. Good-bye, my dears.'

Dotty turned and battled her way through the whirling snow-flakes to the shelter of the cottage. She was not to see her dear hens again for many a long day.

'D'you know what?' demanded Ella, bursting into Dimity's bedroom. 'The whole place is full of dam' snow!'

'Indoors, do you mean?' asked Dimity, wrenched thus brutally from sleep and understandably bewildered.

'No, no, no!' said Ella testily. 'Just everywhere.' She stumped across to Dimity's window, a thickset figure wrapped in her old red dressing-gown, and gazed with dislike at the wintry scene.

'All in the trees,' went on Ella disgustedly, as though this really was the last straw. 'All over the roofs,' she added despairingly.

'It's usual, you know, with snow,' responded Dimity, with unwonted irony. 'How deep is it?' She sat up in bed to get a glimpse of the whirling flakes.

'About a couple of inches, I should say,' answered Ella. 'But plenty more to come. Let's have breakfast in our dressing-gowns, Dim, and then get dressed and clear the paths.'

The thought of action against this infiltrating enemy cheered Ella at once, and the two drank their coffee and ate their habitual toast and marmalade in the snug kitchen and made plans like a pair of generals at the beginning of a campaign.

'We must bring the spades inside tonight,' said Ella briskly, 'in case we have to dig ourselves out tomorrow. It looks quite likely. I'll bring in extra coke, coal and wood, and it might be a good idea for you to take extra milk today. The milkman's on the other side of the green. Let's put a note out now.'

'You think of everything,' said Dimity, with admiration. 'I must put out more food for the birds, poor things, before I go to church.'

'I suppose you have to?' queried Ella. 'It'll be perishing cold, and everyone will be teeming with revolting germs. There's flu about, they tell me.'

'Yes, of course I must go,' said Dimity with quiet firmness. 'Charles would be most upset, if I failed to go.'

Ella's massive hand held the coffee pot arrested in mid-air as she looked at her friend.

'I believe you're right,' she said slowly.

It snowed for two days without ceasing, and an easterly wind, which sprang up during Sunday night, caused drifts several feet deep. Banks of snow reached to the windows of 'The Two Pheasants' and completely covered the white fence at the village school hard by. The lane to Nod and Nidden was impassable by Tuesday, and the two hamlets were cut off from the outside world. The snow ploughs were out along the main road from Lulling to the north, but the steep hill was so slippery that little could be done there. The older inhabitants spoke longingly of the handrail which had once lined the path to the town, as they slithered, with socks over their wellingtons, to gain a foothold on the slope.

The Lulling shops were under-staffed, for many of their assistants lived in outlying villages and were unable to get into the town. Delivery vans were few and far between, and neighbours lent each other cupfuls of sugar and packets of tea as supplies became short.

Influenza had spread in the little town, with such alarming rapidity that the preparatory school attended by Paul and his friend Christopher had closed for a week in the hope that this might arrest the spread of infection.

After the first few days of joy Paul soon became bored. Snow showers continued intermittently throughout the week, and the nights were bitterly cold. His mother only allowed him to play outside for short spells, but towards the end of the week she invited Christopher to play during the hours of daylight, as both boys were in the rudest health and were obviously not going to succumb to the prevailing plague.

Paul was delighted to have company. In the afternoon, a watery sun tried to shine through scudding clouds, and Joan said that they might go out for a time.

'Let's go to the camp,' said Paul as soon as they were outside. 'It's years since we were there.'

They crept through the hole in Harold Shoosmith's hedge, skirted the shrubbery which had protected the path from the worst of the snow and struggled along to the tree.

Here a deep drift made it impossible for them to go further. The snow had been swept into a vast billow delicately patterned with a tracery of whorls and curves. Beyond it stretched the snowy valley, with Dotty's cottage a mere hump in the vastness. The house looked dead. No smoke rose from the chimney, no one moved behind the closed windows and there was no sign of life anywhere.

Paul, used to seeing Dotty pottering about her colourful garden, hearing the squawking of her hens and the companionable mewing of Mrs Curdle as she followed her mistress about, suddenly felt a spasm of inexplicable fear.

'There's nobody there,' he said, gripping Christopher's arm. 'It looks all wrong.'

'Only because of the snow,' said Christopher sturdily. 'It's all this whiteness. Makes you feel sick after a bit, my mother says, because our eyes are used to lots of colours.'

This scientific explanation did not satisfy Paul.

'I don't mean that,' he protested. 'It looks as though Miss Harmer's gone away. But she *never* goes away, Chris. Never! She's got the animals to look after.'

While Paul gazed with anxiety at the house and his friend gazed at him with perplexity, a terrifying thing happened. One of the upstairs windows slowly opened, and a witch-like form, with grey eldritch locks hanging round a paper-white face, sagged over the sill. A skinny arm began to swing an old-fashioned hand-bell, and the eerie notes clanged across the snowy wastes to the frightened boys.

'It can't be Miss Harmer,' whispered Paul, white as a ghost.

'It is!' said Christopher shakily. 'And she's ill or something. She wants help.'

'We can't get through that drift,' answered Paul, with a hint of relief in his voice. 'Let's shout to her and tell her we'll get help.'

They cupped their hands round their mouths and began to call to the small wild figure. The bell kept up its erratic din, now loud, now soft, but the toller gave no sign of hearing the answering cries from the boys.

At that moment, Harold Shoosmith, clad in fishing waders and an oilskin, appeared from his garden and approached the children.

'How long has this been going on?' he asked.

They spoke together in a rush, too relieved to see help to worry about their trespassing.

'It's Miss Harmer—' began Paul.

'She must be ill,' said Christopher. 'She's just come to the window.'

'We were shouting to tell her we'd get help,' continued Paul. 'It's too deep for us to get through.'

'I'll go and get a spade,' said Harold. 'You wait here,' he added, 'I may need you.'

They watched him plough back towards the house. The figure still sagged from the window, the bell hanging silent in one hand.

'Mr Shoosmith's coming!' shouted Paul encouragingly. He felt brave with relief, and almost began to enjoy the adventure.

'We're going to help him!' bellowed Christopher, not to be out-done.

By way of reply it seemed, the bell gave a convulsive ring and fell from the inert hand into the muffling snow below. The figure slid out of sight, presumably to the bedroom floor. Alarm seized the boys again.

'It's the shock,' said Paul aghast. 'We've jolly well killed her!'

For once, Christopher was too stunned to reply. At this moment Harold appeared again, armed with two spades and a coal shovel.

'She's fallen down,' quavered Paul.

'Then there's no time to lose,' said Harold briskly. 'We'll see how we get on, but if it's deeper than we think, one of you must run for more help.'

He set to, and cleared a way through the first deep drift, the boys flinging the snow energetically aside, pink-faced with excitement and exercise. Luckily, they soon came to shallower snow, and Harold proceeded alone, the snow almost to the top of his waders, until the garden gate was reached.

'Stay where you are,' Harold ordered. He struggled over the gate. He was beginning to wonder just what he would find inside the house. No sound had come from it, and he was secretly most alarmed.

He had to dig his way again through the garden. The snow had drifted into grotesque shapes against the hen house and the cottage.

After ten minutes' struggle he reached the back door. He was perspiring with his exertions, and the oilskins were horribly stuffy. He found the door unlocked, and entered the kitchen.

It was very cold and quiet. An unpleasant smell, compounded of stale food, drying herbs and cats, greeted him. The clock had stopped, the barred grate was full of grey ash, and a spider had spun its web from a cold saucepan on the hob to the wall near by.

'Anyone at home?' called Harold. 'Are you there, Miss Harmer?'

There was no reply. Harold stamped the snow from his boots and mounted the stairs. The sound of frantic mewing reached his ears from behind a closed door. He undid the latch and out bolted Mrs Curdle, followed unsteadily by four young kittens. They vanished downstairs, presumably in search of food.

The only other bedroom had its door propped open. There Dotty lay, crumpled on the floor, by the open window.

Harold was relieved to find that her eyes were open and that she was attempting to speak. She looked desperately ill, and her breathing was loud and stertorous. He lifted her on to the untidy bed and covered her gently.

'Just lie there for a moment,' he said. 'Now don't worry about a thing.'

He strode to the window and leant out.

'Cut back home, Paul,' he shouted, 'and ask your mother to ring Doctor Lovell. I'm going to carry Miss Harmer to my house. She's not well.'

'Me too? asked Christopher.

'No. I may need you,' said Harold. 'Hang on there.'

Dotty was becoming agitated, rolling her untidy grey head from side to side restlessly. Harold went closer to hear what she was trying to say.

'Poor cats! Poor chickens! No food!' croaked Dotty.

'What about you?' asked Harold. 'When did you eat last?'

She shook her head.

'I'm going downstairs to get you a hot drink, and I'll see to the animals,' he promised. 'Then we must get you out of this.'

He closed the window, switched on an archaic electric fire, which looked none too safe for his peace of mind, but was better than nothing, and departed downstairs.

The cats mewed plaintively, and he explored the tiny larder. A bottle of milk was now solid cream cheese, but a dozen or more tins of cat food, prudently purchased by Dotty at the onset of the blizzard, cheered him. He opened two, scooped out the contents and let the cats wolf it down. Dotty's provender was harder to find, but he discovered some Bovril and an electric kettle and soon returned to the bedroom with a steaming cup.

The warmth of the bed and the room seemed to have given poor Dotty more strength. She sipped her Bovril gratefully. Harold wondered how she would react to his suggestion that he carry her bodily up the hill to his own house. It was quite apparent that she was desperately ill. Ideally, she should not be moved, but the house was cold, without food, and inaccessible. If he could get her to Thrush Green then Lovell could take over. She was as light as a bird, and the path had been made. It should not be too difficult a journey, but he must wrap her up well. He looked at the shabby coats hanging behind the door with a speculative eye.

'I'm taking you to Thrush Green,' he said, with gentle authority. 'Then Doctor Lovell can have a look at you. You'll have to let me carry you, you know.'

'No need,' wheezed Dotty, surprisingly acquiescent. 'Sledge downstairs.'

'How splendid!' cried Harold. 'I'll go and get it ready.'

He found old Mr Harmer's masterpiece, and some leather straps, hanging in the lean-to. He collected some spare blankets from the room in which Mrs Curdle and her kittens had been incarcerated and made a warm comfortable bed upon the sledge, and then returned for his patient. It seemed most practical and decorous to wrap the old lady in the warm bed-clothes which already surrounded her, and carrying the unwieldy bundle, Harold stepped carefully down the staircase and deposited her on the sledge. He returned for a pillow, and leant from the window to shout to his assistant who was busy making a snow man.

'Be ready,' he called. 'I'm bringing Miss Harmer on a sledge. Are you warm enough?'

'Boiling!' said Christopher, scarlet in the face.

Harold closed the window, switched off the fire, gathered up the pillow and returned downstairs.

'Drink,' said Dotty, looking exhausted.

Harold hurried to get a glass of water.

'Cats!' said Dotty, with weak exasperation. Harold meekly filled a bowl and put it on the floor.

'I promise you,' he said solemnly, 'that someone will come and look after all the animals, as soon as we've got you safely in bed again.' He strapped the small figure safely on to the sledge, tucked an old mackintosh over and under the whole contraption and set off through the snow to Thrush Green.

The journey was comparatively easy, and Dotty stood the jolting well. Harold was glad, however, of Christopher's help, and tireder than he cared to admit when he finally arrived, by way of the garden, at the corner house's back door.

To his relief, Joan Young was there with Paul awaiting him, and he left her to put Dotty to bed in the spare room while they waited for the doctor.

Whisky and soda in hand, he stood at the sitting-room window watching the trees dropping flurries of snow as the wind caught them. If there were much more of this weather, thought Harold gloomily, they would not get Nathaniel's statue erected in time. He resolved to find out more from Edward Young about the progress he had made.

At that moment, young Doctor Lovell appeared and Harold took him upstairs to the patient.

Paul and Christopher were on the landing, gazing from the window. It occurred to Harold that the two boys might well be tired and hungry too.

'Come down to the kitchen,' he said, 'and we'll find some biscuits and a hot drink.'

'Not *hot*,' begged Paul.

'What then?' asked Harold. 'Iced lemonade?' he added amusedly, looking at the bitter world outside.

'Oh please!' breathed the two fervently, following him downstairs. Shuddering, he led them to the refrigerator.

'Hospital job,' said Doctor Lovell, crashing downstairs. 'Can I use your phone?'

'Carry on,' said Harold and waited until all was arranged before making more enquiries.

'Bronchitis, perhaps pneumonia,' said the doctor. 'Basically, of course, it's malnutrition. I shouldn't think she's eaten a square meal for years. But she'll be all right. Keeps fretting about her pets.'

'Tell her I'll go down myself while she's away,' said Harold. 'It's no great distance.'

'You're what's known as a good Samaritan,' said the doctor, making for the door. 'And one who was just in time, I may say. She wouldn't have lasted much longer without attention – and then where would all the pets have been?'

The arrival of the ambulance broke short their conversation. Curtains twitched at several windows on Thrush Green, and one or two bolder spirits emerged from their cottages the better to see who might be the victim. The arrival of Doctor Lovell had not gone unnoticed. The sight of the ambulance increased the excitement. What could have happened to Harold Shoosmith?

It was with considerable mystification that the watchers saw Harold himself striding beside the stretcher a few minutes later. Who could he have been harbouring in his house all these years? Must be a deep one – that newcomer.

After the tedium of several house-bound days it was delightful to speculate about the drama unfolding before their eyes. Here was mystery, here was excitement, here was food for endless gossip! Thrush Green was agog.

Harold Shoosmith was a good Samaritan in more ways than one.

17. Two Clues

Snow shrouded Thrush Green for over a week and throughout that time Harold trudged daily to Dotty's cottage to care for the animals. People were heartily sick of the snow. Travelling was difficult, supplies were getting scarce, influenza spread alarmingly and tempers were sorely frayed.

It was with the utmost relief that the good folk of Lulling and Thrush Green saw their barometers rising and the weather-vanes veering towards the south-west. Soon a warm wind enveloped the Cotswolds and within two days little rivulets ran down the hill to Lulling, the snow slithered with a heartening rushing sound from the steep tiled roofs, and the green grass could be seen again.

People emerged from their houses as joyfully as children let out from school. It was wonderful to smell the earth and grass again, and more wonderful still to feel a gentle warmth blowing instead of the withering east wind.

Dotty Harmer had recovered, and was able to sit up in bed at Lulling Cottage Hospital and receive visitors bearing flowers and little home-made cakes and fruit. Once she had been made to realize that all the animals were being cared for, to the point of cosseting, she had taken a turn for the better. She could not get over Harold's kindness and was delighted to think that her father's sledge had proved so useful.

'I always say,' she told her visitors, more times than they cared to count, 'that it is wise to keep *everything*! There's always a time when one finds a use for things. Father's sledge is a case in point.' To be proved right did more to help Dotty's progress than all the pills which she was persuaded to swallow.

Betty Bell came to see her as soon as the weather released her from her distant cottage, and she resumed work at Dotty's and Harold's again. Another released prisoner was Nelly Tilling who went back to 'The Drovers' Arms' as soon as possible, and flung herself, with joyful abandon, into scrubbing the traces of the weather from the brick floor in the bar. It was the reward of her zealous labours which was to give Albert Piggott the greatest moment of his life.

Nelly set out to see how he had fared during the snowstorm, with a basket on her arm. She carried it carefully, through the darkening afternoon, and looked forward to making a pot of tea for herself and Albert when she reached Thrush Green. It was wet and muddy along the field path past Dotty's cottage and her shoes were soon soaking. She was glad to reach the shelter of Albert's kitchen and take them off. Albert seemed almost pleased to see her, and the kettle was already humming on the hob.

They exchanged news of the storm. Albert described the horrors of the mess he had had to clear up in the church, the ordeals he had undergone to get the coke free from snow and the difficulty he had found in keeping the larder even moderately filled.

Nelly countered with her own privations and – a sly stroke – how much she had worried on Albert's account.

'There I was,' she told him, rolling her dark eyes at him, 'wondering how you was managing without someone to cook you a bite or clean the place up. Kept me awake at nights, it did, hoping you was looking after yourself.'

Albert appeared a little touched by her solicitude, and gave a kindly grunt as she poured his tea.

'I brought something for you to have a look at,' she went on. 'Mrs Allen give it to me for doing a bit extra. It's a little clock she bought cheap, but it won't go. You mended my mother's wrist-watch a rare treat, and you might be able to see to this. It's real pretty.'

She fished in the basket at her feet and produced a newspaper parcel. Albert undid it gingerly and set a little gilt clock on the kitchen table.

'I've seen one like this afore,' said Albert ruminatively. 'Can't think where for the minute.' He turned the pretty thing about in his horny hands.

'It's French,' he said, still musing.

'Mrs Allen bought it off Bella Curdle, you know, Sam's wife—' began Nelly conversationally, but was cut short by a thump of Albert's fist on the kitchen table which made the tea-cups rattle.

'That's it!' cried Albert. 'This is Miss Watson's clock, I'll wager.'

'Never!' gasped Nelly. 'Are you trying to tell me that this is the clock that got stolen? And that Sam was the chap as done it?'

'That's right!' chortled Albert gleefully. 'That's it!'

'But why should Bella sell it if she knew Sam had pinched it? It'd be bound to be found out.'

'Don't suppose Sam told Bella,' pointed out Albert. 'And I bet Bella never told Sam she'd sold it to Mrs Allen. How did it happen, anyway?'

Nelly said that Mrs Allen had told her that Bella was worried because she was behind with her payments for the clothing club. The young woman occasionally helped to dress poultry or do piece-work on the farm and was a frequent visitor to 'The Drovers' Arms'. She had brought the clock one day to Bessie Allen and asked her if she would give her a pound for it. Although Bessie did not want it, she had taken pity on the feckless Bella and had given her a pound and kept the clock. Later, touched by Nelly's arduous efforts after the snow, and knowing that she admired the gilt clock, she had made her a present of it.

'Well, it's Miss Watson's by rights,' insisted Albert. 'Give it here, my gal, and I'll walk along and show her. She'll know well enough.'

'Wait for me,' said Nelly, drawing on her wet shoes again. 'I'll come with you.'

This seemed an admirable opportunity to consolidate her position with the headmistress. For who knew, thought Nelly, shrugging on her coat, how soon she might be living at Thrush Green, conveniently placed to take over the cleaning of the village school?

Unaware of the visitors who were about to descend upon her, Miss Watson sat before her fire pondering upon a most upsetting incident. A pile of history test papers lay on the hearthrug, a red pencil across the top, but Miss Watson could not bring herself to begin marking.

It had happened only an hour or two before, as the children were dressing to go home. The two little Curdle girls were struggling into their coats when their father appeared. He had the van outside, he said, and as the lane was still awash with melted snow he thought he would pick them up as he was passing.

Miss Watson rarely saw Sam. Occasionally Bella met the children, trailing the toddler behind her, but Sam seldom showed his face at the school. He seemed a little disconcerted to see Miss Watson in the cloakroom. Normally Miss Fogerty saw the children off, but today she had left early to keep an appointment with the local dentist.

He bent down to help his younger daughter tie her shoelace. Something in his movements gave Miss Watson a shock. A moment later she had a second shock. Unable to feel the laces properly with his gloves on, Sam had tossed them on the floor beside the child's feet. Miss Watson had seen those gloves before. They were knitted grey ones, bound with leather and they had gripped a heavy stick.

Miss Watson had felt so sick and so faint that she had been unable to speak. Sam had departed with his offspring, wishing her good afternoon civilly. Since then her mind had been in turmoil.

Should she ring the police on this shred of evidence? Was it, in fact, evidence? There must be thousands of pairs of gloves like that. But she was sure that she had recognized Sam as he had bent suddenly in the cloakroom. Was she justified in confiding her suspicions to the police? If only dear Agnes were here, how helpful she could be!

As her agitated thoughts coursed through her throbbing head the bell rang at the front door, and she went to answer it.

'Why, come in, Mr Piggott,' she cried. 'What brings you here?'

*

That evening a police car splashed along the watery lane to Nod and Nidden and stopped outside Sam Curdle's caravan.

The next morning Sam appeared before the magistrates and was told that he would be called before Quarter Sessions at the county town to answer his serious charge.

That same day Albert Piggott was treated to so many pints by the regular customers at 'The Two Pheasants' that he fell asleep in the stoke-hole of St Andrew's at half-past two and did not wake until the great clock above him struck five. It was as well, he thought muzzily, as he stumbled homeward, that Nelly Tilling was spending the day at her sister's.

If Nathaniel Patten's memorial were to be erected in time for his birthday on the fifteenth of March, then haste was needed, said Edward Young, who had been in communication with the young sculptor whom he much admired.

Consequently, a meeting was called of Thrush Green Entertainments Committee, when the design was to be approved and the sculptor definitely commissioned.

The meeting was to have been held, as usual, in the village school, but the tortoise stove had developed a mysterious crack which let out fumes and smoke in the most unpleasant manner. Miss Watson, in some perturbation, had mentioned this to Harold Shoosmith when he called to return three balls, a rubber quoit and a gym shoe which had landed in his garden.

'We'll have it at my house,' he said, with secret relief, for the thought of being wedged into the infants' desks for a hour and a half on a bleak January evening had cast its shadow before. 'There's plenty of room, and I'll send a message round.'

He rang the rector last of all.

'Come and have supper here first,' he said. 'The meeting's not until 8.15, and as far as I can see there will only be about half a dozen of us.'

The rector was delighted to accept. Mrs Butler had just told him that she thought there would be enough of yesterday's corned beef hash left for his evening meal, and he had been resigned to his lot. Although he was not a greedy man, the thought of good food and good company greatly cheered him.

He arrived at a quarter past seven and the two men had a splendid steak and kidney casserole and apple tart which Betty Bell had come back specially to cook. The rector thought wistfully how competently Harold managed his domestic affairs, and remembered his own meagre fare and dismal surroundings which he seemed unable to alter.

'Do you know anything about this young man of Edward's?' enquired Charles Henstock later, as they toasted their toes and waited for the rest of the committee members. 'You know, I'm devoted to Edward, and have the greatest admiration for his work – they tell me he has a wonderful flair for domestic detail in his housing plans. But, just occasionally, I wonder if he is not a trifle too advanced in his ideas for the rest of us. Those walls of his – all different colours – and that pebble-dash square he has let into his doorstep "for excitement of texture", I think it was, seem a little out of this world sometimes. The Thrush Green world, I mean. I suppose we're rather stick-in-the-mud, but we really don't want a jagged piece of metal that looks like a heron with the stomach-ache put up for ever on the green, do we?'

'We certainly don't,' said Harold forcibly. 'But I don't think you need to worry. After all, it's for that very purpose that the committee is meeting tonight. To protect Thrush Green from dyspeptic herons, or – worse still – a bunch of bladders of lard in stone all lumped together and called "Bounty", is *exactly* what we're here for, my dear Charles.'

The rector appeared somewhat comforted and sipped his excellent coffee.

'I must confess,' he said, expanding under the influence of shared confidences, 'that I am relieved that Ella wasn't asked to tackle the job. She is a most gifted person, believe me, *most* gifted. But I find that strong rugged effect in her work a little overpowering. I fear I'm still at the stage of admiring flowered chair covers, and liking water-colours on the wall.'

'And what's wrong with that?' responded Harold sturdily. 'But I agree with you that Ella's well out of it. She would have "had a bash", as she so elegantly put it, I feel positive. She's a brave woman and I can quite see why Dimity relies upon her.'

The rector looked up quickly.

'I sometimes think it is the other way round,' he said. 'Beneath that timid manner of Dimity's there's a very strong and fine character.

For all that Ella bullies her – or appears to – I think she feels a deep affection for Dimity, and takes more notice of her gentle suggestions than we realize.'

'You're probably right,' agreed Harold. 'You're a better judge of character than I am.'

'I've known them both for many years now,' replied the rector. 'I have the greatest respect for them,' he added, with a careful preciseness which reminded Harold of one of Jane Austen's heroes.

'I gather it's reciprocated,' commented Harold drily, 'even if Ella doesn't go to church more than twice a year.'

'One can't expect everyone to be as devoted as Dimity,' answered the rector reasonably.

'She's as devoted to you as she is to the church,' said Harold quietly, and watched his friend's face grow pink and decidedly alarmed.

'I think you do her a wrong there,' said the rector hesitantly. 'She is a deeply religious woman and would attend services whoever might be in charge.'

'I've no doubt about that,' said Harold, rising to his feet to make up the fire. 'But she also finds pleasure in your company.'

He pointed a log at the perturbed rector and waggled it for emphasis.

'You underestimate your charms, Charles, as I've told you before.'

The rector was saved from answering by a thunderous knocking at the front door. They heard Betty Bell hurrying from the washing-up to answer it, and the sound of a booming voice which set the dinner gong vibrating.

'Ella,' said Harold. One did not need to live long at Thrush Green before recognizing that voice.

Ella and Dimity entered, closely followed by Edward Young and Doctor Bailey. The rector greeted them with his usual warmth, hiding his inner agitation with considerable success.

'There are only the six of us,' said Harold. 'Shall we stay by the fire?'

There was a chorus of assent.

'Though that question does remind me of Violet Anderson's last dinner party,' said Ella, 'when she cut a veal pie and said: "I do so hope you like veal" and we all meekly muttered "Yes". As a matter of fact, I very nearly said : "No, I loathe it; so count me out and I'll have a banana," but I bit it back.'

'Good manners frequently drive one to dishonesty,' agreed the rector. 'It's a nice point to consider — whether one should offend one's host or one's conscience.'

Edward Young took out an enormous envelope and began to undo it rather fussily.

'Perhaps it would be as well to look at the designs at once,' he began, a little pompously. .

'I'll read the minutes, and apologies, if I may,' replied the rector mildly, and the younger man bowed his head curtly. As an ambitious man, fast climbing his professional tree, he was beginning to be a little impatient of such petty matters as the minutes of Thrush Green committees.

The rector dispatched the usual business competently, and then looked towards the envelope.

'We're all looking forward to seeing the designs,' he said. 'I take it that the young man is really interested?'

'Oh, very, very,' answered Edward, tugging at the envelope. 'He is an interesting fellow and has just finished some outstanding murals for a new nursery school.'

'Oh, how sweet,' cried Dimity. 'What about? Animals and things?'

'I shouldn't think so,' said Edward, looking as shocked as if Dimity had made an improper suggestion. 'He's very mature in his approach, for his age, and he realizes that young children see through the façade of accepted nursery illustration to the elemental truths.'

'Oh, for pity's sake,' implored Ella, 'stop talking like a second-rate psychologist and let's see what the chap's done! You're putting us off before we start.'

Edward had the grace to turn pink, realizing that the rest of his hearers silently agreed with Ella's forthright plea.

'I made him understand,' he went on, 'that we preferred a traditional bronze figure as near to a photographic resemblance as he could manage. He found the pictures that you sent of great help, sir,' he added, with unusual deference, to Harold.

'Good,' said Harold. 'You seem to have handled it admirably.'

'Well you certainly didn't think we'd stand for a great lump, reeling and writhing and fainting in coils, with holes in its middle, did you?' demanded Ella, still belligerent.

For answer Edward handed her a large sheet of paper and she was momentarily silenced. He passed others to the rest of the gathering and they studied the plans with interest.

Harold saw, with overwhelming relief, that the suggested design was reassuringly life-like. The young man proposed to show Nathaniel in a typical pose, either reading from a book or studying a plan for one of his own mission schools. If the picture were anything to go by, he had exactly caught the chubby amiability of the frock-coated missionary and made an attractive job of it.

'What exactly is an elevation?' asked Dimity.

'What are the arrows for?' asked Ella.

'Is this a different suggestion?' queried the rector.

Edward patiently answered all the questions that were fired at him. There were several designs, each slightly differing in stance and size, but all acceptable to the committee.

Finally they decided upon the one which Harold had liked, and then the important question was asked.

'Can he get it done in time?' asked Harold.

'He says he can,' said Edward. 'He's absolutely free at the moment and he works at white-heat once he starts.'

'More than the local builders will,' commented Ella. 'I suppose they'll be doing the plinth to this young man's design. I bet he's ready first.'

'We haven't settled that incidentally,' replied Edward. 'He gives three suggestions here, if you notice. They're all quite low, to suit the character of the green.'

'Quite right,' said the rector. 'One doesn't fancy a Nelson's column or even a stone armchair perched up by the chestnut trees on Thrush Green. This looks most suitable.'

'Three steps up,' commented Ella, 'and in York stone. Very nice too. Rather like George Washington who used to stand on the grass outside the National Gallery. Still does, for all I know.'

'One can't help feeling it was a trifle tactless of the Americans to present us with a reminder of the general who overcame us,' observed the rector thoughtfully. 'But on the other hand I think we showed exemplary civility in accepting it and giving it such a place of honour in our capital city.'

'A case of no offence meant and none taken, let's say,' said Harold, with a smile. He handed back the papers to Edward Young, who was busily making notes for the sculptor's reference.

'I think we all agree that a bronze statue, in position four, is the best choice?' he asked, looking round the company.

'With plinth number one,' cried Edward, still scribbling rapidly. 'If I may say so, I think you've made an excellent choice, and I can assure you that the work will be first-class. I'll tell him to get on straight away.'

'Please do,' said the rector, 'and tell him we are delighted with his plans.'

Edward Young suddenly looked a little diffident.

'There is the question of money,' he said. 'The materials will be expensive, as you know. I wonder if it would be possible to advance something to this young man?'

'I don't get paid till I've finished,' said Ella flatly.

'But he may be very poor,' pointed out Dimity compassionately.

'I think that would be in order,' said the rector, looking across at Harold Shoosmith. 'It is often done, I know, in this sort of matter. Shall we take a vote on it?'

Ella snorted, but raised her hand with the rest.

'Right,' said Harold briskly, 'I'll see to that, if you like, as I'm treasurer, I believe. You'll have to let me know how much, of course. Meanwhile, what about a drink?'

He made for the corner cupboard where he kept his bottles, and the meeting ended to the clinking of glasses and the chatter of six old friends, all well content with the evening's work.

18. Spring Fever

The day after Dotty Harmer came home from hospital, Ella made her way across Thrush Green, down the little alley between 'The Two Pheasants' and Albert Piggott's cottage, and so reached the footpath that threaded the meadow and finally wound its way to Lulling Woods.

It was one of those clear mild days which come occasionally in mid-winter and lift the spirits with their hint of coming springtime. Catkins were already fluttering on the nut hedge behind Albert's house and the sky was a pale translucent blue, as tender as a thrush's egg-shell.

Two mottled partridges squatted in the grass not far from the pathway, like a pair of fat round bottles. Ella looked upon them with a kindly eye. They mated, she had been told, for life, and though she did not think much of married bliss, yet she approved of constancy.

Her mind turned from the partridges, naturally enough, to the possibility of Dimity marrying. Nothing had been said between the two friends, and Ella often wondered if she had imagined a situation which did not, in fact, exist. But ever since the day when she had faced her own fears she had held fast to her principles. If Dimity chose to leave her, then she must wish her all the happiness in the world and make her going easy for her. It was the least one could do in gratitude for so many years of loyal friendship, and the only basis on which that friendship could continue.

Dotty's door was opened by Betty Bell, who had offered to stay in the cottage until Dotty was fit to live alone again. She still went to work as usual for Harold Shoosmith, for Dotty was quite capable of pottering about and amusing herself, but her friends were relieved to know that Betty slept there and could keep an eye on her eccentric charge.

'Well, tell me all the news,' said Dotty, when Mrs Curdle had been scooped off the armchair and Ella settled in it. 'What's been happening at Thrush Green?'

'You've heard about Sam Curdle, I suppose?' asked Ella. 'He's coming up at the Quarter Sessions next month – and it's a funny thing, Dotty, but it seems that he might have been your egg-thief too.'

'Really?' said Dotty agog. 'Oh, how I wish I'd caught him in father's man trap! No one would have felt in the least sorry if I'd caught Sam Curdle, even if his leg had been broken.'

'A peculiarly unchristian attitude,' pronounced Ella, taking out her shabby tobacco tin in order to roll a cigarette. 'It seems that Paul Young and that fat friend of his – Christopher Someone – have had a hidey-hole in one of Harold Shoosmith's trees, and they saw Sam go to your hen house one afternoon.'

'There!' said Dotty, slapping her thin thigh which was covered by a brown hand-woven skirt. 'What did I tell you? If I'd had my man trap we'd have had this all cleared up months ago.'

She pounced on another aspect of Ella's account.

'But what were the children doing in Harold Shoosmith's garden? Surely they knew they were trespassing? Children seem to have no idea of the difference between right and wrong these days. Not enough caning, my father always said – and he was invariably right. I was caned every Saturday night when I had my hair washed,' added Dotty, with some pride.

'What on earth for?' asked Ella, astonished.

'I screamed, dear. Screamed and screamed, and my father thought it unnecessary.'

'But if you were caned,' persisted Ella, shocked at the thought, 'you probably screamed more.'

'Oh, I did indeed!' Dotty assured her blandly, 'but I think my father felt that I then had something to scream for. It gave him some comfort, I feel sure.'

Ella drew in a large breath of rank smoke and blew it forcefully down her nostrils. Mrs Curdle, who had been hanging about on the hearthrug waiting her chance to get back on the chair, departed in high dudgeon to the kitchen, her tail erect.

'Harold Shoosmith knew they used the trees as a meeting place,' said Ella, 'but he didn't mind. It gave them a lot of innocent fun, he said, and they did no harm.'

Dotty grunted with disgust at such softness.

'Come to that,' continued Ella, taking up the cudgels on Harold's behalf, 'you'd have looked pretty silly if those boys hadn't been trespassing and heard your bell.'

Dotty had the grace to admit it.

'I've sent Mr Shoosmith,' she said conspiratorially, 'half a dozen bottles of last season's home-made wine – all different. Betty Bell took them up this morning and she says he was quite overcome.'

And well he might be, thought Ella grimly. She had sampled Dotty's wine as well as her other concoctions, and knew, to her cost, that the local ailment called 'Dotty's Collywobbles' could be appallingly painful. She made a mental note to warn Harold against sampling his present.

She smoked in silence, while Dotty rattled on, delighted to have someone to talk to.

'I can never thank him enough,' said Dotty warmly. 'So very kind, so attentive – Thrush Green is all the nicer now that he lives here. Does Dimity still see a lot of him?'

The question startled Ella.

'As a matter of fact, they're out together now,' said Ella. 'Otherwise Dim would have come with me. Field Club again, you know. They've gone to see some prehistoric barrows in Bedfordshire, I think. Unless it was Berkshire,' added Ella, who had never been geographically inclined.

'I really think something might come of it,' said Dotty calmly. She picked up a piece of grey knitting from the floor by her chair and began to busy herself with it. Even Ella realized that she had turned the work the wrong way round and was knitting the second half of the row on top of the first half. It accounted, Ella supposed, for the peculiar shape of the garment and for the alarming number of holes. But she was too perturbed by Dotty's last remark to point out her knitting errors.

'Dimity and Harold, d'you mean?' asked Ella gently, all her old fears returning.

'Yes, dear,' said Dotty, needles clashing. 'Most people seem to think there might be a match. I hope so. But what will you do?'

'I think we'd better wait and see,' said Ella, feeling that everything was going rather too fast for her comfort. 'Dimity's never said a word to me, and Harold is charming to everyone he meets, as you know. If I were you I'd scotch these rumours, not spread them.'

'There! And now you're cross,' exclaimed Dotty. 'Well, don't say I didn't warn you. When something's happening right under your nose it's often difficult to see it. But the outsider, you know—'

'Oh, fiddlesticks, Dot!' burst out Ella exasperatedly. 'You're imagining things!'

'We'll see! We'll see!' chanted Dotty, nodding her grey head and squinting at her crazy knitting. She looked more like a witch than ever.

Ella felt she could bear no more. She rose clumsily to her feet, smote her old friend on the back in a comradely manner, and made for the door.

'I'll come again, Dotty, but I must get back now. Take care of yourself, and don't get any more queer ideas in your head.'

She boomed her good-byes to Betty Bell and let herself out into the welcome fresh air.

Sometimes old Dotty made you feel as loopy as she was herself, she thought glumly, as she stumped back along the footpath. But the maddening thing was that the wretched creature was so often right!

With the departure of the snow and a spell of milder weather, preparations began on the site of Nathaniel's statue. A small area was roped off, and a tarpaulin shed housed three cheerful workmen who brewed tea, and sometimes worked, during the short winter day.

The concrete mixer drowned poor Miss Fogerty's voice in the infants' room and she became adept at miming her instructions to her admiring class. Games in the playground received the children's divided attention, as their eyes were directed far more often to the activity on the green than to that on their own territory. Staunch devotee of Nathaniel Patten as Miss Fogerty was, at times she wished him further.

The progress of the work gave the inhabitants of Thrush Green a new interest. Now that something was really happening even the lukewarm members of the community were stirred with anticipation. The butcher from Lulling and his followers, who had aired their protests at Christmas-time, made no further trouble, presumably washing their hands of the whole affair. But Harold and the rector were still worried about the person who should be invited to unveil the memorial. Time was getting short, and since the failure of their mission in Pembrokeshire they had racked their brains to think of someone suitable for the great occasion.

'You'll probably have to do it yourself,' said Harold to the rector.

'Indeed, no!' protested Charles Henstock. 'It would be most un-suitable. We really must try and think of someone – preferably someone connected with the mission station itself, I think.'

'But they'll all be at the jollifications there,' pointed out Harold. 'I told you they were getting ready for the most terrific celebrations before I left.'

The rector sighed gustily.

'I shall go for a long walk this evening,' he said, at last. 'Very often things are made plain to me on a solitary walk. I may perhaps think of something.'

'Let's hope it works tonight,' commented Harold. 'We're running things a bit fine, if you ask me.'

*

Whether the long solitary walk had anything to do with it, or whether the rector, in his parish visiting, had met infection, no one could say; but before the week was out the good man was in bed at the rectory with a high temperature and the most fearsome headache.

Mrs Butler supplied a light diet of lemon water and dry biscuits, arriving at the bedside in a state of exhaustion after each trip upstairs, and with a martyred expression which caused the rector added misery, as indeed it was intended to do.

He had been ill for two days before Harold Shoosmith heard of it, and he went straight over to see his friend. What he saw appalled him. A small oil stove was the only means of heating the lofty room, and this was not only quite inadequate but revoltingly smelly.

'Have you called the doctor?' asked Harold, troubled by the apparent weakness of his friend.

'Oh dear no!' exclaimed the rector. 'He is far too busy with people who are really ill, and Mrs Butler is looking after me very well.'

'I think you should see him,' said Harold. 'This room's far too cold, and I'm sure you should be having more nourishment than those biscuits.'

'I haven't much appetite,' the rector said weakly. 'And I don't feel like troubling Mrs Butler for dishes that might be difficult to cook.'

'A boiled egg and some warm milk shouldn't strain her resources,' commented Harold tartly. 'Could you manage that?'

'I really believe I could now,' confessed the rector. 'I must be over the worst.'

Harold made his way downstairs and gave firm orders to Mrs Butler.

'I'll take it up myself,' he said, with authority. 'He needs careful nursing, I can see. And I shall take it upon myself to give Doctor Lovell a ring.'

It said much for Harold's manner that Mrs Butler complied with his request swiftly and also with willingness.

'He's not too bad,' Doctor Lovell said to Harold, after he had inspected the patient. They were alone downstairs in the rector's chilly sitting-room.

'I think it's that she-dragon of a housekeeper that's at the bottom of this,' continued Doctor Lovell in a cheerful shout which must have been easily heard in the kitchen. 'I've told her to light a fire in his bedroom and to keep the whole house warm. It's a dismal hole, isn't it?'

'I agree,' said Harold. 'Something will have to be done about Mrs Butler. She simply takes advantage of Henstock's good nature.'

'She's pretty tied, at the moment,' said the young doctor thoughtfully. 'It might be a good idea to let her have the afternoons off, let's say, and she might do her stuff more willingly then while the rector's ill. She makes him worse by going into the room with a face like a thunder cloud.'

'That could be easily done,' said Harold. 'I'll come in myself, and I've no doubt other friends will take a turn.'

And so it fell out that for the next ten days, whilst the rector kept to his bedroom and marvelled at the sight of a real fire in that long-cold grate, Harold or Dimity and Ella took it in turns to spend the afternoon at the rectory in order to relieve Mrs Butler.

Charles Henstock found it delightful to settle down to his afternoon sleep with the distant murmur of friends' voices and movements downstairs to keep him company. Somehow the house was alive again, as it had been in his dear wife's time. He had been lonely so long that he had almost forgotten the security and comfort of a shared home. When he awoke, after his brief nap, it warmed his heart to think of the tea party which would take place in his room, and he looked forward to the tinkling of the tea tray advancing up the stairs bearing, more often than not, some particularly attractive morsel cooked by Ella or Dimity.

'I really feel so much better,' said the rector to Harold one afternoon. 'Lovell says I may get up tomorrow. I asked him if I'd be fit to go to the Diocesan Conference next week, but he says he'd rather I didn't.'

He sighed sadly, and pushed a printed sheet towards Harold across the counterpane.

'Two or three excellent speakers, you see. I'd like to have heard this young bishop from West Africa particularly.'

'But I know him!' exclaimed Harold, putting down his teacup hastily. 'The mission station's in his diocese. How long's he staying in England, I wonder? '

'Why?' asked the rector, surprised at his friend's excitement.

'Don't you see? He's the very chap to unveil the memorial! What could be more fortunate?'

The rector's chubby face grew pink with pleasure.

'What an excellent idea! Now, how can we find out? Could you telephone to our own bishop, do you think, and find out more about it?'

'Certainly I will,' said Harold, bolting down a large mouthful of Dimity's sponge-cake. 'I'll do it at once.'

He paused at the door, doubts suddenly assailing him.

'He's a terrific admirer of Nathaniel's,' he added. 'I hope to goodness he's not made plans to celebrate the anniversary at his mission station.'

'I don't think he will have done, somehow,' answered the rector simply. 'I've a feeling this is a direct answer to prayer.'

It certainly looked like it, thought Harold ten minutes later, as he returned up the stairs. The young bishop, he had been informed, was in England for a three months' study course at Oxford. He had been given his address and telephone number, and he waved the paper triumphantly as he entered the bedroom.

'We'll call an emergency meeting of Thrush Green Entertainments Committee,' he said joyfully, 'and see the reaction.'

'We couldn't do better,' answered his friend, with quiet conviction.

19. Albert Piggott is Won

February lived up to its name of 'Fill-Dyke'. The month began with a succession of rainy days, and people began to fear that the end of the winter would be as uncomfortably wet as its early months had been.

Miss Watson and Miss Fogerty looked at the muddy brick floor of the cloakroom at the village school and shook their heads sadly. Their little brood had just rushed homewards through the rain, mad with joy at being released.

'One really can't blame them,' commented Miss Watson, listening to the diminishing screams and shouts as the children tore away. 'They've missed their playtime all this week. And doesn't the school look like it!'

'Mrs Cooke will put it straight,' comforted Miss Fogerty.

'That's just what she won't do!' responded Miss Watson energetically. 'At least, not for long. Look what the child brought this afternoon.'

She handed over a crumpled and grubby note, written apparently on the fly leaf torn from a cheap paper-back novel. It said:

Dear Miss

Shall be late up scool today as doctor wants to see me as baby cumin whitzun will tell you what he say tonite

Yours

Mrs Cooke

'Well!' said Miss Fogerty flabbergasted. 'Would you believe it?'

'Easily,' said Miss Watson flatly. 'And this won't be the last. The problem is, what to do about a reliable caretaker.'

'There's that fat woman,' ventured Miss Fogerty. 'She seems very willing, and I believe she's a wonderful worker.'

'I've been thinking of her myself,' confessed Miss Watson, 'during recitation lesson. We could ask her to take over temporarily from Mrs Cooke and see how things work out.'

'Much the best thing,' agreed Miss Fogerty, in a business-like way. It was still delightful, she found, to be consulted as an equal in school affairs. Sam Curdle, wicked though he was, had inadvertently brought happiness to Miss Fogerty on that wild distant night.

'Come and have tea with me, Agnes dear,' said her headmistress, 'and you can help me compose a letter to Mrs Tilling.'

Much gratified, the little assistant followed her headmistress across the playground to the schoolhouse.

The result was that four days later, with the letter safely stowed in her bag, Nelly cast a triumphant eye over her new territory as she was shown round the school by Miss Watson in the evening. Her heart leapt as she saw the well-stocked cleaning cupboard with its new scrubbing brushes, tins of scouring powder, long bars of neatly stacked yellow soap, and brooms, brushes and dusters in dazzling variety. Her spirits quickened at the sight of the muddy floors, the finger-marked paintwork, the dull brass handles on the scratched cupboards, and the windows so hoary with dirt that some bold, and unobserved, imp had drawn a figure upon one of them and labelled it 'TECHAR' with a mischievous finger. Here indeed was scope for her powers, thought Nelly exultantly!

'The post would certainly be yours for some months,' explained Miss Watson, 'and I think it might well prove permanent, as Mrs Cooke feels that with another baby to think of it might be better to find work nearer her home. It is quite a step here for her.'

'Poor thing,' sympathized Nelly, drawing a finger along a hot-water pipe and surveying the collected dust with much concern, 'she must have been finding it too much for some time.'

'I gather that she might be offered a job at the farm where her husband works,' continued Miss Watson, thinking it best to ignore Nelly's opening. Village schoolmistresses are adept at such strategies. 'She should know very soon, and then we could tell you more. You may find, of course,' continued Miss Watson, 'that you don't like the job here, or that the journey is too far. It's quite a long way from Lulling Woods, particularly in weather like this.'

She gazed through the school window at the drizzle veiling Thrush Green.

'I'll manage,' Nelly assured her robustly. If she played her cards right, she told herself privately, she wouldn't be tramping from Lulling Woods much longer. As for the work, her hands itched to get at it. 'I'll be here at half-past four next Monday,' promised Nelly, 'and make a start.'

She must break the news to Bessie and Ted Allen she told herself as she wished Miss Watson good-bye in the school porch; but meanwhile there was a more important campaign at hand.

Hitching her bag over her arm, Nelly Tilling set out in search of Albert Piggott.

She found him in his kitchen, immersed in the newspaper spread out before him on the table. The odour of fried bacon surrounded him, and a dirty plate and cutlery, pushed to the corner of the table, showed that Albert had just finished his evening meal.

He grunted by way of greeting as the fat widow dumped herself down on the other chair, but did not raise his eyes from his reading.

'It says 'ere,' said Albert, 'that that fellow as robbed the bank yesterday got away with twenty thousand.' His voice held grudging admiration.

'I just been up the school,' answered Nelly, undoing her coat.

'Oh ah?' said Albert, without interest. 'This chap knocked three o' the bank fellows clean to the floor, it says. Alone! Knocked three down, alone!'

'I can 'ave that job if I want it,' said Nelly. 'I've said I'll start Monday. It's a good wage too.'

'"He told our reporter,"' read Albert laboriously, '"that he was lying in a wolter of blood." Think of that!' said Albert ghoulishly. '"A wolter of blood."' He began to pick a back tooth with a black finger-nail, his eyes still fixed upon the print.

'It'll be quite a step every day from Lulling Woods,' went on Nelly, delicately approaching her objective. 'I'm supposed to go in first thing in the mornings too, to light the stoves and dust round.'

'Oh ah?' repeated Albert absently. He withdrew a wet forefinger from his mouth and replaced it damply on a line of print. '"He was detained in hospital with a suspected skull fracture and injuries to the right eye."'

'I wish you'd listen,' said Nelly, exasperation giving an edge to her tone. 'I got something to tell you.'

Albert stopped reading aloud, but his eyes continued to follow his moving forefinger.

'Don't you think the time's come, Albert,' wheedled Nelly, 'when we thought of setting up here together? I mean, we've known each other since we was girl and boy, and we seem to hit it all right, don't we?'

A close observer might have noticed a slight stiffening of Albert's back, but otherwise he gave no sign of hearing. Only his finger moved a little more slowly along the line.

'You've said yourself,' continued Nelly, in cooing tones, 'how nice I cook, and keep the house to rights. You've been alone too long, Albert. What you wants is a bit of home comfort. What about it?'

A slight flush had crept over Albert's unlovely countenance, but still his eyes remained lowered.

'"It is feared,"' Albert read, in an embarrassed mutter, '"that 'is brain 'as suffered damage."'

'And so will yours, my boy!' Nelly burst out, rising swiftly. She lifted Albert's arms from the table, sat herself promptly down on the newspaper in front of Albert and let his arms fall on each side of her.

She put one plump hand under his bristly chin and turned his face up to confront her.

'Now then,' said Nelly, giving him a dark melting glance. 'What about it?'

'What about what?' asked Albert weakly. It was quite apparent that he knew he was a doomed man. At last he was cornered, at last he was caught, but still he struggled feebly.

'You heard what I said,' murmured Nelly seductively, patting his cheek. 'Now I've got the job here, it'd all fit in so nice.'

Albert gazed at her mutely. His eyes were slightly glazed, but there was a certain softening around his drooping mouth.

'You'd have a clean warm house to live in,' went on his temptress, 'and a good hot meal midday, and all your washin' done.'

Albert's eyes brightened a little, but he still said nothing. Nelly put her head provocatively on one side.

'And me here for company, Albert,' she continued, a little breathlessly. Could it be that Albert's eyes dulled a little? She put her plump arms round his shoulders and gazed at him closely.

'Wouldn't you like a good wife?' asked Nelly beseechingly.

Albert gave a great gusty sigh – a farewell, half-sad and half-glad, to all his lonely years – and capitulated.

'All right,' said he. 'But get orf the paper, gal!'

By the end of the week Albert was accepting congratulations from all Thrush Green, with a sheepish grin. The rector was delighted to hear the news when Albert came one evening, twisting his greasy cap round and round in his hands, to mumble that he wanted to put up the banns.

'You're a very lucky fellow,' he told him. 'I've heard nothing but praise about the lady.'

'You'll have to find one for yourself,' answered Albert, emboldened by his master's approbation.

'I really think I shall,' agreed the rector, smiling.

'One thing,' said Ella to Dimity when she heard the news, 'Nelly Tilling will make that cottage smell a bit sweeter – and Albert too, I hope.'

'And what a good thing for Piggott's poor little cat!' exclaimed

Dimity. 'It was such a waif always. Nelly Tilling's bound to fatten it up.'

'Isn't it fortunate?' said Miss Watson to Miss Fogerty. 'To think that she thought of settling in Thrush Green so soon after getting the job!'

'She may, perhaps, have thought of it before,' pointed out Miss Fogerty, with unusual perception.

'Molly Piggott – I mean Curdle – will be pleased,' said Joan Young to her husband Edward. 'It means she won't have to worry too much about the old man while she's so far away.'

'If you ask me,' said Ted Allen to his wife Bessie, sad at the loss of such a good worker at 'The Drovers' Arms', 'she's plain barmy to marry that man!'

'Ah!' breathed Bessie, 'there's no gainsaying Love. Hearts rule heads every time!' She had always been romantic from a girl.

As the month wore on the weather improved, and tempers with it. The workmen, who had been unable to do much in the rain, now returned much refreshed from their rest, and the base of Nathaniel's statue was fast nearing completion. Edward Young brought glowing reports of the progress of the young sculptor and it really seemed as if Thrush Green would be punctual for once and have everything in apple-pie order for the missionary's anniversary on March the fifteenth.

The mild weather allowed the schoolchildren to play outside, much to their teachers' relief. The new school cleaner, whose doughty right arm had scrubbed and polished with considerable effect, also welcomed the dry spell, and the good people of Thrush Green, so long winter-bound, pottered about their gardens, admiring the silver and gold of snowdrops and aconites, and watching the daffodils push their buds above ground.

One sunny afternoon, Ruth Lovell wheeled her infant daughter's pram along the road to Thrush Green. It was wonderful to feel a warm breeze lifting one's hair, and to feel light and strong again. Ruth's spirits rose as she saw the buds on the lilac bushes as fat and plump as green peas. On the other side of the road some willow bushes grew beside a shallow ditch. Already, Ruth could see, the brown buds were showing a fringe of silvery fur, soon to turn to yellow fluff, honey-scented and droning with bees.

But it was the great sticky buds of the horse-chestnut trees which formed the avenue outside her old home on Thrush Green that caused Ruth's heart to stir most strongly. She looked with affection at the sight which had given her joy all her life.

She paused under the trees, her sleeping baby before her, and let her eyes rest upon the familiar scene. On her right, behind the white palings, the children were at play, their distant voices competing with a blackbird's as he trilled and whistled from the Baileys' gate-post on her left. Above her stretched the strong interlacing branches of the chestnut avenue, and higher still a blue and white sky of infinite freshness.

Before her lay the thick green sward upon which her own daughter would be crawling before the summer ended, and there, some fifty yards away, the workmen clanged their tools and whistled, preparing for the great day.

Soon, thought Ruth, joyfully, it would be spring-time again, a time of hope and new life. Before long Mrs Curdle's fair would be assembled on Thrush Green again, and though the old lady would no longer dominate her little world, yet her spirit must surely be with Ben and the great-grandson she had never seen as the fair filled Thrush Green with music and fun on the first day of May.

As she watched the bright scene before her she heard the clang of a distant gate, and saw Ella's sturdy figure emerge from her garden and set off across the green, past St Andrew's, to the alley-way which led to Dotty Harmer's. She was swinging a basket merrily and did not see the motionless figure under the chestnut trees.

'Egg-day!' thought Ruth to herself, and rejoiced at the pleasantness of country life which was so familiar and intimate. 'She'll probably have tea with Dotty, and take great care in choosing her food!'

She watched Ella with affection as she stumped out of sight between 'The Two Pheasants' and Albert's cottage. Unconsciously echoing Mrs Curdle's words on her last visit to Thrush Green, she addressed her sleeping daughter.

'I always feel better for seeing Thrush Green.'

She sighed happily, thinking of the comfort it had brought her through many weeks of misery. It had never failed her. No matter how sore her wounds, the balm of Thrush Green had always soothed them.

She began to push the pram slowly along beneath the trees, over

the road which was bumpy with massive roots just below the
chequered shade on its surface. As she arrived at Joan's gate she took
one last look at the spring sunshine on the green, and caught sight of
the rector in the distance.

He was walking purposefully towards Ella and Dimity's house,
and in his hand was a large bunch of flowers.

20. Coming Home

The rector, as he had intended, found Dimity alone at the house, for
he too had observed Ella striding towards Lulling Woods, basket in
hand, and had remembered that this was the day on which the eggs
were collected.

'Why, Charles!' cried Dimity. 'How lovely to see you! I didn't
know you were allowed out yet.'

'This is my first walk,' admitted the rector. 'But I wanted to come
and thank you properly for all that you have done.' How convenient,
at times, thought the rector, was the English use of the second person
plural!

'Ella's out, I'm afraid,' said Dimity, leading the way to the sitting-
room. 'But I don't think she'll be very long.'

The rector felt a little inner agitation at this news, but did his best
to look disappointed at Ella's temporary absence. He handed Dimity
the flowers with a smile and a small bow.

'Freesias!' breathed Dimity with rapture, thinking how dreadfully
extravagant dear Charles had been, and yet how delicious it was to
have such treasures brought to her. 'How very, very kind, Charles.
They are easily our favourite flowers.'

The rector murmured politely while Dimity unwrapped them.
Their fragrance mingled with the faint smell of wood smoke that
lingered in the room and the rector thought, yet again, how warm
and full of life this small room was. Ella's book lay face downward
on the arm of a chair, her spectacles lodged across it. Dimity's knitting
had been hastily put aside when she answered the door, and decorated
a low table near the fire. The clock ticked merrily, the fire whispered
and crackled, the cat purred upon the window-sill, sitting four-
square and smug after its midday meal.

A feeling of great peace descended upon the rector despite the preoccupations of the errand in hand. Could he ever hope, he wondered, to have such comfort in his own home?

'Do sit down,' said Dimity, 'while I arrange these.'

'I'll come with you,' said Charles, with a glance at the clock. Ella must have reached Dotty's by now.

He followed Dimity into the small kitchen which smelt deliciously of gingerbread.

'There!' gasped Dimity, 'I'd forgotten my cakes in the excitement.' She put down the flowers and opened the oven door.

'Could you pass that skewer, Charles?' she asked, intent on the oven's contents. Obediently, the rector passed it over.

'Harold is coming to tea tomorrow,' said Dimity, 'and he adores gingerbread.' She poked busily at the concoctions, withdrew the tins from the oven and put them on the scrubbed wooden table to cool.

The rector leant against the dresser and watched her as she fetched vases and arranged the freesias. His intentions were clear enough in his own mind, but it was decidedly difficult to make a beginning, particularly when Dimity was so busy.

'I must show you our broad beans,' chattered Dimity, quite unconscious of the turmoil in her old friend's heart. 'They are quite three inches high. Harold gave us some wonderful stuff to keep the slugs off.'

Fond as the rector was of Harold Shoosmith, he found himself disliking his intrusion into the present conversation. Also the subject of slugs, he felt, was not one which made an easy stepping-stone to such delicate matters as he himself had in mind. The kitchen clock reminded him sharply of the passage of time, and urgency lent cunning to the rector's stratagems.

'I should love to see them some time,' said Charles, 'but I wonder if I might sit down for a little? My legs are uncommonly feeble after this flu.'

Dimity was smitten with remorse.

'You poor dear! How thoughtless of me, Charles! Let's take the freesias into the sitting-room and you must have a rest.'

She fluttered ahead, pouring out a little flow of sympathy and self-reproach which fell like music upon the rector's ears.

'Have a cushion behind your head,' said Dimity, when the rector had lowered himself into an armchair. She plumped it up with her thin hands and held it out invitingly. The rector began to feel quite guilty, and refused it firmly.

'Harold says it's the final refinement of relaxation,' said Dimity, and noticed a wince of pain pass over the rector's cherubic face. 'Oh dear, I'm sure you're over-tired! You really shouldn't have ventured so far,' she protested.

'Dimity,' said Charles, taking a deep breath. 'I want to ask you something. Something very important.'

'Yes, Charles?' said Dimity, picking up her knitting busily, and starting to count stitches with her forefinger. The rector, having made a beginning, stuck to his guns manfully.

'Dimity,' he said gently, 'I have a proposal to make.'

Dimity's thin finger continued to gallop along the needle and she frowned with concentration. Inexorably, the little clock on the mantelpiece ticked the precious minutes away. At length she reached the end of the stitches and looked with bright interest at her companion.

'Who from?' she asked briskly. 'The Mothers' Union?'

'*No!*' said the rector, fortissimo. '*Not from the Mothers' Union!*' His voice dropped suddenly. 'The proposal, Dimity, is from me.' And, without more ado, the rector began.

'Oh Charles,' quavered Dimity, when he had ended. Her eyes were full of tears.

'You need not answer now,' said the rector gently, holding one of the thin hands in his own two plump ones. 'But do you think you ever could?'

'Oh Charles,' repeated Dimity, with a huge happy sigh. 'Oh, yes, please!'

When Ella came in, exactly three minutes later, she found them standing on the hearthrug, hand in hand. Before they had time to say a word, she had rushed across the room, enveloped Dimity in a bearhug and kissed her soundly on each cheek.

'Oh Dimity,' said Ella, from her heart, 'I'm so happy!'

'Dash it all, Ella,' protested Charles, 'that's just what *we* were going to say!'

Harold Shoosmith heard the good news from the rector himself, that same evening, and was overjoyed.

'I can't begin to tell you how pleased I am,' he said delightedly, thumping his friend quite painfully in his excitement. 'And now you can get rid of that wretched Mrs Butler.'

'Upon my soul!' exclaimed the rector, his smile vanishing. 'I had quite forgotten all about her. What a dreadful thing!'

'Think nothing of it,' Harold assured him. 'She'll be snapped up in no time by some other poor devil in need of a housekeeper.'

He took a letter from his pocket.

'By the way, I've heard from the bishop.'

'Ours?' asked Charles.

'No – theirs. He says he'll be delighted to unveil the memorial.'

The rector's face glowed happily.

'Isn't that wonderful? I'm most grateful to you, Harold, for arranging all this. Without you Thrush Green would never have remembered Nathaniel at all, I fear.'

'I suggest the bishop stays here overnight,' said Harold, 'and I'll get Betty Bell to cook for a small supper party. Ella and Dimity, of course, and one or two more who would like to meet him.'

'Thank you,' said the rector, 'that would be very kind.' He looked across the green towards Dimity's house. 'It will be a great pleasure to be able to entertain again. The house has been so cheerless I haven't liked to invite anyone to stay. I'm afraid Ella will miss Dimity very much.'

He looked with a speculative eye at his companion.

'I suppose you don't feel towards Ella –' he began.

'Charles, please!' protested Harold faintly, closing his eyes.

Thrush Green wholeheartedly rejoiced in the news of the engagement. The rector's sad plight had been a source of great pity, and Dimity, for all her timid and old-maidish ways, was recognized as a woman of fine character and sweet disposition. Some said that Ella had 'put upon' Miss Dimity too long, and not a few hoped that Ella would regret her past bullyings, and realize that she was at fault.

In actual fact, Ella's spirits were high. Now that the blow had fallen she found that the changed circumstances invigorated her. That Dimity should have chosen the rector still surprised her, for although in the last week or two she had suspected that the rector's feelings were warmer than before, yet she had for so long envisaged Harold Shoosmith as the only real claimant of Dimity's affections that it was difficult to dismiss him from her conjectures.

Within a week of the announcement Ella had decided to move her workbench from the kitchen to the sitting-room and to have a cupboard fitted on the landing for her painting materials. Dimity was equally engrossed in planning her new abode.

The wedding was to take place quietly in the summer, and meanwhile the rectory was to be completely refurbished and decorated as Dimity thought best. It gave the two friends a common interest, and lessened the inevitable pangs of parting after so many years, as they threw themselves wholeheartedly into their preparations.

'It was good while it lasted, Dim,' said Ella philosophically one evening, as they packed some china to be taken across to the rectory. She was thinking of the little house which they had shared.

'It will go on lasting, Ella,' said Dimity. But she was thinking of the friendship which they had shared.

As the fifteenth of March drew near, the inhabitants of Thrush Green turned their attention to the approaching ceremony. The workmen had finished their task in good time, and three fine steps of York stone formed a pleasant cream-coloured plinth for the statue which was due to arrive at any moment.

'The only thing that worries me,' confessed Harold to Charles, 'is whether it will be worth looking at. It would be dreadful to find it looked all wrong on the green after so much effort.'

'The thing that worries me,' answered the rector, 'is finding the rest of the money.'

'But you know—' began Harold, and was cut short.

'Yes, I do know. You're much too generous. But at the moment the fund is only just over a hundred pounds, and I shudder to think of the final cost.'

Harold Shoosmith put his hand on his friend's shoulder.

'Don't you realize that this is the culmination of almost a lifetime's ambitions?' said Harold, with conviction. 'I've dreamt about this for years. Nathaniel Patten meant a great deal to me when I was in Africa. His life and work brought me to Thrush Green – and I hope I'll never leave it. Don't rob me of a very real pleasure, Charles. This statue may be Thrush Green's memorial, but it's also a thank offering on my part for hope when I needed it abroad, and happiness at finding myself in Nathaniel's birthplace.'

'I understand,' said Charles Henstock. 'And thank you.'

★

The statue arrived two days before it was to be unveiled. It was a perfect spring day, warm and sunny, with a great blue and white sky against which the black rooks wheeled and cawed. In the gardens of Thrush Green the velvety polyanthus was in bloom, and a few crocuses spread their yellow and purple petals to disclose dusty orange stamens.

A little knot of people gathered round the lorry to watch the sacking wrappings being removed from the swathed figure. The young sculptor watched anxiously as his masterpiece emerged. He was a well-dressed thickset young man, red of face and bright of eye, and a source of some amazement to various Thrush Green folk who had been expecting someone looking much more pallid and artistic with, possibly, a beard, a beret and sandals.

He helped his workmen hoist the bronze upright on the grass and seemed pleased to hear the little cries of pleasure which greeted the life-size figure. It was indeed a fine piece of work. He had caught exactly the benevolent facial expression and the Pickwickian figure in its cut-away coat. There was something lovable and friendly about its size and its stance, and Thrush Green prepared to welcome Nathaniel warmly.

It took several hours to put the bronze figure securely upon its plinth and by that time all Thrush Green had called to see its new arrival.

'Do you think it should be covered?' asked the rector anxiously of the artist.

'I don't think we need to worry,' smiled the young man. 'He's going to stand on Thrush Green in all weathers for many years, I hope.'

Very early, on the morning of March the fifteenth, before anyone was astir, Harold Shoosmith leant from his bedroom window and looked upon the fulfilment of his dreams. Later in the day, the unveiling would take place, and there would be speeches, cheers and crowds. But now, in the silence of dawn he and his old friend were alone together. Exactly one hundred years ago, on just such a March morning, Nathaniel had been born in a nearby cottage.

A warm finger of sunlight crept across the dewy grass. At last, thought Harold, the long winter at Thrush Green had ended and, exiles no longer, both he and Nathaniel Patten were home again.

NEWS FROM THRUSH GREEN

For Marjorie and Glen
With Love

'You are now collecting your People delightfully, getting them exactly into such a spot as is the delight of my life; 3 or 4 Families in a Country Village is the very thing to work on.'

JANE AUSTEN *in a letter written to her niece Anna who was then writing novels*

Contents

1. For Sale – Tullivers

If you live at Thrush Green you can expect your morning post between 7.30 and 8.15 a.m.

If it is Willie Bond's week to deliver the letters, then they will be early. But if Willie Marchant is the postman then it is no use fretting and fuming. The post will arrive well after eight o'clock, and you may as well resign yourself to the fact.

'It just shows you can't go by looks,' Thrush Green residents tell each other frequently. Willie Bond weighs fifteen stone, is short-legged and short-necked, and puffs in a truly alarming fashion as he pushes his bicycle up the steep hill from the post office at Lulling. His eyes are mere slits in the pink and white moon of his chubby face, and his nickname of Porky is still used by those who were his school-fellows.

Willie Marchant, on the other hand, is a gaunt bean-pole of a fellow with a morose, lined face, and a cigarette stub in the corner of his mouth. He scorns to dismount at Thrush Green's sharp hill, but tacks purposefully back and forth across the road with a fine disregard for the motorists who suffer severe shock when coming upon him suddenly at his manoeuvres. He was once knocked off his bicycle as he made a sharp right-hand turn from one bank to the other, but escaped with a grazed knee and a torn trouser leg.

Dr Bailey, whose house was nearby, had treated both postman and driver, and found that the motorist, though unscarred, was by far the more severely shaken of the two. But despite this mishap, the violent remarks of later motorists and the advice given unstintingly by his clients on Thrush Green, Willie continues to proceed on his erratic course every other week.

The fact that both men have the same Christian name might, at first sight, seem confusing, but there are distinct advantages. As Ella Bembridge remarked once at a Thrush Green cocktail party, in a booming voice heard by all present:

'It's jolly useful when you're upstairs coping with your bust bodice or bloomers, and you hear whoever-it-is plonking down the letters on the hall table! I just shout down: "Thanks, Willie", and you know you'll be all right.'

There had been a sudden burst of animated conversation as Ella's fellow-guests, embarrassed or simply amused by Ella's unguarded remarks, sought to tell each other hastily of their own arrangements for receiving and disposing of their mail.

'I have had to install one of those wire cage things,' said Harold Shoosmith, the bachelor who lives in one of the handsomest houses on the green. 'Since the puppy came, nothing's safe on the floor. He ate a cheque for six pounds ten, and the rates' demand, all in one gulp last Thursday. I didn't mind the latter, naturally, but I hated to see the cheque going down.'

'We leave our letters sticking out of the flap,' said the rector, 'and Willie takes them!'

'Not if it's a north wind,' his wife Dimity reminded him. 'The rain blows in and drenches them. He has to open the door then, and take them from the window-sill.'

Winnie Bailey, the doctor's wife, said she tried to put hers in the post-box on the corner of the green. It made her go for a walk, for one thing, and she sometimes wondered if Willie Bond read the postcards.

'Why not?' said Harold Shoosmith. 'I *always* read postcards; other people's as well as my own. Damn it all, if you don't want a thing to be read you put it in an envelope!'

Someone said, rather coldly, that was exactly why she *never* used postcards. One was at the mercy of unscrupulous busy-bodies. Her letters were left, neatly secured with a rubber band, on the hall table to be collected by whichever Willie was on duty.

Her companion said he left his in a box in the porch. Dotty Harmer, an elderly spinster as erratic as her name implied, vouchsafed the information that she hung hers on the gate in a string bag, and that they had blown away once or twice. Significant glances were exchanged behind the lady's back. What else would you expect of Dotty?

'My new next door neighbour,' remarked Winnie Bailey, 'leaves hers pinned under the knocker, I see. It must weigh seven or eight pounds. It's that great brass dolphin old Admiral Trigg fixed up years ago, you know. Nothing could get blown away from that thing!'

Suddenly, the subject of letters was dropped. Here was something of much greater importance. Who was Winnie Bailey's neighbour? Where did she come from? Would she be staying long?

The party turned expectantly towards Winnie, avid for the latest news from Thrush Green.

The house where the newcomer had recently arrived had been empty for two years. Tullivers, as it was called, had been the home of old Admiral Josiah Trigg and his sister Lucy for almost thirty years, and when he died, suddenly, one hot afternoon, after taking the sharp hill from the town at a spanking pace, his sister continued to muddle along in a vague, amiable daze, for another eighteen months, before succumbing to bronchitis.

'If it's not the dratted hill,' pronounced old Piggott the sexton gloomily, 'that carries off us Thrush Green folks, it's the dratted east wind. You gotter be tough to live 'ere.'

You certainly had to be tough to live at Tullivers after the Admiral had gone, for Lucy Trigg, in her eighties, could not be bothered to have any domestic help, nor could she be bothered to light fires, to cook meals for herself, nor to clean the house and tend the garden.

Winnie Bailey, the soul of tact, did what she could in an unobtrusive way, but knew she was fighting a losing battle. The curtains grew greyer, the window-panes misty with grime, the door-step and path were spattered with bird-droppings, and the docks and nettles rioted in the borders once tended by Lucy's brother and kept trim and shipshape with pinks, pansies and geums neatly confined within immaculate box hedges.

It wasn't as if Lucy Trigg were senile. Her mind, in some ways, was as clear as ever. She played a good game of bridge with her neighbours. She attacked, and overcame, the challenge of the *Daily Telegraph* crossword puzzle each morning, and played her dusty piano with fingers still nimble despite arthritis. It was simply that the squalor of her house did not affect her. Her world had shrunk to the few things which still had interest for her. The rest was ignored.

It was fortunate that Tullivers was a small house with a small garden. Doctor Bailey, as a young man, had been offered the major part of the next door garden by the Admiral's predecessor. He had bought it for thirty pounds, enclosed it with a honey-coloured

Cotswold stone wall, and planted a small but fine orchard, now at the height of its production. Thus the Baileys' garden was L-shaped, and the remaining portion of Tullivers' land, a mere quarter of an acre, allowed room for only a lawn, a few mature lilac and may trees and the flower border which had been the Admiral's particular pride.

An Albertine rose grew splendidly over one end of the house, and winter jasmine starred the front porch in the cold of the year. Inside were two fairly small square rooms, one each side of the front door, with a roomy kitchen built on at the back.

Above stairs were two modest bedrooms and a bathroom with Victorian fittings and a geyser which made threatening rumbles, wheezes and minor explosions when in use.

Tullivers, in its heyday, was always known as 'a snug house' by Thrush Green people. It stood at right angles to the road, and rather nearer it than most of the larger houses which stood back in their well-kept gardens.

It faced south, across the Baileys' front garden, towards the roofs of Lulling in the valley below, a mile distant. It crouched there, as snug as a contented cat, catching the sunshine full on its face.

To see Tullivers so neglected had grieved Thrush Green. Its decay over the past two years had been a constant topic of conversation. It had been left to a nephew of Lucy Trigg's, also a naval man, who put it in the hands of a London estate agent to sell for him whilst he was abroad.

'Pity he didn't let the local chaps have it,' was the general opinion. 'Keep a sharper eye on it. Should have gone within the month.' There had been one or two prospective buyers, pushing their way through the tall weeds, with papers describing the property's charms in their hands, but the general neglect seemed to dishearten them. Heavy snow in January and February kept other possible buyers away, and by the time the crocuses and daffodils were decking the rest of the Thrush Green gardens, Tullivers was looking at its worst.

Birds nested in the porch and in the guttering, and a bold jackdaw started to build in the cold unused chimney. Mice had found shelter in the kitchen, and spiders spun their webs unmolested.

The children at the village school eyed the blank windows speculatively, and the bigger boys fingered the catapults hidden in their pockets, longing to pick up pebbles and let fly at this beautiful sitting target. What could be more exhilarating than the crack of a glass pane, the dramatic starring, the satisfying hole? Two of the most daring had been observed in the garden by Miss Watson, the head-mistress, who lived across the green at the school house, and she had delivered dire warnings during assembly the next morning. The two malefactors had been displayed to the assembled school as 'Trespassers Loitering With Criminal Intent,' and were suitably abashed. Thrush Green parents, fortunately, were still unspoilt by modern educational theories and heartily approved of Miss Watson's strong line. Miss Fogerty, who was in charge of the infants' class, added her own warnings when she regained the classroom, and the infants approached their morning's labours in a suitably sober mood. It says much for the two ladies, and the parents of Thrush Green, that the little house remained safe from children's assaults, despite temptation.

One bright April day, a red Mini stopped outside Tullivers and a tall woman, paper fluttering from a gloved hand, made her way into the house.

Miss Fogerty was on playground duty that morning. Standing on the sheltered side of the school, teacup in hand, she watched with mounting excitement. Around her squealed and shouted the sixty or so pupils of Thrush Green Church of England Primary School. During those delirious fifteen minutes of morning play-time, they were variously space-men, horses, footballers, boxers, cowboys or – among the youthful minority – simply mothers and fathers. The noise was ear-splitting. The bracing Cotswold air produces fine healthy lungs and the rumpus made at play-time could be clearly heard by fond parents who were safely half a mile away.

Agnes Fogerty, quiet and still as a mouse, and not unlike that timid animal in her much-pressed grey flannel skirt and twin-set to match, stood oblivious of the chaos around her. Somehow, she sensed that the stranger would take on Tullivers one day. There was something purposeful about that stride towards the front door, and the deft slipping of the key into the lock – almost as though the house were hers already, thought little Miss Fogerty.

And quite alone! Perhaps she was a single woman? Or perhaps her husband was working and she had decided to look at the place herself before they came down together? Or, of course, she might be a widow? The war had left so many attractive women without husbands. Miss Fogerty gave a small sigh for all that might have been, and then remembered, sharply, that the stranger was much younger than she was herself, and could not have been much more than a baby during the last war.

Not that widowhood could be dismissed quite so neatly, Miss Fogerty comforted herself. After all, the number of young men who succumbed to coronary thrombosis alone, not to mention the annual toll of influenza and road casualties, was quite formidable. On the whole, Miss Fogerty liked the idea of a sensible widow occupying Tullivers. Who knows? She might even become friendly with another well-read woman living nearby, and companionable little tea-parties and visits to each other's houses might blossom. Miss Fogerty, it will be observed, was lonely at times.

Meanwhile, time was getting on. Miss Fogerty consulted her watch, which she hauled up on a chain from beneath her grey jumper, and then clapped her hands for attention. It says much for her discipline that within one minute the playground was quiet enough for her small precise voice to be heard.

'Lead in, children,' she said, 'and *no pushing!*'

She followed the last child towards the arch of the Gothic doorway, pausing there for a last look across the green to Tullivers. The stranger had vanished from view inside the house. The dashing red mini-car waited by the kerb.

Here was something to tell dear Miss Watson! Warm with excitement, Agnes Fogerty entered her accustomed realm, the infants' room. As soon as school dinner was finished, and she and her headmistress were enjoying their cup of instant coffee, she would impart this latest snippet of news to her colleague.

Needless to say, many other people observed the stranger's entry to Tullivers. Thrush Green, to the uninitiated, might have seemed remarkably quiet that morning. The school-children apart, not more than two or three people were to be seen. There were, of course, almost a dozen unseen – hidden behind curtains, screened by garden shrubs, or cocking a curious eye from such vantage points as porches and wood sheds.

Albert Piggott, languidly grubbing up the dead winter grass at the foot of the churchyard railings, kept the stranger comfortably in view. He approved of the red Mini. Must have a bit of money to drive a car, and that great leather handbag had cost something, he shouldn't wonder. He knew a decent bit of leather when he saw it. Plastic never deceived Albert Piggott yet. A handsome gal too, with a nice pair of long legs.

Not like his old woman, he thought sourly. He straightened up slowly, eyes still fixed upon the unsuspecting stranger. What on earth had made him marry that great lump Nelly Tilling? He should have known it would never work. Women were all the same. Wheedled their way into your life, cunning as cats, and once they'd hooked you, the trouble started.

'You ain't washed, Albert! Time you took a bath, Albert! Give over sniffing, Albert! You've got plenty of hankies what want using. I wants more money than this for house-keeping. And you can keep out of the pub, Albert! That's where the money goes!'

His wife's shrill voice echoed in his head. He hadn't had a day's peace since they were wed, and that was God's truth, said the sexton piously to himself.

Marriage never did anyone any good. He'd take a bet that that young woman at Tullivers' front door was single. She could afford to buy a house, to run a car, to keep herself looking nice. Probably one of these career women who'd had the sense to keep out of matrimony.

Albert leant moodily on the railings, a fistful of dead grass against his shirt front, and pondered on the inequality of the bounty supplied by Providence. By now, the stranger had unlocked the door and entered the house.

For the first time that morning Albert became conscious of the warmth of the sun and the song of a bold robin perched upon the tombstone of Lavinia, Wife of Robert Entwistle, Gent., who had left sunshine and birdsong behind her for ever on 3 February 1792.

Nelly might be no beauty. She was certainly a nagger. But he had just remembered that she was preparing a steak and kidney pie when he had left her an hour ago, and Nelly's hand with pastry was unsurpassed.

Cheered by this thought, and by the hopeful signs of spring about him, Albert bent again to his task. Another warming idea occurred to him. Single women often needed a hand with wood-chopping, hedge-trimming and the like. It would be a good thing to have a little extra money coming in. With any luck, he could keep it from Nelly, and spend it as he used to, in his carefree pre-marital days, at 'The Two Pheasants'!

Albert Piggott broke into a rare and rusty whistling.

But it was Ella Bembridge who had the closest look at the new-comer that morning.

She was about to cross from her cottage to the rectory on the green opposite to consult her friend Dimity Henstock about the advisability of having the boiler chimney swept.

Such mundane affairs had always been left to Dimity when the two women shared the cottage where Ella now lived alone. The rector's wife, as well as running her own ungainly house, found herself continuing to keep an eye on her old establishment, for Ella was the most impractical creature alive.

It was Dimity who defrosted Ella's refrigerator before the icy stalactites grew too near the top shelf. It was Dimity who surrepti-tiously threw away the fortnight-old stew which had grown a fine crop of pale blue fur upon its surface, or some shapeless mess which had started out as a fruit mousse and had collapsed into something reminiscent of frogs' spawn. She did not chide her old friend about her slap-dash ways. She loved her too well to hurt her, and recognized that Ella's warm heart and her artistic leanings more than made up for her complete lack of housewifery.

The little red car had just drawn up as Ella was slamming her gate. Ella had no scruples about staring, and she stood now, a sturdy figure, watching unashamedly as the stranger emerged.

The younger woman gave Ella no greeting, as country people are wont to do. In fact, she appeared not to notice the watching figure. She locked the car door (a precaution which most Thrush Green folk forgot to take) and consulted the paper in her hand before walking swiftly towards Tullivers.

Ella waited until the front door closed behind her with a groaning of rusty hinges, and then crossed the road to the rectory where she found Dimity in the kitchen beating up eggs whilst her husband made the mid-morning coffee.

Over their steaming cups Ella gave her account of the new-comer.

'About thirty, I reckon. Looks bright enough – might be useful in the W.I. Nice dog-tooth check suit in brown and white, and stockings with no seams. Come to think of it – they were probably tights. I didn't see any tops when she clambered out of the mini.'

'Ella dear,' protested Charles Henstock mildly. 'Spare my feelings.'

'Nice pair of square-toed shoes, Russell and Bromley probably, and an Italian handbag.'

'How on earth do you know?' expostulated Dimity.

'I can smell Italian leather a mile off,' said Ella, fishing a battered tin from her pocket and beginning to roll a cigarette from the crumpled papers and loose tobacco therein.

'And I'd take a bet her ear-rings were Italian too,' she added, blowing out an acrid cloud of smoke. Dimity quietly moved the egg-custard out of range.

'Ears pierced?' asked the rector, with rare sarcasm.

'Couldn't see,' replied Ella in a matter-of-fact tone. 'But wears good gloves.'

Something sizzled in the oven and Dimity crossed the kitchen to attend to it.

'Not that I really noticed her,' continued Ella. 'Just got a passing glimpse, you know.'

The rector forbore to comment.

'But she's welcome to Tullivers,' went on Ella. 'There's a jackdaw's nest the size of a squirrel's drey in the kitchen chimney. Which reminds me – shall I get the boiler chimney done, Dim?'

Dimity sat back on her heels by the open oven door and looked thoughtful.

'September, October, November, December, January, February, March, April – yes, Ella. Get it swept now.'

'Good,' replied her old friend, rising briskly and dropping her cigarette stub into the sink basket where it smouldered, unpleasantly close to the shredded cabbage soaking in a bowl.

'I got my old hand loom out again last night,' said Ella conversationally. 'Thought I'd run up a few ties ready for the next Bring and Buy Sale and Christmas time.'

She looked speculatively at Charles, who was doing his best to repress a shudder. He already had four ties of Ella's making, each much too short, the colour of over-cooked porridge, and far too thick to knot properly. Fortunately, he wore his clerical collar more often than not, and could safely leave the monstrosities in the drawer without hurting Ella's feelings.

'Lovely, dear,' said Dimity automatically, putting the egg-custard into the oven carefully.

'I'll see you out,' said the rector, following Ella along the cold dark passage to the front door.

Outside, Thrush Green sparkled in the bright April sunshine. It was like emerging from a dark cave in the cliffs on to a sunlit beach, thought Ella. She was thankful that she did not have to live in the rectory. Could anything ever make that north-facing pile of Victorian architecture comfortable?

She looked towards Tullivers, and the rector's gaze followed hers. The shabby little house basked in the sunshine like some small, battered, stray cat grateful for warmth. There was no sign of the stranger, and the red car had gone.

'Oh,' cried the rector, genuinely disappointed, 'I'd hoped to catch sight of her, I must admit.'

'You will,' prophesied Ella, setting off purposefully for her own cottage. 'Mark my words, Charles Henstock, you will!'

2. Who is She?

Two or three weeks later the red car reappeared. This time the young woman had a companion, as sharp eyes on Thrush Green were quick to observe.

A small boy, of about six years of age, clambered out of the car and jumped excitedly up and down on the pavement. He was a well-built child, flaxen-haired and fair-skinned, and seemed delighted with his first glimpse of Thrush Green. He pointed to Tullivers, obviously asking questions. He pointed to the fine statue of Nathaniel Patten, erected a year or two earlier by Thrush Green residents to honour one of their famous men, and he was clearly impressed by the church and the village school across the green.

The woman looked up and down the road, as though waiting for somebody. Her answers to the child appeared perfunctory.

After a few minutes, she led the way to the front door, followed by the boy. Just as it closed behind them, the local builder's battered van screeched to a halt behind the red car, and out tumbled Joe Bush.

'Late as usual!' was the general comment of the hidden onlookers of Thrush Green as they watched him scurry up the path.

By standing on tip-toe, little Miss Fogerty could just see what was going on across the green. The Gothic window was uncomfortably high, installed by its Victorian builders for just that purpose – to make sure that children could not look out easily and so be distracted from their pot-hooks and hangers by the giddy world outside.

The sand-tray was also rather awkwardly placed beneath the window. Miss Fogerty made up her mind to shift it at playtime. This week the sand-tray carried a tiny replica of Thrush Green with plasticine houses, duly labelled with their owners' names, the church, the school, and even a passable representation of Nathaniel Patten's statue. Some of the infants had proudly brought contributions to the scene. Toy lorries, cars, and even an Army tank, had found a place on the roads across the green, and though grossly over-sized for their surroundings they made an imposing addition to the sand-tray. It was unfortunate that the fine avenue of chestnut trees which flanked the north side of the green, had also been constructed of plasticine. The heat from the hot-water pipe nearby had caused them to bow to the ground with flaccid exhaustion. Loving fingers restored them to the upright position a dozen times a day, but Miss Fogerty decided that twigs set in a plasticine base must replace the present avenue without delay.

Miss Fogerty shifted a Virol jar full of paint brushes further along the window-sill, the better to follow the stranger's activities. The little boy aroused her keenest interest. He looked just the right age for her class, and very likely he could read already. What a blessing! And could probably manage his own buttons and shoe-laces too which was more than half her class could accomplish. It was truly disgraceful that Gloria Curdle, at the great age of six, was still unable to tie a bow!

'Which reminds me,' said Miss Fogerty to herself. 'Tears or no tears, that child's tin camel *must* be removed from the Thrush Green model. Looming over the church spire is bad enough, in

all conscience, but having an Asiatic creature like that among the
Cotswolds scenery just Will Not Do!'

Firmly she plucked the offending beast from its alien pastures and
put it safely into her sagging cardigan pocket.

Across the green the little boy was jumping rhythmically.
Good coordination, noted Miss Fogerty approvingly, and plenty
of spring.

'I wonder if there are any more children?' speculated Miss Fogerty.
A tugging at her skirt nearly precipitated her into the sand-tray.

'Child,' cried Miss Fogerty, with unusual sharpness. 'Don't pull
people about in that rude fashion.'

'I can't wait,' said the child, with simple candour.

'Be quick then,' responded Miss Fogerty automatically, returning
reluctantly to her duties, with a last glance at Joe Bush's retreating
back.

'She's back again,' announced Betty Bell to her employer Harold
Shoosmith.

Harold Shoosmith was a comparative newcomer himself to Thrush
Green, having come to live there on his retirement from business in
Africa two or three years earlier. Tall, spare and handsome ... and,
best of all, a bachelor ... he was welcomed warmly by the community.

It had been his idea to honour one of Thrush Green's famous sons,
the missionary Nathaniel Patten, and the splendid statue of their
nineteenth century hero now graced the green.

The fact that Harold was happy to take part in village affairs, and
had the leisure to do so, meant that he was on a dozen or more local
committees. At this moment he was immersed in the Thrush Green
Entertainments Club's accounts. He looked up from his desk. He had
long since given up remonstrating with his slap-dash help about
bursting into occupied rooms. If Betty Bell held a duster in her hand,
she looked upon it as a passport to free passage anywhere in the
house, the bathroom included. Early in their acquaintance she had
bounced in to encounter her employer stark naked, except for an
inadequate face flannel, but had not been a whit abashed. It was
Harold Shoosmith who suffered from shock. After that, he prudently
locked the door when at his ablutions.

'Who's back?' he asked apprehensively. Ella Bembridge, whom he

found most trying, had just left him after delivering the parish magazine, and he feared her return.

'That new party,' responded Betty, flicking an African carving,
knocking it from its shelf and catching it adroitly, all in a second.
Harold, wincing, could not help admiring her deftness. Practice, he
supposed, resignedly.

'Her that's coming to Tullivers,' continued Betty, attacking a
small enamelled clock mercilessly. 'Got a young man with her this
time,' she added archly.

'Husband, I expect,' said Harold, returning to his accounts.

'What! That age?' cried Betty, giggling at the success of her
subtlety. 'He ain't no more'n six, I'll lay.'

She fell energetically upon a window sill. A dozing fly burst into a
frenzy of buzzing as it tried to escape from her onslaught.

'If you was to go out the front and down to the gate you'd get a
good look at her,' advised Betty. 'She's hanging about for someone.
Joe Bush, I expect. That place'll need a proper going-over before it's
fit to live in.'

'I shouldn't dream of staring at the lady,' said Harold sternly.
'And, in any case, I think you are taking a lot for granted. No one
knows if she proposes to buy Tullivers. If she does, then we shall call
in the usual way.'

Betty Bell was not affected by the touch of frost in Harold's
manner. Hoity-toity was her only silent comment, as she gave a final
drubbing to the window sill.

'Wantcher desk done?' she asked cheerfully.

'No thanks,' replied Harold shortly. 'I want to work on it.'

'Okay, okay!' replied his daily help. 'I'll go and put the curry on.
Suit you?'

'Very well, Betty, thank you,' said Harold, his good humour
restored at the thought of her temporary absence.

The door crashed behind her, and soon the sound of clashing
saucepans proclaimed that his lunch was being prepared. Distracting
though the noise was, Harold Shoosmith thanked heaven that it was
at a distance.

He turned again to his accounts.

Across the green, young Doctor Lovell was having trouble too.
The last patient at his morning surgery was Dotty Harmer.

He had to admit, in all fairness, that she did not worry him unduly with her ailments. She preferred to deal with them herself with a variety of herbal remedies ranging from harmlessly wholesome to downright dangerous, in the doctor's opinion.

His senior partner, Doctor Bailey, who was now too frail to take much part in the practice, had warned him about Dotty.

'Eccentric always – plain crazy sometimes,' he summed up succinctly. 'Father was a proper martinet, and taught at the local grammar school. His wife died young, and Dotty kept house for the old Tartar until he died. As you'll see, the place is filthy, full of animals, and the garden is a jungle of herbs from which Dotty brews the most diabolical concoctions. I beg of you, young man, never to eat or drink anything which Dotty has prepared. We have a special complaint at Thrush Green known as "Dotty's Collywobbles". Be warned!'

Since then, the young partner had frequently met those suffering from this disorder. Doctor Bailey, he realized early in their friendship, knew his patients pretty thoroughly.

This morning he examined a long angry gash in Dotty's forearm, caused by the horn of a young goat who was the latest addition to Dotty's motley family.

'Such a sweet disposition really,' said Dotty earnestly. 'It wasn't *meant*, you know. Just playfulness.'

'When was it done?' asked the doctor.

'One day last week, I think,' said Dotty vaguely. 'Or the week before, perhaps. The weeks pass so quickly, don't they? Monday morning it's Saturday afternoon, if you know what I mean. I treated it at once, of course.'

'What with?'

'Now let me see. I think it was one of dear Gerard's. From his Herball, you know. Yes, I remember now, it was All-Heale.'

'All-Heale?' asked Doctor Lovell, whose knowledge of sixteenth-century remedies was shaky.

'As a practising physician,' said Dotty sharply, 'you surely know Clownes Wound-Wort! You simply pound the leaves with a little pure lard and apply the ointment to any open wound. Gerard gives several examples of his success with the cure. I should have thought that all medical men would be conversant with the "poore man of Kent who in mowing of Peason did cut his leg with a sithe". He had the sense to apply All-Heale, and was cured within days.'

'I'll give you a shot of antibiotics,' said Doctor Lovell firmly. He scribbled a prescription, turning a deaf ear to his patient's protestations.

'The lotion should be used twice a day,' he continued, handing her the form, 'and keep the wound covered. Take the tablets night and morning. You'll be fine in a day or two, but come back if it gives any further trouble.'

Dotty took it in her claw-like grasp and surveyed the hieroglyphics with distaste and doubt.

Doctor Lovell relented, and patted her bony shoulder.

'Most of these things are based on the tried herbal recipes, you know,' he said mendaciously.

Dotty looked relieved.

'I hope you're right, young man,' she said, opening the surgery door. Her eye lit upon the red car and Joe Bush's van.

'Have you met your new neighbour?' inquired Dotty.

'First I've heard of one,' said Doctor Lovell.

'You're the only person on Thrush Green who hasn't,' replied Dotty tartly.

Setting off for her cottage half a mile away, Dotty shook her untidy grey head over modern physicians. They seemed to know nothing about their really great forebears, and very little of the immediate world about them. It didn't give a patient much confidence, to be sure.

She fingered the prescription in her coat pocket. For two pins, she'd tear it up and forget it. But just suppose that her arm refused to heal and she was obliged to return to that silly fellow?

It might be prudent to give his nostrums a brief trial. Medical men were so touchy if one ignored their advice.

Nevertheless, as soon as she had traversed the alley by Albert Piggott's house which led to the path to Lulling Woods, and knew that she was out of sight of Thrush Green, Dotty stopped to extract a string bag from her pocket, and advanced purposefully upon a fine collection of weeds growing in the ditch.

'Best to be on the safe side,' said Dotty to herself, thrusting the pungent leaves into the bag.

Swinging it jauntily, she skipped homeward, well satisfied.

3. The Priors Meet Their Neighbours

In the months that followed, Joe Bush's van spent most of its time standing outside Tullivers. Not that the house was a hive of activity – Joe Bush's methods, and those of his two assistants, were both leisurely and erratic. There were frequent trips down the steep hill to Lulling High Street, where lay the builder's yard, for forgotten items. There were a prodigious number of 'brew-ups' during the day, so that work proceeded slowly.

Luckily, perhaps, only the basic repairs seemed to be tackled. Loose roof tiles were replaced, the jackdaw's nest removed from the kitchen chimney, and two faulty windows were rehung. Inside, a few rotting floor-boards were made good and a particularly hideous fireplace removed. Otherwise, it seemed, the house would be put into shape by its owner.

'Cor!' exclaimed Joe Bush, to the landlord of 'The Two Pheasants'. 'She've got plenty to do there, I'll tell you. I shan't get fat on what she's spending, and that's the truth.'

'Maybe she ain't got it to spend,' replied the landlord reasonably. 'She being a widow, I take it.'

'And what makes you think that?' asked Joe, heavily sarcastic. 'She's got a husband all right.'

'Don't show up much,' commented the landlord.

'He's overseas,' replied Joe, putting down his empty glass and making for the door. 'I shouldn't wonder,' he added vaguely.

'Either he is or he isn't,' pointed out the landlord, understandably nettled.

'Well, that's what she told the kid last week when they was down. But you knows women. Crafty as a wagon-load of monkeys. Maybe he's doin' time and she don't want the kid to know.'

'Don't talk out the back of your neck,' begged the landlord. He flapped at the counter with a teacloth in a dismissive fashion. Joe took the hint and vanished.

The absence of a man in the stranger's life certainly intrigued Thrush Green. It was established that the handsome lady was a Mrs Prior, that her son was called Jeremy, and that they lived, at the present time, in a flat in Chelsea.

These interesting facts had been gleaned from the child, rather than from his mother, by Joe Bush's junior assistant, known as Sawny Sam locally, for obvious reasons, although his baptismal name was Samuel Ellerman John Plumb. It was Sawny Sam who held ladders, carried hods, mixed cement, wheeled barrows, fetched forgotten items from the yard, and brewed the tea six times a day.

He had a gentle, kindly disposition, and at seventeen years of age his intelligence was on a par with young Jeremy's. They got on famously, sharing a love of football, animals and stamp collecting.

On several occasions during the summer, Mrs Prior and Jeremy came down at weekends to decorate the interior of Tullivers. While his mother slapped vigorously at the walls with white emulsion paint, the child occupied himself happily in the garden. On Saturday mornings, the builders were at work, and it was then that the friendship grew between Jeremy and Sawny Sam.

'I'm going to that school,' said Jeremy, nodding across to the other side of the green.

'It's ever so nice,' said Sam heavily. 'My cousin Dave went there. He was a monitor.'

'Why didn't you go?'

'I lives up the street. I 'ad to go to St Margaret's School. We 'ad a beast of a 'ead.'

'What did he do?'

''It yer!'

'What for?'

'Anythink. Nothink.'

'He sounds cruel.'

''E were.'

'Is he still?'

'No. He's stopped now.'

'Why?'

'Dead,' said Sam perfunctorily.

He filled the kettle, and Jeremy set out the enamel mugs for the second tea-break of the day. He looked thoughtful.

'Are they cruel over there?'

'Nah!' drawled Sam derisively. 'There's only two old ducks – Miss Watson and Miss Fogerty. Like Aunties, they are. Gives you sweets and that. Friday afternoons you can take any gear you likes to play with.'

'Like stamp albums?' asked Jeremy eagerly.

'Dinky cars, if you want to. Anythink – absolutely *anythink*, Dave said. Except guns and catapults and that. Them two don't 'old with guns. Nothink dangerous.'

They sat companionably, side by side, on a low pile of bricks, and looked across at Jeremy's new school, while the kettle hummed.

'I shall like it,' announced Jeremy, with decision. 'Shall I learn things?'

Sawny Sam's mouth and eyes became three O's in astonishment.

'Learn? 'Course you'll *learn*. Them two'll learn you all right. Poitry, tables –'

'*Tables*?' exclaimed Jeremy. 'What tables? You can't *learn* tables. You eat off 'em.'

'You must go to a pretty soppy school if you ain't 'eard of tables. Multiplication tables! Twice two are four, three twos are six, four twos are eight, five twos are ten. I knows 'em all – well, nearly. Never quite mastered seven times and twelve times,' admitted Sam frankly.

'We work things out like that with milk bottles at my school,' said Jeremy.

'Must take a lotter time,' said Sam.

'And a lot of milk bottles,' responded Jeremy. They relapsed into silence, brooding vaguely upon elementary arithmetic. The kettle lid began to rattle cheerfully and Sam rose to attend to it.

'Tell you one thing,' he said. 'You'll do all right with Miss Fogerty. She learns kids a treat. Been at it a hundred years, I shouldn't wonder. My dad said so.'

It was a comforting thought.

It was that night that Winnie Bailey, next door to Tullivers, woke at two o'clock. In the other bed her husband tossed restlessly.

'Are you all right, Donald?' she asked softly.

'Sorry, my dear, to have woken you,' wheezed the old man. 'Just can't sleep, that's all.'

'I'll go and warm some milk. It will do us both good,' said Winnie, groping for her slippers. She shrugged herself into her comfortable ancient red dressing gown, and made her way downstairs. In the kitchen, as the milk warmed on the stove, she looked out upon the dark garden. In the distance, an owl screeched from Lulling Woods. A frond of jasmine tapped at the window, and turning to the noise, Winnie Bailey had a severe shock. A light was showing in Tullivers.

Could it be that someone had broken in? Could that attractive young woman have left the light switched on? Should she go and investigate? Or ring the police?

An ominous hissing from the milk saucepan interrupted her agitated thoughts. She filled two mugs, put them on a small tray, and then went to look cautiously from the front door across to her new neighbours.

To her surprise, she saw the little red car parked in the short drive to Tullivers. The light, she now perceived, was a very low one. She realized suddenly that it was a night-light, and recalled with a pang, her own children's early years, when a night-light burned comfortingly in a saucer of water to keep away those bogeys which come at night to scare the young.

But what an extraordinary thing, thought Winnie, mounting the stairs carefully. What could those two be sleeping on? And how cheerless it must be in that cold, empty house!

She had spoken once or twice to the young woman who had introduced herself as Phil Prior, but Winnie had felt that the stranger did not welcome overtures too warmly, and so she had decided to 'make haste slowly', as Donald often said. No doubt, the girl had plenty to do in the short time at her disposal on each visit, and any interruptions were frustrating.

But really, thought Winnie, she must see that those two were all right in the morning. Why on earth didn't they put up at 'The Fleece' overnight?

By the time she regained the bedroom, her husband had fallen asleep. She knew better than to disturb him. Sleep was of more value to the frail man than hot milk.

She sipped her own milk thoughtfully, turning over in her mind the conditions of the pair next door. There was something rather sad about them, she felt. Perhaps 'sad' was too strong a word to use about two young and obviously healthy people. On second thoughts, 'forlorn' fitted them better. As though they were faintly neglected – as though they had lost something desperately necessary.

Could it be, thought Winnie, a husband and a father?

She must certainly risk a snub, and speak to Mrs Prior in the morning. Putting her mug gently upon the bedside table, she slipped, within minutes, into troubled slumber.

Winnie Bailey was one of the very few residents of Thrush Green who attended the communion service at eight o'clock at St Andrew's.

No one was stirring at Tullivers as she returned to prepare breakfast, and it was almost ten o'clock before she heard the child's voice from the garden next door. The August sun was already hot, and Thrush Green was going to have a day of shimmering heat. Doctor Bailey was lying in the old wicker chaise-longue, a rug across his legs, and a battered panama hat tilted over his eyes.

He wished, for the thousandth time, that he was not such a useless crock. Doctor Lovell and Winnie had to work far too hard for his liking. There was no doubt about it, the time was fast arriving when young Lovell would need another partner, and a pretty active one too.

A new estate was growing rapidly along the lane leading to Nod and Nidden. Two or three dozen families had moved in already, mainly young couples with one or two babies, and obviously more would come. The practice had almost doubled in size since he arrived there with Winnie in their young days.

How happy they had been, he thought! His mind dwelt on early patients, many now dead, and the welcome they had given him. He remembered, with affection, the matriarchal figure of Mrs Curdle, the gipsy woman who ran the annual one-day fair on Thrush Green every first of May. He hoped that young Ben, her grandson, who was now in charge, would call again next May.

His eye fell upon his pale wasted hands, and he wondered, without self-pity, if he could live long enough to see the fair again. He doubted it. As a medical man, he could gauge his future fairly accurately. Already, he told himself, he was living on borrowed time. And how good it was! Despite weakness and pain, life was still precious, and the companionship of Winnie the mainspring of his days.

He saw her now crossing the garden to the hedge, and heard the little boy from Tullivers answering her questions. Very soon a third voice was added to the conversation, but he could not distinguish the words.

Winnie came up to him and tucked the rug neatly round his legs.

'I've asked our new neighbours to come and have coffee,' she told him. 'It won't tire you?'

'Attractive women never tire me,' said her husband gallantly. An hour later they arrived.

'Please forgive my piebald appearance,' said the young woman, gazing down at her black jeans and sleeveless black blouse. Both were liberally speckled and streaked with white paint. 'It seems to run down my arm and trickle off my elbow.'

'Try a roller,' advised the doctor.

'I simply can't manage one,' confessed the girl, and the comparative merits of brushes and rollers occupied them happily whilst Mrs Bailey went to fetch the tray, accompanied by a chattering Jeremy.

'And when do you hope to move in?'

'In two or three weeks, with luck. The men should have finished by then, they say.'

'Yes – well,' said the doctor, rubbing his bony nose doubtfully. 'That may be so, but if I were you I should move in even if they haven't departed. Joe Bush takes his time.'

'It hadn't escaped me,' replied the young woman, smiling.

Mrs Bailey returned with the tray.

'We've got *two* sorts of biscuits,' announced Jeremy excitedly.

'It's not very polite to comment on other people's food,' his mother told him gently.

'It sounded favourable comment to me,' said Winnie. 'We like that here.'

'We had rather a scratch breakfast,' said Mrs Prior. 'We stayed overnight for the first time.'

Winnie was glad that she had mentioned the burning subject first.

'Were you both comfortable?' she asked.

'Hardly. Our camp beds are the sort that Victorian explorers humped about!'

'Or probably their native bearers humped about,' suggested Doctor Bailey.

'Are they hard?' asked Winnie anxiously. 'We have two spare feather-beds. Or better still, come and sleep here. You would be quite free to come and go when you pleased.'

'You're very kind,' said the girl. She flushed in a way that made her look suddenly young and defenceless.

'Or "The Fleece" is very comfortable, I know,' went on Winnie, intent upon her visitors' well-being.

'Too expensive,' said the girl.

'Hotel prices are ruinous these days,' agreed the doctor. 'Sugar, Mrs Prior?'

'No, thank you. And as we're to be neighbours, do you think you could call me Phil?'

'That would be very nice. Short for Phyllis, I take it? One of my favourite names,' said Doctor Bailey.

'I wish it were.'

'Philippa?' asked Winnie.

'Worse still. My proper name is Phyllida. My parents were hopelessly romantic.'

'Henry Austin Dobson,' said the doctor. 'Born 1840, died 1921.'

'How on earth did you know?'

'My mind is full of completely useless bits and pieces, such as that,' he replied. 'But the things I want to remember – where I left my pipe, or if I gave my partner a certain urgent message, for instance – completely escape me.'

'Well, you're dead right about Austin Dobson. My parents were great readers of poetry and had a weakness for the light fantastic.'

'A pleasant change from the heavy dismal we suffer from everywhere today,' commented Winnie. 'No one seems to laugh any more.'

'I do,' said Jeremy. 'I laugh a lot.'

'Keep it up,' advised the doctor. 'Keep it up.'

'My daddy makes me laugh.' He turned to his mother. 'Doesn't he make me laugh?' he persisted.

'He certainly does,' agreed his mother.

'When's he coming to see the new house?' asked the boy, through a mouthful of ginger biscuit.

'Sometime,' said his mother evasively. She produced a crumpled handkerchief from her jeans' pocket and gave a deft dab at her son's mouth.

'My husband has to be abroad a great deal,' she explained. 'He's in a textile firm. I'm afraid Jeremy hasn't seen much of him this last week or two.'

'More like a month,' began Jeremy.

'It always seems longer than it is,' his mother said swiftly. She looked at a massive wrist-watch.

'Time we went back to our paint pots, young man,' she told him, rising. 'Thank you so much for the coffee. We shall work twice as fast after that.'

Winnie accompanied her to the gate.

'Now, don't forget. If you want to stay overnight, do let us help. We look forward to having you as neighbours.'

'We look forward to coming,' replied the girl. 'A London flat is no place to bring up a growing boy. I was country-bred myself. I know what Jeremy's missing.'

'You'll be happy at Thrush Green,' Winnie assured her. The girl's mouth quivered.

'I'm sure we shall,' she said. 'We'll be here in good time for Jeremy to start school there in September.'

The two women looked across the green. The dew was drying rapidly, and from St Andrew's came the sound of country voices raised in praise. A pigeon clattered out from the avenue of chestnut trees, and landed nearby, strutting aimlessly this way and that, thrusting out its bright coral feet.

The girl sighed.

'It's all very comforting,' she said softly, as though speaking to herself. 'And now we must go home. Thank you again.'

They parted with smiles, and Winnie watched the pair run to Tullivers. It was good to see the little house in use again.

She returned to her own garden thoughtfully. Why did the girl use the word 'comforting' about Thrush Green? From what pain did she seek relief? From what torment was she flying? Who could tell?

4. A Shock for Dotty

Half a mile away Dotty Harmer was in trouble. She had gone down the garden to feed her hens, when she saw something move behind the garden shed.

An open-ended extension had been built on to house Dotty's winter store of logs. An energetic nephew, staying for a week of his vacation, had obligingly set some flag-stones at the entrance, so that his aunt could step from the path to the logs without getting her feet wet.

'Very nice, dear,' she had commented. 'And I can chop up the logs there. And marrow bones. So useful to have what my dear father used to call "an area of hard standing". It will be most useful, dear boy.'

Its use at the moment, when Dotty stood transfixed, henfood in hand, was unorthodox. For, lying in the sun, was a mother cat suckling five well-grown babies.

Charming though the sight was, Dotty's jaw dropped. How on earth could she cope with six cats – nay, six *more* cats! Already she owned two, a mother and daughter which she had prudently had spayed. What would they have to say about this brazen intruder and her progeny?

Dotty peered through her steel-rimmed spectacles at the family. They were a motley crew, to be sure, but how engagingly pretty! The mother was black with white paws, and one of the kittens had the same colouring. There was a fine little tabby, and three tortoise-shell kittens.

Dotty's heart sank again. Ten to one the tortoiseshells would be female. How long before their first litters arrived? Something must be done before the place was over-run with wild cats.

She took a resolute step forward, and the kittens shot into the stack of logs and vanished. One young quivering triangular tail showed for an instant in a gap, and then was gone. The mother cat crouched defensively, facing Dotty, strategically placed between this enemy and her babies. She was pathetically thin and dusty, and Dotty's tender heart went out to this gallant battered small fighter.

'Good puss! Nice little puss!' said Dotty, advancing gently.

The cat retreated slightly, and spat defiance.

Dotty put down the hen food and returned to the house for a dish of milk. Through the kitchen window she witnessed a remarkable sight. The mother cat gave a curious chirruping sound, and the five babies tumbled from the logs, towards the steaming hen food. Within seconds six heads were in the pot, as the cats ate ravenously.

Dotty stood aghast. That cats, so fastidious as a rule, should fling themselves upon cooked peelings, meat scraps and bacon rinds, all bound together with bran, showed to what excess of hunger the poor things were driven.

She watched them lick the pot clean, their eyes half-closed with bliss, and then sit down to wash themselves.

'Well, that's the last of the chicken's mash,' said Dotty aloud, and philosophically reached for the bag of corn instead. Bearing this and the brimming dish of milk she went once more down the garden path. As before, the kittens vanished, but the mother cat stood her ground. Dotty fed the hens, put down the milk, and retreated to the house, there to work out the best way to cope with an embarrassment of cats.

It was a problem which was to puzzle her, and the rest of Thrush Green, for weeks to come.

One still, hot morning, in the week following Dotty's discovery, Albert Piggot was digging a grave. For this melancholy task Albert's glum expression seemed particularly suited; but although the occasion was a sad one, it was not the circumstances of his labours that troubled Albert that morning, but the worsening conditions of his own matrimonial affairs.

He was the first to admit that he was cunningly hooked at the outset. There were a few aspects of married life which, in all fairness, he would agree were an improvement on the single state, for a man in his position. His house was warm and clean. His clothes were washed and mended. And his meals – ah, his meals! – were superb.

But once you'd said that, Albert told himself, squinting along the side of the grave for any unsightly irregularities, you'd said the lot. Nagging, whining and money-grubbing, that's what Nell was, and lately he had detected a new unpleasant note in her diatribes. There was far too much about that oil-man who came with his clanking van every other Thursday, for Albert's liking. A smarmy fellow, if ever there was one, a proper sissy, a regular droopy-drawers! And Nell was taken in by his soft soap, the great fool, and talked about it being 'so nice to see a gentleman for a change, and what a pity it was she had married beneath her'.

Albert set his spade to one side, pushed back his greasy cap and mopped his sweating brow. It was about time Sam Curdle arrived to give him a hand. He could do with it. Cotswold clay makes heavy digging in any weather. On a blazing August morning it was doubly intractable.

Sam Curdle, grandson of Mrs Curdle who once ruled over the Fair, had been released from gaol early in the New Year. Most of Thrush Green thought, and said openly, that Sam Curdle had a nerve to return to the place where he had so misbehaved.

'How he can face that poor Miss Watson he stole from, and battered into the bargain, I really don't know,' they told each other indignantly. 'It's a pity he doesn't take himself off, with that blowsy Bella of his, and find a living elsewhere.' But that is just what Sam was incapable of doing. Here, in Thrush Green, as well he knew, were a few soft-hearted souls who would give him a little work for the sake of the children – and a *little* work was all that Sam Curdle wanted. Bella had found a daily job at a farm at Nidden while he was doing time, and had developed into a passably good worker under the brisk direction of the farmer's wife. They still lived in the battered caravan, converted years ago from a bus, in a sheltered corner of the stackyard. Here the Curdles reckoned themselves well off, with water from an outside tap, free milk, and a dozen or so cracked eggs weekly.

'You can stay there as long as you go straight,' the farmer had told Sam. 'But you try any of your gyppo tricks here, nicking eggs, knocking off the odd hen, and that sort of lark, and you get the boot, pronto!'

And Sam had toed the line.

The rector had found him odd jobs to do, both in his own garden and in the churchyard. Albert Piggott was glad to have an assistant when it came to such tasks as grave-digging and coke-sweeping. The fact that Sam Curdle was a wrongdoer and had been in prison troubled the sexton not at all.

It was Albert himself, in fact, who had helped to bring him to justice. If anything, Albert felt now a certain proprietorial warmth towards the local malefactor. Just bad luck he'd been caught. He'd simply met a master mind, was Albert's opinion. Plenty of people were quite as bad as Sam, but got away with it.

A shadow fell athwart the grave and Albert looked up to see Sam's face peering down at him.

'And about time too,' grunted Albert. He indicated the second shovel with a jerk of his black thumb.

Sam jumped down and began scraping some crumbs of earth together in a languid manner.

'Don't strain yourself,' said Albert tartly.

Sam stirred himself to attack the other end of the grave with rather more vigour. They shovelled together in silence.

A robin hopped about the growing pile of soil looking for worms. The morning sounds of Thrush Green were muffled by the height of the earth walls about them, but in the distance they could hear the children playing on the two swings on the green. There was a rhythmic squeaking as the chains swung to and fro, and occasionally the thud of the see-saw and the cries of excited children.

The two men worked steadily until St Andrew's clock struck twelve above them.

'That's it then,' said Albert, clambering painfully out of the grave. Sam followed him.

'Time for a quick 'en?' asked Sam.

'Who pays?'

'We goes Dutch.'

'Humph!' snorted Albert, but he quickened his pace, nevertheless, as he shambled towards the open door of 'The Two Pheasants'.

But his thirst was not to be slaked immediately, for, directly in his path, stood Dotty Harmer.

'I shan't keep you,' said Dotty briskly, eyeing the pair. 'But I want you to let me know if you hear of anyone wanting a kitten.'

'Well, now miss—' began Albert.

'I know you have a cat,' cut in Dotty. Her tone implied, rightly, that she felt sorry for it. She looked at Sam Curdle with distaste.

'And I know you haven't room for one in the caravan,' she told him dismissively. 'The thing is, I have five to dispose of.'

Sam's face lit up.

'I'd be pleased to drown 'em for you, miss. Any time.'

Dotty looked at him sharply.

'Out of the question. They are far too big to drown.'

'You wouldn't catch 'em anyway,' gloomed Albert. 'Them wild cats never gets caught. Where've you got 'em?'

Dotty told him.

'Never get 'em out o' there,' said Albert, with relish. 'Why, I recollect that there was a widder woman over Lulling Woods way who had two – *just two*, mark you – livin' in her logs, and within the year she'd got *eighteen* kittens!'

'That's why I intend to tame them,' said Dotty firmly. 'I am going to get the mother cat spayed as soon as she has confidence in me.'

'You'll be lucky!' growled Albert. 'Best by far have a cat shoot and get done with the lot.'

'Disgraceful!' snapped Dotty.

'You won't never tame 'em, miss,' Sam said, hoping for five shillings, if not by drowning, then by a little erratic marksmanship.

'I should set a dog on 'em,' advised Albert. 'Rout 'em out, like, and then shoot 'em as they run away.'

'Have you thought,' asked Dotty severely, 'that they might simply be *maimed*, and not killed outright?'

'They'd die eventual,' said Albert casually.

'I am not proposing to harm these kittens, in any way whatsoever,' said Dotty, now dangerously calm. 'I shall do my best to get them tame enough to be accepted into good homes. *Good* homes!' she repeated firmly.

'I am on my way to Mrs Young to see if she will be able to have one,' she added, nodding to one of the five houses behind the chestnut avenue. 'All I wanted to ask you was to let me know if you hear of anyone needing a kitten.'

'Right, miss,' said Albert with rare deference. His dirty finger rose of its own volition to his greasy cap. Plain potty Miss Harmer was, and no doubt about it – but she was still gentry, and some innate, long-stifled instinct to acknowledge the fact had twitched Albert's hand to its unaccustomed position.

'Yes, miss,' added Sam meekly. 'I'll bear it in mind, miss.'

They entered 'The Two Pheasants' for their long awaited drink, the kittens already forgotten.

But Dotty, striding purposefully towards Joan Young's house, seethed with indignation.

'Drowning! Shooting! Setting a dog on them! A pity those two have never heard of reverence for life. I should like to have introduced them to Albert Schweitzer.'

She thought again.

'Or better still, my dear father. He'd have given them the horse-whipping they deserve!'

She reached the Youngs' gate.

'How I do hate cruelty!' said Dotty aloud, making for the front door.

Joan Young was the wife of a local architect. Her sister Ruth, who was lunching with her that day, was married to Doctor Lovell who, at that moment, was attending a cantankerous old bachelor of ninety-two to the south of Lulling.

Lunch was set in the large sunny kitchen. Paul Young was already at the table, waiting impatiently with the voracious hunger of a young schoolboy for the chicken which had just been lifted from the oven.

Opposite him, in his own old high chair, sat his baby cousin Mary banging lustily with her spoon.

'What's that?' asked Paul, as the bell of the front door rang sharply.

'Wozzat?' echoed his cousin, not caring particularly, but glad to try out a new expression.

'Oh, damn!' said Joan, tugging the fork from the bird. 'You carry on, Ruth, while I see to this.'

'You shouldn't swear,' reproved her son. 'Miss Fogerty made Chris wash his mouth out with soapy water once because he swore.'

'Sorry, sorry!' cried his mother, struggling with her apron strings. 'It slipped out.'

'Oh, damn!' echoed the baby thoughtfully. 'Oh, damn!'

The two sisters exchanged resigned looks, but had the wisdom not to comment. The bell split the air again, and Joan hurried to the door.

'Oh, do come in, Miss Harmer,' she cried, doing her best to sound welcoming. Who else but Dotty, she wondered, would call at twenty past twelve, and be clad, on a boiling hot day, in a tweed coat with a fur collar, topped by a purple velour hat, thick with dust, and decorated with a fine diamond brooch which, as Joan knew, had been in the family for generations and, amazingly enough, had not yet been lost by its present scatter-brained owner.

'Will you have a glass of sherry?' asked Joan, ushering her guest into the drawing-room.

'No, thank you, dear. I shall have a glass of rhubarb and ginger wine with my lunch. I find I get so sleepy if I mix my drinks midday.'

She looked sharply about the room.

'No cat?' said Dotty.

'No. Just Flo, the old spaniel, you know.'

'Well,' began Dotty, undoing her coat and settling herself. 'I'll tell you why I've come.'

Joan listened patiently to the saga of the kittens, half her mind on the fast-cooling lunch.

'And so it is essential that I wean the kittens, first and foremost,' she heard her visitor saying. 'Mr Fortescue says he can't possibly operate until the mother cat is *absolutely dry*.'

Dotty embarked on an involved obstetrical account about nursing felines, showing a remarkable grip on the subject for a spinster, thought Joan.

Her attention wandered again, only to be riveted suddenly when she heard Dotty putting a straight question.

'So how many kittens would you like?'

'Heavens!' exclaimed Joan. 'I must think about this! I don't know that Flo would care about a kitten —'

'Be a companion for her,' said Dotty firmly. 'What about Ruth? She'd like one, wouldn't she?'

'I'll ask her,' promised Joan meekly. To her relief, Dotty rose, and began to make her way to the door.

'Well, dear, I hope that's two kittens settled. It's quite a problem. I refuse to allow them to go to any but the nicest homes.'

'Thank you,' said Joan faintly.

'They won't be ready for a month or so,' continued Dotty, now on the doorstep. Joan rallied her failing senses.

'I will ring you before the end of the week,' she promised, 'and let you know if Ruth and I can have one each.'

'And tell your friends,' shouted Dotty from the gate. 'Those that are *definite cat-lovers*.'

Joan nodded her agreement, and watched her eccentric neighbour trotting briskly homeward to her rhubarb and ginger wine.

'What was all that about?' asked Ruth, when she returned to the kitchen.

'I'll tell you later,' said Joan. 'Little pitchers, you know.'

'Have big ears,' said her son. 'It was Miss Harmer, wasn't it? Did she tell you about her kittens? Chris told me. Isn't it smashing?'

He paused, and his mother watched, with mingled amusement and dismay, the light which suddenly broke out upon his countenance.

'Did she say we can have one, mummy? Did she? Oh, *please* let's! Oh, mummy, do let's have one! Please, please!'

Albert Piggott, much refreshed, set out from 'The Two Pheasants' to his nearby cottage. An aroma of boiling bacon wafted towards him as he approached.

Mellowed already by a pint of bitter, Albert's spirits were cheered still further by the thought of pleasures to come. Maybe Nell wasn't such a bad sort, after all!

At that moment, a clattering van appeared at the top of the steep hill from Lulling, and Albert's heart turned once more to stone.

'Oilmen!' He spat viciously into the hedge.

'Women!' He spat again.

Albert Piggott was back to normal.

5. A Problem for Winnie

A rare spell of superb harvest weather was broken early in September by a day of violent rainstorms. Naturally enough, it was the very day on which Mrs Prior and her son moved into Tullivers.

Gusts of wind shook veils of rain across Thrush Green. Sheets of water spread across the ground which was baked hard by weeks of sunny weather. A small river gurgled down the hill to Lulling, and the avenue of chestnut trees dropped showers of raindrops and blown leaves.

Those unfortunate enough to have to brave the weather, routed out long-unused mackintoshes, umbrellas and wellington boots, and splashed their way dejectedly across the green, sparing a sympathetic glance for the removal men, staggering from their van into Tullivers with rain-spattered furniture.

Within the little house Jeremy and his mother did their best to create order from chaos. It was no easy task, for as fast as they wheeled an armchair to its allotted place, a tea-chest would arrive to be dumped in its way.

'Where d'you want this, ma'am?' was the cry continuously, as the men appeared, far too quickly for the poor woman's comfort, with yet another bulky object.

She had thought, when packing up the belongings in Chelsea, that each tea-chest and large piece of furniture had been labelled. As in most moves, only half seemed to bear their place of destination, and soon the kitchen was beginning to become the resting place of all those boxes needing investigation.

'It's like a shop,' said Jeremy happily, surveying the scene.

'Or a lost property office,' said his mother despairingly. At that moment, Mrs Bailey appeared.

'I'm not even going to offer to help,' she said. 'I should be quite useless. But do please both come to lunch. It's only cottage pie, but I'm sure you'll be ready for a break when the men have gone.'

She put up her umbrella again in a flurry of raindrops, waved cheerfully, and set off through the downpour.

By one o'clock the removal van had rumbled away, and Mrs Prior and Jeremy sat thankfully at the doctor's hospitable table.

'I feel as if I'd been through a washing machine,' said the girl. 'Thoroughly soaked, then tumble-dried. I'll never move again!'

'Goody-goody!' commented her son. 'I don't ever want to move away from here.'

'I certainly hope you won't,' replied Mrs Bailey, handing vegetable dishes. 'Runner beans? They're from the garden.'

'That's something I must do,' said the girl. 'I intend to grow as many vegetables as possible. There are some currant and gooseberry bushes in the garden at Tullivers, I see.'

'You may have to replace them,' said the doctor, toying with his tiny helping. 'They must be pretty ancient.'

'Do fruit bushes cost much?'

There was a note of anxiety in the girl's voice which did not escape the doctor's ear.

'More than they used, no doubt. If I were you, I should clear away all those weeds and long grass around them, fork the ground and put in plenty of bone meal. Then see if they give you a decent crop next season. If they do, well and good. If not, out with 'em!'

The girl nodded thoughtfully, acknowledging his advice. Mrs Bailey, watching her eat her cottage pie, noticed how exhausted she looked. It was understandable: the two had made an early start, and a moving day was always bone-wearying. But she seemed thinner, and there were shadows under the lovely eyes, as though she had slept poorly for many nights. Mrs Bailey's motherly heart went out to this quiet young woman in her trouble – for trouble she guessed, correctly, that she had in abundance. But this was no time to force any confidences. Perhaps, one day, the girl would feel ready to speak, and then would be the time for understanding.

At the end of the meal, the girl and her son rose to go.

'It has been simply lovely. You've really restored us both. But now we must go back and tackle the muddle.'

'Thank you for having us,' said Jeremy politely. He stood soberly eyeing the doctor's wife for a few moments, then flung his arms round her waist and gave her a tremendous hug.

'You *are* nice!' he cried. 'Like my granny!' His face was alight with happiness.

Mrs Bailey ruffled the flaxen hair, more touched than she cared to admit.

'Then I *must* be nice,' she agreed. 'Come and see me whenever you like. And put up your umbrella in the porch, or you'll be washed away before you reach home.'

She watched them splash down the path, and then caught sight of Willie Marchant, the postman, tacking erratically back and forth uphill. His black oilskins ran with water, and drops fell from the peak of his cap on to the mackintosh which covered his parcels.

He pulled in to the kerb, propped up his bicycle amidst a shower of drops, and extracted a letter from a bundle.

'One for you, Mrs Bailey,' he grunted gloomily. 'Marvellous, ain't it? Got twice as many this afternoon just because it's raining cats and dogs. That's life, ain't it?'

Mrs Bailey agreed, accepting the letter and studying it with drooping spirits.

Richard again! Now what on earth did he want?

Richard was her sister's boy, and Winnie Bailey had to confess that he was her least favourite nephew. He had always seemed mature, self-centred, and rather smug. Perhaps if he had been blessed with brothers and sisters this unchildlike quality of self-possession would have been mitigated. As it was, as an only child, Winnie Bailey found him uncannily precocious, and at times a trifle supercilious.

As he grew from babyhood to childhood, it was apparent that Richard would make his mark in the world. He was highly intelligent, hard-working, and as efficient on the games field as in the classroom. His school reports were glowing. His parents adored him, and he appeared to be popular with his school fellows. But secretly to his aunt, he was always 'that odd boy'.

To Winnie and her husband he was always punctiliously polite when he saw them. But, thought Winnie, surveying the envelope in her hand, Richard had never given her a warm-hearted hug as young Jeremy had just done!

He had obtained a First in Physics at Oxford, and spent a year or two in America collecting further honours. As he grew older, his manner had become rather more sociable, and his somewhat anaemic looks had blossomed into wiry sparseness as maturity and a passion for walking grew upon him.

He was now a man of thirty-two, engaged upon research so divorced from the ordinary scheme of things that Winnie Bailey and her husband found themselves unable to comprehend the language, let alone the aims, of Richard's studies. They saw little of him, for his travels and lecturing commitments were extensive. Doctor Bailey heard of each academic success with coolness.

'Nothing wrong with his head,' was his comment, 'but he's no heart.'

Perhaps, thought Winnie, making her way to the drawing-room and her reading glasses, that is why she had never really warmed to Richard, but she kept these feelings to herself.

The doctor slept in the afternoon, and it was almost tea-time before she could hand him Richard's letter. The rain still fell relentlessly, drumming upon the roofs of Thrush Green, and drenching the schoolchildren as they straggled from the school porch. Their cries mingled with the spatter of rain on the window panes of the quiet room, as the doctor read the letter.

'Wants something, as usual,' he commented drily. Winnie remembered that this had been her own first unworthy reaction.

'What do you think?'

'It's up to you, my dear. If you feel that you would like to have him here while he is engaged on this particular work at Oxford, then go ahead. But it all means more for you to do, and I'm enough of a burden, I feel.'

'I don't like to refuse him,' began Winnie doubtfully. 'And we've plenty of room.'

She wandered to the window and looked out upon the rain-lashed garden. A few leaves, torn from the lime tree, hopped bird-like about the grass in the onslaught. On the flagged path, shiny with rain, a tawny dead sycamore leaf skidded about on its bent points, like some demented crab. The garden was alive with movement, as branches tossed, flowers quivered, grass shuddered, and drops splashed from roofs and hedges. Winnie Bailey gazed unseeingly upon its wildness, turning over this problem in her mind. Richard, after all, was her nephew, she told herself – probably rather hard up, and simply asking for a bed and the minimum of board. Perhaps, for a little while – ?

'Shall I invite him for a fortnight to see how we all manage?' she asked her husband, now deep in *The Times* crossword puzzle.

'By all means, if you would like to.'

'It wouldn't be a nuisance to you?'

'Of course not. I don't suppose I shall see much of the fellow, anyway, and he was always a quiet sort of chap about the house.'

Winnie sighed, partly with relief and partly because she had a queer premonition that something unusual – something disquieting – might come from Richard's visit.

Time was to prove her right.

During the next week or so the inhabitants of Thrush Green observed their new resident with approval. They watched her tackling Tullivers' neglected garden with considerable energy. The smoke from her bonfire billowed for two days and nights without ceasing, as hedge-trimmings, dead grass, long-defunct cabbage stalks and other kitchen-garden rubbish met their end. The flagged path was sprinkled with weed-killer, and the hinge mended on the gate which had hung slightly awry for three years, wearing a scratched arc on the flag-stone each time the gate was opened or shut.

The gate was also given a coat or two of white paint, and the front door as well. The girl's efforts were generally approved, and Jeremy too was considered an exceptionally well-brought-up little boy.

But the continued absence of Mr Prior was, of course, a cause of disappointment and considerable speculation among the newcomer's neighbours at Thrush Green. He was obliged to be abroad for a few months, went one rumour, getting orders for his firm – variously described as one dealing in French silk, Egyptian cotton, Italian leather and Burmese teak.

Others knew, for a fact, that he was a specialist in television equipment, computers, road-surfacing, bridge-building and sewage works. Betty Bell, however, had it on the highest authority (her own) that he had something to do with advertising, and went overseas to show less advanced countries the best way to sell ball-point pens, wigs, food-mixers, plastic gnomes for the garden, and other necessary adjuncts to modern living.

Albert Piggott, on the other hand, thought that he was probably in hospital with a lingering complaint which would keep him there for many months to come. He said as much to his fat wife Nelly, whose response was typical.

'Trust you to think that, you old misery! More like he's run off with some lively bit. That wife of his don't look much fun to me!'

It certainly seemed nearer the target than some of the wild rumours. Winnie Bailey, who knew her neighbour better than the rest of Thrush Green's inhabitants, had come to much the same conclusion, but kept it to herself.

Young Doctor Lovell, who occasionally caught a glimpse of the newcomer from his surgery window, also wondered if the girl had parted permanently from her husband, and felt sorry for her vaguely forlorn appearance. He spoke about her to Ruth, his wife, and she pleased him by replying:

'Joan and I are going to see her this afternoon. Paul and her little boy would probably get on very well together, and she might be lonely, even if she is up to her eyes in getting that place straight.'

The two sisters were not the only people to welcome Phil Prior. The rector, of course, called a few days after she had arrived, his chubby face glowing with the warmth and kindness he felt for all he met, even such stony-faced parishioners as his own sexton. Ella Bembridge called, bearing a bunch of Michaelmas daisies tied with what appeared to be a length of discarded knicker elastic, and an invitation to 'blow in any time you feel like it'. Harold Shoosmith spoke to the girl over the wall while she was hacking down some formidable stinging nettles, and offered a hand with any heavy clearing up which she might encounter.

Within a fortnight she found that she knew quite well at least two dozen people nearby, and was on speaking terms, country-fashion, with every other soul who passed. When Dimity Henstock called to invite her to a small dinner party, she looked forward to getting to know her Thrush Green neighbours even better.

'But I shall have to find a baby-sitter,' she said, after thanking Dimity. She looked completely at a loss.

'It's all arranged,' Dimity told her. 'Dr Bailey does not go out these days and dear Winnie will be staying in too. She says she will look after Jeremy and Donald that evening, and thoroughly enjoy it.'

'You are all so kind. I shall look forward to it,' the girl said.

And Dimity, who had brought her modest invitation half-expecting to find someone used to much more sophisticated entertainment went away knowing positively that young Mrs Prior was quite sincere in her expressions of pleasure.

On her way back to the rectory, she called into her former home to see her old friend Ella, whom she found standing on a chair far too frail to support her bulky twelve stone of solid flesh. She was struggling to hang a curtain.

'Shan't be a minute, Dim,' she puffed. 'Got too many hooks for the rings, as usual.'

'I'll do it,' said Dimity automatically. Ella thumped heavily to the floor, and Dimity took her place on the chair.

As her neat fingers worked quickly at the muddle created by her friend, she told her about her visit to Tullivers.

'And it really looks a proper home,' she added.

'What d'you expect?' cried Ella, a note of truculence in her voice.

'A single woman can make a comfortable home just as well as a married one. Don't need a man cluttering up the place to make *a home*!' she boomed.

From her perch, Dimity gave an all-embracing glance at yesterday's ashes in the grate, a vase of withered roses and the soft veil of dust upon the furniture.

'You're quite right dear,' she said meekly, threading the last hook into place.

6. A Dinner Party at Thrush Green

'The Fuchsia Bush', which stands well back from the road in Lulling High Street, prides itself on its home-made cakes and artistic furnishings. It is Lulling's only tea-shop, and having no competitor it tends to be a trifle smug.

Ella Bembridge, smoking one of her untidy hand-rolled cigarettes as she waited for her coffee to cool, looked with lack-lustre eye upon the 'Fuchsia Bush's' décor.

The walls had been freshly painted in an unhappy shade of lilac, and the new curtains were purple. The two waitresses wore the habitual garb of the establishment, overalls of pale mauve, with collar, lapels and belt in a dreadful shade of puce. These garments, faded from much washing, now clashed sadly with the new furnishings, and a pot of real fuchsias, on the table by the door, struggled to make the point that what Nature can do successfully cannot always be copied by Man.

A plastic tumbler, pretending to be made of glass, held a sheaf of mauve paper napkins a few inches from Ella's nose. Disgusted, she moved it to a neighbouring table, just as Dotty Harmer entered.

'Come and have a cup of this ghastly drink – coffee I *will not* call it,' shouted Ella cheerfully. The waitresses exchanged supercilious glances. How common could you get? You'd have thought a lady like Miss Bembridge would have had better manners, their look said clearly.

'Thank you, dear. Yes, a cup of coffee,' said Dotty, pulling up one thick speckled stocking which was forming a concertina over the lower part of her skinny leg. A commercial traveller, coffee cup arrested half way between table and moustache, watched with fascinated horror.

'Was going to bob down and see you,' said Ella.

'Eggs?' queried Dotty.

'No, no. Milk.'

'Why, hasn't the milkman called?'

'He's called all right,' said Ella grimly, grinding the stub of her cigarette into the Benares brass ashtray. 'But he won't be calling again.'

'Why not?'

'Because it's not milk he's delivering, but muck!'

Ella began to throw a small heap of tobacco upon a cigarette paper and roll yet another cigarette.

'Whitewash!' she continued vehemently. 'He calls it "Homogenized – ma'am".' Ella's voice rose to a squeaky falsetto as she mimicked her terrified milkman's tone.

'No cream on it at all. What's a woman to put in her coffee?'

'I take mine black,' said Dotty. Ella brushed aside this irrelevancy.

'It's perfectly horrible. No proper taste of milk, fiendishly white, like liquid paper! No! More like that stuff they make you drink in hospital, to see your innards. Begins with S.'

'Barium,' said Dotty, inspecting the plate of cakes.

'That's it – barium! Well, I'm not standing for it. I want milk that *is* milk, with cream on top and honest milk all the way down to the bottom of the jug. Can you spare some?'

'I can't make up my mind,' said Dotty thoughtfully, 'which is less indigestible – a Danish pastry or a doughnut.'

'Danish pastry,' said Ella promptly. Indecision nearly drove her mad.

Dotty took it reluctantly.

'I prefer the doughnut,' said Ella, transferring it swiftly to her own plate. 'I'm slimming.'

'Then you shouldn't be eating at all,' replied Dotty tartly, justifiably irritated by Ella's manoeuvres.

'Shock treatment,' Ella informed her blandly. She lodged her smoking cigarette across the ashtray, and attacked the doughnut energetically.

'I've only got goat's milk,' said Dotty, after a few minutes munching. 'I could spare you a pint a day. Dear Daisy is producing splendidly at the moment, but I have one or two regular customers, as you know, and the kittens are heavy drinkers just now. I'm trying to wean them.'

'I thought you had two goats,' said Ella, wiping sugar from her mouth with a man's khaki handkerchief.

'Dulcie is too young yet,' began Dotty primly. 'She hasn't been mated. After the kids are born —'

'Oh, spare me the obstetric details!' begged Ella. 'A pint of Daisy's daily, would be a godsend, Dotty, if you can spare it. I'll collect, of course. When can we start?'

'This afternoon? After tea?'

'Fine,' said Ella, thrusting her wheel-back chair from the table with an ear-splitting grating on the flagged floor.

'Have you got some milk to go on with?' asked Dotty solicitously.

'Half a pint of hogwash,' said Ella. 'It'll do.'

The two ladies collected their parcels, paid their bills to the less disdainful of the waitresses, and emerged into Lulling High Street.

'If them two wasn't ladies,' said one waitress to the other, 'they'd both be in the mad-house, and that's the honest truth.'

'You can say that again,' agreed her colleague, dusting a plate languidly against her lilac hip, as she watched the two customers disappearing into the distance.

St Andrew's church clock was striking six as Ella crossed the green to fetch the goat's milk. In her basket lay a clean bottle, a copy of last week's *Punch* and a copy of *The Lady*. There was also a paper bag containing half a pound or so of early black plums from the ancient tree in Ella's garden.

The air was warm and soft. The gentle golden light of a fine September evening gilded the Cotswold stone buildings, and turned the windows of the church into sheets of dazzling flame.

Albert Piggott stood motionless in the church porch. With his head out-thrust and his drooping mouth he reminded Ella of a tortoise she had owned as a child.

'Lovely day!' she called.

'Swarmin' with gnats,' responded the sexton gloomily. 'Sign of rain.'

Ella did not pursue the conversation, but strode rapidly down the narrow alley beside the Piggotts' abode to the field path which led to Dotty's cottage some half a mile away.

As she approached the garden gate she became conscious of a voice – Dotty's voice – keeping up a relentless monologue.

'Come on, boys, out you come! Come and get your good suppers! It's no use skulking in there. How d'you expect to get anyone to give you a good home if you behave so foolishly? Be brave now. Show yourselves. No food for cowardly cats. Come out and feed properly, or back it goes into the house!'

Ella waited, out of sight, irresolute.

Dotty's slightly hectoring tone changed to one of maudlin encouragement. Obviously, one brave kitten had emerged from its hiding place.

'Sweet thing!' murmured Dotty. 'Brave puss! Now, don't run away again. There's a good little cat.'

There was a sound of lapping, and Ella approached cautiously. Her shadow fell across the dish of milk, the kitten vanished with a squawk, and Dotty gave a startled squeal of exasperation.

'There now, Ella, you've scared them! Just as they were coming out. What on earth brings you here at just this particularly awkward time?'

'Goat's milk,' said Ella mildly. 'And, dammit all, Dot, I had to come *some* time. How long do you spend here squatting on that uncomfortable log?'

'I try and have half an hour in the morning and another about this time,' replied Dotty, dusting her skirt sketchily. She peered through her steel-rimmed spectacles into the depths of the log shack, but nothing stirred. She sighed sadly.

'Well, that's ruined this evening's session. Come along, Ella, and fetch the milk.'

She led the way into the kitchen, and Ella thought, yet again, what a perfect film set it would make for a witch's background.

Bundles of drying herbs hung from the rafters. A dead chicken, waiting to be plucked, hung upside down against the back of the door. A pungent reek floated from a large copper preserving pan bubbling on the stove, and the kitchen table was crowded with jars, bottles, newspaper cuttings, an enormous ledger with mottled edges, and a butcher's cleaver still sticky with blood.

Add a few living touches, thought Ella, such as frogs and bats, and the place would be complete.

The milk, mercifully, was already bottled, corked, and standing on the cool brick floor in Dotty's larder.

'That looks fine,' said Ella warmly, surveying the beautiful rich colour admiringly. What were a few germs anyway? 'Makes my homogenized muck look pretty silly. Thank you very much, Dotty dear. And what do I owe you?'

'Say sixpence,' said Dotty vaguely.

'Make it a shilling,' replied Ella, slapping the coin down upon the laden table. 'Suits me, if it suits you.'

'Very well,' responded Dotty. 'I must admit the kittens are costing me quite a bit to feed. I'm having to buy tins of stuff called "Pretty-Puss" and "Katsluvit". I don't approve of the names, but the kittens seem to eat everything ravenously. Such a relief! It means that I can take the mother cat to the vet next week.'

'Got homes yet?' asked Ella.

'The Youngs are having one. Paul was persistent, I gather, sensible child. And Dimity is dithering. Frightened of the traffic, I think.'

'I'll speak to her,' said Ella ominously. 'Cats must take their chance these days.'

The two ladies made their farewells, one moving off to Thrush Green, and the other setting out yet again, to try her luck with the interrupted cat-taming in the log shed.

Dimity Henstock's dinner party was an outstanding success right from the start.

Betty Bell was in charge of the kitchen that evening. She was a first-class cook, even if her cleaning and dusting were sketchy, having been trained in a ducal establishment in the north, under a dragon of a cook who had terrified young Betty but had taught her supremely well.

To be able to engage Betty Bell for the evening was a sure foundation for the success of a dinner party, as Thrush Green and Lulling hostesses knew well.

As Dimity looked at the seating arrangements in the dining-room, she could hear Betty singing cheerfully as she coped with leg of mutton, onion sauce, roast potatoes, cauliflower, peas and young

Brussels sprouts. She had also made some attractive shrimp and grapefruit cocktails and set them in place, and insisted on adding a vast apple pie to the delicate orange mousse, which Dimity had made and privately thought quite adequate, for the sweet course.

'You wants more than that for men,' maintained Betty stoutly. 'No *body* to mousse. Men likes a bit of pastry.'

'There will be cheese and biscuits,' Dimity pointed out, 'if they are still hungry.'

'Not the same,' asserted Betty. 'Mrs Furze,' she added, referring to the she-dragon who had taught her all she knew, 'wouldn't dream of putting but the one sweet on the table.'

'Very well,' agreed Dimity. She knew when she was beaten. 'Certainly make an apple pie. I'm sure it will be delicious.'

The dinner table pleased even her over-anxious eye. She had polished the rector's silver candlesticks herself and the light of six candles fell upon the bowl of orange dahlias which formed the centrepiece. For once, the bleak lofty room looked warm and inviting. The carpet was thin and worn, the furniture shabby, but the kindly candlelight hid these things, and Dimity felt proud of her arrangements.

Dimity longed to furnish the rectory as she knew it should be furnished. It needed thick velvet curtains at the tall narrow windows to mitigate the draughts and the gauntness of design. It was a house which cried out for soft carpets and central heating, but there was no money for such luxuries on the rector's stipend, and Dimity loved him far too well to ask him for the impossible. The floors of the bedrooms and the long draughty passages were covered with the dark brown linoleum chosen by a predecessor of Charles Henstock'. It was badly worn, but gleamed with years of polishing. Nevertheless, it wrung Dimity's heart to see her beloved Charles walking barefoot on a winter's morning upon such an inhospitable surface. The few small rugs available lay like tiny rafts upon the glassy sea. Sometimes Dimity envied her husband his Spartan attitude to their surroundings, and there were times when she thought, with secret longing, of the small cosy bedroom under the thatched roof opposite, where she had slept snugly for so many years.

Eight people sat down to enjoy the leg of mutton. The guests were Edward and Joan Young, Doctor Lovell and his wife Ruth, Harold Shoosmith and the newcomer, Phil Prior.

Dimity had selected her visitors with considerable care. She wanted to introduce Mrs Prior to people much of her own age. The Lovells and Youngs were in their early thirties, but try as she might Dimity could find no unattached male of that age to balance her dinner table.

'What a *blessing* Harold is single,' she said to her husband whilst making her preparations. 'We could do with half a dozen more men really in Thrush Green. I mean, if one were going to have a really big affair it would be simple to find a dozen single women – Ella, Dotty, the three Lovelock sisters and so on – but where are the men?'

'Safely married,' replied Charles smugly. 'Like me. You can't have it both ways, my dear.'

'And even dear Harold is a little older than I really wanted,' mused Dimity to herself.

'He's no older than I am,' the rector pointed out mildly, and was amused to see the contrition on his wife's face as she strove to make amends.

In any case, thought Dimity, looking happily about her dinner table, Harold was easily the most handsome man there, and by far the best dressed. Why was it, she wondered, that young men these days appeared so scruffy compared with their elders? Their wives looked so pretty in their silk frocks; one sister in green and the other in striped grey and white, while the newcomer wore a softly-draped frock of very fine wool starred with tiny flowers. A Liberty print, guessed Dimity correctly, thinking how beautifully it set off the girl's dark looks.

She was more animated than Dimity had ever seen her. Among these old friends, so easy with each other, she showed no shyness.

'And how many committees do you find yourself on?' asked Harold.

'Why, none yet.'

'Amazing! I was on *five* before I'd been here a month,' said Harold. 'You see, your turn will come. Which reminds me, Charles, I haven't been able to type the minutes of the Entertainments Committee. My typewriter has collapsed.'

'What's the matter with it?' asked Mrs Prior with genuine interest.

'Asthma, I should imagine, from the rhythmic squeaks it gives out. It's gone in for an overhaul. Poor old thing, it's well over thirty years old and spent most of its life in the tropics, so it's not done too badly.'

'I could type the minutes, if you'd like me to,' offered the girl.

'Do you type too?' asked the rector, in open admiration. 'How clever of you! Without looking at the keys?'

'Of course,' she said, laughing. 'I should have been thrown out of my typing class pretty smartly if I'd dared to look at the keyboard.'

'Well, I've never been able to master a typewriter,' confessed the rector. 'I once tried to type "How doth the little crocodile" on Harold's machine, and it made an awful lot of 8s and halfpennies, I remember. Do you use yours much?'

'I do a column for a girls' weekly,' said Mrs Prior. 'About five hundred words. And a few book reviews.'

This modest disclosure brought forth a buzz of excited comment. Thrush Green had no writers among its inhabitants, and to meet someone who not only wrote, but who actually had those writings published was indeed thrilling.

'I've always thought I could write,' observed Edward Young, adding predictably, 'if I only had the time.'

'I couldn't,' said his brother-in-law honestly. 'It's quite bad enough writing prescriptions. Anything imaginative would floor me completely.'

'When you say "a column",' said Dimity, 'do you mean a short story?'

'A brief article,' answered the girl, 'on some topical matter which would interest girls. Sometimes I make one of the books the subject of the column – that's cheating, I feel, but the editor approves.'

'You must enjoy it.'

'Not always – but it's well paid, and the editor is a sweetie.'

'Mary has just learnt to hold a crayon properly,' said Ruth Lovell proudly, 'and has scribbled on *every page* of the laundry book.' The company agreed that this might, conceivably, show literary promise.

The orange mousse and the apple pie were eaten to the exchange of news about children, and no more was said about the writing until the company were enjoying Dimity's excellent coffee by the drawing-room fire.

Harold Shoosmith, who settled himself next to the girl, asked if she would find it a nuisance to type the minutes.

'Or I could do them myself, if I might borrow the typewriter for half an hour,' he said. 'Whichever is simpler for you. They only take up a page of quarto-size.'

'Bring them in tomorrow,' said the girl. 'I shall be in all day.'

And so the matter was left, and the evening passed very pleasantly in general conversation, except for ten minutes of television news which Edward Young asked if he might see as he had heard that a house he had restored for a wealthy pop singer had just been burned out and it might be shown on the screen.

The company obligingly sat through a student demonstration, plentifully sprinkled with bleeding noses and blasphemies, a multiple car crash on a motorway from which a stretcher, ominously blanketed, was removed, an interview with a distracted mother whose child had been abducted, and the arrival at London airport of a half-naked film star whose long unkempt hair was something of a blessing in view of her neck-line. But Edward Young's burned-out masterpiece was not included among the attractions, and everyone was thankful when the set was switched off.

'I don't call that news, do you?' said Charles Henstock. 'Not by Thrush Green standards anyway. What I mean by news is hearing about Dotty Harmer's kittens, or Albert Piggott's prize onions or meeting a charming newcomer to the village,' he said, bowing slightly to his guest of honour.

'And why should one be subjected to all these horrors on one's own hearth rug?' agreed Doctor Lovell. 'To think we *pay* for it too! It's galling.'

'Too bad about your house,' said Dimity to Edward, 'it probably wasn't ghastly enough to compete with all that violence. I suppose nobody was burned?'

'No one, as far as I know.'

'That accounts for it,' said Dimity reasonably. 'An item of news like that, without so much as a few charred bones, or firemen falling screaming into the blaze, wouldn't stand a chance.'

At eleven o'clock the guests began to make their farewells. Only the Lovells drove home, for their house was a mile away. The rest of the guests lived round the green and walked across the grass together.

Already most of the houses were in darkness, for country people have to be up betimes and midnight is considered a very late hour indeed for going to bed.

But a light shone still at Tullivers, where Winnie Bailey sat sewing, her young charge fast asleep in the bedroom above. She heard his mother's light footsteps on the path, and put down her needlework.

'My word,' she said, looking at the girl's glowing face in the doorway, 'I can see you've had a lovely evening. And so, my dear, have I!'

7. A Question of Divorce

The next morning Harold Shoosmith crossed the green to Tullivers.

He found Mrs Prior alone, her typewriter already on the table and an appetizing smell of steak and kidney casserole floating from the kitchen.

'Jeremy gets home at twelve,' she said, 'and we have our main meal then. It gets cooking over and done with for the day, and I boil an egg or have some cheese and biscuits when Jeremy's in bed.'

'I do much the same,' said Harold, 'though Betty Bell is always willing to come and fatten me up, if given half a chance.'

He put the hand-written minutes on the table.

'Are you sure it's not an imposition?' he asked.

The girl laughed.

'It will be a change from the perils-of-Pauline stuff I'm attempting at the moment. I'm trying to sell some short stories to magazines.'

'Here, or overseas?'

'Here, and in America. They pay most generously over there, but I doubt if my stuff will be suitable.'

Harold Shoosmith gazed thoughtfully through the window.

'I've an editor friend in one of these magazine combines. If I could be of any help –?'

'You're very kind. If I get too many rejections, I'll remember. I'm sorting out old material just now, and trying to bring it up-to-date.'

'Wouldn't it be better to start again?'

'I need some money pretty quickly,' replied the girl frankly. 'This house – as always – has cost far more to put to rights than I bargained for, and if I can sell some stories now, I can get down to some really new stuff while they are being considered. Editors seem to take an unconscionable length of time to make up their minds.'

'If you think I could help by looking through any of your stories to see if they seem to be on the right lines for Frank, I would be only too happy to do so,' said Harold.

'I might be very glad indeed,' replied Phil, 'but let's see how my luck turns out in the next few weeks. In any case I've always got my column to keep the wolf from the door.'

'Yes, indeed,' said Harold, but there was doubt in his tone.

'And my husband is very generous,' the girl added, a shade too swiftly. 'But, of course, one likes to feel independent.'

'Of course,' echoed Harold, obviously bemused, but doing his best to cope with the situation. There was a slight pause. The clock struck eleven, and brought Harold to his senses.

'Well, I must be off. When shall I call for the minutes?'

'Oh, don't bother. I'll pop over after tea, if I may.'

'That would be very kind of you,' said Harold gravely, making for the door.

He crossed the green thoughtfully.

'That devil's left her!' he said to a startled blackbird on his gate-post.

Harold Shoosmith had guessed correctly, but it was Winnie Bailey who heard the truth first from the girl herself.

It was a fine October afternoon, clear and vivid, and Winnie noticed how auburn the chestnut avenue had become since the first few frosts. Her spirits were high as she breathed the keen air.

It was quite two weeks, she told herself, since she had talked to Phil, but this was not surprising. One's next-door neighbours, however dear, tend to be neglected for the plain reason that they *are* next door. It is the friends at a distance whom one makes the effort to meet. But she had caught a glimpse of her at the typewriter, and knew that she was busy.

She was calling now to see if she could persuade her to collect for Poppy Day. The Misses Lovelace who had quartered Lulling and Thrush Green between them for decades, had decided that their arthritis and general frailty would not allow them to continue the good work. To find one noble soul willing to turn out in November to rattle a collecting tin, is hard enough. To find *three* was proving a headache.

Full of hope, Winnie knocked with the late admiral's great brass dolphin on Tullivers' front door. It was opened by Phil herself, white of face and red of eye. Winnie Bailey, used as a doctor's wife to seeing men and women in misery, thought she had never seen quite such a tragic face.

'Phil, tell me!' she said impulsively, and then checked herself. 'No, my dear, let me creep away. You won't want to be bothered with callers just now.'

'Do *please* come in,' cried the girl. 'I need a friend badly.'

She led the way into the little sitting-room and motioned the older woman to take a seat. Winnie watched her as she put two logs on the dying fire. Her hands were trembling and tears were running unheeded down her cheeks.

'What is it?' begged Winnie. 'Someone ill? Or worse?'

'Worse,' choked the girl. 'It's my husband.'

'Not dead!' Winnie whispered.

'Oh no, thank God!' She gave a high, cracked laugh, frightening to hear. 'Though why I should thank God, I don't know. He's left me.'

'You poor dear,' said Winnie, patting the arm that was near her. She felt the gnawing pity and the tragic impotence which captures those who are in the presence of grief which they are powerless to assuage.

The girl fumbled for a damp handkerchief, mopped her eyes, and took a deep shuddering breath.

'He left me almost six months ago. Another woman, of course. A French woman – a buyer for one of the Paris houses. I met her once.'

She stopped, and mopped her eyes again.

'Perhaps it's just an infatuation,' said Winnie. 'Is she very attractive?'

'Not a bit,' cried Phil. She smiled damply. 'Well, I know I'm biased, but I don't think anyone – except John – would find her attractive. She's one of those bony Frenchwomen with a long face like a disapproving horse. Marvellous figure, of course, and dresses superbly, but no glamour-girl, I assure you.

'When he wrote and said that they were in love, I laughed out loud. It seemed so ludicrous, I just couldn't believe it – like some awful unspeakable joke.'

She helped herself to a cigarette, and lit it shakily.

'But it was no joke, as you can imagine. He came back several times to the flat, and was more determined each time to break with me. I tried desperately to keep my head. I was sure he would get tired of her – that it was, as you said, an infatuation. But the day came when he told me flatly that he was going to bring her to live in our house, and I must get out.

'Then I really did grovel! I told him I loved him still. I pleaded for Jeremy's sake. I swore I'd never throw this affair in his face if he'd think again. All useless!'

She stood up and walked restlessly about the little room.

'When I saw it was hopeless, and that she'd won, we made a scratch agreement to part. He gives me a regular amount each month, and he let me take the things I wanted from the Chelsea flat. But I absolutely refuse to give him a divorce. I still hope that he will come to his senses – or she will. Meanwhile, I try to keep it all from Jeremy. He adores John. It turns the knife pretty keenly, as you can imagine, when he prattles on about Daddy.'

She rolled the damp handkerchief into a ball and thrust it into her cardigan pocket.

'But this morning I had another letter. It's so terrible – so terrible –' She shook her head desperately, and a tear flew into the fire and sizzled.

'It's brought it home to me. We simply can't go on like this. I think I must make up my mind to go forward with a divorce. I suppose I've been evading it really – hoping, just stupidly hoping. The very idea of solicitors and courts and settlements and all the other beastly details absolutely revolts me. But I see now I must face it. He's only too pleased to give me grounds,' she added bitterly.

She sat down beside Winnie on the couch and took her hand.

'What would you do? What would you do if you were wretched me?' Winnie put a comforting arm round the girl's shoulders.

'I should wait until tomorrow before doing anything. You've been brave and patient for so long, keep it up for a little longer. By that time it won't hurt so much and you'll tackle things better.'

The girl nodded dumbly.

'Don't write,' cautioned Winnie, 'don't telephone, don't talk to anyone about it until you've slept on it. No one will learn anything from me, I promise you. Then why not talk it over with your parents?'

'They died some years ago. I was an only child.'

'Is there someone else? A cousin, say, or a family friend?'

'Not that I could discuss this with. I would sooner tell our old family solicitor. He's wise and kind ... a real friend.'

'Then why not go to him?'

'I'll do that,' whispered Phil huskily. 'It's keeping up appearances before Jeremy which is so hard. I've cried all day. Thank God he didn't seem to notice much at dinner time.'

'Let me walk across to the school when the children finish,' said Winnie, 'and take him back with me to tea.'

'No, really—'

'Please. I should love it, and it will give you a chance to get over the shock a little. I'll bring him back before half past six.'

She stood up and kissed the girl's pale cheek gently.

'Go and have a warm bath,' she advised. 'Hot water truly is the benison that Rupert Brooke said it was. And then give yourself a tot of something strong. You'll feel twice the girl.'

'You are an angel,' cried Phil, accompanying her to the door. 'I've done nothing but moan; and I haven't given you a chance to tell me what brings you here.'

Silently, Winnie held up the poppy tin.

'Of course I'll do it,' said Phil warmly. 'I can't weep for ever.'

Winnie's nephew Richard arrived the following week. He seemed genuinely grateful for his aunt's hospitality, and set himself out to be exceptionally charming to Doctor Bailey.

To Winnie's eye he looked very fit and lively, having acquired a fine tan in America which set off his pale hair and blue eyes. But it was not long before symptoms of the hypochondria which had always been present showed themselves in strength.

Two small bottles of pills stood by his plate at the first evening meal, and naturally excited the professional interest of his uncle.

'I find them indispensable,' said Richard. 'Otto – Professor Otto Goldstein, you know, the dietician – prescribed them for me. The red ones take care of the cholesterol, and these yellow and black torpedoes check acidity and act as a mild purge. Constipation is a terrible enemy.'

'You need a few prunes,' said the doctor, 'and a bit of roughage.'

'Donald!' protested Winnie. 'Must you? At table?'

'Sorry, my dear, sorry,' said her husband.

'Too bad of me,' apologized Richard. 'Living alone such a lot makes one over-interested perhaps in one's natural functions.'

Winnie felt that this could lead to somewhat alarming disclosures which might be regretted by all. She changed the subject abruptly.

'You must meet our new neighbour,' she said brightly, passing her nephew Brussels sprouts. He held up a stern denying hand.

'Not for me, Aunt Winnie. Not *cooked* greens, I fear. Quite forbidden by Otto because of the gases. You haven't two or three raw ones, by any chance?'

'Not washed,' replied Winnie shortly, passing the rejected dish to her husband. She was keenly aware of the smile which hovered round the old doctor's lips.

'A pity,' murmured Richard, tackling pork chops *en casserole* with faint distaste.

'She plays bridge and whist, and is a very nice person to talk to. She writes.'

'Really?' replied Richard vaguely. Clearly his mind was concerned with his digestive tract.

'Will you have any spare evenings?' pursued Winnie.

Richard gave a gusty sigh, the sigh of one who, over-burdened with work, still enjoys his martyrdom.

'I very much doubt it. I shall be writing the notes on my experiments, of course, and I intend to spend as much time as I can refuting Carslake's idiotic principles. An obstinate fellow, if ever there was one, and a very elusive one too. I must thrash things out with him during the next few months.'

Winnie felt a wave of pity for the absent Professor Carslake. Richard, on the rampage, must be an appalling bore. She decided to put aside the idea of arranging Richard's social life at Thrush Green. Richard obviously did not want it, and was it really fair to her friends to inflict her nephew on them, she added reasonably to herself?

She watched him swallow a red pill and then a yellow and black one. It was quite apparent that he enjoyed them far more than the excellent dinner which Winnie had spent hours in preparing.

'Coffee?' she asked, rising from the table. 'Or does Professor

Goldstein forbid that too?' There was an edge to her tone which did not escape her observant husband.

'No, indeed,' replied Richard, opening the drawing-room door politely. 'He approves of coffee, provided that the berries are really ripe, well roasted and coarsely ground. He doesn't agree with percolators, though. He always strains his through muslin. Do you?'

'Not with Nescafé,' said his aunt, with a hint of triumph, leading the way.

Richard was not the only one at Thrush Green suffering from indigestion. Doctor Lovell gave Albert Piggott a prescription, and then a few words of sound advice.

'Your wife's a fine cook, I know. But have small helpings. Don't forget your stomach was on short commons for years. It can't cope suddenly with all this bounty.'

Nelly tossed her head when Albert relayed this piece of advice.

'Good food never hurt nobody. Who does he think he is – the old Tin-ribs? He could do with a bit of flesh if anyone could. I bet he never gets his teeth into a decent steak-and-kidney pudding with that dreamy wife of his to do for him! Take them dratted pills, if you must, Albert Piggott, but you eat what's put in front of you and be thankful!'

She seemed to surpass herself in the days that followed. Cold fat bacon with pickled onions, fried cod cutlets with chips and peas, ox-tail soup, hot and glutinous, with swedes mashed with butter, all followed each other in succession, flaunting their richness and tempting Albert to fatal indulgences. His liverishness grew: his temper became more morose than ever. Nelly became aggrieved and nagged more and more bitterly.

The oilman began to figure largely in her conversation.

Albert, belching prettily after consuming a plate piled with pickled brawn, beetroot and bubble-and-squeak, spoke his mind.

'Can't you shut up about that ruddy oilman? Any more of it, and I'll tell 'im to stop calling. Givin' 'im cupsertea! Giggling like some fool-girl! I seen you at it – eggin' 'im on!'

'I'll thank you,' said Nelly haughtily, 'to mind your tongue. I only treat him civil. The poor chap's wife's left him.'

'Best day's work she ever done, I shouldn't wonder. You'd best take a leaf outer her book, my gal.'

'It's a pity if I can't have a friendly word with a gentleman without you getting filthy ideas into your head,' snapped Nelly, crashing cutlery about dangerously. 'The Lord alone knows I get little enough pleasure from your company. If you're not down the coke-hole you're in "The Two Pheasants". Why I was ever fool enough to give in to your begging of me to marry you I *cannot think*!'

This complete travesty of the facts of Albert's wooing rendered him speechless. But not for long.

'I *could say*,' said Albert, with a hiccup which marred the heavy solemnity of his utterance, 'exactly the same words, my gal, and with a deal more truth.'

Rumbling dangerously, he left his kitchen for something to settle his stomach next door.

8. Gossip and Gardening

The rapid spread of news through a village is a natural phenomenon which is hard to explain. Phil Prior, after much inward wrestling, sought the advice of a London solicitor as a preliminary step to divorce from her husband.

She said not a word to anyone. Winnie Bailey, true to her promise, breathed not a syllable, not even to her husband. And yet the possibility of a divorce was generally known in Thrush Green.

How did such knowledge get around so swiftly? Winnie Bailey asked herself this, not for the first time. She supposed that someone originally made a shrewd guess, and passed on the surmise to a friend.

The friend then might say: 'I hear that there's talk of a divorce between the Priors.' And the next step would be: 'Have you heard about the Priors' divorce?' After that it was, of course, an accepted fact, despite the usual riders: 'Mind you, it's only what I've *heard*,' or 'It may be only idle gossip,' or 'Don't repeat it unless you hear it confirmed.' And, sure enough the snippet *would* be confirmed within an hour or so. Thus easily does bush-telegraph work in a small community.

Fortunately, Phil Prior, new to country ways, was not conscious of her matrimonial affairs being common gossip. Now that the first wretched step was taken, she felt calmer, and renewed her writing efforts.

Harold Shoosmith proved a wise adviser in literary matters, and the girl frequently called on him to discuss possible markets. Frank, the editor friend, had received one of her stories with guarded enthusiasm, but after keeping it for some time, returned it with the excuse that it 'was not strong enough' but said he would consider it again if she felt she could amend it.

'What does he mean exactly?' asked Phil of Harold Shoosmith. 'Not enough shooting and rape, do you think? I mean, I simply can't write about violence. The only person I ever saw shot, was a neighbour who was peppered in his garden by the boy next door with an air gun. To make matters worse, the wretched boy's feeble excuse was that he thought he was a squirrel! He weighed eighteen stone,' added Phil reminiscently.

'Insult to injury,' agreed Harold. 'I hope the boy had a good hiding on the spot, and was not made the subject of psychiatric reports two months later, when everyone had forgotten all about it.'

'Lord, yes!' cried Phil. 'This was years ago before such refinements were thought of. He was a good friend of mine, and he said he had one beating from his father and was then handed over to the victim of his attack. He didn't seem to bear any grudge about it. He was always a resilient child.'

She turned again to her typescript.

'But how on earth can I make it *stronger*? I wish editors would either reject a thing outright, or take it as it is. I do loathe messing about with a piece of writing which, after all, you have made as near perfect in the first place as you possibly can.'

'I'd be inclined to send him another,' advised Harold, 'while the going's good, and mull over this one for a bit. Tell him you will let him have it later, when you've had a chance to revise it.'

He watched the girl turning the pages, a worried frown creasing her brow. Damn Frank, he thought suddenly! And that wretched husband too! Why should such a nice woman have all this confounded work and worry? She should be enjoying life, not fighting for existence.

'Come and see my last few roses,' he said, rising abruptly. Suddenly, he longed for fresh air and sunshine.

Harold's garden was quite six times the size of Tullivers' but was in a state of exquisite neatness.

'With no help at all?' queried the girl unbelievingly, gazing about her.

'Piggott comes for an hour or so when he needs a little extra drinking money,' said Harold. 'But I find I can keep it fairly trim now that it's in order.'

He snipped another rose to add to the bouquet he was making.

'I wish you would let me help you with your garden,' he continued. 'It would be such a pleasure to me, and if it is straightened up this autumn it should be so much easier to manage next year. As you see, I'm well ahead here, and could easily spare the time, if you would allow me to trespass.'

'You are very, very kind,' said Phil warmly, accepting the bouquet gratefully. 'And these are simply lovely. To be honest, I'd be terribly thankful for a hand with some bramble bushes which seem to have roots from here to Lulling.'

'I'll be over tomorrow afternoon, if that suits you,' said Harold briskly.

They walked together to the gate, and Harold watched her cross the green, the bunch of late roses making a splash of colour against her pale coat.

Another figure was advancing, in the distance, from his right. It was Dotty Harmer, struggling with a large cat basket. Heavy though it appeared to be, Dotty was making good headway, so that Harold, who felt unequal to Dotty's conversation at the moment, retreated strategically to the peace of his study, chiding himself for cowardice and lack of chivalry the while.

Dotty was bound for the Youngs' house, a bewildered ginger kitten mewing its protests as they made the uphill journey together.

She was glad to rest the basket on the doorstep as she rang the bell. The kitten, relieved that the motion had stopped, now sat mute among its blankets, but watched warily.

Paul opened the door, and fell upon his knees in front of the basket adoringly.

'You nice little puss! Are you coming to live here, then? Dear little cat, nice little—'

At this point, Dotty poked him sharply, bringing his ecstasies to an abrupt halt.

'Where are your manners, boy? What about speaking to me before you fuss with the cat!'

Scarlet with shame, Paul struggled to his feet and made apologies, just as his mother arrived.

'Please come in; I'd no idea you were going to bring the kitten. We intended to come and fetch it to save you trouble.'

'No bother,' said Dotty, about to lift the basket again.

'Let Paul do it,' said Joan. 'It really is very sweet of you to have carried it all the way here. What a very pretty one!'

They stood and admired the minute scrap, crouching among its bedding.

'Now, if I were you,' said Dotty, taking charge, 'I should put the basket in an empty warm room, and put its earth box and a saucer of milk there too. Then make sure it cannot get out of the room, open the door of the basket, and let it explore for some hours.'

'What about buttering its paws?' asked Paul, anxious to show his knowledge.

'Fiddlesticks!' snapped Dotty. 'You do as I say, and he'll soon settle down.'

'Do you think it is a he?' asked Joan, with some anxiety.

'That I can't be sure of. Cats are very difficult to sort out. But the vet will cope at six months either way.'

'But I should *like* it to have kittens!' protested Paul. He was on his knees again, one finger stroking the kitten's head through the wire door of the basket.

'Precocious, that child!' said Dotty to his mother, in a dark aside. 'Who said anything about kittens, young man?' she added forthrightly. 'We know what we're about, and what's best for that cat. Just you go and do as I said.'

'Take it up to the spare bedroom,' directed his mother, 'and I'll come up in a moment. Don't undo the door until I come.'

Paul picked up the basket. Without being prompted, he smiled upon Dotty and spoke his thanks.

'That's more like it,' said Dotty grudgingly. 'Remembered your manners after all! Now, take care of that mite. It's the tamest of the litter. It wants plenty of love, warmth and food, in that order. And if I hear you've tormented it *in any way*, I shall *take it back!*'

'Yes, Miss Harmer,' said Paul meekly, and began to mount the stairs with his treasure.

'Not a bad child,' conceded Dotty, watching his departing back.

'We find him fairly satisfactory,' agreed Joan drily. The mild irony was lost upon her guest.

'It's because you haven't kept many animals,' said Dotty. 'Now, they are *completely* satisfactory. Which reminds me, I must return to mine. I've left a saucepan of fish simmering, and I don't want it to boil dry.'

'Nothing worse,' said Joan, 'than the smell of boiling fish, I agree.'

'It's not the smell I worry about,' cried Dotty, stepping out of the front door, 'but the dear cats won't touch fish if it's the slightest bit caught.'

She set off at a fast trot towards the pathway to Lulling Woods and her animal family.

True to his word, Harold Shoosmith made his way to Tullivers the next afternoon. The girl came to the door immediately, for she had seen him pass the window. Papers were spread upon the table, and her typewriter stood among the litter.

'Don't let me stop you,' said Harold. 'I think I know where the brambles are.'

He pointed to the wall which divided Tullivers' garden from the Baileys' orchard. A border lay at its foot, but was so overgrown with many weeds, including the brambles, that it was practically invisible.

'There are some tools in the shed at the back of the house,' said Phil. 'I'll get them for you.'

'No, no! I can find them,' said Harold. 'Don't let me interrupt the writing.'

He made his way round the house as the girl returned to her typing.

He found the shed easily enough, but surveyed the tools with mingled dismay and pity. There were very few of them, and all looked hopelessly inadequate or outworn to Harold's sharp eye. The only fork available was a very large, heavy old veteran with wide flat tines, meant for digging up potatoes. The spade was equally heavy, and coated with dried Cotswold clay. The handle was badly cracked and had been bound, in an amateurish fashion, with string. Two trowels, a rake with a wobbly head, a birch broom, and a rusty bill-hook comprised the rest of the gardening equipment, except for a lawn-mower whose newness simply threw the age of the other tools into sharp relief.

Very quietly, Harold went round the back of the house to the gate, so that he did not need to pass the worker's window, and went to collect his own shining equipment from across the green.

Half an hour with a swinging mattock loosened the worst of the roots, and Harold enjoyed piling up the rubbish on the ashy remains of earlier bonfires. Brambles, elder shoots, and lofty nettles removed, it was possible to see the remains of the border. Among the shorter weeds which clothed the earth, Harold found clumps of irises, peonies and pinks still surviving suffocation. At one time the border had been well-stocked. It would be very rewarding, thought Harold, to see it trim and colourful again.

With his light fork he loosened wild strawberry runners, groundsel, docks, chickweed and yards and yards of matted couch grass roots.

The pile of rubbish grew higher and higher, and Harold was just contemplating the possibility of lighting a bonfire, as he straightened his back, when Phil came out from the house to admire his handi-work.

'And I believe you've got some nerines among those clumps of bulbs,' said Harold enthusiastically. 'It's an ideal spot for them there. Don't disturb them. I'll put a marker by them next time I come.'

'But you can't spend too much time among my weeds,' protested Phil. 'Your own will sneak up on you.'

Harold, flushed with his exertions, looked contentedly at the first few yards of border revealed.

'I'd like to finish this job,' he said. 'Three or four afternoons should see it cleared.'

Phil was looking at his fork with envy.

'Is it stainless steel?'

He said, somewhat apologetically, that it was.

'One gets used to one's own tools, you know. When you replace, my dear, I do advise you to get stainless steel. It is well worth it.'

'I shan't be replacing for some time,' said Phil, laughing. 'But I came to tell you that I had made some tea.'

It was snug in the little house. Harold had been so happy and busy in the garden that he had not noticed the grey clouds scudding ominously from the west. A spatter of rain on the window heralded a wet evening.

Phil nodded at a large envelope, stamped, sealed and ready for the post.

'I've taken your advice,' she said, 'and looked out another story. I do hope he likes this one. I'm going to alter the one he's just sent back. I had a brain-wave last night in bed which might work, I think.'

'Any more luck?'

'A hopeful letter from a women's magazine in America. I sent an article about how to encourage children to take to books. So many don't, you know. Thank heaven Jeremy likes reading!'

'I must be off,' said Harold, rising. 'Thank you for restoring me with tea. I'll be in London for the next two days, but I hope you'll let me tackle the border when I come back.'

'You know I shall be very, very grateful,' Phil replied, opening the front door.

The rain fell heavily, splashing from the admiral's brass dolphin upon the door mat.

Harold picked up his bundle of tools, neatly swathed in a sack.

'Here, give me your letters,' he said, eyeing the downpour. 'I'll put them in the box as I pass. You'll get drenched if you go out, and Willie's due to collect any minute now.'

She put the bundle of letters, including the large packet, into his outstretched hand.

'You really should spit on the big one, for luck,' she called after him as he hurried down the path.

With his tools across his shoulder and the letters in his hand, Harold made his way to the letter box at the corner of Thrush Green. The Cotswold stone glistened with rain around the red oblong.

Harold inserted the small letters, and then carefully threaded the large one into the aperture. It fell with a satisfying plop, and as it vanished Harold wished it luck.

Whistling cheerfully, he splashed beneath the chestnuts to his home, thinking gaily of work well done and the pleasure derived from a good-looking woman's company.

Little did he think that the packet he had so carefully posted would be the cause of much concern for the pair of them.

On that same rainy evening Sam Curdle, who had managed to conduct his affairs in a relatively honest manner for some months, succumbed to temptation.

It so happened that Percy Hodge, the farmer in whose yard the battered Curdle caravan was housed, had seen some fine wallflower plants going cheaply in Lulling market. He bought twelve dozen and left the twelve newspaper-shrouded bundles lodged against the corner of his back porch.

'If you get that lot put in for me tomorrow, Sam,' he told him, 'there's half a sack of spuds for you. Fill up the round bed in the front of the house, and the border under the greenhouse. You'll need the gross, I reckon, to make a tidy show.'

Sam agreed with alacrity. Half a sack of potatoes would be most welcome to the family, and planting out a few wall-flowers was easy work.

It took Sam less than five minutes to plan how he could make a few shillings for himself on the deal. Percy Hodge would be out all day at a sheep sale, Sam knew. By planting the wall-flowers carefully, he reckoned he could keep two, or possibly three, dozen aside for sale elsewhere.

That new woman at Tullivers, he pondered, as he lay beside his snoring Bella that night. She looked the sort who might fall for a few plants, and Lord alone knew that garden of hers was in need of something. Sam surmised, correctly, that she would know little about prices, and would not be the type to haggle.

What should he ask now? Six shillings a dozen? Too steep, perhaps, even for a greenhorn such as that Londoner. He'd heard down at 'The Two Pheasants' that most of the locals were getting twopence a plant. Maybe it would be best to settle for fivepence. After all, he reasoned happily to himself, if he swiped two dozen from Percy Hodge he'd make a clear ten bob. With any luck, though, he could appropriate three dozen. Fifteen bob, now that really would be useful! He might even have a flutter on a horse in the afternoon, and make a bit that way too.

As for Percy Hodge, he'd never notice a few wallflowers missing once the beds were planted. It was a chance too good to miss, Sam told himself.

Well content with his plans, he turned on his side, wrenched rather more of his share of the marital blankets from his wife's recumbent form, and settled to sleep.

9. Sam Curdle Tries His Tricks

On the whole, Winnie Bailey found Richard's stay with them less punishing than she had first feared. Nevertheless, she was becoming heartily sick of his preoccupation with his alimentary canal, and said as much to her husband one day when her nephew was safely in Oxford about his affairs.

'Ignore it,' advised Dr Bailey.

'That's easier said than done,' said Winnie, knitting briskly. 'After all, I have to spend a great deal of time and thought on our meals, and it really is maddening to see him picking about like an old hen.'

'The boy wants more exercise,' said her husband. 'As far as I can see, the walk from the front door to the garage is about the sum total of his exertions. He's bound to be liverish.'

'Have a word with him,' begged Winnie. 'It really can't be good for him to be so introspective about his food, and honestly, it's driving me quite crazy.'

'I'll do my best,' promised her husband, but privately he had little hope of curing a hypochondriac so easily.

His chance came a day or two later when Winnie was out at an evening meeting of the Lulling Field Club, accompanied by her old friend Dotty Harmer. Winnie had left cold chicken and ham, and a fresh green salad for the menfolk, with a delicious orange trifle for their pudding. She herself would be dining on two Marie biscuits and a cup of weak tea, as the Lulling meeting began at 7.00 p.m. and these exciting refreshments would be served at half-time – somewhere about 8.15 p.m. This was the usual pattern of evening meetings

in Lulling and Thrush Green, and accounted for the internal rumb-
lings of hungry stomachs which invariably accompanied local lectures
and whist drives.

Dr Bailey helped his nephew to the meat which his wife had left
neatly sliced on the dish.

'Oh, far less than that, please,' begged Richard. 'Somehow I seem
to be averse to flesh these days.'

The doctor obligingly transferred two small slices to his own
plate.

He watched Richard turning over the salad. Now that Winnie
had made him aware of the young man's foibles, he noticed how
anxiously he picked over the greenery, selecting a lettuce leaf here, a
sprig or two of cress there and taking care to miss the sliced cucumber
which hid among the leaves.

'Averse to cucumber too?' asked the older man pleasantly. 'I always
enjoy cucumber, I must confess.' He helped himself generously.

'Aunt Winnie's food is always delicious, but I don't seem to get as
hungry as I used to do. And then, of course, I like to keep to Otto's
diet. I'm sure he's in advance of his time in these matters.'

'You need more exercise,' said the doctor.

'I agree, my dear uncle. I couldn't agree more. As you know, I've
had to cut down my walking time since I've been engaged on this
Oxford project, and I certainly feel all the worse for it,' replied
Richard vigorously. 'It's one of the reasons why I try to cut down on
my intake of food.'

'You probably worry too much about your work at the moment.
Nothing like worry to deaden the appetite. You should take life
more easily.'

Richard, chewing his lettuce as conscientiously as Mr Gladstone,
looked gratified. Rarely did he get any active encouragement to talk
about his health. To have the attention of a medical man, even a
medical man with ideas as antiquated as his uncle's, was wholly
delightful. He became more confidential, encouraged not only by
the doctor's interest but also by the absence of his aunt.

'I think you are quite right, uncle. Otto seemed to think that I was
a shade too highly-strung. He suggested that marriage might help. It
relieves tension, you know.'

'It can increase it,' observed the doctor drily dabbing his lips with
his napkin. 'A lot depends on one's wife.'

'I have been thinking about it,' continued Richard, brushing aside his uncle's comment. 'It looks as though I shall need to settle in London within the next year or so, and it would be wise, I think, to buy a small house. A wife would be very useful domestically. I'm no hand at cleaning and cooking, I'm afraid.'

'You could always get a housekeeper,' said Dr Bailey, with a touch of asperity.

'I was thinking of Otto's advice. He seemed to think that I needed a comfortable settled background in order to do my best work. And although I don't consciously miss it, busy as I am with my research, he assures me that I am deeply deprived sexually.'

'You could always get a mistress too,' said Dr Bailey, even more frostily. His thin fingers drummed on the edge of the table. Winnie would have known that he was becoming very angry indeed. Richard blundered on.

'I dislike the idea,' he said primly. 'And frankly, uncle, I'm surprised that you suggest it. No, I feel sure that I'm ready for marriage. After all, I shall be thirty-three next birthday. I think it's time I found a wife.'

'You may have some difficulty,' said Dr Bailey.

'Really?' Richard was genuinely surprised. 'I don't want to appear conceited, but I'm reasonably healthy and good-looking, and as for prospects – well, I think I can safely say that I shall be at the top of my particular tree within the next five years.'

The older man hit the table so sharply that the glasses jumped.

'Richard, will you never grow up?'

His nephew looked at him with startled blue eyes.

'You seem to view marriage purely as a panacea for your own ills,' continued the doctor, his cheeks flushed with exasperation. 'You talk as though a wife were a cross between a box of tranquillizing pills and a Hoover. *Not once* have you mentioned affection, respect or mutual happiness. D'you think any girl worth her salt is going to take you on, on your terms? Believe me, Richard, you're the one that will remain single if all you are offering are the attractions you've just mentioned.'

'Uncle –' began Richard, in protest but he was ignored.

'I must say it, my boy, hard though it sounds. You are as bone-selfish now as you were at seven years' old, and you've grown no wiser with the years. Marriage might well do you a power of good –

heaven knows you need humanizing somehow – but I pity the girl who ever takes you on.'

The doctor raised his glass and sipped some water. Across the table his nephew sat transfixed, a slightly sulky look replacing the one of utter surprise.

'I'm sorry I should have upset you,' he said stiffly at last. 'I had no idea I was so objectionable.'

'Oh, tut-tut!' said Dr Bailey testily. 'Don't get in a huff over a bit of straight talking. You've got your good points, my boy, as we all have – but unselfishness is not among them at the moment. You think over what I've said now.'

He reached for the trifle.

'Let me give you a helping of this, Richard. Dr Goldstein would approve, I feel sure.'

But Richard was not to be mollified by a helping of trifle or a quip about his medical adviser. He rose from the table, his whole demeanour expressing acutely wounded dignity.

'No, thank you, uncle. My appetite has completely vanished after those remarks. If you'll excuse me, I will go for a walk.'

'You couldn't do better,' said the doctor cheerfully. 'And take an alka-seltzer before you go to bed. You'll be as right as a trivet in the morning.'

When Winnie returned, Richard was still out.

'Walking somewhere,' said her husband, in answer to her inquiries. 'Getting over the sulks. We had that little talk you suggested.'

'Oh, Donald, you haven't upset him, have you?'

'I rather hope so. We went from food to marriage. Richard seems to think that a wife might be a useful cure for his constipation and save him from doing his own chores.'

'Donald! Is that all?'

'That's what I asked him. He's out now, I fancy, trying to find the answer.'

Next door, at Tullivers, Harold Shoosmith continued his assault on the neglected border. Some days had elapsed since his first visit, and on his second he was surprised to see that the narrow bed under the dining-room window had been planted with healthy wallflower plants.

'Your handiwork?' he asked.

'Yes. Are they put in properly? Not too close, are they?'

'No, they're just right. Very fine specimens too. They put my own to shame. Where did you buy them?'

'As a matter of fact,' said Phil, 'a sandy-haired man came to the door with them while you were in London. I can't remember his name – but he's often about. He helps old Piggott sometimes, I think.'

'Sam Curdle,' said Harold grimly.

Phil looked at him anxiously.

'Why, what's wrong?'

'What did he ask for them?'

'I paid him ten shillings for two dozen. Was that too much?'

'Much too much, my dear. Especially as he probably pinched them in the first place.'

'Damn!' said Phil softly, thrusting her hands into her coat pockets and surveying the border ruefully. 'I might have known. What shall I do? If these have been lifted from someone else's garden, they'll be furious.'

'Leave it to me,' replied Harold. 'I'll have a word with Sam Curdle. He's no business to charge more than two shillings a dozen anyway, and well he knows it. Don't have any dealing with that chap. You'll be done every time.'

'I'll watch him in future,' promised Phil. 'How I do hate to be fooled!'

'Who doesn't?' smiled Harold, moving off to his digging.

Sam Curdle's peccadillo, as it happened, had already been discovered. Percy Hodge had a farmer's sharp eye, and a pretty shrewd idea of how twelve dozen plants would look in the garden beds allotted to Sam's care. It did not take him long to discover that they were fairly sparsely planted. He confronted Sam the morning after the sheep sale.

Sam denied the charge.

'You be allus down on us Curdles,' he complained, a gypsy whine creeping into his voice. 'Every blessed plant as was outside your back door I planted, as God's my Saviour.'

'Fat lot of saving you'll get,' said Percy Hodge roundly. 'There's a good score or more plants missing, and I want them back. Understand?'

'How'm I to get 'em? I tell you, sir, they're all set in, as you can see.'

'You get them back, Curdle, or tell me what's happened to 'em. You can take yourself and your missus off my land if I don't get the rights of this business. You had fair warning when I let you come into the yard.'

'You be a hard man,' whimpered Sam. In truth, he was more frightened of his wife's reaction to the news than his master's threats. Bella could be ferocious in anger, and Sam still bore the scars of marital battle from earlier engagements with his wife.

At that moment, the telephone rang and Percy Hodge strode indoors to answer it, leaving Sam to his thoughts.

For the rest of that day, and the next, Sam puzzled over his problem. Not for a minute did he consider telling the truth. Such a straightforward course was completely foreign to Sam's devious temperament. Somehow he must slide out of this tangle of trouble and, more important still, without Bella finding out.

Fate was against him. Percy Hodge and Harold Shoosmith met on the evening of Harold's discovery at Tullivers. Both men were on their way to the post-box at the corner of Thrush Green. After the usual greetings, and comment on the weather, Harold came to the point.

'Is Sam Curdle still with you?'

'Yes, indeed, the rogue. But he'll not be with me much longer, I fancy. He's up to his old tricks. Pinching wallflower plants this time.'

'I'll show you where they are,' said Harold, and led the way across the road to Tullivers. It was beginning to get dark, but the sturdy plants, so carefully put in by Phil, were clearly to be seen. The two men gazed at them over the gate.

'D'you know what he got for them?' asked Percy, turning away. The two men moved towards the green.

'He fleeced Mrs Prior of ten shillings,' said Harold. 'It's despicable.'

'She must be a green 'un,' commented the farmer. Harold's wrath kindled.

'She is a Londoner. One wouldn't expect her to know the price of plants. And Sam Curdle knew that well enough!'

Percy Hodge looked at his companion curiously.

'No offence, old man. I'm not trying to excuse Sam. He's a twister right enough, and he'll get his marching orders in the morning.'

'I can let you have a couple of dozen plants,' said Harold, more coolly, 'if you're short. It seems a pity to worry Mrs Prior about this. She was upset when I told her my suspicions.'

'Well, that's very handsome of you, but I've got all I need really. Tell the lady to leave them where they are, and not to worry her head about the matter. I'll deal with our Sam, you mark my words.'

They walked across to the Land Rover which the farmer had left in the chestnut avenue, and bade each other a cheerful good night.

'That was a rum thing,' mused Percy Hodge to himself, as he drove up the shadowy lane to Nod and Nidden. 'I shouldn't wonder if old Harold Shoosmith isn't a bit sweet on that young woman. Ah well, no fool like an old fool!'

He trod on the accelerator, keen to confront Sam Curdle with the fruits of this chance encounter.

Suddenly, the thought of his farmyard, free of the Curdle tribe for ever, filled him with pleasurable relief.

Harold Shoosmith's flash of anger surprised the man himself quite as much as it surprised the observant farmer. He returned thoughtfully to his quiet house and sank into an armchair. What exactly was happening to him? He didn't mind admitting that he was attracted to Phil Prior, but then he had been attracted to many girls in the past. He had always enjoyed the company of intelligent women, and if they were pretty, then so much the better. This protective feeling for Phil Prior, he told himself, was the result of her unfortunate circumstances. Anyone with a spark of humanity would want to help a poor girl left defenceless and hard up, especially when she had to cope with the rearing of a young child, single-handed.

Sam Curdle's was such a dirty trick! He grew warm again at the very thought. It was small wonder that he flared up in Hodge's company. Any decent man would.

Or would he? Harold rose from the chair and walked restlessly about the room. Was he really becoming fonder of this girl than he realized? Damn it all, this was absurd! He was a steadfast bachelor and intended to remain so. He was old enough to be Phil's father. Well, nearly —

He walked to the end of the room and studied his reflection in the handsome gilt-framed mirror which lay above the little Sheraton side-table.

He was tall and spare, his eyes bright, and his hair, although silver, still thick. As a young man he had been reckoned good-looking. He supposed now, trying to look at himself dispassionately, he still had a few good points – but he was old, old, old, he told himself sternly. No young woman would consider him now, and quite right too!

He returned to his chair, dismissing these foolish thoughts, and opened the paper. It was as inspiring and exhilarating as ever. Four young men were appearing on charges of peddling drugs, an old lady had had her hand chopped off whilst attempting to retain her purse, containing two and eightpence, and a motorway to end all motorways was proposed which would wipe out six particularly exquisite villages and several hundred miles of countryside.

Harold threw it to the floor, leant back and closed his eyes. How pleasantly quiet it was! The fire whispered. The clock ticked. Somewhere, across the green, a car changed gear as it moved towards Lulling, and hummed away into nothingness. This was what he had looked forward to throughout those long hard years of business life in Africa. He would be mad to try and change his way of life now.

And yet Charles Henstock had found a great deal of happiness in later life since his marriage to Dimity. Charles, Harold pointed out to himself, had nothing to lose when he married. Ruled by that dreadful old harridan Mrs Butler, that desiccated Scotswoman who half-starved the poor rector, enduring the chilly discomfort of that great barn of a rectory all alone – of course marriage was attractive! Besides, Charles was the sort of man who *should* be married: he was not. That was the crux of the matter.

He took up the poker and turned over a log carefully. Watching the flames shoot up the chimney, he told himself firmly that marriage was out of the question. Once that poor girl's divorce was through he hoped that some decent kind *young* man would appear to make her happy, and take some of her present burdens from her.

Meanwhile, he would do what he could to help her, and would frankly face the fact that her presence gave him enormous pleasure. But for her sake, he must guard his feelings, he reminded himself. Thrush Green was adept at putting two and two together and making

five, and she had enough to contend with already, without being
annoyed by foolish gossip.

'Avuncular kindness!' said Harold aloud, and was immediately
revolted by the phrase. He hit the flaring log such a hefty thwack
that it broke in two, dropped the poker, and went to pour himself a
much-needed drink.

10. Harold is in Trouble

Regrettably, but understandably, Thrush Green folk tended to avoid
Dotty Harmer when they saw her approaching. Few had the time to
stand and listen to her diatribes against juvenile delinquency, the
present-day teaching of history, air pollution, the exploitation of
animals or whatever subject happened to be to the fore of Dotty's
raggle-taggle mind.

Now that Dotty had kittens to find homes for, the pursuit of her
neighbours was doubly frightening to them. Even she, unobservant
as she was, began to notice how people hurried away at her approach.

'Can't understand it,' she told Ella, one gloomy November afternoon. She was carrying the daily bottle of goat's milk to her friend's
house.

'Anyone'd think I'd got the plague,' she complained, putting the
damp bottle down upon the freshly-polished dining table. 'What's
wrong?'

'Kittens,' said Ella briefly. 'How many left?'

'Three,' replied Dotty. She looked accusingly at Ella. 'I was relying
on you to help me find homes. What about Dimity? Although I still
think that house is too draughty for cats. They need warmth, you
know.'

'Better a chilly rectory than a watery death,' said Ella downrightly.
'Sam Curdle would drown them for you, I expect, if you're really
stuck.'

Dotty blew out her papery old cheeks with indignation.

'The very idea, Ella Bembridge! If that's your idea of a joke, I
consider it in particularly poor taste!'

'Don't be stuffy,' said Ella, 'and sit down, for Pete's sake, mopping and mowing about, with the door open too. It's downright unnerving.'

She slammed the door shut, and watched Dotty perch herself primly on the edge of a chair, the epitome of one who has taken umbrage and is rather enjoying it.

'To tell you the truth, Dotty, I clean forgot to ask Dim about the cat. Anyway, I've an idea that Charles is allergic to them. He certainly never had one while Mrs Butler was with him.'

'*That* woman,' said Dotty, 'wouldn't have had *anything* in the house if she'd had her way! I certainly shouldn't have let any cat of mine go there with *her* in charge of the domestic arrangements. It would have been fed on cold potato and bread crusts, I have no doubt – with watered milk to drink. A quite dreadful person! She once had the temerity to offer me a helping of bread pudding to take home. She got short shrift from me, I can tell you. "Throw it to the birds, Mrs Butler," I told her. "If they're strong enough to lift it from the ground they are welcome to it." She wasn't very pleased, I remember.'

'She's got a post as cook in a boys' school, I hear,' said Ella conversationally.

'Dotheboys Hall, no doubt,' commented Dotty sharply, unwinding a long woolly scarf from her skinny neck.

'Have a cup of tea,' suggested Ella, glad to see that her old friend's wrath was subsiding.

'Thank you, dear. That would be most acceptable,' said Dotty graciously, unskewering her hat and placing two formidable hat-pins upright in the arm of her chair, where they quivered like antennae.

'Tell you what,' said Ella, using one of her favourite phrases, as she returned from the kitchen with the tray. 'Let's go over to Dimity's when we've had this. And what about that Mrs Prior? She might like a kitten. Have you tried her?'

'Now, that's quite a good idea,' replied Dotty, picking over the biscuits thoughtfully. 'No, dear, not Petit Beurre. I find them rather too rich. Ah, an Osborne! Just what I love, and a happy reminder of dear Victoria!'

She nibbled happily, and Ella thought, not for the first time, that there was something infinitely endearing about Dotty's innocent pleasure in simple things. Anyone who could wax enthusiastic about an Osborne biscuit commanded Ella's respect.

When their light repast was over, the two ladies crossed to the rectory to find the rector and his wife sitting by their fire, winding wool.

'A new waistcoat for Charles,' said Dimity. 'Do sit down.'

Ella, as usual, came to the point at once.

'Forgot to ask you before, but do you want one of Dotty's kittens?'

To her surprise, Dimity looked distressed and gazed at her husband.

'Well–,' she began timidly.

'I should simply love one,' said the rector. 'But Dimity –'

'But I should love one too,' cried his wife, 'but I always thought you disliked cats – that you had hay fever or something when they were in the house. Wasn't that why you never had one here?'

'Mrs Butler was the reason why I didn't have one,' said Charles robustly. 'Somehow, I've always thought *you* didn't really want one, and so I've never mentioned it.'

'For two grown people, you really are pretty stupid,' scolded Ella. 'All this sparing each other's feelings can only lead to misunderstandings, as you see. You should speak your mind.'

'Then I take it,' said Dotty, pulling out a crumpled notebook in a business-like manner, 'that you want one.'

'Yes, please,' said Charles and Dimity in unison, smiling at each other.

'Male or female?'

'Do you know which is which?'

'Well, frankly, no!' confessed Dotty, suddenly becoming less business-like.

'In that case,' said the rector, 'we'll be happy to leave it to the vet, when the time comes.'

'Now, I'm very glad to hear you say that,' said Dotty, lowering the indelible pencil which she had been sucking. Her blue-stained lips and tongue gave added piquancy to her appearance.

'I was so afraid you might have religious scruples, Charles, about interfering with nature. I'm glad to see you are more enlightened.'

'Better to give one doctored cat a home, than twenty kittens an untimely end,' said the rector philosophically.

'Quite, quite!' agreed Dotty, turning the pages of her notebook briskly. 'Well, which is it to be? Ginger with white paws, black with white paws, or plain tabby with exceptionally fine eyes?'

The rector and his wife exchanged amused glances.

'We'll come and see them tomorrow,' promised Dimity, 'and pick ours, shall we?'

'Very well,' said Dotty, stuffing the book untidily into her coat pocket. 'Come to tea – you too, Ella dear – and it will save me bringing up the goat's milk.'

'I think,' said the rector, making his way to the sideboard, 'that this transaction should be celebrated with a drink.'

And so it was.

Harold Shoosmith finished his labour of love on the flower border at Tullivers, just before the first sharp frosts of winter arrived. There was still plenty of work in the garden to warrant many more visits, but he was beginning to wonder if it would be wiser to pay calls less frequently.

His heart-searchings had left him somewhat ruefully amused. He was certainly becoming extremely fond of Phil, and Thrush Green must not know it. Nor, of course, must the girl, particularly with divorce proceedings in the offing. Life, thought Harold, cleaning the prongs of his gardening fork, was quite complicated enough without tangling it even more.

He was admiring the tidy border as Willie Bond, the postman, came with the afternoon letters. Phil came to the door to collect them, then crossed the grass to admire his handiwork.

'It really is splendid,' she said truthfully. 'So neat – and so lovely to find that it's got such a lot of good stuff in it already.'

She waved one of her letters.

'Do you mind if I open this now? It's from your friend Frank. Perhaps he's taken something after all.'

She ripped open the envelope and read the contents. Harold watched her growing pink with excitement. She thrust the letter towards him.

'There! Isn't that marvellous? Fifty guineas! I can't believe it.'

'Congratulations,' said Harold warmly. 'Which story is this?'

'Oh, the one about the two friends and the curate,' said Phil. 'I've a copy on the table if you're interested. When do you think they'll publish it? Shall I get paid on acceptance, do you think?'

'I should tell Frank that's what you want,' replied Harold,

shouldering his tools. 'And, yes, please, I'd love to read the story.'

'You must have brought it luck,' said the girl when she handed it over. 'You posted it for me. Remember?'

'So I did,' said Harold. 'I've a strong share in this success.'

He made his way back across the green, warmed with the thought of the girl's pleasure. When he had changed, and was sitting by his fire, he settled back to read the story.

He turned the typed pages with growing dismay. It was not the telling of the tale which worried him. Phil's style was as crisp and lucid as always, and the suspense was well-sustained. But the characters, in this present story, were far too realistically portrayed for Harold's peace of mind.

Here, for all the world to see, were Ella and Dimity, in the guise of Jean and Phoebe, and Charles Henstock – though far less attractive – under the name of Tobias Fuller, a hearty curate.

Even their appearance fitted. Jean was thickset, Phoebe skinny. Their determined pursuit of the innocent curate was told with a nice sense of the ridiculous which Harold would have appreciated in different circumstances.

He read it through to the end, let the typescript drop to his knees, and gazed thoughtfully at the fire. This simply must not be printed. He must go and see Phil immediately, before she wrote to accept the offer of payment.

But what a kettle of fish! What could have possessed the girl to lift two characters from life so inartistically! He looked through the story again, and sighing, went to the telephone.

Phil answered immediately.

'Do you think I might come over for a few minutes? It's about the story.'

'Of course. Something wrong with it?'

'Frankly, yes.'

There was a short silence. Then Phil spoke briskly.

'Well, bring it over with you, and we'll go through it. I expect it can be altered easily enough.'

She showed him into the sitting-room where a log fire crackled welcomingly.

'No Jeremy?' asked Harold.

'Early bed tonight. He's running a slight temperature. But he's quite happy reading a Paddington Bear book.'

'I'll go and see him, if I may, before I go.'

'He'd love that. But do tell me – you can guess how anxious I am – what's the matter with the story?'

Harold found her bright gaze very difficult to face.

'If you want to continue to live at Thrush Green,' said Harold, 'I'm afraid you'll have to scrap it.'

'Scrap it?' cried Phil, in horror. 'But why?'

'Jean and Phoebe are Ella and Dimity to a T. The curate, though not so near the knuckle, might be Charles Henstock.'

The girl looked aghast.

'I never thought of that,' she whispered. 'Here's a how-d'you-do.'

She looked swiftly at Harold and put a hand upon his arm.

'You surely don't think I did this knowingly? I wrote that story three years ago – long before I knew anyone here. Don't you remember? You said it would be a good idea to send a story I had by me while I altered the new one. This is it.'

'I remember very well.'

'What on earth shall I do?'

'Tell Frank to send it back.'

Phil's face took on a mutinous look.

'I don't really see why I should. I've got a clear conscience. This is pure coincidence. Frank's accepted it, and I'm dam' glad to have earned fifty guineas. Besides Frank won't be particularly anxious to take other things if I mess him about with this effort.'

Harold said nothing.

'Besides,' continued Phil, getting up and walking restlessly about the room, 'how many people in Thrush Green are likely to see this particular magazine? And what the hell does it matter if someone thinks I've written about Ella and Dimity? I wrote that story in good faith, and the money's honestly earned. And, believe me, it's needed. I've just had a further bill from the wretched builders for eighty-five pounds. This isn't the time to start being squeamish about possible hurt feelings.'

Harold let her argue herself to a standstill. Soon enough, he realized, she would be able to cope with this bitter disappointment, and he felt sure that she would decide, eventually, to withdraw the offending story.

'I really think you are fussing about nothing,' she went on standing in front of his chair. 'Why must you be so maddeningly interfering? The implications would never have dawned on me – and I don't suppose, for one minute, that they ever will on any readers in Thrush Green – if there are any. Why did you have to meddle in this?'

'Because I don't want to see you leaving Tullivers,' said Harold drily.

Phil snorted.

'It would take more than a few wagging tongues to oust me from Thrush Green, I can assure you.'

She sat down abruptly in the armchair on the opposite side of the hearth. Harold could see that her fury was fast abating. Far more upsetting, to his tender heart, was the look of hurt bewilderment which began to creep across her countenance.

'What on earth shall I do?' she asked quietly. 'I could, I suppose, have it published under a pen name.'

She sounded near to tears, and Harold began to feel alarmed about his own ability to cope with an emotional situation. If only she weren't so confoundedly pretty, it would be easier, he told himself.

'I feel partly to blame,' he said. 'Shall I have a word with Frank and say that I've noticed this likeness?'

'No, thanks,' replied Phil shortly. 'I can handle it.'

Harold refused to feel rebuffed.

'Very well. But you do see that it would be far wiser to scrap the story?'

'No, I can't say I do. And I'm not making up my mind one way or the other until the morning.'

'I'm glad to hear it.'

'I think you meant well–'

'Thanks,' interjected Harold grimly.

'But I don't relish your interference, I must say. I've nothing to blame myself for, and I need the money. Naturally, I don't want to upset good neighbours, but I'm not keen on upsetting Frank either.'

She stood up, and Harold rose to make his departure.

'No hard feelings?' he said with a smile.

'Of course not.' Her tone was warm.

'And can I see the boy?'

'Yes, indeed. Let's go up.'

But when they reached the bedroom the child was asleep with the open book lodged upon his chest.

Phil removed it quietly, put out the bedside light and they went downstairs.

'By the way,' said the girl. 'We're going to have a cat.'

'One of Dotty's?'

'That's right. Jeremy's thrilled.'

'And what about you?'

'Modified rapture. I love them, but I'm terrified of the traffic, and we're so horribly near the road.'

'Keep your fingers crossed,' said Harold, on the doorstep. He hesitated for a moment.

'Will you be kind enough to let me know how you decide to act?' he said diffidently. 'Perhaps I shouldn't interfere any more.'

'I shall let you know as soon as I've made up my mind,' said Phil stiffly. She watched him make his way to the gate, raised her hand in farewell, and closed the door, with what seemed to Harold, unnecessary firmness.

'Damn!' said Harold, plodding homeward. A much-quoted dictum of his old nurse floated into his perplexed mind.

'What can't be cured must be endured!'

Cold comfort indeed, thought Harold, turning the key in his front door.

Harold Shoosmith was not the only person in the neighbourhood to suffer a disturbed night.

Sam Curdle was receiving the lashing of Bella's tongue, as they packed their few poor belongings in the stuffy caravan. They were off at first light, making for a village north of Southampton.

Bella had learned the bitter truth that they were to depart from the farmer's wife.

'I'm sorry to lose you, Bella,' Mrs Hodge said truthfully. 'You've been a good worker and we've got on well. But my husband won't be done, as you know, and Sam's a fool to try it on.'

Bella had pleaded for leniency, promising to keep an eye on her erring husband, although she knew, in her heart, that he was too slippery a customer even for her control. The poor woman was at her wits' end. There were three children to bring up and she knew that Sam's chances of getting any kind of job in the Thrush Green area were slight indeed.

Mrs Hodge stood firm. It was as much as her life was worth, she said, to oppose Percy. Sam had known from the start that he was allowed in the yard on sufferance. He had flouted the master's demands, and there was an end to it.

A furious scene between Sam and Bella followed. The next day, Bella, slightly less heated, betook herself to the telephone booth at the corner of Thrush Green, a fine assortment of coins in hand.

Unknown to Sam, whom she had left sulking in bed, she put her pride in her pocket and decided to talk to her father who kept a country pub in a village in Hampshire. She had been his barmaid before marriage, and hoped that he and her stepmother would take pity on their plight now.

She disliked the idea of going there intensely, but there seemed to be no alternative. Her father had married some years after the death of Bella's mother, and her step-mother was a hard-working, but tight-fisted woman who had never taken particularly to her blowsy step-daughter. It wouldn't be a very comfortable situation for the Curdle family, Bella knew, remembering her step-mother's sharp tongue, but beggars couldn't be choosers, she told herself, as she dropped the coins in the box.

Her father was a tender-hearted man and responded kindly to her tearful call for help. Yes, they could all come, and the caravan could stand in the backyard. As it happened, his present barmaid was leaving to have a baby, though she would be back in a couple of months, Bella must understand.

And Maud herself, Bella's step-mother, was laid up with a sprained ankle, so Bella would be doubly welcome.

Sam, said her father, with rather less warmth, could find himself a job nearby and could earn a few bob helping him in the evenings with the crates.

'But you can tell him straight, Bella, he's to behave himself. You know what I mean. You and the kids are welcome for a bit, just to tide you over like, but Sam had better get down to a steady job and make a proper home for you all. Tell him I said so.' Bella promised, with some relish, thanked her father sincerely and went back to the caravan to face Sam with the ultimatum.

'Well, we ain't going!' said Sam roundly, when faced with the news.

A dangerous glint appeared in Bella's eye, and Sam began to quail inwardly.

'You speak for yourself, Sam Curdle. Go where you like – it don't trouble me, and that's flat. But me and the kids set off tomorrow for home. I can drive well enough to get us down there, and I reckons I own this caravan more than you do. It's my wages as keeps us going, and we'll all be a dam' sight better off without you.'

'Now, Bella –' began Sam.

Scarlet in the face, Bella rounded upon him.

'Take it or leave it! We're off first thing tomorrow, come rain or shine. Come if you like, or clear off – one or the other!'

And so, next morning, the battered caravan clattered out of Percy Hodge's yard for ever. As it rattled by Harold Shoosmith's house, Willie Bond the postman watched it. At the wheel was a grim-faced Sam. Beside him, arms folded, sat an equally grim-faced Bella. The news that the Curdles were off had already flown around the neighbourhood, but Willie was the only witness to their departure.

'Good riddance to bad rubbish!' said Willie aloud, as the caravan slid out of sight down the steep hill to Lulling.

He echoed the general feelings of Thrush Green.

11. Albert has Suspicions

Harold Shoosmith's bathroom was at the back of the house overlooking the little valley that lay to the west of Thrush Green. In the distance were Lulling Woods, a deep blue smudge against the winter sky.

As he shaved the next morning he gazed beyond the shaving mirror on the window sill observing the bare trees and brindled hedges of winter. The elm trees, near Dotty Harmer's distant cottage, spread their fans of black lace, and a wisp of blue smoke, curling up towards them, showed that Dotty was already astir.

After his restless night, Harold felt out of sorts. He had gone over the irritating affair of Phil's story, time and time again, in the maddening way one does at night. He had almost decided, at one stage, to ignore Phil's request to cease meddling and to ring Frank and explain matters, swearing his old friend to secrecy.

But with morning light, things could be seen more coolly, and

Harold made up his mind to let this business work itself out, without worrying himself unduly. He had made his point. It was Phil's decision, and she had plenty of sense.

He determined to put it at the back of his mind, and went downstairs to brew his coffee and make toast. Nevertheless, he intended to keep within earshot of the telephone. Luckily, Betty Bell came that day to go through the house, like a mighty rushing wind, and she would answer the telephone if Harold were called away unexpectedly.

For the first part of the morning he worked at his desk, the telephone within arm's reach. It rang once and he snatched it up, only to be told that the exchange was testing his line.

Betty Bell burst in, without knocking, at eleven o'clock, bearing half a cup and half a saucerful of far too milky coffee, and two soggy gingernuts.

'Heard the news?' she asked.

'What about?'

'Them Curdles.'

'I heard Percy Hodge had asked them to leave,' said Harold guardedly.

'Fair old rumpus they had, Bella and Sam,' said Betty sitting down on *The Times* which Harold had left in the armchair. 'Willie Bond said they looked as black as thunder going off in that old van. Got a tin bath and the pushchair lashed on top. He said it sounded like Alexander's rag-time band.'

Betty burst into merry laughter, rocking back and forth to the detriment of *The Times*.

'Proper cough-drop old Willie is! You ever heard him sing "I Gotter Motter"?'

'No,' said Harold, pouring the coffee from the saucer into the cup. The biscuits he had wrapped in blotting paper and deposited in the waste-paper basket.

'You ought! You really ought! Brings the house down. Never fails. Always gets an encore, does Willie.'

She got up bouncily.

'Well, this won't buy the baby a new frock, will it? I'm doing you liver and bacon for your dinner. All right?'

Harold nodded. Betty Bell, in full spate, after a poor night, was more than usually exhausting.

She whirled out, crashing the door behind her. Harold sipped his tepid coffee and looked across the green to Tullivers. What was going on there?

A pale wintry sun lit the scene. He decided that he would do some gardening. No point in moping about. Fresh air and exercise would do him good.

'Give an ear to the phone, Betty,' he said casually, as he dragged on his wellingtons. 'I'm expecting a call.'

But it did not come. The morning passed. The liver and bacon were cooked and eaten. Betty Bell departed, leaving her master hoeing the beds beneath the study window where the telephone bell could be heard should it happen to ring.

But it remained silent for the rest of the day, and when evening came Harold shrugged aside the whole stupid incident and bent his energies to solving a much-crumpled crossword puzzle in *The Times*.

The departure of Sam and Bella Curdle had repercussions in the community. John Donne's dictum about no man being an island is truer in a village, perhaps, than in any larger community.

In the first place, Winnie Bailey was expecting him to come to the house to sweep the kitchen chimney. An odd quirk in this structure, necessitated by a by-gone architect's devious design, meant that it needed a sweep's ministrations twice a year. Dr Bailey owned some stout brushes, which were frequently loaned to neighbours, for this purpose, and Sam was always ready to do the job for five shillings.

Albert Piggott was the second person to miss Sam. They had been instructed by the rector to take out some rusty and damaged iron palings from the churchyard fence.

'Children or animals could be injured so easily,' said the rector anxiously. His sexton had snorted, but made no spoken comment. Children and animals, his expression implied, got what they deserved if they meddled.

'It's too bad,' said Mrs Bailey, when she heard that Sam had gone. 'That wretched boiler will start smoking as soon as the wind changes, mark my words. I shall have to get someone up from Lulling, I suppose.'

'No need,' said Richard, sprinkling wheat germ on his plate of Otto-recommended breakfast cereal. 'I'll do it this evening.'

Winnie surveyed her neat nephew with new respect.

'Do you know what to do?'

'Of course. I rather like sweeping chimneys. And cleaning drains. So worthwhile. Instant rewards, you know.'

He poured himself some coffee.

'Think no more of it. I'll be ready for the job after dinner tonight, if that suits you.'

'Wonderful!' cried Winnie. 'I'm most grateful, Richard dear. I'll let the boiler out this afternoon.'

True to his word, Richard tackled the job that evening. He was clad in ex-R.A.F. overalls, once white, but now mottled with the stains of many a year and many a job, from creosoting fences to cleaning out wells.

'They go everywhere with me,' said Richard, stroking his filthy overalls fondly. 'Such a useful rig-out.'

This practical side of Richard's nature was new to his aunt, and she found her respect for the young man growing considerably as she watched him tackling the flue. He was quick and clean. He had had the forethought to spread newspapers at strategic points, and he wasted no time in idle conversation as Sam Curdle did.

While the flue brush was rattling away inside the chimney, Phil Prior called.

'My goodness,' she said, with admiration. 'You're making a splendid job of that.'

'A minor accomplishment,' replied Richard, with a rare smile. 'It's more useful than painting water-colours these days.'

'It certainly is,' agreed the girl. She turned to Mrs Bailey.

'I hate to bother you, but would you come and have a look at Jeremy? He's looking so flushed. He went to sleep as usual, but he's woken up again so crotchety. I don't like to bother Doctor Lovell, but if you think –'

'Let me slip on my coat,' said Mrs Bailey, making for the stairs.

'Ah!' said Richard, with enormous satisfaction. A sizeable piece of hardened soot rattled down the chimney and splintered on the waiting newspaper.

'I think Aunt Winnie wants a different sort of fuel for this contraption.'

He picked up the soot in a blackened hand and studied it with close attention. Phil watched, amused. At last, this young man had come to life! Until then, she had found him cold and a trifle super-cilious.

'Do you often sweep chimneys?' she asked lightly.

'If I'm asked I do,' replied Richard. 'I like mucky jobs. It makes a change from my finicky figure work.'

He looked at her swiftly.

'Do you want anything done?'

'Not chimneys, alas. They were done when we moved in, but—' She hesitated.

'No, nothing really,' she finished lamely.

'It's a waste-pipe,' said Richard shrewdly.

Phil laughed.

'You're clairvoyant! As a matter of fact, it is.'

'Well, I love a good stuffed-up waste-pipe,' said Richard, with relish. 'I'll be over tomorrow evening, if that suits you.'

'There's no hurry — it's the spare room waste-pipe, but I'd be eternally grateful, if you really mean to do it.'

'Mean to do it? Of course, I mean to do it,' said Richard indignantly. 'If not tomorrow, then one evening soon. I'll ring first to see if it's convenient.'

'You are kind,' said Phil gratefully.

Mrs Bailey reappeared and the two women hurried next door. After inspecting Jeremy, Winnie suggested a little milk of magnesia.

'And if he still seems feverish in the morning, send for Doctor Lovell. He'll pop in before morning surgery, no doubt.'

'You've relieved my mind,' said the girl. 'I seem to worry un-necessarily.'

'How are things going?' Winnie ventured.

'Worse,' said Phil. 'By that I mean that the wheels are grinding along. What I *cannot bear* is the thought of Christmas for Jeremy without his father. I must screw myself to telling him before long. I can't tell you how I dread it.'

'Do you hear from him?'

'Sometimes he writes a short note when he sends my cheque. He's in France, at the moment. With her, I imagine.'

The girl sounded dog-tired and hopeless. Winnie felt powerless to help.

'And the writing?' she asked, hoping to find a more cheerful topic.

Phil laughed mirthlessly.

'All in a muddle. I've had an acceptance, but I'm not sure if I want it to be published now. There are plenty of stories, by me, waiting to be read by editors. Something may turn up.'

'I'm sure it will,' said Winnie robustly. 'Now have an early night, and by morning both you and Jeremy will be fighting fit again.'

She kissed her gently, and returned home, shaking her head.

'Poor young thing!' she murmured, opening the kitchen door.

Richard was taking up the newspapers. The stove was back to rights and freshly-washed.

'That's a nice young woman,' observed Richard thoughtfully. 'Is her divorce through yet?'

My goodness, thought Winnie, in some alarm, Richard's touch may be sure enough with chimneys and waste-pipes, but it was surely rather too heavy and direct in his dealings with women!

Albert Piggott did not find help as easily as Winnie Bailey.

He surveyed the cold November day through his cottage window. It was going to be proper bleak tugging up them old railings. Been stuck there, in Cotswold clay, for a hundred years. They'd take some shifting – and no Sam to give him a hand.

He said as much to Nelly, who was whirling about behind him with a tin of polish and a duster. He got short shrift from her.

'A good day's work won't hurt you, Albert. Make a nice change,' she puffed, rubbing energetically at the top of the table. 'Do that liver of yours a power of good.'

Fat lot of sympathy she ever gives me, thought Albert morosely, lifting his greasy cap from the peg behind the door. He dressed slowly, watching his buxom wife attacking the furniture with zest.

All right for some, Albert grumbled to himself, crossing to the windy churchyard. She'd never had a day's illness in her life – strong as a horse, she was – and still game to make eyes at that oilman.

The pain which gnawed intermittently at Albert's inside seemed worse today. Doctor Lovell's pills helped a little, but Nelly's food was too rich, no doubt about it, and he was that starved with hunger when it came to meal times, he ate whatever she provided, dreading too the lash of her tongue if he refused to eat.

He set about the broken railings and found the job as difficult as he had feared. As he tugged he contemplated his marriage. What a fool he'd been! A clean house and good cooking was no exchange for peace and quiet, and that was what he missed. The only times he had the house to himself were Tuesdays and Fridays when Nelly took herself to Bingo at Lulling.

Or did she? A sudden suspicion made Albert straighten his back and look across Thrush Green. Come to think of it, Bingo was on Saturday night. It dawned, with horrible clarity, on Albert's dull mind, that Nelly must be meeting the oilman on Tuesdays and Fridays.

That was it! Tuesday was the oilman's half-day, he remembered, and Friday was his pay-day. It all fitted together.

He bent to his task again, half relishing the scene when he confronted Nelly with his discovery. The pain in his stomach seemed worse, and there was a tight feeling across his chest which he had not suffered before, but he continued tugging with the vigour born of righteous indignation.

He saw Nelly whisk out of the cottage, a basket on her arm, bound for the butcher's down the hill. He gave her no greeting, but watched sourly as her ample back vanished in the distance.

'You wait, my gal,' said Albert grimly. 'You just wait!'

Young Jeremy Prior was no better the next morning and Doctor Lovell called at Tullivers when morning surgery, next door, was over.

'There's measles about,' he told Phil when they were downstairs again, 'but it doesn't look like it at the moment. No rash yet, of course. But keep him in bed, and I'll look in tomorrow.'

He eyed the girl sympathetically. She looked wretchedly tired.

'Did you sleep last night?'

'Not much.'

'Would you like a few tablets?'

'Not really, many thanks. I've a horror of pills, and I know I'll have a good night tonight. It works out that way, I find.'

'Good,' said the young doctor briskly. 'But if I can help, do just say. And don't worry about that young man upstairs. I think we'll find his temperature's down tomorrow.'

Throughout the day the child was unusually demanding and fractious. He wanted his mother with him most of the time, and she was content to shelve her writing and sit beside him reading stories or helping with a gigantic ancient jig-saw puzzle of the Wembley Exhibition, bequeathed to him by Winnie Bailey.

The affair of the story niggled at the back of her mind, but she had little time to give it attention that day. Harold Shoosmith's attitude she still found high-handed, and was annoyed that she cared so much. The fact that he might expect to hear about her decision that day, never entered her head. She had told him that she would let him know what she would do, and this she intended to do in time.

Meanwhile, she kept Jeremy company and watched the activities of her neighbours through the bedroom window. She saw Albert Piggott attacking the church railings, and his fat wife waddling down the road. She saw Charles Henstock walking across the green, bent against the wind, to speak to Albert. Her friend, Joan Young, emerged from the fine house nearby, and battled her way towards Lulling, and across the green she watched the children pour into the playground at mid-morning, shouting and leaping, whilst little Miss Fogerty stood sipping her tea among the tumult.

It reminded Phil that she must let Miss Watson know why Jeremy was away. She would telephone during the dinner hour. She did not want to be out of earshot if Jeremy called.

But in the afternoon, when he fell into a peaceful sleep, she ventured into the garden to get a breath of the cold blustery air. A rose or two still starred the bushes and she picked them to enjoy indoors. The winter jasmine was in bud and already one or two bulbs were poking their green shoots through the earth.

Elsewhere winter held sway. The chestnut trees were bare now, in the avenue, and the dead leaves of the Baileys' beech hedge rustled dryly in the wind. The skeletons of dead plants rattled together like castanets, and the matted ivy on the old wall flapped up and down like a loose curtain.

The Cotswold stone was as grey as the November sky above it. In the distance, the girl could see the dun-coloured meadows of winter and the faraway smudge of Lulling Woods. The grey coldness seemed to echo her own life just now. Would she ever know light and warmth, colour and excitement again? Would this desolation last for ever?

She was tired of the struggling, tired of keeping up a bright front for Jeremy, for the neighbours and for herself. If only something, however insignificant, would happen to give her hope.

12. Albert is Struck Down

The wind increased to a gale during the night, screaming down the hill to Lulling, rattling windows and even shifting some of the heavy stone roof tiles of the town. The few remaining leaves were wrenched from the trees, and an old oak crashed across the road near Percy Hodge's farm, bringing down some telephone wires, and causing more than usual confusion in the Lulling exchange.

It was no better in the morning. Willie Marchant could make no headway on his bicycle in the face of this fierce northerly blast. Even his tacking methods were no use against it, and he was forced to wheel his bicycle up the steep hill, his eyes half shut against the cigarette ash which blew dangerously against his face from the inevitable stub in his mouth.

It was useless to try to prop a bicycle against the kerb in this wind, and when he reached Tullivers he prudently lodged it against the wall while he battled his way up the path.

There was no one about, and he thrust the letters through the flap beneath the admiral's dolphin and continued on his erratic course.

Everywhere he met tales of damage. A flying tile had broken the glass in Joan Young's greenhouse. The school dustbin had been found in the hedge at the end of the playground. Albert Piggott's cat was missing, 'blown to kingdom-come', its owner surmised gloomily.

Little Miss Fogerty did not tell Willie about her own troubles, but they had been severe. Two pairs of sensible long-legged knickers, of a style which she had been brought up to know as 'directoire', had blown from the discreet little clothes line hidden by laurel trees, over the hedge into her neighbour's garden.

Much agitated, she had watched until the man of the house had gone to work, and then had knocked timidly at Mrs Bates' door to explain about her embarrassing loss. Mrs Bates, a kind-hearted woman, forbore to show any coarse amusement, as some less refined Thrush Green folk might have done, rescued the garments from the roof of her hen-house and returned them gravely, wrapping them first in a piece of brown paper. Miss Fogerty was much touched by the delicacy of this gesture, but the horror of the incident haunted her for the rest of the day.

Harold Shoosmith heard about the havoc in the Lulling Woods area when Betty Bell burst into his house at half-past nine.

'I found Miss Harmer's letters all twizzled up in her string bag in the road. Soaking wet, of course, but it never bothered her. "They'll dry, dear," was all she said when I took 'em into her. Willie won't be best pleased, I'll lay. And the roof blew off the hen-house at "The Drovers' Arms" and landed in the pond! My, what a night! Any damage here?'

Harold had to admit that he had found none. Betty looked disappointed. She thrived on daily drama.

It was later that morning that the telephone rang, and Harold's spirits soared when he heard the excitement in Phil's voice.

'Wonderful news! Frank's taken the latest story, and for more money.'

'I'm so glad. Well done!'

'Isn't it splendid? And he wants me to meet him "with a view to further work", so his letter says. I'm going to ring him in a few minutes.'

'You'll find him very easy to talk to,' said Harold. 'What's more, he can explain the sort of thing he wants done, which saves a lot of time and temper.'

He paused, wondering if the girl would tell him about the awkward story. As if she knew his thoughts, she spoke of it next.

'I've decided to scrap that other thing. You were quite right.'

'That's extremely generous of you.'

'Not at all. It could have upset people here – though I still think the chances were slight, particularly if I'd used a pen-name. Anyway, this second acceptance takes care of most of the builder's bill, and I don't feel so hard-pressed.'

'I can't tell you how pleased I am,' said Harold warmly. 'You deserve to succeed. You've worked so hard lately.'

'I hope you weren't expecting a call yesterday,' said Phil suddenly. 'Jeremy was off-colour and I didn't really bother much about the other problem. He's much better this morning, thank goodness, but won't go to school until next week.'

'Well, give the young man my regards,' said Harold. 'Now, I'm not going to hold you up – you must be anxious to get in touch with Frank. Remember me to him, if it enters your head. I hope he'll come down here one day. Meanwhile, the best of luck with all your ploys.'

He put down the receiver, feeling unusually elated. It was a relief to know that the story would never appear, and even more gratifying to know that the girl was having some success. Frank would treat her right, thought Harold robustly!

He went into the windy garden, whistling like a boy, and Betty Bell, well-versed in affairs of the heart, winked at her reflection in the hall mirror as she polished it.

Richard was as good as his word and appeared some evenings later dressed in his working overalls and carrying his drain-clearing equipment. His expression was animated, and when Phil opened the door to him she was struck by his good looks, which she had not noticed before.

'Got plenty of newspaper?' asked Richard, mounting the stairs. 'I like lashings of *really thick* paper to spread about.'

'About a dozen *Telegraphs* and great fat wads of *Sunday Times*,' said Phil. 'And all those lovely Business Supplements no one reads. Absolutely unopened, they are.'

'Good, good! Pity you don't take the *Sunday Express* though. Wonderful powers of absorption for this sort of job.'

He spread the papers busily, patting them down happily, and humming to himself. It was quite obvious to Phil that he would be better alone with his passion.

'I'll get out of your way,' she said diplomatically, 'but shout if you want anything.'

She heard nothing for the next twenty minutes but the sound of running water and Richard's footsteps up and down the stairs as he hurried outside to make sure that the water was flowing without interruption. When he finally appeared in the sitting-room, he looked triumphant.

'As I thought, simply the U-bend. No difficulty at all. Someone has been using a disintegrating face-flannel, I suspect.' 'Not guilty,' smiled Phil. 'Perhaps the admiral's sister? I believe she used that room.'

She indicated a tray of drinks on a low table by the fire.

'What will you have? My goodness, you've earned a drink! I'm so very grateful.'

Richard looked at the pale chair covers, and with rare thoughtfulness began to step out of his filthy overalls. It seemed to Phil, watching him, that this young man wasn't the ogre that Winnie, despite her tact, had portrayed.

'My aunt tells me that you write,' said Richard. He sipped his dry sherry appreciatively. Otto allowed one small sherry a day if it were a dry one, Richard remembered happily.

'Not as successfully as I should like,' admitted Phil, 'but it all helps. I'm hoping for some more work next Wednesday.'

She told him about Frank.

'Wednesday,' repeated Richard. 'I'm going to town myself that day. Let me run you up. What time do you have to meet him?'

Phil told him that she was lunching with Frank and that she had planned to catch the 10.10 train from Lulling, changing at Oxford, as her car was needing attention.

'It will give me time to see Jeremy safely to school and to tidy up here,' she said. 'Joan Young is having him to lunch, and tea, and I shall collect him about 6.'

'I was proposing to leave about 10.30,' said Richard. 'I am spending the night with the Carslakes, so I'm afraid I can't bring you back, but do please give me the pleasure of your company on the journey up.'

'I should love to,' said the girl, and thought how pleasant it was to be talking to a man of her own age again. A jaunt to London would be something to look forward to after the recent drab weeks at Thrush Green, and Richard she found surprisingly interesting.

He stayed for over an hour and was at his most charming. As he returned to the Baileys' house, carrying his impedimenta, he sniffed the frosty air with relish.

He put his head round the sitting room door. His uncle and aunt surveyed him mildly over their spectacles.

'It's a wonderfully bright night,' said Richard. 'Do you mind if I take a brisk walk?'

'Not at all, dear boy,' said Winnie. 'But don't get over-tired.'

'Tired?' echoed Richard in amazement. 'My dear aunt, I could walk ten miles without stopping tonight!' He vanished, and they heard the front door slam.

The doctor lowered his newspaper and looked across at his wife.

'Would you think,' he asked pensively, 'that our Richard is putting some of Otto's theories into practice?'

International crises always seem to occur at week-ends. Domestic crises appear to follow the same pattern.

Certainly, there was a crisis at Albert Piggott's home on the Sunday. Nelly had dished up a boiled hand of pork, broad beans, onions and plenty of parsley sauce. She had also excelled herself by providing a Christmas pudding for the second course with a generous helping of brandy butter.

'I made six full-size ones,' said Nelly, surveying the pudding fondly, 'but this little 'un was for a try-out before Christmas. What d'you think of it?'

'All right, if your stummick's up to it,' replied Albert dourly, turning his spoon about in the rich fruitiness.

'Lord love old Ireland!' cried Nelly, in exasperation. 'Ain't you a misery? Small thanks I gets for slaving away over the stove day in and day out. Wouldn't do you no harm to have bread and water for a week.'

'You're right there,' agreed Albert sarcastically. 'You knows full well the doctor said I was to go easy on rich food. I believes you does it a purpose to upset me.'

Nelly rose from the table with surprising swiftness for one of her bulk. She whisked round the table behind her husband, and before he knew what was afoot, she had thrust his head sharply into his plate of pudding.

'*You besom!*' spluttered Albert emerging with a face smothered in the brown mess, and with a badly-bumped nose. He picked up the plate and threw it at his wife. It clattered to the floor, puddingside down, but miraculously did not break.

Nelly, who had dodged successfully, now broke into peals of hysterical laughter as she watched her husband grope his way to the sink to wash off his dessert.

'You wait till I get my hands on you,' threatened Albert. 'I'll beat the living daylights out of you, my gal! Pity I never done it before. You and that oil man!'

Nelly's shrieks of laughter stopped suddenly.

'You can leave him out of this, Albert Piggott. He knows how to treat a lady.'

'Humph!' grunted Albert, from the depths of the roller-towel on the door. 'I'll bet he knows! I could have the law on him, if I'd a mind, carrying on with another man's wife.'

Nelly adopted a superior aloofness.

'I'm not stopping here to listen to your filthy insinuations,' she said loftily. 'I shall go and have a lay-down, and you can clear up this mess you've made with your tantrums.'

'That I won't!' shouted Albert to her departing back. 'I'm due at church at 2.15 for christenings, and you can dam' well clear up your own kitchen!'

The door, slamming behind Nelly, shook the house, and a minute later Albert heard the springs of the bed above squeak under his wife's considerable weight.

Growling, he flung himself into the chair by the fire, picked up the *News of the World*, and prepared to have a quarter of an hour's peace before going across to St Andrew's for his duties.

Hostilities were not resumed until the early evening. Nelly remained upstairs, but ominous thumps and door-bangings proclaimed that she was active. When she re-appeared, she was dressed in her best hat and coat, and was carrying a large suitcase which she set upon the table, taking care to miss the dirty dinner plates and cutlery with which it was still littered.

'Well, Albert, I've had enough,' said Nelly flatly. 'I'm off!'

If she expected any pleading, or even surprise, from her husband she was disappointed. Albert's morose expression remained unchanged.

'Good riddance!' said Albert. 'You asked yourself here and you can go for all I care. But don't come here whining to be took back when that fancy-man of yours has got fed up with you.'

Nelly drew in an outraged breath.

'Come back here? Not if you went down on your bended knees, Albert Piggott, and begged of me! No, not if it was with your dying breath! You've seen the last of me, I can tell you. I'm going where I shall be appreciated!'

She hoisted the case from the table and struggled to the door. Albert remained seated by the fire, the newspaper across his knees, his face surly and implacable.

He remained so for several long minutes, listening to his wife's footsteps dying away as she walked out of his life for ever. He had no doubt that Nelly spoke the truth. Their ways had parted.

He looked at the kitchen clock. Time he went to ring the bell for Evensong. But when he came to stir himself, the pain across his chest seared him like a red-hot knife. He fell to his knees, his head pillowed on the *News of the World* on the hearth-rug, and was unable to move. The last thing he saw, before the blackness engulfed him, was the remains of the Christmas pudding spattered, dark and glutinous, across the kitchen wall.

The rector, robing in the vestry, realized with alarm, that Piggott was absent.

'You'd better ring the bell,' he told the largest choir-boy. 'Mr Piggott seems to have been held up.' Privately, Charles Henstock feared that his verger might be the worse for drink. It had happened before, but he did not wish to be uncharitable, and he told himself that he must postpone judgement until he had seen the fellow.

Albert did not appear during the service, and as soon as his few parishioners had departed, Charles put out the lights himself, saw that things were in order, and then crossed to Albert's cottage.

The windows were dark, and the rector feared that Albert was indeed in a stupor. Really, drink was a great nuisance!

He knocked and got no reply.

'Anyone at home?' called the rector, opening the door. The sight that met his eyes, in the gloom, frightened him exceedingly.

He found the light switch and surveyed the chaos. Albert's huddled body lay before the dying fire, but his heavy breathing showed that he was still alive.

'Thank God!' said the rector from his heart, kneeling beside the man. He turned him over, into a more comfortable position and put the cushion from the armchair beneath his head.

'Piggott!' he cried sharply. 'Can you hear me, Piggott?'

A growling sound came from Albert's pale lips, and his eyelids fluttered spasmodically.

'Stay there,' cautioned the rector, thinking, as he said it, how idiotic it was. There was small chance of Albert moving far.

'I'm going for help,' he said, making for the door. The man must have a doctor. Should he telephone from home, or run along to Harold Shoosmith's? There was nothing in it as to distance, and he did not wish to alarm Dimity. Harold it should be.

He ran through the darkness, past 'The Two Pheasants' and was soon banging Harold's knocker.

'My dear chap,' said Harold to his breathless friend. 'What is it? Come in, do.'

'It's Piggott. A seizure or something,' puffed Charles. 'Can I use your telephone?'

'I'll ring Lovell,' said Harold, taking command, 'while you go back. I'll follow as soon as I've got through. And don't worry,' he shouted to his retreating friend, 'it's probably only the drink!'

'Not this time, I fear,' called back the rector, hurrying away.

Twenty minutes later Doctor Lovell agreed with the rector as he surveyed his patient.

The three men had carried Albert up the narrow stairs to his bed. He was conscious now, but very weak and pale.

'We've got an ambulance on the way for you, Albert,' said Doctor Lovell. 'I want to have a proper look at those innards of yours. Where's your wife?'

'Gorn,' said Albert, in a whisper. 'For good.'

None of the three men tried to dispute the statement. The signs of a fight downstairs, the empty clothes cupboard in the bedroom, and the general disorder, were plain enough. There had been plenty of talk about the Piggotts' differences, and about the oil man's advances. Albert, they knew, was speaking the truth.

'We'd better let her know anyway,' said the doctor. 'Know her address?'

'No,' said Albert shortly. 'Nor want to.' He closed his eyes.

An hour later he was asleep between the sheets at Lulling Cottage Hospital, and Harold and Charles were telling Dimity what had happened.

'She's bound to come back,' she said. 'She wouldn't leave him just like that – not in hospital, not when she hears that he's ill!'

'I agree that most women would bury the hatchet when they heard that their husbands had been taken ill, but somehow,' said Harold, admiring his whisky against the light, 'I don't think Nelly will return in a hurry.'

'But what will he do?' asked the rector, looking distressed. 'He must have someone to look after him when he comes out of hospital!'

'I know,' said Dimity suddenly. 'I'll write to Molly, his daughter.

She married Ben Curdle, the man who owns the fair,' she told Harold. 'She left here just before you came to live here. A dear girl – we all liked her so much. She should know anyway, and perhaps she will come and look after him.'

'He wasn't very nice to her when she did live with him,' ventured the rector doubtfully. 'And now she has Ben and the baby to look after, I really can't see –'

'Never mind,' said Dimity firmly. 'I shall let her know what has happened, and it is up to her to decide. I must ring Joan Young for her address. I know she keeps in touch. They were such friends when Molly used to be nursemaid to Paul.'

She made her way briskly to the study, and the two men heard her talking to Joan.

The rector gave a loud yawn and checked himself hastily.

'I'm so sorry. I'm unconscionably tired. It's the upset, I suppose. Poor Albert! I feel very distressed for him.'

'You'd feel distressed for Satan himself,' replied Harold affectionately. 'Poor Albert, indeed! I bet he asked for it. I don't blame Nelly for leaving that old devil.'

'I married them myself,' said the rector sadly, gazing at the fire. 'I must admit, I had doubts at the time.'

Dimity returned, a piece of paper fluttering in her hand.

'I've got the address. If I write now, then Willie can take it in the morning.'

'Well, I must be off,' said Harold rising. 'Many thanks for the drink.'

'I've just thought,' cried Dimity, standing transfixed. 'Did you see Albert's cat? I'd better go across and feed it.'

'You leave it till the morning,' advised Harold, patting her thin shoulder. 'It won't hurt tonight. There's plenty of Christmas pudding lying about the kitchen to keep it going.'

13. Christmas Preparations

Signs of Christmas were beginning to appear in Lulling and Thrush Green.

The squat Butter Market cross, beloved by residents and antiquarians from further afield, was being wreathed in coils of wire ready for its garland of coloured lights later on.

In the shops, gifts were on display. Puddocks, the stationers, decked one of their windows with Christmas cards and the other with a fearsome array of table mats arranged round a scarlet typewriter. Ella found the juxtaposition of these articles extremely annoying, and said so to the manager.

'If you're going to show table mats put something like a large dish, or a vase with Christmas decorations in it,' Ella told him, in a voice audible to all his customers.

'Or if you want the ruddy typewriter on show – though who on earth you imagine is going to pay over thirty quid for one Christmas present these days, I'm blessed if I know – then put office stuff round it. Blotters, say, or calendars, or pens and pencils. But to mix up the two just isn't good enough!'

The manager made perfunctory apologies. As a young man he had dreaded Ella's comments. Now that he was grey and tubby he was hardened to this awkward customer's remarks. Ella Bembridge was a byword in the town. No one was going to worry about her little foibles, he told himself.

He directed her attention to the other window.

'I've done my own,' said Ella, scrutinizing the crinolined ladies, the churches in the snow, and the kittens in paper hats, with obvious disgust.

'Appalling, aren't they?' she said cheerfully, and departed before the manager could think of a cutting reply.

The window of the electricity showroom was much admired by the young if not by their elders. It showed an all-electric kitchen with the oven prominently displayed. The oven door stood open, the better to show a dark-brown shiny turkey and some misshapen roast potatoes. At the kitchen table, a smiling woman stirred something which seemed to be Christmas pudding mixture, while a dish of mince-pies stood on the top of the refrigerator beside her.

Quite rightly, the good wives of Lulling found this scene as exasperating as Ella found Puddocks' window.

'Bit late mixin' the pudden,' one said sourly to another.

'And that bird won't get done with the door open,' agreed her friend tartly. 'I shouldn't care to try them spuds either.'

'Nor them mince-pies,' observed another. 'Plaster-a-Paris as plain as a pike staff. Bet some fool of a man arranged that window. I've a good mind to go in and tell 'em.'

The 'Fuchsia Bush' had excelled itself with rows and rows of silver bells, made from tinfoil, which were strung across the ceiling and rustled metallically every time the door opened.

'Come in handy for keeping the birds off the peas later,' observed one practical customer, speaking fortissimo above the din of the dancing bells.

The bow-shaped windows were studded with dabs of cotton-wool to represent snowflakes, and two imposing flower arrangements of dried grasses, seed-pods and fern, all sprayed with silver by the ladies of the Lulling Floral Society, took pride of place in each window.

Thrush Green's preparations were less spectacular, but Dimity took out the figures for the Christmas crib and washed them carefully in luke-warm water well-laced with Lux.

Miss Watson and Miss Fogerty were in the throes of rehearsals for the annual Christmas concert. Miss Fogerty, who was the more realistic of the two and knew the limits of her infants' powers, had wisely plumped for simple carols, sung in unison by the whole class, with 'growlers' tucked strategically at the back of the stage and warned to 'sing very quietly'. A few percussion instruments in the hands of the most competent few, who included young Jeremy Prior, were going to accompany the infant choir.

In fact, Miss Fogerty's main concern was to get the children to pronounce their vowel sounds correctly. Constant repetition of:

'Awy in er-er mynger'

was causing her acute distress.

Miss Watson, who was more ambitious, had decided rashly to stage a nativity play. The ten-year-olds who were the most senior of her pupils and who, it might be supposed, would be competent to play the leading roles, were at the self-conscious stage, and tended to giggle and look sheepish, which Miss Watson found both irritating and irreligious.

She found herself speaking with unusual sharpness.

'Don't mumble into your beard, Joseph. The parents want to hear you, remember. And if you three wise men keep tripping over the rector's spare room curtains I shall be returning them in shreds. Pick your feet up, do! As for you beasts in the stall, for pity's sake stop nodding your masks in that inane way. You'll have them off, and I'm not made of cardboard!'

With such travail was Christmas being welcomed at the school.

'I suppose it will be all right on the day,' said Miss Watson resignedly to Miss Fogerty.

'Of course it will,' Miss Fogerty replied stoutly, watching her children paste paper chains with frenzied brushes, and more chatter than was usually allowed. She dived upon one five-year-old who was twirling his paste-brush energetically in his neighbour's ear, removed the brush, slapped the offender's hand, and lifted the malefactor to the corner where he was obliged to study the weather chart for December, with his back to the class. Throughout the whole incident, Miss Fogerty's face remained calm and kindly.

Miss Watson sighed. Dear Agnes's methods were hopelessly old-fashioned, and she knew quite well that corporal punishment was frowned upon by all enlightened educationalists.

Nevertheless, thought Miss Watson, returning to her own boisterous class, a sharp slap seemed to work wonders now and again, and at times, like this, one surely could be forgiven.

In the houses round the green, more preparations were going on. Ella had looked out half a dozen lumpy ties, ear-marked for male friends such as Charles Henstock. The Christmas cards, a stack of bold woodcuts with a certain rough attraction, waited on the dresser for despatch later.

Her present to Dimity remained to be finished. She was sewing a rug, in a stitch called 'tiedbrick stitch', in gay stripes of scarlet, grey and white. It gave her enormous satisfaction to do, but its bulk was difficult to hide in a hurry, on the occasions when Dimity called unexpectedly to see her.

Harold Shoosmith, efficient as ever, had bought book tokens for all his friends, and had a neat pile waiting in his desk to be written in, and posted on the correct day. Betty Bell had made him a Christmas pudding large enough for a family of ten, and was upset when her employer told her firmly that he refused to countenance her proposal to make him a dozen mince-pies, two trifles and a couple of jellies 'to keep him going'.

'My dear Betty,' he said kindly, 'I'm going to Christmas dinner with the rector and his wife. I have invited them here for Boxing Day evening, as you know, and that delicious Christmas pudding will be ample.'

'You'd best have a trifle as well,' said Betty mutinously. 'Miss Dimity likes trifle.'

'Very well,' sighed Harold capitulating. '*One trifle!* And thank you.'

Across the green, Phil Prior wrapped a few presents for Jeremy and hid them among her clothes, but her heart was not in the coming festivities. The prospect for her was bleak, and any day now she must steel herself to break the news to Jeremy that his father would not be there at Christmas time. The boy would have to know the truth before long. If only she could get it over!

Meanwhile, she worked hard at her writing, and prepared a batch of stories, articles and ideas, which might interest Frank when she met him for the first time on the Wednesday.

The day dawned clear and bright. Phil watched Jeremy eat his breakfast egg, and felt surprisingly excited by the prospect of a day in London.

'And I go straight to Aunt Joan's, don't I?' he said, for the third time. 'She's having sausages because I told her I liked them. Paul said so.'

'Then you're very lucky,' said his mother. 'Don't forget to thank her when you go back to school.'

'And you'll be back to put me to bed?'

'Of course. Probably by tea time, but it just depends how long I have to spend with the editor, and how the trains run.'

'Can't you come back with Richard?'

'No. He's staying in London.'

'D'you like him?' Jeremy's gaze was fixed upon her intently.

'Of course.' Jeremy drained his cup of milky coffee, and wiped away his wet moustache.

'I don't.'

'Why not? He's very kind. He cleared our drain for us, you know.'

'He did that for *you*,' said Jeremy shrewdly. 'Not for me. He doesn't notice me.'

Children! thought Phil, clearing the table swiftly. Too quick by half!

'Why should you mind that?' she answered reasonably. 'Grown-up people have a lot to think about. They don't always take notice of children.'

Jeremy made no reply, but bent to tie his shoelaces. This was a new accomplishment, and gave him great satisfaction.

'Miss Fogerty gave me two sweets the first time I tied my laces,' he said, surveying his shoes proudly.

'Two? Why two?' asked Phil, glad to have the subject changed.

'Dolly mixture,' replied her son briefly.

She helped him on with his coat, and gave him a hug. His soft face smelt sweetly of Morny pink lilac soap, as he kissed her.

'Have a lovely time,' he said cheerfully.

'You too,' said Phil, opening the front door. 'Have a lovely time,' she echoed, when he reached the gate.

She watched him run across the grass and turned back to make her preparations, turning over in her mind the child's comments on their neighbour.

She enjoyed the drive with Richard. He was quick and competent in traffic, and quite unruffled by the antics of bad drivers around him.

They talked of Thrush Green, of books, and of music.

'There's a concert at Oxford just before Christmas,' said Richard. 'Will you come?'

'Thank you,' said Phil. 'If I can get someone to mind Jeremy, I should love to.'

'Aunt Winnie would sit in, I'm sure,' said Richard. 'I'll ask her.'

'No, please don't. She's been so kind—'

'She's always kind. Looks after me too well,' said Richard, and began to tell her about his dietary difficulties.

For the first time, Phil began to see why Winnie Bailey found her nephew something of a trial. It seemed incredible that an intelligent grown man should be quite so worried about himself.

'But who is this Otto?' asked Phil, when the great man's name cropped up yet again.

'The wisest dietician of our time,' pronounced Richard solemnly, swerving to evade a cyclist bent on suicide. He went on to explain

Otto's theories, his methods and his astounding successes. Phil did her best not to yawn.

'Where can I drop you?' asked Richard as they drove along Piccadilly. 'I have to go up Regent Street, if that's any help.'

'Yes, please. Somewhere near Hamley's if it's possible. I want to buy a gadget for Jeremy's train set.'

'Good luck with the editor,' called Richard, when she left the car. He gave her one of his disarming smiles, and Phil momentarily forgot the boredom of his digestive troubles as she thanked him and said good-bye.

The sausages were splendid – crisp and very dark brown – exactly as Jeremy and Paul liked them. As an added attraction, Joan had tucked them into an oblong of mashed potato with only the ends showing.

'Sausages-in-bed,' she told them. Jeremy was entranced with this gastronomic refinement, and determined to tell his mother how much better sausages tasted when so served.

The Youngs' ginger kitten greeted the boys affectionately.

'We're having one too,' Jeremy told Paul, proudly. 'It's coming at the weekend and I'm making a bed for it out of a cardboard box. I've got a piece of a rug to put at the bottom. A car rug my Daddy bought.'

'What's he giving you for Christmas?' asked Paul, a direct child.

'My daddy? I'm not sure.'

'He'll probably bring you a surprise,' said Paul.

'Yes,' agreed Jeremy. There was a slight doubtfulness in his tone which did not escape Joan, who knew the sad circumstances. 'If he comes,' he added thoughtfully.

'Of course he'll come,' scoffed Paul robustly. 'Bound to at Christmas.'

The school bell began to ring, and Joan held up a finger.

'A quick wash, Jeremy, and then off you go. We'll see you after school, my dear.'

Truly saved by the bell, she thought!

She spent the afternoon engaged in her own Christmas preparations. Her sister Ruth Lovell and her husband and baby were coming for Christmas Day. Her parents were arriving on Christmas Eve and

would spend several days at Thrush Green. Mr Bassett, father of
Joan and Ruth, had now retired, and was always threatening – in
the kindest possible way – to turn out the Youngs from their
Thrush Green house. It had been left to him on the death of his
parents, and one day, he promised himself, he would go there to
live.

She busied herself in preparing their room and sorting out bed-
linen and blankets. The time passed so quickly that she was surprised
to hear the shouts of the school children as they emerged at half past
three.

She hurried downstairs to meet young Jeremy who was rushing
up the garden path, unbelievably grubby after two hours in
school.

'Let me wash your face,' she said, 'and then we'll go down to
Lulling to pick up Paul. And shall we buy some crumpets for tea?'

Sitting beside his hostess in the car Jeremy spoke decidedly.

'Next to my house,' he told her, 'I like yours best. If I hadn't got a
home, could I live with you?'

'Anytime,' said Joan sincerely. 'Anytime, Jeremy.'

Travelling back alone, in the train, Phil closed her eyes and
pondered on the day's happenings, well content.

She had liked Frank the moment she saw him. He was tall, heavily-
built, with a beautiful deep voice and very bright eyes of that true
brown which is so rare.

She found him remarkably easy to talk to, and found herself
telling him far more about her circumstances than she intended, over
a splendid lunch.

The work he had in mind, he told her, was similar to that which
she already did for young girls. Would she be interested in writing a
half page for a monthly for slightly younger children of both sexes?
He told her the payment he had in mind, which was extremely
generous.

'And more stories, please,' he said, 'for the women. I like
your touch. Tell me more about the one you want me to suppress.'

She told him the details.

'Harold is far nicer than I am,' she admitted. 'I would have gone
ahead, but it would have upset him, I'm sure.'

'He's a very fine chap,' said Frank. 'And most meticulous. But I can see no real reason why you should stand to lose your proper reward.'

He went on to tell her that his company owned two Scottish evening papers which printed a short story daily.

'No possible chance of Thrush Green eyes seeing them,' he told her. 'And we'll use a pseudonym. Think one up, and let me have it. I liked that tale. You handled the two old ladies beautifully.'

After lunch, they returned to the office where he gave her a number of back copies of the young people's magazine to study at home. They discussed things very thoroughly, and Phil was surprised to find how quickly the time flew past.

'It's so good to be doing something again,' she said. 'You shall have the copy very quickly.'

'Tell Harold I will come and see him when Christmas is over. You will be spending it at home, I suppose?'

'Yes.'

'I'm going to my son's. He's farming in Wales and there are four children, under ten, so I shall be lively enough. It's rather flat being on one's own at Christmas. My boy Robert understands that.'

They wished each other good-bye and Phil set off for Paddington feeling happier than she had done for many a long day.

14. Sudden Death

When Albert Piggott came round in hospital, he was bewildered and resentful. Where was his comfortable feather pillow, familiarly sour-smelling and crumpled? Where was the sides-to-middled sheet, soft with age? And worse still, where was the cane-bottomed chair beside the bed, with the glass for his teeth and his tin of extra strong peppermints?

Everything was wrong. The light was too bright. The ceiling was too clean and too far away. And now that he could focus his aching eyes, why were there other beds around him?

He tried to sit up, but a pain in his head felled him like a log. After a little while, he managed to turn his head on the hard starched pillow and surveyed the occupant of the next bed through half-shut eyes. Outlined against the bright window, the man appeared simply as a dark hulk to Albert, but he was aware that he was being watched closely.

'Comin' round then, Bert?' he said kindly, and Albert's heart sank still further. If it wasn't Ted Allen, who kept 'The Drovers' Arms' at Lulling Woods! And could he talk? Just his luck to be beside an old gas-bag like Ted Allen! Albert shut his eyes tightly.

'Nurse!' shouted Ted, in a bellow that set Albert's head throbbing. 'Mr Piggott's come round. Looks a bit poorly.'

He felt a cool hand on his hot forehead, and another hand holding his wrist. He opened one eye – the one furthest from Ted Allen – with extreme caution.

A fresh-faced young girl smiled down at him beneath her starched cap.

'Feeling better now?' she asked.

'No,' said Albert.

'Like a drink?'

'What of?' asked Albert, with a flicker of interest.

'Water? Cold milk?'

'No thanks,' said Albert disgustedly.

'He could do with a pint of bitter, nurse,' said Ted with hearty jocularity.

Albert winced.

'Now, Mr Allen,' said the nurse severely, 'don't be a tease. Mr Piggott needs his rest. I'm going to put a screen round his bed for an hour or two.'

'Thank God for that,' said Albert, and meant it.

Later, after some hours of fitful dozing, the nurse came back, removed the screen, and lifted him against the pillows.

'Like some supper?' she said brightly.

'What is it?' asked Albert suspiciously.

'You'll see,' said the nurse, with an archness that annoyed Albert.

She whisked away. Bet it wouldn't be anything as good as Nelly cooked him, he thought morosely.

Nelly! What was it about Nelly, that he ought to remember? Something to do with Christmas pudding and shouting and a row. He groaned with the effort of thinking.

'You all right, old chap? Anything I can do?' asked Ted solicitously.

'Shut yer gob,' said Albert rudely.

'Thanks, I'm sure,' said Ted, offended. Blessed silence fell, and Albert tried out his powers of memory again.

Nelly shouting at him. Banging down a suitcase on the table. The oilman! Now he'd got it!

She'd gone! With horror, Albert found his eyes were wet. Within a minute two tears were rolling down his cheeks. What had come over him? He was damned if he was crying about Nelly, he told himself fiercely. Good riddance to bad rubbish, that was! Nothing but everlasting rows and nagging ever since she'd caught him!

Too proud to wipe the tears away with Ted's sharp eyes upon him, Albert watched the tears splash down upon the snowy sheet top, making neat round stains.

The nurse came back bearing a small bowl full of some milky substance.

'Now, now, now!' she scolded him. 'What are we getting upset about?'

She whisked a paper tissue from a box nearby and mopped Albert's face painfully.

'Upsadaisy now!' she said, heaving him a little higher in the bed. 'Cheer up, cheer up! Worse troubles at sea! Have some supper. That'll put new heart into us.'

Albert surveyed the contents of the bowl sourly.

'Don't eat slops,' he said flatly.

'It's all you're going to get for a bit,' said the nurse firmly, 'so you may as well get used to it.'

'Why?' asked Albert, with some spirit. 'What's up with me? What you been doin' to me while I was unconscious?'

'You've had an operation for a very nasty ulcer,' said the nurse primly.

'Bin *cut*, 'ave I?' yelped Albert, outraged.

'Our Mr Pedder-Bennett performed the operation,' said the girl reverently. 'A beautiful bit of work, the theatre sister said.'

'That ol' butcher?' cried Albert indignantly. I'll have the law on the lot of you! Letting that ol' saw-bones loose on a chap as is unconscious. I'll –'

'You'll eat your supper,' said the nurse, deftly thrusting a spoonful into Albert's protesting mouth. 'And stop talking nonsense.'

She lodged the bowl in front of him and bustled out of the ward.

Albert removed the spoon from his mouth and pushed it about in the bowl gloomily. He became conscious of other people eating in the ward, and looked at his companions with some interest.

Ted Allen kept his eyes sedulously upon his tray. His expression was lofty. He wasn't going to waste his time being pleasant to an old misery like Albert Piggott. Let him stew in his own juice!

'What've they given you?' asked Albert, trying to make amends. Ted Allen, good-hearted, quickly forgave his neighbour.

'Some sort of mince,' said Ted. 'Could be anything from rat to rabbit. You name it – this is it!'

'Looks a sight better than this muck,' said Albert, with considerable self-pity.

'You wants to take things careful,' advised Ted. 'You was pretty bad when you come in. And a proper ghastly colour when they brought you back from the operation. Lay there groaning, you did, and snoring horrible.'

'Did I now?' said Albert, brightening. 'Bet you thought I wouldn't come round.'

'That never worried us,' said Ted ambiguously. 'But you kep' us all awake.'

Albert tried another spoonful tentatively and pondered Ted's last remark.

'What you in for?' he asked at length.

'Appendix. Caught me while I was lifting the crates. Good thing Bessie was nearby. She got Doctor Lovell double quick and here we are. I goes out sometime this week.'

'You're lucky,' growled Albert.

Ted Allen looked about him reflectively. 'I don't know. I've quite enjoyed meself, being waited on. Makes a nice change. And people comin' to see you with fruit and papers. I'll be quite sorry to go, what with one thing and another.'

'Don't suppose anyone'll come and see me,' said Albert.

'What about Nelly? She'll be down with a steak-and-kidney pud hidden in her pocket, I'll bet.'

'That she won't,' replied Albert, putting the spoon and bowl on

the locker top. 'She's cleared off!' No point in trying to keep secret
in Lulling, he told himself.

'You don't say!' gasped Ted, registering acute surprise. Bessie had
told him the news twenty-four hours earlier. She had also told him
about the oilman. 'What did she do that for?'

'Gone off her chump over some fellow that's no better than he
should be,' replied Albert austerely. 'That's why.'

'She's a fool then,' said Ted. 'Throwing over a steady chap like you.'

Albert looked mollified. There was one thing about Ted Allen,
blab-mouth though he was. He was a good judge of character,
thought Albert.

The nurse came scurrying down to his bed, and peered into his
bowl.

'That's better. Next time you must finish it all up, but we'll let
you off tonight. Feeling happier now, are we?'

'No,' said Albert.

'Well, you will when I tell you the news,' said the girl, undeterred.
'Your daughter's here to see you.'

'What? Molly?'

'Yes, and her husband. Now, you be nice to them. They've come
a long way.'

She beckoned to two figures at the end of the ward. They advanced
shyly. For one terrible minute, Albert thought that the tears would
come again. Weakness it was, just weakness, he told himself, fighting
for control.

'Dad,' said Molly. 'How are you feeling now?'

'Middlin',' said Albert huskily. She put a small posy of anemones
on the bed.

'They must have cost a pretty penny,' commented Albert un-
gratefully.

'Never mind that,' said Ben. 'You look better than I thought you
would.'

'Been at death's door, I have,' Albert said with pride. 'Ain't I,
Ted?'

'Mr Allen!' cried Molly, turning round. 'And how's your wife,
and "The Drovers' Arms"? Those were happy times!'

They talked for a minute or two, for they were old friends. Molly
had worked there as barmaid before her marriage, and the Allens had
always been good to her.

'You heard about Nelly?' asked Albert.

'Yes, dad. Miss Dimity told me when we got here. I'm sorry. What'll you do?'

'Same as I did before, of course. Look after meself. I ain't helpless, you know.'

'We know that,' said Ben diplomatically. 'But best see how you get over this operation. Maybe, Molly can look after you for a bit until you're on your legs again. I can spare her for a week or two.'

The two young people smiled at each other. It was plain to Albert that they had been making plans before they paid this visit.

Suddenly, he felt ineffably tired. It had been a long day. Seeing the look of exhaustion, Molly rose and nudged Ben.

'We'll be off now, Dad, and come and see you tomorrow before we go back home.'

She kissed his unresponsive face. Ben shook his hand gently, and they departed.

'She's a grand girl,' said Ted Allen, watching them go. 'Always bright and cheerful, as Bessie says.'

'Takes after her old dad,' said Albert drowsily, and fell into a deep sleep.

In the week that followed Phil's trip to town, she worked hard at the writing. It was always difficult to begin a new type of work, and she had never written for children of ten to fourteen for whom the new column was intended.

Nevertheless, she had experience with slightly older readers, and she was comforted by the thought that Frank was the sort of person who would say exactly what was right, or wrong, with a piece of work, and also give her sound advice.

She had passed on his message to Harold who looked pleased at the thought of entertaining his old friend.

'And I think I ought to tell you,' she added, after some hesitation, 'that the story about the two village ladies is to be published after all.'

She explained about the Scottish papers and the pen-name. Harold was elated.

'I'm so glad. I've felt rather wretched over the whole affair. I'm afraid you must have thought me unspeakably stuffy.'

'Well, I was horribly rude. I was so cross,' laughed Phil. 'Still, all's well that ends well, and I really am most terribly grateful to you for introducing me to Frank and all this lovely work. I shall be quite rich in the New Year.'

The next morning, while Phil was tapping busily at her typewriter, Harold appeared at the window, waving a pair of secateurs.

'Would you like me to prune those roses at the end of the garden? We missed them earlier, you remember. I've just finished mine, and thought I'd ask while it was in my mind.'

'I'd be very thankful,' said Phil, 'I'm particularly dim about pruning. I'll give you a call when I'm making coffee. I just want to finish some alterations.'

'Don't disturb yourself on my account,' said Harold cheerfully, departing down the garden.

It was a clear mild December day. Against the house, a flourishing winter jasmine was breaking into yellow stars. A robin eyed Harold speculatively from the top of the wall, hoping for upturned worms. Nearby, a fat thrush jabbed rhythmically at a rotting apple in the grass.

Harold got on with the job, humming happily to himself. It was a relief to know that all was well between himself and Phil, and an even greater relief to know that she was getting steady work which was decently rewarded.

He was making a neat job of the neglected bushes, and stacking the prickly shoots in a pile ready for burning, when he heard the gate click, and looked up.

Stepping up the path was the local policeman, Constable Potter. He hailed him gaily. The officer walked across the grass towards him.

'And what brings you here?' asked Harold lightly. 'Traffic offences?'

The constable remained unsmiling, and Harold felt a sudden constriction in his chest.

'Not bad news, I hope?'

'Afraid so, sir. But I must tell Mrs Prior first. Is she alone, d'you know?'

'Yes. The boy's at school. But can I help?'

'Not yet, sir. But will you be around?'

'Yes, of course. I'll be here, in the garden.'

He watched the burly blue back advance towards Tullivers' front door with heavy foreboding.

For Harold, there followed the longest ten minutes he could remember. Mechanically he snipped at the rose bushes, while the robin whistled to him. He collected handfuls of dried grass which were caught about the lower shoots like grey lace, and added them, unseeing, to his pile of rubbish. What could have happened? Was it something to do with the divorce? Wouldn't her solicitor cope with all that? Why on earth would young Potter want to call?

At length, the front door opened and the two emerged. Constable Potter replaced his cap, and made his farewells in a low voice. He gave one swift anxious look in Harold's direction, raised a hand, and stumped heavily down the path.

Phil, looking pale and stunned, walked across the grass to Harold who hurried towards her. She looked ready to faint, but when she reached him she held up her arms like a bewildered child and clung to him.

'There, there,' Harold heard himself say, as he patted her back. 'Come into the house, my love, and tell me.'

They entered the house, hand in hand, and in silence. When he had settled her in an armchair, he stood waiting, his back to the fire.

'Brandy?' he asked gently.

She shook her head. At last she spoke.

'I can't believe it. He's dead.'

She raised her eyes slowly, and looked mutely at Harold.

'That policeman. He brought a message from Paris. John's been killed in his car.'

'Oh no!' whispered Harold. 'This is terrible news. Terrible!'

'I must go. I must get over there.' She rose unsteadily and leant against the mantelpiece.

'I told the policeman I must go. He left a piece of paper with the times of the flights.'

She began to wander distractedly about the room, searching in an aimless way. Harold saw a piece of paper protruding from her cardigan pocket. He took it out and studied it.

'The next one is at two o'clock,' he told her. 'Let me take you over this afternoon.'

'No, no!' The girl faced him more steadily.

'I'd sooner go alone. I must go alone on this journey.'

'Then let me take you up to Heathrow.'

'I'd be grateful for that. I'll go and get some things together.'

She stopped suddenly.

'But Jeremy? I must arrange something for Jeremy.'

'I'll take charge of that,' said Harold. 'I'll call and see Joan Young, and go and get the car, while you pack.'

He looked at her white face anxiously.

'Have that drop of brandy before you begin,' he said. She nodded, and he fetched her a tot in a glass, standing over her while she gulped it down, shuddering.

'I'll be back in a quarter of an hour,' he told her. 'Wrap up well, and don't forget your passport.'

She nodded again, dumbly, and he hurried across the green on his errands. Still dry-eyed, Phil went upstairs very slowly, like an old, old woman, to prepare for the saddest journey of her life.

She scarcely spoke on the way to the airport but sat with her hands clenched tightly upon the handbag in her lap. They had some time to wait and Harold fetched coffee and sandwiches as they sat in the crowded waiting room. Beside Phil sat two women with the most clownish make-up that Harold had ever encountered. He found his eyes straying to the green eyelids, the black-rimmed eyes, and the curiously luminous lips. His father would have made no bones about labelling them 'strumpets', thought Harold, but apart from their outlandish faces, they seemed normal enough. Their dress was plain, their speech quiet, their apologies sincere when they accidentally jogged Phil's coffee-cup. Harold was baffled.

The food seemed to revive Phil. She smiled tremulously at him, as though she were seeing him for the first time. 'I can never thank you enough for today,' she told him softly. 'You understand how I feel about going to John alone, though?'

'Of course,' he told her.

'I don't really believe it's happened,' she said wonderingly. 'I don't want to cry, because I just don't believe it.'

She turned to him suddenly.

'Look after Jeremy, won't you? Tell Joan what's happened. I'll tell Jeremy later.'

He patted her arm comfortingly.

'Are you all right for money?' he asked.

'I've a cheque book, and about five pounds.'

He took out his wallet and gave her some notes.

'It's simpler to have ready money. You don't know what expenses you'll find. If you want me to come over, just ring. I'm absolutely free to come at any hour, as you know.'

'I'll remember.'

'And I'll meet you here, in any case.'

'Dear Harold,' said Phil softly.

A booming voice above, nasal and distorted, announced that passengers for the flight must now depart. Phil rose hurriedly, and went with Harold to the door.

'Don't wait, please,' she told him. 'You've done so much. Get back to dear Thrush Green.'

She was swallowed up in the crowd of travellers and vanished from his sight.

But Harold did not return to Thrush Green until he had gone to the roof of the building and watched the plane take off. He watched until its greyness merged into the greyness of the December sky, before turning to go home.

15. Harold Takes Charge

The departure of Nelly Piggott from Thrush Green may not have upset her husband unduly, but it certainly distressed Miss Watson and Miss Fogerty.

Every morning and evening Nelly had cleaned Thrush Green school with all the vigour of her thirteen stone. The classrooms, lobbies, windows – even the dingy old map-cupboard – were kept spotless. Nor had Nelly chided the children for stepping in snow or mud.

'So good-hearted,' mourned Miss Watson. 'And so *thorough*.'

She lowered her voice.

'Did you know, Agnes, that she scoured the outside drains every morning? Scrupulously clean – scrupulously!'

'I can't think how poor Albert Piggott will manage without her,' said Miss Fogerty compassionately. 'He'll need someone there when he comes out of hospital.'

'Well now,' began Miss Watson, looking important, 'I heard a rumour that Molly might be back for a bit.'

'Splendid!' cried Miss Fogerty, clapping her small hands together. 'Dear Molly!'

'It's not *definite*, Agnes dear,' said Miss Watson severely. 'Don't repeat it, until we've had it confirmed. As you know, I cannot abide idle gossip. But certainly, that's what I heard.'

'I shan't breathe a word,' promised Miss Fogerty solemnly. 'But I do so hope you heard aright.'

She turned her attention to the hymn book in her hand.

'What shall we have this morning?' she asked her headmistress. '"Jesus bids us shine"?'

'I am afraid it had better be a carol, dear. They still need plenty of practice before the concert. "Away in a manger", perhaps?'

Miss Fogerty winced.

'Not again, please. I have to go through it so often.'

'Very well,' said Miss Watson indulgently. 'You choose, Agnes dear.'

'What about "Once in royal"?'

'Splendid,' said Miss Watson, looking about for a bell-ringer. Her eye lit upon Ben Lane who was engrossed in cleaning the doorknob with a spat-upon handkerchief.

'You may ring the bell, dear,' she said graciously. A tag from her well-worn college notes came into her mind.

'Always direct the child's energies into useful channels.'

Of course, she thought, a minute later, as the school bell rang out its warning to late-comers, we may need the children's labour to keep the school clean now that Nelly's gone. But Ben Lane's methods, of course, *would not* be countenanced.

Nothing had been heard from the departed lady. The oilman had left Lulling without giving anyone an address, so that neighbours put two and two together, as always, and this time came to the right conclusion. The love-birds had flown together.

The local paper had Albert Piggott's story in it. Not, of course, the story of his broken marriage, but a sensational one about his dramatic collapse.

'St Andrew's Sexton Found Unconscious' it said boldly. And in smaller print below: 'Timely Aid by Vicar.'

'I do wish,' said Charles Henstock, quite waspishly for such a

kindly man, 'that papers would get their facts right. Everyone here
knows I'm a *rector*.' He read the rest of the story with an expression
of marked distaste on his chubby countenance, but his comment was
typically Christian.

'Perhaps Nelly will see this, wherever she is, and come back to
him.'

'More fool her if she does,' said Ella who was present.

She voiced the general sentiments of Thrush Green.

But the drama of the Piggotts was soon overshadowed by Phil
Prior's sad news. Despite the fact that her husband seemed to be 'a
proper fast one', as they had observed to each other, Thrush Green
folk were sincerely shocked by the tragedy which had befallen the
newcomer, who had so quickly become one of the community.

Harold Shoosmith, on his return, had gone at once to see Joan
Young. The little boys were playing in the garden with Flo, the old
spaniel, and he could speak openly.

'She's in a pretty bad state of shock, naturally,' he said, 'but wanted
to go through this business alone. She'll ring tomorrow to let us
know what's happening. I've told her to telephone me. I hope you
don't mind? I'm there alone, and it might be awkward for you if the
boys were within earshot.'

'By far the best thing,' agreed Joan. 'I hope she won't feel that she
must hurry to get back to Jeremy – though I know she'll want to, of
course. But he's a dear child, and fits in so happily.'

'There'll be a few formalities to go through, no doubt, but I
should think she'll be back in about two or three days. It depends on
the funeral arrangements.'

He walked to the window and stood staring across the chestnut
avenue to the green. Joan could see how worried he was and, woman-
like, knew why without being told.

'Would you like to come and have dinner here tonight with
us?' she asked impulsively. 'Edward and I would love it, if you are
free.'

As though he knew what was in her mind, he turned quickly and
smiled.

'You're very kind, but I ought to write a letter or two, and I want
to let the Baileys know about this. Winnie will wonder what's
happened when she sees the house in darkness.'

'I understand,' said Joan.

A little later she saw him crossing to the doctor's house, and thought what an attractive man he was.

'Phil could do a lot worse,' she thought, then chided herself for thinking of such things, when poor John Prior was not yet in his grave.

Jeremy had asked only a few questions about his mother's absence, for which Joan was truly thankful.

'Why has she gone to France? To see Daddy?'

'Yes,' said Joan.

'Why so quickly? Why didn't she take me?'

'Daddy had an accident in the car, so she went straight away.'

'He always drives fast,' said Jeremy, proudly. 'Once we did *ninety*. *Ninety!*' he repeated.

'My uncle,' said Paul, 'once did a hundred and thirty. And my friend Chris says his father did *two hundred* on a straight road in Norfolk!'

'Don't boast,' said Joan. But she was glad to have had the subject changed, nevertheless.

Harold found the Baileys, and Richard, taking their ease and watching, in a lack-lustre way, a programme on television. Winnie rose to switch it off as he entered.

'Oh please, don't let me interrupt anything you want to see,' cried Harold.

'It's a relief to switch it off,' said the doctor. 'We've been too idle to do so. It's one of those tiresome interviews where the interviewer is obsessed with the importance of prepositions. You know the sort of thing – "The Minister is here, AT this moment to answer questions ON our policy IN regard TO our commitments." Dreadful stuff!'

'I'm so glad you've come in,' said Winnie. 'I was going to ask you about the garden next door. Do you think there is room for a rose bush or two? We thought we might give Phil a couple for Christmas.'

Harold looked at her quickly, and then at the doctor.

'Yes, I'm sure there's room for the roses. A lovely idea. As a matter of fact, it's Phil I've come about.'

He stopped, and the doctor thought how unusually exhausted he seemed.

'Richard, get us all a drink, there's a good fellow. Sherry, or whisky?'

'Sherry, please,' said Harold. He sat in silence while Richard handed glasses, and then began again.

'I'm afraid she's had bad news of her husband.'

'The divorce is through?' Winnie looked puzzled.

'No. He's had a car crash. In France.'

'Dead, I suppose,' said the doctor quietly.

Harold nodded.

'Poor, poor girl!' said Winnie, her face puckered with distress. 'I must go round at once.'

'No,' said Harold, 'that's what I came to tell you. She's over there already.'

'On her own?' said Richard sharply. 'Surely not on her own.'

'She preferred it that way,' Harold replied.

'Did she fly?'

'Yes. I took her to Heathrow this morning.'

'I'll meet her when she returns,' said Richard. 'I don't like the idea of her being alone through an ordeal like this. I wish I'd known earlier.'

Harold felt some irritation at Richard's assumption that his presence was necessary to Phil's well-being, but he tried to speak calmly.

'The arrangements are settled about her return,' he said. 'Of course, no one knows yet which day it will be.'

'I can be free at any time,' said Richard. Harold decided to ignore the remark, and turned to Winnie.

'Joan is taking care of Jeremy. He seems very cheerful there, and doesn't know the truth yet, of course.'

Doctor Bailey turned his glass thoughtfully round and round in his thin old hands.

'It is a dreadful affair. A young fellow like that. In his thirties, I suppose. She will be badly shaken, despite these last few months of separation.'

He looked up at Harold.

'What about the practical side? This must mean the end of her allowance from him. Is there anything to leave, do you know?'

'I've no idea. They probably hadn't much between them. After all, they haven't been married very long – not long enough to amass much in the way of savings.'

'What about her writing?'

'Chicken feed, I should think,' interjected Richard, who was now walking about, hands in pockets, looking extremely agitated.

'How I wish she had parents to turn to!' cried Winnie. 'She's so alone in the world.'

It was the feeling which was uppermost too in Harold's mind, but he felt unable to speak about it at the moment.

'I thought you should know the news,' he said, rising to go. 'Do you have a key to Tullivers, by any chance? I thought I might go round the house and make sure the switches are off, and the windows closed, and so on. We left pretty hurriedly.'

'I know where one is hidden,' said Winnie. Country folk invariably know where 'the secret key' is kept by their neighbours. On occasions such as this, it is a useful piece of knowledge.

'It's in the garden shed,' continued Winnie, 'on the ledge on the right hand side of the door, by the plant labels.'

'Good,' said Harold, 'I'll go and see to it now before it gets dark.'

'I'll come with you,' said Richard.

There was no earthly reason why he should be prevented, so that the two men walked together through the chilly dusk to Tullivers.

'My God,' said Richard. 'This is a fine thing! How will she manage? D'you think she'll move?'

'I've no idea. I don't think she'll want to.'

They plodded across the grass to the little shed which housed Phil's splendid new mower and the few poor broken tools which had distressed Harold by their uselessness. The key was carefully lodged behind the packet of plant labels, and they made their way to the front door.

Apart from a bathroom heater which had been left on, and a tap dripping at the kitchen sink, everything was in order. The scent of freesias hung about Phil's bedroom, bringing memories of her sharply to Harold.

'I know they didn't get on,' Richard said, as they descended the stairs, 'but this is a real blow for her. So dam' final, death, isn't it?'

Harold made a noise of agreement. Richard's obvious agitation was surprising. He had not met the fellow very often, and had no idea that he knew Phil as well as this concern for her seemed to show. Harold found his anxiety a trifle alarming.

'We can't do anything yet,' he observed reasonably. 'We know nothing. One thing, she's a girl with plenty of courage and good sense. I'm sure she'll do nothing silly, or in a hurry.'

'She'll need advice,' said Richard.

'I understand she has a good solicitor,' replied Harold shortly.

He locked the front door, and put the key in his pocket. He intended to be the one to take charge of Tullivers while its owner was absent.

'If you'll excuse me,' he said politely, to Richard at the gate, 'I must get back.'

He set off homeward at a brisk pace, turning over this new development in Phil's affairs in his mind.

'And to think,' he said to himself as he opened his front door, 'that I chose to come to Thrush Green for a simple life!'

Winnie Bailey was taking coffee with Ella Bembridge the next morning when Dotty arrived bearing a large bundle of magazines, and the daily pint of goat's milk for Ella.

Thrush Green had a very sensible institution, started in war-time, called the magazine club. A number of residents each took a weekly or monthly magazine. They were collected together by one of the members and passed round in turn. In this way everyone saw a dozen or so journals regularly for the price of one. The rota had remained the same for years, only removals, or deaths, altering the system.

Ella took *Punch* although, as she said: 'It ceased to be funny after 1920.' The Baileys took *Country Life*, Harold *The Field*, Charles Henstock *The Church Times*, the Youngs weighed in with the *Spectator* and *The Listener* and Dotty contributed *The Lady* and *History Today*. Less intellectual matter was supplied by Ruth Lovell and various ladies at Lulling, and included 'really readable stuff', according to Dimity, who was no high-brow, such as *Woman, Woman's Own* and *Homes and Gardens*. It was interesting to note that these last three magazines were always the most well-thumbed when they came to be passed on. *The Field, The Church Times* and the *Spectator* remained immaculate for quite a time.

'Heard the news?' enquired Dotty, unwinding a long scarf from her stringy neck, and dropping the bundle of magazines in the process.

The ladies bent down to put the bundle together again, Dotty uttering little cries of self-reproach the while.

'No harm done,' said Ella, straightening up. 'Have some coffee, Dot?'

'Thank you. I must say I was very surprised to hear about it.'

'About what?' asked Winnie carefully. She had just told Ella the sad news about John Prior, but had not realized that it might have reached as far as Lulling Woods already.

'A very good thing really,' continued Dotty. 'It had to come some time.'

'How d'you mean?' asked Winnie cautiously.

'Well, I mean, we're all getting older every day. Can't expect to carry on for ever. Taking the long view we'll all be the better for it.'

'What on earth,' said Ella downrightly, 'are you maundering on about, Dotty?'

Dotty looked hurt.

'Albert Piggott, of course. His wife's gone off with the oilman, though how she could I just don't know. Such a vulgar fellow. Always talking about "the ladies", and "the fair sex", and "being a mere male". If it weren't for the fact that he comes right to the house with the paraffin, and carries very good old-fashioned wax tapers, I shouldn't allow him to call. Father would have shown him the door.'

'Yes, we had heard,' said Winnie. There was an ominous hissing sound from the kitchen.

'Blast! The milk!' cried Ella, stumping off.

'I'm having mine black just now,' Dotty informed her when she returned.

Ella, speechless for once, exchanged a meaning glance with Winnie.

'And had you heard that Molly may be coming back?' asked Dotty. 'I do so hope that she and that nice Curdle boy settle here. Did you know that she taught him to read and write after they were married? He didn't have much schooling, shifting about with the fair. I thought it was so clever of her to do that.'

'And brave of him to try,' agreed Winnie. 'Some men would have been too self-conscious to admit their ignorance.'

The ladies sipped their coffee and Winnie was about to let Dotty know Phil Prior's news when Dotty herself mentioned the girl.

'I'm taking the last of the kittens to Tullivers this weekend. I must say I shall miss them sorely. They've all turned out remarkably well-behaved and intelligent. How's Tabitha doing?'

Dimity and Charles had chosen the tabby with exceptionally fine eyes. Dotty kept a vigilant eye and ear open for news of the various kittens.

'Scoffing down ox liver at four-and-six a pound,' said Ella, 'last time I saw her.'

'Oh. I do so hope dear Dimity isn't over-doing the protein,' cried Dotty. 'A little raw liver is *excellent*, of course, but too much can be rather heating. I must have a word with her.'

She rose to make her departure. Winnie got up too. This seemed the time to break the news.

'I should leave the kitten for a little longer,' said Winnie. 'Phil Prior is away for a few days. In France, in fact.'

'At this time of year?' protested Dotty. 'If anything, the weather's worse than in England.'

'It's no pleasure trip,' Winnie said gravely. 'Her husband had an accident there. I'm sorry to say he has died. She's gone over to see about things.'

Dotty stood transfixed for a moment at the enormity of the news.

When she spoke, it was with her usual breathtaking directness.

'Sad, of course,' said Dotty, picking up the disreputable scarf, 'but it simplifies things a lot. Harold Shoosmith will be able to go ahead now, won't he?'

She preceded a stunned Winnie Bailey to the door, thanked Ella for the coffee, and bustled away down the path, her skinny legs, in their thick speckled stockings, twinkling energetically.

'Sometimes,' said Winnie faintly, 'I wonder if Dotty is clairvoyant.'

'She's an old witch,' responded Ella roundly.

16. Harold Thinks Things Out

Phil Prior was away for four days. She rang Harold and Joan on alternate evenings and was mightily relieved to hear how little Jeremy appeared to miss her.

Everyone was being incredibly kind and helpful, she told them. Formalities had been hurried through, and she would return immediately after the funeral. John's parents had met her out there, and they were doing their best to comfort each other. Her plane was due to arrive at five-thirty, and she was longing to get back to the haven of Thrush Green and all her friends.

During her absence, Harold had plenty of time for thought. This tragedy had quickened his affection and admiration for the girl, and his determination to do all in his power to help her. Whether, in the distant future when she had recovered from the blow, she could ever contemplate marriage again, he had no idea. Whether he himself really wanted to give up his serene bachelorhood, he was not sure. But one thing he did know — if he ever should marry, then the only person he wanted was Phil.

He took several long solitary walks in the few days of Phil's absence, trying to come to terms with this new surprising feeling which so strangely moved him. The weather was mild and quiet, overcast and vaguely depressing, as though the world were in waiting for some momentous happening. Away from the domestic bustle of Christmas, the countryside was infinitely soothing, Harold found.

He found himself noting things with newly-awakened observation and sensibility. Tiny spears of snowdrop leaves were pushing through. Already the honeysuckle showed minute leaf rosettes, and in the still morning air, a thousand droplets quivered on the spikes of the hawthorn hedge.

Percy Hodge's black and white cows gazed at him over the gate, their long eyelashes rimed with mist, their sweet breath forming clouds in the quiet air. A thrush, head cocked sideways, listened intently to the moving of a mole just beneath the surface of the grass verge. In Lulling Woods the trees dripped gently, their trunks striped with moisture, while underfoot the damp leaves deadened every footfall.

He returned from these lonely walks much refreshed in spirit, even if any sort of decision still evaded him. It was good to escape from people, now and again, and a positive relief to be away from Betty Bell's boisterous activities. The coming of Christmas seemed to rouse her to even greater energy, and carpets were beaten within an inch of their lives, pillows shaken until the feathers began to escape, paint was washed, windows polished and all to the accompaniment of joyful singing which Harold had not the heart to suppress.

'Got all your presents tied up?' asked Betty, busily winding up the Hoover cord into an intricate figure-of-eight arrangement, which Harold detested. It was useless to tell her that this was a strain on the covering of the cord cable. Figures-of-eight Betty Bell had always done, and would continue to do until her hand grew too frail to push the Hoover. Harold averted his eyes from the operation.

'Yes, Betty. I think everything's ready.'

'Want a Christmas tree?'

'No thanks.'

'Holly? Ivy? Anythink o' that?'

'Well, perhaps a little holly –'

'Fine. I'll send the kids out. Don't want to waste good money in the market, do you?'

'No,' agreed Harold. 'But only a sprig or two, Betty, please. I can't cope with a lot of stuff.'

'I'll see you right,' Betty assured him, flicking his desk energetically, and knocking his fountain pen to the floor. Harold retrieved it patiently.

'I suppose there's nothing 'eard from that Nelly Tilling? Piggott, I should say.'

'Not as far as I know.'

'Miss Watson's in a fine old taking,' said Betty conversationally. 'Talking of getting that Mrs Cooke back as lives up Nidden way. Must be hard up to want her to take over the school cleaning. Proper slummocky ha'porth, she is. Ever seen her?'

'I don't think so.'

'Once seen never forgotten.' Betty burst into a peal of laughter, as she picked up the Hoover, ready to depart to the kitchen. 'Ugly as sin, and could do with a good wash. You wouldn't fancy anything as she'd cooked, I can tell you. Ham omelette do you?'

'Beautifully,' said Harold. She bore away the Hoover, and slammed the study door with such vigour that it set a silver vase ringing on the mantelpiece.

Harold wandered to the window and looked out upon empty Thrush Green and the quiet countryside beyond. The lines of a hymn floated into his mind.

> Where every prospect please
> And only man is vile

Perhaps not 'vile', Harold thought forgivingly, but distracting certainly.

Two days before Albert Piggott's release from hospital, Molly Curdle arrived at her old home with her little son, George, an energetic toddler.

Ben, who had brought her, was obliged to return to his work, but promised to spend Sunday with his family. It was the first time the couple had been parted since their marriage, and Molly felt forlorn as she watched him drive away.

However, there was plenty to do at the neglected cottage, and she set to with her customary vigour. In the afternoon she was delighted to receive a visit from Joan Young, who was bearing a pretty little Christmas decoration of holly, Christmas roses and variegated ivy, set in a mossy base. The two young women greeted each other affectionately, and George was admired by Joan, as much as the posy was admired by Molly.

'I can't tell you how lovely it is to have you back,' said Joan sincerely. 'How long can you stop?'

'Well, Ben and I hope it won't be for longer than a fortnight, but it depends on Dad. You know what he's like. He'd sooner manage on his own, I know, but he can't do that just yet.'

'No news of Nelly?'

'None. But she won't show up again, I'm positive. And frankly, I don't blame her. We never thought it would last.'

'Bring George to tea tomorrow,' said Joan. 'Paul's longing to see you and to show you off to his new friend Jeremy.'

Molly agreed with pleasure. She had always loved the Youngs' house, and had been very happy working there. She had learnt a great deal about managing children from looking after Paul as a young child, and this experience was standing her in good stead in bringing up George.

The tea party was much enjoyed. There was a rapturous reunion between Paul and Molly, and George enjoyed being the centre of attention. It was the last day of Molly's freedom, for the next morning her father arrived from the hospital and was put comfortably to bed.

She had expected him to be a demanding patient, but was surprised by his docility. Hospital discipline seemed to have improved Albert's manners. At times he was almost grateful for Molly's attentions. It couldn't last for ever, Molly told herself philosophically, but while it did, she enjoyed this rare spell of good behaviour.

His first short walk was across to St Andrew's church. It was not being cared for in the way he thought proper, as he pointed out to the rector when he called, but nevertheless he admitted grudgingly that it could be a lot worse. This was high praise indeed, from Albert, and the rector was suitably impressed.

'I really feel that affliction has mellowed Albert,' he told Dimity on his return to the rectory.

'Don't speak too soon,' his wife replied sagely.

Phil's plane was due to arrive at half-past five and Harold set off from Thrush Green soon after three o'clock.

The same quiet grey weather continued, with a raw coldness in the air which the weather-wise said was a sure sign of snow to come.

But despite the bleak outlook, Harold was in good heart. To be driving to meet Phil again was enough to raise anyone's spirits. How would she be, he wondered? He thought of the numbed silence of the drive to the airport, with the pale girl suffering beside him.

He remembered the two ladies 'painted to the eyes' who had sat beside Phil as they drank their coffee. Out of the blue came the verse which Phil's parents must have had in mind when they chose their daughter's name.

> The ladies of St James's
> They're painted to the eyes,
> Their white it stays for ever,
> Their red it never dies:

> But Phyllida, my Phyllida!
> Her colour comes and goes;
> It trembles to a lily, –
> It wavers to a rose.

Sentimental, maybe, thought Harold as he threaded his way through the traffic, but how light and elegant! He turned the lines over in his mind, relishing their old-fashioned charm. It didn't do, he told himself, to dwell too long on 'trembling to a lily' and 'wavering to a rose'. One might as well say, 'it wobbles to a wallflower –'.

Harold checked his straying thoughts. Whatever the merits of the poem, without doubt his favourite line was:

> But Phyllida, my Phyllida.

The years fell from him as he said it silently to himself. The plane was punctual, and Phil smiled when her eyes lit upon him. She looked wan, and somehow smaller, than when she left, but her voice was steady when she greeted him.

He tucked a rug round her protectively when they reached the car.

'Heavens, how lovely! It's colder here than in France. My parents-in-law are flying back tomorrow and wanted me to stay on for another night, but now that all has been done – all the *awful* things – I wanted to hurry back to Jeremy.'

Harold told her that the boy had been wonderfully cheerful, but was longing to have her back.

'Do you know,' said Phil, as they neared Thrush Green, 'that when the constable told me the ghastly news, my first thought was: "I shan't have to tell Jeremy about the divorce." And then, "Thank God, I shan't have to go through all that wretched court business." It's a shameful thing, I suppose, to admit, but I felt I must tell someone, and you are just about the most understanding person to confess to.'

'It strikes me as a reasonable reaction,' replied Harold soberly. 'You've been dreading breaking the news for months now. It didn't mean that your grief was any the less. That, if I may say so, was quite evident.'

There was a long pause before the girl spoke again.

'It seems as though I've died twice. Once when he left me, and then when I heard of his death. Even now, after all this time apart, I can't imagine life without John. Whatever happens, you simply can't wipe away years of married life. The sense of loss is far, far greater than ever I imagined it would be. It's like losing an arm or a leg – some vital part. I suppose one grows numb with time, and other things happen to cover the scar, but I'm sure it will always be there.

'Thank God I've got Jeremy, and work to do!' she added. 'Without those two things I think I should sink.'

'Never!' said Harold stoutly. 'You'll never sink. You're far too brave for that.'

They climbed the steep hill to Thrush Green. It was dark, and the lighted windows looked welcoming to the tired girl. The lights were on at Tullivers, and she looked inquiringly at Harold.

'Betty Bell and Winnie between them have made you and Jeremy a little supper, I believe. We all thought you'd prefer to be alone the first night, but if you would sooner have company, then do, please, spend the evening with me.'

Phil shook her head, smiling.

'You've thought of everything. I'll never be able to thank you properly. I couldn't have got through this week of nightmare without you, Harold dear.'

He helped her in with her case. In the hall Jeremy and Winnie met her. After painful hugs from her son, Phil stood looking at the welcoming flowers, the fire, and the table set for two.

'Something smells delicious,' she said, sniffing the air.

'Chicken casserole,' said Winnie. 'Betty's left it all ready to serve.'

'I didn't know, until this minute, how hungry I was,' confessed Phil. 'Stop and share it, both of you.'

'No indeed,' said Winnie. 'I'm off to see to my two menfolk.'

'I'll call in the morning,' said Harold. 'Sleep well!'

Phil and Jeremy watched them depart down the path before returning to the firelit dining room.

'It's so lovely to come home,' said Phil. 'I've missed you so much.'

'Me too,' said Jeremy cheerfully, and began to tell her about the wonders of Paul Young's electric railway. The saga continued all through the meal, leaving Phil free to consider the terrible problem of when to break the news. She felt that she really could not face any more that day. It must wait until morning, she decided.

She took the boy upstairs to the bathroom and left him in the bath while she unpacked her case.

When she returned to give him a final inspection, she found him sitting very still, gazing into the distance.

'He's dead, isn't he?' he said softly.

There was no mistaking his meaning, and Phil made no pretence.

'Yes, Jeremy,' she answered. There was silence, broken only by the plopping of water dripping from a tap.

'Tell me, darling,' she said, very gently. 'How did you know?'

He looked up at her, wide-eyed and tearless.

'I saw it in your face.'

17. Richard Contemplates Matrimony

The mild quiet weather continued over the Christmas season, and the inhabitants of Thrush Green were divided in their feelings towards the such unseasonably balmy weather.

The pessimists pulled long faces.

'A green Christmas means a full churchyard,' they pointed out. 'A nice sharp frost or two is what we want. Kills off the germs.'

'Kills off the old 'uns too,' retorted the warmth-lovers. 'Give us a nice mild winter – germs and all!'

The church had been lovingly decked by Winnie, Dimity, Ella and other Thrush Green ladies. Albert Piggott was still kept in bed for most of the day by Doctor Lovell, and his temper was fast deteriorating to its normal stage of moroseness. His condition was not improved by seeing fat Willie Bond, the postman, looking after St Andrew's, while he himself was laid up. There had never been any love lost between the two men since the time that Willie's vegetable marrow had beaten Albert's, by a bare inch in girth and length, at Lulling Flower Show two years earlier.

Molly was beginning to wonder how long she would have to stay with her trying old father. Ben came every weekend, but it was obvious that he was becoming impatient at the delay, and resentful of the old man's carping attitude to his poor hard-working Molly.

'It can't be helped,' Molly said, doing her best to pour oil on troubled waters. 'It won't be much longer, Ben. The minute the doctor says he can be left, I'm flying back to you and our caravan.'

And with such limited consolation Ben had to be content.

Christmas, for Phil Prior, was made less painful by the kindness of her neighbours. Jeremy's natural joy in the festivities found fulfilment at the Youngs' house, where a children's party and innumerable presents helped to put his father's tragedy into the background. The arrival of the long-awaited kitten added to his excitement. But inevitably, it was more difficult for his mother. Memories of past Christmases were inescapable.

She saw again John lighting the red candles on the Christmas tree, with wide-eyed two-year-old Jeremy gazing with wonder at each new flame. John pulling crackers, and showing Jeremy the small fireworks inside – setting fire to the 'serpent's egg', waving a minute sparkler, making a flaming paper balloon rise to the ceiling, whilst Jeremy applauded excitedly. John wrapping her in a scarlet cashmere dressing gown, which she considered madly extravagant, but adorable of him. John had always been at his best at Christmas, gay, funny, sweet, considerate. It was more than Phil could bear to think that he would never again be there to make Christmas sparkle for her.

It was strange, she thought, how the bitterness of the last year was so little remembered. The humiliation, the misery, the wretched effort of keeping things from Jeremy, were all submerged beneath the remembrances of earlier shared happiness. She marvelled at this phenomenon, but was humbly grateful that her mind worked in this way. When the subject of his father cropped up, which was not very often, Phil found that she could speak of him with true affection, keeping alive for the little boy his early memories of a loving father.

She was relieved when the New Year arrived and things returned to normal. Jeremy started school during the first week in January, and she was glad to see him engrossed in his own school affairs and friendships again. Meanwhile, she set herself to work with renewed determination. It was plain that she must work doubly hard. John's affairs had been left tidily, with a will leaving his wife everything unconditionally. But when all had been settled, it seemed that Phil could expect a sum of only about six thousand pounds which included one or two insurances, and the sale of the furniture at the Chelsea flat. The flat itself was rented, and the firm for which he had worked had no pension schemes for dependants. There was no doubt about it

– things were going to be tight if she decided to continue to live at Tullivers.

But she was determined to stay there. She loved the little house and she loved Thrush Green. The friends she had made were the dependable, kindly sort of people whose company would give her pleasure and support in the years to come, as their affection towards her, in these last few terrible weeks, had shown so clearly. She had settled in Thrush Green as snugly as a bird in its nest, and so had Jeremy. Whatever the cost, Tullivers must remain their home.

Winnie Bailey had grown particularly dear to Phil since John's death. Quiet and loving, unobtrusive, but always available, Phil found herself looking upon her as the mother she unconsciously missed. Winnie lived with anxieties herself. She knew, only too well, that her husband could not live much longer. Only constant care and rest had kept him alive so long, and the doctor himself was well aware of the fact.

'I'm living on "borrowed time", as dear old Mrs Curdle used to say,' he said matter-of-factly. 'And very lucky I am to have these few extra years.'

His complete absence of self-pity made things more bearable for Winnie, but the secret sadness was always there, and made her doubly sympathetic towards the young widow next door.

Richard, too, was unusually attentive, and made himself useful by mending a faulty lock, an electric kettle, and a pane of glass broken by Jeremy's football. He would like to have taken Phil to the theatre one evening in Oxford, but decided against it.

'The pantomime is at the New until heaven knows when,' he told his aunt impatiently, 'and the Playhouse have three weeks of something translated from the Czech, by a Frenchman, which is set in near darkness with long sessions of complete silence. I don't think Phil would find it very cheering, at the moment.'

'Take her out to lunch,' said Winnie. 'I think she'd prefer that. I know she likes to be at home when Jeremy gets back after school. He can come here for his lunch that day.'

Richard brightened.

'Kingham Mill, perhaps? "The Old Swan" at Minster Lovell? "The Shaven Crown" at Shipton-under-Wychwood?'

'Ask Phil,' advised Winnie. And so he did.

The day of their jaunt together was clear and cold. There had been a sharp frost, and the grass was still white in the shade when Phil went to the Baileys' for a drink before setting off. She found Winnie and the doctor alone, but sundry thumps overhead proclaimed that Richard was getting ready.

'He's becoming quite a Beau Brummel,' said Winnie. 'You are a good influence, Phil.'

'I don't know about that,' said her husband lightly. 'He's taking the day off for this spree.'

'Heavens!' exclaimed Phil. 'I hope I'm not taking him from his work!'

'Do him good to have a break,' said his aunt firmly.

There was a particularly heavy crash above, as though a drawer had been pulled out, too abruptly and too far, and had landed on the floor.

'It reminds me,' said the doctor ruminatively, 'of the remark made by Dr Thompson, of Cambridge, sometime in the last century. He said of Richard Jebb: "The time that Mr Jebb can spare from the adornment of his person, he devotes to the neglect of his duties." I hope that our Richard will appear as elegantly turned out as his namesake, when he *does* appear.'

He certainly looked uncommonly spruce, Phil thought, when at last he arrived, full of apologies.

'And so bad for the system, fussing and fuming,' he added. 'Otto's paper on the consequences of an overflow of adrenalin upon the digestive system is always present in my mind when I begin to get worked up. Truly horrifying, his findings were! Remind me to lend the pamphlet to you sometime.'

Ella was stumping up the path as the pair made their way to the car. They greeted each other, and Ella watched the car drive away.

'Where are they off?' asked Ella abruptly.

'They're having lunch at "The Swan",' replied Winnie. 'Come in, Ella.'

'They're not making a match of things, are they? "Going steady", as they say?' 'Really!' expostulated Winnie. 'How ridiculous you are, Ella! Richard is simply showing a little kindness to the poor girl.'

'That's a change for Richard,' observed Ella. 'What's he hoping to get out of it?'

Winnie drew a long breath, and then let it out slowly. She had known Ella long enough to forgive her behaviour.

'What can I do for you, dear?' she asked mildly. Winnie's self-control was admirable.

The departure of the two together had been observed by several other people on Thrush Green.

Little Miss Fogerty, taking a physical education period with the infants, noticed Jeremy's mother entering the car. The children were ostensibly playing in four groups with suitable apparatus. Jeremy's group was nearest the playground railings, each child struggling to ply a skipping rope. Most of the little girls were twirling theirs adroitly enough, with expressions of smug superiority on their infant faces.

The boys, including Jeremy, were bouncing energetically but becoming hopelessly entangled with their ropes. It was whilst he was engaged in extricating himself from the loops round his ankles that Jeremy noticed his mother, and rushed to the fence to wave enthusiastically. Miss Fogerty, following his gaze, noted that Mrs Prior was accompanied – and by a bachelor!

'And so soon,' thought Miss Fogerty, sadly shocked.

'There's my mummy!' shouted Jeremy excitedly. 'And Richard! They're going to Minster Lovell. And Mrs Bailey's giving me lunch.'

'Lovely, dear,' said Miss Fogerty primly. But there was something in her tone which made Jeremy look up quickly at her little button mouth.

He resumed his clumsy skipping thoughtfully.

Harold Shoosmith was equally thoughtful. He had waved his hat cheerfully at the distant pair, as he crossed the green on his way to see Charles Henstock, but he could not ignore the involuntary spasm of concern which gripped him. Damn that fellow, Richard! He was making a confounded nuisance of himself.

As for Betty Bell, strategically placed for observation by cleaning the inside of the bedroom windows, her reactions were as straightforward as Ella's.

'*She's* not losing much time!' said Betty tartly.

The keen-eyed watchers of Thrush Green would have been singularly disappointed if they could have witnessed the innocent happenings at Minster Lovell.

The village, peaceful in its winter emptiness, showed little movement. A few wisps of blue smoke curled from the honey-coloured stone chimneys. An aged cocker spaniel, white round the muzzle, ambled vaguely along the green verge, sniffing here at a gatepost, there at a dry-stone wall.

The river Windrush purled placidly along, dimpling under the bridge, the current criss-crossed by the willow branches trailing on its surface. The ancient inn drowsed in the winter sunlight, and welcomed them with a great log fire which whispered, rather than roared. A white-haired old lady, dozing in a leather chair, scarcely stirred as they entered.

The entire village seemed to be wrapped in dreams – an atmosphere which Phil found wholly in keeping with her present state of suspended animation. Since John's death, she had gone about her daily life automatically, as though she were enclosed in an invisible shell which cut her off from everything around her. Her senses were still numbed, her reactions slow, her thoughts, when she wrote or spoke, seemed to drop from her with deadly deliberation, as slowly and stickily as cold treacle from a spoon.

If Richard could have known he would have been surprised and hurt to realize that it was this apathy which had made Phil accept his invitation in the first place. It was easier to accept than to produce an excuse when the young man had pressed her, but in truth she would have been happier getting on with a story which she had in mind.

Nevertheless, she was grateful for Richard's kindness, and believed that Winnie was glad to see them both having a brief break. She would hate to hurt Winnie, after all her concern.

The lunch was excellent, and Phil was content to let Richard do the major part of the talking. She found him interesting and remarkably astute when talking about his work, but incredibly naïve in his attitude to people.

'He's just not interested in them,' thought Phil to herself, watching him demolish caramel custard with a few swift movements. In fact, the only person he ever seemed to mention with any sort of feeling was the redoubtable Doctor Otto Goldstein. And on this subject, Richard was, without any doubt, the most crashing bore, Phil decided.

They had coffee alone by the whispering log fire, which shed a few white flakes of ash every now and again, as if to prove that the natural laws of gravity still held good even in this spell-bound lotus-land. Afterwards, they strolled up the somnolent village street towards the ruined priory. The cocker spaniel, exhausted by his morning exercise, lay sprawled on his side in the shelter of a sunny wall. He did not stir as they passed.

Walking across the shorn grass and ancient stone paths of the ruins, a wonderful sense of peace crept over Phil. Richard stopped to study a map of the site, and she walked alone into the roofless hall and gazed at the tracery of the empty windows framing the pale-blue skies of winter. A lone blackbird was perched upon one of the stone vaultings, and piped a few melancholy notes, as clear as the river water that ran nearby, and as round as the washed pebbles beneath it. What had these venerable walls witnessed in their time, Phil wondered? Passion in plenty, bloodshed without doubt: but also piety, perseverance and simple happiness. How many people had stood here, as she did now, puzzled, unhappy, numb with pain and perplexity? And how many had found comfort in the knowledge of the continuity of life, of being but one link in a long chain of human experience, in this old, old setting?

Somehow, thought Phil, feeling the grey roughness of the ancient stones with her bare cold hand, one's own sufferings were put into perspective in the face of this survivor of the centuries. For the first time, since John had left her, a tiny tremor of hope ran through her – the faint stirring of life renewed.

They drove back slowly. Although it was barely three o'clock, the sun was low on the horizon, and the shadows of the trees lay long and straight across the bare winter fields.

'I've enjoyed it so much,' said Phil. 'It was kind of you to give me such a treat. I feel better for it.'

'I hope we can do this again,' replied Richard. 'But, of course, I shan't be at Thrush Green much longer.'

'Why, is the work nearly finished?'

'Practically. I shall have to go back to London within two or three months.'

There was a pause, while he negotiated a sharp double bend expertly, and then he spoke again.

'Would you think of coming to live in town?'

Instantly, Phil was on her guard. From his tone it was clear that the two words 'with me' might well have been added. The happy daze engendered by Minster Lovell and the sunshine fled instantly, and Phil was suddenly alert. This was a possibility of which she had not really been aware.

'I want to settle in Thrush Green,' she replied carefully. 'Both Jeremy and I are very happy there.'

'I should think you might get bored. Not many people of our age there. Besides, if you were in town you'd be on the spot for meeting your editors, wouldn't you?'

'I go up about once in three weeks to discuss things with Frank,' said Phil. 'It seems quite often enough to plan the work ahead. I'm sure I shouldn't want to call into the office more frequently, even if I were nearer.'

Richard did not reply, and Phil sensed that he was a little put out. The car's speed increased considerably, and a muscle twitched in his cheek.

Really, thought Phil, emotions of any kind were very tiresome. What was more, they were horribly exhausting. She hoped that she was wrong in imagining that Richard was interested in her – or rather, in matrimony.

She pondered on the subject as they neared Thrush Green. No doubt Richard had reached the stage when domesticity had its appeal. She suspected that anyone reasonably attractive and companionable would be eligible to Richard just now, and did not delude herself by thinking that her own personal charms had fired the young man. To be honest, would *anything* fire him?

She recalled Doctor Bailey's words. 'Richard's a cold fish,' he had said to her once. 'I'm afraid the only person Richard considers is – Richard!'

They drove up the hill from Lulling to Thrush Green. The sun had vanished behind Lulling Woods and a sharp little wind reminded the world that it was still January.

Phil sighed. It had been a lovely day, despite this small cloud between them. And whatever happened, she had Richard to thank for taking her to the tranquil ruins of Minster Lovell, and that sudden miraculous glimpse of life again after the long months following John's desertion. For that, she would always be grateful to him.

She thanked him sincerely at her gate, and he did his best to smile in return.

But there was something tight-lipped about the smile, which made it plain that Richard had been crossed, and did not like it.

Albert Piggott was one of those who saw the return of the couple. He was standing at his cottage window gazing gloomily across the green.

Willie Bond had just entered St Andrew's with a slightly pompous air of ownership which Albert found intensely irritating. What was that fat lump going to muck up now, he wondered?

He looked beyond the church to the car from which Phil emerged, his mouth curving downwards with distaste.

'Fine goings-on,' grunted Albert to Molly, who was trying to dress her fidgety son for his afternoon's outing.

'Hold still, do!' said Molly sharply. 'What goings-on, dad?'

'That young widder-woman. Setting her cap at Mrs Bailey's young fellow. Not that he's much catch, Lord alone knows, but it ain't hardly decent to go running after the men with her own poor chap scarce cold in 'is grave.'

'Maybe he's just given her a lift up from the shops,' said Molly reasonably, controlling her temper.

Albert gave a disbelieving snort.

'That's a likely tale!'

Molly buttoned George's coat with unnecessary violence.

'The trouble with you, dad, is you always thinks the worst of folks. You can't wonder you haven't got any friends.'

Albert bridled.

'Whatcher mean, no friends? What about them next door?'

'They sell beer,' said Molly roundly. 'You're a good customer. They're kind-hearted, I know, but you look around – there's not one true friend to your name!'

'That's right!' said Albert, adopting a quavering tone. 'You pitch into your poor ol' dad, just when he's too weak to stand up for hisself. I don't know what the world's comin' to when children turn on their parents. I does my best – ill though I be – to give no trouble, but you've got no proper feelings in you, you wicked hussy!'

Molly bit back the flow of words which she would willingly have poured forth, dumped George from the table to the floor, and tugged him smartly outdoors into the blessed calm of Thrush Green.

This couldn't go on, she fumed to herself, watching George stagger across to the steps which supported the statue of Nathaniel Patten, Thrush Green's famous missionary son. Jumping from the steps was the little boy's favourite activity, and Molly was glad to see him engaged so happily while she studied her problem.

When Ben had come the weekend before, Albert appeared to be rather worse, but whether this was wholly physical, or simply a way of drawing attention to himself, it was difficult to say. In any case, Molly had discussed with Ben the possibility of making their home at the cottage, in order to look after the old man.

Ben's face had clouded.

'Can't be done,' he said slowly. 'I know how you feel, but it's not right for you or George – or me, for that matter.'

He had looked across at the churchyard where his redoubtable old grandmother lay at rest.

'And gran,' he added, 'wouldn't have let me give up her fair. And quite right too.'

'Perhaps just for the winters?' pleaded Molly, torn both ways. 'When the fair's laid up?'

'Well, I'll think about it, my love, but I don't like the idea and that's flat. You'll be nothing but a skivvy, and I'm not having that.'

Now, watching George clambering up the steps on all fours, she knew that Ben was right. She could stand it no longer. Plans would have to be made to see that the old man was provided for, and she would have a good talk with Doctor Lovell to make sure that he was not being left too soon. But go, eventually, she must.

And so, unwittingly, Phil and Richard's jaunt had brought matters to a head, in the cottage across the green, nudging into motion Albert Piggott's particular wheel of fortune.

18. Harold Entertains an Old Friend

One morning in February, Willie Marchant tacked up the hill to Thrush Green and delivered a letter to Harold Shoosmith.

Later that day Harold walked across to see Phil.

'Frank's coming down for the weekend,' he told her. 'I'm so pleased. Now I shall have a chance to repay the dozens of times I stayed at Frank's house when his wife was alive. They were so good to me when I came home on leave.'

'Bring him over for a drink,' invited Phil.

'Thank you. I know he'd love to see the cottage. But I really came to ask you and Jeremy to lunch one day, while he's here. I must get Betty Bell to whip up something rather special. He's thoroughly spoiled by Violet who housekeeps for him.'

'So Richard tells me,' said Phil.

'Richard?' exclaimed Harold. 'How does he know?'

'They belong to the same club, I gather,' said Phil, picking the kitten out of a box of new typing paper in which it was settling for a nap.

'I didn't realize they knew each other,' said Harold, looking a little put out. 'Well, well! Shall we say about twelve o'clock on Saturday?'

'That would be lovely,' agreed Phil. 'And what's more I'll give him my week's work to take back with him, and save postage.'

'That's admirably thrifty,' commented Harold with approval.

'Needs must,' laughed Phil. 'By nature I'm rather like the Flopsy Bunnies, "very improvident and cheerful", but I have to discipline myself these days.'

'How are things going, seriously?' asked Harold, emboldened by her own introduction of ways and means.

'Not too badly. I've had an introduction, through Frank, to an editor who's in charge of a number of local papers in the Midlands, and I'm starting a series of articles for him. Pretty good pay, too.'

'That's cheering news,' said Harold, rising to go. 'But don't work too hard. You ought to be having some fun now and again. What about a day out soon? Jeremy too, of course, if you'd like to bring him.'

'There's nothing I'd enjoy more,' said Phil, and meant it.

Jeremy had found a new interest since the arrival of the kitten. He had called on Dotty Harmer to report the cat's progress, and discovered the wholly delightful mode of life at the old lady's cottage.

There was no nonsense about wiping feet before entry, or having clean hands, or respectable clothing. If you arrived in the middle of one of Dotty's sketchy meals, it didn't seem to matter. As likely as not, she would be consuming a light repast as she stood at her stove or walked about the house on other affairs. As far as Jeremy could see, the meal usually consisted of a piece of brown bread, liberally spread with butter, a rough lump of cheese, and some unidentifiable leaves, by way of a salad. This seemed to be eaten at any time, followed by the crunching of a home-grown apple. Jeremy was always offered one too, and found this largesse much to his liking.

But better by far than the informality of Dotty's welcome, and the present of the apple, was the large number of animals which made up Dotty's family. The goats in particular, fascinated the boy and he even drank the milk whilst it was still warm from the animal, with uncommon relish, which Dotty heartily approved.

One spring Saturday morning he bounded down the path by Albert Piggott's cottage and gained the path leading to Dotty's and finally to Lulling Woods. The air was balmy, his spirits high, and he carried a large bunch of grass and greenery from the hedges as a present for Daisy, the milker, and Dulcie, the younger goat.

Charles Henstock privately thought that Dulcie was poorly named – neither sweet nor gentle, and very quick to use her horns on unsuspecting visitors, as he had found to his cost one wet day. His clerical grey trousers had never completely recovered from their immersion in the puddle in which Dulcie's sly butting had landed him. Jeremy, however, was rather more alert to Dulcie's wiles, and his passion for her was unclouded.

On this particular morning he found Dotty in a somewhat agitated mood. She was having difficulty in fixing a chain to Dulcie's collar. Daisy, taking advantage of the disturbance, was adding gleefully to the chaos by bleating continuously, and rushing round and round in circles so that her tethering chain was soon shortened to a couple of feet. This gave her the opportunity to bleat even more madly, puffing noisily between bleats to prove how sorely she was being tried.

Dulcie, unduly skittish, kicked up her heels every time that Dotty approached her. Dotty, red in the face, greeted Jeremy shortly.

'Get Daisy undone, boy, will you? And give her some of that stuff you've brought to stop her row.'

Jeremy obediently accomplished this task. In the comparative peace that followed, Dotty captured the younger goat, and sighed noisily with relief.

'Where's Dulcie going?' asked Jeremy.

'To be mated,' said Dotty flatly.

'What d'you mean – *mated*?' queried Jeremy.

'Married, then,' said Dotty, hitching up a stocking in a preoccupied way.

'*Married*? But only *people* get married,' exclaimed Jeremy.

'I know that,' said Dotty, nettled. Dulcie began to tug powerfully at her lead.

'But you said –'

'Here, you clear off home,' said Dotty forthrightly. 'I'm up to my eyes this morning, as you can see.'

The boy retreated very slowly backwards.

'Will she have baby goats when she's been mated?'

'*Kids*, you mean,' said Dotty pedantically. 'Do use the right expressions, child.'

'Well, will she?'

'What?' said Dotty, stalling for time.

'Have baby goats. Kids, I mean?'

'Maybe,' said Dotty, with unusual caution. Difficult to know how much children knew about the facts of life these days, and anyway it wasn't her business to enlighten this one.

'Can I have one when they come, Miss Harmer?' begged Jeremy longingly. '*Please*, can I?'

Dotty's slender stock of patience suddenly ran out at her heels like gunpowder. Her voice roared out like a cannon.

'Look, boy! I don't know *if* she'll have kids, *when* she'll have kids, or if your mother would let you have one if she *did* have kids! You're far too inquisitive, and a confounded nuisance. Get off home!'

She raised a skinny, but powerful, arm, and Dulcie, sensing joyous combat, lowered her head for action. In the face of this combined attack, Jeremy fled, but even as he ran determined to come again as soon as things at Dotty's had returned once more to their usual chaotic normality.

Meanwhile, he decided, slackening his pace as the distance between Dotty's and his own breathless form increased, he must set about persuading his mother that a little kid would be very useful for keeping Tullivers' grass down. But, somehow, he sensed that that would be an uphill battle.

Frank arrived the following weekend, in the midst of a torrential rainstorm. Ella Bembridge, struggling to shut an upstairs window to keep out the deluge, was the first to see the beautiful sleek Jaguar creep through Harold's gateway. She knew whose it must be, for Dimity had told her all about Harold's friend, his redoubtable Violet, and the fact that he was a busy editor. If Frank had been aware how much was known about him already at Thrush Green he would have been very surprised.

'What a welcome for you!' exclaimed Harold, opening the front door. 'Come in, my dear fellow, before you are wet through.'

He showed his friend to his bedroom and went downstairs again to prepare drinks. From the kitchen, delicious smells of lunch emanated.

'Not quite up to Violet's standards, I'm afraid,' said Harold, when his friend reappeared, 'but pretty good, nevertheless. By the way, Mrs Prior and her boy are joining us for lunch.'

'How nice!' said Frank. 'Whereabouts is her house?'

Harold pointed out Tullivers through the veils of slashing rain.

'If this doesn't stop, I must fetch her,' said Harold. 'It will save her getting out her car. She could get soaked just going to her garage.'

It occurred to Frank that Harold was rather unduly solicitous.

'Mine's out already,' he said. 'We'll fetch her together.'

But, as it happened, the storm swept away before Phil and Jeremy needed to set out, and by the time they arrived, the sun was turning the puddles on Thrush Green to dazzling mirrors.

Betty Bell, who had heard quite enough of the paragon Violet to be put on her mettle, brought forth a superb steak and kidney pudding swathed in a snowy napkin. The Brussels sprouts, the braised celery and the floury potatoes were all at the peak of perfection, and a truly enormous orange trifle, decorated with almonds and crystallized orange segments made Jeremy sigh with ecstasy.

'And if that Violet can do better than that,' said Betty grimly to herself as she returned to the kitchen, 'I'll eat my hat!'

After lunch, the three friends sat and talked over coffee, while Jeremy lay on the floor with volumes of *Punch* around him. It was a happy relaxed little party, mellowed by Betty's superb cooking and

Harold's good wine, but Frank was alert enough to notice the attentions which his old friend Harold gave to the young woman, and thought that they were perhaps a trifle warmer than ordinary civility dictated. Could this confirmed bachelor, now approaching sixty, have designs on his promising new contributor?

It looked highly probable, thought Frank, sipping his coffee, but who would have suspected it?

Just before three, Phil and Jeremy departed.

'We'll look forward to seeing you both tomorrow about half-past six,' said Phil. 'I've asked the Baileys to come in to meet you. And Richard.'

When they had gone, the two friends settled by the fire again.

'An attractive girl,' said Frank cautiously, 'and very sound as a writer. I have you to thank for introducing her to me, Harold.'

'We're all very fond of her here,' replied Harold. 'I can't make up my mind if her husband's sudden death was a good thing or not. She was dreading the court proceedings, and telling the boy, of course. A messy business – but she was terribly shocked by his death. I wonder if she'll ever get over it.'

'Be married in six months,' said Frank robustly, producing a pipe and ramming home a generous pinch of tobacco. 'Got any eligible young men nearby?'

A faint look of distaste crept over Harold's face, and was observed by the wily Frank.

'There's Richard. You know him, I believe?'

'Slightly. I see him at the club, but he's such a crashing bore about his insides I give him a wide berth, I don't mind admitting.'

'Phil seems to like him, nevertheless.'

'Does she?' said Frank thoughtfully.

They leant back in their armchairs, pondering on the idiosyncrasies of women.

'I shouldn't think he stands a chance,' said Frank, at length. 'She's too much sense to take on a fellow like that. Why, he thinks of no one but himself!'

Harold brightened a little.

'That's how I feel. How I *hope*, perhaps I should say. But then, after all, they are much of an age, and she might think that marriage would improve Richard.'

'Any woman who marries a man expecting to improve him,' said

Frank tartly, 'deserves all she gets – and that's disappointment. No, Phil won't be so foolish, I feel positive.'

He tapped his pipe briskly on the bars of the grate.

'But you say you *hope* she won't marry Richard, Harold,' he went on. 'Perhaps I shouldn't ask, but tell me, are you at all interested?'

There was a little silence before Harold replied. Outside, the rooks cawed above the chestnut avenue, and the sound of distant church bells told of a Saturday afternoon wedding.

'Yes, I am,' said Harold very quietly, looking down at his clasped hands. 'But to be truthful, I find it hard to sort out my feelings. I love my present way of life. I'm not at all sure that marriage would suit me, and in any case, I can't see that it would be fair to ask a young woman like that to take on a man of my age.'

'You're only five years my senior,' pointed out Frank. 'I still look upon myself as a spry young-middle-ager.'

'You've always been young for your years, anyway,' answered Harold. 'I've knocked about such a lot, I sometimes feel older than mine.'

'Try your luck,' said Frank spontaneously.

'Too early yet,' replied Harold. 'Let her get over her tragedy first, I think. Besides, do I really want to get married? That's the test, I think. Surely I should be more whole-hearted about this affair? What do you think, Frank? You know I value your opinions.'

Frank took a long pull at his pipe.

'I hate to give any advice in a case like this. But I do just wonder, Harold, if your kind heart and old-fashioned sense of chivalry are rather pushing you into this offer of marriage. To my mind, you are a perfectly-balanced person on your own – self-sufficient without being self-satisfied, a truly rare combination. You may well find that matrimony complicates your well-ordered existence, and puts more of a strain on you than you had imagined. On the other hand, as I know full well, marriage can make a man. I miss Margaret more than I can say.'

'That I can understand. She was a fine woman in every way. But not having been so blessed, I've no experience. No, Frank, reason tells me that it would not be fair to Phil – she'd probably spend the last few years of my life as a nurse – appalling thought! And I don't think I really want to give up my selfish way of life.'

'Put the whole affair out of your mind for a month or two,' said Frank. 'You'll both know your feelings better by then.'

'Good old Time,' agreed Harold quietly. 'I'm sure you're right.'

He got up and fetched a map from his desk, closing the subject of Phil Prior.

'I thought we'd drive out to Lechlade for a meal tonight,' he said. 'Which way shall we go?'

The two friends held the map between them and plans for the distant future were forgotten in making those for the evening.

The tiny sitting room at Tullivers just held the six grown-ups comfortably, and Jeremy, as the important seventh, made himself useful in passing salted nuts and other delicious morsels to his seniors whilst managing to dispatch a generous selection on his own account.

Frank found Doctor Bailey a fascinating companion. They were both fishing enthusiasts, and the doctor regaled the younger man with tales of past exploits on the Windrush.

'You must come down again and try your luck on the Lechlade stretch,' said the doctor. 'I've several old friends there who would be delighted to give you a day's sport.'

He nodded across the room to Richard.

'Our nephew there,' he continued, 'isn't interested, more's the pity.'

Richard was making himself particularly charming to Phil. Since their outing, she had taken care not to meet him alone, but was glad of this opportunity to repay his invitation in the company of others.

There was no doubt about it, thought Frank privately, Richard showed up to greater advantage here than in town. And he was a personable young man, and certainly going to be a very successful one. Harold seemed to have a rival here.

He watched his hostess's reaction to Richard's attentions, but could perceive nothing more than ordinary politeness on her part.

The cottage he found charming, and delighted Phil by saying so when she showed him round.

'It's the perfect place to work,' she told him. 'Small enough to keep tidy easily, and gives me a peaceful base when Jeremy's at school.'

'I think I've got an American magazine interested in a longish short story from you, sometime in the future. Perhaps a Christmas story? Like the idea?'

'*Rather!*' cried Phil warmly.

'I'll tell you more when you come up next week,' promised Frank.

That evening he said farewell to his old friend Harold, being careful not to mention the confidences which he had been given earlier.

'Come to me for a weekend in April,' were his last words before setting off, and Harold promised that he would.

Frank drove home speedily, his thoughts full of Thrush Green and its inhabitants.

What did the future hold for them, he wondered?

19. Richard Tries His Luck

Spring seemed a long time in coming to Thrush Green, and people were getting heartily sick of being housebound.

Keen gardeners, such as Harold, fretted at the delay in planting early potatoes and vegetable seeds. The lawns were as tousled and rough as unshaven old men, and the mowers, oiled and waiting to be used, had to wait still longer as snow showers and cold rain kept the ground soggy.

Molly's father developed a mild attack of bronchitis which meant that her departure must be delayed.

'Done it a-purpose, I shouldn't wonder,' commented Ben, who was chafing at Molly's enforced absence from her own home.

'Just till he's over this,' Molly pleaded. 'I must stay till he's back on his feet, Ben. I don't relish it, you know that, but who's to do for him?'

At the school, Miss Watson and Miss Fogerty looked forward to the end of term. Measles and mumps had taken their toll in February and March, and the bitter weather had meant that play outside was impossible. Tempers became frayed, and the fact that the school was most sketchily cleaned did not help matters.

Mrs Cooke of Nidden, who had come back temporarily 'to

oblige', was no Nelly Piggott when it came to elbow grease, and Miss Watson and Miss Fogerty were often to be seen sweeping up the classrooms which, in theory, had already been done by Mrs Cooke.

'But what else can we do?' asked Miss Watson despairingly of Miss Fogerty, two days before term ended. 'I had a word with Molly Curdle. She'd be perfect, of course, living so near and being such a good worker, but she's too tied with George and that dreadful old father to consider it. In any case, it would only be a temporary arrangement again.'

Matters came to a head when Mrs Cooke arrived on the last day of term. She wore a look of smug importance, as she carried her broom into Miss Watson's room. The children had departed, excited at the thought of three weeks' holiday, and bearing home their term's drawings to show their resigned mothers. As most of these were executed in chalk, and were being clutched face down against winter coats, their reception at home might be expected to be bleak indeed.

'I thought I'd tell you straight off,' said Mrs Cooke cheerfully, 'that I'm not to do any more work. Doctor's orders.'

'Good heavens!' exclaimed Miss Watson. 'What's the matter?'

'Another little stranger on the way,' replied Mrs Cooke, with immense satisfaction.

Miss Watson's mind was in confusion. Could Mrs Cooke's pleasure really come from the thought of yet another addition to her large, dirty and unruly family? Or was she simply pleased to have a good excuse to leave the school in the lurch? Miss Watson, a realist, was inclined to think that the latter reason caused Mrs Cooke's evident smugness.

'Will you be able to cope with the holiday scrubbing?' asked Miss Watson, knowing the answer before the question was finished.

'Not a hope,' replied Mrs Cooke triumphantly. 'I'm inclined to miscarry if I does too much. It's a weak sort of uterus, you might say. Doctor said something about a prolapse. You know what that is?' asked Mrs Cooke darkly.

'No, I don't,' replied Miss Watson shortly. What a blessing to be a spinster, was her heartfelt thought!

'Well, that's that, I suppose, Mrs Cooke,' she continued resignedly. 'I must thank you for stepping into the breach. You'll sweep up now, will you?'

'I'll oblige,' said Mrs Cooke, inclining her head regally, and set about her limited labours.

'Would you have thought it?' asked Miss Watson of Miss Fogerty later. 'I gather she's still feeding that last baby – Adrian, or Clifford, or whatever it is. Frankly, I lose count of them.'

'It's a common fallacy,' pronounced Miss Fogerty importantly, 'that a woman who is feeding a child cannot fall again.'

Miss Watson looked at her assistant in astonishment.

'Agnes, dear,' she protested, 'how on earth do you know such things?'

'I always read the mothers' page under the dryer at the hairdresser's,' answered little Miss Fogerty imperturbably.

She skewered her good velour hat to her skimpy bun, and the two ladies made their way outside.

'But this doesn't solve our problem, does it?' said Miss Fogerty, pausing in the chilly porch.

Next door, Harold Shoosmith's gate clanged as Betty Bell set off home on her bicycle. Rosy and bright-eyed, as fresh as when she had arrived at work some hours earlier, she waved energetically to the two ladies in the school porch, before pedalling away briskly down the hill.

Miss Watson looked at Miss Fogerty, rather as stout Cortez looked upon the peaks of Darien, so long ago.

'Dare we?' she whispered.

'Why not!' said little Miss Fogerty robustly.

It was in April that Richard's work at Oxford came to an end, and as the time approached, Winnie Bailey was mightily relieved.

In all fairness, she admitted that although Richard had stayed longer than was at first intended, he had really been very little trouble, and had more than pulled his weight by tackling little jobs about the house which were beyond her own understanding and the doctor's strength.

Nevertheless, the thought of having the house to themselves again was heart-lifting. She wondered, sometimes, about the relationship between her nephew and the young widow next door. She had noticed that the outing *à deux* had not been repeated, and that since that day Richard had been unduly restless, but nothing had been said, and in any case, Winnie would not have expected to hear about such a personal matter from Richard.

It was all the more surprising, therefore, when he broached the subject one Sunday morning at breakfast time. The doctor was still in bed, having had a restless night, and Winnie and her nephew lingered over their coffee.

Richard was busy grating a raw apple into a bowl of rolled oats, pine kernels, sultanas and milk – a mixture which he concocted each morning for himself from a recipe of Otto's.

It was a messy business, and Winnie watched the operation resignedly.

'Why don't you eat the apple separately?' she asked.

Richard looked up from his work in some surprise.

'My dear aunt, that would quite defeat Otto's object. The enzymes in the saliva react in a truly magical way upon the mixture of minerals in this bowl. Wonderfully purging, and marvellously toning to the lining of the digestive tract. A friend of Otto's claims to have cured dyspeptic ulcers with this mixture alone.'

He continued to grate energetically, stirred up the mash, and ate it with much relish.

Winnie watched him as she sipped her coffee.

'I've been meaning to tell you about my immediate plans, Aunt Win,' he said, when at last the bowl was empty. 'I really do appreciate your hospitality. You've both been so kind. I hope I haven't been too much of a nuisance.'

Winnie reassured him on this point.

'Well now, I ought to be off in a week or two's time. The point is that the Carslakes have offered me their house while he has a year at Harvard as a visiting professor. They're asking only a nominal rent – they really want someone to keep an eye on things, I gather, and of course it would suit me perfectly.'

'And you are going to accept?'

'It all depends.'

'What on? It seems straightforward enough to me.'

For once in his life Richard appeared discomfited. The vestiges of a blush were apparent to Winnie's sharp eyes.

'The point is,' said Richard, pushing back his chair and walking to the window, 'I've been thinking of getting married, and I suppose the girl would like to see the house first. Hardly fair to take her there if she loathed the place.'

'Quite so,' agreed Winnie. 'And who have you in mind?'

'Why, Phil Prior!' exclaimed Richard. 'Surely you realized that I was interested?'

'I knew you liked her,' said Winnie guardedly, 'but not that you hoped to marry her.'

'Aunt Winnie,' said Richard, returning to the table and looking down at his aunt pleadingly. 'Do you think I've a chance? Has she said anything to you about me?'

'Nothing at all,' confessed Winnie, 'except to say how beautifully you'd cleaned out the drain.'

'Hardly a sufficient basis for marriage!' observed Richard, with a wry smile. 'But I suppose I can count it as half a point in my favour.'

He wandered back to the window, hands in his pockets. Something about the slouched back, the ruffled fair hair and general air of desolation, touched Winnie's kind heart.

'You could always ask her,' she pointed out.

'But what hopes, d'you think?'

'Who knows?' said Winnie. 'But why not try your luck?'

She began to pile the coffee cups on to the tray. Richard continued to stand, glooming out upon the garden with unseeing eyes. She wondered what effect this preoccupation with love would have upon Richard's fickle digestion.

He was certainly not her idea of a husband, thought Winnie, bearing the tray towards the kitchen.

Nor, she thought with some satisfaction, Phil Prior's, if she knew anything about that sensible young woman.

'Here,' cried Betty Bell to her employer one morning. 'Got something to tell you! I've got a new job!'

'Betty!' exclaimed Harold, dumbfounded. As everyone knows, one of the most heinous crimes which can be committed in a small community is inveigling someone else's domestic worker into coming to work for oneself. Many a deep friendship has been wrecked by such perfidy, and Harold could not believe that Betty Bell would be a party to such treachery.

'You're not going to leave me?' pleaded the stricken man.

Betty's hearty peal of laughter set the silver ringing on the side-board.

'Now, would I do a thing like that? No, I was just pulling your leg. Made you sit up though, didn't it, eh?'

'It certainly did. But, tell me, what's all this about?'

Betty settled herself comfortably on the edge of the dining room table. Harold, forewarned, shifted the remains of his breakfast out of harm's way.

'Well, it's like this. Mrs Cooke's expecting again—'

'No!' broke in Harold.

'Strue! Like rabbits, ain't it? Well, as I was saying, she's off work for a bit – if she was ever *on*, if you take my meaning – and them two poor old things next door are up to their hocks in dirt in that school, so they've asked me if I'd help 'em out.'

'Oh,' said Harold, 'and what have you replied?'

Betty suddenly became rather distant and adopted the air of one-who-knew-her-place.

'I said I must ask your permission, sir. They was going to come and have a word with you themselves, but I said let me sound you out. If you was going to be funny about it, I said I'd turn the job down.'

'What does it mean – from my point of view?' asked Harold cautiously.

'If you was willing, I'd come to you half an hour earlier, as soon as I'd done in there in the morning.'

'Humph!' said Harold, considering the matter. It seemed reasonable enough, and he knew Betty could do with the extra money which the school job would provide.

'Very well,' he agreed. 'Let's see how it works out.'

'You're a real gentleman!' cried Betty, bouncing off the table energetically. Harold retrieved a spoon which had been whisked to the floor by her skirt. 'I'll call in next door on my way home and tell the poor old soul!'

'I'll call on Miss Watson myself,' said Harold. 'I'm glad to be of some help to the lady.'

'You'll be mentioned in her prayers tonight,' said Betty heartily. 'And to tell you the truth, in mine too, Mr Shoosmith. Money's not easy to come by these days, and I'm thankful to get a bit of extra work.'

She whirled from the room and very soon Harold heard her voice raised in song as she polished the bathroom floor.

Harold smiled to himself. She really was a wonderful girl. He supposed he must be prepared to share his good luck with Thrush Green School. If Betty Bell took on the job, she would certainly do it splendidly.

It was, in fact, the school's luckiest day, for Betty Bell was to keep it spotless and shining for many a long year.

Two days after Richard's breakfast conversation with his aunt, the young man dressed himself with some care and made his way next door.

Dusk was falling, and although the weather still remained cold, a few early daffodils had braved the April winds, and the sticky buds in the avenue of chestnut trees were beginning to break into leaf.

The birds were busy struggling with wisps of dry grass, feathers, and other nesting material. It seemed a propitious time for a young man to go a-wooing, and Richard approached the late admiral's dolphin knocker in the appropriately nervous condition brought on by mingled hope and ardour.

Phil answered the door with a bath towel thrown over one shoulder, her hair in a state of disarray and a blue streak across one cheek, which had been made, Richard guessed correctly, by a ball-point pen, and would, he had no doubt, be the very devil to remove.

'Do come in,' she said somewhat distractedly. 'I'm just giving Jeremy a quick once-over before he puts on his pyjamas. He's rather like a cat in his ablutions – terribly busy working on one or two square inches, and completely neglecting the rest.'

She led the way to the sitting-room and handed him a decanter and a glass.

'Help yourself, Richard. I'll be back in a tick.'

Richard poured himself an inch of dry sherry. Otto did not approve of alcohol, but Richard felt that on this occasion even the stern Otto would have relaxed his rules. And as he had once said to his disciple, 'If you *must* drink such liver-rotting poison as sherry, then drink the dryest you can find.'

He sat there twirling his little glass disconsolately. Having girded himself for the endeavour, it was doubly hard to have the event postponed, even for a few minutes. He realized that he must approach the delicate proposal with some preliminaries, but he had decided that they must be as short as ordinary civility demanded. He was no speech-maker, and he had wisely made no rehearsals. He felt it best to rely on the spontaneous promptings of his feelings.

When Phil returned, she had combed her hair, miraculously removed the blue streak, and generally looked her usual neat and attractive self.

'May I pour you one?' asked Richard.

'Thanks. I can do with it. I always think that the time between tea-time and bed-time is the most exhausting for mothers. Just when one is most tired is the time when most is demanded.'

She accepted the sherry gratefully, put her feet up on a foot-stool, and sighed happily.

'But what brings you here, Richard? I hear from Winnie you are leaving us very soon. Will you be sorry?'

Such an abrupt approach to the matter in hand took Richard off his guard. He swallowed awkwardly, and set himself spluttering, as a drop of sherry went down the wrong way.

'Let me get you some water,' said Phil, getting to her feet, and viewing her scarlet-faced visitor with concern.

'All right now,' he gasped huskily, still fighting for breath. What a way to go about a proposal of marriage, thought Richard!

Phil resumed her seat.

'I always think it's extraordinary,' she remarked, 'how violently the body reacts to something in the windpipe.'

'Good thing it does,' responded Richard. 'You'd soon croak if it didn't!'

An amicable silence fell. A tiny jet of flame hissed from a crack in the coal in the fireplace. The clock ticked companionably above it, and outside the birds shrilled and piped before going to roost for the night.

Richard, now recovered, felt that he must return to the subject of his departure. He put down his glass carefully.

'You asked if I should miss Thrush Green, and I certainly shall. Uncle Donald and Aunt Winnie have been very patient, and so good to me.'

'They're absolute darlings,' agreed Phil warmly. 'Don't you agree?'

Richard refused to be side-tracked.

'But the person I shall miss most of all,' said Richard firmly, 'will be you.'

'Me?' cried Phil, with mingled surprise and dismay. 'But we've had very little to do with each other, after all.'

'I should like to think,' said Richard, warming to his theme, 'that we could be a great deal together in the future.'

'How do you mean?' asked Phil, her heart sinking. She rose and poured herself another glass of sherry. If this were to be a proposal of marriage, she could do with a little support, she told herself.

Richard launched into a long explanation of the Carslakes' offer of their house for a year, and before he was halfway through the saga, Phil could foresee the outcome.

'And there is no one in the world,' declared Richard, with more warmth in his voice than Phil had ever heard before, 'I should like to share it with, more than you yourself. It may seem a roundabout way of asking you to consider marrying me, but if you could – ?'

His voice faltered to a halt, and his blue eyes were full of pleading. At that moment, Phil found him more alive, more attractive, more lovable than she would ever have thought possible. It was a pity that his Uncle Donald could not see the 'cold fish' now. For this one fleeting moment, Richard was a warm human being. Rare emotion had shaken him into life at long last.

'Could you?' he asked earnestly.

'Oh, Richard!' exclaimed Phil, genuinely moved. 'I hate to upset you – I really do. But it would never work, you know. We're not in the least – what's the word I want – *compatible*.'

'We could try,' said Richard.

Phil shook her head.

'No, we couldn't,' she said gently. Already, the mutinous little-boy-crossed look had come into Richard's face. 'In some ways, I'm so much older than you are. I'm a lot further along the road of experience, for one thing, with a marriage behind me and a boy to bring up. And then, in so many ways, you are much cleverer than I am. I'm afraid you would soon be impatient of my shortcomings. I know nothing of your work You know nothing of mine. There's so little to hold us together, Richard.'

Richard's gaze was downcast. The hissing coal fell from the fire and smouldered, unheeded, on the hearth. Somewhere, on the other side of Thrush Green, a child called to another, and a man went by Tullivers, tapping rhythmically with his walking stick.

These little outside noises seemed to break the spell of silence.

'Well, that's that, I suppose,' said Richard mournfully. 'I'm disappointed, but I'm not surprised. I suppose I'm not what Aunt Winnie would call "much catch". I've never had anyone to consider but myself. It makes a man selfish, but if you had felt you could marry me, I think it would have been the making of me.'

And what about me? was Phil's silent rejoinder. She surveyed the young man for a few moments, wondering if she should speak her mind or not.

She made her decision. She had nothing to lose. Richard, and perhaps another girl one day in the future, had much to gain.

'Richard, of course I'm grateful for being asked to think of marrying you, but do you realize that not once have you said you want me to marry you because you love me? I'm not a romantic woman, heaven knows, but you'll meet a great many who are, and *any* woman will want to be assured that she is loved before she enters marriage. Who on earth is going to get married without it?'

'But you must know that I shouldn't have asked you if I didn't love you!' protested Richard.

'Then say so,' said Phil, with some asperity. 'I think you will marry eventually – probably very soon, but you'll have to put your under-worked heart, as well as your over-worked head, into persuading any normal girl to take you on.'

She paused, and Richard rose to depart. Had she gone too far?

'I'm sorry to hurt you,' she said impulsively, 'but someone must tell you. No hard feelings?'

'Of course not,' said Richard. 'I'll think over what you've said.'

He held out a hand.

'I probably shan't see you again. I'll move into Carslake's place as soon as I can.'

Phil ignored the hand, and kissed him gently on the cheek.

'Dear Richard! Don't take it too badly, and look out for someone who really will make you a good wife one day. Thank you for being so kind, always, to me and Jeremy.'

Richard's blue eyes blinked rapidly as he turned away.

Phil accompanied him to the front door. The green was dark now, and the light at the corner by the pillar box silhouetted the writhing branches of the chestnut trees.

At the gate he turned and raised his hand to his fair hair in the semblance of a salute.

It was to be a very long time before Phil Prior ever saw Richard again.

20. An Engagement

It was May before Molly managed to rejoin Ben. The fair had come as usual to Thrush Green on the first day of that month, but, as the doctor said to Winnie, it wasn't the same without Mrs Curdle to run it.

'And I still expect a bouquet of artificial flowers,' confessed Winnie. 'Embarrassingly large though it was, and really quite hideous, I loved her for bringing it.'

All the children of Thrush Green had spent a hilarious few hours on the simple swings and roundabouts, the coconut shies and side-stalls of Ben Curdle's little fair. Jeremy and Paul had tried everything, and Jeremy had presented his mother with a hard-won vase of shocking pink with heavy gilding, and a very small goldfish in a jam jar. These treasures she had accepted with praiseworthy, if mendacious, expressions of delight.

When the fair closed down that night, after its one-day stand, Ben and Molly sat in Albert's kitchen and talked of their plans. Upstairs, Albert snored noisily. In the next bedroom young George, thumb in mouth, slept just as soundly.

'Doctor Lovell says he can manage pretty well on his own, and I've made arrangements for him to have a hot dinner at "The Two Pheasants" next door every day,' said Molly. 'At least for a bit.'

'And who pays for that?' asked Ben.

Molly looked confused.

'Couldn't we do that, Ben? You know how he's placed and –'

Ben cut her short with a hug.

'Anything to get you back,' he told her cheerfully. 'I'll go round and settle things with them. But knowing your dad, I reckon it would be best to do this a month at a time. See how things go with him. If he gets hitched up again, he won't need it!'

'I can't see anyone being fool enough to take him on,' admitted Molly. 'He's nigh on killed me this last few months.'

And so it was arranged. A week later Molly was ready to go. The cottage was spruce, the larder well stocked, with a fruit cake in the cake tin, and a steak and kidney pie in the larder. Her father's linen was washed, ironed and mended, and Molly said goodbye to him thankfully. She set out with little George on her lap and with Ben at the wheel, to go back to her own life.

They drove slowly across the green, Molly waving to the bent figure of Albert standing pathetically in the cottage doorway. Thrush Green had its newly-washed, innocent, early morning look – the wide grassy spaces bare of figures, the rooks circling lazily above the church.

Molly felt a pang at leaving it all. There was nowhere as dear as Thrush Green, and despite her father's niggardly ways, she felt a certain sympathy with the old man.

Ben, knowing her gentle heart, put a comforting hand on her knee as the car slid down the hill to Lulling.

'He'll do,' said Ben, and added wickedly, 'the devil looks after his own.'

Later that day, the rector found Albert Piggott walking briskly around the churchyard. He carried no walking stick, and although he was thinner and paler than usual, he seemed remarkably spry. He was inspecting old Mrs Curdle's grave. Ben had decked it with tulips and daffodils. At every visit he had thus honoured the memory of his much-loved grandmother, and even Albert's flinty heart was touched.

'Why, Albert,' cried the rector, with genuine joy, 'how well you look! I'd no idea you were getting on so famously!'

Albert acknowledged the kindness with a perfunctory nod.

'Got to do for meself now, sir, so I'd best get used to it. I was thinking I might manage the church again if you're so minded.'

'But, of course!' exclaimed the rector, delighted. 'If you are sure you feel up to it.'

Albert's face took on its usual woebegone and cautious look.

'I don't say as I could do the graves. I'm past that sort of work – but the boiler, now, and any little inside jobs as I used to do, well – I reckons I can struggle along with they.'

'I'm sure we can come to some arrangement with Willie about

the heavy work,' Charles Henstock assured him. 'Now look after yourself, Albert, and don't stay out too long in this treacherous wind.'

He returned to the rectory in high spirits.

'Dimity, my dear,' he declared to his wife, 'Albert Piggott's made a truly remarkable return to health. He was actually walking without a stick! Think of that!'

'I am,' said Dimity drily. 'Now that Molly's gone he can finish with his acting.'

The rector made his way thoughtfully to his study. As a student of human nature, he gave his keen-eyed wife full marks. But who would have thought it?

Sometime later that month, Ella Bembridge strode across the green to collect her goat's milk from Dotty.

At last the weather had relented. May, the loveliest of months, was warm and sunny, and as if to make up for lost time, the leaves and flowers burst out of their sheaths and filled the air with glory.

Butterflies and tortoises emerged from their long hibernation. Bees hummed among the wallflowers, and the cats of Thrush Green sunned themselves on the warm stone walls.

Ella found Dotty watching the antics of Dulcie's new twin kids. They were a skewbald pair, white and brown, and already as nimble and wicked as their proud mother. They skittered away, prancing sideways, their eyes upon Ella as she approached.

'A handsome pair,' commented Ella, wisely keeping her distance from Dulcie. She knew, from painful experience, that Dulcie had a way of running rapidly round a person's legs, trapping them in her chain, and bringing them heavily to the ground. It was a pastime which never palled for Dulcie. The unwilling victims failed to see the joke.

'Got homes for them?' asked Ella.

'I shall keep one,' said Dotty, 'and that Prior child wants one; but whether his mother does, I don't know.'

'Not much room at Tullivers,' observed Ella.

'Well, I suppose she may well be at Harold Shoosmith's before the year's out,' said Dotty reasonably. 'Now Winnie's Richard has left the coast clear, I can't think why Harold doesn't move in for the kill.'

Ella, forthright as she was, could not help feeling that Dotty's expressions were rather stronger than necessary.

'Maybe he doesn't want to get married. And anyway, they may prefer to live at Tullivers, if they do make a match of it.'

'Doubtful,' said Dotty, taking out a man's red and white spotted handkerchief from her skirt pocket, and blowing her nose with a resounding trumpeting. 'Too pokey for Harold. All those cups and things he's got. And he's used to large rooms, living out in Africa, with all those natives fanning him.'

'Got any goat's milk?' asked Ella abruptly. The conversation seemed to be getting out of hand, and Dotty, once started, was deucedly difficult to stop.

'Well, for the kid's sake, I hope they make up their minds quickly,' continued Dotty, leading the way through a rabble of hopeful hens to the house, 'and plump for Harold's place. Plenty of good grass there, and a nice hazel hedge. I shall rely on you, Ella, to do your best to further this affair.'

'Who do you think I am?' cried Ella. 'Dan Cupid? If you ask me, Harold Shoosmith's quite capable of doing his own work. He knows his own mind, mark my words!'

But, if the truth were known, Harold was only now coming to know his own mind.

He had been at Frank's when Richard departed, and learnt from the Baileys about the young man's haste to go, after his visit to Tullivers.

'Sent him away with a flea in his ear,' said the old doctor, with some relish. 'Can't blame her, can you?'

'I think you're misjudging her,' said Winnie. 'She's too kind to deal over-ruthlessly with Richard. But you know how he is – hates to be crossed. He's been hopelessly spoilt ever since he was a child. He was bound to take this badly.'

'How is she?' asked Harold.

'As cheerful as ever. Very busy writing for your friend, as you know. She's said nothing to me about Richard's proposal. Probably thinks I don't know, but he burst in here that night, looking as black as thunder, and simply said: "She won't have me. I'm off next week!" And that was it.'

It certainly brought matters to a head for Harold, and as the days slipped by he studied his feelings as dispassionately as he could. There was no doubt about it. The girl was very dear to him, but the longer he postponed his decision to speak, the more certain he became that marriage was not for him.

All the arguments that he and Frank had discussed, when his friend visited Thrush Green, were gone over again. When Harold had stayed with Frank, only a week or so before, little had been said on the matter, except that Harold had intimated that he felt that he could not expect an attractive young woman like Phil to take him on, and that his own feelings were, perhaps, as Frank had once suggested, a compound of pity and protectiveness.

The more he thought about it, the stronger grew his conviction that he would never be accepted, even if he were brave enough to ask her. Time, his old ally, seemed to be slow in coming to his aid and he was still troubled in his mind when he called at Tullivers, one fine morning at the end of May, to help Phil in her kitchen garden.

Their combined efforts had made it one of the tidiest and most attractive gardens at Thrush Green. Harold surveyed, with pleasure, the double row of sturdy broad beans, and the neat labels which showed where carrots, early potatoes and beetroot had been planted. The currant and gooseberry bushes, which he had rescued from suffocation last autumn, were making vigorous growth, and Phil's fruit trees had plenty of blossom. The walnut tree which grew at the end of the garden, by the Baileys' wall, was in young auburn leaf.

Everything, Harold thought, looked in good heart, and when Phil came from the house to join him, he thought how well she looked too. There was a radiance about her which was new.

Of course, he told himself, he had never known the girl when she had been free of worry. Now, with the winter and its tragedy behind her, she seemed to be responding to the spring with all the natural joy of young things. How easy it would be to take the plunge, to ask her to marry him, to leave it to the gods – and to Phil – to arrange his future!

He realized that she was looking at him, as though she read his thoughts.

She put out a hand and touched his arm, speaking quickly as though she had just come to a decision.

'Come and sit down for a minute. I've something to tell you.'

He followed her to an old garden seat which the admiral had placed years ago in a sunny corner against a southern wall. At Harold's feet an early bee was rolling over and over, its striped furry body entwined with a wallflower blossom from which it was zealously extracting the honey.

'I've some wonderful news,' said Phil, 'and I want you to be the first to know. Can you guess?'

Harold looked at her. He had always thought that poets grossly overstated things when they talked of eyes like stars. Now he began to understand.

'I was never good at guessing,' he confessed.

'I only knew myself yesterday. Frank has asked me to marry him. Say you're pleased.'

Harold took a deep breath. If he felt a pang of jealousy, it vanished at once. Wholeheartedly, he congratulated her.

'He's the luckiest devil in the world,' he told her sincerely, taking her hands in his.

'He's coming here tomorrow to arrange things with the rector,' said Phil. 'We had the longest telephone talk ever known to the Lulling exchange last night. We shall get married this summer.'

She leant forward and kissed Harold on the cheek.

'And will you give me away?' she asked.

'It's like asking me to part with my heart,' replied Harold, half-meaning it, 'but since you ask me, I shall count it an honour, my dear.'

They stood up and gazed across the garden.

'Will you leave Thrush Green?' asked Harold.

'We haven't got that far,' smiled Phil. 'But I don't think I could ever leave Tullivers. We could build on, I suppose.'

She looked about her vaguely, trying to envisage the future, and suddenly became conscious of the wonder of a life which contained such a precious element as sure joy to come.

She turned to Harold wonderingly.

'What is it about Thrush Green which makes it so special? Is it the air, or the green, or the people?'

Harold considered the question seriously before he spoke. In the silence between them they could hear the distant sounds of a Thrush Green morning. Miss Fogerty's children called to each other in the playground, the rooks cawed above St Andrew's elms, and Winnie

Bailey's voice could be heard as she opened a window to the sunshine.

'All those things make Thrush Green,' said Harold, 'and much, much more.'

He thought of his own restless wanderings abroad, and his present joy. Here he had found a home and deep happiness. He knew he shared this feeling with the girl beside him. Thrush Green seemed to have some magic quality which they both recognized instinctively.

'The power of healing,' said Harold softly, as if to himself.